ROBYN YOUNG

ReQUIEM

HODDER &
STOUGHTON

First published in Great Britain in 2008 by Hodder & Stoughton
An Hachette Livre UK company

1

Copyright © Robyn Young 2008

A CIP catalogue record for this title is available from the British Library.

Hardback ISBN 978 0 340 92140 1
Trade Paperback ISBN 978 0 340 92141 8

Map drawn by Sandra Oakins

Typeset in Perpetua by Hewer Text UK Ltd, Edinburgh
Printed and bound in Australia by Griffin Press

Hodder & Stoughton policy is to use papers that are natural, renewable
and recyclable products and made from wood grown in sustainable
forests. The logging and manufacturing processes are expected to
conform to the environmental regulations of the country of origin.

Hodder & Stoughton
338 Euston Road
London NW1 3BH

www.hodder.co.uk

ACKNOWLEDGEMENTS

By the time this book is published, the Brethren trilogy will have been almost a decade in the making. Not only has it taken time to create, but also a great deal of support from family and friends, and from experts who have willingly shared their knowledge along the way. This is a small token of my gratitude to those people.

Thank you to Deborah Druba and all at Univers Poche for the warm welcome to Paris and for introducing me to Joffrey Seguin, who showed me the city's hidden medieval past. Thanks also to Alison Weir for generously sharing her research notes on Philippe IV and to Christine Tomkins for the translation of the French texts.

Many thanks to all those who took the time to talk to me so informatively and passionately about the history of the sites I visited in Scotland, particularly Allan Kennedy at the Bannockburn Heritage Centre, David Frame at Stirling Castle and Sarah at the Berwick-upon-Tweed tourist information centre for help finding a useful history of the town.

My gratitude to Steven Charlton for the unforgettable experiences with his birds of prey. Thanks to Wayne de Strete, Jeff Baker, Karl Alexander, Mark Griffin and Seán George at Stunt Action Specialists for the invasion of Canterbury and for teaching me the best methods of doing away with one's enemies. Thanks also to Mark for the reading suggestions and for checking over the battles.

Much appreciation is due to the Third Monday Club for their editorial support and many thanks go to Dr Mark Philpott at the Centre for Medieval & Renaissance Studies and Keble College, Oxford, for checking over the manuscripts.

A huge thank you goes to my agent, Rupert Heath, for believing in the trilogy from the start and for many laughs along the way. Thanks also to Dan Conaway at Writers House.

I am indebted to everyone at Hodder & Stoughton for the enthusiasm they have brought to the trilogy and for making every step such an enjoyable one. In particular I would like to thank my editor, Nick Sayers, but also Anne, Emma, Tara, Kelly, Laurence, Lucy, Richard, Aslan, Melissa, Laura, Helen and all the Hodder reps. Special thanks go to Toni, Charlotte and Emma for organising the fantastic launch and last, but not least, I want to thank Alasdair Oliver and Larry Rostant for the breathtaking artwork.

Many thanks go to the team at Dutton for their commitment to the trilogy, with much gratitude to my American editor, Julie Doughty. Indeed, I would like to thank all my editors and publishing teams for their hard work.

Lastly, my heartfelt thanks go to my family and friends for allowing me to share with them the highs and lows of this often incredible, frequently challenging, sometimes terrifying, always rewarding process. Most of all, my love to Lee: collaborator, critic, research assistant, fellow celebrator, and so very much more.

CONTENTS

KINGDOM of SCOTLAND

ARGYLL

Stirling
Edinburgh
Berwick-upon-Tweed
Carlisle

KINGDOM of ENGLAND

London

COUNTY of FLANDERS

Courtrai

Paris

KINGDOM of FRANCE

Poitiers

HOLY ROMAN EMPIRE

Bordeaux

DUCHY of GUIENNE

Lyons

GASCONY

NAVARRE

Avignon

KINGDOM of ITALY

Rome

EUROPE

'Requiem aeternam dona eis, domine, et lux perpetua luceat eis.'
Eternal rest give them, O Lord, and let everlasting light shine upon them.

(Introit to the Mass for the Dead)

PROLOGUE

As the young man knelt, the iron cold of the floor seeped through the thin material of his hose. He felt the stone, hard and unyielding, bruising him, but the discomfort was reassuring; the flagstones beneath him were the only thing in the chamber that felt solid. A fog of incense hung in shifting layers, stinging his eyes. It was a bitter smell that reminded him of burning leaves. He didn't know what it was, but it wasn't the serene frankincense that always welcomed him into church. Around him, shadows stole across the walls, nebulous and unfamiliar, as figures passed by candles that sputtered in holders on the ground, placed so far apart that the quivering points of fire cast little real light and served only to blind and disorient him further. A few yards away to his left the floor was spattered with a substance that gleamed wetly. Here, in this dimness, it looked almost black, but in daylight the young man knew it would be a bright, shocking red. He could still smell its sharp, metallic odour, even over the pungent incense, and he swallowed tightly, a plug of nausea clogging his throat.

This wasn't what he had expected. Part of him was glad of that; he might not have gone through with it had he known what would be asked of him this night. The only things that kept him here, doing as he was bid, were the presence of the men in the shadows and the fear of what would happen if he refused. But he didn't want to show weakness. He wanted to do this right, despite his trepidation, and so he stared straight ahead, his chest, bare and pale, thrust forward, hands, slick with sweat, clasped tightly behind his back.

Now the men had stopped moving and the chamber had fallen silent again he could hear faint birdsong coming through the high windows, all covered with heavy black cloth. It must be almost dawn.

There was movement to his left. He saw a figure approaching and his stomach churned with apprehension. It was a man dressed in a shimmering cloak sewn from hundreds of overlapping circles of silk, all different shades of blue and pink: cobalt, sapphire, rose, violet. Here and there the material was shot through with silver thread that glistened whenever the candlelight caught it and created the impression that he was clad in the scales of a fish. The young man knew the figure was male, for he had spoken often during the ceremony, guiding him, commanding him, but so far his face had been concealed by a cowl, fashioned from the same material as the cloak, that hung down almost to his chest. It was surprising he could even see to walk. Under the cowl, his head appeared oddly misshapen and his voice, when he spoke, came out muffled and deep.

'You have chosen the path and it was wisely chosen. You have sworn the oaths and stood fast in the face of temptation and dread. Now is the final test and the most perilous. But obey me as you have pledged and all will be well.' The figure paused. 'Will you obey me now and always?'

'I will,' breathed the young man.

'Then prove it,' snapped the figure, whipping back the cowl and dropping to a crouch before the young man, who recoiled from the grinning skull that was revealed, the candles on the floor up-lighting it, making the bone that much yellower and the huge, hollow eye-sockets that much blacker.

Even though he knew it was just a mask, even though he caught a glimpse of dark human eyes through the sockets of the skull, his terror didn't dissipate, and when a small gold cross was drawn from the folds of the fish-scale cloak and held in front of him, his heart seemed fit to explode in his chest.

'Spit on it.'

'What?'

'Denounce its power over you. Prove you are loyal to me alone, that you speak as one with your brothers.'

The young man's eyes darted left and right as the men moved out of the shadows. They too wore masks: blood red with the image of a white stag's head painted on the front of each.

'Spit!' came the command again.

Feeling the men crowding in around him, blocking out the frail candlelight, the young man leaned forward over the proffered cross. He collected saliva in his dry mouth with difficulty. Closing his eyes, he spat.

PART ONE

I

Bordeaux, the Kingdom of France

23 November 1295 AD

M athieu's palms were slick with sweat. He gripped his broadsword tighter and, seeking reassurance, glanced right to where his commander was hunched in a fighting stance. But the man's gaze was fixed on the double doors at the end of the hall. As Mathieu watched, an oily line of perspiration trickled down the side of his face. The thunderous crash came again, making the doors shudder violently and causing the nine guards lined up in the hall to flinch. In the near hush that followed, their breaths surged, sharp and shallow. Moments later, another brutal impact rocked the wood. This time, there was no brief reprieve. The doors splintered and burst apart, shards of oak exploding into the hall, thumping against tapestries and skittering across the flagstones. There was a wrenching, tearing sound as the iron-headed ram was pulled back out of the wreckage and soldiers poured in through the breach.

Mathieu felt a vertiginous rush of fear. For a second, he was paralysed by it. Incoherent prayers and protestations babbled through his mind. He was only nineteen. This wasn't what he had imagined when his father secured him this post. *Dear God, let me be spared.* Then, hearing his commander yell the order for attack and seeing his comrades racing forth to meet the incoming soldiers, he forced himself forward. A soldier came up on him, all too fast. Mathieu had time to see a kite-shaped shield with an iron boss, rising in a flash of blue and scarlet, matching the surcoat the man wore, then he was cutting up with his broadsword to block the blow that was aimed at his head. All around him, the other guards clashed with their attackers, a chaos of blades and bodies. In the confined space, the clang of steel echoed harshly, along with the ear-splitting cracks of swords striking shields and the ring and stamp of mailed boots. Unlike the soldiers, who were clad in long mail shirts and iron pot helms, the guards wore only studded leather gambesons and padded cuisses to protect their torsos and thighs.

Mathieu gritted his teeth as the soldier swung in again, the ferocious concussion of the blow almost beating the sword from his hand. He wanted to turn and run, but the soldier was forcing him back, cutting and jabbing, and now he was almost at the wall and there was nowhere to go. He let out a cry of frustration as he tried to push the soldier away and the man refused to give ground. Sweat was stinging his eyes, blinding him. There was no room to move. He dodged a rapid lunge aimed at his side, swiped away another that came in at his chest, then struck out clumsily. The soldier ducked left, avoiding the strike. Scarlet and blue filled Mathieu's vision as the soldier's shield, with its iron boss, punched up into his face. He felt pain shout through him. Blood burst from his nose and mouth, and he staggered into the wall, his sword going wide. A moment later there was an awful piercing sensation high up in his side, followed by a sickening agony. The soldier's blade had plunged into the soft flesh below his armpit, where there was none of the leather armour to protect him. Mathieu screamed as the man slammed his gloved palm against the pommel, driving the blade home with a grunt of effort.

He felt his broadsword slip from his fingers. Across the hall, he saw more soldiers forcing their way through the mangled doors to aid the others. But there was little need; his comrades were outnumbered and outmatched. It had all happened so quickly. From the main house they had seen the guards at the gatehouse cut down and the soldiers had come, riding furiously through the grounds, barely giving them time to bolt the doors. The blade in his side was withdrawn with a rush of blood. As he was sinking to the floor, Mathieu saw one of his comrades go down, doubling over the sword that punctured his stomach. The others were scrabbling back in a ragged line towards the stairs that swept up to a gallery. Dimly, he heard shouting somewhere above him, but before he could fathom its source, he collapsed, leaving a red smear on the wall behind him.

The shouting grew louder, sounding over the din in the hall, as a man descended. One by one, the soldiers halted, allowing the fleeing guards to retreat. The man kept on yelling as he sprinted down the last few stairs, his French barely coherent. Brandishing a sword, he moved past his guards up to the soldiers, all of whom had now stopped, their breaths coming fast through their helmets. They held their ground and the man paused several feet from them, taking in their surcoats. The fact that he recognised the uniforms was no comfort. 'What is the meaning of this?' His voice shook with fear as well as anger, but he held the sword steady. 'How dare you assault my property. My men!' He threw a hand towards the bodies of his fallen guards, his eyes lingering briefly on the crumpled form of Mathieu, the youngest. 'Who is your commander? I demand to speak to him.' There was silence. *'Answer me!'*

'You can speak to me, Lord Pierre de Bourg.' A man entered, looking around as he stepped over the debris of the front doors. He appeared to be in his early thirties and had a long face, brown eyes and a sallow, faded complexion, as if he had once been much darker, but hadn't seen sun in a long time. His hair was covered by a white silk coif and he wore a full-length riding cloak that hung neatly from his thin shoulders, making him appear both broader and taller than he actually was. The cloak was plain, but exquisitely tailored, with a small metal boss sewn on either side of the chest through which was looped a silver chain that fastened the garment in place.

'Who are you?' questioned Pierre.

The man removed a pair of silk gloves to reveal blue-veined, spindly hands, his gaze on the lord. 'My name is Guillaume de Nogaret.'

He spoke the *langue d'oïl*, but Pierre detected a softer southern accent filtering through the blunt northern tongue. The soldiers moved aside as Guillaume de Nogaret came forward, but they kept their blades trained on Pierre, whose guards had gathered protectively in behind him.

Nogaret gestured to him. 'Lower your weapon.'

Pierre fought to regain his authority, lost in the face of Nogaret's unnerving calm. 'I will do no such thing. You have broken into my home, killed my people. On whose orders?'

'I am a minister to King Philippe. It is on his orders that I am here.'

Pierre's gaze flicked to the soldiers in their scarlet and blue surcoats: the colours of the royal guard stationed in Bordeaux under the command of the king's brother, Charles de Valois.

'We have been informed,' continued Nogaret, 'that you have been spying on our forces and reporting to the English in Bayonne.'

'Ridiculous! Where have you heard this from? Who is accusing me?'

'You will lower your weapon,' repeated Nogaret, 'or my men will force you to do so.'

There was a long pause before Pierre obeyed.

'Tell your guards to place their weapons on the floor and move back to the wall.'

Pierre turned to his men with a tight nod. As soon as they laid down their swords the room was filled with activity, the royal soldiers moving in to gather the blades and hustle the subdued, embittered guards up against the wall. The bodies of Mathieu and the other dead man were dragged to the side of the hall and dumped.

'How many more people are in this house?' asked Nogaret brusquely.

'Just my family and our servants, but whatever you want with me does not concern them.'

'Search the rooms upstairs,' said Nogaret, motioning to five soldiers. 'Bring down anyone you find. If any resist, use whatever force you deem necessary.'

Pierre looked anguished as they went stamping off up the stairs. 'I beg you, don't hurt them.' He turned to Nogaret. 'Please, my wife and children are up there!'

'Bring him,' said Nogaret, to two of the soldiers. He pointed down a gloomy passage that led off from the entrance hall. 'Does that lead to the kitchens? Does it?' he repeated harshly, when Pierre didn't answer.

Pierre nodded mutely. As he was marched down the passage, Nogaret followed, leaving the remaining soldiers to watch the guards.

The kitchens were expansive, the main chamber divided by a trestle table, upon which sat two pots filled with diced vegetables and a stack of knobbly carrots beside a knife. In a hearth, steam curled from a cauldron and a brace of pheasants dangled from a hook, their bronze and turquoise feathers catching the light from a row of high windows. The place was warm and smelled of herbs.

Nogaret's gaze alighted on the carrots. One was half chopped near the knife, the severed pieces strewn around it. 'Where are the cooks?'

'Upstairs. When the alarm was sounded I sent everyone up there until I could find out what was happening.' Pierre fixed Nogaret with a bitter look. 'But you gave me no time to do that, breaking down my door and attacking my men.'

'Traitors aren't generally given warning and it was your men who refused entry and forced me to break into your home. Your men who rushed at mine before they had a chance to explain themselves.'

'I am no traitor,' responded Pierre fiercely.

'That we shall discover.' Nogaret went to the table and picked up the knife. 'Hold him.'

'Wait . . . please!' cried Pierre, as the soldiers gripped him.

Nogaret inspected the knife. The thin blade was stained with juice from the vegetables. 'We know you have been in contact with English troops in Bayonne, sending them information on our forces in Bordeaux. Our numbers. Defences.'

'I do not know where you have found this information, but I assure you it is false. I have never even met any English soldiers.'

'Come, now,' said Nogaret wryly. 'That cannot be true. When King Edward was residing in the city you must have met many.'

'That isn't what I meant.'

'You paid homage to Edward for your lands when he was in possession of the duchy. You even supplied labourers to help him build his bastide towns.' Nogaret's tone was contemptuous. 'Scattering the area with his little settlements, like a hound marking its territory.'

'Well, as you say, if Edward is my liege lord and I hold my lands in his name, how could I, or any noble in the duchy of Guienne, not have had contact with the English at some point in the past?'

'Edward *was* your liege lord,' responded Nogaret sharply. 'He hasn't been for over a year, not since King Philippe took control of the duchy, and yet it would seem your allegiances, be they merely dutiful or else willing, are as of old.'

'That is not so. I am loyal to my king.' Pierre raised his head higher. 'Despite what he has done here.'

'What he has done here?' echoed Nogaret.

'I am not blind. I know this is happening all over the region. Royal troops still pour in from the north, taking over cities and castles, only now they are also driving out noblemen, seizing their property, their wealth. I have watched these past months and I have borne this with my teeth gritted, but borne it I have. I have had no contact with Edward's forces, nor do I intend to.'

'You have borne it?' Nogaret's voice was low. 'You speak as of a child who has done something tiresome that displeases you, rather than of your king. The sovereign ruler of this kingdom rightfully confiscates the territory of a foreigner, whose own deeds saw them forfeited to the French crown, and you have borne it?' Nogaret's brown eyes were hard. 'Bring him.'

Pierre struggled, but together the soldiers hauled him to the trestle in the centre of the kitchen.

'Put his hand on the table, hold it flat.' Pierre fought wildly as one of the soldiers took hold of his wrist. The other grabbed him around the neck in an arm-lock and squeezed, breaking his ability to resist. The one holding his wrist pushed his hand, palm down, on to the table. Nogaret handed the knife to the soldier who had hold of Pierre's wrist. 'I tell you, Pierre de Bourg, you have borne nothing yet.'

In the passage outside came sounds of a commotion. Nogaret looked round, hearing an indignant and unfamiliar voice. The door opened and a man entered, his flushed face filled with concern. He was around Nogaret's age, short and slight, with a hook nose and a down-turned mouth that drooped over a feeble chin. A royal guard was lingering uncertainly behind him. Nogaret, ignoring the soldier's apology, studied the intruder. He was wearing a voluminous hooded cape lined with brown fur, and underneath a white linen tunic that reached to the floor. A pair of sandals peeked out from under the garment's folds. He was a clergyman.

The intruder forced his gaze from the knife that was held over Pierre. 'I implore you, unhand this man!'

'What do you want here?' demanded Nogaret. 'Who are you?'

'I am Bertrand de Got, Bishop of Comminges.' The bishop looked back at Pierre, who had stopped struggling and was staring at him in hope.

'You are a long way from your diocese.'

'I have been visiting one of my nephews, a priest here in Bordeaux. I was at his church when I learned that royal troops had been sent to arrest Lord de Bourg.'

'What business is it of yours?'

Bertrand took a breath, which steadied his voice. 'Pierre is a generous benefactor of my nephew's church and a well-respected member of this parish. I cannot imagine what he has done to warrant such treatment. A message has been sent to the archbishop, informing him of the disturbance,' he added meaningfully.

Nogaret looked unconcerned. 'This well-respected man is a traitor. He and others in the region have been reporting the movements of our royal troops to the English, who we know are planning more attacks on our positions in an attempt to recapture the duchy.'

'I cannot believe that.'

'It is known he has had close relations with Edward of England. It is not so great a leap to suppose that he might wish to continue to support his former master.'

'But most dignitaries in the area have had dealings with the Lord Edward,' protested Bertrand. 'I myself met the English king on several occasions during his sojourn in Gascony.'

'I have no need to explain myself further to you, *Bishop*.' Nogaret emphasised that last word, his voice revealing something like real emotion for the first time. He spoke to the soldier behind Bertrand. 'Escort him outside. See he is removed from the grounds.'

'This is outrageous.' Bertrand fixed Nogaret with a challenging look. 'The archbishop will not stand for this, not in his province.'

'This house has been seized and is in the possession of the King of France. Leave or I will see you punished for trespassing on royal property.'

'This is not the end of this matter.' Bertrand de Got looked at the lord and shook his head. 'I am sorry, Pierre. I did what I could.'

Pierre strained against the soldiers holding him, his eyes wide. 'Dear God, Bertrand, help me!'

Nogaret went to Pierre, his mouth twisting. 'God isn't the power in these lands any more.'

'*Bertrand!*' shouted Pierre. But the bishop was heading away, compelled by the royal guard, who yanked the door shut, blocking out the sight of the soldier raising his hand and muting Pierre's scream as the knife plunged downwards.

After the torture was done, Nogaret returned to the hall, leaving the half-conscious Pierre with one of the soldiers. The other followed him out, wiping his hands on a kitchen rag. In the hall, more people had been gathered: three men and four girls, servants by their dress, and a slim, pale-faced woman clad in an elegant gown, clutching two boys to her side. One of the boys had his hands balled against his face and was crying.

As Nogaret entered, several of the guards looked up, their faces filled with impotent anger. The woman stared in dumb shock at the blood-stained soldier. One of the servants, an elderly man, started forward, then slumped against the wall as a sword was pointed at him. Nogaret noticed that another guard had been laid out beside the two killed in the initial fight and a royal soldier appeared to have been injured. He crossed to one of the men, whose surcoat was edged with yellow brocade. 'Captain, what happened?'

The captain led him towards the doors, out of earshot of the prisoners. 'When they heard the lord screaming, they tried to attack us. One managed to wrest a sword from one of my men. I hope the traitorous bastard confessed,' he added gruffly.

'Not yet.'

The captain frowned. 'The interrogation sounded very thorough.'

'You did what I asked?' questioned Nogaret, ignoring the comment.

'The wagon is being loaded as we speak.' The captain paused. 'But if he has not confessed should we not wait for confirmation before we proceed? It is possible he was telling the truth. Perhaps our information was wrong?'

'It wasn't,' said Nogaret flatly. 'These people need to be put down before they can compromise us. At present, we are holding well against the English, but we must not allow anything to jeopardise that. They took Blaye and Bayonne from us at the start of the war. With better information they could capture more territory.'

The captain nodded.

'See that the lord and his family are conveyed to the garrison gaol. Their fate will be decided in due course.' Leaving the captain to snap orders at his men, Nogaret headed into the bright November afternoon.

In front of the house there was a great deal of activity around a large wagon. Squires were keeping an eye on the horses, while soldiers tramped back and forth from a side door, carrying an abundance of objects: ornate candelabras, a bundle of trailing silk dresses, the red-faced soldier holding them being jeered by his comrades, stacks of silver plates, armfuls of books, two swords in decorated scabbards, a rosewood spice box.

Nogaret went to the wagon, the soldiers moving around him. He looked inside at the assortment of furniture and clothing. Seeing something glittering on the floor of the wagon, he reached in and pulled out a necklace of glass beads. He tossed the trinket back inside with a scowl. He dearly hoped, when added to the plunder taken from other families, it would be enough to justify the time he had spent here, especially since the seizures had been his idea.

'Minister.'

A soldier was pointing to the main gates. Squinting into the sunlight, Nogaret saw a rider approaching, the horse's hooves pounding up clouds of dust. He wondered for a moment whether the bishop had decided to return, but as the rider came closer Nogaret saw he was clad in a familiar scarlet and black cloak. It was a royal messenger. He recognised the man from Paris.

'Minister de Nogaret,' greeted the rider breathlessly as he drew up. Dismounting, he reached into a dust-streaked leather bag and pulled out a scroll. 'The city garrison told me where to find you.'

Nogaret broke the wax seal and opened it. He scanned the message.

'Minister?' The captain, hearing the hoof-beats, had come out.

There was an anguished cry from the house. The young woman was being dragged through the ruined doorway by two of the guards. She was screaming for her children. 'Finish up here.' Nogaret raised his voice above the din. 'Deliver the wagon directly to Prince Charles. He will see the treasure is conveyed to Lord Philippe.'

'Of course.' The captain glanced questioningly at the messenger. 'Are you leaving us, Minister?'

'I am to return to Paris.' Nogaret snapped his fingers at the squire who held his horse. 'The king has summoned me.'

2
The Banks of the Seine, Paris
19 December 1295 AD

The galley slid haltingly alongside the jetty, grating against the stone. Men grabbed the ropes that were thrown to them and looped them through iron rings, pulling off the slack to steady the vessel. The gangplanks were set down with a clatter and a host of men began to disembark, their faces brown and rough with sun and wind. The white mantles they wore were sodden from the fog that clung to the river and flowed sluggishly around the mast of their ship, where a piebald banner hung limp.

Will Campbell went to the galley's side as the men in front of him made their way down. He scanned the area, the damp, freezing air filling his lungs. The buildings of the Ville stretched away in a confusion of rooftops and spires. The rows of plaster and timber houses, several storeys high, were vague and insubstantial in the misty air, punctuated by the hulking outlines of churches and abbeys. Almost immediately ahead, the Hôtel de Ville: the administrative seat of the provost of the merchants, loomed over the place de la Grève. The imposing structure stood at the centre of a web of workshops, markets and houses that radiated across the city's right bank: the municipal centre of Paris. Will picked out other structures he recognised, but any true sense of the city was disoriented by the fog and by time. It was years since he had stood on these banks. He glanced behind him at the humped shape of the Ile de la Cité that rose out of the Seine, wreathed in white. The heart of France. He caught a glimpse of the palace towers at the western end of the island and his jaw tightened.

'Still looks the same, doesn't it?'

Simon came up and rested his thick arms on the side. His beard had grown bushier during the voyage, but his mop of brown hair was starting to thin on top. Will, who was almost a foot taller than the brawny groom, noticed a bald patch on his crown.

'Robert and I were trying to remember how long it's been. By my reckoning it's over thirty years.'

'Twenty-nine.'

Simon smiled ruefully, revealing his broken front tooth. 'Robert's beaten me then.'

'Did I hear my name?'

They turned. A tall knight with grey eyes and a face that was still boyishly handsome, despite the lines that creased it, headed over.

'You won the wager,' Simon told him.

'I had no doubt.' Robert grinned. 'You couldn't count the fingers on a one-armed man.' He clapped Simon on the back then looked at Will, who had fallen silent and was staring out over the city. 'It is strange to be back, isn't it?' His smile faded. 'So much has happened.'

'You should check on the horses, Simon,' said Will abruptly. He headed for the planks where the last of the knights were disembarking, leaving the sergeants and crew.

Exchanging a look with Simon, Robert went after Will. 'The Grand Master wants us to walk with him at the van. I think he might have actually forgotten how to get to the Temple.'

They descended, the gangplank dipping and flexing. Will stepped on to the stone jetty with a jolt that felt somehow irrevocable. He wanted to turn around and go back, keep on sailing.

Together, they trudged up the jetty, over stinking mud-banks littered with detritus: broken eel pots, a wooden shoe, a dead bird, wings splayed. The banks became harder as they approached the end of the jetty, brown sand and bristly grass, then muddy street. The area was busy with men and women heading to work after morning Mass. A horse-drawn bronette juddered past, conveying two women dressed in fine-looking gowns, the wheels of the carriage skidding in the mud. A group of dirty children ran after it, calling hopefully to the women, who looked the other way with practised indifference. As the children passed, a herd of pigs funnelled out of an alley, followed by a swineherd who guided them with *thwacks* of a stick down to the waterside, near to a wharf where carts were being loaded with timber.

Up ahead, the knights had gathered in a group, at the head of which stood the Grand Master. Jacques de Molay was a bull of a man in his early fifties, with coarse grey hair that fell in thick waves around his shoulders. Like all Templar Knights, he wore a beard, but rather than keeping his clipped and neat, as Will and Robert did, he wore it long, almost to his chest. Will had once heard a knight say that before going into battle the Grand Master would plait it and push it down the front of his shirt. Jacques was addressing a Templar official, his French gruff and guttural. 'Speak to the provost and find out where we should berth our vessel, then have the sergeants follow with our gear. Let us hope my message reached the preceptory and they are expecting us.'

'Yes, my lord.' The official waited for a wagon to trundle past then made his way over to the Hôtel de Ville.

Jacques saw Will and Robert approaching with the last of the knights and motioned to them. 'Commander Campbell, lead the way.'

Pausing to get his bearings, Will led the group of sixty knights towards the Church of St Gervais, whose lofty steeple was lost in fog. Some people stared as the knights marched in a column across the busy street, but many simply hurried past, engrossed in their own business. In Paris, the site of the Order's principal base in the West, Templars were a common sight, as much a part of the community of the city as the professors and scholars of the Sorbonne on the left bank and the royal officials on the Ile de la Cité. Just before the church, Will turned into a narrow side street that wound through a warren of alleys and shallow stairways, where timber-framed buildings crowded in on either side, bowing towards one another. The top storeys of some of the structures were so close the inhabitants could reach out and shake their neighbours' hands. Washing, strung from criss-crossing lines, dripped a steady rain on to the knights' heads as they made their way out on to the rue du Temple. For Will, these gloomy streets were painfully familiar. Around every corner, echoes of the past came back to him, faint in faded signs and peeling shutters, clearer with the appearance of a church spire clustered with gargoyles in a gap between buildings. With familiarity came memories. They hung in the air like ghosts, visible in shop doorways and crumbling façades, in the faces of people who hurried by. Things he had kept at bay on the endless journey from Cyprus, the monotony of travel numbing his mind, now overwhelmed him.

Two butchers lounged in a doorway, aprons brown with blood. A baker chatted animatedly with a woman as he handed her two loaves. Will stared at them, wondering if he would recognise anyone after all this time. Ahead, a young woman hurrying across the street slipped in the mud, dropping the basket she was carrying. As she bent to retrieve it, she flipped back the trailing material of her head veil, revealing copper-gold curls. Will halted. His eyes remained transfixed by her, even as she rose and he saw her face, even as he saw he didn't know her. He started as he felt Robert's hand on his elbow.

'What's wrong?'

Will realised he had stopped. 'Nothing. I forgot which way.'

Robert glanced at the girl as she hastened on, then back at Will, but he said nothing and they continued in silence.

The fog was thinner away from the river and soon they could see the city walls looming ahead, built from pale yellow stone and flanked with towers. Some distance away, near Temple Gate, a crowd had gathered. As they drew closer, the knights could hear someone shouting.

'Weep, my children! Weep for the loss of God's kingdom on Earth! Weep for the fall of Jerusalem and the rise of Babylon! Weep for the men whose sins have led us into this age of darkness!'

Will saw a man standing on the steps of a church. Arms raised, he addressed the crowd in a hoarse voice, as if he had been shouting for some time. He was young and the bald crown of his tonsured head showed pale against his dark hair. His grey robe was shabby and his bare feet were crusted with mud. He was a Franciscan: one of the followers of St Francis of Assisi, who went out into the world as mendicants to preach the gospel, relying on others to provide for their earthly needs. Will hadn't seen one in a long time.

'Weep for your kings and princes, those who traded the Holy City for gold to line their pockets and clad their whores!'

Some of the onlookers moved on uninterested, but more paused to listen as the young friar continued his passionate speech. Some even called their assent.

'But weep most of all for the knights, my children, whose lust for blood is awoken only when it suits their purpose. When it doesn't, these warriors leave mothers and infants, old men and the blind to fend off the swords of the infidel with nothing but prayer!' He flung a hand towards Temple Gate. 'They made a pyre of God's city and turned our dream to ash!'

The calls turned into fervent cheers and there was a smatter of applause.

'What is this?' Jacques moved up behind Will with a questioning frown.

The friar drew a breath to continue, then halted, catching sight of the knights. His eyes lit up, but he scowled. 'These are the men!' He pointed at the knights. 'These are the men whose greed and impiety caused this woe!'

The crowd looked round. Seeing the company approaching, some of the onlookers began to disperse, eyeing the knights' white mantles, each decorated with a splayed red cross. But others stared, accusation plain in their faces.

'These are the men who fled from the Saracens to save their own wealth, leaving women and children to rape and slaughter!'

'Ignore him, my lord,' said one of the Templar officials, as Jacques stepped forward. 'He does not know of what he speaks.'

'Then I will correct him,' growled Jacques, pushing past.

'With me,' said the official, gesturing worriedly to Will and Robert.

'With respect, sir,' said Robert quickly, as the man went to unsheathe his sword, 'I think that might be unnecessary.' All the knights had stopped now. Those near the back were craning their heads, trying to see what the disturbance was. 'These people are unarmed,' continued Robert, as the official hesitated. 'We will only cause a panic.'

'Who are you?' demanded Jacques, striding up to the friar, the crowd parting like water before him. He was a huge figure among them, the large red cross on his back outlined in gold: a blaze of colour amid their drab greys and browns. 'Why do you harangue my men?'

'I am a speaker of truth,' replied the friar defiantly, coming down the steps to confront Jacques. The crowd was stirring with excitement, expecting some drama. 'Every day I come here, telling the people of this city what they need to know.'

'And what is that?'

'That in the final hour, you and your men abandoned the Holy Land.' The friar turned to his audience, his voice rising. 'For two hundred years the mighty Temple has taken not only the money of kings and princes, but also alms from generous, good people such as yourselves, proclaiming it is protecting Christian pilgrims in the East. But these men abandoned those same pilgrims to butchery at the hands of the Saracens, concerned with saving their own lives, their own riches.' He looked back at Jacques. 'Maybe once the Temple did good works, maybe once it served Christendom, but pride and greed and arrogance are your masters now. Your wealth is poured into comfortable lodgings, fine clothing, meat and wine for your tables. Your vows of poverty mean nothing, for even if men are made to give up everything they own to join your Order, they enter lives of luxury.'

Some of the knights started forward, their faces darkening with anger.

'You are a spreader of vicious rumour,' said Jacques. 'That is all. Thousands of knights from this Order lost their lives in the defence of the Holy Land.'

Will, watching the Grand Master address the friar, was struck by an image. He saw himself standing on a platform in a church beside another Grand Master, who was trying to convince a belligerent throng to agree to a peace with the Muslims. The people of Acre hadn't listened; had called that man a traitor, then paid the price in the massacre that followed.

'We could no more hope to hold back the Saracens than we could hope to stop the tide coming in,' continued Jacques, turning his forceful gaze on the crowd. 'When the walls of Acre were breached we gave sanctuary to thousands of Christians, conveying as many as we could to Cyprus and safety.' His voice thickened. 'Our last ship set sail shortly before the Temple fell with more than one hundred refugees, leaving many of our men to death.'

In his mind, Will saw the Mamluk army pouring in over Acre's broken walls. Above the seething mass of men, the sky was black with smoke and the air thick with arrows. Around him his comrades screamed, cut down in the rubble and corpse-strewn street, flesh and hair burning as pots of naphtha exploded. There was chaos and slaughter, and there was fire. Will closed his eyes. Terrible fire.

'Are these the actions of arrogant men? Of cowards?' When no one spoke, Jacques roared at them. '*Are they?*' People began to move away, unable to face the Grand Master's steel gaze. Jacques turned on the friar. 'If I hear your lies spoken again, I'll have you whipped through these streets. My men have been protecting the dream of Christians for decades, fighting and dying for God and for you. You will show them the respect they deserve.'

He began to walk away, but the friar was roused and came after him, pushing through the dispersing crowd. 'If you had done more Acre would not have fallen. While the Saracens were busy gathering an army, you were fighting among yourselves. It is well known your hostilities with the Knights of St John divided and weakened our forces.'

Will's eyes opened as the friar's abrasive voice grated in his ears. Jacques was walking away, but the Franciscan was following, not heeding the warning in the grim faces of the knights.

'You should answer for all those dead children, those murdered women. You should be ashamed! You left them without protection when you should have laid down your lives for them. You call yourselves warriors of Christ? I say Christ will damn you!'

In an instant, Will was rushing at the friar. All he could see was the man's wide mouth, a dark hole opening and closing, emitting that high,

rasping voice. All he could think of was silencing it. 'Were you there?' he
yelled, grabbing hold of the Franciscan's robe. Behind him someone was
shouting, but he was deaf to anything except the friar's cries of protest.
'*Were you there?*' When there was no coherent answer, Will balled his hand
into a fist and slammed it into the man's face. The crunch and the pain in his
knuckles were satisfying, as was the blood that spurted from the friar's
mouth as his head was knocked sideways, a yellowed tooth ripping loose
with the impact. Will drew back for another strike, but felt himself seized.
Someone was hauling him away. Someone else was prising his fingers from
the friar's tunic.

'*Enough!*'

Jacques's voice blasted through Will's fury. He let go of the friar, who
staggered back clutching his bloodied jaw.

Jacques was glaring at him. 'Control yourself, Commander. We do not
brawl in the street like common thugs, no matter the provocation.'

'I am sorry, my lord,' murmured Will, breathing hard. Wiping his
mouth, he found his beard wet with spittle.

'You will do penance for this.'

'Yes, my lord.'

Leaving the friar hunkered in the mud, the company continued in a tense
silence to Temple Gate, where the city guards barred anyone else from
entering or leaving as the knights, who had right of way, passed through in a
sombre white column. Will rested his bruised hand on the pommel of his
falchion, ignoring Robert's glances and feeling his knuckles begin to throb. He
concentrated on the discomfort as they headed over the fosse on to a road that
led past grand manors, a lazar hospital and several inns. The Paris walls had
been built over a century ago, but barely decades later the city had expanded
beyond its ring of stone, with abbeys, houses and vineyards springing up to
become congested suburbs. Further out, wooded hamlets and villages were
surrounded by cornfields. Beyond the stately towers of the Cluniac priory of
Saint-Martin-des-Champs an even larger set of buildings, encircled by a lofty
wall, rose out of the brown expanse of winter fields.

The Temple enclosure greeted Will like an old friend, long-lost, but not
forgotten. Since leaving Acre, he hadn't stayed in any one town long
enough to feel at home. Here in these damp fields, worlds apart from the
dry plains of Palestine, he was surprised by the sense of homecoming that
assailed him, filtering through less welcome memories. He thought about
the other places he had lived in: London and the estate outside Edinburgh
and, for the first time in years, found himself wanting to see them.

The tallest structure within the walls was the great donjon, its turrets stark against the white sky, a piebald banner fluttering from the centre spire. Crowded around it were a dozen or more buildings, the different heights and angles of rooftops making a jagged silhouette. As the knights approached the gatehouse, the sergeants on guard stood to attention. Their eyes transfixed with respectful wonder on the immense figure of Jacques de Molay, they pushed against the gates which creaked open on to a courtyard shadowed by the guardhouse tower. As a sergeant sprinted across the yard to announce the Grand Master's arrival, Will entered, engulfed by memories.

He knew this place so well; every building, every outhouse. He knew the pungent smell of the stables and the overwhelming heat of the kitchens, frenetic with servants. He knew the comforting, yeasty warmth of the bakehouse, the cloying perfume of apples fermenting in the storehouses and the chill of the chapel at dawn, filled with the prayers of five hundred men. He knew the bright pain of drinking water straight from the well, how the ponds near the servants' quarters boiled with fish at feeding time, knew the deafening hammering in the armoury and the bone-jarring hardness of the frost-bitten training field during a frozen November drill. He had come here a rudderless, stubborn sergeant of thirteen, having witnessed the murder of his knight-master. It was here that he had buried Owein, here that he had met Everard, here where so many things had begun. He wanted to race back through time, back through the halls and passages echoing with the sound of boys' laughter and running feet. He wanted to find that troubled boy and tell him not to leave, not to follow Everard's orders. Not to go to the East. Because then he wouldn't be standing here, a man bereft, ghost-walking through his own life, a trail of death and deception behind him.

The company spilled into the courtyard, overlooked by the grandest buildings in the enclosure: the donjon and treasury, the quarters of the officials, the Great Hall and the Chapter House. Servants stopped to stare as Jacques strode in among the men. Somewhere a bell began to clang. Some moments later, the doors of the officials' building swung open and a host of men appeared. At their head was a short, thickset man with oily hair swept austerely back from his face, accentuating a snout-like nose that jutted over thin lips framed by a wiry moustache and beard. Will was drawn out of his thoughts by the transformation in his old comrade. He had last seen Hugues de Pairaud in Acre over ten years ago when they were both in their late thirties. Age had since crept up on the Visitor of the Order, tracing lines of grey through his black hair, loosening the skin of his face, softening the muscles of his heavy frame into a paunch that strained against his surcoat.

Hugues caught Will's eye and gave a reserved nod, then turned his attention to the Grand Master. 'My lord,' he said, bowing. 'It is an honour.'

Jacques nodded impatiently. 'You received my message?'

'Two months ago. We have been awaiting your presence with anticipation. I sent word of your coming to our preceptories throughout the kingdom and to England.'

'It is good to know someone is pleased to see us at least.' When Hugues frowned, Jacques told him of the Franciscan.

'We know of this troublemaker. We have tried to move him on before.'

'Tried? He should have been arrested if he disobeyed your order. There was a time when it was a public offence to insult us. Have things changed so much that a man can stand on a street corner and defame us for all to hear?'

One of the Templar officials beside Hugues answered. 'We did not want to give his sermonising credence by making a fuss. We believed, were we to arrest him, that it might make others think his words held some truth.'

'I can assure you, my lord,' said Hugues, as the Grand Master's eyes narrowed at the official, 'this preacher will be dealt with, if that is your command.'

'My concern is not the man himself, but the attention he seemed to be enjoying. Do the people truly blame us for the loss of the Holy Land?'

'Only a discontented minority,' said Hugues after a considered pause. 'And it is not just us, many others have been blamed: the Hospitallers, the Teutonics' – he laughed disparagingly – 'even the Franciscans for not praying hard enough. When news of the fall of Acre first reached us you have to know there was widespread panic. People thought God had abandoned us. Some even converted to Islam, fled to Granada, others looked for some reason this catastrophe had befallen Christendom and sought who was responsible. But this atmosphere of blame has receded.' Hugues looked as though he had finished, but then continued. 'There have been more immediate concerns in the abdication of Pope Celestine and, of course, the war.'

Jacques breathed sharply through his nostrils. 'Indeed. You mentioned this in the last message I received on Cyprus, but it was difficult to obtain adequate information after we left for Rome. I would welcome a full report.'

'Certainly, my lord. But shall we retire to more comfortable quarters? I will have the servants prepare your private chambers, but until they are ready we may use my solar.'

'My officers will join us. It will save either of us from repeating ourselves. Have the rest of the men shown to lodgings.'

Hugues nodded to two of the knights beside him, who ushered the group of weary men across the courtyard.

Jacques gestured to the six officials gathered around him. 'And you, Campbell,' he said, looking over at Will. 'I'll need a commander to relay any information necessary to the others.'

Leaving Robert to join the knights and Simon to head off with the sergeants, leading the horses that had travelled with them on the ship, Will fell into step behind the officials.

'It was a sore blow indeed when we received word of the passing of Grand Master Gaudin so shortly after his election,' Hugues was saying, 'and that tragedy coming so soon after Guillaume de Beaujeu's death at Acre. But we all rejoiced, my lord,' he added swiftly, 'in your rapid promotion.'

Jacques glanced at him. 'I will be the first to admit my election to this office was a surprise, Visitor de Pairaud. I am a military commander, not a diplomat, as some of my recent predecessors have been.'

'Well, you have certainly had a longer service in the Order than most. You were, I believe, initiated by my uncle, Humbert, when he was Master of England?'

'I was.'

When Jacques didn't elaborate, Hugues changed the subject. 'Your journey from Italy was without incident?'

'Yes. We sailed from Genoa to Montpellier as recommended, although I dearly wished to visit our preceptory at Collioure.'

'It is for the best that you took the eastern route. Since the English forces took possession of Bayonne and Blaye, the royal troops stationed in Guienne under Charles de Valois have become more heavy-handed. There have been reports of increasing violence, especially against inhabitants in and around Gascony. It is rumoured King Philippe has ordered the seizure of property belonging to any nobles connected with the King of England, but since most of the nobility paid homage to Lord Edward when he controlled the duchy this means almost every landed man south of the Garonne River is being arrested.'

Jacques ducked his head as Hugues motioned him through the doors of the officials' building. 'As I am aware this whole situation began with the sinking of a few merchant ships. Surely it could have been resolved?'

'It is unfortunately more complicated than that, my lord,' responded Hugues, leading the way up a flight of polished wooden stairs to a passage lit by torches. Knights and clerks were working up here, all of whom moved to one side to allow the Grand Master and his entourage to pass. Their gazes lingered on Jacques as he swept by, the gold stitching bordering the red cross on his mantle seeming to glow in the torchlight. 'It is over thirty years since King Louis signed the Treaty of Paris with Henry III of England, promising to cede Guienne to him and his heirs. In the south of the duchy lies Gascony, one of the wealthiest regions in France. Our king does not like to share power and to have another monarch ruling a part of his kingdom, especially such a rich area, has been an uncomfortable cross to bear. Edward may only be a vassal, but he wields a formidable might. King Philippe has been reluctant even to acknowledge the Treaty of Paris, employing every method, legal and otherwise, to keep Edward from gaining full control.' Hugues pushed open a set of double doors and entered a large chamber. A table piled with scrolls and charts stood near the window, with a high-backed chair behind. The Temple's banner hung over a hearth, but other than the desk and an enormous armoire pushed up against one wall, the chamber was virtually empty.

Jacques gave the room a cursory inspection and, seemingly satisfied by its austerity, turned back to Hugues. 'You speak as though the war is all Philippe's doing, Pairaud, yet I heard it was English vessels that attacked French merchants and sank their ships.'

A flicker of annoyance passed across Hugues's face at the bluntness of Jacques's address. 'It was and, as you say, that attack should have been settled with the usual reparations. Philippe, however, used it as an excuse to take control of the duchy.'

Will moved closer to the hearth, listening intently, one name in their conversation drawing all his attention.

'Early last year,' Hugues continued, 'Philippe ordered King Edward to come to Paris to answer for the attack. Edward sent his brother, who eventually agreed to the temporary surrender of several towns and the proposition that a small number of French troops would be posted in Bordeaux. As a gesture of peace, Philippe offered Edward the hand of his sister in marriage and promised to continue to cede the duchy if Edward consented to these terms. Edward did and the towns were surrendered, but Philippe's suggestion of a small number of troops was vastly understated. He poured an army into Guienne and, when Edward protested, he confiscated the duchy.'

'So Edward declared war.'

'It was the only thing he could do to regain his French territories.'
Jacques moved to the window.

'And how goes the war?' one of the officials asked Hugues in the silence.

'The two sides are in stalemate. The English have recaptured several
towns, but Bordeaux and the outlying areas of Guienne remain in French
hands. There has been little movement from either camp for some time,
although the arrests of the local nobility by royal troops are a recent
development.' Hugues looked at Jacques, who was staring out over the
enclosure's walls, where wisps of fog drifted across the fields. The cawing
of crows formed a harsh chorus in the trees outside. 'But these are matters
that can be discussed in greater detail when you are rested. I am eager to
know your news, my lord. You were in Rome for the inauguration of the
new pontiff?'

Jacques turned. 'Pope Boniface will be a staunch leader in these troubled
times, I feel.'

'And your mission to gain support for the Order in the West? It has gone
well?'

Will detected a note of wariness in the Visitor's tone.

'There has been interest in my proposals. Indeed, I believe this is why the
council of thirteen chose to elect me on Gaudin's death. It is not diplomacy
we need now. It is strength. In order to return to the Holy Land and
reclaim our territory from the Mamluks we must concentrate our efforts on
bolstering military and financial support from our leaders here. Without
that support any new Crusade will fail. We must act in one unified
movement. To this end, I am beseeching the kings of the West to join me in
raising men and arms for the continuation of our struggle.' Jacques drew his
massive frame upright. 'Then let the people of these kingdoms see that the
Knights of the Temple of Solomon have lost neither their nerve nor their
purpose. I intend to seek the aid of Philippe and Edward. I take it, despite
the troubles, that a meeting with both can be arranged?'

Hugues's expression was unreadable. He paused, seeming reluctant to
answer. 'As it happens, you will be able to speak to Edward shortly.'

'He is coming here?'

Will's heart thudded faster in anticipation of Hugues's answer.

'No, my lord, but it would seem he too received word of your planned
visit to Paris, for last month a royal summons was delivered, asking that
upon your arrival you travel to England to attend a meeting at the London
Temple.'

'A meeting? About what?'

'We do not know, my lord. The message simply said a discussion was needed on a matter of urgency and that the meeting would be attended by a representative of the pope and by King Edward himself.'

One of the officials spoke up, asking if Hugues had any speculations as to the nature of the unusual summons. Engrossed in conversation, no one noticed Will's hand falling to his side to curl around the hilt of his falchion, the skin stretching taut over his bruised knuckles.

3
The Jewish Quarter, Paris
21 December 1295 AD

W ill made his way through the labyrinthine alleys of the Ville to a crowded quarter packed close to the walls on the east side of the city. It was early morning and the strip of sky above the street was a startling shade of blue. His breath pluming before him as he walked, he paused now and again to check the crumpled parchment, then scanned the buildings. Finally, after several wrong turns, he found it. The house, which was painted a burned orange, was nestled between two booksellers. As he approached, he saw that the door was ajar. Faint voices could be heard inside. Will was wondering whether to knock or to head straight through, when two dark-haired children, a boy and a girl, came racing out. He stepped back as they barrelled past, the girl shouting victoriously as she hoisted a leather ball out of the boy's reach. Will called to them. 'Is this the rabbi's house?'

The girl glanced at him. 'Yes. Too slow!' she crowed, dancing away as the boy grasped for the ball.

Leaving them to their game, Will entered.

The warm colour of the house's exterior was continued inside. A dark red rug lined the hallway and vivid tapestries decorated the walls. Faint smells of incense and spices lingered in the air and, for a moment, if not for the bitter chill outside and the dusting of frost on his boots, he could have been back in Acre. A few openings led into shadowy rooms, but light and the voices were coming through a door at the end of the passage.

Beyond, in a small kitchen, three men were in animated discussion. The room was hot, a well-stacked fire roaring in the hearth. Two of the men were red-faced and sweaty. They were so intent in their debate that it was a few moments before the third figure, seated at a table near the fire, noticed Will standing in the doorway.

'Quiet,' he said in a whispery, ancient voice that although insubstantial as smoke was enough to silence the two younger men immediately. He rose slowly from his stool. His hair was white and his face as brown and wrinkled as a dried fig. 'William.' A smile lit up his watery eyes.

'Rabbi Elias,' said one of the men, looking from the old man to Will, whom he eyed with suspicion. 'This matter isn't resolved.'

'It would be if you would admit you are wrong,' countered the other man.

'Enough, Isaac,' said Elias forcefully. 'Come back tomorrow when your tempers have cooled.' He frowned as a crash and a shout echoed in the hallway. 'And please remove your children before they bring down my entire house.'

Both men inclined their heads grudgingly, though respectfully. As they passed, Will saw that each had a wheel shape cut from garish red cloth pinned to the back of his tunic, the mark King Louis IX had decreed all Jews wear to distinguish them from the rest of the population.

'There is always something to put right in this world, isn't there?' Elias crossed to him. 'I heard your new Grand Master was making his progress through Christendom. I was hoping you would be with him.'

As they embraced, Will felt little more than bone beneath the old man's robe. 'You look tired, Elias,' he said, switching into Arabic. The chanting words were strange yet pleasant in his mouth, like a food he used to enjoy but hadn't tasted in a long time.

'Not tired, busy. This place is more crowded than the synagogue some days.' Elias chuckled. 'I cannot complain. When I left Cyprus I had little more than the cloth on my back. I came to this city with nothing and so I am happy to repay, in any way I can, the generosity of friends and neighbours. I have a decent life, helping to train the younger men in the synagogue. But how are you?' The creases in his forehead deepened. 'You look troubled.'

'It is just strange to be back.' Will took off the plain woollen cloak he wore over his surcoat and sat as Elias gestured to an empty stool. 'What about bookselling?'

'I shut myself away too long in Acre, got too comfortable in my little shop.' Elias returned to his place by the fire. 'I lost sight of my duties. It is my task . . . No, my *wish*, to be with my people, teaching them, watching them grow.' He raised a wry eyebrow. 'Mediating in their disputes.' He peered at the passage, hearing the front door shut. 'I don't suppose you even recognised Isaac.'

'Should I?'

'He was one of the men you saved on the harbour at Acre, along with his wife and daughter; the one outside, terrorising my neighbourhood.' Elias sobered. 'You saved a lot of people that day, William. I hope you realise that.'

'I cannot recall it. Any of it.'

Elias frowned as he looked away. 'You don't remember? The battle? Our escape?'

'No,' said Will, forcing himself to meet Elias's gaze. It sounded true when he said it. He didn't understand why Elias was looking at him with that disbelieving expression. It was something he had heard other men say, many others. They spoke, puzzled, of how hours, whole days even of the siege of Acre and the final battle were missing from their minds. Will envied them. For more than four years, those last days had been at the forefront of his thoughts. He could remember every hour, every second with a clarity that was devastating. He was standing on the crumbled eastern mole of the outer harbour, the dark, hungry sea churning beside him. Behind him, the city was in flames. His sword was in his hands, wet and red. A body tumbled away from him into the water and was swallowed.

'William?'

Will looked up. Elias was standing by the hearth where an iron pot hung.

'I asked if you wanted something to drink?'

Will shook his head distractedly. 'I cannot linger. I just wanted to let you know I was in the city.'

Elias unhooked the pot, clamping a rag over the handle, and poured a steaming liquid that smelled of cinnamon and cloves into a bowl. 'Are you planning to stay?' he asked, sitting with a wince.

'That depends on the Grand Master.'

Elias nursed his drink thoughtfully. 'I suppose as your Visitor is one of the Brethren it will not matter where you are. You will have someone looking after your interests here in the West.' When Will said nothing, Elias leaned forward. 'And what of this talk I hear about your Grand Master preparing for another Crusade?'

'It is why he has come: to gather support.'

'What do you plan to do about it?'

'Do?'

'Yes, William,' said Elias sternly, 'as head of the Anima Templi what are you going to do to stop this?' He sighed heavily. 'Admittedly, expulsion from Acre at the hands of the Mamluks wasn't what we wanted. None of us who wished for the years of war to end sought such a bloody, tragic finish to two centuries of conflict between East and West. But you cannot deny the fact that now the Christian forces have been compelled to withdraw from the Holy Land you have a chance to continue the Brethren's work unhindered. Do you not feel the Anima Templi could establish a far stronger relationship with the Muslims than they could have while the Western armies were camped out in Palestine?' Elias's eyes were intense. 'Could the Brethren now be in the best position to establish that hoped-for reconciliation between the three great faiths of the world? Shared knowledge to enlighten us, trade to enrich us, peace to fulfil us? Everard taught us that Muslims, Christians and Jews are all children of one God, even though we give Him different names. In hurting our brothers, he always said, we hurt ourselves.' Elias didn't wait for an answer. 'I imagine the dust has settled enough for an envoy to be sent to the Mamluk sultan. You should open a dialogue at least.' He shook his head. 'Of course, if your Grand Master has his way we will be plunged right back into war. You have to stop this from happening.'

'The Temple alone doesn't have the men or resources to mount an effective campaign in the East,' said Will flatly, unmoved by Elias's impassioned speech. How many times had he heard Everard say those things? They now seemed like an old man's foolish dreams, burned up in the fires and chaos of Acre's fall. It was over one hundred years since the Anima Templi had been created by a former Grand Master of the Temple, but although the Brethren had been instrumental in averting many conflicts in that time, working in secret behind thrones and battle lines, they had never managed to stop the ongoing war between Christians and Muslims. 'From what I've heard, the leaders of the West are too involved in their own disputes to give Jacques what he wants.'

'Then what are your plans for the Anima Templi? Do you agree with me – should an envoy be sent East?'

'In truth, Elias, I haven't had much time to think about it.' Will made a fist on the table. 'I've had other things on my mind.' He saw a face, poised and cold, flint-grey eyes mocking him. In the past two days, since the meeting at the Temple, King Edward had been occupying all his thoughts. His face, his name, were dark clouds building inside him, obscuring everything else.

Elias's eyes narrowed. 'I would have thought time was the one thing you have had. But too much of something can be bad, can it not?' he murmured, half to himself.

'What can I do?' demanded Will. 'More than half the Brethren were killed at Acre and the handful of us left have been scattered across the West. The Temple has had three Grand Masters in the space of four years, all of whom have pulled the Order in different directions, the current one being so bent on a Crusade he has travelled the length and breadth of Christendom looking for anyone who will help him start one. How can the Anima Templi continue in this way? We have no base in the East, we lost all contact with the Muslims when Kalawun died. It is over.'

'If the Temple exists then so does its Soul. How Everard must be writhing in his grave to hear his successor speak in this way! How can the work be over when East and West still glare at one another, waiting for the moment to strike back, avenge their dead, spread their messages of destruction and hatred?' Elias threw a hand towards the door. 'Tell me how it is over when my own people have to wear that badge like a brand upon their backs? If the Anima Templi was formed to bring about reconciliation between our faiths, why do these things still happen?' His voice quietened. 'It was a heavy burden Everard placed upon you and one that has only increased in the years since his death. But it is essential, as leader of the Brethren, that you now continue the work he and others before him started. Our people must find new ways of living together in this changing world. Peace between nations is as important as peace between faiths and that is something we need here and now with France and England at war, and Scotland poised to join the conflict.'

Will looked up sharply. 'Scotland?'

Elias nodded. 'A delegation from Edinburgh has been in Paris in talks with King Philippe. It is said the two kingdoms will join sides against England. Your work is far from over. Indeed, I would say it is only beginning.' He sat back with a long exhalation and finished off his drink. 'But you have just arrived. You must settle in, come to see how the land lies yourself. I can help you with that. Anything you want, as ever, you need only ask.' Elias seemed to relax. 'And how is Rose?'

Will scratched at a mark on the table, preoccupied by the news of his homeland's involvement in the conflict. There was so much he didn't understand about what had been happening here. All he knew were fragments; scraps of news that filtered through to them back in Acre and conflicting and incomplete information received on the road. He realised how foolish it was now, but he had imagined everything would have remained much the same in his absence. Out in the deserts of Palestine and Syria, rocked by war and political convulsions, the thought that he could one day return to solid ground had kept him strong for years. It was disconcerting to find it wasn't so solid after all. He realised Elias was waiting for a response. 'I haven't seen Rose yet. I was planning to go to her after I visited you.'

'Then I will not keep you from that reunion.' Elias got to his feet. He held out his hand. As Will took it, Elias placed his other hand firmly over Will's. 'Do not forget the things that are important to you, William. Do not forget who you are, what you are capable of.'

The Royal Palace, Paris, 21 December 1295 AD

The grass in the royal gardens was brittle with frost. It crunched under Guillaume de Nogaret's riding boots as he crossed the lawns, past fruit trees and clipped yew hedges. Two men were sweeping dead leaves from the pathways. They stopped to let him pass as he headed for an arched opening in a high wall. Moving through, he entered a quadrangle, which formed the end of the palace complex at the very tip of the Ile de la Cité. Several buildings bordered the yard, but most of the space was taken up by a row of wooden huts, fashioned to look like miniature houses, with painted shutters fixed to the front of each. A fence ran around them forming a pen and outside each hut was a perch, occupied by a bird.

Dozens of tiny, glinting eyes followed him as he passed down their line. There were goshawks and sparrow-hawks on bow-shaped perches, merlins, a hobby and a pair of lanners. The huts became more ornate as he reached the gyrfalcons. There were twelve in total, perched on wooden blocks padded with linen. One, her speckled feathers brilliant white in the sunlight, bated suddenly, darting towards him, the silver bells attached to her legs chiming madly. Nogaret stepped back. She strained at her leash, wings beating the air, then settled back gracefully on to her perch, talons sinking into the linen. As he moved on, the gyr gave a shriek that sounded like scornful laughter. Nogaret picked up his pace, his gaze on a group of men ahead. A young man with light brown hair, who stood head and shoulders above the others, turned at his approach. On his wrist, poised on a leather glove, was a peregrine, her powdery grey wings folded back behind her. As Nogaret halted and bowed, two pairs of eyes, one black and ringed with gold above a steel-sharp beak, the other ice blue, set wide and deep in a striking face, fixed on him.

'What has taken you so long?'

'I apologise, my lord, the roads were treacherous with snow.'

King Philippe paused, as if considering the worthiness of the excuse. The other men had fallen silent. One, dressed in the same well-tailored black robe Nogaret himself wore under his travelling cloak, regarded him cagily, lips pursed. Ignoring the disapproving stare of Pierre Flote, king's chancellor and Keeper of the Seals, Nogaret waited.

After a moment, Philippe smiled slightly and the tension dispersed. 'Maiden broke a feather, but it has been mended perfectly.' He raised his fist, causing the peregrine to cry and unfurl her wings in expectation of flight. 'You can scarcely see the join where the new feather was imped. Come now, Nogaret, you'll have to get closer than that. She won't bite. Will she, Flote?' Philippe laughed and the chancellor joined in.

Nogaret tried not to scowl. He still had the scar on his neck where Maiden had plunged that razor beak into his flesh. Philippe had given her a treat, pleased with her fierceness.

'Sir Henri has outdone himself,' said the king, glancing at the man next to him, who wore a spray of dove feathers in his cap.

Sir Henri, the Master Falconer, smiled. 'We'll fly her well this week, my lord, get her strength up.'

'I want her ready for the hunt after the Christ Mass,' said Philippe briskly, passing the bird to Henri, who lifted her expertly on to his glove, grasping the jesses. Sliding off his gauntlet and passing it to one of the squires, Philippe gestured to Nogaret and Flote. 'Come, both of you, we will talk in my chambers.'

The king led the way out of the enclosure and back through the gardens. The walkways through the lawns were narrow, with room for only two abreast. To Flote's visible irritation, Nogaret manoeuvred himself so he could walk at Philippe's side. 'Your brother sends his regards from Bordeaux, my lord. He will shortly be delivering the funds we have secured thus far.'

'How has our plan worked?' enquired Philippe, his long-legged stride causing Nogaret, who was several inches shorter, to quicken his footsteps. 'How much have we acquired through the arrests?'

'By our estimates, enough to keep soldiers in Guienne until late spring next year.'

Philippe halted abruptly and faced him. 'That is all?'

'Much of the wealth in the region is bound up in the estates themselves: properties, vineyards, townships. Monies from these fixed assets will obviously take us longer to garner.'

Philippe set off again. 'I was hoping for better news from you, Nogaret. I need more than this if I am to dislodge that contumacious old crow from my kingdom. There have been significant problems with the building of the fleet. The shipwrights are asking for more funds to complete their work.' As Nogaret started to speak, Philippe raised a hand. 'No, I need to think.' He scowled as he climbed the steps to the royal apartments. The guards at the top pushed open the doors to let him through. 'This is not what I wanted to hear.'

'We could cut back in other areas, my lord,' suggested Flote, moving in to walk at Philippe's left as they marched down a wide passage.

'Are you offering up your own salary?' asked Philippe sourly, heading up the winding flight of stairs that led to his private solar.

'We need to think of ways in which to replenish the royal coffers, not how to limit or, worse, damage the good works we have already started,' said Nogaret, with a glance at Flote. 'Expansion cannot continue without adequate funds and without expansion, without a forceful exertion of royal power in this kingdom, our lord will be as impeded by wilful vassals, bishops and princes as his predecessors before him.' As they reached Philippe's solar, Nogaret went forward to open the doors.

Philippe was nodding as he entered the sunlit chamber. 'Nogaret is right. Expansion is paramount. Under my father the Capetian dynasty lost its potency. In order to regain the authority wielded by my grandfather, I must continue to exert myself.'

'With all due respect, my lord,' said Flote, 'King Louis didn't attain his authority through the purchase of townships and bishoprics. It was through Crusading that he earned his people's respect.'

Nogaret smiled inwardly as Philippe turned to stare at the older minister.

'People say lawyers talk too much. Be careful, Flote, that you do not prove them right, or it will not be your salary that is cut.'

'I am sorry, my lord. I meant no offence.'

Passing a desk that was carefully arranged with parchments, quills and ink pots, none of which looked used, Philippe shrugged off his winter cloak, edged with cloud-soft ermine, and handed it to Flote. Sitting back on a couch that overlooked the gardens, he crossed his long legs. 'While I wish to discuss the matter of Bordeaux further, I have received some disturbing news that requires my immediate attention.' Philippe's blue eyes fixed on Nogaret. 'The Grand Master of the Temple arrived in the city two days ago. Shortly before this, we discovered he has been requested to attend a meeting at the London preceptory with King Edward and a representative of Pope Boniface, a man named Bertrand de Got.'

'The bishop?'

'You know him?'

'In a manner of speaking. I met him in Bordeaux.' Nogaret told the king how the bishop had interfered with one of the arrests. 'He could make things difficult for us, especially if he elicits the support of the archbishop, as he threatened.'

'Bertrand doesn't worry me. I've had dealings with him before. All that interests him is filling Church offices with members of his family. The man is an avaricious little leech who has spent most of the past year since his appointment trying to worm his way into the pope's favour. I doubt he will cause us any real trouble, but if needs be, a well-placed bishopric for one of his nephews will keep him pliant. No, it is the reason for this meeting that concerns me. I fear Edward may try to use the Templars against me.'

Nogaret's brow furrowed. 'I do not see how. Edward cannot command them. The Temple answers only to the pope.'

'Exactly,' said Philippe, rising suddenly. 'Which is surely why Bertrand de Got, as Boniface's representative, will be in attendance? My forces can hold against the English at present, but against the full might of the Temple?' He shook his head grimly.

'Even if the English Templars joined forces with Edward, the French would not, neither would those in the Maritime States, or Germany, or Portugal. They rely on kings and princes across the West for donations and privileges. They wouldn't want to jeopardise that.'

'I have to agree with Nogaret,' interjected Flote.

'What purpose do the knights have now the Crusades have ended?' demanded Philippe. 'What are they if not an army looking for a war? As a unified force they could take Guienne in a matter of weeks.'

'They aren't a unified force,' responded Flote. 'Half their Order is camped out on Cyprus, the other half dispersed throughout Christendom. Since the fall of Acre, they have spent most of their energy increasing their monopoly over the wool trade and from what we know, Jacques de Molay has come seeking support for a Crusade, not to fight someone else's war.'

'Nonetheless, I would know for certain that I have nothing to be concerned about. Perhaps the Temple would not fight a war for Edward, but he might persuade them to support him financially. I know he is struggling to maintain a strong presence in Gascony and the revolt in Wales must have taxed him heavily.'

'And if they do support him?' ventured Nogaret.

'Then I will have to find the money for my fleet from somewhere. I may have to bring my plans for an invasion of England forward.' Philippe turned to Nogaret. 'You will go to London. I will arrange for you to leave as soon as possible in order that you are there ahead of Jacques de Molay. You will discover the purpose of the meeting.'

'Surely, my lord, one of our usual sources would be better equipped for such a task,' said Nogaret, affronted by the idea that he, king's lawyer and a former professor of one of the finest universities in France, would be trailing about London like some common sneak. He looked at Flote, wondering if he had suggested this. But the chancellor didn't meet his gaze.

'No,' said Philippe. 'I want this information quickly. When you arrive go directly to the royal palace at Westminster. Say you are there to visit my mother-in-law, that you have an urgent message from her daughter. This should allow you to avoid the formalities of an official visit, although I doubt anyone will know who you are and become suspicious in any case. Have her find out whatever she can.'

'With King Edward's brother leading the English in Bayonne that could be difficult. The queen mother may not know anything.'

'She is a woman in a royal court, Nogaret. Her husband will not be her only source of information, certainly.'

Before Nogaret could answer, there was a knock at the door. A clerk appeared. 'The Scottish envoys are preparing to leave, my lord.'

'I will be there shortly.'

'Scottish envoys?' questioned Nogaret, as the clerk closed the door.

'They arrived while you were away, seeking an alliance against Edward for his continuing interference in their realm. Two months ago I signed a treaty agreeing to aid them.'

'The Scots are a nation of barbarians,' said Nogaret derisively. 'Still living in mud-huts and warring with one another over who will be chief.'

'That they may be, but they are enemies of Edward and that makes them allies of mine. They will keep him occupied on the borders of his kingdom, while I continue to beat back his forces here. With his army divided in such a way, I expect he will not be able to hold out much longer in Gascony. Edward will almost certainly have learned of this alliance by now, which may be precisely why he has requested this meeting with the Templars, and which is why this matter now takes precedence over your task in Bordeaux.' Philippe drew a breath. 'Now leave me, both of you. I wish to change before bidding our barbarian friends farewell.'

When the ministers had gone, Philippe crossed the chamber to a full-length silver mirror. He removed the gold circlet from his head and placed it on the desk. Next, slowly, deliberately, he unfastened the belt embossed with silver that pulled in the wine-coloured robe at his waist. Drawing the folds of the robe over his muscled torso, he took it off and draped it on the arm of the couch. All the while, he kept his eyes on the dazzling surface of the mirror, watching himself with cool detachment, as if he were observing someone else. Beneath the robe, Philippe wore a hair shirt. The tight-fitting garment was fashioned from coarse goat hair and gave off a repugnant odour, which worsened when he sweated. He noticed the weave was looking a little flat and reminded himself to have his tailor make a new one. He wore it most days and the stiff hairs tended to lose some of their abrasiveness over time, smoothed by the movements of his body and the constant rubbing against his skin. As he unlaced the leather thongs, the garment loosened, coming away from his chest with a feeling of such intense relief that it took all his effort not to tear the thing away. Undoing the rest of the ties, he removed the hair shirt and laid it carefully beside his robe. In the mirror, Philippe examined the results of the day's penance. His skin was irritated a feverish red. As he turned to one side, a fresh line of welts showed where he had been bitten by the lice that tended to breed in the garment. On his back, scars made patterns of his skin. Some were old and silvery white, others were newer, scabbing wherever the flagellum had drawn blood. The mortifications were vivid in the daylight, running down to disappear beneath the line of his hose and up as far as his shoulder blades. There they stopped. From the neck up, Philippe's skin was pale and smooth, all the way to his unblemished face. The contrast was startling. It was as if the face and the body belonged to two different people.

For a moment, he allowed himself to stand bare-chested in the window, the cold air numbing his flesh. His gaze wandered over the gardens, where men were working. It gave him a sense of satisfaction, watching them. Ascending the throne at seventeen, Philippe had worried that the household staff wouldn't obey him as readily as they had his father or stalwart grandfather and even though he had been king for ten years he still sometimes wondered if they respected him enough. It was one of the reasons he had surrounded himself with ministers like Nogaret, men nearer his own age. With them, he felt superior.

Movement directly below caught his eye. A woman was heading through the yard, towards the servants' gate in the palace wall. She was walking quickly, her skirts bunched in one hand to keep them from trailing. Something about the way she kept looking back over her shoulder focused his attention. As Philippe watched, intrigued, the woman slipped through the gate and was gone. She vanished for a minute, hidden by the high outer wall, then reappeared on the riverbank beyond. She had removed her coif and her tawny hair hung loose around her shoulders. Philippe frowned as he saw a man waiting on the narrow bank that tumbled down to the water. The man approached the serving girl and they embraced. As she pulled away, glancing back at the palace, Philippe's keen eyes picked out the features of her face. Turning from the window, he locked them in his mind. He would speak to the steward, have the woman expelled for improper behaviour. A servant who flouted the rules was an infection, sowing seeds of disobedience throughout the household. It was something his father had told him. Philippe hadn't taken much of what his father, a weak, directionless man, had said to heart, but that piece of advice had stuck in his mind. The royal household was an extension of himself. Whatever his staff did reflected on him and he would allow no one to tarnish his reputation. He was the grandson of Louis IX. His subjects would know only his greatness. Going to the couch, Philippe picked up the hair shirt. He drew it back on, ignoring the stinging discomfort as he pulled the thongs tight.

The Banks of the Seine, Paris, 21 December 1295 AD

Over an hour had passed since he had crossed the Grand Pont on to the banks of the Ile and Will was beginning to wonder if the servant had delivered the message. The palace walls loomed over him, sheer and impassive. Dramatic changes had occurred within them. There were two new towers a short distance up river from the bridge, flanking an impressive gateway. Beyond the walls, along with the grey steeples of the royal apartments and administrative buildings that he recognised, a tight jumble of structures had sprung up, the sharp angles of rooftops carving the spaces between soaring turrets, adorned with colourful flags. On the far side of the complex rose the majestic Sainte-Chapelle. The chapel, built by Louis IX to enclose a fragment of Christ's crown of thorns, lent beauty to a place that, to Will, appeared more imposing and fortress-like than it ever had before.

He looked round, seeing a girl heading down the muddy banks towards him. Will's breath caught as she came closer and he saw his mistake, for she was no longer a girl, but a woman. The white tunic she wore over a linen gown was drawn in at her waist, accentuating her height and the slimness of her figure. Her gold hair whipped about her in the breeze coming off the water and she pushed it back in a swift, impatient movement. Her face was pallid and a little gaunt, prominent cheekbones emphasising a strong chin. The sight of that face hurt him; both in its strangeness and familiarity, it hurt him somewhere vital.

'Rose.'

She stopped short, but he went the rest of the way and drew her to him. Her hair was soft and smelled of wood-smoke. It was two years since he'd held her, but felt much longer.

'I was starting to wonder if you were coming.'

'I have duties,' she replied, pulling away with a glance at the palace.

Will drew in a slow breath. He shouldn't have expected her to come rushing to meet him; their parting had not been easy and in the time he'd spent on the road since he'd had no chance to contact her. 'How are you?' He tried to sound bright, but regretted the question immediately. It was so formal, so insipid.

Rose gave a tight shrug.

'Because Andreas assured me you would be given a good position here. In his letter he said he had written to the queen, asking if something suitable could be found for you.' Will stared at the muddy ground, unable to look at her rigid face. 'He promised me you would be taken care of, that he had the influence to make certain of this.'

'Then I suppose it must be fine,' she retorted.

The wind lifted her hair and she pushed it back again. As she did so, Will saw the scars on her hand, where she had been burned. Her skin was raw-looking and shrivelled. She caught him looking at it and folded her arms. 'I want to know that you're happy,' Will said, aware of how helpless he sounded.

She made a sharp, scornful noise. 'So you don't have to think about me any more.' Her dark blue eyes were cloudy with anger. 'So you don't have to feel guilty for sending me away.'

Her words stung him, filled with venom and truth. He put his hands on her shoulders. She had grown tall. How old was she now? Seventeen? No, she would have turned eighteen last month. 'I know these past few years must have been difficult for you, but . . .'

'Difficult? You have no idea! As soon as we landed on Cyprus you left me. I hardly saw you for months.'

'What else could I do?' said Will quietly. 'On the ship from Acre people just assumed you were another orphan rescued from the city, but when we reached Cyprus I had no choice but to leave you.' He stared out across the green Seine flowing silently beside them. 'I would have been expelled if the others had found out about you, if they knew I had a daughter. You know that.' He looked back at her. 'But I made sure you would be cared for.'

She scoffed again.

Will's expression hardened. 'I did the best I could. You had a good life with Elias.'

'Yes! And then you forced me to come to Paris!'

'Elias had told me he was planning to come here and Grand Master de Molay began preparing his progress through Christendom as soon as he was elected. I couldn't abandon you in Limassol knowing we would all be leaving. Paris offered you the best chance. I knew Andreas would be able to use his contacts with the royal family to help you find decent work.' Will shook his head. 'Other children who survived Acre weren't so fortunate, Rose. They lost both their parents and were forced to beg on the streets. Or worse.'

'I know how they feel. I lost my parents too.'

Will felt as though she'd just slapped him. He was silent, staring as she half turned away, unable to meet his gaze, her cheeks flushing pink. He tried not to say it, but couldn't help himself. 'What is that supposed to mean?'

'Nothing,' murmured Rose.

'I want to know what you meant by that.' He didn't. Yet, still, he asked the question again.

Rose turned on him. 'It means my parents died at Acre. Both of them!'

For a moment, Will saw someone else looking back at him out of those stormy sea eyes, mocking him, and right then he wanted to strike her. The wall inside him cracked apart and his hand squeezed into a fist, all his rage and pain and impotence flooding into it. He wanted to push it into her, into the woman in front of him who shouldn't even be a woman, who had grown up without him into this perfect picture of her mother; his hurt made manifest, standing here before him, reminding him of that great betrayal, those dark blue eyes not his, not her mother's, but someone else's. A name he couldn't even say.

As Rose began to walk away, Will took a step forward, reaching out as if to grasp her. Then he faltered, his hand falling, as the distance between them grew too great. He waited, but she didn't look back. Entering the servants' passage, she disappeared. Will lifted his head and stared into the sky, until the sunlight blinded him.

By the time he crossed the Grand Pont and made his way back up the rue du Temple, the sun spots in his vision had cleared and the familiar numbness was enclosing him once more. Having returned to the preceptory, he was making his way through the knights' quarters, when Hugues and Robert found him.

'We need to talk,' said the Visitor.

Robert noted the cloak bundled under Will's arm with a quizzical frown.

'Come,' said Hugues, not seeing Robert's look. He led the way to the officials' building and up to his room. 'We do not have long. It will soon be Nones and Jacques has arranged a special service to address the men.' He closed the door as they entered. 'This morning I received word from our brother in London. As soon as the summons for the Grand Master arrived, I had Thomas try to find out the purpose of it.' Hugues's mouth flattened in a line. 'It would appear the pope is proposing to merge together the Temple and the Hospital. The plan is to send both Orders back to the Holy Land as one united force on a Crusade we will fund together.'

Will's brow furrowed, but he shook his head. 'That will never happen.'

'You don't know that,' said Robert, a little sharply.

Will looked at him, then back at Hugues. 'Does Jacques know?'

'I told him this morning. I said I found out from the Master of England, which is partly true. Thomas intercepted a message from King Edward to the Master which spoke of the pope's intentions. Edward, it seems, was requested to attend, as a man of influence who has close relations with the Temple. Presumably the pope wants him to support this plan.'

'What was Jacques's reaction?'

'Jacques wants a Crusade, certainly, and is prepared to pay for it. I fear he would quite willingly bankrupt the Order for one. But he wants any move eastwards conducted under his own terms. He will not work with the Knights of St John and I do not blame him. From a military point of view it would be a disaster. Any possibility of harmony between our Orders ended years ago.'

Will knew Hugues was referring to the Temple's assault on the Knights of St John in Acre. The assault, which followed a dispute between opposing royal factions, had happened decades ago, but the Hospitallers had never forgiven them for it. In every disagreement between Western forces in the Holy Land since, they and the Templars had stood on opposite sides. The only time there was any unification was at the fall of Acre, when the two

Grand Masters rode out together to face the Mamluk hordes. But Will doubted, in this convoluted arena of Western politics, where battle lines weren't clear and alliances seemed built on sand, that any such event could unite them again. Too many in the Knights of St John remembered the stories of brothers begging to allow the sick and dying through the Temple's barricades in Acre and the Templars' jeers at their pleas. Conversely, the Templars maintained they had been in the right and the Hospitallers' quarrel with them was born less out of vengeance and more out of an ongoing attempt to undermine them in the hope of gaining control of Templar territories and assets. It was hardly, as Hugues said, grounds for a merging of the Orders.

'But if Pope Boniface commands it?' Robert asked the Visitor.

'Then we may have a struggle on our hands, though the fact he is sending a mere bishop as his representative tells me this isn't a particularly pressing matter for him at this juncture. Perhaps he simply wishes to gauge our response to such a proposition? From what you have told me, the pontiff didn't mention anything of this during your time in Rome.'

'No,' acceded Will, 'but that isn't surprising. Pope Boniface's election wasn't popular with everyone in the Sacred College and while we were there he was kept busy placating his rivals. Jacques was away for months, visiting the king in Naples and our preceptories in Venice and Genoa, so other than a few meetings in the spring, we hardly saw his holiness at all.'

'You said the summons came from Edward,' said Robert. 'So it can only be assumed he does support the pope? This is what we've been afraid of, ever since he started demanding money from Everard. The old man feared it would only be a matter of time before the king acted on his ambitions for the Holy Land and now, with the Grand Master bent on returning . . .' Robert hefted his shoulders. 'Though I cannot say I blame him. There are times I wish we could avenge what was done to us at Acre, times I feel so consumed by fury I cannot imagine how I ever saw any Muslim as a brother.' He looked at them. 'But the Crusades are over and despite what was lost that is a good thing. King Edward pledged himself to the cause of the Brethren. He should be with the Brethren in seeing the cessation of hostilities as an opportunity for continued peace between East and West, not planning to deliver us all back into war, even at the bidding of the pope.'

Will was quiet. His comrade had no idea of the lengths Edward would go to in securing what he wanted. Edward only cared for peace when it suited him. He made alliances and broke them with utter disregard for any who might be ruined by his actions and he did it all with a shrewdness and a ruthlessness that were staggering.

'You spoke of your concerns over Edward when you inducted me into the Brethren,' Hugues was saying. 'But Edward has made no move east in all the years since he signed a truce with the Muslims. How can you be so certain he is working against us? If there had been any doubt in Everard's mind over the king's intentions he never would have elected him as our Guardian. True, I never really knew the priest, but one thing was clear during the time I spent with our brothers in Acre: Everard believed in the Anima Templi above all else and would not have done anything to endanger it.'

'Everard made a mistake,' said Will in a low voice. 'We were almost destroyed with the theft of the Book of the Grail. He was eager to replenish our strength and he chose the wrong man. He regretted it until the day he died.'

'We don't know why Edward will be at the meeting,' continued Hugues. 'He had dealings with Bertrand de Got in Gascony. Perhaps he plans to be our advocate? If anyone could dissuade the pope and the bishop from this course of action it is him.'

Will's tone was steel. 'Edward is not our ally. He has betrayed us again and again.'

'How?' pressed Hugues. 'Other than some requests for funds that may well have been innocent appeals, what has he done? I have read Everard's writings that you sent to me before the fall of Acre. There was no reference to any betrayals, just Everard's fear, formed mostly through your own suspicions I might add, that the king wasn't seeking peace when he agreed to be our Guardian, but a source of revenue to fund a war in Wales. But even if that is true, the subjugation of Wales was a necessary venture. Just because a man believes in peace, does not mean he can maintain it in the face of rebels and warmongers.'

'And his aggressions on Scotland?' demanded Will. 'He has been seeking control of the kingdom for years and now he's crushed Wales there is nothing standing in his way.'

'Scotland was in chaos after the death of King Alexander, with the magnates all vying for the throne. Edward offered to help them.'

'Yes, by attempting to marry his five-year-old son to Alexander's heir so that England could take control of the crown!'

'And if the Maid of Norway had survived then our two kingdoms would now be united in peace through that union.' Hugues shook his head at

Will's belligerent expression. 'If the Scots hadn't trusted Edward they wouldn't have promoted him as their overlord upon the infant queen's death. He has been endeavouring to restore order in their realm ever since, fortifying castles, setting garrisons in towns where tension between rival families was greatest. How do the Scots repay him? They could have entered into talks, negotiated their differences. Instead, they signed a treaty with his enemy.'

'Just when did you become English, Hugues?' asked Robert, eyeing his friend with resentment.

'I'm merely trying to see it from Edward's point of view,' replied Hugues calmly. 'And to understand where this suspicion of him comes from. We are brothers are we not?' He spread his hands to the two angry men in front of him. 'We are on the same side. I just want to make sure, whatever happens, that the Temple is safeguarded. These are unsettled times. Our Grand Master wants to launch a Crusade and the pope wants to join us with our rivals. Either of these possibilities could have a devastating impact on us. Jacques plans to leave for London after the Christ Mass. The three of us will be in his company. I've made sure of it.'

'We are going?' said Will.

'Yes, and I believe we should look upon Edward as our friend in this matter.'

'Then this discussion is over,' said Will, crossing to the door.

Hugues stared after him. Fury flooded his face in a red rush. 'You will halt, Commander! How dare you turn your back on me!'

Will rounded on him, the violence in his eyes making Hugues pause. 'We were discussing Anima Templi business. In case you had forgotten, I am its head. If I say our meeting is ended, it is ended.'

'God damn him,' murmured Hugues, as Will left the room. Robert went to speak, but the Visitor silenced him. 'No, Robert, do not excuse him. If he speaks to me like that again I'll have him expelled from this Order.'

4

New Temple, London

7 January 1296 AD

T he city was on fire. Pillars of black smoke billowed into the dawn sky,
   obscuring the sun. Boulders tossed up by the siege engines smashed
through the walls, pulverising rock into rubble, crushing men. Women and
children, faces dust-streaked, crowded on the harbour wall, desperate for
the few boats to take their swelling numbers to the last galleys out in the
harbour. Will spurred his horse through them, his attention fixed on a
distant figure stumbling along the broken eastern mole.

*It was always Edward pulling the strings. And I dangled limply in his grip, while
all my dreams faded and died around me, and all yours came true.*

Will sat up as the sound of Garin's bitter words filled his mind. There
was a pressure in his chest, making it hard to breathe.

*I had been Edward's puppet for so long that I danced to his tune even when he
wasn't controlling me.*

He rose and crossed the empty dormitory to the window. Planting his
hands on the ledge, Will looked out over a square of grass, bordered by
cloisters. On the air, he smelled the marshy Thames. This place was
crowded with memories, but fainter, less substantial than those that
surrounded him in Paris. He had spent only two summers at New Temple,
although the fact that this was the last place he had seen his father held a
certain nostalgic pain. It felt as though he were retracing his steps: Paris to
London. Thoughts of Scotland, his birthplace, were stronger here. He still
had the letter from his sister, Ysenda, folded in his sack. Both she and his
elder sister Ede were, as far as he knew, still alive.

Three Templar sergeants headed across the lawn, black tunics loose on
their lean frames, young muscles not yet toughened from labour or
combat. He had been like them once, green with youth, in awe of the
knights who towered above him like fierce angels in their sinless mantles.
He recalled days spent helping Simon in the stables, winter mornings

loping around the training field, Garin running at his side. It seemed like another life.

As the preceptory bell began to clang, the sergeants picked up their pace and disappeared under the arches. Will went back to the pallet. Crouching, he pulled his sack from under the bed. He paused, his hand hovering above it.

It's over, Will. Don't you see? It's over for both of us. We've lost everything. All we can do is die!

As Garin's voice echoed back to him, he reached into the sack, his fingers closing over the folds of his spare undershirt that was wrapped around something hard. He withdrew it, peeling back the shirt until the knife lay naked on his palm. He had taken it from the preceptory kitchen yesterday evening when most of the men were at Vespers. No one commented on his tardiness when he slipped into the chapel to join them. The Master of England and his officials were preoccupied with welcoming the Grand Master and if any of the knights had noticed they hadn't questioned him. After all, he was a commander. The blade was long and thin, embedded in a stout wooden handle. It was easy to conceal. No one would see him draw it.

Garin had been a pawn, a fatal one at that, but still, just a pawn. Edward was the player, the one pushing the pieces across the board, winning with every move, from Owein's murder at Honfleur and his own degradation in a Paris brothel, a death in its own way, to the ambush outside Mecca and the fire in Andreas's house. He may not have dirtied his hands in the process, but Edward had been the driving force behind all Garin's actions. That was as clear to Will as if the king had ground his own seal into each and every cruel moment that had been spun around his intentions. He had killed, connived and lied his way to gaining the things he wanted, throughout it all wearing a veneer of honour that had fooled even Everard. It was because of Edward that Will had lost almost everything that was precious to him in life. He couldn't live with that injustice any longer.

He had sworn revenge on the deck of the *Phoenix* as they had sailed out, leaving Acre in ruins behind them. His fury then had been pure, a raging fire, but in the years since it had turned to ashes inside him, grey and stagnant, polluting his thoughts. With his return to the West that fire had been rekindled and now, so near to the king's seat of power, so close to the man himself, it blazed hotter than ever, that arrogant face a beacon in his mind.

Will's fingers reached out, ready to wrap around the handle of the knife. But he stopped short of touching the blade. He exhaled sharply, aware that he had been holding his breath. Growling a curse, he stuffed the shirt around the blade and bundled it back into the sack. He would return it to the kitchen later, before anyone missed it.

The door opened and Robert entered. 'What are you doing in here?'

Will kicked the sack under his pallet. 'Nothing.'

'Didn't you hear the bell?'

Will realised the monotonous clanging was continuing outside.

'He's here,' said Robert grimly. 'You should come.'

Will crossed to the door. He glanced back at the pallet, then headed out.

The main courtyard of the London Temple, which led on to Akeman Street, was crowded with men. A group of finely caparisoned horses was being led towards the stables. Will halted. Walking towards him beside the Master of England, was Edward.

If age had altered Will's comrades, that was nothing compared with what the years had wrought upon the English king. They had taken the haughty young man he had last seen twenty-three years ago and changed him beyond recognition. True, he retained his athletic figure and his impressive height that lifted him above most other men, but there the similarity ended. Will had been imagining a face still framed by dark hair, but now, at fifty-six, Edward's hair was as white as a swan's feathers. His beard was silvery, clipped close to the line of his jaw, underlining the hardness of his face, and the slight droop in his eye had become more prominent. He looked a little stiff as he walked, although with his broadsword slung from his hip and his stride purposeful, he seemed as vigorous as all the younger men around him.

As Edward approached, followed by a multitude of royal guards and advisors, his eyes fell on Will. For a few seconds there was no sign of recognition, then his face filled with alertness. 'Campbell.'

The Master of England, a youthful, energetic man with black curly hair called Brian le Jay, looked from the king to Will, who, unlike the other knights, didn't bow as Edward paused. 'You know one of our brothers, my lord?'

'Of old,' said Edward, not taking his eyes off Will. His French was poised and perfect.

'Commander.'

Will glanced to Edward's right and saw Hugues staring at him intently.

'*Bow*,' mouthed the Visitor.

They were all looking at him. A frown was creasing Brian le Jay's face. Hugues's command was unassailable. Setting his jaw, Will inclined his head in Edward's direction. A flicker of satisfaction appeared in the king's eyes, then le Jay moved in and the frozen moment passed.

'My lord,' said the English Master, motioning Edward to the Chapter House. 'Grand Master de Molay is waiting. We should join him.'

Will followed, Robert close at his side. His eyes didn't leave Edward as they filed into the chamber. The Grand Master was seated on a dais beside a small man with a tonsured head, who Will guessed was Bertrand de Got. Jacques rose to greet Edward as the king ascended the dais and took his place on one of the empty seats, along with Brian le Jay and Hugues, while the knights and royal advisors crammed into benches on the floor. Jacques remained standing as the Chapter House doors were shut.

'Almost two hundred years ago, Hugues de Payns journeyed east with eight fellow knights. The first Crusaders had captured Jerusalem for Christendom and the Holy City had become a place of pilgrimage. Here, Hugues, a young nobleman under the vassalage of the Count of Champagne, saw the perils confronting so many Christians who wished to travel to the holy places. Determined that these men and women should be allowed to tread the sands where Christ himself had walked, freely, without fear of assault or death at the hands of the Saracens, he established an Order of knights, whose purpose it would be to safeguard these pilgrims.' Jacques's voice was resonant. The men were silent, listening to the familiar story. 'Hugues de Payns was the first Grand Master and although our Order expanded from those beginnings into the realms of politics and trade, growing more influential every year, his mission remained at our core. We are the guardians of the Holy Land. It is what we were created for. It is our sole purpose.' He shook his head. 'No, the purpose of our *soul*.'

Will was surprised. Jacques, a man of sparse words who, like many men in the Temple, could neither read nor write, wasn't normally given to such articulacy. He noticed that the Grand Master's scribe, seated in the front row, was nodding in time with the speech, and guessed he'd had a lot to do with it.

'And that is why our task there is not ended. I am proud to be the twenty-third Grand Master of this Order and, as all those before me, I will not rest until the Holy Land is liberated for God and for Christendom.'

Applause followed his words. The expressions of the men on the dais, however, were mixed. Brian le Jay was listening with respectful interest, Hugues was staring pensively at the floor, Bertrand de Got was nodding vigorously, while Edward's face, cool and impassive, revealed nothing of his thoughts at all.

Jacques turned to the bishop. 'I believe I and Pope Boniface want the same things.'

Bertrand rose, smoothing down his robe. 'That is true, Master de Molay, and you speak most eloquently in echoing the papacy's desires. But I have talked at length with his holiness and we feel your men alone cannot accomplish the enormous task of reclaiming the Holy Land from the Saracens and that is why he proposes the Temple joins forces with the Hospital; that both these noble, ancient Orders might, in strength, achieve this aim.'

Murmurs of discontent rippled through the Chapter House, although nothing like the outrage Will had expected, leading him to believe that most of the men already knew the purpose of the assembly.

Jacques was silent for a moment. 'That can never happen.'

Bertrand looked taken aback at the change in Jacques, from graceful orator into gruff commander. 'But, Master de Molay, this is why we have met, to discuss this. Surely you will hear my thoughts?'

'I do not need to. I have made up my mind. I would welcome the Knights of St John joining us in a new Crusade, but as a separate Order, as we have always been.'

'There is a fear that your rivalry with the Hospitallers may have contributed to the loss of the Holy Land.' Bertrand raised his hands as some of the knights protested. 'I merely state what others perceive to be true.'

'Our rivalry was a help, not a hindrance. It pushed our Orders to compete to do the best for Christendom. On the field of battle, one of us would command the van, the other would take the rear.'

'This would all remain the same,' argued the bishop. 'The only difference being that you would be carrying the same banners.' A stony silence greeted his words. 'Surely?'

'And what about my men?' questioned Jacques, motioning to Hugues and Brian le Jay. 'We could not have two Visitors, two Masters of England. What about myself? I can say with certainty that the Grand Master of the Hospital would be as loath as I to give up his position. Many would be demoted and knights used to one commander would find themselves reporting to someone new whom they may have previously considered a rival. What you propose would not result in a unified force, but a discontented, disorganised rabble that would get as far as Marseille before it started attacking itself.'

Bertrand pursed his lips. Looking around, seeking assistance, his gaze fell on Edward. 'My lord, you were an advocate for this debate. What are your thoughts?' Bertrand returned to his place, looking relieved, as the king took the stage.

'I would welcome a Crusade.'

Watching Edward, Will felt blood begin to pound in his temples. He sat forward.

'But presently, I am preoccupied with other matters.' The king turned to Jacques as Bertrand frowned. 'As you may be aware, the Scots under John Balliol have signed a treaty with King Philippe of France. I had hoped we would be able to settle this reasonably, as civilised men. Now I see that when it comes to these people such a thing is impossible. The treaty constitutes a declaration of war, one I must answer swiftly and resolutely. Yesterday I ordered that all Scots in England be arrested.'

Will gripped the bench.

'My lord,' Jacques interjected, 'we have Scotsmen among our number.'

'Templars will be exempt from this.' Edward kept his flint eyes on Jacques. 'You must understand the necessity of this. The Scots have agreed with Philippe to take aggressive action against me. I cannot allow them any safe haven within the bounds of my kingdom from where they might strike.'

After a pause, the Grand Master nodded. 'No. Indeed.'

Bertrand was staring bewildered at Edward, as if he had expected the king to say something else entirely. 'My lord, with respect, you are talking here of going to war with another Christian nation, when what we have gathered to discuss is the recapture of the Holy Land from the hands of non-believers. This must be our priority!'

'Unlike the Church, Bishop, I do not have the luxury of choosing my enemies. Philippe and the Scots have raised arms against me. I would be failing my people and my position if I did not respond.' Edward looked back at Jacques. 'I am preparing to head north to counter Balliol, but with my brother leading English forces in Gascony and others of my commanders overseeing the suppression of the Welsh revolt, I am diminished. I have need of disciplined warriors and heavy cavalry. To this end, I seek the support of the Temple.'

Will was relieved to see that the Grand Master looked unimpressed.

'The very reason I have journeyed here, my lord, is to ask the aid of kings in raising men and arms. I did not expect to have to answer such a request myself. My men are needed in the East.'

Edward's brow creased. He went to speak, but Hugues stood.

'My lords, might I suggest we bring this meeting to a close? With these unexpected matters now requiring our attention it would be prudent if we each are given time to think before making hasty decisions.' He looked at Jacques. 'We could reconvene tomorrow.'

The Grand Master nodded. 'Very well, Visitor de Pairaud. My lord?'

Edward paused, then inclined his head.

'I too am in favour of this,' said Bertrand stiffly, shooting an aggrieved look at the king.

As the company began to rise, the knights talking among themselves, Will sat back, his eyes on Edward, who swept down the aisle and out of the Chapter House, followed by his train of officials and guards.

Someone in Paris had signed a piece of parchment. Now, England and Scotland were at war.

The Tower, London, 7 January 1296 AD

Hugues paused at the top of the stairs that curled down into darkness. A putrid smell of decay drifted up to him. He glanced at the man beside him.

'Down there, sir,' insisted the guard, jerking his head towards the stairs.

Taking them carefully, Hugues descended. For a moment, he found himself in pitch blackness and had to feel his way down the steep, uneven steps, his fingers pressing into the damp stone to either side. Gradually, the ruddy glow of torchlight stained the way ahead and he could see again. Stepping confidently down the last few steps, he entered an arched passageway. The smell here was overwhelming, a thick, animal reek. Hugues breathed thinly through his mouth. At the end of the passage, the torchlight was brighter and he could see figures moving. Five rough-looking guards turned to him as he headed into a wider corridor, the right-hand side of which was lined with stout doors. 'I was told to come here,' said Hugues, in awkward English. He heard a muffled scream from somewhere.

'I'll take you to him, sir,' said one of the guards. 'He's expecting you.' As Hugues followed, the guard motioned to the left. 'Keep to this side and watch where you're walking.'

Glancing down, the Visitor saw that the passage floor was sloped, with a channel cut out of the stone running through the centre. It was filled with viscous, oily liquid.

'You don't want to step in their filth, sir.'

Knowing the source of the stench made it worse. Hugues resisted the urge to clamp his hand over his nostrils as the guard stopped at one of the doors, unhooked a set of keys from his belt and dug one in the lock. There was another scream, this time much closer. The guard pushed open the door.

Beyond, in a cramped cell, were four men. Three of them looked round as Hugues entered, but the fourth, who was hanging by his wrists from a chain looped through a hook on the ceiling, didn't raise his head. There was a burned, meaty smell in the confined chamber that reminded Hugues uncomfortably of roasted pork.

'Visitor de Pairaud.'

Hugues bowed, looking from King Edward to the figure dangling limply from the chain in front of him. The man wore only a stained loincloth and his bare skin was livid, soaked with sweat in the scorching heat coming from a brazier of burning coals. The sand on the floor around him was congealed with blood. It ran thickly down his torso from cuts that marked his chest alongside several charred wounds. Hugues guessed the burned patches had been made by the branding iron one of the other two men, both guards, was wielding and the meaty smell made him feel suddenly nauseous. 'Should I return later, my lord?'

'No,' replied Edward curtly. 'I will speak to you now.'

Hugues's nose wrinkled as the prisoner coughed bloody drool into the sand. 'Who is he?'

'A Scottish spy.' Edward moved to the side of the cell and nodded to the guard, who thrust the iron into the heart of the glowing coals. Sparks crackled and fizzed. A deep shudder ran through the prisoner at the sound. 'He crawled his way like a maggot into my household months ago. He has been spying on me, waiting to report back to his masters. It is a good thing my men unearthed him when they did, or the Scots might have known my battle strategy before the vanguard left London.'

'That isn't true,' rasped the prisoner. 'I'm innocent!'

Edward snapped his fingers at the guard, who withdrew the brand, its tip now smouldering orange. 'Again.'

The man howled as the guard pressed the fiery brand to his chest. Hairs burned and flesh bubbled. He swung forward, his legs giving out. 'Dear God. No . . . m . . . more!' He was panting harshly.

Edward leaned in. 'Then tell me what I want to hear. Did you get word to Balliol? Does he know of my plans?'

'No,' breathed the man. There was silence for a long moment. Slowly, the man raised his head. 'But it does not matter. He will still be ready for you.'

'There, you see,' Edward murmured.

'My people will slaughter you, you false-hearted bastard.' The man clenched his eyes shut and threw back his head. 'Long live King John!'

'Kill him.'

One of the guards stepped forward, his sword rasping in his scabbard as he unsheathed it. He plunged it into the man's belly, ripping through muscle and bowel with one cruel twist.

'These people came to me for help,' said Edward, as the man buckled over the sword and began to grunt. 'They came to me after the death of their king and his only heir, and begged for my help. At great expense to myself, I set up a trial to determine the rightful claimant to their throne.' He turned to Hugues. 'Once John Balliol was chosen and enthroned, order was restored to their kingdom. I believed they would be grateful. I was mistaken.' The prisoner sagged forward as the sword was withdrawn, in a rush of blood and fluid. Edward moved to the door, which was opened for him by the other guard. 'I need the Temple's assistance. You must persuade Jacques to give me the men to put down Balliol's rebellion.'

Tearing his gaze from the dying man, Hugues followed Edward into the passageway. 'That may be difficult, my lord. Jacques is set on his Crusade. I doubt he will want any resources deviated from that cause.' Hugues squinted against the growing light as they headed up to a windswept courtyard, dominated by a huge shed which housed the royal menagerie.

Edward turned abruptly, stopping Hugues at the top step. 'He might, if all talk of merging the Temple with the Knights of St John was silenced.'

'What are you suggesting?'

'I know Bertrand de Got. He may appear a feeble pedant, but he does have the ear of the pope. He could persuade Boniface from this proposition, given the right encouragement from me. We have always had good relations in the past, you and I. You have given me aid when I have asked for it before. Do not fail me now.'

'What of your pledge to me, my lord? With Acre lost, the Temple needs a secure base. The Hospitallers are established on Cyprus and the Teutonic Knights now have a firm hold on Prussia. We must follow their example and seek an empire of our own, safe from the interference of secular authorities and the whim of the Church. We have always relied on our reputation to generate support: funds and potential recruits from the nobility, special privileges from kings. Now our standing is diminished we must look to things of greater permanence to ensure the continuation of our Order. Foremost of our needs is land.'

'And I will be in a much better position to help you secure this when the Scottish rebels are put down. Perhaps Scotland could even provide a useful base for your Order? You already have preceptories there. I'm sure we could come to some arrangement.'

Hugues was quiet. 'I will do what I can,' he said finally. 'I will try to persuade Jacques to aid you. But in return, all talk of us being merged with the Hospital must stop. The whereabouts of our new base can be decided in due course.'

Edward moved out into the yard, allowing Hugues to step into the daylight. The braying of an animal in pain sounded from the shed. 'What of Campbell? He is your head and more of Everard's stock. I doubt he will agree to this. He is Scottish, after all.'

'Campbell may be head of the Brethren, but I am Visitor. He will yield to my authority.'

5
New Temple, London
8 January 1296 AD

A s Will entered the Chapter House with the other knights, he scanned the chamber. Hugues was at the front with Jacques. Seating himself on one of the benches near the dais, Will tried to catch the Visitor's eye.

Following yesterday's assembly, he had called an urgent meeting of the Brethren, but only Robert and Thomas, their English brother, had attended. Will had been distracted, by both Edward's demands and Hugues's troubling absence, and their discussion ended unsatisfactorily with nothing decided. Afterwards, he looked for Hugues in the Great Hall at supper, but there was no sign of him and he went to his dormitory after Compline, plagued by concerns. He had lain awake long into the night, the knife that remained beneath his pallet a tangible presence in the gloom.

As Hugues moved to sit beside Brian le Jay, his gaze fell on Will, but if he noticed the questioning look he showed no sign of it, his eyes flicking away as King Edward took his place.

Jacques looked weary, but his voice was resolute as he addressed the assembly. 'I have spent many hours in discussion with my officials, but my conclusion remains the same. To unite our Order with the Knights of St John would do the ongoing struggle for the Holy Land more harm than good. I cannot agree to this,' he said, turning to Bertrand de Got.

The bishop, who appeared pale and drained, stood. 'I too have had time to think upon this matter.' He hesitated. Will frowned, seeing him glance at Edward. 'I have had time to think,' Bertrand repeated. 'And I believe you are right.'

Murmurs of surprised approval greeted his words. Jacques silenced them.

'For now, Master Templar,' continued Bertrand, looking at the Grand Master with something like regret, 'I will defer to your experience and shall return to Rome to pass my recommendation to his holiness that the Temple and the Hospital remain as separate Orders, each working individually towards a new Crusade.'

Will was as taken aback as the rest of the knights at this abrupt change of heart on the bishop's part, but unlike the others he wasn't glad. He felt uneasy. Something else, some other agenda, was playing out on the stage in front of him, he just didn't know what it was. The answer wasn't long in coming.

The Grand Master remained standing as Bertrand sat. 'On the matter that was raised yesterday by Lord Edward, I also have a response.' The Grand Master nodded to the king. 'The Temple will give you what you ask for. We will support your move against Scotland.'

Will jerked to his feet. A few of the men sitting beside him glanced at him, but he only had eyes for Edward, who appeared cool, composed and not at all surprised by the Grand Master's decision.

'Master le Jay will work with you to this end, but only knights from English preceptories will form part of your force. I will not anger the Temple's allies in France and elsewhere.'

Edward inclined his head to Jacques. 'That is certainly understandable, although it would be advantageous for me to use your principal preceptory in Scotland as a base. I plan to have crossed the Tweed above Berwick by Easter. Once the town has capitulated, the gateway to Scotland will be open and I will advance north. Balantrodoch will be a useful staging post in which to rest my troops and from where I could proceed directly into Edinburgh.'

'This can be arranged.'

'I presume the knights at Balantrodoch will agree to this, no matter any partisan inclinations they may have?' As the king spoke, his eyes fell on Will, who was still standing.

'They will obey any order that comes from me,' responded Jacques. 'In addition to fifty knights from this preceptory, we will send one hundred sergeants to augment your infantry. Master le Jay will agree the rest of the details with you. He will command our forces personally.'

'I welcome your commitment,' said Edward smoothly. 'And, with your pledged assistance, I believe this battle is already won.'

The Grand Master added a few words about how he was looking forward to discussing his Crusade with the king, once the troubles in Scotland had been resolved, but Will wasn't listening.

As the meeting drew to a close, Edward got up to speak to one of his advisors. 'Summon the magnates. We meet at Newcastle on the first day of March. From there we head north.'

Seeing Hugues walking down the aisle towards the doors, Will pushed past the men on the bench and followed him into the courtyard. 'Hugues!'

Hugues turned angrily. 'You will address me in the proper manner, Commander.'

'What happened? Why did Jacques agree to this?'

'Keep your voice down,' snapped Hugues, as knights filed out of the Chapter House behind them. He gestured to the officials' building. 'In there.' When they entered Hugues's chambers Will went to speak, but the Visitor beat him to it. 'You need to stop this. Your behaviour is starting to be noticed. It's been four years since Acre. It was devastating, yes, but it is time you ceased dwelling on it.'

'I know we haven't always seen eye to eye, Hugues, but I respect you and your position, which is why I initiated you into the Anima Templi. You have to talk to Jacques. You have to persuade him from this course of action.'

'I cannot do that.'

'Why not?' Will stared after him as he strode to the window.

Hugues looked down on the courtyard. Edward's tall form was moving among the knights, the circlet on his head a halo of gold in the sunlight. 'I tried to tell you in Paris, but you wouldn't listen.' He turned. 'The West is changing. Jacques is part of an old Order, still looking to the East, still holding the cross to Jerusalem. We cannot allow him to drag the Temple with him.'

'I agree. You and I, we will talk to him.'

'I've known him less than a month and I already see he will not be persuaded from this course. Jacques is a military man, a general through and through. You've been on the road with him beating the drums of war for two years. If he could have been converted from this aim, you surely would have done so by now.' Hugues went on as Will faltered. 'Listen to me. Jacques will go his own way if he has to take up his sword and march east alone. We cannot stop him, but we can safeguard the Order. In this changing world, territory is everything. It is what Philippe and Edward are fighting so fiercely for. With territory comes power and with power comes autonomy. We stood beyond the laws of kings and princes for almost two centuries because only the pope had control over us, but now the pope's power is waning. God's Vicar on Earth does not own enough of it to match the rising authority of these warrior kings. If we do not cut ourselves away from the papacy we may find our strength diminished. But with a secure base of our own we can continue to expand and grow. We can continue to be one of the most powerful and affluent brotherhoods on this Earth.' Hugues's eyes were bright. 'We can control kings, keep royal treasuries, hold sway on sea and land, whether selling our wool at the trade fairs or protecting merchant ships, just as we did at the height of our power. With the Crusades over, we no longer have purpose in the eyes of the world. We must make our own purpose, or someone else will decide it for us. It has already begun, with the pope's desire to merge us with the Hospitallers.'

Will was shaking his head. 'And what of the Anima Templi? What of its aims?'

'The Brethren have no real power or direction any more.' Hugues continued. 'You know that, Will, or else you would have started to rebuild us as soon as Acre fell. What have you done to restore us?' He raised a hand. 'I'm not blaming you. Indeed, what could you have done? After the Holy Land was lost, how could the Anima Templi continue its aims?'

Will didn't answer. Hugues's words just echoed what he had been asking himself all this time: what now was the point in the Anima Templi? He remembered the Seneschal, the man he had always thought would become Everard's successor, charging him to continue their work in the West and to safeguard the Temple from all enemies, within and without. But the Seneschal couldn't have known what an impossible task this would be. *He sacrificed himself for this*, a small voice said, but Will forced it away.

Hugues was nodding at his silence, taking it for acceptance. 'But with the Temple's future secured, we can rebuild the Anima Templi, continue those aims. You've said it a thousand times: the Brethren cannot exist without the Temple, without the money and resources it provides us, albeit unknowingly. If we allow the Order to be taken over by other forces, we will find ourselves crushed within the fist of someone else's ambition.' Hugues paused. 'Edward can help us achieve what we want, Will. Indeed, he could be our greatest ally.'

Will felt something leaden go through him. 'Dear God, Hugues. What have you done?'

'What I had to.'

'It wasn't Jacques who agreed to aid Edward's war. It was you. You persuaded the Grand Master to go along with it.'

Hugues thrust out his chest. 'Yes.'

'Whatever Edward promised you is a lie. He's using you.'

'He has already helped us. In return for military assistance in Scotland, he pledged to dissuade Bishop de Got from merging the Orders. That has happened. When order is returned to Scotland, he will help us find a permanent base, a place from which we can decide our own future.'

'You said it yourself, Hugues: Edward wants territory for himself! Do you really believe he'll create a state for a mighty, untouchable army, where it can grow even more powerful? Cruel deceiver and ambitious tyrant Edward may be, but fool he is not.'

'He will see the benefits of having an alliance with such a brotherhood,' insisted Hugues.

'Yes, as a personal army he can call on at will. You're playing right into his hands!' Will crossed to him. 'Hugues, I swear this will be the end of us. You aren't saving the Temple with this alliance, you're destroying it!' He faltered. 'You remember Garin de Lyons?'

'How could I forget? He stole the Book of the Grail and almost exposed the Anima Templi. Robert told me all about him'

'What Robert doesn't know, what *no one* else knows, is who he did it for. At the fall of Acre, Garin confessed he had been working for Edward. The attack on the Templar party conveying the crown jewels to Paris: that was Edward. His plan to retake the jewels failed and when Garin told him about the Book Edward used him to hunt it down. The king was planning to blackmail the Brethren to help him expand his kingdom. He knew we controlled the Temple, its wealth and power, and he was going to use our resources for himself. His attempts to capture the Book also failed and maybe that would have been the end of it only Everard misguidedly made him Guardian of the Anima Templi. Edward tried to use this position to fund his war against Wales, but by then Everard and I had become suspicious of him and we endeavoured to cut ourselves away from his influence.' Will's words were coming in a rush. 'Edward sent Garin to force us to yield and while he was in the Holy Land, trying to worm his way into my life, Garin discovered Grand Master de Beaujeu's plan to steal the Black Stone of Mecca.' He watched the emotions changing on Hugues's face: surprise, shock, incredulity. 'On Edward's behalf, he worked against me, trying to get the Stone. In holding the Muslims' holy relic to ransom, he believed Edward would get what he wanted: money for a future assault on Scotland and his own Crusade.'

Hugues moved away. 'Garin told you this?' he asked finally.

'Yes.'

'Where is he now? What happened to him?'

'He died at Acre.'

'You are sure?'

When Will nodded, Hugues sighed roughly. 'Then none of this can be proven. Garin may have been lying to you. Is there other proof?'

Will went to speak, then shook his head. 'No,' he admitted, frustrated, 'but—'

'Do you know what I think this is about?' Hugues went to his desk and leaned against it, arms folded. 'I think this is about your own dislike of Edward. It was you, not Everard, who came to the conclusion that Edward was working against us. Everard said as much in his writings. He was careful about what he did reveal, but reading between the lines that much at least was evident. He spoke of Garin as a wayward arrow and believed he was working for himself in the Holy Land. If you confronted Garin, no doubt he would have implicated someone else, so as not to take the blame, which, from everything everyone has told me about him, seems very likely.'

'No, that isn't—'

'I think,' Hugues cut across him, 'that there was some part of you that was jealous when the priest, your mentor, appointed Edward as Guardian. Until then, you had been his closest confidant. With the arrival of Edward that changed. And of course there are your ties with Scotland. I know you still have family there and I know this decision to go to war in your homeland must be hard for you to accept, but you cannot let personal feelings cloud your judgement of the wider implications here. Edward could very well be the Temple's only chance for survival. I cannot allow anything to jeopardise that. I'm sorry, Will. I have to trust my instincts and my instincts tell me it was Garin, and Garin alone, who betrayed us.'

Will felt the weight of doom pushing down on him. 'You cannot do this!'

'My decision is final.'

'I am head here!' shouted Will, reaching for his sword.

Hugues's eyes narrowed. 'Head of a secret brotherhood no one knows exists.' He took a step towards Will, his hand falling to his own sword. 'I am Visitor of the Temple, second only to the Grand Master. Tell me, whose power is the greater? You will accept this, or I will have you removed from this Order.' His tone softened. 'Once Edward puts down these few rebels in Scotland, the realm will be the better for it and we will have what we need to safeguard the Temple.'

'Edward is carving himself a nation out of flesh and blood.'

'What was Everard's expression? Did he not say peace sometimes has to be bought with blood? We have to acknowledge that in the pursuit of freedom some things have to be sacrificed.' Hugues took his hand from his sword hilt. 'Come, Will. Support me in this. Do not make me exercise my authority over you.'

Will turned and made for the door. Not heeding Hugues's calls, he raced down the passageway. Bursting out of the officials' building, he sprinted across the yard. Horses were being led out of the stables. Edward was still there, talking with Jacques. Entering the knights' quarters, Will took the stairs to his dormitory two at a time. He threw open the door, went to his pallet and pulled out his sack. His mind was filled with the face of his father, a proud Scot and a Templar, but above all a man of peace. Will tipped the contents of the bag on to his bed. A pair of hose tumbled out, along with a pendant on a tarnished chain, the creased letter from his sister, a couple of quills and his undershirt. Will grabbed the shirt and shook it out. Even as he did so it felt wrong, too light.

'Is this what you're after?'

Will jerked round to see Robert in the doorway, holding the knife. He stood. 'You don't know what is happening, Robert.'

'No? So you're not planning to murder a king? I saw you,' Robert said sharply in response to Will's silence. 'Saw you kick that sack under there with a face full of guilt yesterday. You've been planning it since Hugues told you we were coming here, haven't you?'

Will hesitated. Was that true? He didn't know his own thoughts any more. This numbness, shot through with unexpected jolts of pain and memory, was unbearable.

'I know you blame Edward for Garin's actions, Will, but no matter what wrong he has done, no matter his ambitions for a Crusade and his attempts to use the Anima Templi, it was Garin, not him, who was responsible for what happened to Elwen. Garin, not Edward, who started that fire.'

'Don't say her name, God damn you!'

'You didn't want to speak of it, but Simon and Rose talked to me a little on the voyage to Cyprus. I don't understand all of what happened, but I know this has to stop. We've been walking around you as if on thin ice since we left Acre, me, Simon, all of us. But this has gone too far.' Robert shook his head. 'It is my fault in part. I should have spoken to you about it, but I was scared of your reaction. Jesus, Will, can you not see what you have become?' He took a step forward. 'What you're planning is regicide. You'll go to hell.'

'I'm already halfway there.'

'The Brethren were formed to keep the peace through diplomacy, not violence. If you go down into that courtyard with this knife all of that ends. You will destroy yourself and the Anima Templi. What Robert de Sablé and the others after him – your father, Hasan, Everard – created is greater than you or me, greater than hatred or revenge.'

Will was pacing, his hands pushing through his hair.

Robert watched him. 'You'll draw that knife and one of two things will happen. You will kill Edward and be killed yourself, or else be cut down before you get to him. Either way, it will mean your death and maybe some part of you wants that, but you'll be damning us all. Who will lead us? Who will continue the work?'

Will stopped pacing. 'The Anima Templi is already damned. It was Hugues, not Jacques, who pledged to support Edward.'

Robert frowned, but he pressed on. 'We'll talk to him.'

'Hugues doesn't know Edward like I do and neither do you.' Will sat heavily on his pallet, his head in his hands. He told Robert about Garin's confession. 'I should have told you before,' he said in response to the knight's stunned expression. 'But I couldn't bring myself to speak of it.'

Robert went to him and crouched down. 'Let me talk to Hugues.'

'It is too late. Jacques and le Jay are in this now. The time for diplomacy is past. I will not let what my father died trying to protect and what Everard spent his life building become used for Edward's ambition. Peace is not worth that price. I would rather see the Anima Templi ended than become a pawn for him. He has ruined my life. I will give him nothing more.' Will looked at the knife in Robert's hand. 'If I do not do this, he will destroy Scotland and we will help him.'

Robert stood. 'You're not a killer, Will.'

Will looked away. He was on that mole again, his sword stabbing out. He felt that pure shock of elated triumph as the blade punched into Garin's back. Elias had told him not to forget what he was capable of, but he was all too aware of that. Deception, selfishness, weakness, murder: they were the things he was capable of. He drew his falchion. Maybe this blade was more fitting; maybe it was good that Edward would see him coming.

'Don't,' said Robert. 'The king has surrounded himself with men who share his ambitions for expansion. His son is too young to rule without their counsel. Scotland will still fall under the steel of an English army and you'll have done nothing to stop it. The only thing you can do is try to persuade Hugues to end this alliance.'

Will stared at the sword in his hands. It was a Scottish blade. It had belonged to his father and his grandfather. He looked down at his things, strewn across his bed. Was this all he was left with after a lifetime of struggle?

'Edward won't stop his war if we refuse to give him the men. He'll just find his soldiers from somewhere else. He'll still lead his army north. He'll still . . .' Will trailed off.

Robert was speaking again, but Will wasn't listening. It wasn't true: he did have something. He had information. He knew Edward's plans, or at least enough of them to give the Scottish forces a chance.

Robert stared at him as he sheathed his sword and unhooked the clasp of his mantle. 'What are you doing?'

Will pulled the white garment, emblazoned with its red cross, from his shoulders and let it fall to the floor. He felt lighter than he had in years. He tugged off his surcoat and tossed it aside. Bending down, he stuffed his belongings back into his sack and grabbed the plain woollen cloak from the head of the pallet, which he'd been using as a pillow. He shrugged it on over his hauberk. 'I'm going home.'

Robert's confusion turned to disbelief. 'No, Will, for God's sake!'

'If the only option I have is to hinder his war, make it harder for him to get what he wants, that is what I'll do.'

'Do this and you'll be betraying your own men! You won't find justice where you're going,' Robert shouted, as Will slung his pack over his shoulder. 'You'll only find war.'

'Peace sometimes has to be bought with blood, Everard was right. And it'll be with Edward's blood that I'll buy it.'

'What about Rose?'

Will halted in the doorway. His daughter's words rang in his mind. *I lost my parents. Both of them.* She didn't even believe he was her father. 'She will have a better life without me,' he murmured. 'You will watch out for her? You and Simon?'

'Your father ran from his family, from you. It haunts you still. Do not do the same to her.'

'My father left to do something good and right in this world. I failed to continue his dream. Perhaps we should have done more in the Holy Land. Maybe we should have stood firmer in the face of our enemies, used our swords more and our tongues less.'

'We use our swords only when all hope of diplomacy is past.'

'And that is now.'

Robert went to him and took his arm. 'You cannot come back from this, Will. You'll be imprisoned as a deserter. Do you understand? You cannot come back.'

'I do not want to.' As he said it, Will felt his new-found sense of purpose solidify. Pulling away from Robert, he stepped through the door.

6

The Royal Palace, Paris

14 January 1296 AD

Philippe raised his head as the door to his bedchamber opened. His wife entered, followed by two handmaidens carrying her embroidery materials. Philippe returned to his study of the parchment he was holding then looked up again, his eyes fixing on one of the handmaidens, who placed several spools of silk on a table near the ornate bed that dominated the chamber. He stared after her as she headed out, the door clicking shut behind her.

'What is it?' asked Jeanne, following Philippe's intent gaze. Her voice was soft and low.

'Who was that girl?' he demanded, setting the parchment on his desk and rising.

'Marguerite?'

'Not her. The other one. Who is she?'

The queen frowned at his tone. 'Her name is Rose. She has been a servant here for some time. I have just promoted her to my staff.'

'I saw her last month. She was meeting a man outside the palace. The steward was supposed to have expelled her.' Philippe strode to the door.

'Wait.' Jeanne crossed to him, placing a gentle hand on his arm. 'It was a misunderstanding. The man you saw wasn't her lover, as you told the steward. It was her father.'

'Why would she be meeting him in secret on the riverbank like some bawd?'

'He is a Templar.'

Philippe arched an eyebrow. 'A Knight Templar with a daughter?'

'Her mother was a handmaiden to your grandmother, here in the palace. Andreas di Paolo, the Venetian mercer who supplies my tailor, wrote to me asking if I could find her work. He always struck me as a man of good judgement on the occasions he had an audience with me.' Jeanne went to the table where Rose had deposited the silks. She picked up a vibrant blue spool. 'She rarely speaks of her family. I think her mother died at Acre. The other girls say she sometimes cries in the night.' Sighing, the queen set down the silk. 'I suppose I felt sorry for her.'

Philippe's brow furrowed. Going to her, he put his hands on her shoulders and looked down into her brown eyes, always so expressive, so filled with emotion. He traced a finger across her face that was as soft and round as the rest of her. There was nothing hard about Jeanne. She was a woman of curves and contours with dark, slightly heavy features and thick black hair, inherited from her native Navarre. She had grown even fuller after the birth of their sixth child, a girl called Isabella, but to Philippe she was as lovely as she had been since he had first known her. They were betrothed twelve years ago, when she was eleven and he was sixteen, but before that they had grown up together in the royal house at Vincennes. Jeanne, who inherited the throne of Navarre as a baby, had been placed in the royal household by her widowed mother and the two children had grown close, Philippe taking on the protective role of older brother.

Drawing her to him, he stroked her hair. 'I hate to see you sad.' He felt her arms come up, her hands sliding across his back and he winced when her fingers brushed a fresh laceration.

Jeanne lifted her cheek from his chest as he tensed. 'I wish you wouldn't mortify yourself,' she murmured, the concern in her eyes now all for him.

Philippe pulled away. 'Guillaume de Paris believes it necessary.'

'Your new confessor seems to be a difficult man to please, more difficult perhaps than faith demands?'

'I am king, Jeanne. God demands much of a man in my position.' He scowled. 'As does this kingdom. My grandfather has not even been canonised, yet the people proclaim him a saint. Can I command such respect?'

'Give them time. Once they know you as I do, they will love you as they loved Louis.'

Philippe looked over at the desk, littered with the parchments Flote had given him that morning. They were rolls from the treasury, listing his expenses in Guienne and his treasurer's estimations of what it would take to keep his army in the duchy over the coming months. Everywhere he turned another lord was trying to keep him from consolidating his kingdom: Edward, rapacious dukes in the south, stubborn counts in neighbouring Flanders. If he couldn't find the funds to control them he might as well just call himself King of the Ile de la Cité and be done with it. 'The people will only see my greatness in deeds, Jeanne. To be seen as a great king, I must act as one.' He kissed her brow. 'But, here.' He picked up the blue spool of silk and placed it in his wife's hands. 'Do not burden yourself with my worries.'

Leaving Jeanne to take up her embroidery, Philippe moved pensively through the grand passageways of the royal apartments, servants bowing as he passed. He headed through a set of doors and stepped out on to a covered balcony that ran round to an ornate portal, leading into the upper level of the Sainte-Chapelle. Below, in the courtyard, courtiers and officials hurried about their business, not noticing their king come to a rigid halt before the chapel doors and stand there, eyes on the stone Christ that guarded the threshold. Philippe's gaze moved over the statue to the pier above, which depicted a scene from the Last Judgement. A seething mass of men and women were cut out of the stone, each blow of the masons' chisels carving another expression of anguish or horror from their writhing forms, while in their midst the angel, Michael, weighed their souls. If he looked at them long enough, they seemed to move. His heart quickened as he stepped towards the doors, swallowing back the rising dryness in his mouth. Reaching out, Philippe placed his hands on the wood. Steeling himself, he pushed. The doors opened into a vast, empty space, filled with glass and echoing silence.

'My lord.'

Philippe started at the voice. He turned, angry to be caught unawares, to see Flote behind him, but his anger thawed, replaced by eagerness, as his eyes flicked to the figure at the chancellor's side.

Guillaume de Nogaret bowed. 'I bring news from London, my lord.'

With greater relief than the two men could know, Philippe grasped the chapel's doors and pulled them firmly closed, shutting off the sight of the cavernous space beyond. He crossed to his ministers, pulling his fur-lined cloak tighter around his shoulders. 'Well?'

'Edward did make an alliance with the Temple, as you feared,' answered Guillaume, 'but against Scotland, not you. According to the queen mother, the meeting was initially called to discuss the pope's proposition to merge the Temple and the Hospital, but Edward's designs on Scotland took precedence. She sends her regards to her daughter,' Guillaume added, when Philippe remained silent.

'I will pass them to Jeanne,' replied Philippe distractedly. He looked at Flote. 'What are your thoughts?'

'I would say this is good news, my lord. Your fears that Edward would ally with the Temple against you have been assuaged.'

'But that they would ally with him at all still concerns me.' Philippe toyed with his lower lip, rolling it between thumb and forefinger. 'Did you manage to find out anything else, Nogaret? Edward's plans for Gascony? Troop movements?'

'Unfortunately, Blanche hasn't been privy to any reports her husband has sent to Edward. It seems the king is wary of her presence in his household and has kept her under close scrutiny since his brother left for Gascony. Edward is more intent on his plans for Scotland at present; that much was plain. From what I could ascertain, he intends to put down the rebellion under King John before making any further move in your territory. We could use his distraction to step up our own efforts in the region.'

Philippe was nodding, but Flote quickly interjected. 'My lord, if you had a chance to study the rolls I sent to you this morning, you will see that we simply do not have the revenue for any extension of our forces in the area. We are already stretched to the limits. Perhaps a temporary truce with Edward might be the best way forward, at least while he is preoccupied in Scotland? This will allow us time to consolidate our resources and—'

'No,' argued Nogaret, 'the king must show his strength. Any display of weakness at this point could prove fatal. The English must not know how precarious our situation is.'

'What do you suggest we do?' countered Flote. 'Bankrupt the realm?'

'Tax the clergy again, my lord,' said Nogaret to the king.

Flote shook his head. 'We cannot make an enemy of the Church. The taxes were extremely unpopular when they were levied last year. Many bishops simply refused to comply.'

'Then use force this time,' said Nogaret harshly. 'The clergy are rich and greedy. When did you last see a poorly dressed bishop? Or a thin cardinal?'

'The Franciscans,' snapped Flote. 'The Dominicans.'

'Formed because their founders felt the Church's use of its own wealth was abhorrent!'

'Enough.' Philippe nodded. 'It is a good idea. Chancellor, you will draw up a proclamation immediately.' He spoke on as Flote went to protest. 'The clergy will come to thank me in time if this kingdom is made stronger by their sacrifices. You are dismissed, both of you.'

Nogaret bowed and headed off, but Flote hung back.

'What is it, Chancellor?'

'My lord, this idea will only work in the short term. We need to put other strategies in place.' Flote's voice lowered. 'Nogaret is young and ambitious, but his lack of faith or respect for the Church perturbs me. I advise you most strongly against listening too closely to his counsel. We both know the hatred that drives him.'

'This has nothing to do with that. Nogaret sees how the balance of power is shifting. The Church is the mother: the teacher, the consoler. The state is the father: the law-giver, the protector. Let the bishops worry about the souls of my people and I will worry about the defence of their country.' Philippe began to walk along the balcony towards his apartments. 'The world is changing, Flote. It is the men of the law who are taking control now. I would have thought this would please you?'

'It does, my lord. But that should not mean we become Godless.'

Philippe stopped.

Flote halted, frowning at the king who was staring at the closed chapel doors. 'My lord?'

'No,' murmured Philippe. He glanced at Flote. 'Draw up that proclamation.' Turning, he forced himself to walk back towards the chapel.

Midlothian, Scotland, 7 February 1296 AD

It was late afternoon and the light was fading fast. He drove the horse on relentlessly, whenever its pace began to flag. The beast's hooves sank into the boggy ground with every stride and kicked free with a spray of muddy slush that splattered its flanks and his legs. Once or twice, the horse splintered through a layer of ice and plunged into a pocket of black mud, threatening to jolt him from the saddle. Still he didn't slow. He was almost there. Just a few more miles and he would see it.

It was thirty days since he discarded his mantle and stole the palfrey from the stables at New Temple. Thirty days since he deserted.

Leaving London by Ermine Street, Will had made good speed through the sprawling forests of the hunting shires, travelling by day from hamlet to hamlet, keeping a wary eye out for robbers and cut-throats, aware of the attractive target he made: a lone rider on a well-bred horse, the glint of mail beneath his cloak a tempting challenge. The days were short and gloomy under the canopy of trees, and even when the forests gave way to rolling miles of crop fields it rarely got light, the sky growing greyer and heavier, until finally it opened and the first snows began to fall, leaching the last of the colour from the land. The wide road was treacherous with wagon ruts and potholes that were soon concealed beneath the rising drifts and he went from covering twenty-odd miles a day to barely fifteen. Coupled with this, he had to take several detours to ford rivers, avoiding the tolls on bridges. As a Templar he was exempt from such taxes and could have found free lodgings all along the route, but he was a knight no longer and had no proof that he had ever been. Cursing himself for not having the foresight to have kept his mantle, the bold gesture now seeming foolish, he was forced, on the second day, to sell the only thing of value he owned, other than his sword.

He sat for a time on the steps of a church in the town of St Albans, cold-numbed fingers rubbing at the tarnished pendant. Beneath the layers of grime, the figure of St George gradually appeared. Elwen had stood on her toes to put it on. He could still recall her breath, warm on the back of his neck, as she fastened the chain. He thought it might break his heart to sell it, but in truth it was a relief to hand the pendant to the trader. It was one more burden to be rid of, one more memory to release. In return he had been given enough coins, so long as he was careful, to see him in food and board all the way to Edinburgh.

The land changed slowly, forests and farmlands giving way to towns. Fields scraped bare by the plough, the autumn wheat buried beneath the snow, were replaced by warehouses and mills and the road grew crowded with merchants. In the inns he stayed at Will expected to hear much talk of the coming conflict, but other than the odd snatch of conversation, one man saying the English in Scotland were being arrested, another that the Scots were planning to invade, there was no mention of it. Life in the villages and towns of England went on as normal and if people were aware they were now at war, they showed no sign of it. It wasn't until he crossed the crumbling wall built by the Romans to imprison the wild north that the atmosphere began to change. It was subtle at first; the men in the taverns were more guarded and conversation was hard to come by, then he began to notice travellers were moving in caravans, many with armed escorts. In the windswept uplands of Northumberland, where hills and sky seemed to marry in whiteness, hospitality became positively scarce and he was forced to sleep on the hillside in stone shelters that he shared with huddles of sheep.

A week ago the snows had stopped and a red wintry sun appeared. Four days after that, he crossed the Tweed and the Teviot at Kelso and entered the Borders. Here, the tension was palpable. There was a heavy presence of soldiers in the towns, the gates guarded and often barred. Will was stopped and questioned several times, but his knowledge of the area granted him passage. Beneath the tension, he began to sense confidence. These men appeared ready for war, some even seemed eager for it, gathered in tight groups outside newly erected palisades, joking about the soft English. Hearing their laughter, Will spurred his exhausted palfrey on towards Edinburgh. Their assurance disturbed him. He knew what was coming.

The earls and barons summoned to the king's service would be leaving their estates with their knights, marching in armoured lines all along the roads of England to converge, in three weeks, on the city of Newcastle. Together, under the banner of the lions, this feudal host would move north as one vast army, the like of which Scotland hadn't seen in a hundred years. These young men with their wooden clubs and scornful jokes weren't ready at all.

But despite the pressing need, Will was unable to ignore the strange familiarity of the landscape surrounding him. The closer he came to Edinburgh, following the curve of shallow, stony rivers, the more he felt the pull of home, until late that morning, barely seven miles from the royal city, he changed direction, swerving west over the hills.

He urged his horse on, up over a steep bank to join a track pocked with hoof prints and sheltered on one side by a high, snow-dusted verge. After fifty or so yards, he turned a corner. In the distance, at the track's end, was the house he had been born in. Part of him had almost wondered if it would still be there, as if, like so many of those who had lived within its walls, it would have faded into memory. It was a surprise to see it in front of him, unchanged, a low wall ringing the main house, several outbuildings and a paddock. Will slowed the horse, its flared nostrils snorting clouds into the air. Limbs rigid with cold, he slid from the saddle and led the horse off the track. The estate had been owned by the Temple since his father had been knighted, his mother and sisters having been delivered to a nunnery near Edinburgh. He doubted news of his desertion would have travelled quicker than he had, but he didn't want to meet anyone out here if he didn't have to.

Will clambered down the hillside, heading for the copse his father had used for firewood. Entering the trees, he looped the reins over a branch and crept out of the cover, keeping low as he came up alongside the wall. In the paddock a few goats were grazing and in the barn beyond he could see the ponderous shapes of cattle. He ducked as a man came out lugging a pail and disappeared behind the house. Will moved along the wall. The herbs in the garden his mother had planted were bushier, but otherwise the place looked the same. He crouched down, assailed by images from his childhood: his mother's hands filled with sage, the fragrance drifting around her, his younger sister Mary in the paddock spinning round and round, his father lifting him on to his horse, his elder sister, Alycie, singing by firelight. She had followed the others to the grave some years ago.

After a time, his legs began to ache and he went to stand. There was movement behind him. Will turned. He had time to see a young man's face, fierce with fear, a snatch of blond hair and a raised hand with something lodged in the fist, before the hand came down and the object in it smashed into his forehead.

7
Midlothian, Scotland
7 February 1296 AD

There were voices nearby, but faint and muffled as if he were hearing them through water. Slowly, his vision came into focus. Ahead, through a doorway, Will could see several pairs of feet. The perspective seemed strange until he realised he was slumped on the floor. Someone had removed his cloak, which was hanging on a hook adjacent to a hearth, in which a fire blazed. His head was thrumming and he could feel something sticky on the side of his face. When he tried to move he found his hands were bound behind his back. The voices stopped and someone strode into the room. Will's gaze travelled dazedly upwards. A beefy man with dark hair was staring down at him. Behind him was a blond youth, thumbs thrust defiantly through a leather belt.

'He's awake,' the beefy man called over his shoulder. His accent was thick Scots.

Will recognised him as the man he had seen carrying the pail from the barn. The youth was the one who had attacked him. Almost at the same moment, he realised where he was. This was the kitchen of his old home. Even some of the furniture was the same.

'Who are you?'

Bracing himself against the throbbing in his head, Will brought his knees up and pushed himself to his feet. Both men started back.

'Get a knife, David!' Will heard a woman call fearfully.

'Tell me,' he said groggily, taking a few steps towards the men, 'do you treat all visitors this way?'

'Only English spies,' replied the older man, as the blond youth scanned the nearby shelves, presumably for a knife.

'Well, as I'm neither perhaps you could untie me and allow me to explain myself?'

'You aren't gagged, are you?'

Will leaned against the wall to steady himself. 'I used to live here. I was on my way to Edinburgh and I decided to pass by. I mean neither you nor your property any harm. I merely wanted to see the place I was born in.'

'He's lying.'

Another voice, this one older, sounded from the doorway. A woman entered. She looked to be in her late thirties and was tall and lean with sandy-coloured hair wound in two plaits that were pinned to either side of her head. Her eyes were dark green, much the same shade as his own, and her face, long and angular, was somehow familiar.

'Stay back, mistress,' said the beefy man.

'The Knights Templar owned this property for thirty years,' said the woman, ignoring the warning. 'Before that it was in the possession of only one family, a family I know. You look no older than forty years, so tell me, how could you have been born here?'

'I'm forty-nine,' Will corrected her. 'And I know the family you speak of, for I was the eldest son.'

The woman fell silent. Her hands rose to her face, leaving only her green eyes visible, eyes that now grew bright. 'Sweet God,' she whispered.

'Who is he, Mama?' said a young woman, stepping in from the hallway to stare at Will. At her back was another girl, barely in her teens, who scowled as she was stopped from entering the kitchen, the older girl's hand firm on her chest.

'He is my brother.'

Will felt something tighten in his chest as he realised the woman before him, who shared his eyes, was the sister he hadn't seen since he was eleven and she was four months old, a mewing, wrinkled thing in his mother's arms. The shocking reality of time passed, of encroaching death, of summers lost were all there, displayed in her. He looked from her to the three figures, drawing protectively around her. Her children? He let out a breath. His nephew and nieces. 'Ysenda.'

The woman waved a hand at the beefy man. 'Please, Tom, untie him.'

Tom's brow knotted, but he went to Will warily.

Will winced, flexing his sore shoulder muscles as his hands came free.

'Mama thought you were dead,' said the younger girl to Will, creeping in behind her sister.

'Hoped,' corrected the older girl harshly.

'Out,' said Ysenda suddenly. 'All of you.'

'Mother!'

'Out. And you, Tom.'

Ysenda closed the door as Tom disappeared through it. As she walked towards him, Will thought she was going to embrace him, but she stopped at the table and pulled a stool from under it. She sat, hands clasped rigidly on the table. 'Are you going to stand?'

He bent and took a stool on the opposite side, facing her. He wasn't sure what to say, so he said the first thing that came to mind. 'How is it that you're living here?'

'The Templars at Balantrodoch leased the estate to a tenant, a sheep farmer. He died a year ago and they decided to sell the place rather than rent it again.' Ysenda seemed to relax a little, unclasping her hands. 'I still have contact with a priest at the preceptory who befriended Mother. When I found out the estate was going to be sold, I asked my husband to buy it.'

'You must have a wealthy husband.'

'Duncan thought it was a good investment and with him spending so much time in Edinburgh of late, it has proved more convenient than we could have hoped.' She rose and went to a trestle stacked with bowls. A row of candles dripped molten tallow from a shelf above. Outside, the sky was the colour of slate. Taking a rag, Ysenda dunked it in a pail of water by the door. She squeezed it out and handed it to Will. 'Here,' she said briskly, nodding to his head.

'Your son has a mighty swing in his arm,' said Will, pressing at the wound and rubbing away the sticky blood. 'He would make a fine knight.'

'I expect he'll be dubbed next year, when he turns eighteen.'

'As a Templar?' asked Will, lowering the rag.

'No,' she said abruptly.

'I still have your letter. The one about our mother.' Will faltered. 'Was her passing peaceful?'

'Her passing, yes. It is a pity the same cannot be said for her life. Why did you not return?'

'I couldn't.'

'Couldn't or wouldn't?'

Will felt a stab of guilt, although for a more recent abandonment. 'I was eleven years old when I left, Ysenda. I did not have much say in the matter.'

'Mother would never tell me why you and Father left us, but when I was older Alycie and Ede did. They told me you killed their sister, Mary.'

'It was an accident. And she was my sister too.' He thrust a hand through his hair. 'God, if I could take that day back I would. But I cannot. It is something I've had to live with.'

Ysenda was quiet for a time. 'Mother used to tell me I looked like Mary.'

'You do, a little.'

'It was a hard face to wear.'

They both fell silent.

'Is Ede still . . . ?' Will paused, unsure how to ask. He felt like a stranger, not wanting to intrude on someone else's life, someone else's family.

'Alive?' Ysenda nodded. 'She moved with her husband to Elgin a few years ago. Since the troubles began it's been hard for us to get word to one another. But I believe she is well. She has three boys, all grown now.' Ysenda drew a breath. 'What was he like?'

'Who?'

'Our father.'

'That would take longer than I have at this moment to tell you and do any justice to the telling.'

She frowned, staring behind him at the cloak hanging by the fire. 'Where is your mantle? David found your horse in the thicket, but there were no Templar garments in your pack.'

'I've left the Temple.' Will stood as she opened her mouth. 'I was on my way to Edinburgh. I have information for King John I must deliver. King Edward's army is less than a month behind me.'

'Then it is happening? They're coming for us?' Her hand drifted absently to her throat, where a delicate silver cross hung.

'King John needs to hear my information. It may help him.'

'John Balliol isn't the power in this realm any more. A council of magnates took control when he refused to oppose Edward's demands. He says he will now, but at present he defers to them.'

'They will be at Edinburgh?'

'They are inspecting the border defences. The king is with them. They are gathering our men for war. The fiery cross has been sent through the kingdom.' She paused. 'But my husband is at Edinburgh. You can give the information to him.'

'With respect, Ysenda, I must give it to someone who can use it.'

'Duncan is a knight of Sir Patrick Graham of Kincardine, a powerful man. He will see that his lord hears what you have to say. I'll send David with you tomorrow at first light. It is too late to leave now,' she said firmly, as he began to protest. 'And I would hear more about you . . . brother.'

The Royal Castle, Edinburgh, 3 March 1296 AD

The sun glimmered on the wet rooftops of the tightly packed buildings that tumbled down the spine of the hill towards Holyrood Abbey, a faint silhouette against the backdrop of the craggy mountain that rose behind it to glower over the city. Will shaded his eyes against the glare as he stood on the ramparts, buffeted by the wind coming off the Firth of Forth that whistled through the arrow slits, chasing straw and dust into the air.

'Sir William!'

Will turned, holding the hood of his cloak as the wind tried to flick it over his head. Two men were walking towards him down the steep path that led under an arched gate, beyond which the main buildings were clustered on the highest point of the castle rock. David smiled as he approached, but the expression of the man beside him remained cool. 'It is just William now,' Will reminded his nephew. 'I'm not a knight.'

'You were a commander, a *Templar* commander. Whether you wear the uniform or not, you should still call yourself a knight.' David shrugged. 'I would.'

'You wanted to see me,' said the man, placing a hand on David's shoulder.

Will's gaze moved to his brother-in-law, a stocky, dour version of his nephew. 'I want to know what the delay is, Duncan. I have been waiting three weeks. You know what I gave up to bring this information here. I would hate to think my sacrifice was in vain.'

Duncan wasn't moved. 'As I told you, until my lord returns there is nothing I can do.'

'What about the sheriff? The constable? The English host will have arrived at Newcastle. Edward planned to be at Berwick by Easter. That's less than a month away.'

'The castle is jammed to the rafters with soldiers, the stores are being filled, the defences bolstered and there're weapons' inspection reports coming in from all over the shire. They don't have time for audiences.'

'Even when the audience could save their kingdom?'

When Duncan remained silent, Will pressed him. 'You do believe me?'

'The truth or accuracy of your information isn't for me to decide. You'll get your audience as soon as Sir Patrick returns. I am a man of my word,' Duncan added stiffly.

'What am I supposed to do in the meantime?'

'You can wait. The rest of us have work to do.'

Will bit back his anger as Duncan headed away up the path, leading a reluctant David. He understood the man's hostility and suspicion; he was a stranger here, who had connections to the enemy and who had abandoned the woman Duncan loved, failing even to contact her until now. He understood, but it frustrated him beyond belief. For years he had been respected, feared even, able to command armies and negotiate with kings. Now, all because he had removed that mantle, he was reduced to nothing. He had no uniform, no money. No power. The only thing he could claim to be was a Campbell, but the family his grandfather had left years ago was based far away in the west and he'd never had any contact with them.

Feeling stung and irritated, Will rested his arms on the ramparts. Out in the estuary, four ships were gliding towards the port of Leith. The stretch of water was black, reflecting the towering cloudbanks, but glittered gold wherever the sun burst through in great, sweeping rays. Everything about this place was vast and wild. It had a strange energy, a brooding, primitive power, visible in the dark volcanic stone that had splintered its way up out of the earth, upon which the Scots had built their indomitable fastness. There was something defiant about the castle and the town below; a bold gesture in the face of the inhospitable terrain that hemmed them in on all sides.

His father had brought him to the castle once when he was a boy. They had come with a company of Templars from Balantrodoch to see King Alexander, something to do with rents from what he could remember. Back then, the royal apartments and administrative buildings, in which the king's constable and the Sheriff of Edinburgh resided with their staff, had mostly been built of timber. Now, many of the buildings had been replaced by larger, stone structures. Work was going on around some of them, the wooden scaffolds shuddering in the wind.

Sensing someone move up alongside him, Will looked round to see David. 'I ought to watch my back. You're as stealthy as a fox.' He tapped his forehead, where he had a faint scar.

David grinned ruefully and leaned against the damp stone. 'You have to be if you want your supper out on the estate.'

'A knight and a hunter.'

'Well, a knight soon,' said David, unself-consciously. 'Don't mind my father,' he added, looking out over the estuary. 'He is just trying to protect Mother.'

'I suppose she was upset with me for a long time?'

David gave a shrug. 'She didn't speak about you much, but after Grandmamma died she cried a lot and I sometimes heard her and Father talking of you and Grandfather. She used to say Grandmamma died of a broken heart.'

Will looked away.

David fiddled with his belt, then glanced at him. 'Did you really save a Grand Master's life?'

'A long time ago.'

'Tell me more about Acre.'

Will smiled. It had become a pact of sorts. He told David about the Holy Land and in return David told him of Scotland and the struggle with Edward, filling in the gaps in his knowledge.

His nephew had spoken at length of the day a decade ago when King Alexander died, breaking his neck in a fall from his horse. In grave tones, that sounded to Will like echoes of Duncan, David told him how the king's granddaughter, the Maid of Norway, passed away shortly after, and Scotland's woes had begun. More than fourteen competitors came forward following her death, each citing a claim to the throne. With civil war threatening, Edward, Alexander's brother-in-law, was requested to intervene. He arranged to conduct a trial to determine the rightful candidate, but Edward had ulterior motives, motives that soon became apparent when he demanded the Scots recognise him as superior overlord, surrendering to him the royal towns and castles. With little option but to comply, the Scottish magnates agreed on the promise that once a king was crowned, Edward would relinquish any hold on the realm.

After a year-long trial, Edward chose John Balliol to be Alexander's successor and, for a time, Scotland's peace was regained. But then slyly, skilfully, Edward began to undermine Balliol's power. As king, it was Balliol's sovereign right to administer justice in his realm, but Edward insisted legal claims that should have been settled in Scotland be heard in England. This continued for several years, Balliol increasingly humiliated, on one occasion even being called to defend himself at Westminster. By this action, Edward was showing that the king was merely a vassal, subject to the English crown and bound by English authority. Things, David told Will, finally came to a head last year when the Scottish magnates, angered by Edward's actions and Balliol's weakness, formed a council to govern in his stead and sent envoys to Philippe to ask for his aid.

David's retelling of these events had only served to increase Will's hatred of Edward. Deserting the Temple to warn the Scots of his plans had felt like a direct and satisfying action against the man who had destroyed his life, but with no one willing to listen to his information, he had begun to feel ever more impotent.

'I would see it myself one day.'

Will, lost in his thoughts, stared at his nephew uncomprehendingly.

'Acre,' said David, laughing at his blank expression. 'Were you even listening to—' He broke off as a horn blew on the walls above them and leaned out, shielding his eyes against the sun. 'Look!'

Following his nephew's finger, Will saw a column of riders moving fast up the hill, pennants flying out behind them in wisps of colour. On the wind, he heard the throb of hooves.

'It's the king.' Grabbing Will's arm, David drew him from the battlements. 'Come, let's tell Father. You'll get your audience now.'

But his nephew's prediction proved premature, for as Balliol's party came sweeping up the track to the castle, funnelling through the arched gates into the courtyard, Will found himself pushed roughly aside by a guard. He caught a glimpse of the king as he was helped down from his horse by a squire, but was afforded no more royal attention than the grooms who came forward to take the tired horses, as Balliol and the magnates headed quickly through the doors of the Great Hall, which thudded shut behind them.

Almost five hours later, Will was pacing the courtyard near the castle stables. There had been a great deal of coming and going since King John's arrival: servants and messengers hurrying in and out of the hall, occasionally followed by an earl or a lord, surrounded by knights. As the hours crawled by, it had been all he could do to stop himself striding in and demanding to speak to the king.

'Campbell.'

Will turned. His hopes rose momentarily at the sight of Duncan, then sank as he saw the expression on his brother-in-law's face. 'Did you speak to Sir Patrick?'

Duncan nodded.

'Well?'

'They wouldn't listen.' Duncan had the grace to sound apologetic as he delivered the crushing news.

Will pushed on, refusing to believe that all he had done had been for nothing; that these men could be so obtuse. 'You relayed my words exactly? You told him Edward intends to take Berwick, then, using Balantrodoch as a staging post, he'll take Edinburgh?'

'Sir Patrick gave the information to Balliol, but the king and his men have made their plans and they're going to keep to them.'

Will slumped on one of the water barrels stacked outside the stables. Duncan heaved a sigh. 'For what it's worth, I think they're wrong.'

Will couldn't even summon the energy to feel grateful for this unexpected support. 'It was all for nothing.'

Duncan sat beside him and folded his muscled arms. 'They've been working towards this for months, Campbell. Everything has been put in place. The treaty with France has been agreed, the border defences have been bolstered.'

'All their defences will count for nothing if Edward punches his way through at Berwick.'

'Sir William Douglas will be defending Berwick. He is one of the most fearless knights in this realm. If what you say is true and Edward will attack the town first, he'll have a hard task on his hands.'

'If what I say is true?' echoed Will. 'They believed me, didn't they?'

'They were suspicious,' admitted Duncan. 'They had a spy in Edward's household trying to find information on his strategy, but it is feared he was discovered. Several of the magnates thought you could have been sent by Edward to sow seeds of confusion, getting us to move our forces into one town, leaving the rest undefended. Some thought you should be arrested.'

Will stared at him.

'But Sir Patrick vouched for you on my pledge.' Duncan shook his head. 'I hope you don't prove either of us wrong.' He stood. 'The magnates are planning to attack Carlisle. For the past year, it has been defended by the Bruce family, who have betrayed their country to fight for Edward. It seems they weren't willing to relinquish the estates they own in England. Seven earls will be going and I'll be leaving soon with my lord, but I've secured David a place here, helping to defend the castle. He's not ready for this battle, not yet.' His chin jutted. 'I want you to bring my wife and daughters here. If Edward does attack Berwick and if . . .' He inhaled quickly. 'I want to know they'll be safe.'

'You want me to be their guard?'

'You owe Ysenda that.' Seeing the defeated agreement in Will's eyes, Duncan nodded, then walked away.

Will rose, about to head in the direction of the barracks, where he'd been stationed in a cramped, draughty dormitory with forty soldiers, when a man, who had been watching his exchange with Duncan, approached.

'William Campbell?'

Will nodded warily, eyeing the large sword strapped to the man's back and wondering if Duncan's promise that he wouldn't be arrested would hold true.

The man, who had thick reddish hair and brown eyes, had a gravelly voice. 'I am Sir Patrick Graham.'

Surprised, Will inclined his head.

Sir Patrick smiled. 'If all I hear of you from my man and his son is true, it is I who should be bowing. Unfortunately, most of my countrymen do not share my gratitude for your sacrifice in coming here to warn us. I did what I could to convince them otherwise, but they are set on their course.'

'I thank you for your support. I know it was a risk to give it.'

'The risk to our kingdom is greater.' Patrick sighed hard. 'I fear the enmity of the magnates towards King Edward has made them too eager for battle. That eagerness has grown into confidence. True, the men of the realm are doughty fighters and the magnates have spent the past few weeks rousing their battle-lust, but it is all a question of numbers in the end. Something I believe your father, being a bookkeeper, would have under-stood?' His smile broadened at Will's astonishment.

'How did you know him?' Will studied Patrick's face. The man didn't look much older than thirty-five and his father had been dead for almost as many years.

'I didn't. My father had business with the Templars at Balantrodoch over the grant of a piece of land. James Campbell brokered the deal on behalf of the Master of Scotland. My father was grateful for his impartiality during the negotiations and, after the deal was done, swore he was in James's debt. They kept in contact for several years before James left Scotland. My father never heard from him again, but years later he still remembered his assistance with gratitude, for when he pronounced me his heir he told me that I held part of my lands in thanks to James. Your father never called upon that debt and when Duncan told me who you were and why you had come, I felt I should honour it.'

'Thank you,' murmured Will, unsure whether he was thanking Patrick for his backing, or for the uplifting memory of his father his words had stirred.

'I am afraid that we do not have the troops to defend ourselves adequately against Edward's army. Unfortunately, neither one of us can do anything about that now. All we can do is fight and pray God is on our side. To that end, I would have you with us, Campbell. At the very least you are an experienced soldier. Add to that your knowledge of Edward and his strategy and I believe you could prove yourself most useful. I will see that you are given a suitable position in the defence of Edinburgh, if you will stand with us?'

Robert's words came back to him, telling him he wouldn't find justice, only war, but Will pushed them aside. 'I'll do more than stand.'

8

Berwick-upon-Tweed, Scotland

30 March 1296 AD

T ogether, the four boys scrabbled up the ramparts, hands digging into
the hard-packed soil, which was covered with bristly grass that
scratched their bare knees. The mound stretched left towards the castle,
perched over the banks of the Tweed, and right in a broad earthen ring
around the town, all the way to the sea gate. It was crowned with a timber
palisade, set deep in the ground, with slits for lookouts at intervals between
the stakes. The boys crowded around one of these slits, their breaths
misting the air. Before them, the ground fell steeply into a narrow fosse that
had been dug out to encircle the town. Beyond this trench, fields rolled
gently away, dotted with houses and farms. It was a damp, dull morning,
but with no fog to obscure the landscape the view was clear, all the way to
the army that covered a shallow hill, less than a mile to the north-east. At
this distance, the boys couldn't pick out details. All they saw was a mass of
men and horses, interwoven with vivid banners and the glint of steel.

'How many?' whispered the youngest, who wore a red felt cap.

One of his comrades squinted, as if trying to count. On the still air, they
could hear faint sounds of shouting, baying dogs and the metal discord of a
host of armoured men moving into position. 'Hundred thousand,' he
pronounced, after a moment.

The youngest boy's mouth opened in an astonished circle, but his
brother, the oldest of them, shoved the one who had spoken. 'Fool.
There're no more than ten.'

'Ten thousand?' whispered the youngest, the discrepancy between the
two numbers offering no consolation.

'They won't get near,' said his brother scornfully, yanking the red cap
down over his eyes. 'Our archers will shoot them down.' He dug a stone
out of the earth by his knee. Standing on his toes, he lobbed it over the
palisade in the direction of the army. 'English dogs!' he yelled at the top

of his lungs, as the stone disappeared in a patch of bushes just beyond the fosse.

The other two grinned and got to their feet. They had heard some soldiers shouting insults at the host on their way to the ramparts. Hands clinging to the top of the stakes for purchase, they hauled themselves up until they could peer over the top. Their voices joined with his.

'English dogs! English dogs! Come here and we'll cut your tails off!'

The youngest pushed the cap back on his head. Their voices were high-pitched, strained. Even as they laughed, he sensed the fear beneath their bravado. Suddenly, the top of the stake his brother was clinging to snapped off. He was only saved from falling backwards down the ramparts by grabbing the boy next to him. As he steadied himself, they fell silent, staring at the piece of timber in his hand, the rot within visible in the crumbling edges of the shard.

'You up there!'

The boys whipped round to see a company of soldiers below, wearing the colours of the town garrison, under the command of William Douglas.

'Get down,' barked one of the soldiers.

They half clambered, half slithered down the mound on to the muddy street.

'Maybe they could take our place?' suggested one of the men, chuckling.

'Get away home to your mothers,' snapped another, cuffing the oldest boy round the head.

Outside Berwick-upon-Tweed, Scotland, 30 March 1296 AD

King Edward's face was set as he surveyed the earthen ramparts of the town. There was a pressure behind his eyes, a mild, burrowing pain. He sniffed once, hard. The dank cold of the north didn't agree with him and he'd come down with a sickness several days into the campaign. He wasn't often ill and the lingering ache in his head was making him irritable. There were hoof-beats behind him as Anthony Bek, the Bishop of Durham, rode up to join him on the hillock half a mile from the town. The bishop's violet robe was swept back over one bulky shoulder, revealing a splendid coat of mail and a broad-bladed sword, sheathed at his hip.

'The ships are ready in the estuary, my lord. They await your signal.'

Edward glanced at him. Iron-willed man of the Church Bek might be, but war suited him even more. He displayed all the pomp and swagger of a military general in his command of the army he had brought with him from

St Cuthbert's Land. Bek was a virtual king in his bishopric, his territories forming part of the northernmost defences of England. Edward had appointed the bishop lieutenant of Scotland six years earlier, when his son was set to marry the Maid of Norway. Bek had since been instrumental in the planning of the war.

Edward turned his attention back to the town, with its maze of timber buildings huddled behind the palisade, interspersed here and there with squat, stone churches. Beyond, the North Sea was a slice of pale silver, fading into the ashen sky. It was hard to imagine this humble burgh, bordered on the far side by the sluggish Tweed and the mud-flats of the estuary, was the richest town in Scotland. The inhabitants, twelve thousand or so, were made up of Scots and a thriving community of foreign merchants, many from the Low Countries, who shipped the hide and wool from the area to Flanders and Germany, in return bringing back cog-loads of red Flemish bricks.

'Some of the men have heard the townsfolk shouting insults.' Bek's nose wrinkled as he surveyed the town. 'These people have no idea of chivalry.'

'Then we shall show them,' responded Edward. He raised a gloved hand and pointed at Berwick. 'There.'

Bek strained his eyes against the distance. 'The ramparts are lower,' he observed.

Edward nodded. 'The scouts have found a path has been built up across the fosse, covered in animal tracks. I expect it's where they lead cattle to pasture. It is where we will enter.' With a firm nudge of his calf and a tug on the reins, the king turned his warhorse, Bayard. The beast's massive head was encased in armour. 'Come. It is time to knight the new-bloods.'

With faint jeers from the town following them on the wind, the two men rode back to the broad slope where the English army was arrayed for battle.

The bulk of the cavalry and infantry was made up of two hundred of Edward's tenants, who, according to the laws of feudal service, had each brought a fully equipped company of knights. This force, more than eight thousand strong, was augmented by conscripts of Welsh bowmen and the Templars under Brian le Jay. All of them were eager to shake the morning chill from their stiff bones, keen to prove themselves to their king.

They had advanced on Berwick three days after Easter, slightly later than Edward planned, due to a brief skirmish at the town of Wark. Here, the campaign began inauspiciously when the town's lord, an English nobleman, deserted to the Scottish side. First blood was spilled by the Scots, who made an attack on Wark, forcing the king to divert his army to relieve the town.

This done, Edward forded the Tweed at the village of Coldstream, swearing to make an end of what the Scots had begun. Berwick's great bridge had been washed away in a flood two years earlier and the village was the nearest crossing point. Following the English army by sea were more than forty galleys that had sailed up the coast from East Anglia. They were now lurking in the mouth of the Tweed, below the town.

Last night, messengers had come with news that the Scottish army was heading for Carlisle, far to the south-west, but Edward diverted no forces. Carlisle was a well-defended city, commanded by one of his staunchest Scottish vassals, Bruce of Annandale. He believed it would hold, but even if it didn't it provided a useful and unexpected diversion for the Scottish army, who had left the way to Edinburgh wide open. The only thing that stood in the king's way was this colony of Scots and foreigners. For Edward, the sooner they were crushed and his campaign was advancing to victory, the better. He hated the cold north and it vexed him greatly that if Alexander III's granddaughter hadn't died none of this would have been necessary.

Six years earlier, with the approval of the pope and the wary agreement of the Scottish magnates, he arranged the marriage of his son and heir, Edward of Caernarvon, with the infant queen, ensuring England's future dominion over the realm. But with her unexpected death, all his plans came to nothing and instead he was compelled to exert years of effort and money in securing his hold on the kingdom. He thought by choosing Balliol, whom his spies had assured him was the weakest of the claimants, his control over the Scottish throne would be set and it might well have been if the magnates hadn't risen against him in rebellion. Now he would have to subdue them by muscle rather than guile, as he'd been forced to do with the Welsh, and he despised them all the more for it.

Like King Philippe, his cousin and rival, Edward had a desire for control. As King of England, he saw it as his right to subdue his disorganised neighbours and bring them into his dominion, creating one strong feudal empire, to be ruled over by his heirs for generations to come. A senior royal clerk, a domineering, yet efficient man named Hugh Cressingham, had spoken of it as smoothing out the ruffles on a cloak; straightening the hems. Edward liked the description. And, by the end of this day, the crease that was Berwick would be levelled.

On the slope in front of the vanguard, which was commanded by the Earl of Surrey, thirty young men were waiting, restless with excitement. They fell silent as Edward and Bek approached. Edward dismounted, ignoring the

proffered hands of the squires. After finalising the plans for the assault with
the Earl of Surrey and the other commanders, the king strode up to the
youths, noble sons of landed men all. They dropped to their knees, heads
bowed, as he unsheathed his sword. The army fell into a near hush for the
solemn moment, disturbed by the barking of dogs, the clink of weapons and
the snorting of horses. Edward moved up to the first, his sword naked in his
hand. Two clerks lingered at the king's side, to discreetly remind him of the
youths' names. Edward raised his sword and laid it on the young man's
shoulder, who swore the oath of fealty faultlessly in a clear voice that
carried to the men behind. Dubbed, he rose; a knight, and a man, as yet un-
blooded, but ready to prove his worth. A cheer rose from the ranks and he
grinned broadly. As the cheer died away, a distant chant could be heard,
coming from the ramparts of Berwick. The king frowned as he approached
the second youth. He lifted his sword, but paused distractedly as he heard
his name within the chant. He cocked his head, listening intently. It came
again.

'*Edward of England, march home on your longshanks! Edward Longshanks, turn
your tail, you English dog!*'

The youth looked around uncertainly as a flush mottled Edward's
cheeks.

Bishop Bek gestured to the officers behind him. 'Cheer for your king,' he
growled. 'You,' he snapped at the man who bore the king's banner,
emblazoned with its three golden lions. 'Get that up!'

The banner-bearer stared at him bemusedly, unused to being given
orders by a bishop. Bek strode over to him. Already cheers were rising,
spreading out like ripples in a pond. 'Get that flag up, or I'll ram the pole up
your arse!'

The banner-bearer lifted the king's flag and began waving it frantically.
The cheers grew louder, drowning out the taunting chants from Berwick.
Edward turned back to the youth and brought down the flat of his blade, his
jaw locked in anger.

The dubbing continued for some time, each man's knighthood ushered in
with louder, more fervent applause than the last, until the plain around
Berwick resounded with the roar of eight thousand men. It was the Earl of
Surrey who first noticed the ships gliding into the estuary beyond the town.
He frowned, rising in his stirrups to get a better look, then swore and
kicked his horse towards Edward, who was knighting the last of the youths.

'My lord!' The earl pulled his horse up, pointing to the ships as he caught
the king's attention.

Edward's grey eyes widened at the sight.

Bek was hurrying over, having also seen them. 'Why are they attacking? We haven't given the signal!'

'The cheering,' said Edward suddenly, 'the banners. They think we've begun the assault.' Barking orders to the nearest commanders, he strode to Bayard.

There was a general scrabble as word spread, men rushing to their horses, those who were already mounted tightening shield straps. The newly knighted youths sprinted for their chargers, hearts hammering with anticipation. Archers pulled arrows from quivers and infantry drew swords or hefted maces as the knights moved into position, warhorses stamping and jostling.

In the distance, down by the Tweed, the sky brightened as a hail of flaming arrows went shooting into the air from the town. They arced silently towards the lead ship. Edward strained forward in his saddle. Even at this distance, he could tell something was wrong: the ship was stalled, dead in the water. He swore viciously as he guessed the vessel had run aground on the mud-banks. As the fiery missiles struck, the white mainsail went up like a torch. 'With me!' Edward roared at his commanders, digging his spurs into Bayard's muscular sides.

The English cavalry followed, cantering down the broad slope towards the town. The Earl of Surrey led the vanguard with the king, the two of them streaking ahead. Their right flank was headed by Brian le Jay and the Templars, white mantles flowing, the hooves of their horses drumming the earth. The left was commanded by Bek and the warriors of St Cuthbert's Land, the bishop's cloak blooming behind him, violet as a bruise. The archers loped along behind, heading for a point just beyond the small hillock where Edward had surveyed the town. From there, they would cover the knights and the infantry, now pouring down the hill. On the Tweed, the ship's decks were burning, yellow flames billowing, fanned by the breeze coming off the sea. Screams drifted on the air, but Edward and his men didn't hear them over the thunder of their charge.

Two more ships were moving in to aid the first, but Berwick's soldiers were racing from a postern gate on to the mud, where they hacked the men fleeing the burning ship to pieces. More arrows sprang into the air, hissing into the water around the approaching vessels. Another ship ran aground and the defenders yelled in triumph. After the arrows, bundles of flaming wood were tossed over the sides of the floundering galleys by the men on the banks. They struck the decks and began to smoulder. Dry timbers crackled into life, faster than the crew, themselves trying to dodge the arrows, could extinguish. Men jumped overboard to escape the flames, only to find themselves sucked into the sticky mud by the weight of their mail. Smoke was pouring off the first vessel, making it harder for the English to see the soldiers rushing towards them, their lightweight leather armour allowing them to cross the waterlogged mud-flats in safety.

Edward steered Bayard straight, heading for the point where the broad ramparts dipped down, creating a gateway in the defences that led on to a narrow path, banked up with earth and stones from the fosse. The gate that had been set there was tall and wide to compensate, but a timber barrier couldn't keep out eight thousand men, especially men whose honour had been challenged. Edward's temper burned, striking livid colour in his cheeks. The insults of the townsfolk rang in his ears and the sight of his own ships blazing on the river drove him into a fury that would only be quenched with blood. All chance of mercy that Berwick's citizens might have hoped for had gone. Now, they would suffer his wrath in full.

As the men neared the ramparts, arrows slammed down around them. One struck a knight in the chest. He arched backwards with the force and tumbled from his mount, to be trampled by the destriers that rode on over him. Other arrows clattered off helmets, or stuck fast in mail shirts and coifs. Several hit horses, which wheeled and bucked, throwing their riders violently from the saddles and crashing into the mud. Edward raised his shield, but the missiles streaked past, none coming close. Behind them, the Welsh archers began to launch at the earthen ramparts, sending arrows curving over the palisade to stab down at the defenders huddled behind. Drawing closer to the fosse, Edward slowed his horse, allowing two of his commanders to ride on ahead with their best knights and the new-bloods. It was hard for him to do so; his rage made him want to spur Bayard on to punch through that stockade himself, but the thirty knighted youths were as keen as hounds, nostrils filled with the scent of quarry. He would use that eagerness. These young men only knew the controlled thrill of the tournament field. They hadn't yet experienced the chaos of a battlefield; hadn't learned to fear it. They were arrogant, bold and reckless. They would tear through the barrier to get at the meat inside, or die trying.

Bek and a veteran commander of many a battle under Edward, including Lewes and those in Wales, ordered four of their knights on across the bank that spanned the fosse. All had grappling hooks ready in their hands. One took an arrow in the neck and fell from his horse, still holding the reins. He tumbled down the steep embankment with a cry that was cut short as his horse, squealing in terror, collapsed on top of him. The other three knights launched their hooks at the top of the gates. Arrows whistled over the ramparts from the Welsh archers. There were screams beyond the stockade as they struck home. The grappling hooks held fast and, lashing the ropes around the pommels of their saddles, the knights spurred their horses back across the fosse. The ropes snapped taut. One of the grappling irons broke clean through the rotting timbers and flew down to bounce along the ground behind the mounted knight. The other two held for a split second, then pulled free with a sharp crack, bringing the top half of the gate with them to reveal the startled faces of several soldiers.

'The gate's rotten!' yelled one knight, as behind the ruined barricade some of the defenders began to flee. Others held fast, drawing back bowstrings to propel arrows through the breach.

'On!' shouted Bek, driving his horse towards the gate. The beast leapt up at the last moment, launching itself over the jagged timbers. One of its hooves caught on part of the gate but smashed straight through it as the horse went hurtling into the street beyond. The archers within scattered as Bek's men followed, one by one, charging up and over. Behind came the new knights, baying for blood, racing one another to be the first in. One horse baulked at the last minute and veered around, crashing into the side of the gate that had remained intact. The wood buckled with the impact, although the gate didn't break, and the rider lost control of the beast, which stumbled down the embankment, taking him with it. After him, two more knights faltered, both managing to wheel their horses around and back across the path.

Edward's impatience exploded into urgency. Kicking into Bayard's sides, he stormed the gate. The massive destrier leapt the broken barrier in one graceful movement. Seeing their king enter, the knights drove themselves madly forward, one armoured horse punching straight through, the remaining weakened timbers spraying inwards, leaving a splintered gap, through which the stream of men became a flood.

The confidence of Berwick's young soldiers, who had been taunting the English from the ramparts, melted into horror as the metal-clad knights plunged into the streets around them, faces hidden behind expressionless steel or else snarling with savage glee as they brought sword blades and axe heads swinging into skulls and necks. They weren't used to the giant destriers, which the knights used against them as weapons – toppling, crushing, trampling – and their armour consisted mostly of leather; only their knight-commanders had mail. Flesh, pale and vulnerable, was exposed to the iron of arrow tips and spear heads. The defenders' backward scrabble became a rout as the knights overwhelmed them.

One soldier sprinted away, blowing hard on a horn. Two young knights followed him, eyes alight with the exhilaration of the chase. The first pounded up behind him, his sword chopping down at the defender's back. The man veered off at the last moment, darting into a narrow side street. The knight cursed as he barrelled past the opening and his comrade took up the pursuit, using the channel of the street like a jousting list, couching his lance in the crook of his arm, bracing himself for impact. He caught the fleeing soldier in the back, between his shoulder blades, the tip of the lance piercing leather, muscle and bone, driving clean through him. The momentum swept the man off his feet for a few seconds, the knight still holding the lance, until the strain was too much and he was forced to let go. The lance crashed to the floor and, as the knight rode on, one of the iron-shod hooves of the destrier came down on the man's head, bursting it like fruit. Another landed on the horn and shattered it. The knight rode on into the streets, drawing his sword and following his comrades, eager for another target with which to prove his prowess.

The horn had signalled a general alarm, but the garrison who rallied and rode out under the command of William Douglas were too late to stop what had started. Doughty they might be, but there were only two hundred men under Douglas. Against eight thousand they were a row of pebbles set against the incoming tide. With a lack of coordinated soldiers to fight, the English cavalry blooded themselves elsewhere, chasing the defenders, many of them farmers and fishermen, into the narrow streets, where the butchery began in earnest. In their wake, infantry broke down the doors of houses, pushing and shoving one another to get inside, the lure of plunder, rape and slaughter urging them on. Veteran commanders directed younger knights to herd the fleeing inhabitants into open squares so the rest of the knights could get at them more easily. Some locals had erected barricades, from behind which they shot arrows and stones at the knights, but for every man they felled, ten of them were killed, struck by hurled spears and axes. The defenders on the mud-flats of the Tweed attacking the ships, three of which were now aflame, drew back as more vessels glided in, cautiously now, the captains aware of the treacherous mud, and the crews disembarked to storm the weak defences along the banks.

No one found on the streets of Berwick was spared the sword, whether young or old, man or woman. A group of boys raced through a riddle of alleys, followed by whooping soldiers. They cried out in terror, skidding to a halt at a dead-end behind a church. One crouched against the wall, making himself as small as he could, as the seven knights chasing them brought their snorting warhorses to a halt at the mouth of the alley. One of the knights called out, promising to spare them if they surrendered. The boys crowded in around one another, panting with fear. One bent and picked up a stone, but didn't throw it. The knight called out again. Warily, the boys stepped towards the knights, all but the youngest, who remained huddled against the wall. He watched as the others reached the end of the alley. He kept on watching as the knights steered their horses in around them, locking them into a killing zone. Swords rose and fell and blood sprayed across the walls of the buildings as the boys were cut down. The youngest sprang to his feet and, in desperation, tried to climb the church wall. He made it halfway, his fingertips tearing on the rough stone, before the sound of hooves clattered up behind him and he felt something punch solidly into his back. As he fell, his red felt cap slipped from his head.

The killing continued throughout the day and on into the night. Edward himself, along with the Earl of Surrey and five hundred knights, pushed Douglas and his soldiers back hard, until they were forced to retreat inside the castle. Douglas was one of the last through the gates, his roars of frustration sounding above the screams that echoed across Berwick. Inside the Church of St Mary's, bodies of the townsfolk who had sought sanctuary and who had been butchered when the knights had broken through, were dragged out into the street to make way for the king, who set up camp inside as evening drew in. Around the town fires raged, pushing back the darkness. The bloodstained faces of the knights were ghoulish in the crimson light.

By dawn, the Red Hall, owned by the Flemish merchants, was aflame. Inside, over forty men huddled together, hands clasped over their mouths against the suffocating smoke, eyes weeping. They had held firm against the English, shooting volleys of arrows from the upper windows of their Hall into the ranks on the street below. One man, more by luck than judgement, had launched an arrow that shot straight through the slit of one knight's helm and pierced his eye, killing him instantly. The merchants' relish over his feat became all the greater when word went up that the knight killed was none other than a cousin of King Edward. But with no chance for surrender and nowhere to run, they were no more than prisoners in the Hall. Now, over the fierce crackle of flames, the merchants could hear the knights who had barricaded the doors and set the fires laughing and shouting abuse.

As morning dawned, pale and cold, Berwick lay shrouded in smoke. Bodies choked the narrow streets and the stink from opened corpses was revolting, turning even the hardest warriors' stomachs as their horses slipped and skidded in the gore. So much blood had been spilled that it had run down on to the banks of the Tweed where, as the dawn tide rose, the river turned red. The butchery had become weary now, almost perfunctory. The knights and their mounts were tired; battle-lust faded, fury spent, honour regained. But still, Edward refused to give the order to halt the assault.

After hearing Mass in St Mary's and breaking his fast, the king rode out to survey the carnage. Bishop Bek went with him as did Brian le Jay who, several hours earlier, had asked the king to bring an end to the butchery.

'My lord,' the English Master had reasoned, 'this town is on its knees. Is it not time to finish it?'

'We must make an example here,' the king had replied. 'Let all Scotland know what awaits them if they insist on challenging my authority.'

Le Jay had gone to protest, but Bek warned him away with a quiet reminder of Edward's violent temper and what had befallen other men who had argued with him when he was in such a black mood.

The Templar Master now rode at Edward's side in a tense silence, his knights riding behind him, steering their horses around the carcasses that littered the ground.

Ahead, a blood-curdling scream rent the air. It was impossible to tell whether it was male or female, but whoever had uttered it was obviously in horrendous pain. The company rode on towards the noise, which stopped momentarily, then started again. It was a terrible, almost animal sound, filled with agony. As the knights trotted their horses around the side of a building, they saw its cause. A young woman was dragging herself along the street towards a shoemaker's, the doorway of which had been battered down, leaving a gaping hole that led into darkness. Her belly was huge and swung from side to side as she crawled forward on her hands and knees. The back of her white dress was scarlet with blood, although whether this was caused by the wound to her side, visible through the rips in the gown, or the act of childbirth in which she was clearly engaged, wasn't certain. Behind her a soldier picked himself up off the floor, where he seemed to have fallen, or to have been pushed and with a shout of anger snatched up his sword, lying several feet away. Before any of the company could call out, he ran forward and began to hack at the woman. Her screams cut off as the sword rose and fell.

Sickened by the display of mindless savagery, le Jay turned to Edward. 'End this, my lord. Call off the assault and rein in your men.'

The king, who had sent two of his men to pull the blood-splattered soldier back from his frenzied attack on the woman, arched an eyebrow at the English Master. 'Are you giving me an order?'

'I am giving you a choice,' replied le Jay harshly. 'Call off the assault or I'll withdraw my support. You will have to continue this war without my men and without the use of Balantrodoch.'

'Your Grand Master commanded you to aid me.'

'Grand Master de Molay commanded me to help you put down a rebellion, not murder pregnant women in the street.'

There was silence, broken only by the sound of the soldier's sword clattering to the ground and the noises of his retching as he bent over beside the mutilated woman and her half-born child and began to vomit.

'My lord,' said Bek, his voice quiet with caution. 'Perhaps this has gone on long enough. We mustn't spend ourselves on one town, not when we have other battles ahead.'

Edward glanced at him, something shifting in his grey eyes, some spark of reason entering his flat stare. After a long moment, he nodded. 'Send orders to the men that the assault is ended, then deliver word to Douglas that if he surrenders himself to me I will spare the lives of his soldiers. Search the houses. Any women and children you find alive are free to go, but you will kill any man who will fetch no ransom. These people will breed no more sons to defy me.' Turning his horse, he paused beside Brian le Jay. 'You have your way today,' he murmured, 'but talk back to me again and I'll have your head.' His voice rose as he addressed Bek and the others. 'When the streets are cleared we will begin work on refortifying the defences. Berwick will be rebuilt as an English town.'

Later that morning, the scattered forces, exhausted and bloodstained, came to order as the word went out for the assault to be raised. Men dressed their wounds, said prayers over dead comrades. Others returned to their captains with saddlebags stuffed with jewellery and silver. Down on the riverbanks, men worked in lines, tossing corpses into the Tweed. It was back-breaking work, for over eight thousand inhabitants had perished. The bodies tumbled slowly over one another in the current, clogging the estuary like thousands of enormous dead fish. Gulls and crows swooped and dived, picking a feast from the waves.

9

The Temple, Paris

23 April 1296 AD

'The troughs need cleaning again, Etienne.' Simon motioned to a spotty-faced sergeant as they filed out of the Great Hall. 'And this time,' he added gruffly, 'if I can't see your face in that water, I'll see it in the dung heap.'

'Yes, sir,' murmured Etienne, trudging off towards the stables.

Simon chuckled to himself, still tickled by the fact that the younger ones called him that. He was the son of a tanner from Cheapside and a sergeant like them. But as one of the senior grooms he was beneath only the stable master in rank, a position that granted him almost as much respect as the knights themselves. His mirth faded as he caught sight of a tall figure with silvery-blond hair heading into a building on the other side of the quadrangle. 'Sir Robert!' he called, hastening after the knight, ignoring the glare of disapproval his shout elicited from a passing priest. As Robert disappeared inside, Simon followed. He caught up with him in the cloisters that connected the knights' quarters to the Grand Master's palace.

This time, Robert turned at his call. The knight greeted him tersely, halting in a patch of sunlight that was streaming through the arches, making stark shadows on the wall behind.

Simon thought he looked old suddenly, old and tired. 'I heard you'd all returned this morning, but I've been looking for Will and no one knows where he is.' When Robert didn't answer, Simon added, 'I didn't think you'd be gone so long.'

'The Grand Master wanted to visit several preceptories in England.'

'Will's friend from Acre, the rabbi, has been asking after him. He was aggrieved Will hadn't been to see him.'

'Elias?' Robert nodded wearily. 'I'll visit him when I get the opportunity. Explain what has happened.'

'Explain what?' When Robert looked away, the burly groom took a step towards him. 'What's happened? Where's Will?'

'In Scotland, I believe,' said Robert, lowering his voice as two knights walked by. He exhaled roughly. 'He's gone, Simon. I couldn't stop him.'

Simon remained silent as Robert told him what had happened in London. 'This has to be a mistake,' he murmured, when the knight finished. 'Will wouldn't desert the Order.' He frowned at Robert's uncompromising expression. 'He wouldn't,' he repeated. 'And he certainly wouldn't leave Rose. You must have got it wrong. Maybe he just meant to see that his sister was safe, then planned to come back?'

'I watched him take off his mantle.' Robert's face was tight. 'He's not coming back.'

'It's Elwen. That's why he's gone. He's mad with grief. Did he say anything else? Did he give you any message for Rose?' The lines in Simon's forehead deepened. 'Or me?'

'Only that he wanted us to keep a watch on her.'

Simon sat down on the wall that ringed the cloisters. 'Has the Grand Master sent anyone after him?'

'Hugues managed to cover his disappearance saying Will was running a message to Scotland. No one but the two of us, and now you, know he's deserted, although I doubt we will be able to keep it hidden indefinitely.'

'I always thought the Visitor was a stickler for the rules?'

Robert hesitated. 'The Visitor thinks Will has gone for the sake of his family; to warn them the English are coming.' His tone was quiet, but firm. 'I never spoke of Will's intention to inform the Scots of Edward's plans and you mustn't either. For deserting he could be imprisoned, but for that he could be executed. He's threatening the lives of our own men with this action.' His jaw tightened further. 'Not that this seemed to matter to him.'

'As I told you,' said Simon staunchly, 'he's mad with grief. He doesn't know what he's doing.' He was silent for some moments. 'I'll go after him.'

'What?'

'I'll go to Scotland, talk some sense into him.'

'Don't be a fool.'

'What's foolish about it? Don't you want him to come back?'

'What makes you think you could persuade him when I couldn't?'

'Isn't it worth a try?' demanded Simon, rising to face the knight.

Robert stared at Simon's dogged expression. He smiled slightly, but it faded quickly. 'How can you leave without arousing anyone's suspicions?'

'You can get me posted to Balantrodoch. I don't even have to go to the preceptory, just send me with the papers. I'll find Will and convince him to come back with me and you can make sure I'm transferred back here. You can do this, Robert,' pressed Simon, when the knight didn't answer. 'I know it.'

'Oh yes, very easily,' retorted Robert. But he saw the look of determination in Simon's face. 'It would be dangerous. The war.'

'He'd do the same for us.'

'And if he doesn't want to come back?'

'He will, if I tell him Rose needs him.'

After a long pause, the knight exhaled. 'I'll think on it.'

Leaving Simon to head to the stables, Robert continued towards the officials' buildings. His mood, which had lifted briefly with the groom's stubborn optimism, dampened again. For the past few months, he had gone over and over that conversation in New Temple, wondering if he could have done more, said something that would have made Will change his mind. He had come to the conclusion that he couldn't have, but he still blamed himself for not acting more decisively as he watched Will's descent into darkness after Acre. Had he said or done something earlier then perhaps Will would never have gone this far. Will wasn't just a comrade, a brother-in-arms: he was responsible for the Anima Templi. His desertion from that cause rendered Robert's own pledge and sacrifices for the Brethren somehow meaningless. But Will and Simon had been close since they were boys in New Temple, and he knew the depth of the groom's feelings. If there was a chance Simon could succeed where he had failed, shouldn't he let him take it?

'You're late,' said Hugues, as Robert entered the solar. He rose from behind his desk, briskly rolling up a scroll. 'Shut the door.'

Robert pushed down an urge to retort. He didn't think Hugues would take kindly to his mocking these days.

'I had an audience with the Grand Master this morning,' said Hugues. 'He intends to leave for Cyprus in the next few weeks to begin planning his Crusade. He hopes the support the leaders of the West have promised him will materialise in time for a move east by the spring of next year.'

'You don't sound convinced.'

'You've seen how entangled in their own conflicts they are. Once King Edward has subdued Scotland, he'll lock horns with Philippe over Gascony again, no doubt using the support he's managed to obtain from the Count of Flanders, who is desperate to stop Philippe attempting to annex his territory. King Philippe meanwhile seems intent on making an enemy of the Church with these new taxes he has been demanding from the clergy. I hear a priest was killed in a skirmish with royal guards. Apparently, they tried to take his collection box and he refused to allow them. The royal household has sent out criers to dispel the rumours, saying the priest attacked one of the guards, but only the most gullible Parisians will be convinced by that.' Hugues set the scroll on the desk and moved over to him. 'Which is why I have asked the Grand Master to allow you to stay here with me when he returns to Cyprus.' He placed a hand on Robert's shoulder. 'These are troubled times.'

'The Grand Master agreed to this?'

'I was persuasive. I need someone I can trust to help me in my capacity as head of the Anima Templi, as well as in the day-to-day running of the Order.'

'You've made yourself head?' murmured Robert, staring at his old comrade, who seemed more and more changed from the man he thought he knew.

'Someone needed to fill the position. It was vacant after all.'

'What if Will returns?' ventured Robert.

Hugues scowled. 'Campbell gave up any right to hold that position when he deserted. He chose his family over the Brethren.' He hesitated. 'But if he returns and makes amends for his disobedience he may assume a position under me.'

As Hugues turned away, Robert saw the look on his face and wasn't so sure Will would be welcomed. He thought of Simon's comments about the Visitor being a stickler for the rules. He hadn't spoken his mind to the groom, who was unaware of the Anima Templi, but privately thought he knew why Hugues had agreed to let Will's desertion go unchallenged. The Visitor wasn't used to sharing power and it was clear that he had his own vision for the future of the Brethren and the Order; a vision that ran counter to Will's. Robert's fears were compounded as he recalled Will's belief that Edward had played them for fools all these years and his concern over how easily Hugues had fallen into bed with the king.

'I have need of good men with me here, Robert. Together, we must do everything possible to ensure that the Order retains its authority.' Hugues returned to his desk. 'When Jacques has gone we can begin looking to a new future, one in which the Temple can survive beyond his outdated war.'

*   *   *

The Lateran Palace, Rome, 14 May 1296 AD

Bertrand de Got had to hurry to keep up as the cleric marched through the square towards the main palace building, past the entrance to the Lateran Church. It was a dazzlingly bright day and, to the west of the palace, the city of Rome sparkled like a gem, elegant towers and voluptuous domes of churches thrusting above the rooftops. Beyond, the Tiber was a blue ribbon, curling languidly around newly built palazzos and the crumbling remains of the ancient civilisation that once ruled the Earth.

Bertrand found himself short of breath and sweaty inside his travelling cloak as the cleric escorted him up the wide marble steps, into the cool shade of the palace's interior, bustling with officials from the papal curia.

'I have to warn you, Bishop, you may find his holiness to be troubled of spirit.' The cleric exhaled sharply. 'The death of Celestine has caused him some unexpected difficulties.'

'Celestine is dead?'

The cleric frowned at Bertrand's expression. 'You had not heard?'

'I have only just arrived.'

The cleric halted, glancing around. Bertrand was relieved at the chance to catch his breath.

'Celestine died in his prison cell a fortnight ago,' continued the cleric in a quiet voice. 'No sooner had his body been brought out than Giacomo and Pietro Colonna were demanding an investigation. His death was declared to be the result of natural causes, as of course it was.' The cleric dropped his voice further. 'But that didn't stop the Colonnas spreading vicious rumours that his holiness had been the architect of Celestine's demise.'

'The Colonna cardinals have accused the pope of murder?' said Bertrand, astonished.

'Not openly, of course, but there is no doubt in the minds of many that these rumours originated with Cardinal Giacomo. He has been an enemy of the pope ever since his holiness imprisoned Celestine for abdicating the papal throne. He even once charged him with persuading Celestine to step down so that he could take the papal tiara. But Giacomo was not concerned for Celestine. It was himself he was thinking of. He has always been bitter that Boniface was elected over—' Two black-robed officials from the chancery swept past and the cleric broke off abruptly. 'Come,' he said, after the officials had passed, 'but I advise you to refrain from saying anything that may vex his holiness.'

Bertrand thought of the news he had brought with him and had a sinking feeling as the cleric led him up several curving stairways and along a stately corridor towards a set of colossal doors. The cleric rapped smartly and pushed them open.

The expansive chamber was crammed with sumptuous furnishings, all arresting in their opulence, and it was some moments before Bertrand, scanning the room, caught sight of its occupant. Pope Boniface VIII was seated in a large, cushioned chair by an arched window. Behind him, a barber worked an ivory comb through his hair. At sixty-two, Boniface still had a full head of it, although it was dove white and thinning at the edges of his neat tonsure. His dark eyes flicked to Bertrand, who glanced round as the cleric shut the doors behind him.

'Bishop,' Boniface greeted, in a voice laced with self-assurance. 'That will do.'

Bertrand halted, then realised the second address had been to the barber, who took the cloth Boniface pulled from his shoulders, bowed deeply and padded across the rugs to a smaller door on the other side of the chamber. As Boniface rose and extended a hand, Bertrand went towards him, feeling a tingle of colour in his cheeks. He forgot how the pope always managed to make him feel like a clumsy acolyte. Steeling himself, he bent, his lips brushing the gold ring.

Boniface withdrew and strode to a marble table, his robes, blood-red Venetian silk, whispering across the floor. 'I thought you might have come sooner,' he remarked, picking up a jewel-encrusted tiara and placing it on his head.

'I apologise, your holiness. I was kept from my diocese for many months and I desired to see that all was well with my people before making the journey here.'

'And your mission in England?' The pope straightened the tiara in an ornate mirror. 'How did you fare?'

'Not as well as I had hoped,' admitted Bertrand. 'After I wrote to King Edward to suggest the merging of the Knight Orders I heard nothing for some time, then I received a message asking me to join him in London for a meeting with Jacques de Molay.' Bertrand was aware of the peevishness in his tone, but couldn't help it; he wanted Boniface to be as angry at the English king as he was. He was still sour over Edward's change of face and his own naivety in not seeing it coming. 'In this message, the king seemed keen to discuss my proposition, but no sooner had the meeting begun than he commandeered it for his own purposes.'

Boniface's reflection frowned. 'His own purposes?'

'He wanted the Temple to aid him in his war against Scotland. I warned him how unhappy you would be at the prospect of him warring with another Christian nation rather than with the Saracens, but he would not listen.'

'I'm glad you felt free to speak my mind,' said Boniface, looking round. His eyes locked on the bishop, who shuffled under his gaze.

'Your holiness, I . . .' But he didn't continue; the pope's stare wasn't getting any gentler and besides, Edward had promised to get Bertrand's nephew a more profitable benefice when he regained his lands in Guienne, if Bertrand complied with his wishes. Swallowing his anger, he met the pope's gaze. 'Edward did, however, say that he would lead a new Crusade as soon as the trouble in Scotland was ended and Jacques de Molay is still determined to head east. Our hopes for regaining Jerusalem are not ended.'

'Well, those hopes may have to wait for now. Pass me the ferula.'

Bertrand followed the pope's finger to a long, ornate chest beneath the window. Crossing to it, he opened the lid. The papal cross was lying on a white cloth inside. As Bertrand's fingers closed around the shaft and he withdrew it, the gold caught the light coming through the window and glittered. 'Wait?' he echoed, handing the ferula to the pope.

'I have received disturbing reports from the clergy in France, telling of recent tax demands by King Philippe. The king and his ministers have employed increasingly violent means. Priests who have protested against his intolerable demands have been robbed, beaten even. I warned Philippe of making an enemy of the Church when he did this last year. It seems he did not take my warning seriously. This time, I will not let it go unchallenged.'

'What will you do?'

'I have already done it. I have drawn up a bull, *Clericis laicos*. In it I have forbidden the taxing of the clergy by laymen, without papal permission. Any who engage in this activity shall be pronounced excommunicate.'

Bertrand was unable to cover his surprise. 'But the kings of France and other nations have always drawn monies from the Church with which to fund their military engagements.'

'And now they shall be subject to my will in such matters and must ask for aid, at which time I will be the judge of whether it should be given or not.'

'Do the cardinals know of this?' asked Bertrand, wondering how the pope's rivals in the Sacred College had taken the news. The Colonna family, he knew, were supporters of France and Bertrand doubted they would have remained quiet at the proclamation of this provocative bull, especially not in light of what the cleric had told him.

'Most of them know,' said Boniface staunchly. 'And those that don't will in the next hour. I am making an address in the consistory.' He studied Bertrand's worried expression. 'Do not fear, Bishop de Got,' he said coolly. 'My will shall prevail. I am the successor of St Peter, acting under the direct authority of God. Philippe will learn this soon enough.' Wielding the papal cross in both hands, Boniface appraised his imposing reflection. 'As shall all who oppose me.'

10

The Royal Castle, Edinburgh

15 May 1296 AD

W ill came awake with a start to see his nephew looming over him. 'What is it?' he groaned, pushing the youth away. He had been on watch on the walls of the castle for two days straight without sleep and had collapsed on his pallet barely an hour earlier, not bothering to take off his boots. He sat up, massaging his face.

David sat back on his heels. 'It's Father. He's returned.'

Will's tiredness faded at David's expression. Kicking off the rough blanket, he stood. As he pulled on his hauberk and cloak, David reached down and picked up his falchion. Without a word, he handed it to him. Will pulled the belt tight around his waist as he followed his nephew out of the dormitory and down into the courtyard.

It was almost dawn and the star-strewn sky glowed turquoise in the east. Everything below the rock was shrouded in mist. It was as though the castle were a ship, sailing on a phantom sea. The air was chilly and smelled of the acrid smoke from burning torches. There was a large crowd in the courtyard and thirty or so horses gathered near the stables. Squires were removing saddles and hastening to fetch water. Will saw several stretchers laid out on the ground, two of which were occupied by injured men. One had lost a leg. The injury didn't look particularly fresh, the wound was bound tightly and dried blood and dirt had stained the binding black. In the light of the torch flames, the soldier's face was slick and had an ill-looking greenish tint to it. Will recognised the signs of infection and guessed he didn't have long. He spotted Duncan talking with the Sheriff of Edinburgh. As he pushed through the agitated crowd, he caught snatches of conversation.

'Fallen?'

'. . . don't know how many we lost, we were scattered.'

'. . . most of them dead.'

Approaching, Will saw that Duncan was also wounded, a nasty gash running down the side of his face. The split skin had been crudely sewn back together with thread, between which beads of blood had welled and scabbed over. It looked absurdly like a large black caterpillar had crawled up his cheek, with stitches for legs. His cloak and mail were covered with blood and reeked of it. As Duncan turned from the sheriff, Will saw the look in his eyes. His brother-in-law wasn't the stalwart, unshakeable man he had last seen leaving the town with Patrick Graham and the feudal host of Scotland over two months ago. He was haggard, haunted. David went silently to his side, eyes lingering on his father's scarred face.

Duncan glanced at Will, then spoke to his son. 'Did you wake your mother?'

David shook his head.

'Good lad.' Duncan looked down at his clothes. 'I want to get this red off me before I see her.' He attempted a smile, which was more of a grimace.

'What happened?' Will had to raise his voice over the men around him. More people were hurrying into the courtyard, woken by the commotion. The injured men were being hefted up and carried towards the infirmary.

Duncan faltered, as if uncertain where to begin. 'We were at Dunbar,' he said eventually, 'almost three weeks ago. Our forces were unable to take Carlisle. The Bruces held firm against us, so we pushed on into northern England.' Duncan lowered his voice, glancing around him. 'Our men contented themselves with burning villages and monasteries, pillaging estates, destroying crops and livestock. They near enough spent themselves on this futility while Edward and his army remained in Berwick, like carrion crouched over their meal.' It was a moment before he could gather himself to continue. Will understood. Edinburgh had learned of the sack of Berwick a month ago, but the shock of it was still reverberating around the city. 'Leaving Northumberland, laden with plunder for the cause, we circled around to Dunbar. The Earl of Dunbar had sided with Edward.' Duncan's jaw clenched. 'These bastards call themselves Scots, but their blood runs thinner than water. Fortunately for us, his wife was of stronger heart and opened his castle to a company of loyalist troops, but her treachery and the word that we were on our way soon roused the English.

'They came under the command of John de Warenne, Earl of Surrey. He put some of his knights before the castle to stop our men there joining with us, then turned to face us. We had the higher ground. We had the advantage.' Duncan shook his head and stared up at the lightening sky. 'All of us were maddened by the fate of Berwick, desperate to spill English blood, avenge our dead. The English columns were advancing downhill into a steep valley. We couldn't see it from our position, but there was a burn at the bottom. The English started to separate. I suppose they must have been deploying to cross the burn, but I swear to God it looked like they were scattering, fleeing the field. Seeing them disordered we stormed down that hill as if the hosts of Heaven were with us, Christ Himself urging us on. But when we reached the bottom we found the English all in a line, ready for us. Too late to stop the charge, we smashed into their steel like the sea against a cliff. Many cavalry were lost in the first moments and as the English led their own attack our foot-soldiers were cut down in the hundreds.' His hand drifted absently to his wound. 'After this, we were in chaos, forced to flee or be killed where we stood.' His voice shook. 'But my lord wouldn't leave that field. He was unhorsed and fighting three English knights, roaring like a lion. Last I saw was him going down under their blades.'

Will had known Patrick Graham for only a brief moment, yet the sorrow he felt for the knight's death was disproportionately sharp.

'Most of us who fled the field headed for the shelter of Selkirk Forest. I stayed there with the survivors of my company for several days, tending wounded, burying dead. Word came to us that many of our leaders had been taken prisoner during the battle, including three earls.'

'What about Sir Patrick's son?' asked David suddenly.

'Sir David Graham was captured. All the prisoners have been sent to gaols throughout England. Unless ransoms can be paid, I doubt we will see them again.' Duncan squeezed his son's shoulder. 'I'm sorry, I know you were friends. The sheriff was telling me there's been no word from King John for some weeks,' he said to Will.

'It's thought he might be at Stirling, or further north. No one is sure.'

They fell quiet. Around them, disbelief and anguish gradually gave way to heavy silence, as everyone tried to take in the news Duncan's ragged band had brought.

After the massacre at Berwick, the atmosphere in Scotland had changed. They had all felt it. Their earlier confidence slipped away to be replaced by a grim determination. The wanton butchery of thousands of their country-men had a profound effect on the mood of the nation. Men who had previously snubbed King John and his weakness in the face of Edward's demands, now banded together beneath his banner. A rallying cry went up across the kingdom, ushered in by the voices of the few men and women who had fled Berwick with their lives and who brought with them the livid horrors that had befallen fathers, brothers, sons and daughters. What started as a whimper became a roar.

But now, here in the hushed castle courtyard, with the red light of dawn bleeding in the east, there was just the crushing sense of inevitability. How could they fight without their leaders? It was a question visible on every man's face.

The silence was broken by a door banging open as Ysenda came running into the yard, snatching a shawl around her. Her hair was unbound and flew about her shoulders as she raced towards Duncan, her face filled with relief, which quickly turned to shock at the sight of his torn face. 'Dear God. Duncan?'

'I'm all right, woman,' he said gruffly, pulling her to him. 'I'm all right.' She drew back to grasp his bloody face and kiss his mouth.

Will looked away, discomforted that their fierce affection, which should please him, just made him feel bitter.

As Duncan hugged Ysenda, he caught Will's eye. 'It is rumoured Roxburgh Castle has fallen,' he told him over her shoulder. 'They'll be coming for us next.'

The Royal Castle, Edinburgh, 7 June 1296 AD

There was a muffled thud. Dust and grit showered from the ceiling. In the darkness, someone sneezed. A baby was wailing, the shrill sound echoing maddeningly around the cavernous chamber that was hewn into the rock at the base of the castle tower. People raised their voices from whispers to murmurs over the noise. There was another thud that vibrated through the stone. Will took the skin Ysenda handed to him. Taking a swig, he swilled water around his mouth and spat, clearing the dust from his lips.

'How is it up there?' she murmured, as he returned the skin.

'We're holding.' Will glanced around at the women and children, crammed into the storeroom. A few candles flickered fitfully, but most of the chamber was in shadows, just the outlines of bodies and the glitter of hundreds of eyes visible in the gloom. It was unbearably stuffy. Just being down here for a few moments made Will feel claustrophobic and he wondered how they could have stood it for seven days and nights, trapped together with barely space to lie down among the sacks of grain and barrels of ale, breathing one another's stale air. As another thud came, he saw his younger niece, Alice, wince. Leaning in, he tweaked her chin. 'These walls are as solid as the Earth they're built from.'

Alice smiled weakly back at him and rested her head against Ysenda's shoulder.

Her sister, Margaret, put a protective arm around her and gave Will a cold look.

'Do you need that dressed?'

Seeing Ysenda staring at his hand, Will looked down. Half the skin had been scraped off his knuckles. The wound was weeping, the skin peeling away from the edges. He didn't even remember doing it. 'It's nothing.'

'Please tell me you're both looking out for David.' Her face was ashen in the candles' glow.

'Don't worry.' Will gave a small smile. 'He wanted to be up on the fighting top, but Duncan has made sure he's keeping to the courtyard. I have to get back up there.' He went to rise, but she grabbed his wrist.

'Look out for yourself too.'

He nodded and squeezed her hand. Heading through the hush, careful not to step on any stray fingers or legs, Will made his way up the stairs. He came out of the tower in the courtyard, where the air, although thick with dust, was still a great deal fresher than below. After the tense silence, the commotion out here was disorienting.

The place was packed with soldiers and castle officials, as well as shepherds and farmers and shopkeepers, who had crowded into the castle from the town. Troops spilled out of the Great Hall, pulling on armour. Messengers scurried through their ranks, passing orders between commanders and the men on the walls. Under the eaves of the constable's residence, the injured lay sprawled on pallets. The two physicians were moving between them, faces grey with exhaustion, as they called for the women who were attending them to fetch more water, or summon a priest. Outside St Margaret's Chapel, the ground was lined with bodies. Some were draped with sacking, others had been left exposed, the bloody punctures made by arrows tempting the flies that swarmed in black clouds. The most damaged corpses, those that were crushed beyond all recognition of the human form, were inside the chapel, hidden from view.

Steeling himself, Will strode into the chaos, as other thuds and crashes echoed around the walls. Out here they were louder, occasionally followed by the hammering rain of falling masonry and the cries of men. The ground below the ramparts was strewn with rubble. Boys raced between the legs of the soldiers, snatching falling arrows to take up to the archers. There were a few fresh bodies scattered here and there, which no one had had time to move.

Swerving right as a huge boulder came smashing down, sending splinters of stone flying out, Will sprinted to the steps that led up to the ramparts. Here and there, the walkway was shattered, where boulders had broken through. Above, there was a groan of timbers, followed by a *crack* as one of the mangonels on the fighting top let fire its load. A few of the men manning the machine glanced round as Will came up. At the start of the siege they had all looked quite different, but now faces and features were indistinct, each of them covered in stone dust, their hair and beards powdered with it.

Will moved in to help two of the men heft a stone from the pile beside the mangonel and drop it into the cup that was hollowed out of the engine's pivoted beam. The pile was getting smaller. This stone was badly chipped and of a different colour to the ones they had been using at the beginning of the week. Will guessed it was one of the stones that had landed in the enceinte. Now they would send it back. The three of them moved aside and the other men, who had hold of the ropes attached to the shorter end of the beam, steadied themselves. Their commander raised his hand, then let it fall.

'Fire!'

Together, the men hauled on the ropes. The beam swung towards them, the end with the stone nestled in the hollow springing up to slam against a crossbar, the stone hurling itself out of sight. Will rushed to the ramparts and stared through the arrow slit, his eyes following the boulder as it sailed down. His anticipation vanished in defeat as the boulder hit the grass below the castle rock and bounced harmlessly downhill. His eyes moved beyond it to the six huge trebuchets set out on the flat. Every few moments, one of the beams of these engines would swing and an answering stone would fly up towards the castle to strike the walls, or sail right over. The Scots had watched those engines appear in the valley seven days earlier, each one pulled by a team of twenty oxen at the head of the English army.

The trebuchets used slings rather than cups, which the castle garrison quickly learned were far more accurate than their own rigid machines. But, at first, the Scots had laughed when they had seen them, wondering how the English could hope to do anything more than smash the rocks beneath. The answer soon become clear when the English began to construct tall tower platforms for each of the engines, bringing up cart-loads of timber from their fleet, visible as a patch of darkness on the Forth. Around the engines, wooden screens had been set to protect the engineers, each covered with vinegar-soaked hides, making it virtually impossible for the archers on the

ramparts to set them alight. In a gap between two of the trebuchets lay the
remnants of the Scots' only victory: a jagged tower and the broken parts of
an engine, hit successively by three large stones. That was on the second day
of the siege, and they hadn't cheered like that since.

Beyond the bulk of the army, hundreds of tents were spread out. Outside
the largest, striped blue and white, a red banner fluttered. At this distance,
the emblems sewn into it were just blotches of colour, but Will knew that
close up they would be three golden lions. However impossibly far out of
range that tent was it hadn't stopped him trying to hit it all week, some
childish part of him futilely hoping his will would be enough to propel the
shot that extra distance. One lucky strike, one God-driven miracle, and this
would all be over.

Taking his eyes from the failed stone, Will went back to help the others
prime the engine once more. A stone flew up and smashed through the
walkway a few yards away, taking the archer crouched behind the wall
down into the enceinte with a thundering hail of rubble. Will set his jaw as
the beam of the engine pivoted and the shot sailed off. Moments later, a
shout rose. Two soldiers wearing the colours of the sheriff's men were
sprinting along the walkway.

'Cease your fire!' one of them was shouting. 'Cease!'

The soldiers with Will paused, two of them letting the stone they were
heaving fall back on to the pile.

'Sir?' called the engine's commander in confusion.

One of the sheriff's men paused, but the other ran on shouting for the
men at the rest of the engines to hold their fire. 'We're surrendering.'

Will stepped in front of him. 'What? We can't.'

'It's already done. The sheriff has gone out to negotiate terms.'

The other men were moving back from the engines, looking around at
one another. Somewhere, a trumpet was sounding. Archers were downing
bows, peering through the slits.

Will went to the wall as the soldier headed off. He saw a mounted
company riding from the English camp towards the castle. The royal
banner was raised above them. He caught sight of a figure riding in the
centre of the group, not a helmet on his head, but a gold circlet.
Turning, he crossed to the pile of stones. 'Help me!' he shouted to the
others, who stared bemused as he grasped one and tried to lift it. His
arms strained and veins stood out on his neck. His teeth were bared with
the effort.

'Stop,' said the commander. 'You heard the order.'

Groaning with the weight of it, Will hauled the stone to the engine and dropped it with a shout into the cup. Pushing past the men, he grabbed one of the ropes now trailing loose from the beam.

The commander crossed to him. 'I said stop!'

Will shoved him back. As he hauled on the rope, he felt a hand grabbing his shoulder, pulling him round. A fist flew in and struck him in the face. Reeling backwards, Will's foot caught on part of the mangonel and he went down.

The commander was above him. 'If I give you an order, you'll obey it.'

Will pushed himself up, swiped at his bloody mouth and moved in, enraged. He was stopped by Duncan.

'What the hell are you doing?' growled his brother-in-law, slamming him up against the rampart wall. 'Let me deal with this, sir,' he said, turning to the commander.

'We can't surrender,' Will seethed. 'Not to him.'

'The sheriff and constable are in agreement. We've lost over a hundred men.'

'If we surrender then he has won!'

'But we can keep our lives and maybe our lands too.'

'Father?'

Duncan glanced round to see his son coming up behind him. 'Stay back.'

Will faltered at the worry in Duncan's voice. His eyes focused on his nephew, who was bleeding from a cut on his forehead. 'I will not let him win.' His face twisted as he looked back at Duncan. 'I *cannot!*'

'You have no choice.' Duncan took his hands from Will's chest. 'Not today.' He stepped back, leaving Will to slide down the wall and slump amid the rubble.

Outside the Castle Walls, Edinburgh, 8 June 1296 AD

As Edward looked into the water, his reflection stared back. Truly, he was a man in the winter of his life. Snowy hair hung down, framing a face that was becoming gaunt. The lines were carved across his brow, webbing thickly around his eyes. He could count a new one for every year since the death of his beloved wife, Eleanor. He had outlived her and most of his children. You don't have much time, a quiet voice said. Not much time left to consolidate your rule, subdue those who oppose you, make a strong kingdom for your son. *Be remembered.* His reflection distorted into ripples as the page holding the silver basin shifted on his knees.

'Keep still,' ordered Edward irritably, leaning forward to dip the white linen cloth he held into the water. He withdrew it and dabbed at his face. It was uncomfortably humid, the tent seeming to have collected the heat of the past few days. He had told the pages to light incense to mask the smell of sweat and steel that clung to the air over the encampment, but even so the place still reeked. Edward glanced over at John de Warenne, who was reclining on a cushioned stool tearing greedily at a chicken leg. There were brown sweat rings under his arms, staining his tunic. Edward had a sudden urge to have the page toss the basin of water over the earl, who must be a primary source of the stink.

The tent flaps parted and a portly man in black robes entered. It was Hugh Cressingham, the senior clerk. 'My lord,' he greeted, in his shrill voice, 'the last of them are coming down.'

Edward dropped the cloth in the basin and rose. Pushing past the page he strode outside. In the distance, beyond the siege platforms, which were being dismantled, a line of people were filing down the steep hill from the castle gate. Shading his eyes, Edward could just distinguish the garish colours of his guards' uniforms from the dreary dress of the locals. He looked beyond them to the castle walls where plumes of smoke curled.

'Bishop Bek is making sure the place is searched for any stragglers,' Cressingham informed him, as John de Warenne came out to stand beside them.

Tossing the gnawed chicken leg to a hound sprawled in the sun, the earl wiped his greasy fingers on his robe. 'Bek is becoming quite the little emperor,' he remarked, belching.

Cressingham, who always kept himself impeccably neat, frowned disdainfully, his chubby chin dimpling as his lips pursed.

Unaware of Cressingham's disgust, de Warenne swiped viciously at a fly. 'Well, just as long as he's making them hurry. The sooner we leave this dung heap the better. God damn these flies! Why do they torment me?'

Cressingham looked as if he wanted to answer, but glancing at the king seemed to think better of it. 'Are you going to let all the survivors go, my lord?'

Edward clasped his hands behind his back as he surveyed the men, women and children trudging down the hill. 'Of course. Who else will plough the fields and mill the grain and collect the wool that will help to fill our coffers? We must leave a labour force.'

'A good point,' said de Warenne.

Edward kept his eyes on the survivors. 'From here we continue to Stirling. It is the last obstacle.'

'The last?' asked Cressingham.

'Stirling is the key to the north,' de Warenne answered. 'Its castle guards the crossing over the Forth. If we take Stirling, we take Scotland.' He smiled contentedly.

'Before the feast of St Michael I want this kingdom on its knee before me.' Edward turned to them. 'When it is subdued I shall make a progress through the towns and cities so that every man will see their new lord and do me honour. Our labourers from Northumberland will soon be finished building Berwick's fortifications. When the town is rebuilt it will serve as our headquarters here in the north. I want both of you to take up chief positions.'

John de Warenne's smile faded. Cressingham, however, looked like an eager schoolboy who has just been told he has passed his examinations.

'We will talk more when . . .' Edward trailed off, seeing two royal guards approaching. Between them they were holding a man. He had a leather bag over one shoulder. 'What is this?'

'A messenger, my lord,' said one of the guards. 'He says he has come from Balliol's camp.'

Edward studied the messenger, who was looking at him grimly. 'What is the message?'

The guard handed over a scroll. As Edward gestured, Cressingham stepped forward to take it. He read the text.

'Well?' said Edward impatiently.

'Balliol says he will renounce the treaty he made with Philippe.' Cressingham looked up at the king. 'He offers unconditional surrender.'

A smile twitched at the corners of Edward's mouth. 'By St Michael's Mass did I say?' He glanced at the earl. 'I think it may be sooner. Write a response immediately,' he said to Cressingham. 'Tell him we accept his surrender. Once I have stripped that rebel of his crown I will have every man of noble birth in this kingdom come to pay homage to me.'

'And then, my lord?'

'Then I will return to England,' replied Edward with a frown, as if the answer was obvious. His gaze moved back to the grim-faced messenger and now the smile spread full across his face. 'Truly, a man does good business when he relieves himself of shit.'

II

Midlothian, Scotland

5 July 1297 AD

T he forest was cool and shaded, its dense canopy an effective barrier
against the midday sun. Insects hummed in an air drowsy with the
sweet smells of summer. In a clearing, a hart was grazing. As it lowered its
head to the grass, antlers smooth as bone, Will edged his horse closer. The
lymer, tethered to the horse's crupper by a long leash, gave a barely audible
whine. Silencing the hound with a tap of his crop, Will checked the hart.
The beast had raised its head and stood poised, scenting the air. One of its
dark eyes fixed on him, positioned a short distance upwind by a patch of
nettles. He sat still in the saddle, letting his horse graze, his green tunic and
hose making him one with the trees, his face masked by leaves strung from a
circlet of bound twigs on his head. A faint breeze rustled the undergrowth
and the leaves fluttered against his forehead. The hart returned to the grass,
but it was wary now, muscles tensed. It had caught Will's scent on that
breeze. As he inched the horse nearer with gentle nudges of his knees, the
hart began to move slowly downwind, in the direction Will intended. It
was troubled, but had no face for its fear, just another four-legged beast that
moved close by and showed no sign of aggression. Will, all his attention on
the hart, his peripheral vision obscured by the mask of leaves, didn't see the
trailing branch until it switched past his face. He raised his hand instinctively
and in so doing knocked off the circlet. The hart's head jerked up at the
movement. Then it was off, hurtling through the trees.

Will swore and kicked his horse after it. 'It's heading straight for you!'
he shouted, narrowly avoiding smashing his kneecap into a tree trunk, as his
horse cantered on through the wood, the lymer streaking excitedly behind.

David, some distance downwind, his back pressed against the tree,
glanced to his left at the shout. The hart was charging towards his hiding
place. He set his jaw as he drew the yew bow, which curved taut with a soft
creak, the arrow fixed and ready. Suddenly, the hart veered off its course

and headed right. David drew in a breath and turned, the bow, almost six feet in length, swinging round in front of him. Narrowing his eyes, his vision fixing on a point just ahead of the animal, he let go. The arrow sprang forward, straight into the hart's path as it careened through the undergrowth. The barbed tip plunged into its side, punching through its ribcage. It bellowed and reared up, then crashed down on to its side, twigs snapping beneath it. David ran across, drawing a dagger with his free hand ready to despatch the animal, but the hart was dead, its hind legs twitching spasmodically.

'A clean kill,' he said, rising and stowing the dagger in its sheath as Will pulled up alongside.

Dismounting, Will shook his head admiringly. 'You shouldn't have even hit it the way it came at you.'

David shrugged, but flushed with pride.

'It was my fault,' Will admitted, as they trussed the animal's legs and, together, heaved the carcass over the saddle. 'I'm afraid I'm still more of a hindrance than a help.'

David reached into a leather bag strung from his belt and brought out a piece of soft yellowed cheese, which he fed to the lymer, ruffling its long ears. 'It just takes a while.'

'A while? You've been teaching me for a year.' Will laughed.

David grinned. 'Well, I suppose you are a bit slow, being so ancient.' He shouted and tried to duck as Will cuffed him about the head.

'This old bag of bones could still best you in a fight, boy.'

David's laughter faded. As he turned away, Will cursed inwardly.

'We should get home,' murmured his nephew, taking the hound's leash.

Leading the horse, the hart's head swinging lifelessly, Will followed him through the trees. 'Did I ever tell you I was kept back from my knighthood?' he said, after they had been walking for a while.

David glanced over his shoulder. 'What?'

'When I was your age, I was kept back.'

David stopped walking. 'Why?'

'I pilfered the Eucharist,' said Will with a half-smile, remembering Everard kicking him awake as he lay curled in the sacristy of the Paris Temple, the priest's wrinkled face glowering down at the empty chalice and crumbs of the host scattered around him.

David didn't return the smile. 'Then it was a punishment?' He shook his head, a hank of blond hair falling into his eyes. 'It isn't the same. I've done nothing wrong.' He carried on walking, pulling hard at the leash as the lymer tried to launch itself after a rabbit that went bolting off between the trees.

'It will happen, when things change.'

'When will that be?' David demanded. 'When are things going to change? How?'

Will didn't have an answer for him. They lapsed into a taut silence broken only by twigs splintering under their feet and the startled chirping of birds.

As they made their way out of the forest into the languid heat of the afternoon, Will was struck again by how strange it was that everything around them seemed so peaceful; the hills bathed in golden light, tall grasses swaying, flowers dusting their clothes with pollen. It was all so markedly at odds with the events of the past year that it felt almost offensive for the landscape to carry on as if nothing had altered. Yet the seasons still turned and the days flowed by, and it was only in Scotland's people where the changes were etched. For some, it was true, life went on mostly as it had, except now it was just that little bit tougher. For others it was harder by far. But for everyone there was a sense of things having paused, as if they were all waiting for something, refusing to believe what had happened, unable to move forward, even though it was now a year since Edinburgh had fallen to Edward's army. A year since Scotland had become an English fief.

While Will had left Edinburgh with his sister's family, heading for the Midlothian estate, the English army moved on to Stirling. They later learned the castle had been abandoned by everyone but the gatekeeper, who handed over the keys to an undoubtedly triumphant Edward. With the crossing over the Forth secured and the last of Scottish resistance broken, the king advanced north as far as Elgin on a royal progress, making sure that at each town and castle he rested at, every prominent landlord in the area came to pay him homage. They heard that Edward received Balliol at Montrose, where the Scottish king gave his formal surrender and was stripped of his royal arms. The man Edward chose to be his puppet king, who had rebelled and cut free of his master's strings, was sent, subdued and humiliated, to the Tower in London. With him went the seal of Scotland, broken in four. In one final, devastating act, Edward had the Stone of Destiny removed from Scone Abbey and conveyed to Westminster. This ancient rock, the seat of crowning for the kings of Scotland for over four hundred years, was more than just a relic: it was the symbol of a nation and with its removal and interment in England, Edward thus sealed his conquest. By the autumn, Berwick's fortifications were complete and the town, rebuilt over the mass graves of its people, became the new centre of government. Leaving John de Warenne as lieutenant of the realm and Hugh Cressingham as treasurer, along with a vast number of English bureaucrats and officials to run the country, Edward returned to England.

One saving grace, that came later, was the release of a number of the Scottish magnates imprisoned in England, David Graham, Sir Patrick's heir, among them. These men, along with fifteen hundred of their countrymen, had been forced to do fealty to Edward and now owned their estates in his name, but minor landowners, such as Duncan, had been allowed to keep their holdings running much as they had before. For most of the time, Ysenda and the children remained at the Midlothian estate, rather than in Kincardine with Duncan, having found that it was far enough away from the main centres not to be taken much notice of by the English justices under the hated Cressingham.

Approaching the house up the steep track, sweating with the climb, Will and David saw a plume of smoke rising into the haze.

'Looks like our supper's on,' said Will, feeling his stomach growl at the promise of food.

'Go on in,' said David, taking the horse's reins. 'I'll see to the unmaking.'

Sensing his nephew, who had been quiet since leaving the forest, needed to be on his own, Will let him lead the horse with its burden to the barn, the lymer barking exuberantly at his heels. In the paddock, Tom, their manservant, who had remained at the estate all through the war, was feeding their two goats. They had lost three during the winter and hadn't yet been able to replace them. Food had been scarce, most of the harvests either having been destroyed or else having withered in the fields while the men were away at war.

Heading round to the back of the main house, through the herb garden his mother had planted, Will pushed open the door.

Ysenda was chopping sage at the kitchen table. She looked up as he entered. 'Did you catch anything?'

'Your son did. A hart.'

She smiled. 'That should last us a good long while.'

Will kicked off his boots. Pulling up a stool, he sat at the table, rubbing the sweat out of his eyes. His skin felt tight. 'Duncan's not back?'

Ysenda shook her head as she scraped the sage into an iron pot where a broth was bubbling away. Her sandy hair curled around her forehead in the heat.

The herb smell reminded Will of his mother and, for a moment, he closed his eyes, listening to the knife grate against the wood, held within the memory. Everyone else here had their tasks that kept them busy, kept them from thinking about the past, or the future. David had his hunting, Ysenda the running of the estate, Duncan his work under Sir David Graham in Kincardine, Tom and the girls their allotted duties. They all had a place, something to do. He was the only one who didn't fit, who flitted from task to task, helping each of them in turn, but ultimately aimless. He felt suspended, hanging frozen like the rest of Scotland, waiting for something to change. For the string to snap.

'Is the food ready?'

Will raised his head from his hands at the singsong voice to see Alice come skipping into the kitchen. He smiled at his niece, then went still, his gaze locking on a tiny silver pendant that swung to and fro from her neck. He stood, the stool tipping to clatter back behind him. Alice halted at the sight of his rigid face, her own smile fading. Ysenda looked round.

'Brother—' she started to say, but the rest of her words were cut off as Will strode to Alice.

'Where did you get that?' he demanded.

'What?' Alice's eyes grew wide.

'The pendant! Where did you get it? Have you been looking through my things, girl?'

'Will!' exclaimed Ysenda, setting down the stack of bowls she was carrying.

'It was Margaret's,' said Alice, clearly terrified as Will loomed over her and snatched up the pendant from where it hung against her chest. 'She gave it to me last month when I turned thirteen. Father gave it to her when she was my age.' Alice looked round as Margaret came into the kitchen. 'It was yours, wasn't it!' she blurted.

Even as she was speaking, Will turned the pendant over in his hands and realised his mistake. Instead of a man with his foot on a serpent, there was the delicate outline of a woman, crowned by a cross. St Margaret of Scotland. He remembered now: her sister presenting it to her with much ceremony and a rare smile from Duncan.

Margaret plucked the pendant from his palm. Holding her sister's shoulders protectively, she glared at him.

'What is wrong with you?' said Ysenda in a low, fierce voice, coming up alongside him.

'I'm sorry,' Will murmured. 'I thought it was . . . I'm sorry.'
Returning to the table he righted the stool. He sat, recalling the moment
when he had handed the St George pendant to the trader in St Albans, the
day after his desertion. How could he have forgotten? Ysenda returned to
the broth, but her eyes kept flicking to Will as she stirred it. Margaret took
up the bowls and began to set them around the table as Alice slid on to a
stool, fiddling self-consciously with the pendant. Margaret slammed Will's
bowl down in front of him, making him wince. He had only just started to
form a bond with his elder niece and now he had gone and ruined it.

The door opened and David entered, his earlier despondency replaced by
a broad grin. 'Look who I found.'

'Father!' said Alice, as Duncan headed in behind his son. She threw
herself into his arms and he staggered back with a grunt of surprise.

'Anyone would think I'd been gone for a month.'

'It feels like it,' said Ysenda, kissing his cheek.

The tension in the room dispersed gradually, Duncan shrugging off his
travelling cloak and David standing his bow up by the back door, while
Ysenda spooned broth into the bowls.

'Venison soon,' she said, with a smile towards David as she sat. 'We'll
feast like kings.'

'We're the lucky ones,' said Duncan wearily. 'God be thanked.' They all
bowed their heads as he murmured a prayer.

Will raised his spoon, then let it fall, finding his hunger had gone.

'It must be better now the harvests are coming in?' asked Ysenda,
watching her husband eat.

'It would be, if the treacherer let people keep enough to feed
themselves.'

David smiled coldly as his father used the nickname most Scots were
calling the treasurer, Hugh Cressingham.

'But no sooner has the grain come in than most of it goes out again, all
going south, along with our rents and our wool. I've seen families bled dry
in Kincardine, unable to feed their children, and it's getting worse since the
fighting broke out. The English sheriffs are coming down harder and harder
on all of us because of these rebels.' Duncan glowered into his broth. 'They
should be out in the fields bringing home what they can like the rest of us,
not disrupting what little peace we still have.'

David's smile vanished. 'We have no peace, Father. Not under the
English.' He set down his spoon. 'We should be *joining* the rebels, not
criticising them.'

Ysenda shot him a warning look. 'Don't talk to your father like that.'

'But it's true.' David glanced at Will. 'You agree with me, uncle, I know you do. You don't want to be sitting here doing nothing, pretending everything is fine, do you?' He looked back at his father, who had gone silent. 'When Tom was in Edinburgh he heard Wallace killed the Sheriff of Lanark and overthrew the justiciar at Scone. Sir William Douglas is said to have joined with him, others too. Don't you want to do something? Don't you have any pride?'

Duncan jerked to his feet, his face scarlet. He raised his hand to strike David, but faltered at a shocked cry from Alice.

The back door opened and Tom entered. He frowned at the frozen tableau, then nodded tentatively to Duncan. 'There're men coming up the track, sir. Five of them.'

'I'll come out in a moment,' murmured Duncan, staring at his defiant son. 'Go and greet them.'

'Who would it be?' asked Ysenda, as Tom headed out.

Duncan picked up a cloth and wiped his hands. 'I don't know,' he said, crossing to the door. 'I'll go alone,' he added sharply, when Will rose. 'I'm still lord of this estate.'

Duncan headed into the oppressive afternoon, anger hot in his veins. But beneath that was an uncomfortable sense of shame. His son was right. He shouldn't be out with Sir David Graham each week, travelling the length and breadth of his young lord's lands, both of them under the yoke of the English, draining the people of Kincardine of their food and their money. He should be standing firm with his countrymen against this tyranny. His pride, however, was fighting a more powerful urge to protect his family.

Coming around the house, he saw Tom greeting the riders. Duncan's heart sank as he saw their mail armour. English soldiers. One of the five was dressed differently, in a fine cloak of green and gold brocade. He remained on his horse while the soldiers dismounted. 'Good day to you,' called Duncan, bracing himself as he approached.

'Who is the lord here?' asked the man in the cloak, staring imperiously down. His accent was thick and treacly, the words seeming to stick together as he spoke. The horse tried to toss its head, but he jerked hard on the reins.

Duncan's eyes moved to the sword that was hanging from the man's hip, beside a large leather pouch. 'I am.'

'I've come to collect this quarter's rents.'

Duncan shook his head. 'There must be a mistake. I've already paid. A collector came last month.'

'Unfortunately the rents have risen since then.'

'By how much?' asked Duncan, straining to keep his voice calm.

'Father?'

Duncan glanced round as David came out of the house. 'How much?' he said incredulously, turning back as the collector answered him. 'That's out of the question. I cannot pay that.'

'We can take other forms of payment,' responded the collector. He nodded to the paddock, where Duncan's horse, a silky-coated piebald, was tethered. 'That's a fine beast.'

Duncan clenched his teeth. 'I need a horse in order to travel to my lord's lands so I can help seize his tenants' assets for your lord.'

The collector's brow furrowed. 'Is King Edward, not *our* lord?'

Duncan glanced at the soldiers, who were surveying the house in an appraising way that made him feel uneasy. He wished suddenly that he'd brought his sword out with him. 'Go back inside, David,' he called, hearing footsteps coming up behind him.

'Is this your son?' asked the collector. 'A healthy-looking lad. Well fed too. Wouldn't you say so?' he commented to one of the soldiers.

The man smiled unpleasantly. 'Yes, sir.'

Glaring at the collector, Tom stepped in front of the soldier who had answered.

'Times are hard,' continued the collector, shrugging at Duncan. 'If you want to blame anyone, blame your countrymen. If they weren't rebelling against Lord Edward we wouldn't have to raise the rents. The funds to crush their little mutiny have to come from somewhere. They fight and you and yours pay for it.'

'Sounds like they have enough to win that *little* mutiny, what with the plunder Wallace and his men took from your justiciar at Scone.'

Duncan whipped round as David's voice rang out. 'Go back inside, will you!'

The collector's eyes narrowed. 'I would keep your son on a shorter leash if I were you. I can always raise the rents some more, should I see fit.' He kept his gaze on Duncan. 'But I'm a fair man. Have your manservant here bring me your horse and we'll leave it at that for today.'

'I've told you, I cannot do that.' Duncan took a few steps towards him and lowered his voice. 'I will give you more next time. I'm a knight of Sir David Graham, he will vouch for me.'

'This is the last time I will ask you.'

'Listen to me, damn you!' shouted Duncan, frustration getting the better of him.

'Kill him,' said the collector, gesturing at Tom.

Duncan and David shouted at the same time as one of the soldiers drew his sword. Lunging forward, the man thrust it into Tom's belly. The manservant looked more surprised than anything as the length of steel entered him. The soldier twisted the blade and withdrew it in two brutal movements. Tom crumpled, clutching his stomach, blood pumping thickly between his fingers. He stared at Duncan in disbelief as he sagged sideways, his face screwing up in agony. Before he even hit the ground, Duncan was hurtling at the soldier. At the same time, the other soldiers went for their weapons and David raced towards Tom. There was a scream from the house as Ysenda came rushing out to see Tom go down and her husband running at the man who had struck him.

Duncan ducked under the sword as the soldier lashed out, then barrelled into him with a roar, sending him flying. The sword sailed from the man's hand and his helmet strap snapped as Duncan crashed down on top of him, the impact on the parched soil winding them both. As the soldier's helmet went rolling away, Duncan, deaf to the screams of his wife and the shouts from his son, grabbed the man's hair in his fists and slammed his head into the ground with all his strength, his only thought to disable the soldier long enough to seize the fallen blade. As the man went limp, Duncan hauled himself forward and snatched up the sword. He rolled off him as one of the other men came at him. Blocking the first strike while still on the ground, Duncan launched himself up at the second soldier. The force of his blow caused the man to take a few stumbling steps back. Losing his footing on the uneven ground, his sword went wide, only for a moment, but it was all the time Duncan needed to run him through. He pulled the sword free, hearing hoof-beats behind him and a harsh shout from his son, then felt something punch into his back, between his shoulder blades. His fingers went dead, the weapon slipping from them to thump on the ground. Duncan saw his wife freeze, her arms rising into the air, as if she were about to dance, or pray. Then he felt pain like he'd never imagined driving through him, propelling him to his knees, down into the earth.

The tax collector, towering above Duncan on the horse, withdrew his sword, streaked red. 'Kill them!' he was yelling. 'Kill them!'

David fell back in terror as one of the soldiers came at him, but as he turned to run his feet caught in the legs of the man his father had felled and he went down hard. The other soldier made for Ysenda, who was sprinting towards her son.

A shout tore through the air.

Will was coming around the house, David's bow in his hands. The arrow was aimed at the tax collector, who had turned in his saddle at the shout. His sword was aloft, Duncan's blood running down to the hilt, and his horse was stamping, agitated. Beneath the hooves, Duncan lay prone, sprawled on top of the man he'd knocked unconscious. The two remaining soldiers paused, eyes flicking from Will to their master.

Snarling, the collector kicked the horse at Will, who let the arrow spring free.

The collector threw himself sideways in the saddle to avoid it, but Will wasn't aiming for him. He caught the horse in the neck, the tip ripping through the soft tissue. The horse reared up, then fell, taking the collector down with it. The beast landed on top of him, crushing his leg, still caught in the stirrup. He let out a scream. The soldier going after Ysenda checked himself and raced back to help him. Will yanked another arrow from the quiver on his back, fitted it and fired at the man who now turned on David, still sprawled on the ground. It missed, driving into the soil a few feet away. Will cursed and dropped the bow. Wrenching his falchion from its scabbard, he began to run.

David twisted away as the soldier's sword hacked down at him. Scrabbling on to his hands and knees, he threw himself forward and snatched at the arrow embedded in the ground. The soldier lunged in. Ysenda screamed. Turning, seeing the sword come stabbing towards him, David curved his body and thrust the arrow up into the man's groin, above the padding protecting his thighs. He shouted in rage, feeling the barb slice through flesh, going deeper as he pushed. The soldier howled and dropped to his knees. Will came charging up behind. As the soldier tried to lift his sword, he rammed the point of his falchion through the man's neck, sunburned and dirty beneath the lip of the helmet. David recoiled as the tip punched out of the soldier's throat and he coughed a spray of blood. Will kicked the soldier in the back, yanking his sword free as the man fell forward, then went for the soldier who was trying to haul the tax collector out from under the horse. Wrapping his arm around the man's head, pulling it back, he ripped the short blade across his neck.

'No!' the collector shouted as Will loomed over him. 'Please! I—'

But his words cut off as Will stabbed him through the throat, the blade plunging into the earth beneath him. Afterwards, he strode to the unconscious soldier lying under Duncan and, carefully rolling his brother-in-law off him, ran the man through. Lastly, he despatched the horse, still thrashing and snorting in pain. It was the only kill he felt any remorse for.

Ysenda, who had run to David and was hugging him to her, turned as Will wiped his blade on the soldier's tunic. Her face crumpled as she saw Duncan on his back, arms splayed on the dry grass. She crossed to him and crouched, clutching his face in her hands, crying his name. When he didn't move, her cries became louder; an incoherent torrent she let loose at the sky. David, white-faced and blood-splattered, went to her and grabbed hold of her.

Will sheathed his sword and pushed his hands through his hair, slick with sweat. It dripped from his nose into his beard. 'Sweet Jesus,' he murmured between breaths. 'Sweet Jesus.' It was all he allowed himself.

He crossed to the house. Margaret was hunkered down in the doorway, her palms pushed against the frame to either side of her. Her lips were moving, but no sound was coming out. Will coaxed her up, gently but firmly. She didn't resist, but her eyes remained staring past him at her mother and brother draped over her father's body.

'Margaret, listen to me, you have to fetch whatever money Duncan has here, also blankets, food and water-skins. Get Alice to help you. Don't let her come out here.'

She wasn't listening.

Gritting his teeth, Will shook her. 'Margaret!' She focused on him. 'Do it!' he ordered, turning her forcibly and marching her into the hall. As she stumbled away from him, he headed back outside and went to Ysenda and David. He took hold of his nephew.

David lashed out and struck him on the chin.

Will rolled with the punch. 'I need you to be a knight now, David. Do you understand?' David was panting hard, but he had stopped struggling. 'You're going to saddle both the horses and get your bow and your father's sword and shield. Then you're going to help me get these bodies into the trees.' Will nodded down the hill to the copse. 'Can you do that?'

David pulled roughly away. 'Yes.'

Will waited until his nephew began to walk to the house, then knelt by Ysenda, still crouched over Duncan. His sister's cries were ragged. Unbearable. He knew that grief all too well. It pierced him as he pulled her to him, wrapping his arms around her. 'We have to leave,' he murmured. 'Those men will be missed and others will come looking. There will be no fair trial for this. They'll come down hard.'

'I cannot leave my husband,' wept Ysenda, her words muffled against his chest. '*I cannot!*'

'For the sake of your children, you have to.'

'Where will we go?' she sobbed. 'Oh, dear God, where will we go?'

'We'll go into Selkirk,' said Will, after a pause. 'It's not far. We can find shelter there until the dust settles. With any luck, the English will have more than enough to worry about than the death of some bureaucrat.'

She looked up at him, her eyes swollen. 'Kincardine. Sir David Graham. I want to go to him.'

'They can track us too easily there. It's the most likely place we would go.' Will rose and looked south across the hills, which faded into a green haze. 'We go into the Forest.'

The Tower, London, 6 July 1297 AD

'Send word to Earl de Warenne immediately.'

'Certainly, my lord king,' said the clerk, struggling to keep up as Edward strode along the passage.

'He'll be at his Yorkshire estate no doubt,' said Edward sourly. 'If he imagines he can play at lieutenant from the comfort of his manor he has another think coming. Order him to meet Cressingham at Berwick. They will lead a force from there.' The king's face was taut. 'If these rebels want a war, by God I will send one their way. Tell the earl I want their uprising crushed and the ringleaders' heads on London Bridge by the time I return.'

Dismissing the clerk, who scurried off, Edward continued along the passage and down a long set of steps, wincing as his joints creaked. The news of the rebellion in Scotland, which had been joined by some of the nobles he had freed earlier in the year, had vexed him greatly. But he had more pressing matters to concern himself with. While he had been preoccupied north of the border, Philippe had strengthened his hold on Guienne. Some of the barons were growing restless with the flagging war in France and had refused to fight in his service. They were gaining support within the royal court and he knew how dangerous mutinous barons could be. Simon de Montfort had taught him that.

Heading into the stifling heat of the afternoon, Edward was met in the courtyard by two of his advisors.

'Your ship is ready, my lord,' said one, as they fell into step beside him. 'We can leave when you wish.'

'I want to be in Flanders by the end of the week.' Edward looked back at the Tower rising above him, white and imperious. 'Let us see what my dear cousin's enemies are willing to do to end France's dominion over them.'

12

Selkirk Forest, Scotland

20 July 1297 AD

W ill brushed the sweat from his face with the crook of his arm as he
reached the top of the incline. He turned, offering a hand to David,
who was scrabbling up behind him. His nephew paused, looking at his
outstretched hand, then grasped it, allowing Will to haul him the last few
feet. The swollen water-skins sloshing against their legs, they made their
way back through the trees, the bubbling of the stream at the bottom of the
gully fading behind them.

As they approached the clearing, Will felt his spirits, lifted by the
practical task of fetching water, begin to sink again. They had been camped
there for only three days, but already he had come to loathe the stuffy
space, enclosed by pines and thorny bushes. Ysenda was fussing over Alice,
who had been crotchety following a fall several days earlier. It was a shock
more than anything. Her ankle had been sore and inflamed, but although it
soon went down, Will using his spare undershirt to make a compress, she
complained about it more and more bitterly, until finally she sat down in
tears, refusing to walk another step.

Ysenda glanced round as they entered the clearing, then returned her
attention to her daughter. Tossing the skins by their packs, David threw
himself down in the shade of an enormous red-trunked pine, where his
lymer was curled, panting in the heat. Close by, the horses switched their
tails at the flies that plagued the air, sticky with the pine smell. Margaret
was hunched on a log by the dying fire, jabbing at the embers with a stick.
She had lost her coif and her hair hung loose and ratty around her shoulders.
Will noticed, with a stab of annoyance, that she hadn't fetched the wood
he'd asked her to.

'I need some water,' Ysenda called.

When David didn't stir, Will gritted his teeth and crossed to her. Alice
was sitting with her back against a tree, her face screwed up. Ysenda had

removed the compress and was holding her foot carefully. Handing his sister the water-skin, Will saw that his niece's ankle was unblemished.

As Ysenda poured some of the icy water from the skin on to it, the girl gasped. 'Does that hurt?' Ysenda asked worriedly.

'It's just cold,' said Will, harder than he meant to.

Alice looked up at him and her pained expression, which turned instantly to one of petulant dislike, told him all he needed to know.

'How would you know?' the girl challenged. 'It isn't your foot that's hurt.'

'Neither is yours, Alice.' He tried to keep his voice gentle, though irritation made him want to shout. 'Not any more. It wasn't even a sprain.'

Alice's hot little face flushed a brighter shade of red. She went to speak, then burst into tears.

'How dare you!' Ysenda rose to face him, her cheeks streaked with sweat and grime. Will noticed a line of bites running under her collarbones like a necklace. Some of them were weeping where she had scratched them. Since entering Selkirk Forest, they had all suffered with the midges and ticks, but Ysenda had fared the worst. 'If she says it hurts, it hurts! You're not a physician.'

'She says it hurts because she doesn't want to go on,' retorted Will, raising his voice over Alice's sobs, 'and if you hadn't pandered to her tantrums we would be miles away by now.' He had wanted to say this for days, but they had hardly spoken since leaving the estate and he hadn't wanted to break the leaden silence with argument. It was too late for that now.

'Miles away!' Her voice became a yell. 'Miles away where?' She flung a hand at the dense trees that hemmed them in on all sides. 'You've been leading us blind for two weeks. Where are we supposed to be going, exactly?' Will went to speak, but she drove on, not wanting to hear an answer. 'I said we should go to Sir David Graham for help, but you forced me to leave everything I owned and flee into the Forest like some outlaw!' She whirled away from him and began stomping around the camp. Margaret had dropped the stick and was holding her head in her hands. David was whistling a loud, jaunty tune. The lymer had sat bolt upright and was barking. 'You let me think this was our only choice, but it wasn't!' Ysenda crouched and began stuffing blankets into one of the horse panniers.

'I told you, Ysenda, if the English want justice, Sir David Graham's lands are the first place they'll seek us.'

'We'll go north to Elgin then. Ede will shelter us gladly. By God, you turn up out of nowhere after all these years and I'm fool enough to listen to you!'

'You don't even know if Ede is still there,' said Will sharply. 'There's been no word from her.'

'Stop it!' Margaret yelled, leaping to her feet. 'Stop it, both of you! I cannot bear this!'

Ysenda rounded on Will. 'You made me take my children away from their home! From their *father*!' As her voice cracked and broke on that last word, Margaret dashed off into the trees.

'*No!*' shouted Alice, who had risen and was standing with her back pressed against the tree, staring terrified at her wild-faced mother.

'Let her go,' said David suddenly, 'there'll be more food for the rest of us.'

Ysenda stormed over to him. David shouted and tried to fend her off as she slapped him. The sound of her open palm striking his face ricocheted. The lymer's barking rose to a frantic pitch and it thrashed against its leash. David grabbed hold of his mother's wrists. They were both yelling.

As Will went to pull them apart, he was halted by a scream echoing through the woods a short distance away.

Ysenda froze. Her eyes flicked to Will, but he was already running for his sword, lying on his blanket in its scabbard.

Unsheathing it, he set off through the trees in the direction of the scream. As he fought his way through the undergrowth, twigs and branches scratching at his face and clothes, he wasn't certain he was going the right way, then the scream came again, this time closer. Up ahead rose a steep bank, carpeted with pine cones and spiny needles. Will saw a figure at the top, arms outstretched, silhouetted in a shaft of sun.

'Margaret!'

She whipped round with a cry of relief. At that moment, her foot slipped and she fell backwards with a scream that cut off as she hit the ground and tumbled head over heels, sending up a storm of twigs and pine needles. Dropping his sword, Will charged up the bank. Throwing his arm around the trunk of a tree, he grabbed at her. His hand caught hold of the back of her dress. He was yanked downwards with her momentum, his arm locking around the trunk with painful force. There was a ripping sound as her dress tore, but she was brought to a lurching stop. Letting go of the tree, balancing precariously on his knees, Will grasped Margaret's hand and pulled her upright. He glanced down the slope to where the trees drew in tight. The speed she was going she would have been knocked senseless had she hit them. Broken bones. No physician. He shook away the thoughts. Margaret's hair was full of pine needles and her cheek had a graze on it, but other than this and the tear in her gown she looked unhurt. 'Dear God, girl, it's a good thing you weigh next to nothing or I might be holding your dress without you in it.'

Margaret wasn't listening. Her eyes were fixed on a point up the bank behind him.

Even as he turned, Will heard shouts for them to stand. The reason for Margaret's screams now became clear as three men scrabbled down the bank, wielding clubs. Four others remained at the top, bows in their hands, the arrows fixed on him and Margaret. Another two were moving quickly through the trees to his right. One was heading for his falchion.

The Royal Palace, Paris, 20 July 1297 AD

'This is excellent news, my lord. A triumph.'

Philippe smiled, his pale blue eyes shining in the light coming through the window of his solar. 'It is,' he agreed, placing the parchment on his desk and sitting back, his gaze on Guillaume de Nogaret. His smile faded. 'Of course, it should have been done years ago. But, still, late is better than never.' He looked at the parchment again, the pope's seal, attached to the skin, a mark of his victory. He had an urge to hang it in the porch of Notre Dame, where all the citizens of Paris could view it. In it they would see the power of their king and word of his great achievement would spread. The people of France may have called his grandfather a saint, but it was through his deeds, *his*, Philippe's, that he had finally been canonised. Now, when they lit candles for St Louis in churches across the kingdom they would think of their king and praise him too. He imagined their prayers like tiny winged birds, all spiralling up into the choirs of churches, up, up into the face of God. Philippe's thoughts were pulled back into the room as the door opened and Pierre Flote entered.

'My lord,' greeted the chancellor. He was out of breath.

Philippe picked up the parchment. 'Have you heard, Flote?' he said, rising. 'Pope Boniface has given in to my demands. My grandfather is to be canonised.'

'My lord, I—'

'See here.' Philippe cut across him, striding to the chancellor and showing him the document. 'Nogaret was right, we needed only to hold our nerve in the face of his proclamations and he would yield.' The king sobered, glancing at Nogaret. 'It was a good idea, forbidding the export of gold and silver from France.' His tone stiffened at the praise, as if he couldn't bring himself to commit fully to the minister's achievement. 'Faced with the inability to collect the revenues from French churches, the pope had no choice but to back down.'

'And a holy fool he made of himself in the process,' said Nogaret, smiling, contemptuous. 'Proclaiming *Clericis laicos* far and wide with all the pomp he could muster, only to retract this order meekly when he realised we could do him far more damage. He knows his place now though, my lord. We have Boniface exactly where we want him.'

'My lord!'

Philippe turned back to the chancellor with a frown. 'Do not shout at me, Flote.'

'I beg your pardon, but I have just received word from England that King Edward has set sail for Flanders.'

'Flanders?' questioned Nogaret, the triumph falling from his face.

Flote didn't look at the minister. 'It is said that he seeks to build upon the Nuremburg alliance with the marriage of his son to the daughter of Guy de Dampierre.'

Philippe's hand dropped to his side, the parchment crumpling in his fist. He looked down at it, then tossed it on to his desk and went to the window where he stood in silence, his back to them.

'Damn him,' murmured Nogaret.

'These tidings are not without hope,' said Flote, addressing the king's tall silhouette, framed in the sunlit window. 'Edward's barons are rebelling against his war in Gascony, refusing to fight in his service, forcing him to seek military support elsewhere. This move to join with the Count of Flanders is perhaps more desperate than it appears.'

'No,' said Philippe, turning. 'My cousin plays my game. He intends for me to fight a war on two fronts, dividing my troops between Guienne and Flanders. It was just such a predicament I intended for him when I signed the treaty with Scotland.'

'But in Edward's case he does not have a secondary force to place in the field,' said Nogaret, frowning pensively. 'He too must divide his army. He weakens himself with this action.'

Philippe wasn't listening. 'Meanwhile, the delays on my fleet continue and money still dribbles daily from my coffers.' He sat behind his desk, glowering at the parchment with Boniface's seal on it, which now seemed to mock him. His conflict with the pope had ultimately been just another protracted venture that had kept him occupied this past year. He felt like a piece of meat being fought over by his enemies. They all had their teeth in him, dragging him this way and that, leaving him divided, unable to focus on any one of them at once.

He thought he had dealt with the alliance at Nuremburg, formed between Edward and the rulers of the Low Countries three years ago. After learning of it, he immediately persuaded the Count of Holland, with monetary enticements, to withdraw his support, undermining the entire coalition. Philippe had known he still faced fierce opposition from Guy de Dampierre, who had been resisting his attempts to bring Flanders fully under French control, supported by the powerful textile guilds whose workers made up a large percentage of the Flemish population. But he had thought he would be able to deal with the count once the English in Guienne had been defeated. That his two enemies would join forces against him now was an unexpected blow. 'I should have seen it coming.' He looked up, his eyes narrowing on his advisors. 'You should have seen it coming.'

'My lord, how could we?' asked Nogaret.

'I agree,' said Flote, silencing the minister, 'we should have, even without the warning of the Nuremburg alliance.' He turned his gaze on Nogaret. 'Flanders' predominant industry is weaving and England's greatest export is wool. The two have been natural allies for many years, far longer than the counts of Flanders have been vassals of French kings. Their relationship has been cemented by royal marriages before. That Edward would attempt to strengthen his country's friendship with his closest ally by such means was, I would say, inevitable.' He looked at Philippe. 'The question now becomes what can be done to stop this?'

'Perhaps if we—' began Nogaret.

'If I put a new force in the field,' Philippe asked Flote, 'for how long could they be adequately supplied?'

Flote pursed his lips. 'I would need to speak to the treasurer, but I would think, with the monies we extracted from the Church taxes, a good few months.'

Philippe perched on the edge of his desk, all his attention on the chancellor. 'If we take decisive action now, before this Anglo-Flemish union has time to solidify, we might kill several birds with one stone. A victory would mean I could take control of Flanders, firmly establishing our wealthy neighbour as a French domain. But it would also mean the destruction of part of Edward's army.' Philippe smiled, clasping his palms together and setting his fingertips to his lips. 'And with it the rest of his waning reputation.'

'And if you abandon the building of the fleet for the time being, my lord,' added Flote, 'you could equip an army in the north-east for the rest of this year if needs be.'

'We do it,' said Philippe. 'We send an army as soon as it can be raised, forcing the English and Flemish to counter before they can consummate the marriage. With luck, one strike will be all that's needed to break them.'

Nogaret stepped in. 'My lord, I am concerned by the thought that we would abandon the fleet after so much time and money has already been spent on it.'

'I would say, Minister de Nogaret,' said Flote, before the king could answer, 'that the fact so much time and money has been spent on it would be grounds alone for its abandonment.'

Nogaret's dark eyes glittered, colour blooming in his waxy cheeks.

In the pause, the king moved past them to the door. 'Flote, arrange a meeting with my staff for tomorrow after Nones. I will set these plans in motion.'

'Yes, my lord.'

Nogaret stared after Flote, who followed the king out of the solar. A breeze drifted through the window, ruffling the parchment proclaiming the canonisation of King Louis, forgotten on the desk.

Philippe remained deep in thought as he headed for his bedchamber. Even through his fury at Edward, forcing him into this corner from where he could only fight, he felt oddly jubilant. If the English king thought he could rattle his nerve by this endeavour he was wrong. Hadn't he, Philippe, just defeated the pope? A ripple of unease passed through him at this thought, or, more precisely, at the satisfaction he felt. He must not allow himself to be like Nogaret and gloat in his victory over the Church. He must feel regret for his actions, actions he was forced to commit because of the pontiff's own failings. He would be the penitent shepherd, not the crowing conqueror. He would arrange to see his confessor at once; submit to penance, cleanse himself of any stain.

Reaching his bedchamber, Philippe pushed open the doors. The first thing he saw was a woman standing in front of a full-length silver mirror, dressed in one of his wife's gowns. The second thing he saw was that she wasn't his wife.

Rose gave a cry and whirled to face him, her arms flying up to cover her chest as if she were naked and trying to hide herself, as well she might for the laces that criss-crossed the back of the crimson gown were wide open, revealing a triangle of flesh, all the way to the cleft of her buttocks, plainly visible in the mirror behind her. In the few seconds during which Philippe took this in, Rose hopped towards the bed, where a plain white dress lay crumpled. 'My lord, I . . .' She snatched up the dress and crushed it to her chest. 'I'm sorry, I thought—'

'Where is Jeanne?' Philippe demanded. His wife's gown was far too big for the handmaiden's thin frame. It hung off her like a red bell. 'What are you doing wearing that?'

'A tear,' said Rose suddenly. 'My lady thought she found a tear. I couldn't see it. I thought – I thought if I put it on I might be able to see clearer.'

Philippe's jaw pulsed in recognition of the lie. He felt furious, yet also flustered. This wasn't his domain. He didn't know how to punish this young woman, standing here in his wife's clothes, brazenly lying to him. He would tell Jeanne, have her deal with this. He had a war to concern himself with. 'Leave,' he commanded, thrusting a finger towards the door that led into the room where the handmaidens slept.

Rose, her cheeks burning, fled, one hand grasping her own dress, the other trying to hold the back of the queen's gown closed as she passed him. Before the door banged shut, he caught another glimpse of her naked back, pale against the crimson silk.

Selkirk Forest, Scotland, 20 July 1297 AD

'What will they do with us?'

Will glanced round at the whisper. His sister's eyes were wide, but she walked erect at his side as if to hide her fear, from her children or the nine men surrounding them he wasn't sure. 'I do not think we are in any immediate danger,' he murmured, looking at their captors, who were an odd group all told.

Three of them had taken point, two leading the horses with their packs strapped to them and the lymer leashed to the crupper of the piebald. The third, a burly, unkempt man, barefoot and clad only in shabby leather breeches, wielded a club and looked as if he had lived in the Forest most of his life, his broad chest and arms riddled with scars. The other two were slighter of build and much better dressed in short coats of mail and well-tailored surcoats. They carried bows with slender baskets attached to their belts to hold arrows. To either side of Will and his family marched another four men, one with a long spear and three who looked more like shepherds than soldiers. Bringing up the rear were two in Highlander dress: dyed woollen tunics that reached to their thighs. These last two looked very at ease with their long-handled Lochaber axes in their fists and Will and Duncan's swords slung from their belts.

'How can you be sure we aren't in danger?' Ysenda bowed her head to disguise her words, although the sounds of twigs cracking under the footfalls of the men were loud enough to cover her whisper. Alice and Margaret were in front of her and David was walking at Will's side. Margaret kept looking round at them, but Alice was staring straight ahead as she walked, all pretence of her injury ended. She hadn't said a word since the men entered their camp, having discovered it when David came racing out of the trees after Will and Margaret.

'If they intended to rob us they would have taken our supplies and left us.' Will didn't add 'for dead'. 'And if they meant to harm us they would have done so by now. From what I overheard when they were gathering up our gear they are taking us to their camp.'

'Camp?'

'They are part of the resistance, I think.'

Ysenda stared at him. 'You knew they would be here.'

'Tom told me the rebels had set up a base in the Forest, yes.'

'That's why you brought us here? To join them!'

'Quiet,' warned the spear-holder.

Ysenda's cheeks were livid. As the man looked away, she hissed the words through her teeth. 'You've led my children, *your nieces*, into a den of thieves and cut-throats, all with prices on their heads, because you want to continue your fight!' She put her hands on Margaret and Alice's shoulders.

'Your children will be safer here than anywhere,' Will murmured. 'If we had stayed in the open sooner or later we would have been found. You've heard the same rumours I have, of how the English soldiery treat those who defy them, let alone anyone who kills one of their officials. Chivalry isn't worth as much this side of the border. I could not even say your daughters would be safe from their punishments.'

But Ysenda didn't want to hear it. She quickened her pace, pushing Alice and Margaret in front of her. 'David,' she snapped, her stare commanding him to follow.

David shook his head.

'Keep moving,' ordered one of the men, forcing Ysenda to face forward, leaving David walking at Will's side.

Almost an hour later, as the golden light dappling the ground began to fade and the snatches of sky above them turned dusky purple, they began to hear distant sounds of civilisation. The burly man gave three sharp whistles. Hearing an answering sound, Will noticed indistinct figures half hidden in bushes and behind trees. He caught glimpses of bows and the glint of knives and guessed that if the man hadn't signalled they wouldn't have made it much further. Ahead, the low hum of many voices was punctuated by calls and laughter, the *thock* of an axe blade, the barking of dogs and whinnies of horses. Through the trees, they saw people moving, smelled wood-smoke and food. Ysenda gathered her daughters closer as their captors led them into the midst of a huge camp that stretched off between the pines.

Men clad in many different styles of dress, bearing all manner of weapons, stood about in groups by fire pits, or sat on logs eating from wooden bowls. Some tended animals: pigs, sheep, goats and cattle, penned in corrals. Others lounged on the mossy ground beneath cloth canopies strung between trees. More permanent structures, fashioned from bound branches and twigs and covered with turf, were visible further in. There were even a few tents. Many eyes followed Will and his family as they were led through the fringes of the camp, heading deeper in. One man whistled lewdly at Margaret, raising a laugh from his companions. Margaret lowered her head and Ysenda threw a barbed look over her shoulder at Will. Her look changed when a young woman ducked out from a shelter, clouted the whistler on the arm and nodded apologetically to her. Ysenda frowned curiously after the woman as they continued on, making for a circle of tents in the centre of a clearing. Glancing back, Will realised some of their captors had melted away.

As they approached the tents, the burly man called out and a boy scrabbled out of one of them. The archers handed the boy the reins of the horses, then moved off as the burly man pushed his way into a large green and white striped tent, leaving Will and the others guarded by the two Highlanders. Their escort reappeared a few moments later with a short, stocky man. He looked to be no more than thirty, although his hair, cut brutally close to his head, was already dusted white. His brown, weathered face was almost as scarred as his comrade's and he wore a leather gambeson, and had a keen-looking dirk strapped to his belt. His gaze moved uninterestedly over Ysenda and the girls, lingered briefly on David, then came to rest on Will.

'They had this on them, Gray,' said the burly man, handing over the pouch he had taken when he searched their packs. It was the pouch Will had cut from the tax collector's belt and was bulging with coin, Duncan's money having been added to it before they fled the estate.

The man called Gray hefted it appreciatively. 'A good weight.'

'That's my father's,' said David, taking a step forward.

The burly man lifted his club and Ysenda made a sharp sound at her son.

'Your father should tell you to mind your mouth,' said Gray, his gaze moving back to Will.

David scowled. 'He's my uncle.'

'What brings such an unlikely company into the wilds of Selkirk, with bags stuffed with gold, two horses and a knight's armour? These are dangerous times to be moving abroad without protection.' Gray glanced at his companion with a crooked grin. 'Never know who you might run into, eh, Adam?'

'We have protection,' retorted David, before Will could answer.

'Who?' Gray laughed as David's eyes darted towards Will. 'Him? Looks like he's three winters short of a graveyard. Of course, it's hard to tell under all that beard. Lost your razor, old man?'

'We mean no trouble here,' said Will, placing a warning hand on David's shoulder. He could feel the tension coiled in his nephew's body. 'We were forced to seek shelter in the Forest after an altercation with an English tax collector.'

'Must have been some altercation to bring you in here with your women.'

'The collector was killed, along with his men.'

The man smiled, but caution showed in his eyes. 'By you?'

When Will inclined his head, Adam gave a snort. 'And what army?'

'He doesn't need one,' said David roughly. 'He's a Templar.'

Gray's smile vanished. He stared at Will, then motioned to his comrade. 'Guard them.' Turning, he strode into the gloom.

'I'm sorry,' murmured David in response to Will's black expression. He lifted his shoulders stubbornly. 'But they would have found out.'

They waited in silence for what seemed like a long time, but was probably only minutes, until out of the trees came two figures. One was

Gray, his expression now wary. The other was one of the largest men Will had ever seen.

Not only was the man of exceptional height, but he was also broad; his arms and legs roped with muscle, his neck thick, his head square and rather brutish. Despite his great size, however, he had an agile stride and moved with an almost languid confidence. He wore a plain, dark blue tunic, under which Will picked out the bulk of armour, and his brown hair hung loose, curling with sweat around his temples. He looked to be in his mid-twenties.

'I think it's him,' David said under his breath at Will's side, eyes wide with a mixture of respect and apprehension.

The giant came to a halt before them. He appraised Will for an uncomfortable length of time before speaking. 'What is your name?'

'Campbell?' questioned the stocky man, when Will answered. 'From where?'

'Quiet, Gray,' said the giant.

'My grandfather left his family's lands in Argyll a long time ago,' replied Will. 'And I left Scotland as a boy.'

'Gray tells me you're a Templar.' The giant glanced at Ysenda, who was hugging Alice to her and biting her lip. 'Where is your mantle?'

Will didn't want to tell this stranger anything about himself. He felt weary, hungry and mistrustful, but he had little choice. Besides, wasn't this what he had come here for? Ysenda was right: he had wanted to meet these men.

Slowly, he began to speak, telling them of his service in the Holy Land as a Templar commander, his return to the West and his desertion. It was odd, talking to these outlaws of such things, here in the depths of the Forest with dusk gathering around them. Now and then, the giant would interrupt and his probing questions reminded Will of the examination during his inception twenty-seven years earlier. This was an altogether cruder, more simplistic interrogation, but the outlaws took it as seriously as if they were knights of an Order, checking his worthiness for admission. By the time he had spoken of his part in the siege of Edinburgh and the death of Duncan, the shadows were solid around them and the flickering points of light from torches hovered like fireflies between the trees.

'Why did you come here?'

The giant's voice hadn't changed in its gruffness, but Will noticed something new in the young man's eyes: a spark of recognition, or understanding perhaps.

'I cannot shelter you.' The man spread a large hand at the camp. 'Everyone works here. Even those who do not fight have tasks.'

'Does this force not continue to grow, as more men join the resistance? You must welcome them, surely?'

'I welcome able soldiers,' said the giant, nodding at David. He looked to Ysenda and the girls. 'But I cannot carry deadweight.' There was nothing malicious in his tone, only frankness. All the same, Ysenda looked wrathful.

Whether that was because he had just recruited her son, or abandoned her daughters Will wasn't sure. 'My sister and nieces aren't without skills. They are well educated. They can cook and sew, read and write.'

The giant didn't answer.

Gray spoke up in the silence. 'We could use a few more to help with the food. Adam's wife would burn snow if she were cooking it.'

The burly man gave him a bored look.

After another lengthy pause, the giant nodded. 'Very well. But you'll pull your weight. All of you,' he added, with a meaningful glance at Alice, who hid her face in Ysenda's shoulder. 'Gray, show them somewhere they can sleep. Not you,' he said to Will. 'You can help me with something first. Come.' He strode off in the opposite direction, ducking his head under the lower branches of the trees.

Giving David an assured nod, Will followed, noticing that Adam fell into step behind him.

'When Gray told me you were a Templar, I thought you might have come for him. We have one from your Order here,' the giant explained.

Will halted. 'Then it would be best I do not meet him. As I told you, I'm a deserter.'

'He is a captive, not a guest. We were planning to ransom him, but I'd like to know how much he would fetch.' The giant plucked a torch from the ground and headed for an area away from the main encampment.

They passed a few men, who stood to attention at their approach, adding to Will's speculation that David might be right: the giant, who hadn't yet offered his name, might well be William Wallace, the leader of the Scottish resistance. Up ahead, Will saw a cage of wooden stakes, built around several trees. Inside, visible as the pool of yellow light from the torch spilled towards them, were about a dozen figures, some slumped on the ground, others sitting with their backs against the trees, to which Will saw they had been roped.

One of them tried to stand, but the tether around his leg was too short and he could only get to his knees. 'I demand to speak to your leader! Do you have any idea who I am?'

'Shut your hole, English dog,' growled Adam, coming up behind Will.

'Wake him,' said the giant, motioning to a figure curled on the ground a little way from the others.

One of the men guarding the cage went over and poked his spear through the stakes at the prone form. As the spear prodded him, the figure jerked upright with a shout.

Will caught a flash of red on a black tunic, saw terrified brown eyes under a thatch of hair, a face smudged with dirt and an unkempt bushy beard. He started forward. 'Simon?'

'You know him?' demanded the giant, at once alert.

Will looked round, feeling Adam close in behind him, brandishing his club.

'Are you here to rescue him? Are there more of you?'

'No.' Will glanced at Simon, who was on his knees, staring at him in amazement. He turned back to the man he thought was Wallace. 'I haven't seen him since I left Paris, eighteen months ago. You have my word.'

Wallace scrutinised him, his eyes glittering in the torchlight, then nodded to Adam, who lowered the club.

'Where did you find him?' Will found he couldn't bring himself to look at Simon, who was calling to him, his voice hoarse with relief.

'A scouting party picked him up a few months back. He refused to tell us what he was doing on his own in the wild and so we took him for a spy. Fortunately, my men had the foresight to bring him blinded into our camp for questioning. We may have got nothing but screams for our efforts, but it will mean we can still exchange him for gold without compromising our position. I was going to ask you how much you thought a sergeant would be worth to them, but as you know him you can tell me if he is favoured in the Order.'

'He is a groom. Not a spy.'

'What would a groom from Paris be doing here?'

Now Will did look at Simon, his face hard. 'I expect he was looking for me.'

Simon was too far to hear what they were saying, but he strained forward as Will turned to him. 'Will! Tell them to release me!' The other prisoners were stirring now, some adding their pleas to Simon's.

'I can vouch for him,' Will told Wallace. 'He'll cause you no trouble.'

'He's English,' growled Adam, 'he can cause nothing else.'

Wallace said nothing.

'You have the money I brought, along with my brother-in-law's horse and armour,' continued Will. 'That's worth ten sergeants at least.'

'Like you say, we have that,' responded Adam. 'And with him, we can get more. You said he was a groom. That must make him valuable.'

'Exactly.' Will thrust a hand at Simon, but kept his eyes on Wallace. 'No one knows horse lore like he does. You said you've had him for a few months, so you cannot be that desperate to ransom him. At least let him prove his worth. He would be an asset. If not, you can keep my gold and sell us both back to the Temple with nothing lost.'

'Unchain the prisoner,' said Wallace, gesturing to one of the guards by the cage.

'William, no,' protested Adam.

'I've been around English soldiers long enough to know something of deception, cousin,' Wallace said. 'I believe he is telling the truth.'

The other prisoners began to complain as Simon was released, but were soon silenced by the guards' spears.

Simon limped out of the cage. Faded bruises on his face were visible as darker patches beneath the dirt as he entered the sphere of torchlight. 'Will. Thank God.'

Will grasped him by the arm, ignoring his wince at the contact, and led him as far as he dared from Wallace and the others, who continued to watch him closely. 'What are you doing here?'

'I came looking for you. Robert got me transferred to Balantrodoch.'

Will gritted his teeth at the way Simon said it, as if the groom were surprised he would even ask this; as if it were a foregone conclusion. 'Why?'

Simon's relief turned to puzzlement. 'You left the Temple, Will. Did you think I wouldn't want to know the reason?'

'I had hoped you would respect my decision.'

'Respect?' demanded Simon, puzzlement giving way to anger. 'What was there to respect? You abandoned the Order, your brothers, your friends, your *daughter*. I know you were grieving for Elwen, but that's no cause for you to desert your duties like a coward and—' Simon's words were cut off as Will struck him in the face. He reeled back into a tree, which he clung to for support.

Will went still as Simon clutched his face. Blood trickled on to his tunic, loose on a frame wasted by ill-treatment and lack of food. Shame rose in Will and his fists unclenched. 'Simon.' He took a step towards him, then stopped, the apology sticking in his throat. To utter it would admit that Simon was in some way right. And he couldn't do that, not after all this time; after the supreme effort it had taken to bury his past. He hadn't asked him to come searching for him like some pining hound. He didn't want him here. Leaving Simon sagged against the tree, Will turned and walked away.

I 3
Selkirk Forest, Scotland

25 August 1297 AD

Simon walked purposefully through the camp, heading for Will's shelter. Even before he reached it, he could see that it was empty, a coarse blanket lying crumpled under the screen of twigs and leaves. He halted outside and stared around. Here and there men sat in groups, tending fires, or else moved between the rows of shelters, carrying wood or pails of water. There was no sign of Will. After a moment, Simon sat down on a patch of dewy grass and slumped against a tree. He had been awake for hours going over what he would say and he had been ready, eager even, to talk. Now, all the words were gumming up inside him.

It was over a month since Will had entered the rebels' camp and secured his release from Wallace's prison. In the weeks that followed, his friend had hardly said two words to him, avoiding his gaze at meal-times, sitting on the opposite side of the fire. Secretly, Simon had taken this for guilt. The bruise on his face took some weeks to heal and he had hoped that when it faded so too would Will's detachment. But, if anything, Will just avoided him more, until Simon began to realise his hope had been unfounded. Will truly did not want him here and that punch had been intentional.

Last night, going over what he should do, he had pondered, briefly, the idea of returning to Paris, but however much he would rather be back in the stables, in comfort and safety, he knew he couldn't make that choice. If he left now, he doubted he would ever see Will again and that wasn't something he wanted to live with. He loved Will as a brother and in other ways he had never fully understood, and a life without him in it seemed unthinkable. The only thing he could do was to persuade Will to return with him to Paris and the only way to do that was to gain his trust again.

In the early hours, it had dawned on Simon that to do this he would have to submit to Will's choices. He would have to go where he went and do what he did, even if that meant fighting in the battle everyone said was coming. He had followed Will into a war before and survived. His experiences in Acre, as well as his torture and imprisonment at the hands of the Scots, had toughened him. True, he wasn't a skilled fighter, but he had more strength than many men and knew how to use it. He hadn't come all this way to turn around now.

Simon looked up as a shadow fell across him.

It was David. The young man was holding a bow. 'Do you want to come hunting?'

Simon glanced at the empty shelter, then pushed himself up and brushed down his hose. He would come back later to tell Will his decision.

The water splashed on Will's face and neck, numbing his skin. He let it drip on to his bare chest as the water in the bowl grew still and his reflection settled. Slowly, he raised the blade and set it to his cheek, the metal colder than the water. He scraped it against his jaw, removing the last of the black bristles, drawing beads of blood whenever he pressed too hard.

When it was done, he cleaned the blade, feeling strangely naked and exposed. He hadn't seen himself without a full beard since he was eighteen. But only old men wore them, old men and Templars, and he was neither.

Picking up his shirt, Will walked down through the quiet glade and along the banks of the river. Dawn had brought a mist and an amber haze lingered between the trees, the sun struggling to pierce the canopy. The air was humid, fragrant with the smell of grass. Ahead, he heard laughter and splashing. A group of women were gathered on the rocks around one of the deep pools into which the river bubbled, washing clothes. There were a fair number of women in the camp and not a few children, most of them wives and daughters of those men who had been proclaimed outlaws and who feared for their families' safety in the towns they left behind, crawling with English soldiers. Alice and Margaret were sitting together, rubbing wet shirts on the stones, each pass and press of their hands making *slap-slapping* sounds on the rocks. Ysenda was a little way away beside a young woman with red hair, plaited thickly down her back.

Outwardly, his sister seemed to be enduring her grief for Duncan's death, but Will guessed she had been shielding the girls from the depth of her sorrow in an effort to lessen their own. Still, he did sense she had found some solace in the Forest; a world away from her old life and the violence that had brought her here, sheltered in this haven of routines and camaraderie. Even Alice and Margaret were calmer now, settling into the rhythm of the days.

The women looked up at his approach. Ysenda's eyes widened at his changed appearance. The young, red-haired woman, who was called Christian, smiled. Nodding to them, Will headed away from the river towards an area cleared of trees, where sounds of sawing and hammering grated on the stillness. In the clearing, huge shapes reared out of the mists; outlines of half-built siege engines. The air was green with pine resin. There was a shout and a creaking groan as a tree toppled and crashed into the undergrowth. He moved on, passing a line of men with short bows shooting targets pinned to distant trees and a knot of youths being instructed in the use of the long spear by a thickset Highlander.

Reaching his area of the camp, Will threw his undershirt over a branch. He saw David and Simon's shelters were empty and guessed they had gone hunting. After handing the blade to the man he had borrowed it from, he knelt on the mossy ground and murmured the Paternosters he had been taught to say whenever he was in the field and unable to hear the seven offices. There were some things he would not give up.

As he was reciting the last prayer, Will sensed someone move up behind him. Turning, he saw a whip-lean man in a hooded robe. 'Good morning, Father.' He rose to tower over the man, who had been introduced to him a fortnight ago as John Blair, Wallace's chaplain.

'I'm sorry to disturb your prayers,' said John, in his quiet voice.

'I was finished.'

'I was wondering, William, why do you not join the others for Mass in my chapel? You would be welcome.'

Will tried to hide his mockery at John's use of the word; the chaplain's church was a clearing in the Forest with a tree stump for an altar. 'I am used to praying on my own, but thank you.'

'Then perhaps you might speak to the men of the Holy Land at one of my sermons?' ventured John, as Will went to head off. 'You could inspire them.'

'Inspire them?' Will turned back. 'The Holy Land isn't the Paradise men want it to be. When we went there with our crosses and swords we defiled it. What would I say to inspire them, when all I could speak of are death and horror? If what the scouts say is true and the English army is on its way? Well, these men will soon see enough of that for themselves.'

John frowned. 'These men have held out so far, against forces greater than their own.'

Will lowered his voice. 'I do not dismiss their bravery, but their battles have been won through guile; ambushes against ill-prepared garrisons and supply lines.'

'They took Perth and Glasgow.' John's placid tone deepened. 'Routed the English justice at Scone, overthrew that bastard, the Sheriff of Lanark, and slew fifty of his soldiers.'

Will had heard tell of these events almost every night he had been in the camp and with each telling and every cask of wine that was opened, many of which had admittedly been stolen from English troops, the tales got more lurid and outlandish. At first, Will had been impressed. Out on the estate, little news had come to them and he'd had no idea how widespread and effective the resistance had been.

The uprising had begun in earnest in the spring, headed by Wallace in the south and in the north by a young nobleman named Andrew de Moray, whose father had been the Justiciar of Scotland. Before long, most of the realm was in open revolt. Wallace and his forces struck out on daring assaults against Perth, Glasgow and other English-held towns, then melted back into the vast wilds of Selkirk, laden with plunder. Now, the magnates of Scotland were starting to take notice, some even forsaking their English estates to join the rebellion.

Will wanted to be buoyed up by the triumphs of Wallace and his men, feel that same confidence, flowing hot and determined in him. This was what he had sought by coming here: a new sense of purpose, a way to continue his fight against Edward, and perhaps he could have had it, but for Simon. The groom had entered his world like a shadow, a reminder of everything he had tried to shut out: the pain, the memories, discarded obligations and burdens of duty. Now, staring into John Blair's enquiring face, Will felt more of that same unwanted pressure bearing down on him. 'Wallace and his men have taken towns crowded with abused people, desperate to be rid of the English. They haven't stood on an open field against a thousand heavy cavalry.'

'Our liberty is not an easy task,' replied John, after a pause. 'Each of us knows this. We have bled hard for it already, in body and spirit.' The chaplain's eyes were thoughtful, almost sad. 'But each man here has something on his side. Something I think you might have lost.'

'And what is that?'

'Belief.' John inclined his head before Will could answer. 'My chapel is always open should you change your mind. Good day to you.'

Will watched him go, part of him struggling against his doubts, wanting to believe the chaplain was right and the Scots could win through, for he was desperate for a victory after the defeat at Edinburgh. But ever since word had come that the English army under Cressingham and de Warenne had set out from Berwick, he had felt only a creeping unease. He had seen that force. Unlike Wallace and his close comrades, sons of knights, trained to fight, most of the men were shepherds and farmers, blacksmiths, merchants. However valiant their leaders, this ragged band could not match the English might.

Pulling a dry shirt over his breeches, Will headed for the circle of tents near the centre of the camp, resolved to speak to Wallace. He found the young giant with his generals. They were a motley crew, all battle-scarred and dirty, but laughing, relaxed, seated together around a spitting fire, over which an iron pot was suspended. Will smelled venison and herbs and his stomach groaned. David had killed the hart the week before. Wallace, his nephew told him elatedly, had said it was one of the best shots he had ever seen.

'No,' Adam was saying, shaking his head. 'It was that time in Ayr. That wrestler.'

Gray chuckled. Wallace smiled, but said nothing. Will paused a short distance away, reluctant to talk while the others were there.

'What happened?' The rasping voice belonged to a man called Stephen, a warrior from Ireland.

'There was an English soldier in the town, a wrestler, who wagered he could beat any opponent,' said Adam. 'You had to pay to fight him. What was it, cousin?' he asked, looking over at Wallace. 'Three pennies?'

'Four,' answered Gray, before Wallace could speak.

'Well, William paid eight,' Adam went on, smirking. 'And broke the idiot's back.'

'Jesus,' muttered Stephen.

'The man's comrades then set upon him and William killed seven.'

'I killed three,' said Wallace, his deep voice silencing them, 'and you left out the part where they threw me in gaol. They tortured me for five weeks. Starved and beat me. I felt my life draining with every day that passed until finally . . .' He shrugged. 'I slipped away.'

The men were hushed. 'It is said you died,' ventured a comrade of Stephen's.

'It's true,' responded Adam soberly.

'Whether I did or not, the English thought I had,' said Wallace, taking a water-skin one of the men passed to him. 'They tossed me in a dung heap.'

'Bastards,' growled one soldier.

'As fortune would have it,' said Adam, picking up the story, 'an old woman who was a friend of William's mother heard of his death, for the

English were crowing about it. She found his body and had her sons put him on a cart to take him for burial. But as she was laying William out in his shroud, she saw his eyes moving. She took him into her house and nursed him back to health, her and her young daughter.' He grinned at Wallace. 'Tell them, cousin.'

Wallace took a swig from the skin. 'The old woman tried to feed me, but I was too weak to take a spoon, so she had her daughter do it.' His own mouth began to twitch. 'She'd just had a baby and was still suckling.'

Gray roared with laughter and some of the others joined in, guessing what was coming.

'Let us say I woke up with a mouthful,' finished Wallace.

'What did she do?'

'She gave a start, then smiled down at me, told me she was almost drained and popped the other one in.'

'God, but you're a hook for the women, Wallace,' complained Stephen. 'How is it they all love such a brute?'

'It's the size of his sword,' said Adam, nodding to the enormous claymore propped against the tree beside Wallace. The blade, almost six feet from pommel to tip, was taller than most of the men in the camp.

There were more roars, but Wallace had gone silent at Stephen's comment. His fading smile was like the sun going in behind a cloud, his face drawing in on itself. He got to his feet, took up a couple of skins and moved off, leaving the men to continue the conversation.

After a pause, Will followed, heading in a wide circle around the tents, so as to avoid the notice of the others. Quickening his pace, he caught up with Wallace, who was headed for the river.

Wallace turned swiftly, reaching for his dirk, then relaxed. 'What do you want?'

'To talk.' When Wallace kept on walking, Will went after him. 'You have a lot of stories, you and your men, tales of courage and skill.'

'They aren't stories.'

'Oh, I believe they happened. But perhaps you have all come to rely on your past accomplishments too much?'

'You should get back to your training, Campbell. The English army won't be long in coming and you've been out of the field for some time, so your nephew tells me.'

'Listen to me,' said Will, moving round in front of Wallace, forcing him to stop. 'Beating guards in a street brawl is not the same as commanding an army on a field. I do not think your men fully understand what they will be asked to face in this war, or the sacrifices they might have to make.'

'Sacrifices?' demanded Wallace, anger leaping into his eyes. 'It is you who does not understand. We tell the stories that hearten us, sustain us. You have not heard the others, the ones that wake us in the night, clawing at our souls. I had a wife once. I used to visit her in Lanark in disguise after I was outlawed for killing an Englishman who tried to take my uncle's horse. Marion understood. Her brother had been killed by English soldiers, as had my father. She was eighteen and heir to her father's estate, but I wed her for her spirit, not for any dowry as the English put about.' His voice was glacial. 'After we married in secret she bore me a daughter. During one of our meetings, I was followed by soldiers and Marion helped me escape. When she refused to give me up to the Sheriff of Lanark, he had her and my daughter killed and so I broke into his house and slew him in his bed. You do not know me, Templar, me or my men.'

'I'm not a knight,' said Will quietly, finding no comfort in the similarities between his life and Wallace's.

'You think shaving your beard changes who you are?' Wallace shook his head. 'You're still a Templar who has lost his way and I'm still the widowed son of a nobleman who died trying to free his country. The Forest hides these things, but it does not alter them. When you've been in here long enough you'll discover that.'

As he walked away, Will went after him. 'You and your men haven't faced the English in full force. You have three thousand. They will have twenty, at least. Do you really believe you can beat them? Or is this just revenge?'

'Even before Balliol was stripped of his arms, even before he rebelled against the English, Edward's men were ravaging our lands. While you have been fighting for God on foreign sands, we have been at war for seven years.' Wallace's voice grew rough and impassioned. 'When the magnates of Scotland swore fealty to Edward as their overlord, they let a wolf into our lands. A hungry, savage wolf. English soldiers crowded into the towns and castles. They treated it as their land and us as slaves. They called us coarse, uncivilised. We complained and they silenced us, with threats, then fists, then swords. The magnates of Scotland looked the other way as the violence grew, unwilling to endanger their fortunes.

'Six years ago, near my family's home in Ayrshire, some children were throwing stones at a castle where English troops were garrisoned. The English knights on the battlements shot them. Four boys and a girl. The oldest was twelve. That night a force of men, including my father and brother, overpowered a company of knights from the castle. Some of them managed to flee, but five were caught. They were hanged from a tree in the middle of the town. After that, the English pursued us in strength. There was a battle at a place called Loudoun Hill. In the struggle, my father was killed, his legs cut away from under him.' Wallace paused. 'You do not know what it is we fight for. How could you? You haven't been here.'

Some distance behind them, they heard the pounding of hooves and the calls of men. Wallace pushed his way back through the undergrowth, Will close behind him. Ahead, they saw two men dismounting from horses, surrounded by Gray and the others.

'What is it?' called Wallace.

'We have news of the English,' said Adam, heading over, with a suspicious look at Will. 'The English army under the treacherer and John de Warenne are headed for Stirling.'

'They will cross the Forth there,' said Wallace, nodding, 'head north to try to undo what we have done. I imagine they will attempt to win Perth first, then relieve Dundee.' He drew a breath, his voice steady again. 'Then Stirling is where we shall meet them.'

'The scouts bring other tidings,' continued Adam, his scarred face filling with exhilarated triumph. 'Andrew de Moray and his army wish to join forces with us against them.'

A fierce smile broke across Wallace's face. 'Gather the men, cousin.' He glanced back at Will. 'We ride out.'

14
The English Camp, Stirling, Scotland
11 September 1297 AD

♊

John de Warenne, Earl of Surrey, frowned across the land from the saddle of his destrier. The morning was glowing, golden. The grass beneath his horse's hooves sparkled and the glints of light playing on the deep waters of the Forth dazzled him. There was a freshness in the air that hinted at autumn and the earl was glad of the heavy mantle of blue and gold brocade he wore over his surcoat and armour. He felt the cold more these days, since coming down with a fever during a hunting expedition. It had developed into a sickness in his lungs he hadn't fully recovered from and the last place he wanted to be was astride his horse in this accursed country, the English army restless at his back.

'The Dominicans should have returned,' rang a loud voice. 'We cannot delay any longer.'

De Warenne's brow knotted further as Hugh Cressingham pulled up alongside on a bay-coloured stallion. It was a sturdy, thick-legged beast, which it needed to be considering its charge.

In the time since his appointment as Treasurer of Scotland, Cressingham had turned from a podgy, pompous clerk into an obese, arrogant official. It had taken four men to hoist him on to the horse, a group of sniggering Welsh archers watching as the squires heaved and strained. Stuffed in the oversized saddle in his bright mail hauberk, Cressingham looked like an enormous, shiny slug. His face was oily with sweat despite the cool and the strap of his helmet had disappeared between two of his chins. De Warenne himself wasn't the wiry man he had been in his youth, but beneath his old man's paunch he was still slabbed with muscle. The flabby toad beside him had no business wearing the garb of a warrior, let alone sharing command of the thousands who crowded the plains between the banks of the Forth and the royal burgh of Stirling.

'We go when I give the order,' the earl said gruffly.

Cressingham arched an eyebrow. 'Is that so? Because I was under the impression you had already given that?'

De Warenne scowled, but couldn't argue; Cressingham was right, he had given the order last night and that morning, as dawn broke, the first ranks passed dutifully over the wooden bridge that spanned the river. Three hundred Welsh archers were followed by five thousand infantry, all stomping across the long, narrow bridge above the inky waters. By the time they had crossed the sun had risen, but de Warenne was still at rest in his tent. With no sign of support from the bulk of the army, the advance had turned around and marched back across, the men muttering, irritable.

The earl blamed his illness for his torpor, but although this was true in part, there had been a more prevailing factor in his delay in sending the rest of the force across. For the past two days since their arrival at Stirling the weather had been drizzly, the land wreathed in mists that clung to the hills, obscuring the view. With this crisp morning had come a clearer picture of the terrain that faced them, and de Warenne's resolve had faltered.

On the flat plains beneath Stirling Castle, soaring high on its rock, the ground was firm and level. But once over the bridge, itself a difficulty in terms of how few men could cross at once, the fields by the broad, looping river became soft and spongy, unsuitable for heavy cavalry. From the head of the bridge a causeway ran across these boggy fields, all the way to a rocky outcrop known as Abbey Craig, visible in the near distance. On this causeway there was room for only four horsemen to ride abreast. As the sun had begun to flash on the distant tips of spear heads and helmets, it became clear that the Scots had positioned themselves on some shallow slopes less than a mile to the north, just left of Abbey Craig. Rising behind the Scottish army, the dark mass of the Ochil Hills were bald and scarred in the morning light. To reach their enemy, de Warenne's army would have to funnel itself over the bridge, make its way across the exposed, narrow causeway surrounded by waterlogged meadows, then fight uphill. It was an unenviable prospect.

'The longer we dally, the more resources are drained,' said Cressingham, into de Warenne's taut silence. 'Lord Edward wants this rebellion crushed quickly, so he can concentrate his efforts in Flanders. Those were our orders. Besides, the men are impatient.' He flung a stubby hand behind him. 'The young bloods are keen to fight. Let us loosen their leashes.'

The earl wanted nothing more than to kick the fat treasurer from his saddle, but he bit back his temper. Cressingham had launched himself with gusto into his appointment and even with rumours that he was scraping a percentage off the revenues his sheriffs collected, he was still favoured by Edward. De Warenne, on the other hand, had spent most of his time as Lieutenant of Scotland on his Yorkshire estates, hunting and feasting, with little thought for the realm he was governing. In his notable absence, Cressingham had become Edward's eyes and ears in Scotland and, however much he loathed the official, de Warenne now had no choice but to heed his counsel. Cressingham had already sent a company of reinforcements back to Berwick to save funds. He had the authority to do more damage, if pushed.

'We will give it another hour. If the Dominicans haven't returned by then, we cross.' Not allowing Cressingham time to reply, John de Warenne wheeled his destrier around and rode back to where his knights were waiting. Despite his tension, he was confident that the two friars he had sent to parley with the Scots would return. He was also confident of the answer they would bring and that this would settle any further debate. The Scots were outnumbered and outmatched. They were peasants, led by outlaws and thieves. What contest were they against the cream of England's nobility? They would surrender.

But although the Dominicans did return, their ragged robes whipping about them as they crossed the causeway like birds of ill omen, they did not bear the tidings the Earl of Surrey expected.

The generals of the English army gathered on foot outside de Warenne's tent to hear the verdict, the wet grass staining the hems of their surcoats and glistening on their mailed boots.

'Well?' demanded Cressingham, as the friars approached. 'What did the brigands say?'

'The Scots will not surrender,' replied one of the friars grimly. 'They want to fight.'

One voice rose above the exclamations of angry surprise. '*Want* to fight?' scoffed Henry Percy, an ambitious young lord, whose star was rising in the English royal court, along with his fortunes. 'Do the churls even know what faces them?'

'They know,' replied the second friar. 'But their leader, Wallace, said they would rather die than live another day under English rule.'

This time, along with the mutters, were snorts of laughter.

'Wallace said they were there to avenge their country and their dead,' continued the Dominican gravely, 'not to make peace with tyrants. He said he would prove this to our very beards.'

The snorts died away. A couple of younger lords spoke up.

'Then let us give them what they want!'

'Prove it to our beards? We'll prove it in their gullets!'

De Warenne, whose spirits had sunk with the news, now stirred, his resolve settling in him. 'Their decision has been made and let the Scots rue it. Our decision rests on where to make their graves. In their present position, they have the advantage.' He turned to one of the friars. 'Was our guess of their numbers correct?'

'They have many foot-soldiers. But only a handful of cavalry.'

A couple of the generals offered their opinions, but over them all Cressingham's shrill voice rang. 'I do not see what decision there is to be made. You already gave the order to cross the bridge,' he added to de Warenne. 'Let the men now follow that command and have at it! Enough money and time has been wasted with all this vacillation.'

De Warenne's cheeks darkened, but before he could respond, an officer from Percy's retinue spoke.

'I understand Earl de Warenne's reluctance,' he said, inclining his head to the brooding earl. 'The bridge is narrow and the terrain beyond treacherous. But there is a ford not far upriver, where at low tide many more men could cross at once. The area is heavily wooded and we could approach from the north in secret. While our infantry cross here, luring the Scots to attack, we can come at them from behind.'

De Warenne frowned thoughtfully at this suggestion, but it was hard enough to think with his head thick from a bad night's sleep, harder still with all the generals shouting over one another.

Yet again, Cressingham's was the voice that prevailed. 'No. Waiting for low tide will add hours more to this needless delay. Let us stop arguing and cross the damn river! Once the Scots see us marching, they will most likely turn tail and flee. If not, we will destroy them where they stand. They had the advantage at Dunbar,' he said shortly, to de Warenne, 'and you made butchery of them there. And that was the feudal host of Scotland, not a gang of ill-disciplined peasants.'

'I agree,' said Percy determinedly.

No one dared disagree with two of their leaders. All eyes now turned to de Warenne, who looked from the young lord to Cressingham. Not only was Percy favoured in court and fired with ambition, he had also brought three hundred knights and eight thousand foot to the battlefield. To fight Cressingham and his tight purse strings was risky, to fight Percy as well was folly. Besides, he had given the order for the army to cross last night; he had thought it the best way then. The earl rubbed irately at his brow. He wanted to lie down for a few more hours until he could think clearly. But he needed to make a decision. 'Very well,' he growled. 'We cross the bridge.'

The Scottish Camp, Near Stirling, Scotland, 11 September 1297 AD

Will shortened the reins as his horse, a smoke-grey gelding, tossed its head agitatedly. All the mounts were growing restless, feeling the tension in their riders, lined up on a gentle slope, watching the English cross the river.

It was an awe-inspiring sight.

First across the bridge came the Welsh archers with their longbows, the deadly range and power of which was just becoming known, and dreaded. In their midst, banner-bearers marched, hoisting the flags and pennants of their leaders high. The colours shone: blue and purple, yellow and red, the flags adorned with stags and lions, griffins and eagles. Behind rode great barons and lords, surrounded by knights and squires, the iron-shod hooves of their armoured destriers pounding a tattoo across the wooden bridge, the waters of the Forth swirling dark beneath them. Next came the foot-soldiers, their helmets and swords a sea of bobbing light, channelling across the bridge then fanning out to flood the fields around the causeway. Once over the bridge, a company of horsemen, fifty strong, broke off from the main host, now heading down the causeway towards Abbey Craig. This company lined up in tight formation on the edge of the bank to cover the advance. It was slow, steady progress. Behind, on the south side of the river beneath Stirling Castle, the bulk of the English army waited, ranks drawn up, thousands upon thousands, ready to cross when the lines in front had gone on ahead. Over the rumble of the hooves, horns bellowed, resounding across the plain, all the way to the Scottish host waiting on the hillside.

Will squinted against the sun's glare. Even at this distance and with the enormous mass of men, he couldn't see the distinctive white block that would indicate a company of Templars anywhere in the English force. The lack of them made him wonder briefly if Edward was getting less support for his war, but he thought it more likely that the king felt so confident of the outcome of the campaign he hadn't called upon the Order's service. Edward hadn't even come himself. It was rumoured he was in Flanders, fighting the French.

'Mother of God.'

Will glanced round at the murmur. A young Irishman, mounted at his side, was staring at the advancing army in appalled fascination. He was one of Stephen's men.

The man caught Will's eye. 'Have you ever seen anything like it?' Will thought of Antioch and Acre.

When he nodded, the Irishman blew through his cheeks. 'Mother of God,' he said again, his gaze pulled back to the English host.

He wasn't the only one showing his nerves. Everywhere Will looked, he saw wide eyes and rigid faces, veins pulsing in necks locked with tension, hunched shoulders, glistening lines of sweat. Fear was infectious. It seeped from the one hundred and sixty cavalry into their horses and spread out across the slopes creeping over the ten thousand foot-soldiers arrayed there, under the joint command of William Wallace and Andrew de Moray.

Last night had been different. Listening to the men around the blazing campfires, their laughter and their songs, Will sensed only their confidence. But rather than concerning him, as it had the previous year when he rode into Scotland to discover a nation keen, but sorely unprepared, he found himself lifted by it. They had learned their lessons hard during Edward's invasion, from the brutal sack of Berwick to the imprisonment of their king and their own persecution. Their confidence now was tougher, born partly out of the remarkable victories achieved by Wallace and de Moray, but more from a growing patriotism that unified them in common cause, binding them in loss and longing. More than anything else, that sense of unity had been visible to Will last night, hearing these lowborn men, brought together from across the realm, talking of their families and homes. Unlike the English soldiery, many of whom had been pressed or enticed into service, these Scottish peasants had come freely to these sunlit hills. They weren't landed knights or mighty earls, few of them wore the mail armour donned by the English; some were even barefoot and bare-chested, clutching spears and axes, dirks and clubs. But against the odds and despite their fear, they stood there all the same, ranged before one of the most formidable armies in the world.

Somewhere in the throng were David and Simon. Will scanned the sprawling infantry lines, but couldn't see them. He prayed fervently that whatever happened to him, his nephew would live through this. Their leaving had hit Ysenda hard, David forced to pull himself out of her embrace, leaving her weeping bitterly in Christian's arms, as the Scottish host rode out of Selkirk Forest.

Turning back to watch the English come, Will felt his heart settle into a determined rhythm that beat in time with their drums. As the inexperienced troops around him fidgeted and murmured, toyed with weapons and needed to piss, he felt his own nerves falling away to be replaced by solid calm. There was a peace that came with the decision to fight. It was like a stone falling in the centre of him; a heavy resolve, grounding him. No turning back now. Soon that calm would rise into anticipation. His heart would pick up pace and the blood would throb in his temples. Then it would begin to feel like a thrill and he would grin as he couched his lance, fixed his eyes on a target. Aimed.

The sun was rising higher. It was almost mid-morning. Will guessed around seven thousand had crossed the bridge. The signal would come any moment. In expectation, he raised his eyes to the rocky summit of Abbey Craig, where he knew Wallace and de Moray, along with their generals, would be watching the English advance. They had set their trap late last night in a closed war council. Will, hearing the audacious plan as he was given his orders that morning, began to understand just how Wallace, the younger son of a minor knight, had accomplished what he had these past years. Despite the fact that the young giant was almost half his age, he found himself as inspired by him as he once was by men like his father, Owein and Everard.

'*We are here to fight in the name of King John!*' Wallace had roared at the troops as they had drawn up. '*We are here to fight for the sons and daughters of Scotland, crushed beneath the heels of tyrants!*'

As a blast from a deep-voiced horn rang from the top of Abbey Craig, Will felt a rush of blood go through him. The sound resonated across the hills, drowning the English trumpets and sending a shiver of anticipation through the Scots. Will levelled his spear, bracing it against his body, as battle cries sounded all around him.

We are here to fight for our lands and our livelihoods.

Together, the Scottish force charged. First the cavalry, Will among them, sweeping down from the shallow hills towards the head of the causeway, beneath the shadow of Abbey Craig.

We are here to fight for our liberty.

Behind came the infantry, a huge, ragged wave, surging over the fields. The right wing of this force, made up of spearmen, split away from the main group at a shout from one of their commanders. They sprinted hard to the south, making for Stirling Bridge, where the fifty horsemen were lined up covering the English troops, still advancing.

As Will rode, the world rushing past, his body jarred by the ferocious stride of his horse, Wallace's words reverberated in him. They echoed, louder and faster, until they became his own. His fight. His reasons for being there. Like this small Scottish force against the English might, like

David and Goliath, it was him against Edward; a knight against a king. Edward wasn't here, but his army, his *pride* was. That was something. That was enough. Hatred swelled in him, firing his blood, making him slam his spurs into the sides of his horse, his lips pulling back in a savage grin inside his helmet. The lines of soldiers ahead were coming rapidly up before him, horses wheeling around, shields raising, lances levelling. They were the soldier who had run Tom through like he was nothing and the tax collector who had stabbed Duncan in the back. They were no longer men, but pieces of Edward to be hacked away.

Arrows stabbed down as the Welsh archers on the causeway let fire. But the Scots came on, fast and furious. Horses leapt up and over as some mounts crashed into the earth, baying in pain, struck by the feathered missiles. Men lurched from saddles and were slammed into the ground. Some rolled and staggered to their feet. Others didn't. From the lower slopes of Abbey Craig, the generals, led by Wallace and de Moray, swept on to the plain to join the main force. Wallace roared as he rode, whirling a massive axe.

With a convulsive clang of swords and spears, armour and shields, the Scottish cavalry punched into the English on the causeway. Their own horses, lighter and sturdier, fared better on the boggy ground than the English war-chargers, weighed down by armour and trappings. Will fixed on a man in a faceless helmet and thrust out with his spear. His momentum carried the iron tip straight through the man's mail shirt, snapping rings apart, to sink through the padding beneath and into his chest. As the man was thrown back, the spear was wrenched from Will's hand. Drawing his falchion he continued on, driving into the English ranks. His grandfather's blade, although much shorter than a cavalry sword, was nonetheless effective in these close quarters. Pressed in by men on all sides, there was little room to manoeuvre, let alone swing a broadsword, but with the falchion he could jab and stab at those around him. His horse was knocked in the press. It reared up, eyes rolling, and crashed into another beside it. A sword whistled past Will, missing his neck by inches, another smashed into his helmet, concussing him. Guiding his horse with his knees, he raised his wooden shield to block impact after impact, the blows jarring his arm.

Wallace, meanwhile, had cut a bloody swathe through half a dozen English knights, to thunder into the lines of Welsh archers, still firing at the Scottish infantry sprinting across the fields. The archers scattered as he charged them, his axe felling men as if they were stalks of corn.

As this fierce combat settled in around the north end of the causeway, the Scottish infantry barrelled into the English foot-soldiers, now fanning out to meet them. Among them ran David, his thoughts burning with his father's image and fuelled by the need for revenge. He held a long spear that he pointed at the men speeding up to meet him, holding it balanced as Wallace had taught him. Close behind was Simon, no longer in his sergeant's garb. He, too, wielded a spear.

Ten thousand foot-soldiers slammed into the English advance with shocking force. Men screamed as they were lanced with spears. Exposed flesh was slashed open, skulls crushed. Their feet churned the boggy ground into a slick, black mud as they pushed against one another, face to snarling face. But the English were outnumbered and many of the infantry were pushed back towards the Forth, the banks of which crumbled away behind them. The water was deep and those who fell or were pushed drowned trying to swim to the far shore, weighed under by armour. The English knights and commanders, stretched thinly along the causeway, were too far apart and too involved in the battle to marshal their scattering infantry effectively.

While the main Scottish force struck at the advance, the right wing of spearmen who broke away at the start of the charge were slicing a path through the fifty English cavalry protecting the bridge. The ground here was even marshier and the knights floundered in the mud, their horses slipping and stumbling as they led a futile charge against the incoming Scots. A few tried to ride back across the bridge to escape the ferocious onslaught. This caused a violent stampede as men on the other side surged forward to aid their comrades and those being hacked at by the Scots tried to retreat. Horses bucked and reared in the mêlée, trampling men beneath hooves or knocking them from the bridge. There were several huge splashes as horses tumbled in, their riders throwing themselves from saddles to plunge into the swirling waters. Men flailed for a moment, mouths gasping, before sinking. Others clung to the bridge piers, but were pierced by spears launched from the Scots crowding the banks.

Will blocked the sword of a knight with his shield, hefted the blade away, then stuck the man through the throat. As the knight slipped from his saddle and caught in the stirrup, his horse bolted. In the gap, Will spurred his mount up on to the causeway, now littered with bodies. Sweat stung his eyes as he drove through a group of English foot-soldiers. Ahead, he saw Wallace. The young giant had been unhorsed and fought on foot, swinging his claymore in two-handed strokes. The blade carved through anyone who stood against him, ripping through armour and flesh. He was covered in blood and his eyes were wild. Adam fought at his side, slick with sweat and splattered with mud, his club swinging out, pulverising jaws and skulls. Together, the cousins were a fearsome sight. As he kicked his horse towards the fray, Will saw an archer rising to his feet, bow in his hands. Swiping an arrow from his quiver, the man fixed it and aimed at Wallace.

Will turned his horse sharply as the archer pulled the bow taut. Thundering up behind, he leaned out in the saddle and chopped down with his sword. The archer whirled around, hearing the drumming hooves and Will caught him in the shoulder. The blade cut through the man's armour and sliced into the flesh beneath. The archer shrieked in agony and let go of the bow. The arrow sprang into the air to curve harmlessly into the river. The man went down a second later, kicked in the back by another rider. It was Gray.

He had lost his helmet and his white bristly hair was covered in blood from a wound on his scalp, but he grinned savagely at Will. 'On them!' he yelled, thrusting his blade towards the tattered English lines. 'On them! They fail!'

As the Scottish spearmen closed in to take the bridge, John de Warenne stared in horror from the other side of the river. His mighty army had been neatly split in two, the head severed from the body. Now, with the Scots barring entry to the causeway with a wall of spears, he could only watch, impotent, as nearly six thousand of his men were butchered before his eyes. His archers might have been able to ward off the Scots long enough for him to clear the crush on the bridge and lead a charge. But they had gone with Cressingham in the vanguard. Unable to use their deadly weapons at such short range, they were being cut down in the hundreds. De Warenne couldn't see the treasurer's banner any more. He opened his mouth to shout orders to his troops, but no words came. The din of battle would drown anything he could say.

'My lord,' one of his knights murmured at his side, his face pale. 'What shall we do?'

John de Warenne, one of the most powerful men in England, veteran commander of more than a dozen campaigns, shook his head. 'I do not know,' he said hoarsely. 'I . . .' He faltered, his vision filling with the sight of armoured knights jumping into the river, herded and jabbed at by the Scots. The last of the men on the bridge were surging back across it, some crawling on hands and knees, others dragging comrades. A few Scottish spearmen were advancing slowly along it, finishing off the dying, but they seemed wary about coming too far down. 'Burn it,' rasped de Warenne. 'Burn the bridge and sound the retreat.'

Leaving the last of their men to be cut down behind them and the bridge going up in flames, the rest of the English army, led by John de Warenne, turned their backs on the Forth and departed.

In less than an hour, the battle was over, the Scots triumphant beyond measure. The gruesome work of despatching the wounded continued for a while longer, but soon, the only things living in the churned-up fields were the victors. Over one hundred English knights had perished along with more than five thousand infantry and a large contingent of Welsh archers. All the dead were relieved of their weapons and armour, and pushed into the river. Very few Scots had perished, although Andrew de Moray sustained a bad wound to his chest and was carried from the field by his men. The bloated body of Hugh Cressingham was found among the dead, his stomach ripped open by a spear. Grimly, the Scots stripped their hated treasurer, whose taxes had drained them to the point of starvation, jostling one another to get at the fleshy corpse. One man took his blade and with a savage cry sliced off the treasurer's genitals to the fierce cheers of his comrades. This signalled a frenzied attack as others, all desperate to prove to their countrymen what they had achieved this day, drew daggers and knives and began to hack and flay Cressingham's body, each bloody scrap of his skin a token of their victory, hard won and long in coming.

Will found David in the fields near the river, where Stirling Bridge was blazing. Black smoke belched into the sky, making their eyes smart. Both of them were sweat-drenched and bloody. Pulling off his helmet, Will embraced his nephew fiercely, then drew back to see Simon limping up, covered in mud and leaning on his spear, a cut on his thigh. Will, who had hardly said two words to the groom since securing his release from Wallace's prison, held out his hand. Simon clasped it as the breathless cheers of the Scots echoed around them.

After finding someone to tend Simon's wound, Will slumped exhausted on the causeway. His shield-arm and shoulder burned and his sword-arm was throbbing. Sitting there in the midday sun, the stink of death in his nostrils, he closed his eyes and imagined Edward's face as he was told how his mighty army had been defeated by peasants and outlaws. He savoured the image, rejoiced in it. A shadow fell across him and Will opened his eyes to see Wallace standing before him, drenched in gore.

'Gray tells me I am to thank you. You covered my back.'

'I need no thanks.'

Wallace smiled. 'Come.' He held out his hand. As Will took it, Wallace pulled him to his feet. 'It isn't over yet.'

As the tide turned on the Forth, Wallace and his generals roused their weary men and led the cavalry down to the lower ford where they crossed the river. From there they pursued the retreating English army relentlessly, picking off lagging foot-soldiers and snatching pack-horses, all the way to the Borders.

It was later said John de Warenne rode so furiously to escape them, he didn't stop to rest his horse until he reached Berwick.

15
Selkirk Forest, Scotland
21 June 1298 AD

R emoving his shirt and rolling up his breeches, Will made his way
across the mossy stones and stepped into the pool. In contrast to the
heat in the air, the water was freezing. Bending, he dunked the bowl in and,
using a fistful of soapwort, began to wipe away the grease from last night's
meal, the rush of the river loud in his ears.

'Good morning.'

Will looked up to see Christian heading down the bank, her arms piled
with wooden bowls. He gave a nod.

She smiled as she pushed up the sleeves of her pale green dress and
plunged one of the bowls into the foaming water. Sunlight, filtering
through the leaves of the alders and wych elms that bordered the river,
played on her face. 'It's going to be hot again today.' As she looked back at
Will, her smile became curious. 'Who did that to you?'

When she pointed to his back, Will realised she was referring to the faint
silvery lines that criss-crossed his spine, made when Everard whipped him,
all those years ago. 'An old master.'

Christian set the bowl on the grass and sat back, drawing her knees up.
She was in her early thirties, but sitting there like that, her red hair tousled
from sleep, she could have passed for eighteen. Will realised he was staring
and thrust the bowl back into the water, even though it was now clean.

'And that one?' Christian nodded to his knee, where his breeches were
rolled up over a lumpy riddle of scar tissue.

'I fell down a well,' he murmured, recalling Angelo Vitturi's blistered
face, twisted in triumph, disappearing above him as he slipped back into
nothing. The leg, which had broken in two places, still pained him, usually
in winter; a lingering ache that sometimes woke him in the night.

'Those I know,' said Christian, gesturing to his forehead, shoulder and
calf, marked with wounds from more recent injuries, borne over the past

year since the battle at Stirling Bridge. 'And . . .' She squinted in scrutiny, then shook her head. 'That is it. I cannot see any— No, wait. There is one more, on your arm.'

Will stared at the pinkish patch of skin on the side of his arm, the bowl forgotten in his hand. The scar was barely visible. He was surprised she had seen it at all. He had thrown his arm up against the billowing flames. Blazing embers rained down on him and a wall of fire raged in front of him as he tried to climb the staircase. The hairs on his arm had burned away, the skin beginning to blister. Yet the scar was so small, so insignificant. Pathetic. If he had something more disfiguring, he might have felt better. But every time he saw that patch of hairless pink skin he was mocked by how feeble his efforts to save his wife had been. *You wanted her to burn because of Garin, because of what she did with him. She betrayed you and you wanted her to suffer.* 'No.' Realising, by the frown on Christian's face, that he'd spoken out loud, Will straightened and shook the water from the bowl. But his fingers were trembling as he tried to wipe it on his breeches and he dropped it. The bowl hit the water and spun away from him, bobbing like a toy boat.

Christian lifted her dress and stepped down the shallow bank, wincing as stones crunched beneath her bare feet.

'I can do it,' said Will, as she waded in, one arm outstretched for balance, the other holding her dress above her knees. 'Careful, it gets deeper here.' He went towards her, his feet tentative on the slippery stones.

'There,' she said, gasping with the cold, as she plucked it from the pool. The water was almost up to her thighs. Her dress was trailing in it, darkening as it soaked into the thin material. She held the bowl out, but as Will went to take it she slipped. The bowl flew up from her hand and he grabbed her wrist instead. Christian caught her balance and steadied with a breathless laugh. She looked up at him and a flush of colour leapt into her cheeks.

Beneath his thumb, Will felt her pulse flicker, agitated.

'Will, I—'

'You've dropped your bowl.'

Looking over her shoulder, Will saw Simon and David on the bank. The groom was staring at him enquiringly. David was grinning. Will let go of Christian's wrist and fished out the bowl.

'Sir William Wallace wants to see you,' said David, as he climbed out of the pool, Christian close behind. 'If you're not too busy,' he added.

'Does it look as though I'm busy?' Will glanced at Christian, who had wrung out her dress and was bent over the stack of dirty bowls, her back to him. He snatched up his shirt and pulled it on.

As they set off through the trees towards the main camp, David moved in alongside him. 'Don't play the fool, uncle. We saw you.'

Will halted and turned to him. 'Whatever you thought you saw, you are mistaken.'

David's smile faded. 'I'm sorry, I—'

'Just get back to your training, will you. It isn't as if you don't need the practice.'

David stared at him. 'If I'm so incompetent, why did Sir William dub me?' He pushed his way through the undergrowth.

Will went to call after him, but stopped and shook his head.

'Making friends?'

'I shouldn't have said that, I know.'

'I meant back there,' said Simon, nodding towards the river.

Will's brow creased. 'You as well?'

'When you live on top of one another, things get noticed,' said Simon, hastening to keep up as Will strode off. 'I'd be careful if I were you. You don't want to go making an enemy of her brother.'

'She was married to Gray's brother,' said Will tightly. 'That makes him her brother-in-law.'

'Well, whatever, he's very protective of her. Ysenda said when Christian's husband was dying, Gray pledged to take care of her.'

'Christ, Simon, she came to wash dishes. What was I supposed to do? Ignore her?'

'What are you doing here, Will?' said Simon suddenly. 'It's been over a year. How long are you going to keep hiding in this place, acting as if there's not a world outside you've left behind?'

'Hiding?' Will faced him. 'I've been fighting a war!'

'Someone else's war. This is Wallace's fight. Him, Gray, the others, even David. This is their home.'

'As it is mine.'

'You spent longer in the Holy Land.'

'And do years make a place home?'

'No. *We* make a place home. We make it home when we are settled, when a place gives us joy and comfort. I know you, Will. I've known you since you were eleven years old and I know you aren't happy, or comfortable, or settled here.'

'I don't want to talk about this. How many times do I have to tell you that?'

Simon followed when he moved off. 'I'll stop asking when you give me an honest answer and tell me when we'll leave.'

'I'll leave when Edward is defeated.'

'Is that what you think you were doing in England? Defeating Edward? Making him pay for what he did here?' Simon's brown eyes were hard. 'Because I thought you were robbing and murdering.'

Will rounded on him. 'I never killed anyone. I'm not like . . .' He trailed off.

'Who? These men you call comrades?'

'Wallace tried to stop the ones who were taking it too far. You know he did.' Will shook his head. 'You cannot blame them, Simon. They wanted revenge; revenge for seven years of rape and slaughter, revenge for Berwick, Edinburgh. But more than that, they wanted to survive. Scotland was on its knees after Stirling. While we were trying to save the kingdom, the harvests were dying in the fields. Victory couldn't make the corn grow taller or the cattle fatten, could it? We had to invade England or the country would have starved.'

'And the people of Northumberland and Cumbria? What did they eat through the winter?'

'Most of them found shelter in Newcastle and Carlisle,' said Will gruffly. But his words were hollow.

After the battle at Stirling Bridge the resistance hadn't stopped. It had grown. News of the incredible victory over the English spread like wildfire, blazing in the hearts and minds of the Scots. The English were no longer a terrifying, unstoppable force. They were just men, vulnerable men. Even after the death of Andrew de Moray, who succumbed to the wound sustained in the battle, the Scots continued to flock to Wallace's banner, until, barely weeks later, the scent of blood still fresh, the fierce young giant led his army into England.

Sweeping down over the Tweed into Northumberland, they destroyed crops and livestock, burned monasteries, looted towns, slaughtered inhabitants. The people of northern England, most of whom had taken no part in the sack of their neighbour, paid the price for their king's brutality. And paid in full. Those who fled before the marauding Scots returned to their homes once the horde moved on, only to find they had no food or shelter for the coming winter. Newcastle was soon packed to the walls with the homeless and the destitute. The Scots stripped the county bare and everything they took was conveyed back across the border to feed the starving families they left behind.

With no one to oppose them, the Scots vented years of pent-up anger on towns and villages. Wallace and his generals attempted to restore order, even resorting to hanging in the worst cases of unnecessary violence, but they had broken a dam at Stirling and unleashed a tide that couldn't be stopped, until it had drained. Wallace's men called him William the Conqueror and his name was quickly taken south, rippling through all the shires of England, where the fear and hatred of him and his men grew. But their king was still in Flanders and there was no protection for his subjects. The reprieve for the people of northern England only came at midwinter, when the first snows began to fall, forcing the Scots back across the Tweed.

'You gave me your word you would think about returning with me to France,' said Simon, watching the emotions change on Will's face. 'Robert might be able to get you back into the Temple. You don't know for sure that Hugues will prevent you. He used to be your friend. But either way you have to make amends for the oaths you have broken. You cannot stay here, pretending you were never a knight. It was all you ever wanted to be. You cannot let your grief for what happened to Elwen ruin everything you ever were. And I know you miss your daughter. I can see it in your eyes every time you see Ysenda embrace Alice, or scold Margaret, or praise David. God damn it, *I* miss Rose! I miss our comrades, our home.'

'I don't believe she's mine, Simon.' The words came in a rush and Will looked surprised after he'd uttered them.

Simon was silent. 'Garin?' he said finally, following Will with his eyes as he turned away. 'I wondered after the fire at Andreas's, with what he was saying. Do you know for certain she is his?'

Will opened his mouth to speak, then pressed his lips together. 'I promised to think about returning to France before word came that Edward and his army were on the march. I cannot leave now. I am needed here.'

'You are needed more elsewhere,' the groom called as he walked away. But this time he didn't follow.

The words ringing in his ears, Will made his way to Wallace's tent. Following their reconciliation at Stirling, he had found himself glad of Simon's company, the familiarity of their friendship a relief after so long with strangers. But after the invasion of England, Simon once again started questioning him on when they would return to their old lives, as if it were inevitable. Simon didn't understand. The groom thought he had left the Temple and fled to Scotland because of grief over Elwen and concern for his family. Will couldn't tell him the truth, because then he would have to explain about the Brethren and Edward; would have to tell Simon he had been lying to him all these years and that the groom didn't really know him at all. That it hadn't been a stray Mamluk arrow that had sent Garin into hell. That it had been his sword.

'Campbell,' Wallace greeted tersely, as Will approached the circle of tents. He was standing by the fire holding a ragged map. Adam and Gray were poring over it. In the past year since his great victory, Wallace had grown gruffer. The deaths of comrades and enemies were marked in him, visible in his eyes, and in his face and arms, carved with more scars. 'We've had news.'

'The English?'

'They are headed for Roxburgh. The vanguard should reach it in a matter of days. Their king will not be far behind.'

'Do we know numbers?'

'The scouts reckon seven thousand horse, with large contingents led by Bek and de Warenne.'

'The earl's no doubt trying to make up for his cowardice at Stirling,' said Adam scornfully.

'And more than twenty thousand foot,' finished Wallace.

'Dear God,' murmured Will.

Gray nodded. 'The bastard means to teach us a lesson.'

'We've also had word,' continued Wallace, looking at Will, 'that the Templars are to allow the army to rest at their preceptory at Liston. Knights from England, under the command of Brian le Jay, are coming north with him.'

Will felt a heaviness enter him.

'The loyalty of the Bishop of Durham and the Earl of Surrey is unquestionable. But you told me when we first met that the Templars were compelled by Edward to aid his invasion. Will they fight for him willingly in this campaign?'

Will nodded reluctantly. 'If the Grand Master has commanded Brian le Jay then, yes, the Templars will fight.'

'More heavy cavalry than we can shake our sticks at,' muttered Adam. 'And we've fewer than a thousand horse.'

Wallace's blue eyes went to him. 'We knew this day would come. What do you think we have spent the past year raising troops and training our spearmen for? None of this changes anything. We keep to the plan.' Wallace turned to Will. 'I want you with Gray to supervise the razing of the lands south and east. Most of the inhabitants of the towns there have made it into the Forest. We gave them enough warning. Those who linger will soon make haste when you lay waste to their fields and homes.' Wallace's jaw was set. 'I want every grain of corn burned, every drop of water poisoned, every beast of the fields herded into the woods. I want the very earth where Edward leads his army to be scorched and dead. When you are done, ride north. We will be camped near Stirling.'

'Are you sure Edward will lead his army that way?' asked Gray.

Will answered before Wallace. 'The Temple's preceptory at Liston lies on the route north. If Edward means to camp there it is almost certain Stirling is his goal. Not only is it strategically vital, it is the site of his worst defeat. He will want to avenge himself.'

'We will let hunger and thirst do their work in this heat,' murmured Wallace, staring into the leaden blue sky. 'When his army is weakened and demoralised, we will strike.'

'And then let the rest of our kingdom's nobility fall at your feet in gratitude,' said Gray fiercely.

Wallace didn't answer.

Will, watching him, wasn't sure whether he would welcome this. Wallace seemed uncomfortable with his reputation, which had grown so great after Stirling that even the powerful magnates of Scotland were forced to acknowledge his success, and to reward him for it, in the form of a knighthood.

Robert Bruce, the Earl of Carrick, performed the ceremony. This young man had defied his father, who held Carlisle for Edward, and changed sides to fight for the Scottish cause. A number of lords and bishops, following Bruce's example, proclaimed Wallace as Guardian of the Realm, but even with his new-found rank he remained in Selkirk Forest, living rough with his men. When Will asked him why, Wallace said the trappings of nobility were a dangerous thing, for it was this love of wealth and possessions that had led the nobles of Scotland to forsake their country, and he would not make the same mistake. His righteous defiance did not endear him to all the nobility. Many of them, it was widely known, resented his rise to their ranks and feared his power and the growing army of men under his command.

'We had better get going if we're to outrun the English,' Gray said.

Will hung back as Wallace called to him.

'Are you going to be able to fight your Templar brothers?'

Will paused, surprised by the question and the sternness with which it was spoken. 'Are you questioning my loyalty?'

'I know you are loyal to me, Campbell. You have proven that more than once this past year. But you were a Templar far longer than you have been a man in my army. I would understand if warring against men you swore your life to would cause you to waver.'

Will thought of the battlefield to come. But all he could see was Edward's arrogant face. All he could feel was a rising sense of anticipation, eagerness even, to meet him on that field. He shook his head. 'I know where my allegiance lies.'

Temple Liston, Scotland, 21 July 1298 AD

Edward closed his eyes and tried to rest. Sweat trickled in lines down his back and his silk robes clung to his skin. The air coming through the window was oven hot. Beyond the preceptory wall, sounds of men and beasts were a constant drone. Closer, the jangling notes of a harp climbed and fell. The music was supposed to soothe him, but he found it intrusive. After a moment, Edward rose from the bed. 'Enough.'

The music stopped.

'A drink, my lord?' A page came forward with a goblet of wine.

Edward grimaced as he sipped. 'This is hot.'

'I'm sorry, my lord. The casks were in the sun too long.'

Edward flung the goblet aside, splattering the wall and another page in red wine. 'The royal menagerie would have been more use to me! Get out of my sight!'

Needing little encouragement, the pages hastened out, leaving Edward pacing the stifling chamber. His mind was tormented. Worries crowded in on top of one another, clogging his thoughts. He didn't understand how events could have taken such a turn. Only a month ago, he had been marching at the head of a vast army, filled with fervent conviction.

Edward had pulled the support of his entire kingdom behind him for this war; almost a holy war with the zeal his clerics and criers had stirred up. While he conscripted foot-soldiers and archers from Wales and Ireland, called horsemen and crossbowmen from Gascony and summoned his vassals, they whipped his subjects into a frenzy of hatred. The clerics sent word to every corner of the realm, telling of the evil of Wallace and his men. The Scots were ogres. They ate babies, molested nuns, butchered priests. By the time Edward and his army were on the move, the prayers of all England were with them. They would crush the hated Scots, avenge the atrocities of Northumberland and Cumbria. Kill the monster, Wallace, and his devil followers.

Once over the border, they advanced towards Edinburgh, one of only a handful of castles that had withstood the Scots' insurrection. But instead of terrified populations to slake their vengeance on and towns to loot for plunder, the king and his men found an empty, desolate land. At first it surprised them. Then, as the days dragged beneath the scorching sun, with the aching drudgery of long marches, it came to disturb and then to madden them.

From Roxburgh to Temple Liston, every village the host passed through was abandoned. Little wattle and daub houses stood empty, doors open on silent interiors. English soldiers barged in, kicking over furniture, upending barrels, opening chests. Finding nothing of value and nothing to eat, they moved on through barren fields where poppies bloomed like blood, mailed boots scuffing up dust. Men sweated and toiled under the metal-blue sky. Armour chafed, lips cracked and bled, blisters bubbled up on feet. Rations ran low, then ran out. Sometimes they passed smoking remains of farmsteads, the cornfields scorched and black. Archers shot crows circling the rotting corpses of a few cattle and the bitter meat was divided surreptitiously between a few lucky companies. But for most men, each exhausting march ended with a hollow belly and increasingly fitful dreams of food.

None of them knew where the enemy was, for there were no people to offer information on Wallace's location. Scouts were sent out and returned without news. Many men spent sleepless nights, staring into the darkness beyond the campfires, waiting for the glint of steel in the starlight. Two days before they reached Edinburgh, thunderheads built in the north and a searing wind whipped grit in their faces. That evening they watched as lightning ripped across the sky, mirrored in the distant sea. Edward had organised a fleet of vessels to follow them up the east coast, due to meet them at Leith to deliver much needed supplies. But when the army reached Edinburgh, instead of ships filled with grain and meat, they found the docks deserted. Word filtered through that the storm had forced them to turn back and starvation loomed like a spectre. The next day, three cogs limped into the port, but other than a few sacks of grain, which went straight to the royal guards and commanders, their holds were just filled with casks of wine. As the troops moved on to Temple Liston, men began to sicken. The Welsh and Irish, who had been surviving on the barest of rations even before these ran out, were forced to eat grass and bark from trees. The king had sent Anthony Bek to besiege two nearby castles that threatened their flank, but that was almost a week ago and he had heard no word from the bishop.

Edward stopped pacing and sank on to his bed, transported from his headquarters at York and erected inside the Templars' manor. Everyone had been stunned by the defeat at Stirling last year, no one expected that. But it was barely months later that events at Flanders had unfolded like a nightmare before his eyes.

On arriving in Ghent the previous autumn, Edward had met with Guy de Dampierre to form the alliance against the French. When King Philippe's soldiers were reported to be marching on Flanders, this Anglo-Flemish force had set out to meet them at Vyve-Saint-Bavon. In less than an hour they had been utterly routed by the French. Shortly afterwards, with survivors still limping back into Ghent, Edward learned of the battle at Stirling. Leaving Guy de Dampierre to face the victorious French alone, the wedding proposal terminated, he returned to England to avenge his loss. But he was painfully aware how incompetent he was beginning to look. The barons had rallied around him for this campaign, but he feared, unless he could offer them a decisive victory, their earlier murmurs of discontent would swiftly grow louder.

The prospect of civil war entered Edward's mind like a poison, seeping, weakening. He had told his generals several months ago, in an imperious speech during a council in York, that when he died the inscription on his tomb would read *Scottorum Malleus*. The Hammer of the Scots.

Now, his army starving and mutinous outside, those words came back to mock him.

'My lord king?' The door opened and the Earl of Surrey entered.

The loss at Stirling had aged John de Warenne beyond his years. He looked haggard and grey, and walked with a stiff-legged limp, tormented by gout. Behind him came Brian le Jay. The Templar Master's face was burned by the sun, his nose beginning to peel. Neither man had endeared himself to Edward. All he saw when he looked at de Warenne was defeat and le Jay had been more of a hindrance than a help, following orders reluctantly and questioning almost all his decisions.

'The Templars have distributed the last of their grain, my lord,' said de Warenne, in his rasping tones. 'There is no more.'

'And their personal stores? What about them?' Edward stared at le Jay.

'We must keep enough provisions for ourselves, my lord,' responded the Templar Master firmly. 'Else we will be no use to you on the field of battle.'

'What field?' snapped Edward. 'What battle? Is there no news?'

John de Warenne shook his head. 'Nothing.'

'Then you can tell the scouts if they have nothing to report they may as well not bother returning at all!'

'My lord,' murmured de Warenne, 'the men are restless. We cannot keep this up. They will start deserting unless we fill their bellies and give them a visible target to fight. We may need to consider turning back, just to Edinburgh. We've more chance of finding food there.'

'No,' said Edward abruptly. 'We stay until Bek returns. If successful, he will bring supplies from the castles.' He paused, his eyes alighting on a wine cask. There were more outside the preceptory walls, many more, loaded on wagons. 'In the meantime, have the wine we took from the cogs delivered to the troops. It will hearten their spirits.'

De Warenne nodded, but le Jay spoke up. 'Wine, my lord? Most of the men haven't eaten properly in days. Combined with this heat it will—'

'Do not challenge me on this, le Jay,' responded Edward. 'Or I swear I shall turn my army towards your preceptory. The promise of meat and ale within should make them sufficiently motivated.'

Brian le Jay's eyes filled with angry surprise. But biting back a response, he nodded stiffly and strode from the room.

An hour later, weary cheers rose as the casks of rich Gascony wine were taken out around the camp. Men, half delirious from sun and exhaustion, drank it by the bowlful. Some pushed comrades aside to get at the sweet liquid that stung their parched throats and stained their mouths. Brian le Jay and the Templar Master of Scotland watched in grim silence from behind the gates of their preceptory as soldiers reeled and staggered in the fields, some vomiting almost immediately with the effects of the wine on their empty stomachs. Cheers and drunken laughter quickly turned to shouts and arguments. A large company of Welsh foot-soldiers, angered by their meagre rations, tried to storm the supply wagons of the royal guard. English soldiers barred the way and a brawl began. A group of priests tried to stop it, getting in between the companies to beg them to see sense. But in the confusion several were killed.

As the drunken brawl descended into a riot, barons sent their knights to quell the fighting, but the appearance of armoured men on horseback did nothing to subdue the struggle. The Welsh came to the aid of their beleaguered comrades and the English to theirs, until half the infantry were at war with one another. The English had far greater numbers, however, and soon the Welsh were routed from the camp. They fled to a nearby wood, leaving almost one hundred of their fellows dead on the grass, now littered with empty casks.

Edward looked out upon the devastation from the gates of the preceptory. Evening was drawing in, the sun throwing red light across everything. A pit had been dug and the dead were being hauled into it. De Warenne had come to inform him that the Welsh had sent a message threatening to go over to the Scots. Edward blustered at this, proclaiming that his enemies could do what they wished, for he would crush them all on the same field soon enough. But despair had begun to creep in, chilling him in the evening's warmth. For one foolish decision, he could lose the last of his failing authority.

It was then that Anthony Bek returned, riding down the road towards the preceptory with the warriors of St Cuthbert's Land, back-lit by the flaming sun.

Edward started forward, seeing carts being drawn behind the company, loaded with crates and barrels. His hope turned to elation as the Bishop of Durham met him at the Temple's gates and informed him of his victory over the two castles. He had also received word from Edinburgh that the supply ships had made it into Leith and the food shipments would be with them shortly. But, most promising of all, the enemy had been sighted by Bek's scouts. Wallace and his men were only thirteen miles away, just south of Stirling, near a town called Falkirk.

Falkirk, Scotland, 22 July 1298 AD

The air was dead, without even a whisper of breeze, as the English army formed up in front of a narrow stream. Beyond, on the slopes of a moor, Wallace was deploying his troops. It was past ten in the morning and the sun was full in the faces of the soldiers, the sky flat and white, leached of colour by the blaze.

Lines of infantry were jogging out of the woods that crowned the moor, clutching twelve-foot-long spears. Following the orders of Wallace and his generals, they trickled down the hillside to pool in four huge circles. The outer ring of soldiers in each immediately knelt, one knee on the scrubby grass, the other wedging their spear in place, the butt on the ground and the shaft slanting outwards. The men behind stayed standing, their spears also pointing out, until these shield rings, known as schiltrons, bristled on the hillside. Between each, companies of archers stood ready and behind this forest of spikes and arrows the Scottish cavalry formed up. Alongside

Wallace and his men were earls and lords, companies of knights gathered around them, but the nobles were still a small force in comparison to the army of commoners who made up the schiltrons.

The soldiers were nervous, watching the enemy at the foot of the moor, but they stood firm to a man. Most of Scotland was back in their hands. Here, now, they had so much more to lose than they had on that summer day a year earlier on the slopes of the Ochil Hills, and so much to gain. If they could defeat the English one more time, before the very eyes of their tyrant king, it could be the last blow needed.

Wallace rode before them, his voice booming across their ranks. He fortified them, filled them with strength and conviction. Then, at the last, with a fierce grin, he goaded them. *'I have brought you to the ring! Now let us see if you can dance!'*

A resounding cheer answered him.

Edward looked round as the roar from the Scots cascaded down the hillside. His jaw pulsed, but he made no comment as he ordered his generals to take their positions. The English, eyeing the stream and the rising slope beyond with caution, had moved into their companies. Wallace had chosen the battlefield well; he would fight on higher ground with the cover of a wood behind. They would attack uphill with water at their backs. But, despite this, Edward's men were eager for battle. Along with the massive force of infantry, there were four main cavalry regiments, under the earls of Lincoln, Norfolk and Hereford, and the Bishop of Durham. These were augmented by the knights with John de Warenne and English Templars under Brian le Jay. There was also a corps of horsemen from Gascony and a large number of smaller companies, led by barons and lords, called to do their feudal duty. Edward himself had almost a thousand royal guards at his command, all clad in scarlet surcoats, matching his banner.

After Bek brought the news of the Scots' location the previous night, all dissension in the English ranks vanished. The Welsh drifted back into camp, grumbling, but lured by the promise of food. With their target found and fixed upon, the army left Temple Liston as evening drew in. It was past midsummer, but the nights remained light and the army made it all the way to Linlithgow before Edward called for camp to be made, the men bedding down on the warm grass. With the anticipation of battle, a hush descended as the soldiers prepared themselves; tightening armour, checking blades and bows, reciting prayers. Just before dawn, they set out once more. As they neared the town of Falkirk, a line of spears was spotted on a nearby hill.

Knowing the position of the enemy, Edward called a halt for Mass to be said. Afterwards, he wanted the last of their supplies divided among the troops, but the generals were so keen for the fight that they refused to break their fast and, despite their growling hunger, insisted on riding on.

Now, at a wail from the trumpets, their horses snorting and stamping the ground, the English cavalry began to move. They crossed the stream, the knights leaning back in their saddles as their mounts descended the banks into the brown water then hauled themselves up the other side and set off at a confident trot. But with all their attention fixed on the Scots on the slopes above, the knights didn't see the bog that lay ahead until the front lines had ridden right into it. Horses went plunging into the sucking black mud, treacherously concealed by reedy grass and wild flowers. Knights cried out in surprise and fear as their mounts panicked and lunged forward, searching for surer ground, only to take them deeper into the mire. Men clung desperately to saddles as the beasts bucked in the stinking slime. All the while, the Scots on the hillside jeered and laughed to see the trap so easily fallen into.

Surveying his troops in such embarrassing disarray, Edward launched his destrier, Bayard, across the stream to bellow orders at his commanders. Slowly, the front lines began to pull back from the bog. Bishop Bek, riding with his men between the stream and the marsh, shouted that the ground was firmer to the east. Another company, under the earls of Hereford and Norfolk, found the same to be true to the west. The Scots fell silent as the English cavalry re-ordered itself and charged left and right, sweeping round to meet them.

'Archers!' came Wallace's yell, as he stood in his saddle on the crest of the moor.

The Scottish archers, set between the schiltrons, fixed their arrows and let them spring in two dark arcs at the converging arms of the English, who were bypassing the schiltrons and heading straight for Wallace and the cavalry. But unlike the Welsh longbow, the strength and accuracy of which could propel an arrow clean through armour, the shorter Scottish bows didn't have the force to puncture the metal hides of the English. A few shots caught horses, but for every one man who fell, thousands more rode on, picking up speed as they crested the hill and thundered towards the Scottish cavalry. The faces of Wallace's troops filled with fear as this steel horde came crashing towards them, lances thrust forward. As a few turned their mounts and rode for the woods, Wallace cried at them to stand firm, but the courage of those who remained was a futile gesture. Now, truly for the first time, the Scots understood the terrible power of an English cavalry charge.

The English host slammed into them like a wall of iron, making a shambles of their thin line of defence, slicing through those who stood against them, scattering the rest. Quickly, it became a rout. The Scottish peasants in their tight schiltrons watched aghast as their commanders abandoned them on the field, fleeing into the safety of the woods, where the trees would hamper the pursuit of the English on their armoured destriers. Only Wallace and a handful of his men remained. Seeing the battle on the hilltop was lost, they cantered recklessly down the slope to their infantry. Abandoning his mount, Wallace threw down his axe, grabbed a spear and wedged himself in the front line of one of the schiltrons, yelling orders until he was hoarse, as the English knights turned and surged towards the Scottish archers. The foot-soldiers watched, helplessly, as the archers were divided by the cavalry charge, then pursued like frightened rabbits across the hillside. Knights yelled as they gave chase, the first few knocking men down with sword blows or lance thrusts, their comrades behind riding on over them, pounding bodies into the black soil, bones and spines snapping like twigs. In less than fifteen minutes, the only part of the Scottish army left standing were the four huge schiltrons that braced themselves for impact as the English circled around and came at them.

'Hold!' Wallace bellowed as the knights careened towards them. '*Hold!*'

From the safety of the woods, Will sat forward in his saddle, his breath in his throat, as the English charged the schiltrons. There was a second of confusion as the lines struck; a blur of metal, colour and motion, then the air was rent with the screams of horses and men. The Scots had stood fast and the English had barrelled straight into their out-thrust spears. The English lines wheeled around and retreated, leaving dead and dying comrades. Horses had been pierced and had collapsed, crushing their riders, or else had thrown them into the thicket of spears. As the wounded tried to haul themselves to their feet, the Scots in the row behind stabbed down, finishing them off. There were murmurs of relief around Will, as the men with him realised the schiltrons had held.

'Uncle!'

Will turned to see David riding up with Adam. Both were drenched in sweat.

'You're hurt,' said David, staring at Will's upper arm.

His tunic was ripped and the rings of mail beneath had been rent in a jagged line, through which he could see torn flesh. An English knight had caught him with a slicing cut during the charge. 'I'll live.' Will looked at Adam. 'The earls?'

'Most have fled, taking their knights with them. Gone through the woods, back towards Stirling. They said there was no point us all losing our lives.' Adam spat on the ground. '*Bastards*.'

Will stared between the trees at the remainder of Wallace's cavalry, who had scattered into the woods when the English charged them. All were watching the English hurl themselves at the shield rings. There were probably fewer than five hundred of them. Half were wounded, some mortally, and thirty or so had been unhorsed. 'We can only hope the schiltrons hold. This heat will soon weaken the English charge. If our men can hold, the knights will have to fall back sooner or later.'

'And if they can't?' growled Adam.

Will didn't answer. He turned his gaze back to the schiltrons.

Time and time again, the English launched themselves at the rings of spears, growing more and more frustrated as they were pushed back, losing men and horses. They hurled axes and lances into the rings, but even when one man fell, those to either side of him, well drilled by Wallace, drew in tight. Soon there was a pile of English weapons lying useless in the centre of each schiltron.

Before long, trumpets sounded and the knights, angered, began to withdraw. Will, watching closely with the rest of the cavalry from the fringes of the wood, saw the commanders heading towards Edward's scarlet banner, raised high to the right of the field. He guessed the king was there, moving amid the mass of men and flags, and felt frustration prickle inside him. The Scots in the woods became hushed as the Welsh longbowmen were drawn up on the hillside in front of the defeated cavalry. Together they took aim, and fired.

The arrows entered the schiltrons with lethal speed, driving through clothes and armour, piercing necks and raised arms, slamming into skulls and chests, throwing men backwards with the force. Slowly, but surely, gaps began to appear in the shield rings. A second trumpet sounded and the English cavalry began to charge.

'*God, no*,' murmured Will, seeing the schiltrons begin to break apart as men panicked and ran. Wallace was down in those lines, as was Gray and a hundred other men who had become his brothers-in-arms over the past year. Worst of all, Simon was there. Not thinking, only feeling, Will slammed his heels into the sides of his horse and charged out of the woods.

He wasn't the only one. Scores of men, seeing their comrades in danger, rode out with him, David and Adam among them. A few English knights, observing this ragged band surging down the hillside, broke away to confront them, but most focused their attention on the scattering schiltrons. The butchery began in earnest, the English making bloody work of the fleeing Scots, many of whom ran blindly down the hillside into the very bog they had intended the enemy to fall foul of. Men flailed in the black mud, trapped like flies in honey.

Brian le Jay thundered grimly after four Scots, broadsword swinging. But he misjudged the ground and his horse pitched into the mire, the blade flying from his hand. One of the Scots, scrabbling on hands and knees across the bog, clutched at the fallen blade as it landed nearby. Seeing the Templar Master struggling vainly with his horse, the beast almost up to its stomach in mud, the Scot crawled back, sword in hand. Le Jay saw him coming. He pulled his foot from the stirrup, his mailed boot coming out of the mud with a sucking sound, and kicked at the man. The movement further unbalanced his horse, which staggered sideways, taking him down. At the same moment, the Scot thrust up with the sword, sinking it into Brian le Jay's neck.

Will rode furiously for the schiltron on the far left of the field, where he knew Simon had been placed, his breaths coming short and sharp through his helmet. His eyes fixed on the mass of men, he didn't see the rider coming straight at him. The first Will knew of him was the impact of the man's lance in the flank of his horse. The beast reared in mid-flight and crashed down, sending him flying from the saddle. He smashed into the ground and bounced, over and over, his helmet snapping free.

Coming to a dazed stop, Will lay on his back, panting, the sun in his eyes. He rolled over with a groan, then pushed himself up on his hands in time to see his assailant wheel around and come riding back. Staggering to his feet as he drew his sword, Will caught a flash of red on the knight's white mantle and realised, as he crouched to spring, that it was a Templar. Then he was throwing himself aside, cutting his falchion in a savage arc that slashed across the horse's front legs. It tumbled forward, throwing its rider over its head. The knight hit the ground with a thud and lay there unmoving. Not giving him the chance to get up, Will sprinted to him and stabbed down, hard and fast, through the eye slit in the knight's helmet. Blood spurted up and the man's body jerked for a few seconds, until Will withdrew the blade and slumped on the grass.

The sounds of battle and slaughter seemed to fade away as Will stared at the knight, whose white mantle was awash with blood, trickling out from beneath his helmet. Will suddenly went forward on his knees, wanting to see the man inside, wanting to know that under that featureless helm wasn't the face of anyone he knew. His heart lurched into his throat as images of Robert and Jacques, even Hugues, filled his mind, although he knew no French knights, let alone the Grand Master, would be on this field. Before he reached the dead man, he heard his name being shouted, somewhere close by. There was a drum of hooves. Will stood. As he turned he saw a broad blade come sweeping towards him, wielded by another Templar, come to avenge his brother. Will raised his falchion to block it. There was a flash of light as the sword caught the sun, then a clash of metal, followed by a wrenching sensation as his arm was thrown wide. At the last there was an abrupt feeling of release. The knight went riding past and Will reeled backwards. As he fell, he saw the falchion in his hand. It was broken. Then the ground came rapidly up behind him and cracked against his skull.

16

Falkirk Battleground, Scotland

22 July 1298 AD

Sky, ground, up, down; everything was distorted. His mouth was full of blood and earth. He tried to spit, but there was no saliva. His body felt ruined and his head was hammering. He could almost hear it.

Raising himself on his hands, mail gloves digging into the soil, Will pushed himself up until he was sagged on all fours, dizzy and nauseous. There was an appalling stench saturating the dead air, making it hard to breathe. As his vision sharpened he saw its cause. The hillside was covered with corpses. Men lay curled and broken, reduced to a mess of parts. Limbs, still covered in scraps of clothing, were strewn beside bodies at impossible angles. Heads, severed from necks, stared at the sky. One man, close by, was half buried beneath his own entrails, bursting from a gash in his stomach. Will felt a rush of bitterness in his throat and hung there weakly as vomit poured out of him in a vile stream. Wiping his mouth on his torn sleeve, he heard the hammering in his head again. After a second, he realised the sound was external. It was echoing everywhere.

Across the slopes of the moors, English soldiers were wading through the corpses, despatching the wounded, chopping at bodies like firewood with axe and sword. Cavalry were pursuing survivors, struggling for the woods. Will remembered spurring his horse down to the schiltrons as they broke apart, the Templar attacking him, falling from his horse. Then . . . He twisted round, feeling on the grass for his falchion. He found it beneath him. Holding it up, he stared numbly at the blade, which came to a jagged stop less than a foot from the hilt. As he turned it, he recalled someone shouting his name, just before the second Templar struck. The recognition of that voice was like a punch in his chest. David. Sticking the broken falchion in his scabbard, he went forward, pain grinding in his body. The stink assaulted him as he crawled through the piles of dead. Here and there bodies moved beneath him, squirming in agony. A few times, he put his hand in something sticky and the padding on the palms of his gloves was soon soaked red. Someone grabbed his wrist, making him start.

The soldier's glazed eyes focused. 'Please, help me. I can't feel my legs.'

Will's gaze moved from the man's face down to the place where his legs should have been. He ended at the torso. 'I'm sorry,' he said thickly, pulling his hand away. As he crawled on, the air around him shuddered with screams and whimpers. The lines of English soldiers moving up the hillside were closer.

Becoming frantic, he began lifting men's heads by the hair to check the faces. Some were just a bloody pulp. The sun beat on his neck and everywhere flies buzzed over the dead and dying. Will halted. Several paces ahead, he saw a horse, its great head lying limp. Sprawled over its rump was a burly man with shaggy hair, matted with blood. It was Adam. As Will went to him, he saw his skull had been caved in. He sat back on his heels, feeling the last of his strength draining. Someone grasped his tunic. He jerked round to see his nephew's face, bloody, but whole, in front of him.

David's teeth were chattering. 'I tried to wake him,' he said, staring at Adam. 'He saved me.'

'We've got to move,' groaned Will, dragging himself to his feet.

'I want the Master found. Who saw him last?'

As the imperious voice rang out, Will saw a figure some distance away, astride a war-charger. Even though the man wore a coif of mail that hid his hair and part of his face, Will would recognise that voice anywhere. It was Edward. There were several men with the king, including a Templar.

David was pulling at him. 'Will, come on!'

The Templar was heading for the body of the knight Will had slain, the white mantle stark against the drab clothing of the Scots.

For a moment, Will was rooted to the spot, his gaze moving between the dead knight and the king.

David hauled on his arm. '*Will!*'

The Templar was heading straight for his fallen brother, paying no attention to them, but one of the other men with the king had spotted the two Scots and now kicked his horse towards them, sword out.

At once, Will began to move, pushing David in front of him. 'Run!' he yelled, hearing hooves striking the ground behind.

'*Wait!*'

As the command snapped out, Will stumbled on the corpse of a spearman and dropped to his knees. The rider checked himself and went storming past.

'I want them alive! Bring them to me.'

Raising his head, Will saw men dismounting. They came towards him, swords drawn. The rider had circled around to block David's escape. He felt hands pulling him up, dragging him towards the king. He heard David struggling, then a cry of pain.

Edward towered above him on the warhorse. In his aged grey eyes Will saw surprise.

'My lord!'

Edward turned, glaring at the interruption.

A soldier in a scarlet surcoat rode up to him. 'We've found the Templar Master. It seems he drowned in the marsh.'

'Very well. Call off the search.' Edward looked back at Will, then gestured to the men holding him and David. 'They are my prisoners.'

The Dominican College, Stirling, Scotland, 28 July 1298 AD

The door opened and a wooden bowl was kicked into the room. Half the contents slopped out and a voice called, 'You can eat off the floor, dog.'

As the door banged shut, Will crawled to the bowl. A few spoonfuls of grain floated in water. One by one, he carefully picked up the handful that had soaked into the dust and returned them to the bowl. Clutching it, he slid back to the far wall, where a patch of sunlight warmed the grey stones. The grain tasted bitter, but it was the first meal he'd had in days and every seed strengthened him. When he had finished eating, he set the bowl to his lips and drained the water, the feel of it bathing his parched throat the sweetest sensation imaginable. As he licked the last drops, his tongue rasped over a deep groove in the bottom. Studying it, he saw a crack zigzagging through the wood. Taking hold of the bowl, he forced the sides until it snapped in his hands and he was left with two jagged pieces. It wasn't much, but it was something.

Stowing the halves of the bowl in the bucket they had given him for his toilet, he slumped against the wall, the stone chilly against his spine. His breeches were the only thing they had left him with. His mail coat, tunic, boots, the broken falchion: all had been stripped from him at Falkirk. They had beaten him then, as Edward rode away, two royal guards in scarlet, their mailed fists punching into the wounds he had sustained in the battle. A third held him, so he couldn't shield himself, and he was barely conscious when they threw him on the back of a cart. He had seen David senseless beside him and a few other men in similar states. After that, he remembered little, until the English army entered Stirling.

Will had smelled the smoke before they reached the town, its acrid odour drawing him from his stupor. His eyes, gummed with blood, cracked open and he squinted against the glare as the cart jolted along the road. Stirling had been razed. The houses that clung to the rock below the castle were burned-out shells, skeins of smoke drifting between them like ghosts. The castle walls were blackened from the fire that had gutted it. Listening to the angry mutters of the soldiers, Will felt hope rise in him. If this devastation wasn't the work of the English, it must have been done by the Scots. His hope grew as he recognised Wallace's tactics and prayed this was a sign he had made it from the field. Certainly, Wallace wasn't among the captives in the cart, two of whom had died and been dumped on the road. David was asleep, or unconscious. Will wanted to reach over to him, but didn't dare. Instead, he lay motionless as the vanguard marched into Stirling.

While the rest of the army wearily set up camp on the plains around the ruined town, Edward and his generals took over the only building left untouched by fire: a college belonging to the Dominicans. Will was dragged from the cart and hauled inside. The place was deserted, although there were signs that people had been there recently: a sack of grain left in the corridor, its seam split, a helmet lying in an empty hall, the dull glint of a coin underfoot. He was taken into a chamber on the second floor, which he guessed was one of the monks' cells. There was a barred window that looked out over cloisters. The soldiers removed the only furniture: a wooden pallet, a chest and a stool. Then, beating him again, they left him curled in a pool of blood, his eyes on a crucifix pinned to a wall.

He thought that had been two days ago, but couldn't be certain. Pain distorted time, made it hard to keep track of anything external. The world had become a place inside him. In strange seas, where he drifted in delirium, were islands of hurt. He was aware of all of them, but they seemed far apart, the throbbing in his head a long way from the delicate agony in his fractured fingers and the twinges in his broken ribs. The meal, however meagre, brought an uncomfortable lucidity in which both his injuries and his thoughts became clearer. At the forefront of his mind was David. The night before, clinging to the window bars, he had called softly into the darkness, hoping his nephew might be in one of the adjacent cells. But no voice came back to reassure him. Will had been living so closely with Wallace and the men for so long that the silence was unbearable. Left alone with his thoughts, bereft of distractions, they clamoured in him, tormenting him.

If it wasn't for him, his nephew wouldn't be here. He was the one who had taken his family into Selkirk, seeking the rebels. He was the one who deserted the Temple without a word to Simon, his loyal comrade for so many years, who came looking for him out of concern and friendship, and whom he had treated like dirt. Was Simon lying on the battlefield at Falkirk, his body invaded by worms? And what of the Templar he had killed, whose face would remain forever hidden beneath that helmet? Was he there too, or had he been buried by his brothers? It might have been Thomas, one of the last members of the Anima Templi. He might have killed one of the Brethren. The faces of his father and Everard swarmed before him, eyes filled with accusation. He had betrayed them. He had broken his oaths and abandoned his duties, his brothers. His daughter.

The door crashed open. Will barely had time to look up, before men were grasping his arms and yanking him to his feet.

King Edward entered. His mail coat and coif had been replaced by a crimson robe and a gold circlet. The soldiers marched Will into the centre of the chamber. One kicked him viciously in the back of the leg, forcing him to his knees. They stepped away at a gesture from the king.

'Leave me.'

'My lord, the prisoner—' began one.

'Cannot even stand. Leave me.'

Bowing, the soldiers left the room. Edward looked down at Will, then crossed to the window, leaving him kneeling on the floor.

Even through the pain, Will felt his muscles tighten. After all these years, haunted, *obsessed* by this prospect, he was now alone with his enemy. His eyes flicked to the bucket, where the jagged halves of the bowl were half hidden beneath a layer of piss.

'Have you looked out of your cell today?' When Will didn't answer, Edward turned. 'You should. There is a rather elaborate construction out there.'

Will remembered hearing hammering that morning. Trying to save his strength, he hadn't got up.

'Do you know what it is?'

A sick feeling slid through him, but Will managed to keep any emotion from his face. 'My guess is a gallows.' His voice, unused for days, was a throaty whisper.

Edward returned to stand before him. 'Have you ever seen a man hang, Campbell? It is not a pleasant sight. The face turns red, then purple. It bulges, horribly. The tongue distends and swells. The eyes protrude until you imagine they will pop from the sockets. The neck stretches, about so far.' Edward spread his hands to show the distance. 'It can last almost half an hour. In this time, the bladder will void, then the bowels. The final indignity, for men, will be a hardening of the penis and the inevitable release. And all the while the crowd watch on.' He studied Will's face. 'I can save you from such a fate.'

Will glanced up at him, then grunted. 'You aren't going to let me leave here alive.'

'No. But I can offer you a noble death: a swift execution at the point of a sword, rather than the slow torture of the gallows. I *will* offer this, if you tell me why you are here, in Scotland.'

Will looked at the floor to cover his surprise. He had imagined of all the people who might know of his desertion, Edward would be one. The only reason he wouldn't was if he'd had no contact with Hugues since the meeting in London. This was entirely possible; Edward had been pre-occupied in Flanders as well as in Scotland in that time. The question was could he somehow use this to his advantage? He tried to think through the fog in his brain, but Edward was speaking again.

'Why are you here? Answer me! Did the Temple send you to make contact with Wallace? Is the Order working against me?'

Will's mind cleared. Edward had no idea he had left the Temple, but what was more, he doubted the Order's loyalty. He wondered what had happened to give rise to this. Had Hugues come to his senses and ended their alliance? Or was it something else? He thought of the king's callous response to the reported death of Brian le Jay. Perhaps not all the masters were comfortable with the Order's support of Edward and his war. 'I will tell you everything you want to know,' he said slowly, 'if you let the man who was with me go free.'

'Who is he? Another knight?' Edward was contemptuous. 'Set him free to report back to his masters? I am not a fool. You will both die here. The only choice you have is how.'

'Then you will never know the reason I came.' Will lifted his head, fortified by the knowledge that David was at least still alive. 'I know about Honfleur, Edward.' The king's eyes narrowed, whether at the revelation, or the insultingly familiar use of his name, Will wasn't sure. Either way, Edward's visible anger satisfied him. 'I know you tried to steal the crown jewels, pawned to us by your father. I know you forced Garin to get the Book of the Grail. I know you used Everard, just like you used Hugues. I know all about your treachery.'

Edward rounded on him. 'None of that matters. Thanks to your Visitor, Jacques de Molay gave me what I wanted, when I wanted it.' His voice was saturated with venom. 'My men estimate ten thousand died on the hills of Falkirk. Whatever you told Hugues de Pairaud, whatever he knows, does not matter. I do not need the Temple. I can destroy the Scots on my own. I have proven that. The barons will support me fully now.'

'And when your war here is done, do you believe the Order will be content to let you play them for fools? Do you think there will be no repercussions for your actions? Your betrayal of the Anima Templi?'

Edward gave a bark of laughter. 'Repercussions? The Temple is finished. That fool de Pairaud practically got down on his knees and begged me to help him rebuild it! The time of knights has passed. Now is the time of kings.' His eyes blazed. 'Of empires.'

'Even the greatest king can become the victim of a determined man. You are still flesh and blood.'

Edward went still. 'Is that it?' he murmured. 'Is that why you are here?'

Summoning the last of his strength, Will lunged for the bucket.

Even as Will was thrusting his hand inside, Edward was shouting for his guards. As Will threw himself at the king, the door burst open and two soldiers entered. His hand arced through the air, the broken bowl in his fist. The king staggered back, the jagged edge missing his neck by inches, just as the guards barrelled into Will, slamming him back into the wall.

He cried out as his broken ribs ground against one another, the piece of bowl slipping from his fingers. Soon, that pain disappeared as a dozen other agonies burst into life all over his body, the soldiers bombarding him with punches.

'*Enough!*'

Through streaming eyes, Will saw Edward coming towards him.

'I want him alive,' the king said breathlessly. 'When his death comes, I want him to live through every suffering imaginable. Not just the gallows,' he said, his grey eyes wide. 'That is too swift.' He came closer. 'Before you die on the scaffold, I will have you cut down. Your wrists will be bound and tied to horses that will draw you apart until your arms are dislocated. But still, you will not die.' He was almost face to face with Will, whose head was being held up by one of the soldiers, who had hold of his hair. 'You will be laid out on a table, for all my men to see. A spectacle. There you will be opened, from neck to groin and every part of you removed and burned before your eyes. Then, and only then, will the axe end your torments in this life. In the next, they will just be beginning.'

Will saw a line of muddy-coloured droplets staining Edward's cheek. He realised, dimly, that when he attacked with the bowl he had splattered the king's face with piss. His lips curled back, revealing bloody gums and a grin.

When he regained consciousness, some time later, it was dark, the square of sky in the window dusted with stars. Will lay there, letting some of the feeling return to his limbs. They had taken the bucket and the fragments of the bowl; the only things left, four bare walls and the crucifix. The bravado he had shown Edward was long gone. Now he just felt a profound sense of despair. He had damned himself and David to the worst death imaginable. He would die, most likely tomorrow, with a hundred stains on his soul and no chance of repentance and forgiveness. The oaths he had made before God were broken and Edward's last words rang in his mind like a judgement. His only hope, however faint, was that the king would be so intent on making him suffer that less attention would be paid to David's trial.

Will crawled to the wall. Digging his bloodied fingertips into the stone he pulled himself up and grasped the crucifix. He tugged it from its nail and slid to the floor, clutching it. 'O Lord, have mercy upon me for I . . .' But although his mouth still moved, no more words came. He wasn't ready to say them. There were so many other words needed first; so many atonements.

He stared at the door. They would feed him again before the end. Edward would want him awake and aware for the torture. His mind mocked him, asking how he planned to subdue armed guards when he could barely walk, but he pushed the question away. Making the decision that he wouldn't give Edward the satisfaction of his slow death, he inched across the chamber and sagged beside the door. He would fight his way free, or die trying. But his eyes kept closing, his head lolling on to his chest then jerking upright as he fought the exhaustion, and despite all his efforts he was soon asleep.

Will woke with a start. His eyes, hooded with sleep, rolled to the closed door, then opened fully as he heard several muffled thumps. There was a louder thud, this time right against the wood. Will dragged himself up the wall, holding the crucifix like a dagger. The door opened and a head appeared. He slammed the wooden cross down as hard as he could and the figure dropped with a shout, lifting an arm to fend off further blows as Will scrabbled over him, lunging for the corridor. Before he got past the door a large hand wrapped around his throat, cutting off his air and his voice. As he was forced back into the room, he saw part of a jaw, the face shadowed by a cowl, then he was striking out again with the crucifix. The figure grabbed his wrist and squeezed. Will's fingers went numb and he dropped the cross. At the same time, he realised the man was hissing his name. The cowl inched back and in the gloom he made out the face of William Wallace. The man by the door, rising to his feet, clutching his head, was Gray. There were dark outlines of more men out in the corridor, a brief flash of steel.

'How——' Will began.

Wallace shook his head. 'Later. Is Adam here?'

'Adam?'

'They know he's my cousin,' said Wallace impatiently. 'They would have brought him with the other prisoners. Gray said he saw him with you on the field.'

Will faltered. 'Adam's dead,' he said, after a pause.

Wallace stared at him.

Gray's voice sounded from the doorway. 'Let's go!'

Slinging an arm around Will's waist to hold him up, Wallace led him out into the corridor.

Will recognised Stephen of Ireland among his rescuers. There were also a couple of prisoners, who had been on the cart with him. They were in better shape and had been given weapons. The bodies of the English soldiers guarding the cells were crumpled shadows on the floor.

'Wait,' breathed Will. 'They have David. I have to——' He stopped as another two figures appeared from a door on the opposite side of the passage. One was David, badly bruised, but limping on his own. The other was Simon. The groom met his gaze as he wrapped his cloak around David's bare shoulders. Before Will could say anything, he was being bundled down the corridor. He noticed that a man in monk's robes was leading the company.

Gray took point as they descended a spiralling staircase, stepping over another dead soldier at the bottom. They pushed through doors leading out into the cloisters and raced across the starlit lawn, past the scaffold erected in the centre. The nooses hung dark against the sky. Behind them there was a shout as three royal guards appeared. Two sprinted down the cloistered passage after them. The third dashed back through the doors and continued shouting, raising the alarm. Wallace let go of Will, who stumbled and almost fell, before Simon caught hold of him. Drawing the massive claymore from the scabbard on his back, Wallace charged the soldiers. Steel chimed on the quiet and there were more calls as other soldiers came running.

'Quickly!' yelled Gray, leading them through an archway with steps heading down.

Will smelled stale food and guessed they were going down into the monastery's kitchens. He grasped Simon's arm, teeth gritted. Wallace sprinted down behind them, his sword dripping blood. He snatched a torch from the wall as a bell began to clang.

The party barrelled through the kitchens, Stephen pausing to kick a heavy sack of grain in front of the door. The monk led them into a storeroom. There was a trapdoor in the floor, which Gray wrenched back. As Wallace moved in with the torch, Will caught sight of a dark hole, stacked barrels, an earth floor, then men were jumping down and arms were lifting him, tugging him. He gasped as the pain overwhelmed him, felt himself falling into blackness.

Near Perth, Scotland, 5 August 1298 AD

'Can we speak?'

Wallace glanced round, then continued poking the fire with the stick he held. A charred log disintegrated into ashes as he jabbed it. 'I didn't think you'd be walking for a while.'

'It looks worse than it is.' Will sat on one of the logs around the fire with a grimace and Wallace raised an eyebrow. The murmurs of men drifted between the trees, but it was early and most were asleep, huddled on the ground beside fires. 'Did everyone make it out?'

'You don't remember?'

'Just fragments. I hear the Dominicans helped us.'

Wallace nodded. 'Soon after it was known captives had been taken to the monastery the monks came to tell us about the tunnel. The rock beneath Stirling Castle is riddled with them, most of them natural, but some must have been cut out as escape routes from the foundations. One leads to their college.'

'It was brave of them, risking themselves.'

Wallace shrugged. 'They owed us. The monastery was the only building we didn't burn down when we razed the town. Fortunately for you. If it hadn't been there, you'd have been out in a field surrounded by the English army and we'd never have got to you.'

'I'm sorry about Adam.'

Wallace shook his head, but remained quiet.

'I wanted to thank you, all of you. Not just for me, for David.'

'I thought my cousin might be there.' Wallace's jaw pulsed. He tossed the stick into the fire where it began to smoulder. 'But I owed you my life, Campbell, so I need no thanks.'

'Simon tells me you've razed Perth.'

'The English will most likely head there from Stirling. The only thing we can do now is waste the land before them. Our scouts have been keeping track of their movements, which is how we knew they'd taken prisoners at Falkirk. We know the English have run out of the rations they received by sea. If we can cut off their access to food and shelter, sooner or later they will have to turn back.' Wallace stared into the fire. 'Edward's victory will only sustain his troops so long.'

'He thinks he has won.'

Wallace looked up. 'He hasn't. He may have destroyed my infantry, but I've still got most of my cavalry.'

'And the earls?'

'They didn't return to the English side, whatever cowardice they showed at Falkirk. What is more, at Perth I heard a rumour that Earl Robert Bruce is attacking Carlisle.' Wallace rested his broad arms on his knees. His hands were black with bruises from the shield ring. He hefted his shoulders. 'Maybe others are fighting their own battles, all over Scotland?'

Will was silent. He had been thinking these things over since he had come round the day before, but he still wasn't sure how to broach the subject with Wallace. 'You know you cannot win like this,' he said, deciding candidness was best.

'We won at Stirling.'

'They'll not make that mistake again. They'll make us fight these pitched battles and we will lose. This isn't the way to defeat Edward. On a battlefield, he will always be superior.'

'What are you saying? That I should give up?'

'I'm saying you need to attack him in a different way. The alliance with France,' Will continued, before Wallace could speak, 'the treaty made by the council when King John was in power, does it still stand?'

Wallace nodded. 'When I was made Guardian of the Realm I wrote to King Philippe, telling him I wished to continue the friendship and trade our kingdoms have enjoyed.'

'Then use it now. Go to Philippe and the pope. Enlist the aid of men Edward is threatened by, men who can put pressure on him to stop this war. This is where he is weak.' Will ran a hand through his hair. 'It was all so clear to me when I was in that cell with him. I've known Edward for many years and I know what he's capable of. But I've never seen him afraid, until he thought the Temple was working against him.'

Wallace's eyebrows lifted. 'Is it?'

'I do not think so, not if Brian le Jay and the others were at Falkirk, but it did seem Edward wasn't on good terms with the English Master. My guess is he wouldn't believe I'd have left the Temple. He thought I was there as a knight and it worried him.' Will looked down at his hands. 'But whatever his relations with the Order, it was clear he fears threats to his power. We know his barons have been angered by his war in Gascony and being bested by Philippe in Flanders must have meant he had to work hard to regain their support. The victory here will raise his esteem for a time, but if Philippe and the pope put pressure on him the barons would soon react. The threat of excommunication is a powerful one.' Will spread his hands. 'To be outcast, alone and vulnerable to attack, all treaties suspended, all trade agreements rescinded: it could cripple a nation.'

Wallace was quiet, his blue eyes fixed on Will.

There was a cough behind them as Gray headed over. He spat in the fire, then nodded to Will. 'You're alive then.' He picked up a water-skin and sat. 'Stephen's brother died in the night,' he added, looking at Wallace. 'How many more sons of Scotland do you think God will take from us?'

Wallace didn't answer. The three of them lapsed into silence, broken now and then by Gray's coughing.

Seeing Wallace wasn't going to talk while Gray was there, Will rose unsteadily. 'I'm sorry about that,' he said, tapping his forehead, where Gray still had a purple bruise from the crucifix.

'Just prove you're worth saving . . . brother.'

Wondering if that was some allusion to Christian, Will headed off.

'I'll think about what you said,' came Wallace's voice behind him.

Will made his way slowly through the trees, pausing to catch his breath. His body had never felt so feeble. A couple of men he passed greeted him, but most were silent, subdued by the defeat and scale of the slaughter at Falkirk. Everyone had lost someone they knew, comrade or kin.

As he headed for a clearing on the edge of the camp, Will saw Simon coming towards him, carrying a sack.

'I woke up and saw you gone,' said the groom, looking relieved. 'For a moment, I thought . . .' He shrugged. 'Well, never mind.'

'What's that?'

Simon held out the sack. 'I was going to give it to you when you'd recovered, but as you're up . . .'

Will frowned as he took it. Opening it, he saw a belt curled up inside, a leather scabbard attached. His heart skipped. Taking hold of the hilt of the falchion, he pulled it free, letting the sack fall. 'How did you find it?' he murmured, studying the broken blade.

'One of the cells we looked in at the monastery was empty, but for a pile of clothes and weapons. I recognised the scabbard. I don't know if it can be mended.'

'Neither do I.' Will met Simon's gaze. 'Thank you.' He shook his head. 'I've been a fool, Simon, a true fool. But I intend to make it right. I'm going back to Paris. I've spoken to Wallace of an idea I've had. He might come with me, but either way I'm going, as soon as possible. I think there are things I can do there, and things I must do.'

'Rose?'

'Leaving her was one of my greatest mistakes, that and my treatment of you.'

Simon stuffed his thumbs in his belt and looked away, his eyes bright. 'You want me to come?'

'Yes.'

'And David? Ysenda?'

'They will stay. It is possible my sister, Ede, is still in the north. If she can be found, they will have somewhere to go.'

'You know David won't be happy.'

'I'll talk to him today, but there is something I must do first.' Will handed him the sword. 'Keep it for me, for now.'

Leaving Simon with the broken blade, Will continued to the clearing, where he had heard a host of men whispering the Paternoster the evening before. It was almost time for morning Mass. Sure enough, John Blair was there, washing his hands in the stream that trickled through the woods on the edge of the glade.

The priest turned as he approached. He eyed Will with some surprise, but gave a nod. 'Good day to you,' he said, walking to where a leather-bound Bible was laid out beside a smoking censer.

'Will you hear my confession, Father?'

John studied him. 'Of course.'

There in the wooded glade, Will knelt on the grass before the chaplain. John was silent, listening, as he began to speak, haltingly at first, then faster, louder. His words at times broke in his throat as he told the priest of his love for Elwen and the violation of his vows as a knight, their secret marriage and the birth of their daughter. He spoke of her betrayal with Garin, his failed attempt to save her from the burning house, the fall of Acre. Then, at the last, the words coming up and out of him like bile, he spoke of his murder of Garin, his former comrade, and the killing of the Templar at Falkirk. His sins, old and new, stagnant and raw, seemed to dissipate like smoke in the golden light that bathed them, as John put his hands on Will's bowed head and absolved him.

17

The Docks, Paris

17 September 1299

It was a bright, windy afternoon. The birds circling the towers of Notre Dame struggled against the gusts that buffeted them and sent ripples across the Seine. The trees swaying on the banks were tinged with the first blush of autumn. In just a few months it would be the end of the year and the beginning of a new century.

Will turned to Simon. 'This is where we part.' He smiled. 'For now.'

Simon stared over his shoulder in the direction of the Temple. 'It's going to be strange returning, after everything.'

'Just find Robert. He knows what you went to Scotland for, so you can tell him what you wish. If anyone else asks, say you transferred to Balantrodoch, but got caught up in the war.'

Simon blew out his cheeks. 'I suppose that's almost the truth.'

'It doesn't matter. No one will check. Even if they did, the Temple in Britain would have been thrown into confusion with the death of Brian le Jay. Records could have been misplaced, mistakes made.' Will grasped Simon's shoulder. 'Don't worry.'

'And you? Will you see Robert?'

Will looked round as Wallace hailed him. The rest of the party had gathered their packs from the boat and were waiting on the dockside. 'In time.'

Leaving the groom to walk alone up the muddy banks, Will headed to Wallace, hefting his pack on his shoulder.

After being questioned by the guards at the Grand Châtelet, the six men crossed the Grand Pont on to the Ile de la Cité. A few people stared as they passed. Wallace's height always drew attention and although his woollen tunic and cloak were well made and his boots polished, he couldn't quite shake off the look of an outlaw. His long hair was tied back, revealing his scarred face. As he strode along the bridge, past flower sellers and chattering shopkeepers, Will thought how notable Gray's absence was from his side. The general had stayed behind to command the army and, without him, Wallace seemed at once alone. But rather than diminishing him, this solitariness gave him an aura of power that increased as he marched towards the royal palace.

Will led them to the entrance, between the towering walls of the Tour d'Argent and the Tour de César. The men standing sentry eyed the rough company suspiciously, but accepted the parchment Wallace handed over, marked with the seal of the King of France. As they scanned it, Will stared up at the slit windows of the towers and rubbed at his chin. He had scraped himself raw shaving that morning on the boat. He doubted anyone from the Temple would be in the royal palace, but he felt exposed nonetheless and pulled his hood lower as the royal guards ushered them into the Salles des Gardes; he wasn't so certain he would receive the forgiveness Simon still believed he would for his desertion. But despite his trepidation it was a relief to be finally walking in through these doors.

Having made the decision to return to Paris the previous year, Will had been impatient to be under way with the journey, but Wallace had been more circumspect, wanting things to be done properly. His first act was to resign his position as Guardian of the Realm. That heavy cloak and the intricate robes of politics that came with it had never fitted him anyway. He was always more comfortable in the wild, living by his own rules. Some time later, they learned Robert Bruce and a man named John Comyn had taken over as joint Guardians. Wallace had been satisfied with the choice.

While this was happening, Edward was leading the English army on through Scotland, securing castles, invading towns. There were several minor skirmishes, but nothing decisive and by the end of the summer, his men growing mutinous, he was forced to retreat across the border. He had won a bloody victory at Falkirk, but it cost him dear. The Scots were grimly satisfied by reports from their scouts informing them that the English were forced to feed on their dying horses to survive the journey home. The war had paused. But it wasn't over.

As autumn drew in, Wallace wrote to Pope Boniface and King Philippe, requesting an audience. By the following spring, he received replies from both, inviting him to meet them to discuss the future of the nation, for John Balliol remained in Edward's custody and Scotland was still without a king. Wallace made his final preparations during the summer, amid disturbing rumours of a truce being formed between Edward and Philippe.

These were strange days for Will, assailed by mixed feelings of anticipation and sadness, though the wrench he expected to feel leaving his family was lessened by the timely arrival of a message from his elder sister. A letter Ysenda had sent to Elgin with one of Wallace's scouts had found its way into the hands of an old neighbour of Ede's, who knew she had taken up residence in a new dwelling close by. The scout returned with Ede's elated reply and Ysenda at once made to journey north with her children. David agreed to go with her, but on the day they left pledged solemnly to Wallace that he would fight by his side once more when he returned. David then clasped Will's hand for a time, neither of them speaking. Alice and Margaret embraced him in turn, but Ysenda held him the longest. After this, there was one more farewell for Will. He said it down by the river in Selkirk Forest late one afternoon, the wych elms shedding gold from their branches. What words passed between him and Christian he spoke of to no one, but kept hidden, locked inside.

As the royal guards showed them into the grand reception hall, sending a servant hastening through one of the doors to inform the king of their arrival, Will stared around him at the marble pillars and silk hangings. Pages and officials moved briskly through, some frowning curiously at Wallace and his men. This chamber hadn't even been here when he had last visited the palace, a youth of David's years. The same age, he realised with a discomforting jolt, his daughter would be now. After ten minutes, the door the servant had disappeared through opened and a thin man with a sallow complexion came to greet them, eying them all with wary disdain.

'Sir William Wallace, the king will see you in his private chambers.'

Rose knelt before the door, fingers splayed against the wood. Her heart knocked in her chest as she placed her eye to the keyhole, catching movement in the room beyond. Philippe strode across the chamber, unlacing his shirt. She winced as he shrugged it over his shoulders, revealing the web of scars that traced his back. She once heard Jeanne say to one of the handmaidens that when she touched him it felt as though all his veins were on the outside. As he took a silk robe from the bed and pulled it on, she imagined tracing those lines with her fingertips. *Philip the Fair.* She formed the words with her mouth in silence, her breath warm on the wood. His people had given him that name. At least, his ministers had, but the royal household had learned to say it, repeating it often in business with visiting dignitaries, until now all of France knew him by it. It was best in the *langue d'oïl.* In English it came across as coarse, in Italian, which she had spoken most in her childhood, it sounded gregarious and showy. But in French it was subtle. Seductive. You could whisper the words, let your tongue flick over your teeth to make the softer sounds.

Philippe le Bel.

Rose stiffened, hearing footsteps in the passage outside her room. She looked round, poised to spring should the handle to the dormitory begin to turn. A door somewhere close by was rapped. She pressed her eye back to the keyhole to see Philippe look round, placing his circlet over his light brown hair. He stood there, hands clasped behind his back, his gaze on the door. After a measured pause, he spoke.

'Enter.'

Rose watched as a group of men filed into the king's private chamber. Guillaume de Nogaret entered first. Her eyes narrowed with dislike on his pinched face, then moved to the newcomers. The first was startling: a colossus of a man, against whom even Philippe looked short. He wore a tunic of dyed wool and had a menacingly large sword in a scabbard strapped to his back. She wondered if this might be William Wallace. There had been rumours flying around the palace for weeks of his impending arrival, this ogre from the wild north. She saw him bow to Philippe, then extend his hand with an easy smile, as though the king were an old friend.

Philippe stared at the plate-sized palm outstretched before him, then coughed politely.

'A drink for you and your men, Sir William?' questioned Nogaret, stepping forward. He snapped his fingers at a servant by the door.

The giant let his hand fall. 'Thank you.'

The awkward moment passed as the servant busied himself pouring wine into goblets.

'Please,' said Philippe, gesturing to the table near the bed, where two stools were placed. 'You must be weary from your journey.'

Accepting a goblet from the servant, Wallace sat. Rose watched the stool, wondering if it would hold his weight. She sighed with irritation as the other men crowded in around the table, blocking her view of Philippe. Three, dressed like Wallace in woollen cloaks, had their backs to her, but Nogaret remained in plain sight.

They began to talk; the usual formalities men felt it necessary to work their way through before discussing business. She found it was like swordplay, each man studying his opponent's reactions to simple questions and statements, finding weak spots for the real duel to come. Philippe, she had observed, was very good at it. But his practice today was short-lived, the giant coming quickly to the point.

'What of this treaty with England, my lord?' Wallace drained his goblet. 'Are the rumours true? Have you agreed to a peace with Edward?'

One of the men blocking her view shifted on his feet and she saw Philippe throw a swift glance at Nogaret, before the Scot moved in again.

'News travels faster than I would have thought to your borders,' Rose heard the king say. There was a pause. 'The rumours are true, but I can assure you it is a peace of convenience alone. I have no intention of keeping any truce with my cousin. The war in Gascony has paused momentarily while I concentrate on the more immediate problem posed by Flanders. Unfortunately, Guy de Dampierre is continuing to resist our attempts to negotiate the joining of our territories.'

Rose's gaze flicked to Nogaret, who looked sour. She had overheard many conversations about *the problem of Flanders* over the past year: at dinner in the Great Hall, filing out of the Sainte-Chapelle, through this very keyhole. She knew the plan to annex the count's territory had been Pierre Flote's. Nogaret hadn't wanted to abandon Gascony after all the effort they had put into the region, but in the end the chancellor had won the argument. There were still royal troops stationed in and around Guienne, but the conflict had halted.

Wallace was talking again. He seemed relieved. 'Then I shall look forward to discussing the future of my nation in greater detail, my lord.'

'You may stay as long as you wish. Our Scottish friends will always be welcome here.'

'I thank you for the kind offer, but I must accept your gracious hospitality for one night only. Tomorrow I plan to continue to Rome to speak to his holiness, the pope. I will return when I am able, but in the meantime one of my men will stay to begin those discussions with you.' Wallace gestured to a Scot, who still had his back to Rose. 'If that pleases you?'

'That can be arranged certainly, but let us speak more over dinner.' There was a scrape of the stool as Philippe rose. 'I insist that you join me.'

Seeing the meeting was over, Rose was about to stand, when she heard her name spoken. She put her eye back to the keyhole, thinking she must have been mistaken, then started back, seeing one of the servants coming towards the door. Vaulting to her bed, she tugged off her shoe. As the servant opened the door, she pretended to be pulling it on, then stood, bowing her head, partly in respect, partly to hide her flushed cheeks.

'Rose.'

She looked up, her eyes locking on Philippe, framed in the doorway, then flicking to the figure beside him. As her gaze came to rest on the man's face, all the colour drained from hers. He was clean-shaven and looked younger without a beard. But his face was still the same. A host of disconnected feelings, loss, sadness, joy and hate, leapt in her at once.

Nogaret's voice sounded from the king's chamber. 'My lord?'

Philippe turned to Will. 'I will see you at dinner,' he said, heading back into the room, the servant closing the door.

Rose pressed herself against the wall as her father came towards her. 'What are you doing here?' she whispered. He began to speak, but she held up her hands as if his words were wasps, swarming in to sting her. 'No. I don't want to hear it. No!' She scrabbled over the bed as he reached towards her.

'Rose, please!'

She stopped at the door and whirled around, spitting words of hate at him in French. It could be a hissing, seething language as well. A language of curses and judgements. She used every one she knew on him, before wrenching open the door.

PART TWO

18

Notre Dame, Paris

10 April 1302 AD

P hilippe's fingers tightened on the arms of the throne, conveyed from the palace that morning and placed on the dais, as Nogaret's voice resounded. The rain lashing the arched windows sounded like stones being pelted against the stained glass and every now and then a growl of thunder drowned the minister's words. It was mid-afternoon, but the sky, boiling with clouds, was black as night. A blaze of torches lit the long aisle of Notre Dame, although their shifting luminescence reached only as far as the first gallery and the angels above, hovering on their stone pillars, were shadows stretching into impenetrable space.

Philippe remembered the first time he set foot in the cathedral. His father had brought him from the royal estate at Vincennes. He couldn't have been more than six years old. As he walked through the doors, his breath had been knocked from him at the vastness of it. Bending his neck back to stare at the ceiling, he wondered that he couldn't see clouds drifting there, so close to heaven those heights seemed. He remembered, too, the discomfort he felt, standing in God's house, how small and insignificant; an insect on the floor of a cavern. He felt it now, magnified by the gravity of the occasion, as Nogaret addressed the throng that packed the aisles.

'. . . and so, we have called upon you, men of the realm, to give your aid. For the very future and freedom of our kingdom is at stake.' Nogaret paused, letting murmurs whisper through the crowd. He motioned to the bench positioned to the right of Philippe's throne. 'My colleague, Pierre Flote, Lord Chancellor and Keeper of the Seals, shall now clarify for you the papal bull, *Ausculta fili*, that you may fully understand the severity of the Holy See's actions against you and your king.'

There was an awkward moment before Pierre Flote rose, a roll of parchment gripped in his liver-spotted hands. His gaze lingered on Nogaret, who seated himself at the king's side. Then, his voice lifting tremulously over the howling storm, the chancellor began to speak. 'Pope Boniface has written to our gracious lord, King Philippe le Bel, grandson of St Louis, pronouncing that he stands above our monarch in the temporal as well as spiritual realm, giving lie to the fact that a king is sovereign in his kingdom. He has demanded the release of the heretic, Bernard Saisset, Bishop of Pamiers, a man who stands justly accused of treason against the crown. By this demand, the pope ignores the fact that our king remains, by law and right, master of all internal policies within his kingdom.' Flote stopped to clear his throat and seemed to struggle to make himself heard against the authority of the storm. 'Furthermore, he has called for a synod at Rome, to be attended by all the bishops of France, at which he intends to charge our king with such heinous and unfounded abuses as debasing the kingdom's coinage, suppressing subjects through violent measures and taxing the clergy without need or reason.' Flote looked down at the parchment. His voice became even quieter, causing Nogaret to shift on the bench and frown. 'But what of Boniface's abuses? What of the heavy tithes placed upon the churches of our land, which bleed their lifeblood into the coffers of Rome without sign of benefit? What of the pope's suppression of his subjects, seen clearly in his groundless defamations of our noble king and his interference in secular affairs?'

As the charges against the pope were listed in Flote's quavering tone, Philippe gripped the arms of his throne even tighter. His body felt as though it were being pressed in on itself by the immensity of the space around him, in which a thousand images of God and Christ, angels and saints could be seen, in statues and stained glass, murals and hangings, all glowering down at him. His throat felt constricted and he was sweating. He should feel proud, powerful, for the scene playing out around him was unprecedented in the history of France. It was the first time the three Estates – Church, nobility and commoners – had been assembled in this way and Notre Dame was packed with prelates, bishops, counts and dukes, lords and guild heads. But Philippe just felt queasy.

Events had moved swiftly since his arrest of the outspoken bishop, Bernard Saisset, too swiftly for him to retain control over, with Nogaret and Flote pulling him in different directions. He wished briefly that he had held this council in the palace. The statement being made by the location in which he now moved openly against the Holy See wasn't worth this terrible, crushing sensation. But despite his discomfort, he knew it had been the right decision. The clergy, the First Estate, were the men most likely to resist his action against the pope and they needed to be shown that he, Philippe, raised on the dais in this soaring cathedral, was invested not only with the power of the state, but of God. He had already been given assurances in secret that the nobility and the burghers of the principal towns would support him, but even though it had been made plain to the clergy that they would become enemies of the crown should they oppose him, he still wasn't convinced he would have their cooperation.

'In conclusion,' finished Flote, 'we implore you to aid us in the defence of our liberties. Noblemen and burghers of the towns, we ask that you provide us with letters, signed by your representatives, that we may pass on to the pope and his cardinals, stating France will not become the puppet of Rome. Bishops and priests, give us your word that you will not attend the synod to which Boniface has summoned you, in protest at his unjust charges against your gentle king. Lord Philippe will hear your decisions within the hour.'

Philippe stood. All eyes were upon him as he walked across the dais, his robes sweeping behind him. As he disappeared in the shadows beyond the choir aisle, Nogaret followed, leaving Flote and the rest of the royal ministers to attend the throng, now stirring into agitated life.

Philippe touched his damp brow as one of the canons escorted him into the private chambers of the cathedral.

Nogaret's face was livid, but he waited until the canon had retreated before turning to Philippe. 'My lord, I feel obliged to lodge a protest against Chancellor Flote. He deliberately attempted to undermine our argument with that' – Nogaret's teeth clenched – '*limp* oration.'

'Did I do the right thing?'

Nogaret halted. 'My lord? Is everything all right? You look pale.'

Philippe met his gaze. 'Answer me, Nogaret. Did I do the right thing? Should I have arrested Saisset?'

'Without doubt. He was fomenting unrest against you, confronting decisions you have made, ridiculing your rule. The man defamed your character, calling you a stupid owl, a witless—'

'All right,' snapped Philippe. He drew in a breath. 'But there was no evidence of heresy. My confessor, Guillaume de Paris, believes the bishop to be innocent of such an unspeakable crime.'

Nogaret sucked his lip contemplatively. 'We discussed this, my lord,' he began slowly. 'The people are still led by the Church, by the old ways. They needed a strong reason, a reason they would understand for your arrest of a prominent man of the cloth. And they understand heresy very well.'

'As do you,' retorted Philippe.

Nogaret went still, his pallid face frozen in the candlelight. Outside, rain hammered on the windows. When the minister spoke, his voice was low. 'I do what is best for you, my lord, and what is best for the realm. My advice has always been to this end. If you wish to reign supreme in your kingdom, you must show yourself to be greater than priests and bishops, greater even than the pope, or your power will always be limited to what the Church is willing to dole out. Do you not want your people to proclaim you as a saint? To revere you in name and deed, as they did your grandfather?'

Philippe's eyes fixed on a tapestry beyond Nogaret, which showed the Virgin and Child. From within the safety of Mary's enfolding arms, the infant Christ stretched out a finger. His eyes were two black pools. 'Yes,' Philippe whispered. 'Yes, I do.'

'Then stand fast, my lord, and I swear I will help you achieve this.'

The council reconvened before the hour was up. The nobles and burghers gave elaborate speeches, announcing their full support, and read aloud letters of protest that would be sent to Rome. Philippe tensed when the Bishop of Paris rose to speak for the clergy. The bishop spoke haltingly, as if choosing his words carefully, but it soon became clear the clergy would stand with their king and Philippe eased back in his throne.

Surveying the clergymen, he saw anger and discontent on the faces of many, but also resignation. They had to obey him, or risk their benefices. His eyes fell on Bertrand de Got, standing near the front. The small man, dwarfed by his ecclesiastical robes, looked wan and weary, but showed no signs of rage. This pleased Philippe. De Got had been elected Archbishop of Bordeaux two years ago and now had real power in the heart of Guienne, still in contention despite the truce with Edward. As much as he disliked the archbishop, Philippe needed to keep him on his side.

The Bishop of Paris finished speaking and, after an imperious address from Nogaret thanking the men of France for their support, the first assembly of the Estates-General was brought to a close.

'What did you think you were doing, Chancellor?' murmured Nogaret, catching Pierre Flote's arm as the mass of men filed out of Notre Dame into the storm.

Flote glared at the minister and shrugged off his hand. 'I did what I had to.'

'It was what our king *commanded* of you. You should have afforded it every importance and presented it with all skill. Instead you sounded like a timid choirboy at his first recital!'

'How dare you—'

'The only thing we can be grateful for is that you didn't damage the verdict.'

Flote scoffed. 'Verdict? We knew what it would be before the assembly began!'

'There was still danger from the Church. You could have jeopardised everything we have been working towards.'

Flote's eyes went wide. 'You talk to me about jeopardy? You are going to destroy *France*!' He led Nogaret into one of the side aisles. 'Why are you conducting this travesty of a trial against Saisset? Is it some foolish display of power because I persuaded the king to concentrate on Flanders when you wanted to remain in Guienne?'

'I admit, I believe we should have continued our drive to regain control of the duchy, but that isn't what—'

'I cannot believe you still don't see the sense in this action! Flanders is just as wealthy, but far more controllable. It is ruled by a French vassal, not a foreign king, and whereas we have reached a stalemate with the English in Gascony, in Flanders we already stand victorious in battle. Now that our troops are stationed in Bruges and Ghent we have a far greater chance to bring the territory under our dominion.' Flote continued quickly when Nogaret went to interrupt. 'If we control Flanders, we can influence King Edward. England relies on Flanders for the wool trade. We can gain power over them with this, perhaps come to an arrangement over Guienne. Can you not see the wisdom in this, Guillaume?'

Nogaret's rigid expression didn't change. 'This isn't about Flanders, or Gascony. This is about punishing men who commit treason. Saisset was damaging our lord's reputation. He had to be arrested.'

'Have you forgotten your training? By that action you violated the laws of the Church! Bishops can only be judged in the Roman curia. Pope Boniface had every right to demand Saisset's release.' Flote's voice dropped to a murmur. 'And every man in this cathedral knew that, whatever they said to appease our lord. All that is happening now will only serve to widen the schism growing between the royal and papal courts.'

'The wider the better. You heard the reports of Boniface's Jubilee ceremony. A quarter of a million pilgrims journeyed to St Peter's at his promise of a remission of their sins to be confronted by the spectacle of the pope planted on his throne, holding sword and sceptre, yelling, *I am Caesar!*' Nogaret's tone was scathing. 'And now he has exiled or imprisoned as many of the Colonna family as he can find, Boniface has no one left to oppose his swelling arrogance. If he lived to usher in another new century, no doubt his cry would be, *I am God!*'

Flote winced. 'This isn't a game, Nogaret. Your actions have seriously threatened France.' He held up the bull he'd had in his hands during his speech. 'Did you even read this? The pope promises that unless Saisset is released, he will suspend all privileges granted to our kingdom by the Holy See.' He unrolled the parchment. '*Come back, my dear son,*' he read, '*to the path of God, from which you have strayed, by your own faults, or else by evil counsel. Do not believe that you are without superior or free from my dominion as vicar of the Earth. This indeed would be madness, for whosoever held such a belief would be an infidel, cut off from the flock.*' Flote looked up. 'Cut off from the flock. Don't you see? He threatens excommunication.'

'He wouldn't dare. Boniface needs the monies the Church in France provides him. That much was clear when we removed those funds and forced him to withdraw *Clericis laicos*. He backed down then. If we hold our nerve he will back down again. Now,' finished Nogaret, 'I believe we both have our orders.' He moved to walk away.

Rage sparked in Flote, making him forget where he was. 'You're a Godless beast, Nogaret. A son of heretics! And I will do everything in my power to bring an end to your malign influence over our king.'

Nogaret turned back, his dark eyes fixing on Flote's scarlet face. 'I would be very careful, Chancellor, about exciting yourself in this way. You are not a young man any more.'

St-Gervais-St-Protais Church, Paris, 25 May 1302 AD

Taking a candle, Will held the wick in the flame of another until it sputtered into life. He placed it among the others before the altar and spoke a prayer, while the ivory statues of saints Gervais and Protais, the twin brothers martyred during the reign of Nero, looked sadly down. He felt someone move in beside him. A hand reached out from under a white mantle and chose a candle from the pile.

'Shall we sit?'

Will met Robert's gaze, then motioned to the benches.

As they sat, a sacristan headed to the altar with a knife and tray. He smiled uncertainly at the two men, one a Templar, the other indistinct in a plain woollen cloak, then knelt beneath the candles and began to scrape wax from the floor. It was late afternoon, between Nones and Vespers. Apart from a couple of people seated near the front, heads bowed, the church was empty. The only sound was the rasp of the sacristan's knife against the stone.

'I wasn't sure you were still in the city,' said Robert quietly. 'I thought perhaps you'd returned to Scotland.'

'Simon would have told you.'

'Simon only tells me when you wish to meet. Most of the time, he avoids me. I think he is worried I'll ask questions and the wrong people will overhear.' Robert pushed a hand through his hair, which was silvery white and receding. 'Either that or he doesn't trust me to keep your secret.'

'I'm certain that's not the case,' said Will, with a frown. 'But it is good he is cautious.'

'I wouldn't worry. Hugues thinks you're long gone and as most of the knights who knew you returned to Cyprus with the Grand Master, there are not many left who would recognise you. As long as you keep your distance from the preceptory, it is doubtful you'll be noticed.'

'Still, I need to be careful.'

'Wouldn't want anything to endanger your important work,' murmured Robert.

Will exhaled. 'I presumed you understood.'

'No,' responded Robert sharply, 'you hoped I did to ease your guilt.' The sacristan glanced over, but returned to his industrious scraping when Robert's gaze flicked to him.

'What is this about, Robert? I thought we were—'

'What?' Robert cut in. 'Friends?'

'Are we not?'

'I don't know what we are. You appeared after three years with no word and expected things to go back to the way they were. But how can they? You left the Temple and you left others with this great burden that wasn't theirs to bear. You were Everard's successor. You pledged yourself to the Brethren.'

'As did you.'

'After you dragged me into it.' Robert paused at Will's pained expression, then looked away. 'What do you expect? You send for me every six months or so as if I'm your servant, wanting to know if the Temple has any information on this or that. You don't even ask about the Anima Templi. I almost didn't come today. I found myself asking who it is you call these meetings for and realised I didn't know the answer. Is it William Wallace? Or King Philippe? Or do you work for anyone these days – a mercenary?'

'You know I'm not that.'

'No? Simon didn't tell me everything when he returned from Scotland, but I know you both fought at Falkirk. Templars died there. The Master of England died there.' Robert followed Will with his eyes as he turned away. 'Perhaps you chose the wrong side.'

'I never changed, Robert. It was the Temple that did. I'm still working against the man who betrayed our ideals, who used us for his own ends.'

'And how exactly are you doing that as Philippe's bloodhound?'

'The king and the pope are the only men who can exercise any power over Edward. Already one of his campaigns has been halted by their intervention. Wallace must continue to keep them on his side if the war against Scotland is to end.'

'I thought you said you were doing this for the Temple,' said Robert, a little cuttingly.

'All the while Edward is tied up in his political and military entanglements he will most likely leave the Temple alone. And I still have family in Scotland, so of course if I can protect them through my work here I will.'

Robert fell silent for a time. 'If you are in Paris on Wallace's behalf, why are you running errands for Philippe?'

'While the rule of the duchy of Guienne remains in dispute, the king needs the Scots. He can use them to mount offences against England, designed to occupy Edward's forces. That is why he is still sending money to the Scots, albeit nowhere near as much as we need. But should the balance ever shift?' Will raised his shoulders wearily. 'Let us just say I am making sure Philippe continues to find the services of a former Templar as useful as possible. It is one of the reasons Wallace left me here when he returned to Scotland: to keep in with him.'

'One of?'

'I asked to stay. Rose,' Will explained. 'Mostly, I make sure messages and the little money Philippe can spare find their way safely into Wallace's hands.'

'I heard a rumour Wallace is dead.'

'No. But he has gone to ground. Edward is intent on hunting him down. He has Scottish nobles scouring the realm for him. Some of them are willing, but most have had their families threatened unless they obey.'

'Have you spoken to Philippe of the Anima Templi?'

'No. He knows I deserted over the Temple's support of Edward and that I was a commander. But that is all.' Will paused as the sacristan passed by, his tray full of yellow shards of wax. 'How are things in the Brethren? Is Hugues still in contact with Edward?'

'Messages pass between them, but infrequently and they contain nothing more than the usual political pledges and assurances as far as I know. In truth, the Brethren don't do much at all these days.'

Will's surprise was followed by a jab of anger. 'Nothing?'

'It is just Hugues and me in Paris, and Thomas in London now. What on earth can the three of us do?' Robert snorted. 'Reconcile the faiths of the world at our annual meeting?'

'Enlist more members?' suggested Will, irritated by his tone.

'Hugues is kept occupied with the running of the Order: expanding our wool trade, recruiting knights, building ships, collecting donations. In turn, I am busy helping him. Among other things.'

Will sensed he was holding something back. 'Other things?'

'It is nothing, just some rumours I've been trying to get to the bottom of.'

'Rumours?'

Robert shook his head. 'I am sure it isn't anything to be concerned about. You know how the younger sergeants can be, always trying to frighten one another about their initiations.' He looked round as a priest headed out of the sacristy, followed by two acolytes bearing a breviary. 'If you have questions the king needs answers to, you should ask them. It will be Vespers soon.'

Will sat back. 'I didn't come for Philippe, I came for me. It's Rose, Robert. I cannot get through to her.'

'Can you blame her?'

'It's been over two years and still she acts as if I don't exist. When we pass in the palace halls she pretends not to see me. If I ask her a question she ignores me. I don't know how many more apologies I can make. She is so distant.' Will's brow furrowed. 'Not just from me, from everyone. I'm worried.'

'I don't see how I can help.'

'You've known her since she was a baby and she has always respected you. I need her to understand why I did what I did.'

'I'm not sure I understand it.'

'Please,' said Will quietly, as Robert turned away.

The knight looked down at his hands, then let out a rough sigh. 'All right. I'll speak to her. Get a message to Simon, telling me where and when. But I cannot promise she will listen.'

19

The Sainte-Chapelle, Paris

30 May 1302 AD

'For I am the resurrection and the life. Whoever believes in me will live, even though he dies, and whoever lives and believes in me will never die.'

Rose raised her eyes, but kept her head bowed, as the priest read from the gospel. The upper chapel of the Sainte-Chapelle was bathed with many colours, as the diffused morning sunlight streamed through the stained glass. It was like standing in the centre of an enormous jewel.

Rose loved the chapel, not for the splendour of its architecture, or the importance of the relics it housed, but for the daily moments it afforded her to look, unobserved, upon the object of her devotion. The dormitory was usually occupied with other handmaidens and offered few occasions for spying, and during meals in the Great Hall there were too many other roving eyes and scrutinising glances for her to stare unnoticed. But here, with all the heads of the royal court bowed in reverence, she was free to drink in every aspect. It gave her a thrilling sense of power, to be the only one seeing him in such a private moment. She shifted on her feet, her skin tingling in the heat coming through the windows.

Today, the king wore a black velvet cloak, which flowed down his back like ink to pool on the floor, where he stood before the priest. His hair was the colour of burned honey in the sunlight and part of it had fallen over his shoulder, exposing a triangle of flesh at the back of his neck. Rose fixed on that surface, letting her imagination wander across it, envisioning the warmth of it, the pulse of blood beneath, the softness under fingertips, lips. Sometimes, such thoughts would become unbearable. Her heart would quicken, her face would flame and her body would tremble until it felt as if a thousand bees were trapped inside her. She felt the sting in her skin and in places unexplored.

There was movement at Philippe's side and her gaze fell on Jeanne's broad back, tightly laced in a sapphire-blue gown. The queen's thick black hair was wound in plaits that Rose had braided and pinned that morning. Jeanne's plump shoulder was now touching Philippe's arm, ruining the reverie. To Jeanne's side stood their five children: the heir, Louis, at thirteen, then Philippe, Charles, Robert and the youngest, Isabella, a darkly beautiful child of seven and their only surviving daughter. Rose glanced over their profiles without interest, before moving back to the king. As she did so, she locked gazes with Guillaume de Nogaret, standing to her right, just behind Philippe. He was looking straight at her. Rose dipped her head to stare, shaken, at the floor, as the priest finished his reading.

Philippe was first to leave, followed by his family, then his closest ministers. The handmaidens and other attendants filed out on to the balcony last. When she was an anonymous servant, Rose heard daily services in the lower chapel and ate her meals in the chamber beneath the Great Hall, with its labyrinth of white marble pillars. Both were plainer, the ribbed ceilings low, claustrophobic in comparison to the upper rooms which were light and airy, without limits. She found these physical reminders of the levels of status sinister, as if they represented more the divides between Heaven and hell.

The light hurt her eyes as she stepped through the doors. The queen and a nursemaid were ushering the children into the royal apartments, but the king had halted on the balcony with Nogaret and Flote. There was a man there, clad in scarlet and black: a royal messenger. Rose glanced at Philippe as she passed, hoping he would look back, but his expression was troubled and he was listening too intently to the messenger to pay her any attention.

'Massacred?' Philippe shook his head. 'How soon can we send reinforcements to assist the survivors?'

The royal messenger looked uncomfortable. 'I'm afraid you misunderstand me, my lord. There was only one survivor. The rest of the garrison were killed. He fled to Courtrai and alerted our men there. I was despatched to inform you immediately.'

Philippe went to the stone balustrade and planted his hands on it. 'How did this happen?' His eyes moved to Flote and Nogaret, standing in silence. 'How?' He turned back to the messenger. 'They were soldiers for Christ's sake! They had swords, horses, armour. How did weavers and butchers massacre four thousand French troops?'

'The textile guilds formed their own militias some time ago to protect their interests from the local nobility,' answered the messenger. 'They are made up of able-bodied men from the working classes, armed by the guild leaders. It was these men who attacked our soldiers. The assault in Bruges was carefully planned. It came just before Matins, when most of the garrison were in the lodgings we had commandeered. The marauders went from door to door with weapons concealed. When the doors were opened they demanded each man speak a phrase: Friend of the Guilds. It is difficult to pronounce in their language. Those who couldn't were considered to be French and killed on the spot. Most of our men weren't even dressed, let alone armed.'

'Four thousand?' breathed Philippe. '*Four thousand.*' He turned to Flote. 'My rule will suffer for this, Chancellor.' He struck the balustrade. 'I barely convinced my people that I am powerful enough to challenge the pope. Now, they will all see my might can be broken. And by peasants!'

'We must send in more troops, my lord,' said Flote, going to him. 'I'm afraid the trouble in Flanders is only just beginning.'

Flote looked round at the messenger.

'The Matins of Bruges, as the Flemish are calling it, has signalled a revolt across the region. The guild militia is on the march and their numbers are growing. As I left Courtrai, it was rumoured they were on their way to the castle, recently captured by our men. It is believed they intend to storm it.'

'Can Guy de Dampierre not be reasoned with?' Nogaret said into the silence. 'Can we offer him some olive branch that will induce him to take control of these men?'

'We took the count hostage when we occupied Bruges,' responded Flote in a caustic tone. 'I doubt he will be in any mood to listen to our pleas.' The chancellor met Philippe's gaze. 'The decision has been made for us by the actions of the guild workers, my lord.'

Philippe nodded. 'Withdraw more troops from Guienne,' he said quietly, his face rigid. 'Send them to Flanders with forces from Artois under Count Robert. Flote, I want you—'

'My lord—' began Nogaret.

'Our king was speaking, Minister,' Flote cut in. 'Hold your tongue.'

'I want you there, Chancellor,' said Philippe, taking no notice of the exchange. 'I want you to go to Flanders and see that this is done. You will be my eyes. My voice.'

Pierre Flote bowed. 'Of course.'

'These peasants may have found it easy to kill unarmed soldiers,' murmured Philippe. 'But we shall see how they fare against the flower of French chivalry. Let them taste the lily.'

The Ville, Paris, 4 June 1302 AD

As Rose tugged off her coif, a few strands of hair dragged free of their pins. Brushing them back, she fanned herself with the cap. The air was sticky and all the smells of the marketplace seemed trapped in it, the reek of dung and food mixed together making her feel nauseous. A group of men passed and glanced over at her appraisingly. Ignoring them, Rose carried on waving the coif in front of her face, the breath of wind a sweet relief.

'What are you doing? Cover your head!'

Rose turned to see Marguerite, the oldest of the queen's handmaidens, staring at her. 'I needed to cool myself.'

'When on business for the queen you will behave as a lady of standing should.'

Rose pulled the coif over her hair, leaving several wisps clinging to her damp skin.

Marguerite turned to the petite, dark-haired handmaiden at her side, called Blanche. 'I always said it would be impossible to make gold from straw.' She flicked her gaze back to Rose.

Blanche put her hand to her mouth to stifle a giggle and Marguerite looped an arm through hers. 'Come, we still have the gingerbread to buy. Prince Louis will not be happy if we return without it and if the prince is not happy, neither is madam.' Together, the two of them strolled off through the market, leaving Rose to trail in their wake.

As they passed several flower sellers, who called hopefully to the three young women in their finely tailored gowns, a couple of dirty-faced children came running over, hands outstretched. Marguerite shooed them away and picked up her pace, Blanche close at her side.

'Please,' implored one of the children, planting himself before Rose. 'Spare me a coin.'

Rose stared down at the grubby child. Many of these street children she knew were sent out by their parents to tug the heartstrings of the rich. The boy, who couldn't have been more than eight, had two fingers missing. There was a knobbly stump of skin where they should have been. She had heard tales of beggars mutilating themselves to get more sympathy and wondered whether the child's disfigurement had been accidental. She shook her head, feeling faint in the heat. 'I'm sorry, I have none.' She spread her hands to prove it and her long sleeves fell back.

The boy's face hardened. His eyes fell on her withered hand. '*Ugly*,' he sneered, before running after his comrades.

Rose stood there, feeling as though the boy had just kicked her. She saw one of the flower sellers look over, so she tugged down her sleeve to cover the burn scars and hastened on. The market was packed and she had lost sight of the handmaidens. Feeling tears prickling in her eyes, she spun in a circle, trying to spot them. As she did so she saw a Templar heading towards her. It was Robert de Paris. She hadn't seen him in over a year.

'Rose,' he called, smiling in greeting. 'Can I speak to you?'

She started to shake her head. 'I have to—'

'Please. It won't take long.'

Numbly, she let him escort her away from the centre of the market and into a quiet side street. 'How did you know I—' She halted. 'He told you where I would be, didn't he? He sent you.' She shook her head furiously. 'I don't want to hear it, whatever message he sent you with.'

'He just wants a chance to explain why he left the way he did.' Robert caught her arm as she went to walk away. 'He's your father, Rose. He deserves that at least.'

She wrenched away from his grip. 'He's not my father! I owe him nothing! *Garin*,' she hissed at his bemused expression. 'Garin de Lyons. He was my father. My mother lay with him and . . .' Rose stopped, her eyes filling up.

Robert looked stunned. He put his hands on her shoulders, searching her face. 'Are you certain? Did Elwen . . . Did your mother tell you this?'

'The day she died, my mother and Garin were arguing in Andreas's house, before the fire. She said she didn't know.' Rose met his gaze. 'She didn't know which of them was my father.'

'Then you don't either,' said Robert gently.

'Do you know the worst thing? The worst thing is remembering how it was to feel loved. If I could choose, I would rather have been some orphan at the mercy of the streets than to wake each day and remember I once had a family who loved me. I had a home.' She held out her scarred hand. 'I was whole. Now my mother is dead, my home long gone, and every time I look upon the man who might have been my father I am reminded of what was taken away.' Rose's hands came up to hide her face as her tears fell.

Robert drew her to him and held her, his hand stroking her back, until her sobs began to ease.

Rose closed her eyes, feeling Robert's arms, strong as bands of iron around her. His mantle was warm against her cheek and smelled of smoke and straw. He stirred as if to move and she clutched at his surcoat to keep him there. He was speaking about her father, about how he loved her still and was desperate for her forgiveness. Rose squeezed her eyes tighter, blocking out the words and concentrating on the feeling of that strong hand rolling over the bumps of her spine. She felt encircled, safe in a way she hadn't felt in years. Keeping her eyes closed, she moved her arms around his back, feeling the muscles shift under his mantle as she slid her fingers towards his neck. Robert had stopped talking. His hand was now still, flat against her back. She could feel his heart. It was thrumming. As her fingertips met the hot skin at the nape of his neck, she felt a shudder go through him. Rising on to her toes, her tears drying cold on her cheeks, Rose pressed her mouth to his. She felt the warmth of his breath, the roughness of his beard, then a slight wetness as his lips parted that sent a delirious rush of shock through her.

It was over in a second.

Robert pulled back. 'Rose . . .'

She stared at him, feeling all the grief and anger rush back into her. Then, turning, she ran down the street to be swallowed by the bustle of the market, leaving Robert standing there, breathless.

Outside Notre Dame, Paris, 4 June 1302 AD

'Make sure it is done exactly as I say.'

The soldier held out his hand. 'It will be,' he assured, when the man in front of him hesitated. He smiled humourlessly. 'Believe me, when arrows start flying and swords start swinging, no one will notice a stray blow.'

'He may not become directly involved in the fighting.'

The soldier shrugged. 'If what you say is true, he'll be on the field. Anything can happen then.' His smile became one of satisfaction as the pouch sank on to his palm.

'I'll give you the rest when I receive the report of his death.'

Guillaume de Nogaret watched the soldier disappear between the confusion of buildings that crowded in around the cathedral. He felt a sense of release, as though something constraining him had snapped free and he could finally move. He knew how to secure Philippe all the wealth he needed to ensure his dominion over France and, at the same time, control the Church. He had known for some while now. Only, he had also known the chancellor would never allow it to happen. Nogaret was mildly surprised by the ease with which he had executed the plan. But then, it wasn't the first time he had caused death through his actions.

A wagon rolled by, puffing up dust, leaving the air dirty yellow in its wake. Nogaret squinted at the sun, sweat dribbling down his cheeks. He would never get used to this humidity. In the south, the summers had been hotter, but it was a dryer, purer heat, the air refreshed by breezes from the coast and the mountains. It was summer when he left his home for the last time. He could still recall the scent of the ground baking in the sun, the grapes swelling to burst black from the vines, the click of insects. The smell of smoke. Of flesh burning. Nogaret closed his eyes. His sister was shrieking, crying for their mother as the fire crackled around her feet, consuming the wood. But his mother's head was already hanging forward, the flames up to her thighs. The material of her dress burned away suddenly, scattering embers on the smoky air and affording the crowd a brief, indecent glimpse of her sex, before her body began to burn.

'God is most grateful to His loyal sons, Guillaume,' the Dominican at his side had said, placing a solemn hand upon his shoulder. 'You will be rewarded for the sacrifice you have made here today. Heresy must be rooted out wherever it is found. It is for the good of us all that we do this.'

20

Near Bordeaux, the Kingdom of France

18 July 1302 AD

'Wait with the horses, Gaillard.' Bertrand de Got winced as he dismounted and handed the reins to his squire. 'I will not be long.'

Grasping the package he had carried from Bordeaux, damp in his sweaty hands, Bertrand made his way to the little white house on the brow of the hill. The sky was azure and limitless, with barely a breeze to ruffle his cloak, as he puffed and panted his way up the dusty track. He turned before he reached the house and was rewarded with a breathtaking view across pastures and vineyards, all the way to Bordeaux. He could just make out the spire of the cathedral and, for a moment, he wondered if someone in the bell tower could look all the way across the valley to where he stood. It was a dizzying thought and he was glad to strike his knuckles on the solid door behind him.

A young woman he didn't recognise opened it. 'Yes, sir?' she ventured, staring at his sumptuous clerical vestments.

'Is that you, your grace?' came a voice from down the hall. A stout woman with coarse features bustled the girl out of the way. 'Back to the kitchen, Marie.'

'Yes, madam.'

The woman watched the girl slip off, then turned to Bertrand. 'I'm sorry, your grace, I've instructed her not to answer the door.'

Bertrand waited until the woman led him into a small, but well-furnished room before he unleashed his anger. 'What is she doing here, Yolande?' he hissed, as she closed the door behind them. 'Who is she?'

'A serving girl, that is all.'

'That is all?' Bertrand seethed, feeling light-headed from the climb and the shock. 'She has seen me! Do you have any comprehension what it would mean if she ever told anyone?' He tossed the rumpled package on to a table.

'She doesn't know who you are,' said Yolande placidly. 'And anyway, she lives here now. Who is there to tell?' The woman folded her hands calmly and watched Bertrand sink on to a stool by the window. 'I need help now the boys are getting older.'

'I said I would find you someone,' he muttered, rubbing at his slick forehead. He grimaced as a lance of pain drove through his stomach.

'You said that months ago.'

'You have a house, woman. What more do you want from me?'

'This is not the life I would have chosen,' said Yolande stiffly. 'If I had my way my husband would still be alive and I would be living with him. Instead I am out here all alone, raising my child and yours.' Yolande pursed her lips. 'I can always leave.'

Bertrand looked up quickly. 'No.' He shook his head. 'No, Yolande. But you must promise me this girl will say nothing. I would have found you someone suitable myself, but things have not been easy for me since my election.'

Yolande seemed to relax, seeing she had won, and went to pour a goblet of wine from a jug she had set out.

'King Philippe has not withdrawn all his troops from Guienne, despite the truce he signed with Edward of England.' Bertrand sighed, then winced at a fresh stab of pain inside. He accepted the clay goblet she handed to him. 'Though half the garrison in Bordeaux were pulled out last month and sent to Flanders, so perhaps we may yet see an easing of the conflict now the king is occupied elsewhere.'

Yolande nodded, entirely without interest in a conversation about politics. 'Raoul has been looking forward to seeing you. Shall I fetch him?'

'Yes.' Bertrand sat back, thankful for the breeze coming through the window as she shuffled from the room. He mused that perhaps it wouldn't be so bad, having a younger woman around. Yolande had her own child late and was able to suckle the boy through infancy, but the years were showing on her now the milk had stopped flowing. Raoul was supposed to have had a young mother to care for him. He would have, had he not killed her during the labour.

Bertrand had met Heloise five years ago, during a visit to his nephew's church near Bordeaux. She was the seventeen-year-old daughter of a local lord, plain, but sweet as honey, and the first and only woman he had loved. After the first moment of passion, Bertrand vowed it would never happen again. But it had, again and often, until Heloise came to him one afternoon and tearfully told him she was pregnant. To conceive a child outside wedlock was sinful. To conceive a child at all as a man of the cloth was anathema. During the Church reforms of Pope Gregory VII, priests and bishops had their nuptials forcibly annulled, their wives condemned as concubines and their children declared bastards. Marriage had been denied to the clergy ever since.

The irony of his lover's name wasn't lost on Bertrand. Two hundred years earlier, Heloise had been the young lover of Abelard, brilliant theologian in the schools in Paris. For his sins, Abelard had been castrated and Bertrand, fearing more than just the loss of his benefice, had persuaded Heloise to run away from her family before the child started to show. He bought the little farmhouse on the hill with funds from his diocese and it was here, miles from anywhere, that Heloise gave birth to their son, prematurely. Yolande, recently widowed, had been there to look after the house and help nurse the infant. She had no experience of midwifery. Bertrand arrived late one evening to find his lover stone cold in a pool of congealed birth-blood, and Yolande hugging a screaming boy.

He buried Heloise in the woods beyond the house, cursing himself. Cursing God. He thought at the time that he was being punished, but as the months went on and he watched his son grow he couldn't believe God had given him anything other than a gift in Raoul. After his election as Archbishop of Bordeaux, a post he had fought for ruthlessly, it became easier to siphon off funds to pay for his son's keep. He knew how to disguise his accounts and as many in his familia were relatives, they would not question his administration. Heloise became a sad memory, but so distant that sometimes he thought of Raoul as a miracle, a child born without parents, who would grow up to change the world. It would be through his son that his sins would be expunged.

The door opened and Yolande entered, leading a toddling boy with brown hair and large black eyes like his mother and a hooked nose like his. Raoul was gripping a worn leather ball and pouted as Yolande took it from him and pointed towards Bertrand. 'Here's your papa to see you, dear one.'

Bertrand frowned in dismay as Raoul clung to Yolande's leg. 'What is wrong with him?'

'He's just shy,' she said, scooping the boy up and depositing him on Bertrand's knee. 'You must visit more often,' she admonished, 'then he will know you better.'

'I have a gift for you, Raoul,' said Bertrand, as his son squirmed and tried to get off his lap. 'Here.' He picked the package off the table. The cloth covering it was still damp. Raoul stopped wriggling and grasped it greedily. 'Let me take this off.' Bertrand unwrapped the cloth to reveal a small, embroidered scene of a domed church on a rock, surrounded by tiny white buildings, crowned with a blue sky. 'One of my young acolytes made this for me.'

Raoul stared at it with a heavy frown. 'Picture,' he said, jabbing a finger at it.

'It is not just any picture. This is Jerusalem.' Bertrand spoke the word in such a soft, reverent tone, that Raoul went still, suddenly interested. Neither of them noticed as Yolande slipped out of the room. 'This is the city where our saviour, Jesus Christ, once lived. One day, I will take you there, Raoul,' he murmured into his son's pink ear. 'One day, I promise we will see this together.'

An hour later, Bertrand left the house and made his way back down the track to where his squire was waiting with the horses in the shelter of a clump of trees. The climb down was made easier by the spring in his step and even the pain in his stomach, affecting him for some weeks now, seemed dulled. Gaillard, the only person other than Yolande who knew his secret, didn't say a word, but dutifully laced his hands to help the archbishop into the saddle.

As he rode slowly back through the hot afternoon towards Bordeaux, Bertrand's joy at seeing his son was soon obscured by thoughts of the promise he had made to the boy. Reports had begun to come through from the Holy Land, where Jacques de Molay had been heading a Crusade. After some initial hope the previous year, borne on the news that the Crusaders had joined forces with the Mongols against the Mamluks, more recent reports revealed the campaign had suffered massive failure. It was said the Templars' last stronghold on the island of Ruad had been captured by Muslim forces and that the Grand Master and his commanders had fallen back to Cyprus. With the Hospitallers unwilling to work with their rivals, the Teutonics fully occupied in their conquest of pagan Prussia and King Edward's promise forgotten in the recent wars, there seemed to be few fighting men left to continue the struggle.

Bertrand had never set foot in the Holy Land, but it called to him like a prayer he yearned to answer. To walk in God's footsteps, to see the places where the Saviour of mankind had lived and breathed: this was what he aspired to. He could have gone on pilgrimage in his youth, indeed had considered it, but the thought of the turmoil on those far shores had stopped him from making the journey. He had heard the stories of the First Crusade, of streets awash with blood and piled with corpses. He didn't want to see it in that way. He wanted to enter a golden city, smell the fragrant olive trees and hear the song of birds as he wound his way up the hill to the Church of the Holy Sepulchre, surely the most hallowed ground on Earth. It was the task of rulers to conquer and soldiers to fight. But it was his task to lead God's faithful into the gates of a liberated Jerusalem.

'What are they doing?'

Bertrand was stirred from his thoughts by Gaillard's voice. The squire was looking towards a huge oak, rising like a green tower from a cornfield. Bertrand saw a group of men heading for it. He realised he could hear shouts over the rushing of the wheat. It looked as if the group were dragging something. It was . . . ? Bertrand's brow creased. Two people.

'Should we intervene, your grace?'

Bertrand started to shake his head, but went still as he saw that the figures were writhing, fighting against the men hauling them towards the oak. He caught a flash of metal and guessed the captors were armed.

'Royal soldiers,' said Gaillard suddenly. 'Your grace, those men are royal soldiers.'

'My God,' Bertrand murmured, as he realised the two struggling men were clad in the vivid scarlet and blue surcoats worn by the troops stationed in Bordeaux. One of their captors threw a rope over the branch of the tree. The archbishop's hand went to the jewelled cross around his neck as he knew with a sick feeling that he was about to witness a murder.

'We have to stop them, your grace.'

'I cannot! They might ask what I am doing out here.' Bertrand glanced back to where the house was still visible on the hill. 'My son,' he said helplessly. 'You go, Gaillard. Find out what is happening. Make them stop this.'

Gaillard looked afraid, but he spurred his horse off the track and into the cornfield, cutting a path through the gold. Bertrand watched two of the group break off to challenge the squire as he galloped towards them. He saw them raise swords. A second rope had been thrown over the branch and the soldiers were being hoisted up. Their shouts came to him, sharp with fear. Gaillard had dismounted and was confronting one of the captors. Bertrand sucked in a breath as the man pointed a sword at him. Gaillard backed away and mounted his horse.

Bertrand looked on, aghast, as the soldiers were drawn haltingly into the air by their necks, the mob heaving on the ropes.

'Your grace,' panted Gaillard, hauling his horse to a stop alongside him. 'I tried, but they . . .' He shook his head, looking back across the cornfield. 'There was nothing I could do.'

Bertrand said nothing, his gaze transfixed by the jerking soldiers.

'They say there is an uprising against King Philippe's occupation,' said Gaillard, 'that they do not accept the truce Edward of England has made with him. They said they will drive out the royal forces themselves, like the Flemish have done in Bruges. They say others are doing the same, all over the duchy.'

The Louvre, Paris, 10 August 1302 AD

'Lord Philippe is aware of your situation, but as you are one of the principal moneylenders in Paris, he cannot help but be surprised by your inefficiency in paying this year's tribute.'

'What more can I do, my lord?' implored the elderly Jew, stepping past the royal treasurer and holding out his hands to Philippe, who was seated in a high-backed chair behind a table covered with rolls of parchment. 'I have done everything in my power to collect the monies owed to me, but there are still many debts outstanding. As you can see.' He unfurled several of the rolls and pointed to the lists of numbers. 'If I could have more time?'

'You have had five months already,' said Philippe, before the treasurer could speak. He leaned forward, resting his elbows on the table. 'I am disappointed, Samuel. Steps may have to be taken.'

'My lord, the laws imposed upon my people by your grandfather, King Louis, have made it increasingly difficult for us to collect unpaid sums from Christian debtors. There is no real incentive for them to pay their debts. They cannot even be imprisoned if they refuse!'

'I would be very careful,' said Philippe ominously, 'about disparaging *St Louis* in any way.'

'My lord, I am certain Samuel meant no offence.'

Philippe glanced up at the whispery voice. He stared at the frail, white-haired Jew with the foreign accent. 'I still do not see your part in this. Why are you here?'

'Rabbi Elias is here to vouch for me,' interjected Samuel. 'He has agreed to act as my guarantor in this matter.'

'I can assure you, my lord,' said Elias, calmly meeting the king's hostile gaze, 'Samuel will pay his tribute to you as soon as—' He broke off at a rapping on the chamber door.

Philippe looked round. 'I said I wasn't to be disturbed.'

'I will deal with it,' responded Nogaret, pushing himself from the wall, where he had been watching the dispute in silence. He moved past the treasurer and pulled open the door.

Philippe frowned, hearing a muttered exchange. 'Who is it, Nogaret?'

'A messenger and an official from the palace, my lord. They say it is urgent.'

'Be quick,' Philippe ordered testily, as the two men entered the chamber. 'I have enough business to get through today without interruptions.'

'I bring news from Flanders, my lord.' The messenger said nothing more, but handed Philippe a scroll.

The king unrolled it. As he read, his expression changed from one of impatience to one of disbelief. When he came to the end, his hand fell to his side. The parchment slipped from his fingers to curl into a roll on the flagstones.

'My lord?' questioned Nogaret. When the king didn't answer, Nogaret crossed to the scroll and swiped it up.

'When our forces arrived at Courtrai, we found the Flemish laying siege to the castle,' the messenger said into the hush. 'Their army was composed of infantry alone, but they outnumbered us. They were led by guild heads and the sons of Guy de Dampierre.' Nogaret was still reading. Philippe had flattened his palm on the table, crumpling one of the parchments Samuel had set out. 'Our knights led a charge, but were hampered by the marshy terrain and by Flemish archers. Those who managed to get close enough to their lines were beaten from their horses by the enemies' clubs.'

'Destroyed?' muttered Nogaret, his eyes still moving over the scroll.

'We estimate more than one thousand knights were slain. A full list of casualties will be delivered shortly, but I was asked to inform you directly of two deaths. Count Robert d'Artois was surrounded on the field. I'm afraid our soldiers couldn't reach him. The other . . .' The messenger bowed his head, not meeting Philippe's stare. 'The other was Chancellor Flote. He was found with his throat cut, some way from the centre of the battle.' Now the messenger did look at Philippe, his eyes bright with anger. 'They took the spurs of our dead knights as trophies, my lord. It is rumoured they hung them in a church in Courtrai.'

Still, Philippe said nothing. Elias and Samuel were looking uncertainly at the treasurer, who was wringing his hands.

'I'm afraid these are not the only black tidings, my lord,' said the royal official, stepping forward. 'Just this past hour the palace has received a report of a rebellion against royal forces in the Guienne region. It isn't clear as yet how widespread the insurrection is, but we know some soldiers have been murdered and—'

'Leave.' Philippe rose, his hands planted on the table.

'My lord?'

'Leave!' Philippe thrust a hand towards the door. 'All of you. Get out!'

'Please,' began Samuel hesitantly, 'I—'

'*Get out!*'

As the messenger and the official left, Nogaret steered the two Jews and the treasurer towards the door and hustled them out. He grasped the handle to close it, but halted at a sharp summons from the king.

'Not you, Nogaret.'

Leaving the door ajar, the minister moved back into the chamber. He inhaled and folded his arms across his thin chest. 'My lord, this is dire news, I cannot pretend otherwise, but we can repair this damage. We just need time to gather more forces.'

'Time?' murmured Philippe. 'Time I have. Funds I do not. How can this be repaired? And now Flote is gone?' He swept a hand carelessly across the table, sending parchments scattering. 'You heard what the treasurer had to say. The royal coffers are all but empty. How do I fight a war on two fronts, put down these rebellions, avenge our noble dead, when I cannot afford to put an army in the field?' Philippe rose and began to pace. 'And yet I must. Somehow I must. If I do not take action, my people will think me feeble. The power I gained in the assembly of the Estates is slipping. When word of this gets out and I sit here and do nothing, I will lose it altogether. Who knows, Nogaret, how many other enemies are out there, waiting to attack me while I am weak. Dukes? Counts? Bishops?' He turned to the minister. 'My grandfather never would have let this happen. He would have found the funds any way he could; sent a host to subdue Flanders and avenge Courtrai, strung these Gascon rebels from the gibbet. I am defeated.' Philippe shivered and clutched at the collar of his black cloak. 'There is no salvation.'

'My lord, there is one . . .'

'I must think, Nogaret.' Philippe thrust his hands into his hair. 'I cannot tax the clergy. It will take too long and I mustn't give Pope Boniface any more chances to build support for his case against me.'

Nogaret took a step forward, trying to distract Philippe's feverish concentration.

'The Jews!' Philippe snatched a parchment from the floor and brand-
ished it at Nogaret. 'My grandfather did this when he needed funds.'

'What, my lord?'

'He exiled the Jews. Confiscated their money and their property, drove
them from the kingdom.' Philippe's eyes grew distant. 'I can remember my
father speaking of it; wagons of treasure being drawn into the palace yard,
gold coins spilling from the sides. This is what we do, Nogaret. We will
send royal guards to evict them, then sell their homes and possessions at
auction. The gold and any treasure I will keep. We will contact their
debtors about any outstanding loans.' Philippe held up the parchment. 'And
we will make certain they repay them.'

Nogaret had been nodding thoughtfully. 'The plan has merit and it will
generate a large income quickly, enough I would wager to mount a campaign
in Flanders. But it is,' he went on carefully, 'only a short-term measure. The
funds would dry up quickly and we would have to forsake the yearly tribute
the Jews pay us. In the end, we may end up losing more than we gain. Execute
this plan by all means, my lord, but concern yourself with longer-term
strategies. The Jews are rich, certainly, but they are a relatively small group.
How do you obtain enough wealth to sustain the royal domains you have
already secured, as well as expand your territories in the coming years?'
Nogaret smiled when Philippe shook his head. 'The Templars.' Philippe
frowned, but Nogaret continued swiftly. 'The Church aside, the Temple is
the largest, most affluent organisation in Christendom. The Order owns
property throughout Europe, hundreds of manors and estates, many of which
generate their own income through farming. They even govern several small
towns.' Nogaret was pacing now, animated. 'They own mills and bake-
houses, shops and vineyards. They are moneylenders, given special dispensa-
tion from the pope to collect interest, as the Jews do, on those debts. Your
fleet was never completed, my lord? Well, then, take theirs!'

'Nogaret,' murmured Philippe.

The minister spoke on, not hearing. 'They have great influence in the
wool trade, charge for passage on their ships and act as protectors for
merchants. No doubt they possess vaults full of treasures and holy relics
which could create revenue from pilgrims. My lord, they keep the
treasuries of kings!'

'Nogaret!' repeated Philippe roughly. 'This is fruitless. I cannot touch
the Temple. The Jews, yes, for no one in the kingdom will mourn their
expulsion. But the warriors of Christ?' He shook his head. 'There would be
uproar.'

'Would there?' questioned Nogaret doggedly. 'You know how many people blamed the knights for the loss of the Holy Land when we first learned of Acre's fall.'

'Be that as it may, the Grand Master is the only one in Christendom endeavouring to recapture that territory.'

'And we know, once again, that the knights are failing in that task. My lord, the people do not care for Crusading any more, nor do they care for knights and their holy quests. They care for business and money, power and land. They care that their kingdom is strong and safe from attack.'

'You are right.' As Philippe said this, Nogaret halted, a keen look on his face, but his triumph soon faded as the king continued. 'The Temple is a powerful, affluent organisation. Why? Because in the two centuries since their creation the knights have had no interference. They stand outside the influence of kings. Indeed, it is the knights who have controlled monarchs over the years. The pope is the only power on this Earth who has any authority over them.'

Nogaret nodded and moved away from the king. 'I am aware of that.' He glanced at Philippe. 'But with a man of our own mind on the papal throne, that might not be an issue.'

Philippe grew still, staring at the minister.

'We could deal with two problems at once,' said Nogaret. 'Our dwindling fortunes. And Boniface.'

'I cannot think about this.' Philippe turned from him. 'It isn't even possible.'

'Anything is possible, my lord. He is just a man and a corrupt one at that. You've seen how he abuses his office. We could make sure that a better man took his place. You would be saving Christendom by such an action, not harming it.' Nogaret went to the king. 'I have thought about this long and hard. Taking the wealth of the Order will provide you with enough funds to continue your expansion and maintain the security of your kingdom. The pope will be our axe. One swing in the right place at the right time and the Temple shall fall.'

Elias made his way quickly across the courtyard of the royal fortress to where Samuel stood waiting. The elderly Jew hailed him with a question, but the rabbi was so deep in thought he didn't hear what it was. 'I am sorry, Samuel,' he murmured distractedly, as he approached. 'What did you say?'

Samuel's face was troubled as he scanned Elias's empty hands. 'I said, would he not give them to you? My accounts,' he pressed, when Elias didn't answer. 'Did he refuse to return them?' He started to move past the rabbi. 'Then I will ask him myself. I need those rolls!'

Roused from his preoccupation, Elias caught the old man's arm. 'I did not have the chance to ask him, Samuel. Come,' he said hastily, as the man protested, 'we will talk to the treasurer. I am sure he will be able to retrieve them. The king was in a meeting with one of his ministers. I did not want to interrupt.'

21

The Royal Palace, Paris

21 August 1302 AD

W ill slowed his horse as a figure stepped out in front of him. 'Simon?'
he called in surprise, his voice barely audible over the rain that
poured down, pummelling the ground and turning the street into a river. A
mist rose from rooftops, baking in midday sun only an hour earlier. The
groom wasn't wearing a cloak and his thinning hair was plastered to his
head. Swinging his leg over the saddle, Will dismounted, stiff from the
morning's ride. 'What are you doing here?'

'I've been waiting for you. A servant at the palace said you were due to
return today.' Simon glanced at the bags strapped to Will's saddle. 'Where
have you been?'

'Delivering a message for the king.' Will frowned at Simon's grim
expression. 'What is it? What has happened?' His eyes moved to the palace,
the towers of which dominated the way ahead. 'Rose?'

'It's your friend the rabbi.'

'Elias?'

'He's been trying to find you. He was – well, troubled isn't the word.
When I told him you were most likely off on business for the king if you
weren't at the palace he demanded to speak to Sir Robert, but he's been out
with the Visitor this past week. The rabbi made me swear I'd come and see
you as soon as you returned, give you a message.'

'What message?'

Simon glanced round as two men hurried past, feet splashing in the wet.
'He said, *You are in the lair of a wolf.*'

'That's it?'

'And you had to go to him. Only,' added Simon, catching Will's arm as
he dug his foot into the stirrup, 'that might be difficult. Will, the whole city
has been alive with the news all morning. On my way here I heard some
dozen people talking about it.'

'What?'

'Royal guards have stormed the Jewish Quarter. The king has declared they be exiled.'

'From Paris?' said Will incredulously.

'From France.'

'I knew nothing of this,' Will murmured. He looked at Simon. 'When did it start?'

'Dawn, from what people were saying.' The groom took a step forward as Will hauled himself into the saddle, the horse's hooves squelching in the mud as it shifted its weight. 'Do you want me to come?'

'I'll be faster on my own.' Digging his knees into the beast's sides, Will urged the horse into a canter.

The streets were almost deserted in the downpour. As he rode, Will thought of Elias's ominous message and spurred the horse on faster, across the Grand Pont and into the confusion of streets that led to the Jewish Quarter.

Even before he reached it, he encountered signs of the eviction. Streams of people were hurrying past, all marked with the red wheel. He saw one man carrying a boy in his arms. Another child was clinging to his shoulders, red-faced and screaming. A woman struggled behind, dragging a sack through the sludge. Two girls, clutching one another, were crying as they stumbled along, long hair dripping down their backs. The street here was churned up, many people having passed through recently. Will glimpsed a couple of shoes, sucked from feet by the mud, the owners in too much haste to go back for them. A few people leaned out of windows, watching the exodus. Will caught one man cheering half-heartedly, but the sound was soon drowned in the tumult of the rain as he rode on into the quarter.

The place was crawling with royal guards. Will pulled up, his horse snorting and veering agitatedly. A woman screamed as a soldier pushed the man she was with to the ground and kicked at him. The man tried to rise and fend off the blows, but two more soldiers ran in to aid their comrade and the man curled up, disappearing under their mailed boots. Another was grasping a sack to his chest, yelling at a soldier who was trying to wrest it from him. Sounds of shouting and things breaking echoed from the interior of houses, many of whose doors had been broken open. People's possessions were strewn across the mud: a red cloak, a golden candelabra, a silver bowl, rain bouncing off it. Further down the street, Will caught sight of what looked like a pile of clothing, but realised it was a body. Male, female, dead or unconscious, he couldn't tell. There were carts piled high with treasures, the harnessed oxen lowing in the rain. He looked round as a royal guard, coming out of a building, challenged him. Ignoring the soldier's shouts for him to halt, Will steered his horse off down a narrow side street heading for Elias's house, past a synagogue where threads of smoke were creeping through the smashed shutters.

Approaching, he saw that the door of the orange house was hanging open. Fear swelled in his mind. This street was quieter, but signs of devastation were all around him and there were more bodies here. Will tethered the horse to a post outside one of the booksellers', then entered the dark hallway. Hearing noises beyond the kitchen door, he drew his broadsword. The balance was still awkward in his hand. The blade had been given to him by Wallace, after his falchion had been broken at Falkirk. Since then he'd rarely had cause to use it and he wasn't yet comfortable with it. With his attention fixed on the closed door, he didn't see the overturned stool in front of him. It skidded on the tiles as his leg connected with it and the noises in the kitchen stopped. Cursing, he shoved open the door and barged in.

The first thing he saw was a wide-eyed old woman, pressed against the wall behind a man, who looked no less terrified, but was standing protectively in front of her, wielding a kitchen knife. Crouched near the fireplace were three more men. They were surrounding a fourth figure, stretched out on the floor. Will had time to see blood splatters on the tiles and on the prone figure's robes, before he recognised him.

'Dear God.' He sheathed his sword. 'Elias?'

'Get back!' commanded one of the Jews, rising to face him.

'William?' came a withered voice from the floor.

'Try not to move,' said one man, pressing a hand on the rabbi's chest.

The Jew barring Will's way moved aside reluctantly, as he pushed past. Will felt anguish slam through him as he saw the cause of the rabbi's prostration. The old man had been blinded. Both eyes had been removed, leaving ragged holes that wept blood on to his cheeks. He knelt and grasped the old man's hand. 'Who did this, Elias? What is happening here?'

'Royal soldiers,' answered one of the men, before the rabbi could speak. Will thought he had seen him before. His hands were fists on his knees. 'They came before dawn. We had no warning. They said we were being banished on the orders of King Philippe, that all our possessions and properties were forfeit to the crown. Anyone who protested was wounded, some were killed. Elias tried to reason with them.'

'I must speak.'

The men looked round at the whisper. Elias was trying to sit.

'Rabbi, please!'

'No, Isaac. I must speak to William. Alone.'

Hearing the order in that voice, however frail, the men and the woman began to move out reluctantly. Isaac touched Will's shoulder on the way past. Bending down, he spoke into his ear. 'We came back for him when the soldiers moved on.' He glanced at Elias. 'But I do not think he has long and we must leave the city.'

'I will stay with him.' As they left, Will stared down at Elias, unable to believe the old bookseller, who had always seemed so filled with life, could be reduced to this. He had seen a lot of death in his years, but there was something so utterly senseless about this violence that it struck at the core of him, demanding explanation. Justice. 'I am so sorry,' he murmured. 'Simon gave me your message. If I had known anything of this attack on your people, I would have—'

'This wasn't what that was about,' croaked Elias. His head turned in Will's direction, causing more blood to dribble down his cheeks. 'I did not expect this. My message was about the Temple. I needed to warn you.'

Will clutched Elias's hand as his head fell back with a soft thud on the tiles.

After a moment, he heaved out a breath. 'I was at the palace and I heard one of the ministers talking with the king. A lawyer called de Nogaret.'

Elias's voice was so quiet Will had to put his head close to the rabbi's mouth to hear him.

'I heard him say the pope will be their axe.'

'Their axe?' Will questioned, when Elias failed to continue. 'What did he mean?'

'One swing,' murmured the rabbi. 'One swing at the right time and the Temple shall fall.' His head jerked up, causing Will to sit back. 'His coffers are empty. That is why he did this, here today.'

'Are you saying he intends to attack the Order?' Will asked urgently.

'I do not know,' breathed Elias. 'That was all I heard of their conversation. It was the lawyer who said it.'

'It won't happen,' said Will, after a pause. 'It cannot. The pope is hardly an ally of the king's.'

'Perhaps they mean to put pressure on him. Or worse?'

The question loomed in the hush. Will answered it quickly. 'Yes, the king is in dispute with Boniface, but it is purely political. He would never move against Rome.'

'You can look upon me, upon what they did on his orders, and say that with such certainty?'

Will felt the accusation like a blow. He looked away from Elias's ravaged face.

'Philippe is not the answer to your prayers, William.' Elias was grimacing, as if every word hurt him. 'There is a devil behind that throne. But you cannot see it. You do not want to see it, because the king has promised to be your ally, your instrument of vengeance. Where will the money for your Scottish cause come from next?' Elias raised his hand weakly and brought it towards his face. 'It will come from me. From the blood of my people.'

Will closed his eyes.

'Shame on you, William! Shame on you for refusing to see the truth. You let yourself be taken over by revenge, by its selfish, empty promise. You abandoned everything you swore to serve, everyone you pledged to protect. For more than a century men have given their lives in service to the ideals of the Brethren, those who worked directly for it and those who supported it. And for a personal vendetta, you throw all that away.' Elias was wheezing, but he gripped Will's hand with startling strength. 'You should have remained in the Temple as head of the Anima Templi. Instead, you left, doing nothing to prevent the Grand Master following his Crusade, nothing to stop the Brethren losing their purpose. But it wasn't your cause to abandon. It was the cause of a hundred men before you. It was Everard's and your father's. *Kalawun's*. Mine. How dare you squander our hopes, our blood, on hatred and weakness! How dare you, William!' Elias wrenched his hand from Will's and turned away, teeth clenching.

Will was mortified. 'Don't say that, Elias. I didn't . . .' But he couldn't finish. All his excuses for deserting the Temple and abandoning the Brethren stuck in his throat.

'You were a commander in the Temple, a man of honour. You were, Everard always told me, your father's son. You were elected head of a brotherhood of men whose ideals lifted them above the prejudice of their age, who worked for the benefit of all people, no matter their faith. You were these things. What have you become? A bitter man. A mercenary. An errand runner for a tyrant king, who abuses his people, steals and lies.'

'Elias. Please.'

'In using Philippe against Edward you have been trying to fight darkness with darkness. What will come of that? No light, that is for certain.'

Will hung his head. He thought of the sense of purpose he felt coming into Paris with Wallace at his side and then the months that trundled into years since then, drawn along by Philippe's promises of more aid for Scotland and his insistence, despite the truce, that his feud with Edward was far from over. He thought of the scraps of money the king had given to their cause; token gestures, designed to keep the friendship of the Scots, should he ever need them to occupy Edward's forces in the north. He had known this, but hadn't let himself think about it. He had been treading water for more than two years, drifting, unable to move against the currents that surrounded him, pulling him this way and that. Elias had just pushed him under. 'I . . .' His jaw tightened. 'I do not know what to do. Hugues de Pairaud has taken over the Anima Templi and allied himself with Edward. My personal hatred of the man aside, I know the king has corrupted the Brethren and used them for his own ends. But Hugues would never let me back in, I'm certain of it. The only ally I have left in the Temple is Robert de Paris and he can hardly look at me these days. The things I have done.' Will stared at his hands, almost expecting to see the stains. 'My daughter will not speak to me. And the war I fought and bled for is stalled, Wallace and his men gone to ground.' He shook his head slowly. 'I have lost my way.'

'Then you must find it.' Elias sought Will's hands with his own. He held them, weakly now. 'Swear you will. Swear it on the lives of those who have gone before you, on the lives of those men and their hopes for this world. Do not let those hopes die with you. Make sure we go on.'

'But how can . . . ?' Will sat forward as Elias's hands slipped from his. 'Elias?' He grasped the rabbi's shoulders. 'I swear it. Do you hear me, Elias? I swear it!'

But the rabbi was dead and there was nothing but silence to answer him.

The Temple, Paris, 28 August 1302 AD

'After forty days, Perceval came to a land, blackened and scorched by a savage sun. And in the distance, he beheld a ruined tower.'

As the figure in the glittering fish-scale cloak stretched out his arm, Martin de Floyran followed with his eyes. In the candlelight, shadows swayed on the wall and the young man felt he could almost see a tower rising dark behind one of the masked men who lined the chamber. The air was stifling, but he shivered, trying to resist the urge to wrap his arms around his bare chest. He wore a loincloth, but felt naked under the hooded gazes of the others. There was a sick feeling in his stomach. It had begun during his night in vigil, fear and excitement bubbling up through him in the waiting darkness where he had knelt alone. He had longed for this moment and its arrival was the culmination of years of hopes and expectations, only the reality was far from what he had imagined. His uncle had told him this would be the proudest day of his life. But Martin felt no pride, just a mounting sense of fear, the sick feeling overwhelming him.

'Perceval entered the tower and by a winding stair came to the top-most chamber. He found himself in an empty room, the floor and walls scarred and bare. On a crumbling dais stood a broken throne. Windows looked upon a desert, parched and desolate. The floor around the dais was scattered with the bones and skulls of men.'

The cloaked figure stepped aside and Martin drew in a sharp breath as he saw the floor behind him was indeed littered with bones. Candlelight threw a ruddy glow across them.

'Upon the throne there was a man. His head was bowed, his body withered by famine.'

Two of the masked men moved forward and drew apart what Martin had thought was a wall, but now realised was a black cloth. Beyond was a recess. It was filled with a wooden dais, on which stood a battered throne, occupied by a hunched figure in a hooded cloak. As Martin watched, his breath suspended, the figure rose and lurched down from the dais, hands held out, palms upraised.

'Join me,' it whispered, in a scabrous voice. 'My men are dead, my army defeated. Join me.'

Martin looked around him at the men in masks, searching for comfort. But fifty-four white stags' heads stared back dispassionately. The figure stumbled towards him and now he could smell something unpleasant coming from it.

'Join me!' The figure shrugged the cloak from his shoulders.

Martin barely managed to bite back a cry. Under the cloak the man was naked, except for a ragged loincloth. His skin glistened in the candlelight. From head to foot, he was slick with blood. It dripped from his scalp, where his hair was matted with it, and trickled down his cheeks. Already, a pool was collecting on the floor around him. Martin saw a bloody trail leading from the throne.

'What say you, Perceval?' demanded the figure in the glittering cloak. 'Will you join him? Fight for him?'

'No,' said Martin, shaking his head. 'No!'

The bloodied figure sank to the floor and was hidden from view, the cloaked man moving in front of him. 'And when Perceval denied the bloody king, day turned at once to darkness.'

Martin couldn't stop the trembling in his body as around him all the men crouched and extinguished the candles in front of them. The only sounds in the darkness were the whispering of hems on the stones and Martin's rapid breaths. He knelt there, poised for the unknown, desperate for the trial to be over.

'Then all at once, dawn broke. And it was soft and beautiful.' The cloaked figure's voice was hushed, reverent. A muted glow lit his cowl. It grew brighter as he took his hand from the candle, the flame of which he had been cupping. 'The tower had gone and Perceval found himself in a verdant forest. A noble white hart, its antlers slender and new, was cropping the turf. Between the trees, Perceval glimpsed a proud fortress of many spires and turrets. Flags of every colour blazed in the morning light and faint on the breeze he could hear the fair call of trumpets. Perceval yearned to go to it, for he felt inside he would find shelter and comrades. But the fortress was surrounded by a broad moat and the drawbridge was raised. Before him on the bank stood a knight, his white surcoat unstained by blood or toil.'

Another man moved in at the figure's side and held a candle to the flame. As the wick flared, Martin saw it was a tall knight, dressed in a plain white surcoat and faceless helm. With the change in atmosphere and the growing light, Martin's heart slowed.

'Will you join me, Perceval?' asked the knight. 'Together, we can ford this river and cross to the castle beyond. Inside, we will at last find safety. Will you join me?'

Martin nodded uncertainly. 'Yes,' he whispered, when he realised the knight was waiting for a more definite response. 'I will join you.' He raised his voice and lifted his head, starting to wonder if he had been terrified for nothing. He felt worried, thinking what impression he had made. Had anyone heard his cry of fear? Seen his quaking body?

'You have chosen the path,' said the man in the glittering cloak. 'And it was wisely chosen. You have sworn the oaths and stood fast in the face of temptation and dread. Now comes the final test and the most perilous. But obey me and all will be well. Will you obey me, Perceval?'

'I will obey you.'

'Then prove it!' The figure dropped to a crouch and snatched back the cowl to reveal a grinning skull.

Martin shrank back in terror as the man produced a small golden cross and held it out before him.

'Spit on this. Prove you are loyal to me alone. Prove you are one with your brethren. Do it now! Or suffer the consequences.'

Martin leaned over and let a glob of spit fall from his lips on to the cross. He closed his eyes as he did it, the Paternoster rolling over and over in his mind.

The figure stowed the cross inside his fish-scale cloak. He placed the candle on the floor, then raised his hand and gripped the protruding chin of the skull mask. For a moment, Martin thought he was going to remove it. But instead, the figure turned the mask and a different visage appeared. It was a smooth, white face, with the prominent cheekbones – perhaps carved from wood – and strong chin of a young man. Brown hair dangled to either side of it, fixed to the top of the mask. Martin thought he could see part of a third face, behind the hair, but his gaze was distracted as the figure spoke.

'You have passed the test. Arise, Sir Martin de Floyran, for you are now a knight and in the presence of brothers.'

The figure stepped back as Martin rose unsteadily. The men lining the chamber came forward to embrace him and kiss his cheeks. But all Martin could see was his saliva dribbling down to desecrate the symbol of Christ.

2 2

Near Château Vincennes, the Kingdom of France

20 June 1303 AD

D own on the marshy flats where pale gold reeds lined the banks of the meandering river, a heron stood sentry, watching for fish. A breeze swept the blue waters. Ducks bobbed on the eddying surface, their raucous calls like mad laughter. Above, smaller birds struggled against the gusts, feathery white clouds racing high beyond them.

Some distance from the river, the company of men, almost one hundred strong, drew up on the firmer ground. The varlets kept the hounds on short leashes, tapping their hinds with sticks whenever one uttered a low keening sound. The dogs' ears were pressed flat against their heads, nerves tightening as they sensed the quarry arrayed before them. Behind the dogs and huntsmen, the courtiers lined up astride their jostling mounts: ministers and high officials, lords and princes, gaudy in their fine velvet cloaks and hats, many of which were crowned with peacock or swan feathers. In between the horses, pages and squires moved about, adjusting girth straps, passing skins of wine or water up to their masters.

Sir Henri, the Master Falconer, steered his horse to the front to order the two cadgers to the edge of the field. Inside the cadges, which were strapped to the backs of the men, were over a dozen birds, leashed to padded perches. All were hooded, their small heads flicking this way and that as they caught the calls of the ducks. There were gyrfalcons, a couple of goshawks, an elegant saker and several powdery-grey peregrines. The cadgers waited patiently as the hunting party decided which birds would fly together. They had been out for several hours already and had flown the goshawks and four falcons. The corpses of three mallards, two hares and one pheasant were stuffed into the hunting bags.

'Sir Henri?' called King Philippe, mounted on his sleek black mare. 'Shall we test the skills of your new acquisition?'

There were grins among the courtiers as Henri inclined his head and nodded to an aide, who crossed to one of the cadges. Opening the frame, he unleashed the dappled saker and coaxed her on to his gloved hand, keeping a tight hold on the jesses as he withdrew her and passed her to Sir Henri. No bird was given to Philippe, who already had Maiden poised on his wrist. The peregrine wore a hood of soft calfskin, decorated with the gossamer feather of a dove she had killed the week before. Philippe nudged his mare with his knees and walked her down to meet Henri. He glanced at the river. The ducks had moved a little way downstream, but the heron was still stalking the marshy bank.

Sir Henri offered up a prayer for the success of the hunt and the safety of the birds. '*In nomine Domini, volatilia celi erunt sub pedibus tuis.*'

In the name of the Lord, the birds of the heavens shall be beneath thy feet.

'On the count of three,' said Philippe, smiling confidently.

At the same moment, the two men pulled the hoods from the birds, then cast them from their wrists. The silver bells attached to the jesses jingled, causing the smaller birds in the sky to dart in different directions. The saker went soaring up and left, veering away from the water as the wind lifted under her wings. Henri cursed beneath his breath. Maiden flew up to a nearby tree and settled gracefully on a branch. Philippe watched patiently as she beat her smoke-coloured wings and roused herself, settling her feathers, priming herself for the flight. Some moments later, she ascended into the sky. All the party watched as she rose, riding the air currents in looping, lazy circles, towering higher and higher, heading for the base of the clouds and cover. The saker, struggling to gain control, followed in her upward path. The ducks had fallen quiet, sensing danger, but the heron hadn't yet glimpsed the two predators that were now specks in the wide, racing sky.

'She is a true joy to watch, my lord,' said Will, moving his horse up alongside Philippe.

Philippe smiled, but said nothing, his wintry eyes fixed on the peregrine's distant position.

'How long did it take Sir Henri to train her?'

Philippe glanced at him. 'I trained her myself. It took me twenty-five days.'

'The shortest time I've ever known an eyass to be tamed,' commented Sir Henri, who was in earshot.

'I wanted to thank you, my lord,' continued Will, 'for introducing me to the sport. I never knew how exhilarating it would prove. The Temple forbade us from hunting of any kind. The only beast we were allowed to pursue was the lion.'

'A taming of the pride,' observed Philippe wryly.

'Just one of their many outdated Rules.'

Philippe took his attention from Maiden and fixed it on Will. 'I wonder, Campbell, since you are so disparaging about the Order, why you remained within its ranks for so long?'

Will held the king's gaze, but inside he was concerned by that searching look. For some while, he had been trying to work his way into Philippe's trust, but the king had spent the first half of the year on campaign in Flanders and there had been scant opportunity for him to do so.

Having acquired enough funds from the auction of the Jews' property to equip an army, the king set out to avenge his defeat at Courtrai and, finally, secured a victory over the Flemish. A truce was signed, which was more of a constraint than an agreement, the Flemish belligerent, but finally subdued under the French crown. Philippe, who did not enter the battle himself, returned triumphant to Paris whereupon he transferred his court to the royal estate at Vincennes, his childhood home.

'Duty,' Will answered finally. 'Family obligations.' He shrugged. 'I was brought up by the Temple. The Order was all I knew. It can take time to see the truth of what you are closest to, to view it with new eyes, and when I started to realise that I didn't agree with their ideals and Rules any more, that the Order had become diluted, weakened by petty leaders gazing back at a golden past that would never come again, I was afraid to leave it. It took their alliance with Edward against my homeland to give me the courage to do what I had contemplated for so long.'

Philippe nodded and looked away, seemingly satisfied. 'I hear you received word from Scotland last week. I take it our friend, Sir William, is well?'

Now it was Will's turn to study Philippe. Was the king keeping a closer eye on him too? 'It wasn't from Wallace. It was from my sister.' He looked away across the water, not wanting to be drawn on the subject.

Ysenda's letter, the first he'd received in years, had been a mixed blessing. His sister spent much of it speaking of the marriage of Margaret to a nephew of Ede's husband. When Will read she was with child, he noticed the letter was dated five months earlier and wondered if his niece had given birth already. David had returned to Wallace in Selkirk for a time, but when the warrior went to ground, his nephew moved back to Elgin, where he entered the household guard of a prominent lord. He had won two tournaments and Alice was courting one of his friends. At the end Will read with a pang of envy that Gray had sent Christian to live with them, fearing for her safety as Edward's bloodhounds continued to pursue the rebels.

Since Elias's death, he had felt more alone than ever, tormented by guilt, anger and indecision. The letter's arrival made him want to leave France and return to his family. He had lost them once, through the passing of years. He couldn't bear to do so again, a fear that was worsened because of Rose, who still refused even to acknowledge his presence. She was a spirit, a thin, insubstantial figure that drifted past him in the passageways, not turning as he called to her. Gradually, his calls became hopeful smiles, which eventually faded into courteous nods until now they just passed one another in silence.

But even through Will's turmoil one thing remained constant, growing stronger with every day that passed: his promise to Elias. The rabbi's dying words had provoked something unexpected in him, something powerful and compelling. He realised, despite the breaking of his oaths and his desertion, that he still believed in the Anima Templi and its aims, and he still felt like their leader. No one had stripped him of that title but himself and slowly, tentatively, Will began to pull that mantle back around him, spending nights in the palace lying awake, wondering what Everard and the Seneschal, his father and the others would do. After a long, reluctant silence, their ghosts began to crowd in, whispering suggestions. He knew the first thing he must do was find out the veracity of what Elias had heard.

The courtiers were murmuring excitedly, heads lifted to the sky, eyes shielded from the glare. Will could see the saker, circling the base of a cloud, but there was no sign of Maiden.

'Have the lures ready,' Philippe called to the squires. 'Just in case.'

'I did hear from Sir William Wallace in your absence,' ventured Will. 'There is a rumour that Edward is to begin a new campaign in Scotland this summer. Wallace was keen to have your assurance that we can continue to count on you for funds to defend ourselves and to put pressure on Edward, along with the pope.'

Philippe's face closed up at the mention of Boniface and Will cursed himself. The dispute between the king and the pope had escalated and the two were currently locked in a grim battle of wills. He was trying to think of a way to re-engage the king in conversation and steer it back to the Temple, when one of the squires shouted.

There was a flash of movement in the sky. Maiden came out of the sun in a ferocious stoop, fast as a lightning strike, a grey missile bearing down on the unsuspecting heron. The hunting party cheered as she dropped like a stone to land on the heron's head, those razor talons sinking into flesh and brain, crushing the life out of the bird. Philippe barked a command at the varlets as the heron unfurled its wings and tried to fight. Two of the hounds were unleashed and went streaking across the grass to aid the falcon in pinning the quarry down. The animals had lived and worked together for years and moved as a finely tuned instrument, the dogs creeping in to bite and pull at the heron's legs, while Maiden finished the kill. The saker was swooping down to join them, but the peregrine was the victor and she would receive the heart as a treat.

Will turned from the struggling heron, now in its death throes as the dogs gripped and tugged, to look at Philippe. There was an expression of fierce joy on the king's face. Will was struck by the admiration in that look; it was the admiration that comes from shared skill and passion. Maiden's ability to go after something with such single-minded savagery, to pursue a target so much bigger than she was and cling to it until she or it were dead, these were things Philippe respected. The king had gone after Pope Boniface in the same way and had similarly pursued Flanders and Gascony, the insurrection in Guienne having been brutally put down, the truce with Edward cemented. For the first time since Elias had revealed to him the conversation overheard between Philippe and Nogaret, Will felt a chill of fear. If Philippe did indeed mean to go after the Temple, he would do so relentlessly.

As if hearing his thoughts, Guillaume de Nogaret materialised, trotting his horse down to the king. The minister wore the same black robes he always did, although now his cloak had a trim of scarlet around the collar and hem, the same colour as the royal seals he had become the keeper of after Flote's death.

'My lord,' Nogaret called, throwing a mistrustful look at Will, 'the scouts believe they have caught the tracks of a boar leading into the woods.'

'Have they?' Philippe turned to his chattering courtiers. 'What do you say? One more pursuit before the day ends and we feast?'

A hearty cheer answered him. Philippe grinned, dug his spurs in and set off at Nogaret's side, leaving Will to fall in with the rest of the hunting party, thwarted and troubled.

Château Vincennes, the Kingdom of France, 20 June 1303 AD

Rose drew the comb through the queen's thick black hair. Now and then, the teeth snagged on tiny knots and she slowed the movement, working the tangles apart until the comb carried on through. Jeanne's face floated in the mirror, like the moon in a pool. Her eyes were closed, giving Rose an opportunity to study her. The queen had been unusually subdued since they arrived at the château two weeks ago. Rose had sensed a strain between her and the king, who had been away on campaign and hadn't wanted his wife to join him. Jeanne's face was pale in the sunlight coming through the window and Rose could see a prominent dusting of black hair across her upper lip. Marguerite had delicately offered to use the tweezers on it, but the queen had brushed aside the suggestion.

Jeanne had always been more concerned about books and learning than the same chores of beauty other noble women in the court seemed to spend their lives performing: buying perfumed soaps, ivory combs and sparkling necklaces from Venetian traders in the markets, admiring one another's gowns in the hallways then talking snidely behind each other's backs at dinner in the Great Hall. As a handmaiden, important enough to be in the same chambers as these noble ladies, but unimportant enough not to be noticed, Rose heard it all. Marguerite and the other girls used their status as the queen's attendants to charm trinkets out of Jeanne, so they could play at being princesses, floating about like pretty, flimsy butterflies, provoking the attention of eligible lords and officials. Rose, more invisible than the others, had once spotted Blanche with one of the steward's aides in a gloomy corridor of the palace. She had been pressed to a wall, the aide pushed against her, his mouth on her neck and his hand up her bunched dress. Blanche's head had been twisted to the side, the expression on her flushed face somewhere between ecstasy and embarrassment.

'I wonder what they have caught on the hunt?'

Rose gave a start, realising the queen's eyes were open and she was staring at her.

'I heard Sir Henri say there could be boar,' answered Marguerite, bustling around the room, gathering the queen's garments and handing them to Blanche who placed them dutifully on the bed. 'What do you wish to wear at the feast tonight, madam?'

'You choose.'

In the mirror, Rose saw Marguerite smile.

'I think the red and the gold. Yes. That will look beautiful.' Marguerite's smile widened. 'The king will not be able to take his eyes off you.'

Rose noticed Marguerite's gaze dart to her, the handmaiden's face becoming hostile. She wondered what the look meant, but was distracted as the queen spoke.

'Leave me for a moment. I wish to speak to Rose.'

Rose's puzzlement gave way to unease.

'Of course, madam,' said Marguerite. Throwing another look, this one almost triumphant, in Rose's direction, she left, hustling Blanche and the three other handmaidens in front of her.

Rose forced herself to continue combing, trying to keep her hands steady as she coaxed and teased the tangles.

'I grew up in this house, Rose,' began Jeanne, her soft voice taking on a dreamy quality. Her eyes were closed again. 'I was an infant when I came here, after the death of my father. Philippe was with me when I learned to read and to ride a horse, with me when my mother married again and moved to England. He was with me all the way up to the point where he ceased being as a brother to me and became my husband. I've loved him from that first day.' Jeanne's eyes opened. Her hand came up and gripped Rose's wrist, halting the comb. 'I know my husband is a handsome man. But I fear your infatuation is turning into obsession. It must stop.'

Rose wanted to deny what the queen was saying, but her guilt was there in the mirror, caught in her flaming red face; a sun behind Jeanne's pale moon.

Jeanne let go of her wrist. 'You may go. Send Marguerite in. She can finish my hair.'

Rose set the comb on the table and walked unsteadily to the door. Entering the dormitory beyond, she saw the handmaidens huddled in a tight circle that parted as she came in. From the look on Marguerite's face, she realised they knew what the queen wanted to speak to her about. She felt as though the queen had just made her strip off and stand before them all, naked and ashamed. She prayed to God Philippe didn't know. The thought made her squirm inside.

Marguerite flounced towards the queen's chamber. 'Did you really believe he would ever look at you?' she whispered as she passed, her gaze going pointedly to Rose's scarred hand.

As the other girls followed her, Rose went to the window and pretended to look out. She felt someone move in behind her.

'You should be careful, Rose,' came Blanche's quiet voice. 'The queen is most displeased. If I were you I would focus my affection elsewhere. There are plenty of handsome men in the royal court. Even if you do not want them you can pretend, so madam thinks you have forgotten your amour.'

Rose rounded on her. 'And then what? Should I let one grope me in the shadows to make the pretence complete?'

The colour drained from Blanche's face. Turning, she fled. As the door banged shut, Rose flung herself on to her narrow bed. Anger coursed through her, molten, insatiable. She was angry at herself for letting her desires become noticed, at Marguerite and her snide ways, at Blanche for thinking she had any idea how she felt. Most of all she was angry at the queen and her dour, pasty face. Closing her eyes, she imagined Jeanne falling from her horse in a terrible accident. Her neck snapping as she hit the ground. A swift, painless, tragic death. Philippe at her funeral, silent and strong. Her hand, later, a comfort on his arm. Him burying his head in her breast, letting his tears come. Their falling would be slow and tender, as the period of mourning was observed, but it would only make the passion more intense when they finally admitted their love.

Château Vincennes, the Kingdom of France, 21 June 1303 AD

'This cannot be our only option?'

Nogaret frowned as Pierre Dubois, one of the five other men in the chamber, voiced his doubts again. 'We have been over this, Minister.'

'Yes, but we are still not all in agreement,' replied Dubois sharply, looking at Nogaret.

'What else are we supposed to do? The pope has made his intentions apparent in his latest bull: bow down to him or risk excommunication. If we do not take a stand now we might as well let Rome tie its leash around our neck and France will become its obedient dog.'

'Are we certain excommunication is threatened in the pope's proclamation?' The quiet voice belonged to a prematurely grey, austere minister named Guillaume de Plaisans. He collected the bull from the table, decorated with the pope's seal, which was starting to crack, the bull having been studied often during the past six months since its arrival in the royal court. 'It is an odd letter indeed, full of biblical allusions, but few clear intentions. Nowhere does Boniface even mention France.'

Nogaret leaned over the minister's shoulder. 'Here,' he said, pointing to the parchment. '*When the Greeks and others claim not to be subject to Peter and his successors, by the same claim they affirm that they are not members of the flock of Christ. For there shall be one fold and one shepherd.* And others?' said Nogaret. 'I think it is clear enough. If we are not part of the flock we do not come under the authority or protection of the Church. We stand alone.'

'Sir Pierre Flote feared this very threat,' commented Dubois darkly. 'We should have listened to his counsel more closely.'

'Flote is dead,' responded Nogaret. 'His speculations are no longer relevant.'

'Enough, Chancellor de Nogaret,' said Philippe, as Dubois and a couple of the others made to retort, anger rising in their faces. 'You will show your predecessor the respect he deserves.'

'My lord,' submitted Nogaret.

'But the chancellor is right,' Philippe continued, studying the men clustered around the table. 'We must remain strong or France will suffer.' The king's eyes went to the bull in Plaisans's hand. '*Unam Sanctam* is his most pompous edict yet. You are correct, Minister de Plaisans, it isn't entirely transparent in its intentions, but Pope Boniface's belief in his own superiority has never been clearer.' Philippe paused, recalling the words he had read so often he knew them by heart. '*Therefore, we declare, state, define and pronounce that it is altogether necessary to salvation for every human creature to be subject to the Roman Pontiff.*' The king exhaled suddenly. 'He has given me no choice,' he murmured, no longer looking at them.

'We must act as one in this matter,' insisted Nogaret, turning to the ministers. 'Next month in Paris, we will hold a second council of the Estates to gain the support of our subjects. At the assembly, we will denounce *Unam Sanctam* and proclaim Boniface as a heretic. Further-more,' he continued harshly, as Dubois shook his head and looked away, 'you will no longer call the pope by the name he chose, in conversation or on paper. You will call him by his secular name, Benedict Caetani. We no longer recognise him as our spiritual leader on this Earth. The ban on the export of money to Rome is once again in place, but we will extend that ban to include the clergy themselves. For the time being, none of them will be allowed to leave France. It will stop the pope from acquiring funds or information from those bishops still loyal to him.'

'Does all this have your blessing, my lord?' said Dubois, moving past Nogaret and planting his hands on the king's table.

Philippe looked up. 'It does,' he said, after a pause. He waved his hand. 'Go, all of you, I wish to speak to Nogaret alone. Go!' he ordered, when Dubois seemed reluctant to move. The king stood when the door had shut and went to the window. He looked out over the forest, spread below him. The freedom he had felt yesterday on the hunt was long gone. He felt trapped in the prison of his mind. It was a dark cell, filled with painful things that worried at him in the blackness. 'We will do it.'

'My lord?'

'As soon as we denounce him, the pope will excommunicate me. There is no other way for this conflict to end. You are right, we can perhaps damage Boniface's reputation by naming him a heretic, but in the end he still holds the power. If France is excommunicated all the treaties we have formed, with Edward, Flanders, Scotland and elsewhere will be declared invalid. The agreements for the territories I have bought will be rescinded. Trade in or out of the kingdom will cease. Any French citizen abroad will be open to arrest or harm, ships seized, cargo taken.' Philippe turned to Nogaret. 'I will not let my reign suffer through his actions. We do it, Nogaret. We execute your plan.'

Nogaret's eyes filled with triumph. 'It is the right decision. And with Boniface gone and a more sympathetic pope on the throne, we can make our move against the Temple. You have been forced to put your plans for expansion on hold for almost seven years, my lord. Finally, you can make your reign as great as your grandfather's and France as powerful as it once was under your Capetian ancestors.' He smiled. 'Warrior kings of a mighty empire.'

Philippe returned to the table and sat. 'When the assembly of the Estates is over, you will go to Italy. Boniface resides for most of the time in Anagni, only travelling into Rome for councils and ceremonies. He will be more easily open to attack there, but you will need help, for he has many allies in the city of his birth.'

'I have already thought about this. We will contact the Colonnas. Most of them fled to France when the pope exiled them, but they are still powerful and have supporters in Italy.'

Philippe nodded. 'It is a good plan. You will take a small force from here who will assist you in arresting the pope and bringing him back to France.'

'Arresting him?' Nogaret's brow furrowed. 'My lord, I beg your pardon, but perhaps you misunderstand me. I did not mean for him to face a trial. I meant for us to finish him.'

'Killing him in an attack will achieve nothing. Arresting him for heresy, bringing him back to France to face trial and judgement? These things will irrevocably damage the reputation of the Church in the eyes of the West. It will render the papacy and the man who fills that office fallible, and that I will be the one to expose this will make my throne the more dominant of the two. Church will stand beneath state, beneath France.' Philippe clasped his hands tightly on the table. 'As it should be, should it not?' He looked up at Nogaret. 'The Church should care for my people's souls, not their earthly needs. It should not be allowed to determine royal policy.'

'No,' said Nogaret firmly. 'It should not.' He hesitated. 'But a trial could be a protracted, complicated affair and we run the risk of losing support by—'

'Boniface will never reach Paris. You will make it appear as an accident. But make it quick. I do not want him to suffer.'

A slow smile spread across Nogaret's face as he understood. 'Poison could—'

Philippe rose swiftly. 'I do not wish to know the method. That Boniface was arrested for heresy and was on his way to face a trial should be enough to elevate our position over the Church. We will say his heart gave out; it was diseased by the evil in it, the corruption in his mind had spread to his body. Afterwards, you will travel to Rome and contact our supporters in the Sacred College. Since the Estates backed our move against the pope last year, we have gained more allies there. Make certain, through them, that I have a say in who is to wear the papal crown.'

'Boniface's undoing will be your making, my lord,' said Nogaret, quiet now, his victory set.

Philippe said nothing, but folded the papal bull and placed it under a stack of parchments on the table. 'You will take a company of my personal guards with you to Anagni.' He counted off a list of six names. 'And William Campbell.'

Nogaret frowned. 'Why the Scot?'

'He was once a high-ranking Templar. I think we could use him.'

'We hardly know him.'

'He has performed every errand I have sent him on.'

'The exchange of messages and money, simple deliveries, nothing more. How do we know we can trust him? Especially given his links to the Order?'

'He has no love of the Temple, that much is clear, and I do not know if I can trust him which is why I want you to take him with you. Get to know him, but do not tell him of our plans, or the other guards for that matter. They will only be told of the arrest. You will do the deed alone.'

'My lord -'

'When I make my move against the Temple I do not want any surprises. If he can be trusted, Campbell can provide us with invaluable information on the Order. He knows the Temple's inner workings, details of their assets and property.' Philippe raised his hand as Nogaret opened his mouth. 'My decision is final.'

'Yes.'

'Now leave me. I wish to pray.'

When the door shut, Philippe crossed the chamber. His limbs felt leaden as he drew aside the black curtains, embroidered with the arms of France, and entered his private chapel. The tiny recess contained a small altar with a crucifix nailed to the wall. He knelt on the stone and put his palms together. His skin was clammy. 'Most gracious lord, forgive me for the mortal sin that will be committed at my command. But there is a man on St Peter's throne, who seeks only dominance for himself and who has corrupted that holy office through his actions against your most faithful sons and daughters. The pope must be stopped, for the good of all my subjects and indeed for the people of Christendom. The world is changing, Father. We must change with it.' Philippe pressed his hands tighter, until they were slick with sweat. 'I know this must be your will, for why else would you have sent Nogaret to me? Why else would you allow this to happen?' He opened his eyes and stared at the crucifix. 'If I am wrong in this action give me a sign. Show me that I am wrong. Speak and I shall hear it. Command and I shall listen.' Philippe pushed himself to his feet and placed his palms on the wall to either side of the crucifix. 'Stay my hand, Father,' he implored. 'As . . . as you did with Abraham. Send a sign to me. Anything!'

But no voice resounded in his head, no angel descended, no tears slipped from the wooden Christ. There was nothing but cold, hard silence, an abyss of it echoing into empty eternity. It was all he ever heard.

23
Ferentino, Italy
4 September 1303 AD

W ill stood in the window and watched another line of men riding up the dusty track towards the castle gate. They had been arriving in companies of varying sizes for the past two days and the courtyard was crammed with horses and men. Soldiers slumped in the shade, drinking water from skins and conversing restlessly, their knight-masters having retired to chambers. The fresh scent of olive and eucalyptus trees drifted from the rocky hills that tumbled around the town of Ferentino and, closer, the tang of wild herbs was a relief from the stink of horse dung that pervaded the sweltering air. Will glanced down at a rapid movement beneath him to see a black lizard dart across the window ledge. The sun was starting to sink towards the hills and the busy drone of cicadas rose in the blush of evening.

As a bell clanged hollowly in the town below, Will's gaze moved to the nearby church tower, then drifted to a line of cypress trees that marched up the slope below the castle gate. He raked the branches with his stare, thinking maybe he had missed it. But despite all his wanting, he didn't see what he hoped to. His impatience, bubbling beneath the surface of his thoughts, rose quickly to the fore. It was four days and still he'd had no word. Time was running out with every company that filed up the hillside to swell the castle garrison.

Behind him, the door clattered open. Will turned to see Gautier, one of the royal guards he had travelled from Paris with.

'Minister de Nogaret wants us in the Great Hall. Colonna has arrived.'

Leaving the dormitory where he had been billeted, Will followed Gautier down through the upper levels of the castle, his impatience replaced with apprehension. The last pieces of Nogaret's plan were coming together. Heading along a narrow passageway, he could hear the sound of many voices through the open doors of the Great Hall. Inside, sixty or so men stood about in groups talking animatedly. The last of the sunlight slanted in through the arched windows, staining the walls red, and servants bustled around lighting torches. Spotting Nogaret's white silk cap and black robe, Will crossed to him through the crowd.

The minister's face had darkened the further south they had ridden, since leaving Paris in July. Oddly, as the colour returned to his cheeks, the subtle trace of his old accent became more distinct, filtering through the northern tongue. Nogaret looked younger, fitter and more at ease than Will had seen him before and he showed not one shred of doubt over what he was about to do. If he didn't know his hatred of the Church, Will would have said Nogaret was on a holy mission with all the zeal he was displaying in his undertaking of this treacherous plan.

Standing with Nogaret were the five other French guards they had travelled with, the captain of Ferentino and several local knights and lords. There was also a tall, well-built man in a wine-dark cloak whom Will didn't recognise, but who was generating enough attention for him to suspect this must be the eagerly anticipated Sciarra Colonna. The man had a hard, tanned face and coal-black eyes that swept the crowd with a keen intensity, a faint smile flickering at the corners of his mouth. He looked like a man about to go into battle, who believes he has already won.

'There are a few more companies yet to arrive,' Rainald, the captain of Ferentino, was saying. 'But we should be ready to move tomorrow, the next day at the latest.'

'It is good to have you with us, Sciarra,' said Nogaret, glancing round as Will and Gautier joined them. 'His graciousness, King Philippe, wanted me to pass on his gratitude for your assistance in this delicate matter. He is aware how much you risk by returning here. I knew, of course, that your aid would be invaluable to the task ahead.' Nogaret gave a gratified smile as he surveyed the busy hall. 'Although I must say I did not expect even you to be able to mobilise such a force in so short a time.'

'I have been waiting for this moment for a long time, Minister de Nogaret.' Sciarra's voice was rich and dark, his French heavily laced with his native accent. 'And I have been planning for it. Had you never contacted me, I would have made this move myself. My family has more cause than most for wanting our persecutor toppled from his throne.'

'All of us here have suffered equally under Boniface's rule, Sciarra,' said Rainald, a note of resentment in his voice.

'Indeed,' spoke up a portly nobleman beside him.

Sciarra's black eyes swung to them. 'Equally? Your sister was divorced by one of the Caetanis, Rainald. And you, Niccolo,' he said to the portly lord, 'your family was dispossessed of their town. These are legitimate grievances. But they are negligible in comparison to what has been done to my family.' Sciarra's face was filled with hatred; it glittered in his eyes and seethed in his voice. 'My uncle, Giacomo, and my brother, Pietro, were pre-eminent cardinals in the Sacred College. Under Pope Celestine, they were granted innumerable privileges and greatly favoured for their commitment to the papacy. When the pope began to question his ability to fulfil adequately the office to which he had been elected, my family were the ones who supported him. It was Boniface who whispered poison in his ear and persuaded him that he was not fit to sit upon the papal throne and who convinced Celestine to abdicate and then secured his own election. It was Boniface who imprisoned Celestine for the very thing he had convinced him to do and had him murdered in his cell.'

Around the Great Hall a hush was growing as Sciarra's voice rose and other men stopped talking to listen.

'When my family spoke out against this outrage, Boniface had my uncle and brother deposed, their benefices and their vestments stripped from them. He then had all property and possessions belonging to the Colonna family confiscated and all of us proclaimed excommunicate. All our wealth, earned over generations, was lost. Not content with this, Boniface proclaimed a Crusade against my family and all our supporters, offering the same indulgences to any who waged war upon us as those offered to men who take up the Cross against the Saracens. Finally, five years ago, when my family was virtually destroyed, those who weren't killed or imprisoned forced to flee to France, papal forces stormed Palestrina, our last stronghold, not thirty miles from here.' Sciarra turned to Nogaret. 'When we come to Anagni, you will see it, Minister. What was once a proud and noble town is a ruin on a hilltop. Boniface had every building razed, except for a single church, left as reminder of who had done this to us. The earth was salted so nothing would grow there again. Every morning, Boniface can open the shutters of his palace and look out upon our defeat and every morning, for the past five years, I have looked out upon a foreign land. It is long past Judgement Day.'

Will glanced round to see nods of agreement and the same shining hatred in the faces of Sciarra's men and allies. There was a pucker of a frown on Nogaret's brow as he surveyed the crowd, a look of caution in his eyes, perhaps even some concern. Will understood why. The minister had asked for military support. He had got a mob.

'We must act swiftly,' Nogaret said, looking back at Sciarra. 'On our arrival news came to us that the pope is moving to excommunicate King Philippe. With the knights you have brought our number totals more than one thousand, although most of those are infantry. We have a hard task ahead of us. Not only does the pope have the support of family in Anagni, but many of the cardinals have residences there also. I am told the town is well defended, positioned on a hill and surrounded by strong Roman walls. Without siege equipment it may take us some time to gain entry, longer if the town garrison is well organised.'

Will shifted restlessly and worried again whether his hope was in vain.

Sciarra, however, didn't look in the least concerned. 'You need not trouble yourself with that, Minister de Nogaret. We require no siege-craft. We have a man inside Anagni who will make certain the gates are opened for us.'

'Who is this man?' questioned Nogaret, surprised. 'Does he have the ability to organise this?'

'His name is Godfrey Bussa,' replied Sciarra. 'And yes, he has the ability. He is the commander of the papal guard.'

Will barely managed to keep his shock from showing.

Nogaret's surprise hovered on his face for a moment, before he smiled. 'Then we will perhaps make shorter work of this than I thought possible.'

'Boniface and his family have made many enemies over the past few years,' interjected Rainald. 'The local communes are primed for an uprising against the Caetanis. Even in Anagni, even among those closest to him, there are many who wish to see him gone.'

'And their support will be gratefully received,' responded Nogaret. 'But we must make certain that the pope himself is protected from harm. It must be made clear to all that we are here to arrest him for heresy in the name of France.'

Sciarra inclined his head, but said nothing.

His reticence gave Will a deeper feeling of unease. Looking at the faces of Colonna and the other men, he didn't see the need for justice. He saw the need for revenge. He knew that look well; had worn it often enough on his own face to recognise it.

The men remained in the Great Hall, discussing the details of the assault on Anagni for some time. Will stood in silence at Nogaret's side, filled with foreboding, until the meeting drew to a close. When the servants were called in to prepare the hall for the evening's feast, he was able to slip away.

Climbing the stairs to his dormitory, he was so preoccupied he almost missed it. Passing one of the arched windows, which looked down over the torchlit enceinte and the castle walls, Will glanced automatically at the line of cypress trees beyond the walls. The flash of red burst into his brain several moments after he had seen it and he had to descend three stairs and return to the window to check. He thought for a second his eyes had been playing tricks on him. But no. There, caught in the glow of the torches on the ramparts, tied to the lower branches of the tree furthest from the gate, was a fluttering scrap of red cloth, bright as a berry against the green.

Swiftly, Will retraced his steps, down through the tower, into the castle courtyard. The night was sultry and filled with the conversation of men. He wove through the crowd and, ducking through an archway, entered the outer enceinte, where soldiers stood sentry at the gates. A dark shape skimmed his head as a bat darted into the sky. Moths tilted at the torches, which threw an amber glow over the sun-baked stones. Whenever one got too close, there was a flicker of fire as its wings caught and it was consumed.

'Campbell.'

Will turned at the sharp voice to see Nogaret behind him, framed in the archway.

'Where are you going?'

Will gave him a relaxed smile. 'I need to piss. The latrines are full.'

'Don't go far. I want you and the others with me at the table tonight.' Nogaret glanced behind him and lowered his voice. 'We need to make certain this goes the way we want.'

'I won't be long.' Will waited until the minister had disappeared, before striding to the gate.

He still had no idea why the king had sent him on this *critical assignment*, as Philippe had called it when he ordered Will to accompany Nogaret. That had been early in July, shortly after the second assembly of the Estates-General where the men of the realm supported Philippe's decision to denounce Boniface and proclaim him a heretic. Will learned this in the days following the assembly, but hadn't connected the disturbing announcement to the assignment until they had left Paris and were on the road south. Out of the city, safe from spies, Nogaret informed Will and the six palace guards what their task was and where they were going. It was clear, from the minister's attitude, that it hadn't been his idea for Will to be a part of the group. But the reasons for his involvement were almost immediately obscured by the realisation that the pope's arrest could well be the king and Nogaret's first step towards the Temple. Perhaps Boniface's arrest and trial in France was designed to make him comply with their wishes? Maybe they would offer to release him and end the trial if he gave them power over the Temple? Whatever the reason, Will he knew he must do everything in his power to stop Boniface from being sent to Paris, which was why, when they arrived in Ferentino, under the pretence of scouting the area, he had gone to the nearest church to seek aid.

Nodding to the guards on the gate, he headed out and down the dusty track to where the cypress trees bordered the steep hillside, which disappeared into a tangle of bushes, alive with the buzz of insects. With a glance behind him to the ramparts, he pushed his way through the trees and scrabbled down into the undergrowth, scanning the shadows. After several moments of searching, thorns scratching his clothes and face, he was beginning to wonder if there was anyone here at all when he heard a whisper off to his left and a young man's face appeared in the gloom, pinched with fear.

'You're late,' murmured Will, as the acolyte struggled towards him, his robes catching on bushes.

'I'm sorry,' the man replied in Latin. 'I could not leave for some days.'

'Did you send the message?'

The acolyte nodded nervously. 'My brother took it to Rome.'

'When?'

'The evening you came to me.'

Will thought. Rome was a two-day ride. It was cutting it fine and even if they managed to get to Anagni before Nogaret and Sciarra, now he knew the men had help inside it seemed increasingly doubtful that they would be able to stop this from happening. His only hope was that they would decide to move the pope to Rome before the attack took place. He nodded to the acolyte. 'You did well.'

'Will they get there in time?' whispered the acolyte, as Will turned to climb back up towards the castle gate. 'Will the Temple be able to save his holiness?'

'For their sake, I hope so.'

The Temple, Paris, 4 September 1303 AD

Esquin de Floyran hurried along the cloisters towards the officials' building. He waved a hand distractedly as someone called to him, but didn't stop to talk. The Paris preceptory was packed with hundreds of masters and knights who had journeyed from across the kingdom, summoned to attend the annual Chapter General to discuss Templar business in France. They had been in session since Prime, only pausing to recite the Paternosters for the offices of Terce and Sext, and it was now past Nones.

In the short break, men gathered in the sun, debating various matters that had arisen. Most of the snatches of conversation Esquin caught as he bustled through were centred on the failure of the Grand Master's Crusade. The officials of the Order were concerned, but with Jacques de Molay encamped on Cyprus and the Crusade halted, there was little they could do except concentrate on matters at home: legal proceedings against knight-brothers, requests for funds to renovate various preceptories, disputes over territory, the acquisition of new holdings. In between the discussions, men stifled yawns and speculated over what delicacies would be on offer at the evening's grand feast. One old master was reminiscing on the year King Louis IX had sent a gift of seven swans to the preceptory for the Chapter General.

Esquin hastened through the doorway of the officials' building and breathlessly climbed the stairs, his short legs aching with the effort, the hem of his mantle trailing up behind him.

As he rapped on the large door at the end of the passage, he heard an irate voice beyond.

'Enter.'

Steeling himself, Esquin pushed open the doors.

Hugues de Pairaud was standing at a desk between two clerics, who were sorting through piles of parchments. He glanced up with an impatient frown, which didn't get any less irritated as his gaze fixed on Esquin. 'Yes?'

'Visitor de Pairaud,' Esquin began quickly, 'I am aware this is a rather inopportune moment in which to request an audience, but as I shall be travelling back to Montfaucon tomorrow on an urgent matter to which I must attend I thought this may prove to be the only opportunity I shall get to speak to you.'

The Visitor was shaking his head. 'And you are?'

'Esquin de Floyran, prior of the Montfaucon preceptory,' replied Esquin, a little bemusedly.

'Of course,' said Hugues absently, as one of the clerics passed him a skin.

Esquin ploughed on, despite the fact that the Visitor now seemed to be engrossed in the parchment he had been handed. 'It is a family matter for which I seek your aid, Visitor de Pairaud. My nephew was admitted into the Temple as a knight here in Paris last year. As far as I and his father were aware, he was to return to my preceptory to serve under me, but he was told after his inception that he would remain in Paris. I am proud he should be posted in our principal preceptory, but in recent years I have seen a decline in the number of noble men wishing to join the Order, a decline that has left me with only a small staff, many of whom are laymen. Coupled with this, I have received many messages from my nephew in recent months beseeching me to apply for his transfer home. And so I am here to ask for your agreement that Martin return with me to Montfaucon.' Esquin shook his head, troubled. 'I do not think he is well. There is something that troubles him, but he refuses to speak of it.'

Hugues had stopped reading. The second cleric was holding out another parchment, but the Visitor hadn't taken it. 'Martin?'

'Martin de Floyran. As I said, he is my nephew and—'

'I am sorry, I cannot agree to your request. De Floyran is a valuable addition to this preceptory. As a knight, he will serve wherever he is posted, as was explained to him during his initiation.' Hugues's face soured. 'Despite how *homesick* he may be.'

'But, Visitor de Pairaud,' protested Esquin, when Hugues snatched the skin from the cleric and headed for the door. 'I simply do not have enough knights to defend Montfaucon adequately. Surely my nephew would be serving the Order admirably were he to—'

Hugues turned abruptly as he reached the door. 'This is not a matter for discussion. My decision is final. He stays.'

Esquin stared after him as he swept out with the clerics. Outside, a bell began to chime, summoning the men back to the Chapter. Frowning pensively, Esquin made his way down the stairs and out into the courtyard. The officials were beginning to file towards the Chapter House, but it would take the press of men a little while to get settled once inside. Turning from the slow-moving crowd, Esquin hurried towards the knights' quarters.

He was sweating inside his mantle by the time he reached the dormitory. His nephew was standing by the window in the empty room. He turned with a start.

Martin's expression filled with such hope that Esquin felt a wrench in his gut. Martin studied his face for a long moment, then turned back to the window.

'He denied you, didn't he?'

Esquin crossed to him. 'I am sorry, Martin, but it is clear Visitor de Pairaud needs you here and for that you should be proud. It is an honour to serve him.' When Martin said nothing, Esquin exhaled. 'I know it is difficult, being away from your family and familiar surroundings, but I promise in time you will—'

'Please, uncle. Please take me with you when you leave tomorrow. I have to come home. I cannot stay here.'

Esquin looked on hopelessly as the young man put his head in his hands. 'I cannot appeal against Hugues de Pairaud's decision, other than by going to the Grand Master himself.' He gripped his nephew's shoulders. 'All this fuss? All those letters you sent? Yet still you will not tell me what is wrong. If you perhaps explained what it is that—'

'No,' said Martin swiftly. He pulled away, his jaw set. 'No. I cannot.' He glanced around as if fearing someone might overhear. 'Not here.'

Esquin tutted as the bell ceased its chimes. 'I must return to the Chapter now and there are matters I must attend to back home.' He paused, then nodded determinedly. 'But I am going to come back as soon as I can. If I do, will you meet me? Martin?' He pressed, when the youth didn't answer.

After a long silence, Martin nodded.

Esquin smiled encouragingly and patted his shoulder. 'Then we shall see what all this is about.'

Anagni, Italy, 7 September 1303 AD

The sky was midnight blue. Soldiers scrabbled silently over the rocks that littered the sides of the track, carrying swords and daggers. There was no moon and it was by starlight that they moved, shrouded in velvet gloom. The hooves of the three hundred horses were muffled on the dusty ground, but the clink of bridles and armour echoed unavoidably in the hush and the company's commanders were poised for the alarm to rise, any moment, from the sleeping town perched on the hill above. They needn't have worried, for the high Roman walls surrounding Anagni shielded its citizens from any disturbing night noises as well as potential attackers and their advance went undetected as they climbed steadily up the hillside towards the Porta Tufoli.

Sciarra Colonna, riding at the vanguard, sent two of his men ahead as the company approached the gate. Nogaret craned his neck to watch as the knights trotted their horses towards the arched entrance. Two torches flickered in brackets, throwing long shadows up the walls. Turning, one of the knights signalled. A smile crossed Sciarra's face before he pulled on his helmet and urged his horse forward. Men threw relieved, jubilant glances at one another as they saw the gate was not only open, but completely undefended. Sciarra snatched one of the torches from its bracket. Swinging his foot out of his stirrup, he kicked at the wooden barricade as he passed through, holding the brand aloft. The gate shuddered wider with a groan. Behind him, the rest of the cavalry poured in.

Once inside the walls, their stealth ended. Sciarra wanted the townsfolk to know who had come and why. His voice struck the quiet, rising over the rumble of hooves on the steep, narrow streets. 'Good people of Anagni! Arise! Awake! By order of the King of France, Pope Boniface is to be arrested as a heretic and taken hence to trial!'

As his voice resounded off the walls of the grand palazzos around the Porta Tufoli, many of them home to the cardinals of the Sacred College, shutters and doors began to open all over the lower town. Citizens started from sleep, pulling cloaks around them. The hoof-beats clattered in the night and mothers dashed to check on children, huddled wide-eyed as the shadows of riders and swords drifted past on bedroom walls. Soldiers, loping along beside the mounted knights, raised sputtering torches, bringing early dawn to the streets that wound up towards the cathedral and the papal palace. Birds flew chattering into the sky.

'Arise! Awake! We are here to arrest the heretic pope!'

The fear in the faces of men and women that appeared in the doorways turned to curiosity as they realised this army hadn't come for them. While some barricaded their doors and began to hide gold and jewels under floorboards, others wandered into the streets, gazing bemused at the knightly procession, as if it were a saint's day and these men were parading some holy relic through their town. Soon a stream of people, half of whom were still in their nightshirts, were following Sciarra's company. A few absently clutched the weapons they wielded when they had opened their doors thinking to defend themselves. As the company passed a church, Sciarra barked an order. A group of soldiers broke away and, pushing aside the priest who had been gawping in the doorway, entered the building. The priest hastened in behind them, protesting. Several moments later, the bell in the tower began to toll.

Will looked up as he passed beneath the church, watching the bell swing to and fro, waking the rest of the town. Glancing over his shoulder, he saw the stream of people had become a flood. To the east, behind the black humps of the hills, the sky was lightening. Beside him, Nogaret looked tense in the torchlight as the crowd gathered in around them, all wanting to be part of the action. Rainald was right: Boniface had made many enemies, and now his own people turned on him for anything they felt he was responsible for; whether the tithes he had levied, or the fact that he once ignored their plea for alms, or the time one of his nephews teased their son in church. Will, riding in their midst, listening to their complaints, could only bob along in the tide, a cork on an ocean. Nogaret had spoken briefly to him and the French guards during the night ride from Ferentino and, in a hushed voice, had given them their orders.

Keep the pope alive. Keep him away from Sciarra.

Will's hope, dashed by the ease with which they had entered Anagni, now lay in the possibility that if the pope survived long enough for Nogaret to arrest him, he might somehow be able to facilitate Boniface's escape on the journey back to Paris.

As they neared the cathedral, Will stared at the distant walls of the papal palace, praying to see an army there, arrayed in white, but the windows of the buildings were dark and shuttered. Sciarra turned off, leading the mob towards the town's marketplace. When they arrived, they found many more people clustered there. There must have been five, maybe six thousand. No one in Anagni wanted to be left out, it seemed; to wake up tomorrow and find history had been made without them.

In the centre of the market square beside a large well a tall, muscular man with a trident-shaped beard and a coat of glittering mail, over which he wore a purple cloak, was waiting with a dozen other men, all of whom wore similar uniforms.

Rainald was the first to dismount. 'Sir Godfrey,' he greeted, striding to the tall man.

Guessing this must be Godfrey Bussa, the commander of the papal guard, Will jumped down from his saddle. Nogaret had already dismounted and was jostling his way between Niccolo and the other local lords, following Sciarra and Rainald. Will pushed through to stand behind the lawyer.

The crowd were all around them, babbling excitedly and Sciarra had to raise his voice. 'We saw no lights in the windows of the palace. I take it the pope is still inside?'

Godfrey's face was grave. 'I believe so, but we cannot be sure. The evening before last my men and I returned to the palace to find the gates barred. I had been out, organising the details of the assault. I called to those of the guard I had left behind, but received no answer.'

'What makes you think Boniface is still there?' interjected Rainald.

'We have seen movement behind the shutters. There are definitely people inside.' Godfrey shook his head. 'The pope must have somehow learned of the attack and barricaded himself in. Perhaps one of my men informed on me?' He lifted his shoulders. 'I cannot be sure.'

'Who is defending him?' asked Nogaret, before Sciarra could speak.

'Most likely those in the papal guard who remain loyal to him, his staff and his family, two cardinals. The majority of the Sacred College is in Rome and we warned three cardinals who support us to leave Anagni before the assault.'

Sciarra went quiet as the men around him continued to question Godfrey. Suddenly, he pushed through them to the well and climbed on to its edge, holding one of the posts for support. 'People of Anagni!' he yelled at the crowd, who at once fell into a hush. 'My name is Sciarra Colonna, brother of Pietro, nephew of Giacomo, wrongfully deposed by the usurper who calls himself Pope Boniface. This man, who has lived among you growing fat on your generosity, is a heretic and a blasphemer!'

Murmurs of fear and assent swelled from the throng. Children were hoisted on to shoulders to watch.

'In the name of the King of France, we are here to arrest him for his crimes. But rather than face us, rather even than deny our accusations, the pope cowers in his palace like the guilty man he is. Good people, I promise you, if you help us liberate your town, I will distribute the wealth of his palace among you. The gold and the relics of the papal treasury! In return for your aid in bringing this evil-doer to justice, you will be made rich beyond your dreams!'

There was silence, his words hanging in the air. Then, a roar rose. Will cursed as the mob surged towards the papal palace, ready to tear the gates apart with their bare hands. Sciarra jumped down from the well and swung up into his saddle with a shout to his men.

The afternoon was dragging on, the sun glaring white on the walls of the buildings. Ahead, across the street, the gates of the papal palace were shut and barred. The wood was splintered and dented in places, but the damage had occurred in the initial attack and since then there had been no further attempt to break through. Around the gates, the ground was littered with bodies. The nightgown of a young woman, lying crumpled near the walls, fluttered in the hot wind like a flag, stained with her blood, the arrow that killed her a black exclamation from her chest.

The assault on the palace had been chaos. The mob flowed through the town, riding or running up the steep alleys to converge on the compound, which contained the pope's residence, the homes of his family and the cathedral, all enclosed behind stout walls, the hillside tumbling sheer beyond. Knights, soldiers and townsfolk vied to be the first in, lest the glory or bounty be taken by others. Despite the fierce commands of Sciarra Colonna and Godfrey Bussa, and the discipline of their immediate troops, this unruly mass had pushed forward, unheeding. Horses reared and people were shoved to the ground. As the first attackers reached the gates and began battering them with fists and weapons there were flashes of motion in the dawn sky. Screams sounded. But it was some moments before the crowd realised arrows were shooting down into them from the palace walls.

The crush at the gates became a rout as people started to flee. The mounted knights had been the first away, followed by soldiers lifting shields over their heads. It was the people of Anagni, untrained and unarmed, who bore the brunt of the palace's defence. Those who didn't fall fled back into the alleys they had poured out of or else broke their way into houses to take cover. Remaining grimly efficient throughout the confusion, Sciarra brought his men to order and regrouped in the streets beyond the walls.

It was shortly after this, when the sky was turning pearlescent blue, that a loud voice had sounded from the walls, demanding to know the meaning of the assault. When Sciarra made to answer, Nogaret beat him to it, so desperate to regain control of the situation he walked right out into the corpse-strewn street without shield or weapon.

'By order of Lord Philippe le Bel, King of France,' the minister had called out, 'Boniface is to be arrested for the crime of heresy. He will submit and be taken to Paris to stand trial.'

'We wish to negotiate a truce,' the anonymous voice responded.

'You have until an hour after Nones,' Sciarra had replied, riding out beside Nogaret. 'At that time you will answer the following demands. In his last action as pope, Boniface will reinstate Giacomo and Pietro Colonna in the Sacred College. After this he will deliver the papal treasury to the remaining cardinals and give himself up to the authority of France.'

The truce agreed, Sciarra's knights settled in to wait. Men were sent to scout the area around the palace walls, while Colonna and Bussa set up base in a chapel to plan for a potential assault. The townsfolk, disregarded by the knights, drifted away, embittered. They had lost over a dozen of their own in the attack and these trespassers were ignoring their sacrifice. The pledge of the division of the treasury became an empty promise in the clear light of dawn and although many returned dazedly to their homes a rebellious gang, several thousand strong, went on the rampage, anxious to receive the riches they had been sworn. Rioting through Anagni's streets, they stormed the grand palazzos of the cardinals. Late into the day, Sciarra and his men heard screams and saw smoke rising in the lower town as the looting continued.

On the hour the truce was due to end, the pope's response came to them. Boniface would not submit. Angry, but prepared, Sciarra made ready for a second assault.

Will watched the group of soldiers heft the tree trunk. As they set out into the street, holding shields over their heads with their free hands, he heard one of the French guards questioning Nogaret.

'Can we be certain the pope is even inside? For all we know this is a diversion. If the pope was aware of the attack perhaps he escaped before it took place?'

Nogaret's gaze didn't leave the soldiers, now tramping towards the palace gates with their heavy burden. 'No, we cannot be certain, but from what Bussa told us, Boniface would have had scant opportunity in which to leave unnoticed. We can only hope he is still there. Whatever happens, we must be the first in.'

As the guard nodded brusquely, Will turned back to watch the soldiers' progress. Arrows began to stab down from the walls. A man shrieked as one pierced his boot and embedded itself in his foot. Letting go of the tree trunk and his shield, he collapsed in the street, hands grasping at the shaft. Another caught him in the shoulder, slamming him into the dust. He writhed feebly, before a third finished him. Whoever they were, the archers inside were no amateurs. From behind the safety of a makeshift barricade erected across the street, another man darted forward at Sciarra's command to take the dead man's place. More arrows rained down, but the missiles were coming sporadically and only from six or seven positions on the walls, revealing the limited ability of the defence, however accurate. The remaining soldiers made it to the gates and began swinging the trunk into the wood, each strike causing the barriers to shudder and shake.

'Minister!'

Nogaret turned as one of his men hastened over.

The guard was out of breath. 'I was using the latrine,' he panted, pointing to one of the buildings up the street. 'The windows look out over the palace and I saw a company of men making their way around the hillside beneath the walls. They were wearing the colours of Sciarra's knights.'

'How many?'

'Forty or so.'

Nogaret hastened to Sciarra, who was at the barricade barking orders. 'Colonna! Did you send a company around the walls?'

Sciarra looked surprised, but gave a curt nod. 'Yes. They will try to gain entry from the rear. Bussa believes the gate by the cathedral will be the least defended.'

'Why wasn't I informed?'

Sciarra scowled. 'You involved me in your plot because you wanted military support. I am doing what I was brought here to do. Let me do it.'

'I told you I was to be the first inside!'

'Be my guest,' responded Sciarra witheringly, gesturing to the street where two more soldiers had fallen foul of the defenders' arrows. The rest were grimly battering away at the gates. A large crack had appeared in the centre.

Nogaret strode back to Will and the French guards. 'Get your horses,' he said fiercely. 'Be ready.' He eyed Sciarra vehemently. 'He'll not destroy Boniface before me.'

The guards were already hastening to where they had tethered their mounts. Will had turned, but he stopped short at Nogaret's last words.

The minister looked round at his hesitation. 'What are you waiting for, Campbell?' he snapped, not seeming to realise he had said anything unusual.

Any question Will might have formed over what Nogaret meant was forgotten as dimly, in the few seconds' pause between the crashing of the ram, cries of alarm sounded beyond the palace walls.

Sciarra's knights had broken into the compound.

The next moments were a blur of confusion. Orders rang out as commanders sprang into action. Men mounted horses, grabbed shields and weapons from squires. Soldiers, waiting in the shade, scrambled to their feet, unsheathing swords. Over everything, the ram continued to boom against the gates, now beginning to sag under the furious attack. Arrows had ceased to lance down from the walls and some of the soldiers now tossed aside their shields and renewed their attack with greater fervour. Will hauled himself into his saddle and rode to the barricade with the rest of the French guards, leaving Nogaret to sprint to his horse. Suddenly, the gates grated open and the faces of Sciarra's knights appeared beyond. Hurling away the tree trunk, the soldiers on the ram piled in, closely followed by Sciarra who led his men on a ferocious charge across the street and into the palace.

On the other side of the wall, a few archers were sprawled on the ramparts, others, shot down by Sciarra's knights, lay twisted on the

ground. Some still gripped bows in death-locked fists. There was movement on the balconies of the palace as a few defenders raced to barricade
themselves inside. In the inner courtyard, beyond which the cathedral
loomed, fighting was still going on. The cathedral doors were thrown open
and sounds of swords clashing echoed within. The first wave of soldiers
went straight to the buildings that housed the pope's family. Those who
wielded axes began to hack at the painted shutters on the lower floors.
Others made quick work of doors, kicking or shouldering their way
through. Screams rang inside.

Will was carried in through the gates on the crest of the cavalry charge.
He had left Nogaret and the French guards behind. All his vision was
channelled forward through the slits in his helmet. He saw the backs of the
men riding in front, the flash of swords, blinding in the sun, shields lifted.
He saw Sciarra heading for a grand palazzo across the courtyard. Steering
his horse expertly through the press, Will pursued him, all his thoughts
fixed on protecting the pope. When Sciarra dismounted, ordering soldiers
to set smouldering torches against the base of the doors, Will followed suit,
slapping his horse on the rump to send it clear of the confusion. The doors
began to blacken and then to burn. Will gripped his sword, feeling men all
around him breathing hard in anticipation. Shielding their faces, several
knights went forward to aim kicks at the doors. Finally, one man broke
through, half the door collapsing inwards in a burst of embers. Will fought
his way to the front as the company surged into a wide corridor, choked
with smoke. Men sprinted in different directions, wanting to be the first to
find the pope and his treasury.

Sciarra made straight for a set of stairs at the end of the passage, seeming
to know where he was going. Hoping none of Colonna's men would dare
make a move without him, Will followed. Elbowing knights out of his path,
he barrelled up the stairs behind Sciarra, who was much younger than he
was and had already disappeared. The stairwell filled with the clanking and
jangling of armour. Up and round Will climbed, his sword occasionally
scraping against the wall, his lungs burning, thighs throbbing with the
effort. Just as he was starting to slow, he reached the top. Gathering the last
of his strength, he raced down a marble passageway. Sciarra was now far
ahead, surrounded by knights, his sword bobbing at the front of the
company heading towards a set of doors.

'Christ, help me,' panted Will, battling down behind, as the doors were
flung open and the host swarmed into a chamber beyond.

There they stopped.

On a throne, wearing a jewel-encrusted tiara and the ornate robes of his office, sat Pope Boniface. In one hand he held a solid gold cross, in the other a sword with a crystal pommel. His broad, lined face was grey with fatigue and fear, but set with obstinate determination, as well it might be, for the pope was not alone. Standing before him, arrayed in white, blades held out before them, were twenty-seven Templars.

24
Anagni, Italy
7 September 1303 AD

A s he sprinted into the throne room, Will felt a fierce pulse of joy at the sight of the knights in their protective ring around the pope. They had come.

For a second, he wanted to pitch himself into their line and turn to face Sciarra and his men. But he forced aside the desire and halted on the opposite side of the chamber, pointing his blade towards the knights, along with all the others around him, while inside he was shouting, exalted. Sounds of the continuing attack on the papal compound came in through the windows, the chime of swords followed by cries, wood splintering, glass breaking.

Sciarra wrenched off his helmet and let it clang to the floor, as if wanting the pope to see the face of his enemy.

Boniface rose. 'What are you waiting for, Colonna? Here is my neck! Here is my head!'

Sciarra took a step at the challenge, his hand flexing around his sword hilt. But his eyes darted to the knights, who tensed at his movement, all their gazes fixed on him.

'What is happening? Where is the pope?' Nogaret's breathless voice sounded from the back of the crowd blocking the doors. 'Let me through!' The soldiers parted reluctantly and the minister appeared. He too tugged off his helmet, the better to see by. His face registered shock, then fury as he saw the Templars and the pope beyond. 'What is this?'

'Keep out of it, Nogaret,' growled Sciarra. 'This isn't your fight any more.'

The cries outside were growing louder. There was a tang of smoke on the air.

'Guillaume de Nogaret?' The pope's voice was glacial. 'So, you are the serpent who has hissed venom in the ear of your king? Whose poison now threatens the very Church?' Boniface's eyes glittered. 'You should have been thrown on to that fire with your mother and father, you blasphemous wretch!'

Nogaret started forward, his face contorting with hatred. Two of Sciarra's men, poised to fight, caught his movement. Thinking it was a general attack, they rushed towards the line of knights. Sciarra shouted, but his warning came too late. Two Templars stepped out to meet the men. One knight ducked under his attacker's strike, then punched in with his sword, ramming it through the man's side. The other knight swung his opponent's blade away with a downward curve of his sword, then ran him through. Leaving the bodies bleeding on the marble floor, the knights moved back into the line. Boniface sat heavily on his throne, shaken by the confrontation. His expression grew even more bewildered as Godfrey Bussa stumbled into the chamber.

The commander's face was white and he was clutching his arm. Blood was pumping between his fingers. He went straight to Sciarra. 'The citizens are rioting,' he said through clenched teeth. 'They followed us in. More are coming up from the town. They've overrun the compound.'

'Godfrey?' whispered the pope. He stood, the sword limp in his grasp. 'The Templars told me local men were involved, but I did not imagine it would be you.' Boniface's expression hardened. 'And to think I was concerned for you when they made me bar the gates and refuse entry to anyone. How many more are against me?' he cried, throwing his head back.

Yells and the clamour of many footsteps erupted in the corridor. The soldiers by the doors turned, adding their own shouts to the commotion as a tide of people swept towards them. The people of Anagni had come for their reward.

Buoyed up by their victories against the palazzos of the cardinals, drunk on stolen wine and heady with the promise of even greater spoils, they raced towards the men crammed in the doorway of the throne room. Some carried blades, wrested from soldiers overpowered outside, others had sticks or rocks. Sciarra's men levelled their swords, but the stampede had picked up too much momentum to stop and the front rows were carried into the bristling line by the impetus of those behind. Men kicked and stabbed, elbowed and punched. The rasp of blades vanished almost at once to be replaced by heavy grunts and gurgling screams that boiled up in the tight scrum.

Sciarra, who had turned to yell orders at his soldiers, now gave a cry of rage as the Templars jostled the pope down from his throne and out through a door in the far wall of the chamber. As Sciarra charged recklessly, Nogaret raced after him. A handful of Templars broke away from the main group and came at them. Will made to follow the minister, who was tackled by one of the knights, but the people of Anagni forced their way through the press of soldiers and burst into the throne room. Smoke was threading through the tall windows, sharpening the air. A building opposite was on fire. Will caught sight of a face, suspended in the black, boiling clouds, before a man came at him, brandishing a club.

The pope and his escort of knights had gone. Sciarra had killed one Templar and was battling a second, his face apoplectic. Nogaret howled as the knight he was fighting got inside his defences and lanced him through the shoulder. The Templar tugged the blade free and brought the sword round in a massive two-handed swing that would have struck off Nogaret's head had two townsmen not barrelled into him, sending him flying. The Templar grunted in frustration as more people rushed past, all trying to get to the throne, where Boniface's crystal-pommel sword and solid gold cross had been abandoned.

Will dodged a clumsy blow aimed by the man with the club and fended off another easily, but more and more men were scrabbling into the throne room to get at the treasures.

'Retreat!' someone was yelling. 'Retreat!'

Sciarra's knights, outnumbered by the mob, began to force their way out, away from the Templars, who were hacking indiscriminately through the press. One man was dragging Sciarra back. Nogaret, wounded, had lost his sword and was groping his way to the doors, trying to escape the knight who was coming after him. Will pushed his way out, using his fist and the hilt of his sword to clout people away.

A general call for retreat went up as thousands of townspeople poured in. The Templars, unable to take the pope safely through the chaos, barricaded him in a tower of the palace as Sciarra's army fled into the amber evening, leaving the people of Anagni to rip down priceless tapestries, brawl over silver plates, haul relics from the treasury and guzzle Communion wine late into the night.

Palestrina, Italy, 8 September 1303 AD

Men threw themselves down on the scrubby ground, gasping for breath. Faces shone with sweat in the early morning light and blood bloomed on torn strips of clothing tied hastily around wounds. Some gulped voraciously from water-skins, then upended them over their heads, closing their eyes as the liquid poured out. Horses gnashed at their bits, mouths frothing with thirst. A few had been injured in the night flight from Anagni and there were piteous screams as soldiers despatched the lame beasts.

Will leaned back against a crumbling wall and watched the stragglers, most of them on foot, trudging up the steep, overgrown track. He still felt exhausted, but at least he'd had a chance to rest, having reached the ruined town of Palestrina a few hours earlier, with those of the cavalry who had made it out of the papal palace. From what he could see, they were still missing at least half of their company. No one knew where Rainald and the men from Ferentino were. No one had seen them since they had entered the palace in the first wave of the attack. Sciarra, Godfrey Bussa and Nogaret were all present, although the minister had lost two of the guards who had travelled with him from France and Bussa was lying in the shade, his face grey with blood-loss.

There was a shrill cry as an eagle drifted overhead, its gold wings glinting. Several others followed, circling warily, disturbed by the intruders. After Boniface had the Colonnas' stronghold razed, it was left abandoned, nature moving in eagerly to take their place. There was scant evidence of the buildings that once crowned the hilltop; any stone or timber not scavenged by locals was covered over by creeping vines and trailing grasses. Now, all that remained were broken stumps and jagged lines of walls, poking here and there through the rambling undergrowth. The chapel was the only building left standing, a forlorn marker of vanished humanity in the wilderness. Tree roots had forced their way in through cracks in the walls, the floor was crusty with bat droppings and spiders' webs floated like fragile curtains in the choir aisle, sprinkled with flies.

Will found it strange that Sciarra had led them here, the site of his family's last defeat at the hands of the pope. But Colonna had wanted a place to regroup, unseen by allies of Boniface, and Palestrina had perhaps seemed the safest option. Maybe Sciarra even hoped for some sense of comfort here; familiar surroundings in which to lick his wounds and nurse his losses. Either way, it wasn't over. That much was clear.

As a shadow fell across him, Will shielded his eyes and looked up to see Nogaret.

The minister's robes were sticky with blood from the gash in his shoulder, which had been crudely bandaged by one of the guards. 'You weren't injured.'

In his flat tone it didn't sound like a question, but Will answered. 'Not much.' He raised his hands. The knuckles were torn and bruised where he had punched his way through the crowd.

'It was a disaster.'

Will pushed himself up with a wince. He was almost a foot taller than Nogaret, but the man continued to look him belligerently in the eye. 'The townspeople shouldn't have been involved.' Will glanced at Sciarra, who was hunched in the shade of a tree near the chapel. 'I've seen mobs form before. It doesn't take much to turn them into a mindless horde, intent on plunder and random slaughter. They are a dangerous tool. Unpredictable.'

'I'll tell you what else was unpredictable, Campbell.'

Will looked back, hearing a note of menace in the minister's tone.

'The pope's white-clad saviours.' Anger broke through to seethe in Nogaret's voice. 'My first question would be how did Boniface know of our assault? Clearly it wasn't from any of Bussa's men, for he was obviously shocked by his commander's part in the revolt. Indeed, the pope said it was the Templars who warned him local men might be involved. So my second question would be, how did the knights know?'

'As Bussa said, it is possible the pope was warned by one of his loyal guards.' Will continued to meet Nogaret's gaze, even though the minister's dark eyes were boring into him, filled with suspicion, hungry for blame. 'The pope may have got word to the Templars in Rome, asking for their protection.'

'That makes no sense. If he thought he would be attacked he would have left Anagni.'

'Perhaps he didn't take the threat that seriously and the knights' protection was just a precaution.' Will shrugged. 'It is even possible the Temple got wind of it and went there of their own accord.' He shook his head. 'I doubt we'll ever find out.'

'Perhaps,' murmured Nogaret. He seemed about to say something further, but was distracted as a troop of horsemen came riding into the ruined town. It was Rainald and the men of Ferentino.

Sciarra got to his feet and crossed the grass to greet them. 'I didn't think you made it out of Anagni,' said Colonna, grasping the captain's hand.

'We were forced to split up. We came when we could.'

Sciarra was nodding. 'And Boniface? Do you know what happened to him? None of my scouts has returned.'

'One of them gave me a message for you. He learned the Templars are to escort the pope to Rome. They planned to leave at first light.' Rainald looked up at the sun. 'I expect they are on their way.'

A slow smile spread across Sciarra's face. 'As I had hoped.'

To Will it was suddenly clear why the Italian had retreated to the ruined town. Palestrina lay on the road to Rome. There was a certain bleak poetry in it: Sciarra riding down out of his former home to wreak vengeance on the man who had destroyed it.

As Rainald accepted a skin someone handed to him and drank gratefully, Nogaret grasped Sciarra by the arm. 'I need to speak to you.'

Sciarra pulled away from his grip, but seemed to see something uncompromising in Nogaret's stare, for he nodded to Rainald and turned to follow the minister into the chapel.

A couple of men watched them curiously as they disappeared inside, but soon moved off to help the newcomers, leading horses to a cleared area of grass, handing over scraps of food, listening to accounts of escape.

Will lingered, his mind filled with questions and uncertainties. Nogaret's words, forgotten in the turmoil of Anagni, returned to him, filled with foreboding. *He'll not destroy Boniface before me.* Until now, he had been focusing on keeping the pope safe from Sciarra. But what if Colonna wasn't the only danger? Picking up an empty skin, he made his way around the back of the chapel. 'I'm going to fetch water,' he told one of the French guards, who nodded disinterestedly.

Making sure he wasn't observed, Will crept alongside the wall. There were plenty of cracks and crannies, but most had trees or flowers growing out of them. He hastened on, then found what he was looking for: a line in the stone cladding, jagged as a lightning bolt, through which he could glimpse the interior.

Entering, Nogaret stalked down to the choir aisle, swiping cobwebs out of his way.

'What do you want?' asked Sciarra, following, his voice brisk with impatience.

Nogaret turned suddenly and backhanded him viciously across the face. '*You fool!*'

Sciarra stumbled away. His hand moved to his cheek, then stopped halfway and went instead for his sword, which he wrenched free.

Nogaret didn't flinch as the sword came up, the tip wavering inches from his throat. 'You think your family had it hard when Boniface declared war on them? That is nothing in comparison to what my lord, Philippe, could do. France is their home now, yes? Their safe haven? We would make it their grave!'

The sword point faltered, but Sciarra didn't lower the blade. His cheek was scarlet. 'I am not a man moved by threats.'

'It is not a threat.'

Sciarra hesitated. Slowly, he brought the blade down.

'You ruined the entire assignment,' hissed Nogaret, pacing the aisle, webs snapping and trailing in his wake. 'Boniface was supposed to be on his way to Paris, a pope cowed and beaten by the might of France, taken in chains to face his accusers and their judgement!'

'I couldn't let him leave this place alive,' Sciarra replied in a low voice, watching him. 'You have no idea of the extent of his crimes against my family.' He beat his breast. 'No idea how fervently we hate him. I didn't want him to languish in luxury in a palace tower, while lawyers fought over his future. I wanted him to have no future! I wanted him dead!'

'As did we!' Nogaret shouted, turning back. He halted as Sciarra's sword flicked out again, but held his ground. 'The pope wouldn't have made it to Paris. I was to poison him on the way.'

Sciarra looked astonished. 'Why didn't you tell me this?'

'I swore to my lord that no other would know of it. Not even my own men were informed. We would have said the pope died of the burden of his crimes. There would have been no evidence of murder.' Nogaret leaned against a scarred pillar. 'Now, all is finished, because of your rashness. The moment the pope enters Rome, he will excommunicate all of us and King Philippe, if, indeed, he has not done so already.'

'We still have a chance,' said Sciarra, after a silence. 'We know he is coming this way.'

Nogaret shook his head. 'If we kill him on the road it will be known that it was murder and, for that matter, who his killers are.'

'Not if there are no witnesses. Even with our losses, my men greatly outnumber his Templar escort. We will distract them so you can get to the pope.'

'There will be no evidence, no body. No one will know anything, except that the pope never made it to Rome.'

'The violence in Anagni will confuse accounts. You can still say you came to arrest the pope for heresy, which is known, and that he evaded you. You can also say he died from the weight of his crimes, or however you wish to phrase it, during his flight to the city.' Sciarra was frowning, thinking it through. 'A few of Bussa's men made it here. What if they took the pope's body to Rome with the story of what happened? No one there would know his own guards had turned against him. They would believe them.'

'What of the Templars? Even if we managed to kill them all, the Order would know where they had gone and why. They would no doubt send more knights when they didn't return.'

'Let them,' said Sciarra flatly. 'They would find nothing of them in these hills. Bussa's men could say the party was intercepted, but that they got away. The Templars stayed behind to sacrifice themselves for the heretic pope.' He lifted his shoulders carelessly. 'Who but the Order would mourn them?'

The Road to Rome, Italy, 8 September 1303 AD

Boniface huddled in the wagon on cushions and furs, his gloved hand grasping the side as the wheels bumped and jolted over the rough road. It was late afternoon and the sun glowed through the red cloth covering the wagon, rendering it almost translucent, like skin. Boniface had the disquieting impression he was in the belly of some beast that was lurching its way towards Rome. The hooves of the Templars' horses striking the hard-packed ground echoed all around. The sound drummed in his mind, building the ache in his head to a crescendo of pain. He patted his brow with a silk cloth. The righteous anger that erupted in him when he first learned of the attack and the subsequent rage that overwhelmed him at the sight of his own people with that viper, Colonna, had dissipated. Now, he just felt like a scared old man. Wounded and betrayed.

His home had almost been destroyed. It would have been, had the riots not died away soon after Sciarra's escape, the citizens sobering up, coming to their senses. He made an impassioned plea from the palace balcony and many, seeing him there surrounded by the Templars, had lain down their weapons. Some even returned the treasures they had stolen. The miracle was that none of his family had been killed, although many servants and guards perished in the assault. The knights had told him how fortunate he was; if they hadn't been there he would most likely be dead, or in the custody of that heretic, Nogaret.

Boniface realised his hand, holding the cloth, was trembling. As he let it fall into his lap, he heard a harsh shout come from outside. It was quickly followed by others and the alarmed neighing of horses. Boniface caught the rasp of swords, then the wagon jerked forward violently. Thrown off balance, he toppled. The furs gave him a soft landing, but the wagon was jolting so precariously it was all he could do to push himself up on his hands. He hung there, helpless, bouncing about like a sack of apples, hearing the approaching thunder of many hooves. There were more shouts, crashing and thudding sounds and the screaming of horses and men.

Clawing his way forward on his hands and knees, Boniface made it to the opening at the back of the wagon. He gripped the cloth, just as the wagon rocked into a pothole, almost tipping over. Boniface swung sideways with a cry and the material ripped in his fists. He thumped on to the bare wood, bruising his knuckles. Raising his head, he stared out of the tear. Through clouds of dust, he saw the road behind him was filled with men. Hundreds of them were riding down the scrubby hillside, yelling as they charged the Templars. Among those shouts, Boniface heard the name of Colonna raised. There were at least four Templars still with him, riding furiously, but even as he watched, wild-eyed with terror, the men on the hillside outflanked them. A black missile came shooting towards him. Boniface threw himself backwards, but the arrow wasn't aimed at him. It caught the rear of one of the horses sending the beast reeling into the side of the wagon. Another caught the driver, who tumbled from his seat. The wagon rocked and jumped as the wheels rolled over his body, then veered off course, the horses pulling off the track and down a steep embankment into a field of white flowers. Boniface cracked his head on one of the chests piled against the side and lay there dazed as the wagon rolled to a stop, the horses stamping and grunting, exhausted.

The sounds of battle continued to reverberate. Boniface hauled himself to the opening before the horses could bolt again. Just as he reached it, a face appeared, shining with sweat and triumph. He cried out and struggled back as Nogaret climbed in. The minister had a dagger in his hand.

'Get away from me! Get away, in the name of God!'

Nogaret advanced, his dark eyes alight.

'How dare you attack me!' Boniface shouted. 'I am God's vicar! St Peter's successor!'

'You're an old fool, standing on the top of a crumbling edifice, trying to hold it up by will alone. The Church's power is waning. The people will soon put their faith in the temporal and the spiritual will be nothing more than fantasy.'

'Why?' breathed Boniface. 'Why would you want this?'

'You are riddled with corruption,' spat Nogaret. 'All of you. Nothing but hypocrites! You kill in the name of your God, but it is your hand that smites down your enemies, not His! You use your faith as an excuse to destroy any who oppose you and your beliefs. What I do, here today, will cleanse the world of your pollution.'

'It was not I who ordered your family to the fire, Nogaret,' said Boniface, stopping short as he came up against the back of the wagon. He struggled on to his knees. 'If you allow me to I can absolve them, clear their names and yours.'

Nogaret was shaking his head.

'I can lift the order of excommunication I have put on you and on France.' Boniface held out his hands as the minister paused. 'I will do all this tonight. If you let me live.'

Nogaret stood hunched in the wagon, poised over the pope, his black robes blocking out the sun. The sounds of battle were growing faint and sporadic. 'The next pope will do this for us,' he said bluntly, thrusting the dagger towards the pope's neck.

As Boniface screamed, Nogaret rammed the phial he clutched in his free hand into the pope's mouth. The old man's eyes went wide as the bitter liquid splashed into his throat. His hands came up and grasped Nogaret's wrist. He choked, tried to turn his head, but it was too late; he had already swallowed half of it. Just then, riders came cantering down from the track, startling the beasts tethered to the wagon. As they jolted forward, Boniface kicked Nogaret in the stomach. The minister staggered backwards and fell out of the wagon as the horses took off across the field. He landed on his back in the grass.

Will shouted in frustration as he saw Nogaret climb inside the wagon, alone in a sea of gold-tinged grass. He slashed savagely at the Templar in front of him, trying to disarm him and get past. But the knight, who couldn't have been more than twenty, was a canny fighter and although he grimaced as he countered Will's mighty strokes, he kept tight hold of his blade and shield. Most of the knights were dead on the roadside, just a few, like this brave youth, battled on determinedly. Will heard a desperate cry come from the wagon. It distracted him and he lost his balance. It was only for a second, but it was enough for the knight to lunge in, kick the sword out of his grip and drive his own weapon home. The blade stopped short. Will, who had crashed to his knees, saw an arrow embedded in the young man's throat. His eyes still fixed on Will, he let his sword fall. It clanked in the dust. The knight collapsed as one of the French guards came riding up, a bow now empty in his hand.

Numbly, Will pushed himself to his feet to see Nogaret come tumbling out of the back of the wagon, which rumbled away across the field. It didn't get far before some of Sciarra's men cornered it. Seeing Nogaret stand and walk towards it unhurriedly, Will knew it was over. As he stared at the young Templar, whose eyes were empty reflections of the darkening sky, the ghosts inside him shifted, whispering and afraid.

St Julien le Pauvre, Paris, 20 November 1303 AD

Esquin de Floyran turned as the church doors creaked open. His heart lifted in relief as his nephew entered. His relief became a frown when he saw the young man was wearing a servant's brown robe and had a bundle on his back. A row of candles in front of an altar lit his face as he hastened down the aisle to where Esquin was waiting. In the pallid light, Martin looked sick with fear.

Esquin pulled his plain cloak tighter around him as his white mantle slipped into view. The priest had been a little too interested in him, a stranger in his church, and there was no sense making the man more intrigued by revealing what he was. 'Martin?' he queried, as the young man came towards him. 'What is this?' He gestured at the bundle.

'I'm leaving the Order. I'm coming home to Montfaucon with you. Tonight.'

Esquin's concern was overcome by a rush of anger. 'That is out of the question! Your father and I didn't spend all those years training you to have you run away at the first sign of difficulty. I came to meet you tonight to try to help you, not escape your troubles, but face them.'

Martin sank on to the floor, the bundle slipping off his shoulder to sag in his lap.

Esquin drew a breath and knelt beside him. 'Martin, please. You must tell me what is wrong. Is . . . ?' He steeled himself, part of him not wanting his worst fears confirmed. He had heard this went on in some preceptories: masters abusing their positions in the most despicable ways, and dreaded this was the cause of his nephew's despair. 'Is a master treating you badly? Or doing anything . . . improper?'

Martin's eyes that flicked to him, full of fear, seemed to verify this. Esquin felt queasy. He wasn't sure what to say next, but before he could find the words, his nephew began to speak.

'I never wanted to do it. I swear. But I thought . . . I thought it was what happened at initiations. I thought everyone must do it and that you and Father had done it too. But I wanted to know for sure and so I began asking some of the knights who were friends of mine.' Martin's face was slack and grey. 'They said they never did that.'

'What?' pressed Esquin, when the young knight paused. 'Never did what?'

'They told me I would be part of something great, something that would change the Order. They said it was . . . *good*.' Martin's voice grew fierce. 'But how can it be good? They made me drink blood and choose a path, and I thought they just wanted to make me frightened, to test my strength and my nerve, but then . . .' He hung his head, in his mind's eye seeing it happening again. 'Then they made me spit on the cross.'

Esquin stared at his nephew, unable to believe what he was hearing. These men he was talking about were Templars, warriors of Christ. *Christians*. But he saw no lie in the youth's eyes, just desperate fear. 'Who made you do this? Who initiated you? Which master was it?'

'He wore a skull,' said Martin in a hoarse voice, his hands wrapping around the bundle. 'A mask of a skull. It had other faces too.' He looked at his uncle suddenly. 'They all wore masks. When we initiated more knights I wore one too. I cannot stop seeing the ceremonies.' He pressed his knuckles to his eyes. 'I dream of it. I hear God's voice telling me I am damned. Telling me my soul is lost to Satan, that I have allied myself with worshippers of evil, pledged myself to them, drunk their blood!' He took his hands away and clutched his uncle's arm. 'Please, uncle. Tell me what to do.'

Esquin grasped his shoulders. 'Who did this, Martin? Answer me. Who are these men?'

'Can I help?'

Esquin looked round to see the priest heading over. 'Thank you. We just need a moment of peace.'

A rush of wind made the candles by the altar shiver. The priest frowned at the door. Esquin, still looking up at him, saw his face change.

The priest's jaw slackened and his hand rose to the wooden cross around his neck. 'Dear Lord.'

Esquin turned in the direction of his gaze and saw men, twenty or more, funnelling into the church. All wore masks, painted red with a white stag's head on each, and a plain white mantle. As the last entered, pulling his mask down and shutting the door, Esquin glimpsed part of a face: a square of jaw, a clipped black beard. Then his attention was drawn to those at the front, who had unsheathed their swords.

Martin had leapt to his feet and was backed up against the pillar. 'Please, no,' he was whispering. 'No.'

Esquin didn't look round as footsteps slapped away behind him. The priest had fled. He reached for his own sword and drew it, planting himself in front of his nephew. 'Stay back,' he warned the front row of men, advancing. 'Stay back!'

'Our master feared you would betray us, Martin,' said one at the front. 'But I thought better of you. I thought you would honour the oaths you swore.'

'Honour?' growled Esquin. 'How dare you speak of honour! I know what you made him do. What perversions you had him commit, endangering his soul! What has our Order come to that men like you infect it? You should be thrown into Merlan. All of you!'

'You do not understand,' answered the man, his words flat, muffled through the mask. 'But you will.' He pointed his sword at Martin. 'Seize him.'

'Run, Martin!' shouted Esquin, shoving his nephew away and meeting the ringleader. He gritted his teeth as he clashed with the masked man, who flicked his blade aside easily.

'Don't be a fool, de Floyran. Put down your weapon.'

Esquin lunged. The man ducked to the left, grabbed his arm and, pulling his sword-arm wide, brought his knee up into Esquin's stomach. Esquin dropped the blade and sank to his knees, wheezing. Through smarting eyes, he saw men coming towards him. One held a black hood.

'Don't hurt him,' the ringleader warned. 'Our master will want to question him. The traitor you can kill.'

Martin entered the sacristy and banged the door shut behind him, jamming the bolt home. Gasping with fear, he dragged a chest in front of it, then stared around wildly. Behind a clothes-perch, from which hung several robes, he saw a small black door, the wood scarred with age. It looked as if it hadn't been opened in years. Faintly, he heard his uncle cry out, then heavy footsteps approaching fast. As the door began to rattle in its frame, Martin threw the clothes-perch aside. The exit was locked and there was no key to be seen. He started as a crash sounded behind him, then slammed his shoulder into the wood. The door shuddered, but held. Gritting his teeth, he tried again, shouting in desperation. The crashing was loud and steady. It sounded as though the knights had picked up a bench and were ramming their way through. He took several steps back, then launched himself at the black door. The wood, brittle and rotten, burst apart. Martin fell into the alleyway outside, just as the bolt on the sacristy door tore away from the frame. He threw himself forward, his hands sliding in mud and decaying rubbish, rats scurrying away before him. Pushing himself to his feet, he began to run.

Martin made it halfway down the alley before he saw torch flames appear ahead. The knights had come around the side of the church to cut off his escape. He turned to run back, then skidded to a halt as he saw men piling out of the sacristy behind him. He sank to his knees, his will leaving him, as they came towards him. Raising his head to Heaven, he saw, in the blue slice of evening sky far above, a single star, burning bright. Martin clasped his hands together. 'Hail Mary, full of Grace. The Lord is with thee,' he breathed, closing his eyes as the swords swung in.

25

The Royal Palace, Paris

20 November 1303 AD

'You never should have involved Colonna.'

'I see that now,' answered Nogaret, watching Philippe's face as they walked through the royal gardens. Servants were sweeping dead leaves into piles and two bonfires had been lit, the spiralling flames pushing back the evening. The North Star glinted coldly and the air was bitter with smoke and frost. The minister gave a shrug. 'But in the end, my lord, everything went as planned. Boniface was charged with heresy and died of shock, at least to all concerned. His body was taken to Rome, where his crimes were listed by the cardinals who support us, and the Sacred College elected Niccolo Boccassino.'

'I would have preferred to choose the candidate myself,' said Philippe, as they continued across the lawn towards the mews.

'That was impossible. The Sacred College understandably wanted to move quickly to replace Boniface. There was simply no way of halting that process long enough for me to return here to advise you.'

'How can we be certain this new pope will do as we wish?' Philippe halted, turning to the minister. 'This has been a trial for me, Nogaret. I want things to go back to the way they were. I want a good relationship with Rome again.' He started walking. 'But we can heal these wounds, yes?' He didn't wait for an answer, but ploughed on, lacing his hands as if about to pray. 'It was an ugly business, but necessary for the future of the kingdom.'

'Benedict XI, as he named himself, is weak and ailing. Our allies in the Sacred College felt, of all the possible candidates, he would be the most easily manipulated. As it is, he has already bowed to the pressure of lifting the order of excommunication placed on you by Boniface. France is safe.'

'But he refused to lift the orders placed on you and Sciarra Colonna.'

Nogaret's mouth curled. 'Unfortunately, Boccassino was one of the cardinals who remained in Anagni during the riot. He holds Colonna and me responsible for the damage done that day. But,' he added stiffly, 'I am certain he can be mollified in time.'

'And Campbell?' ventured Philippe, ducking through the archway in the garden wall and entering the enclosure. 'How did he fare?'

Nogaret's brow tightened as he walked with the king down the line of mews houses. Most of the birds were inside, the perches empty. There were torches burning at the far end, outside the lodgings of Sir Henri and his staff. 'He did as he was told, if that is what you mean, but I do not trust him.'

'The Templars?'

'I cannot help thinking it very coincidental. We arrive to arrest the pope and he is surrounded by knights.'

'If Boniface suspected an attack the Templars or the Hospitallers would have been the most likely choice for military protection. Was there any proof Campbell was involved in their arrival? Anything else that made you suspect him?'

'No,' Nogaret admitted.

'So he did as he was bid? Fought alongside you against the knights?'

'My lord, whatever use you feel he would be to our plan for the Temple is surely outweighed by the question of whether we can trust him or not. It is an unnecessary risk. I would advise you to send him back to Scotland, him and that daughter of his. I spoke to the queen before I left for Italy. The girl is clearly enamoured of you and by all accounts has been for some time. The queen seemed troubled and—'

'Answer my question.'

'Yes,' said the minister finally. 'He fought with us, but even so, I . . .' He stopped as Sir Henri came out to meet them.

'I want you to bring Campbell to me,' said Philippe.

'Now?'

'Yes, now, Nogaret. Sir Henri!' Philippe called, his tone becoming lighter. 'Is Maiden still awake?'

'Yes, my lord. Shall I fetch her food?'

'No need,' replied Philippe, holding up a cloth parcel. 'I had the palace cooks put some meat aside for her tirings.'

Nogaret hesitated, wanting to put Philippe off his decision, but the king was already following the falconer to Maiden's mews and his orders were clear.

*   *   *

Will stood outside the dormitory door, his hand curled in a fist, poised to knock. He lifted it, then stopped as two servants came hurrying down the passage. He waited until they passed, then raised his hand again. Still, he paused. Finally, angered by his hesitation, he went to strike the wood, but was stopped by a sharp voice. Looking round, he saw Guillaume de Nogaret in the shadows at the end of the passage.

'The king wants to see you.'

With a last glance at Rose's door, Will headed to the minister, all at once alert. They had arrived in Paris that afternoon and he had expected the king to question them on the assignment, but something in Nogaret's tone and expression told him this was more than a simple report.

He followed the minister through the palace, out into the royal gardens, where the wind was whipping the flames of the groundsmen's fires high into the darkness. Philippe was in the mews enclosure, Maiden perched on his gloved hand, tearing feathers and flesh from a chicken leg. The king glanced up as Will and Nogaret entered the ruddy pool of torchlight.

'My lord.' Will bowed.

Philippe didn't acknowledge him for a moment, but watched Maiden rip apart the meat. Will could feel the tension coming off Nogaret, standing stock-still at his side.

'I imagine you must have questions about the events in Italy, Campbell,' said the king finally. 'Questions, perhaps, over the morality of what was done and the reasons for it?'

'I have a few, my lord,' responded Will slowly.

'Do you believe that the end justifies the means?' enquired Philippe, frowning pensively, as if wondering about the answer himself. 'That sometimes we may be forced to do unthinkable things that many may benefit?'

'I would say that would depend on the circumstances, but having fought in the Crusades I am well aware that sacrifices must sometimes be made for the greater good.'

Philippe nodded. The silence was filled with cracking sounds as Maiden dug her beak into the bone to get at the marrow. 'Boniface was a dangerous man, disturbed even. He was intent on ruining my reputation and, with it, destroying France. That was in part why you were sent to arrest him, although as you must now be aware, his arrest was a cover for his death.' He let out a breath and stared into the sky. 'I did not want it to come to this, but he gave me no choice. Boniface's sacrifice was for the good of France, which in turn will be good for the rest of Christendom. Your homeland included,' he added, looking back at Will. 'You may not have heard, but King Edward is advancing north on another campaign. The victories won by Sir William Wallace and his men are being eroded by his continuing war. Edward calls himself Hammer of the Scots.'

Will clenched his jaw, feeling more removed than ever from his homeland and its fight to survive, further still from his old enemy and his ability to find justice.

'I can help your kingdom, but only if I have the power to do so. Power these days is governed not by the Church, as it once was, but by money and territory. Any king in Christendom will tell you the same. By helping your country, by warring against Edward and his allies in Flanders, I have severely limited my ability to preserve either funds or land. Despite recent victories over my enemies and the confiscation of the Jews' property, my coffers remain diminished. They must be filled or my capacity to give aid to Scotland and, indeed, my own people will suffer. Now that there is, we hope, a more reasonable man upon the papal throne,' continued Philippe, 'I plan to set in motion something myself and Nogaret decided upon some months ago.' He paused, as Maiden tossed back her head to swallow down the bones and feathers. 'I plan to bring down the Temple and to take its wealth. In doing this I will secure the future of France and make this kingdom great again. As great as it was in the days of St Louis.'

Will felt Nogaret's gaze on him. He knew the minister didn't trust him, but in Philippe's scrutinising stare he also saw uncertainty, suspicion even. Perhaps the king didn't trust him either. Perhaps this was a test. He felt certain, if he failed, he would be killed. He could almost sense Nogaret's hand curling round the hilt of his sword, ready to strike the life from him. All at once, something settled inside him. It was the same sensation he got whenever he was about to go into battle; the same resolve, grounding him. For years, he had been drifting from one place to another, different masters, different causes. Now, the path ahead was clear.

Simon had been right, all that time ago in Selkirk: the war for Scotland wasn't his war; it was Wallace's and Gray's, his nephew's. The fight for the Temple, the Anima Templi, the struggle to protect both from enemies within and without, as the oaths he swore had instructed, this was his conflict. The ghosts inside him quietened, falling into an expectant hush, as he put his foot out and stepped on to the path from which he had strayed for so long. 'You will need the pope to support you for this,' he told Philippe. 'The only way you could secure the Order's wealth would be through him.'

'Does this not make you uncomfortable?' asked Nogaret quickly. 'No matter that you left them, you were a Templar for many years, brought up by them. You must have friends within their ranks still?'

Will turned to look at him. 'Whatever loyalty I owed to the Order vanished when they allied themselves with Edward. Why do you imagine I deserted?'

'You may be able to help us,' said Philippe. 'As a former member, who knows the workings of their organisation: details of their defences, resources, assets. Would you be willing to aid us?'

Will took his gaze from Nogaret and focused on the king. 'On the condition that you end this truce with King Edward. In return for helping you bring down the Temple, I want you to protect Scotland.'

As the last of the suspicion died in Philippe's eyes, Will knew he had won the king's trust.

'As I have told you, Campbell, my peace with Edward was only ever temporary. You have my word. When the Temple falls, Scotland shall be free.'

The Temple, Paris, 20 November 1303 AD

Robert knocked again and waited. Still there was no answer from within the solar. He glanced at the faint glow of candles glimmering beneath the door. Perhaps Hugues had forgotten to extinguish them? It was a risk to leave them burning. Snapping down the latch, he entered.

The fire had turned to embers in the hearth and the only light in the draughty chamber came from Hugues's desk, where the flames of three candles switched and fluttered in the wind threading its way around the cloth covering the windows. The Visitor's desk was a chaos of scrolls and parchments, some of which had slipped off to scatter the floor around it. Robert took a step forward, then stopped. Half hidden behind the papers was a figure, head on the desk, one arm flung out in front of him. By the thinning grey hair, he could tell it was Hugues. For a shocked second, he thought the Visitor was dead, then he heard a grunt and saw Hugues's back rise and fall.

Smiling to himself, Robert crossed the chamber. He saw maps among the strewn papers on the table. One, partially unrolled, was of Prussia. Lying next to it was a parchment decorated with a white cross on black: the mark of the Teutonics. There was another with the insignia of the Hospitallers and a whole stack adorned with the great seal of the Temple, showing two knights on a single horse. Robert caught a mention of the island of Rhodes and something about future intentions, before his foot crackled on a stray parchment and Hugues jerked awake.

'Christ,' growled Hugues, scrabbling to set the desk in order.

'Sorry,' said Robert, moving to help. 'I didn't mean to startle you.'

Hugues paused, his gaze flicking over the maps. 'What were you doing?'

'I needed to speak to you.' Robert was surprised by his comrade's tone and the intensity of his stare.

'It is late.'

'I realise that, but I saw the light in your window and thought you were awake.' Robert watched as Hugues began stacking the papers face down on his desk. 'I hoped I might take the opportunity to speak to you while you weren't in a meeting or away on business.'

Hugues glanced at Robert as he picked up the pile of parchments decorated with the Templar seal. 'Some days I feel I am running this Order single-handedly.'

'You've had word from the Grand Master?' questioned Robert, his eyes on the skins.

'I prayed, when Ruad fell, that would be the end of his fruitless Crusade.' Hugues's tone was bitter. 'Yet still he lingers on Cyprus and every month, it seems, demands I send more knights, more horses, more funds for his campaign.' The Visitor's voice was rising. 'I have told him, time and time again, that I need men here. Does he not see this? England and Scotland are still at war and France has become increasingly unstable, with uprisings and border skirmishes, and trouble with Rome. All this, I have told him, yet he bleeds our Order dry of the very things that will safeguard it in these uncertain times. I need men. I need resources. Why does he not understand this?' Hugues seemed to realise he had said too much, for he stopped short, then tossed the rest of the papers on the desk. 'It is late, brother,' he repeated wearily. 'What do you want?'

Robert hesitated, reluctant to add to Hugues's burden. But he had been waiting for answers for months. 'I was wondering if you looked any further into that matter I brought to your attention earlier in the year? The rumours surrounding the initiations?'

Hugues sighed roughly. 'I told you then, it was most likely just idle gossip among the sergeants.'

'All the same, I believe it warranted our attention. The rumours were disturbing and even if there was no substance to them it would be best they ceased. There has always been a certain mistrustful speculation, both in and out of the Temple, about what goes on at the inceptions of knights, especially given the secrecy that surrounds the ceremonies. It could be damaging to the Order's reputation if outsiders were somehow given the impression we are up to no good.'

'Well, I am grateful for your vigilance, but I looked into it and found nothing.'

'Nothing at all? No clue even as to the source of the rumours?'

'Brother, I really have more than enough to concern myself with, without picking through the furtive imaginations of our younger members for absolutely no good reason I can think of.' Hugues lifted his hand as Robert went to speak. 'That is the end of it. I have work to finish.'

'But perhaps if I—'

'I said that is the end of it!' snapped Hugues, banging his fist on the desk. 'Now, leave me!'

Gritting his teeth, Robert bowed and left the chamber. If Hugues did not want to continue the investigation then there wasn't much more he could do. By the time he stepped out into the chill night air, he had more or less convinced himself that the Visitor was most probably right. The rumours were nothing more than sergeants' stories.

26

Outside Bordeaux, the Kingdom of France

11 February 1305 AD

T he soldier knuckled the water from his eyes as the wind whipped
through the undergrowth, stinging his face. On that wind, he could
smell the Garonne, salty and sour.

'How much longer, Gilles?'

'Get down,' growled the soldier, thumping his comrade in the thigh,
making him drop with a wince. 'Do you want to be seen?'

'They can't see us all the way up there, surely.'

'Not them, Ponsard, you idiot.' Gilles frowned irritably and pointed to a
distant clump of trees where two horses were cropping the frost-bitten
ground. There was a man with them. He was stamping in a circle,
presumably to ward off the chill. 'Him.'

Ponsard's gaze moved from the man up the hill to the little white house
on the brow. 'The others are getting restless. We've been here for hours.
Perhaps it's some distant relative he's here to see?' He hefted his broad
shoulders. 'He's got enough of them round here.'

'Then why all the secrecy? The altered accounts? Why does no one
we've asked know where he goes on these journeys?' Gilles's face was set as
he looked back at the house. 'There's something up there he doesn't want
anyone to find out about.'

A grin crept across Ponsard's face as he studied Gilles's intent expression. 'You've got an idea what it is, haven't you?'

'I have my suspicions.'

'Here,' said Ponsard, nudging Gilles. 'Is that him?'

Gilles squinted into the distance. 'I think so,' he murmured, watching
a man step out of the front door, robes flapping. He spoke momentarily
with someone on the threshold Gilles couldn't make out, then descended the track towards the trees, bent against the wind. 'Get the
others,' said Gilles, watching as the man was helped into his saddle by

his squire. 'Let's go and see for ourselves what the archbishop is so keen to hide.'

The five soldiers waited until Bertrand de Got disappeared from view, heading back the way he had come, towards Bordeaux. Then, keeping low to the rushing grasses, they crept up the hillside.

Gilles drew his sword as he approached the house, ducking under the windows. 'Stay outside,' he mouthed to two of the men, 'guard the perimeter.'

They nodded and backed up against the whitewashed walls, where moss sprouted green from cracks in the stone. Gilles went to the front door, Ponsard and another soldier close behind him. He paused, checking they were all in position, then rapped on the door.

There were footsteps on the other side. A bolt slid back and the door opened, revealing a pretty young woman. Gilles grinned, his suspicions confirmed. Her eyes went from the scarlet and blue tunic, visible beneath his riding cloak, to the sword in his hand. Even as her face was registering surprise and the first jolt of fear, Gilles kicked in the door, knocking her backwards. She sprawled on the floor and let out a scream as he pushed his way in. Reaching down with his free hand, Gilles grabbed the front of her dress and hauled her to her feet. Turning her in one rough movement, he wrapped his arm around her throat, pinning her to him. 'I'll bet he knows a new heaven with you,' he growled, then stopped as another woman appeared, this one bulky and ugly. Gilles thrust his sword towards her.

'Who are you?' The woman had planted herself in the passage, but she looked terrified. 'What do you want?'

'Answers to questions,' responded Gilles. 'Such as why Archbishop de Got makes his way so frequently to a house in the middle of nowhere? Which one of you is he swiving?'

The large woman's face reddened. 'How dare you! Archbishop de Got is an honourable man! He has been a close friend of my family's for years. I have been ill for some time and find it hard to get to church. He comes to hear my confession.'

Gilles laughed. It was a cruel sound. 'Been practising that lie, crone?' His muscled arm squeezed the young woman's throat. 'Tell me who he sees out here. The truth! Or I'll snap her neck.'

'Lady Heloise!' blurted his captive, her thin voice constricted. 'It was Lady Heloise!'

'Quiet, Marie!'

'No, Marie, continue,' insisted Gilles, tightening his hold. 'Where is this Heloise?'

'Dead, sir. Dead for years now!'

Gilles frowned. He was about to question her further, when Ponsard let out a shout.

'We've got something!'

Twisting his head round, Gilles saw one of the guards he had stationed outside coming towards the door. He was carrying two struggling boys, one under each arm.

'Found these two trying to sneak away down the hill, sir.'

'No!' The bulky woman started forward, her face filled with horror.

Gilles turned back. 'Why does de Got come here? Answer me!' he shouted, as the hallway filled with the boys' cries.

'To see his son,' blurted the woman, dropping to her knees. 'Please!' she begged. 'Please don't hurt them!'

Gilles studied the yelling children. His eyes quickly dismissed the stocky, older boy, who looked distinctly like the fat woman and went instead to the smaller of the two, who had dark hair, a feeble chin and, now he looked closer, a startling resemblance to the archbishop. Gilles felt a surge of triumph. 'You will go to Paris immediately,' he said, turning to two of the guards. 'We cannot waste any time in this matter. Tell Minister de Nogaret we have found what he's been looking for.'

The Royal Palace, Paris, 2 March 1305 AD

Nogaret hastened through the palace corridors, ignoring the respectful nods and greetings his presence drew from servants and officials alike. He wanted to grin; this had been long in coming and even though he hadn't given up hope of finding something useful, he never expected it would be so advantageous, or, indeed, quite so . . . delicious. But, despite his satisfaction, he made sure his face was set with solemnity as he approached the royal chambers.

Philippe was seated at a table, nursing a steaming bowl of soup. His nose was red where he had been wiping it, his eyes bloodshot. He had been afflicted with the fever for several weeks and his mood was increasingly sour because of it. He glanced up as Nogaret shut the door.

'We have found it, my lord, at last we have found it. The key that will unlock the Temple.'

Philippe set down his spoon. 'What?'

'The companies of men we sent out to look for evidence of corruption. Tools of manipulation. One of them has uncovered something on a potential candidate.'

'Who is it?'

Nogaret had to clamp down a renewed urge to smirk. 'Bertrand de Got.'

'The Archbishop of Bordeaux?' Philippe rose, pushing his soup aside, virtually untouched, and went to the hearth, where the fire was roaring. He shivered. 'What has he done?'

'Conceived a child.'

Philippe turned quickly. 'This is certain?'

'Our soldiers have imprisoned the boy in his house. De Got was apparently involved in a tryst with a young noblewoman seven years ago. She died in labour, but he has been providing for the child ever since. All out of Church funds,' added Nogaret, with relish.

Philippe's face was taut with contemplation. 'The archbishop wouldn't want this to be known, certainly. His career would be damaged irrevocably and the Church might decide to imprison him, or worse. The fear of his secret being divulged would make him obedient in the short term. But what about later? How could this be used then?' Philippe looked at Nogaret, the hope dying in his eyes. 'It couldn't. There would be a risk the Sacred College would remove him for such an offence and then where would we be?' His tone was flat. 'Right back where we started.'

'I am not talking about divulging his secret. I'm talking about using the child.' Nogaret crossed to Philippe. 'We keep the boy in our custody until de Got fulfils our obligations. He clearly cares for his son. Why else would he visit the child so frequently, risking his position, his life even? Any threat to the boy would make him compliant. I am sure.'

Philippe was shaking his head. 'No. I will not sanction that. An innocent child?' He shivered. 'There has been too much blood shed, Nogaret. Too much. Where does it end? Dear God.' He raised a trembling hand to his brow. 'Where does it end?'

'Those deaths were necessary, my lord,' murmured Nogaret. 'And you need not fear. You had no hand in either.'

'Does the bow take no part in releasing the arrow?'

'Boniface would have destroyed France. He was deranged.' Nogaret was stalking, emphatic. 'A heretic. Corrupt and murderous. He deserved death. We gave the world a blessing.'

'Are you starting to believe your own propaganda, Minister?' Philippe's voice was low. 'What about Pope Benedict? Are you going to tell me that feeble old man deserved death, when his only crime was to deny my requests?' He lurched into his chair, folding his arms about his chest and closing his eyes. 'All I can think of is Benedict's soul winging its way to Heaven, his lips, tainted with poison, opening to hiss my name at the gates.'

'You weren't to blame, my lord. If any name was on his lips it was mine.'

Philippe's eyes opened. 'Why did you do it, Nogaret? Why? You were only supposed to have forced him, coerced him.' He rose. 'God, but I think I should have had you executed for such wicked insubordination.'

'You asked Pope Benedict to lift the excommunication order on me and he refused. You requested that he proclaim Boniface a heretic and launch a trial against him, posthumously, and he refused. The old man had more backbone than our allies in the Sacred College realised. None of us was going to get what we wanted from him, least of all the Temple. As soon as I met with him I realised that. What I did was in your interests, my lord, yours and our kingdom's. There was no evidence it was murder. When he left me for a moment, I poured the poison into some figs he had been eating. His death was proclaimed to be from natural causes. The only two people who know any different are you and me.'

'Three,' snapped Philippe. 'There are three who know. You. Me. And God.' He rounded on the minister. 'What would you have done had the Sacred College elected a new pope immediately? Would you have stayed in Perugia to poison more until they chose someone who would serve our will?'

'That was an unlikely prospect with so many who support us established in the College. Thanks to the work we have done over the past year, electing archbishops of our choosing as cardinals, the curia stands divided. One half supports France, the other Rome. None of our cardinals was going to elect anyone who wasn't sanctioned by you. You made a decision, my lord,' Nogaret continued, anger making his voice rise. 'A decision to make France great. Do you believe your grandfather never spilled blood or broke a law in his pursuit of that aim? You are a king, ordained by God. You stand above the law! Louis didn't become a saint by being weak. He took up the Cross, put hundreds to death, exiled the Jews, levied taxes. He fought for his kingdom, his people. The sooner you realise this, the more like him you will become.'

Philippe stared at his minister in silence. After a long moment, he sat. 'I will not sanction any more murders.' He raised his eyes. 'If you disobey me again, Nogaret, I will not hesitate to have you put to death. We will keep the child in our custody for the time being and send word to our allies in the Sacred College that we have found a candidate who is to our liking.'

'Do not forget de Got has connections with King Edward that may make him useful in other ways,' added Nogaret, relieved that the king was once again primed and ready to act.

'What if the other cardinals vote against him?'

Nogaret shook his head. 'This long interregnum hasn't been to anyone's liking. Everyone in the College will be glad to see someone installed on the papal throne. I think it will help that Bertrand is outside any of their influences. That is why we had to look beyond the College for suitable candidates; neither faction would support the other's nominee.'

'That and they were all either too close to Boniface or Benedict, or too strong-willed to be useful,' added Philippe grimly. 'If de Got is accepted by the others, it will be our responsibility to ensure he complies with our wishes without the need for further bloodshed. We will use the child, but only as a tool. No harm must come to the boy. Is that understood?'

'Of course, my lord.'

'We will meet de Got immediately. I want to make certain he will do as we wish. I want to know this key can be turned.'

27

Château Vincennes, the Kingdom of France

4 March 1305 AD

R ose climbed the stairs slowly, the smell of the herbs in her hands rising pungent around her. As the sun passed out of a cloud, a shaft of light blazed down the stairwell from the arched window at the top. She paused in its silvery brightness, feeling in that glow a whisper of lighter days and warmth. A moan sounded from above. Opening her eyes, steeling herself, she continued climbing.

The royal chamber was dark, the velvet drapes drawn across the day. An acrid odour lingered in the air, issuing from a toilet bowl placed beside the large bed. Laying the herbs on a table beside the queen's combs and ointments, Rose padded across to the window and parted the drapes a little, letting the breeze freshen the room. There was another moan. The bedcovers shifted and rolled as Jeanne turned over, wincing at the daylight.

'What is that smell?' she complained.

'Rosemary, rue and yarrow, madam. For your bath.'

The queen's eyes, puffy with sleep, focused on Rose. 'Where is Marguerite?'

Rose paused. 'In Paris, madam,' she said hesitantly. 'Do you not remember? She was ill and stayed behind when we left yesterday.' As the queen struggled to sit up, Rose hurried to bolster the pillows at her back. The queen's face was ashen. 'Perhaps I should call for the physician?' Rose suggested, worried the queen's memory loss was some new symptom of her malady.

'No, I am fine. Just tired.'

Rose moved back from the bed and stood there, waiting for an order. The silence seemed to thicken and swell. Hearing footfalls on the stairs, she looked round, relieved to see a host of servants appear, carrying buckets. They crossed to where the bath had been set near the fire and began pouring water in.

Jeanne struggled out of the bed when the servants had gone. 'Where is Blanche?' she questioned, not looking at Rose as she lifted her nightgown and squatted over the toilet bowl.

Rose averted her gaze. She heard a brief trickle and a gasp of pain as the queen emptied her bladder. 'Lord Philippe sent her and the others to pick more herbs for your medicine. He wanted you to have enough while he was away.'

'I want Blanche,' murmured the queen, crossing to the bath, her hand pressed to her back. 'Blanche always bathes me.'

'She won't be back for a while yet.' Rose went to the toilet bowl, gritting her teeth as the foul odour rose to assault her. As she took it to the window to empty it, she noticed a red hue to the fluid, which, for the past few days, had been a dark, cloudy yellow. Thinking the physician might want to test it, she placed the bowl under the table. 'You do not want your bath to get cold, madam,' she insisted, collecting the bundle of herbs. She rubbed them together, the bitter fragrance bursting between her palms, then dunked them into the bath, as the physician had instructed Blanche the day before. The water was tepid, having cooled quickly in the walk from the kitchens, but the servants had stacked the fire and the blaze had taken the chill out of the air. Pushing up her sleeve, Rose swirled the herbs around. 'This will help,' she said, soft and coaxing as if she were talking to a child, even though, at twenty-seven, she was five years younger than Jeanne. 'And after your bath I will fetch you more medicine and some watered wine to help you rest.'

Morose, but pliable, Jeanne allowed Rose to remove her nightgown and help her into the bath. Rose had seen the queen naked before, but never so close, Marguerite and Blanche having always been the ones favoured to dress and bathe her. She found it hard not to stare at Jeanne's body, so different to her own: her rounded thighs and hips, olive-skinned, covered in downy black hair, her stomach lumpy, webbed with purple lines where the skin had stretched over seven children, her huge breasts, the nipples fat and dark, swinging pendulously as she bent to sit in the water, the bushy black triangle that covered her sex. The queen lay back, shuddering as the water closed over her shoulders.

Rose took up a cloth that had been draped over the side. She walked around to the head of the bath, dipped in the cloth and, crouching down, dabbed at Jeanne's forehead. Tiny beads of sweat had broken out across her skin, either from the fever or the heat of the fire. As Rose brushed them gently away, the queen gave a sigh. After a moment, it faded into a protracted grimace.

Jeanne's hand slid down to her abdomen. She rubbed it fretfully. 'Why will it not stop? The medicine isn't helping. There is a burning inside me. I can feel it. Why won't it stop?'

'I am sure it will.' Rose reached in to dab at the queen's face, but Jeanne sat up suddenly, a wave of herbs and water sloshing around her.

'Don't touch me!'

Rose sat back on her heels. 'Madam?'

Jeanne had turned to look at her, her black eyes glittering. 'This is your doing. Somehow, you have done this. Sorcery, is it?' She rose, water pouring off her, running between her breasts, dripping from her hair. A sprig of rosemary clung to her inner thigh.

Rose stared up at her, speechless.

'You charm me with your smiles, beguile me into keeping you. I should have thrown you out the moment I knew you desired my husband.' Jeanne stepped out of the bath to tower over Rose, still crouched on the floor. 'You little witch! What have you done to me?'

'Madam, please! I don't . . . I wouldn't . . .'

'What is happening?'

Jeanne and Rose turned at the voice to see Philippe enter the chamber. He rushed to the queen who fell into his arms.

'Pass me her gown,' the king ordered, pointing to the bed, where a red, velvet robe lay crumpled.

At his command, Rose jerked to her feet and fetched the garment. As Philippe took it, his fingers brushed hers. She started back, clutching her hand as if he had burned her. The king didn't seem to notice, but wrapped the gown around his wife's body and led her carefully to the bed.

'What happened?' he repeated.

Rose followed. 'She said it felt as though there was a burning inside her. Then she started saying . . . She said these things to me . . .' Rose trailed off, unable to repeat the words in front of him, terrified the queen, who was weeping, might do so at any moment.

Philippe nodded as he helped his wife on to the bed and wrapped her in the covers. 'The physician said the fever might make her delirious. I will have him examine her again.'

'No!' Jeanne grabbed him as he went to move. 'It hurts. I don't want him to touch again. Please, Philippe, please just stay with me.'

He held her to him, stroking her hair and rocking her gently. 'It will pass, my love. Soon it will pass.'

'Say you'll stay,' murmured Jeanne, gripping his tunic. 'Don't leave me.'

'I have to,' Philippe said quietly. 'There is something I must do. But I will not be gone long.' He bent and kissed her hair. 'And when I return you will be better.'

Jeanne sniffed and looked up at him, her eyes red. 'Do you promise?'

'I promise.'

There were footfalls on the stairs as Blanche and the other handmaidens returned with the herbs. The queen's daughter Isabella followed them in, clutching a bunch of bright flowers. Jeanne's face softened as she took them and Philippe lifted the girl on to the bed, with a laugh at how heavy she was becoming. Rose retreated until her back pressed against the far wall while the handmaidens fussed around the royal couple.

After Jeanne discovered her secret, she had hidden it away so deeply that no one, including the queen, had ever mentioned it again. She rarely spoke with the king, except to answer his questions, and always kept her head lowered in his presence, afraid even to look at him lest her face betray her. She did as she was told and worked through her chores meticulously, the most obedient and quiet of all the queen's attendants. Only at night or alone did she allow her desires to live. In shadows and solitude they bloomed, becoming darker, yet more resilient, like weeds that grow in shade. Now, in this gloomy chamber, filled with the smells of sweat and flowers, those fantasies rose before her; a spectre with Jeanne's voice and a finger outstretched in accusation. How often had she imagined the queen sickening and dying, that her desires might live?

Temple Gate, Paris, 5 March 1305 AD

'Why in God's name have you kept all this from me?'

Will looked away across the fields as Robert stared at him, his grey eyes stormy.

The knight moved into his line of sight. 'Indeed, why tell me now? Why not carry on fighting your own battles? The mercenary, as ever.'

'I thought it was over. After Nogaret killed Boniface and Benedict took the papal throne I waited, biding my time until I knew for certain they had secured the pope's support for their plan. When I realised Benedict had defied them, I thought their plot had been halted. I had no idea the lawyer would go so far.' Will shook his head. 'Boniface was the king's personal enemy. Ignoring the fact that they wouldn't have been able to control him and consummate their plan, he could have destroyed Philippe. He was a danger to France. But Benedict . . . ?'

'You know for certain the king's minister murdered him?' asked Robert sharply.

'No. But I think it far beyond coincidence that the pope died during Nogaret's visit, given what I know of Boniface's demise and their plans.'

A cart rumbled towards the gate. They stepped out of the road to let it pass. Robert looked at the Temple, rising white from the bare fields. 'I cannot believe the king would do this.'

'Philippe has gone after every possible opportunity to procure wealth during his reign. The clergy. The Jews. Gascony and Flanders. Even so, his coffers are empty and his plans for expansion remain unfulfilled. His subjects are growing resentful. The king's aggressive methods and the rise in taxes, especially given the poor harvests of recent years, are making them question his ability to rule. Guienne and Flanders are under his yoke, but they are anything but stable. Philippe needs to give his people something more tangible, else their support will start to crumble. He needs to exert himself, but to do that he needs money. This king is not afraid, Robert, of who he might have to step over on his way to sainthood.'

'We must go to Hugues. Tell him everything.'

'No. I don't want anyone else involved.'

'You cannot mean that? This is too much, Will, for either of us to contend with. If the King of France intends to bring down the Temple, the rest of the Order must be informed at once.' Robert's brow knotted in thought. 'The Grand Master will have to be recalled from Cyprus. Most of the officials are out there with him. They will all need to return.'

'And then what? What will Jacques de Molay and Hugues and the others do? Storm the palace? Kill the king?'

'They will meet him. Reason with him. You said it yourself: the king is losing the support of his subjects. Can you imagine what would happen if he went after the Temple? There would be riots in the streets.'

'Would there?' Will shook his head. 'You're still on the inside, Robert. You still see the Temple through the eyes of a knight. Out on the streets, among the people, I see a different Temple. I see a brotherhood corrupted with pride and greed. I see rich and powerful men above the law, arrogant, untouchable. Suspicious men who work in secrecy, their aims unknown.'

'You think that?'

'I am telling you what others see. For years, the Temple has hidden behind its walls, unwilling to involve itself in the affairs of others, unless interfering in them. Now the Grand Master is off fighting a Crusade the people of Christendom no longer believe in things are worse. You know it yourself. The Temple has lost its way.' Will exhaled. 'Since the war that almost destroyed the Christian empire in the East was started by a Templar Grand Master, the Brethren have fought to keep the Order on course, following the path to peace. With Grand Masters Armand de Périgord and Guillaume de Beaujeu we faltered, but through the efforts of Everard, Hasan, my father, through the efforts of you and me, Robert, we didn't fail.'

'Acre wasn't exactly part of our plan,' said Robert in a low voice, moving with Will off the road as a group of monks from Saint-Martin-des-Champs passed solemnly by, followed by a band of raucous youths.

'Acre needed to fall. Elias made me realise that. How could a lasting truce between Christians and Muslims be built upon the foundation of the Crusades? We went there to conquer. It was no basis for peace. We have a much better chance of working towards reconciliation with our armies withdrawn from the Holy Land. We need to send diplomats, not soldiers. Jacques de Molay is wrong. We must steer him right.'

'We?' said Robert sourly. 'You left the Temple, Will.'

'But not its Soul.' Will turned to him. 'I admit my reasons for deserting the Order were self-serving. I wanted revenge on Edward. I still do. But something else has surpassed that desire: the need to rebuild the Anima Templi and set the Temple on its true path. I pledged my life to the Brethren's aims along with many other men, men I respected and believed in, and that means saving the Anima Templi from itself.'

'Saving it from——?'

'Hugues de Pairaud was elected into the Brethren, but he was never made its master. He took that role for himself when I left. None of you voted him into that position. I would not feel so bitter about that had he the vision to lead you, but what has he done to fulfil any of its aims in the years since? You have said it yourself: the Anima Templi does nothing. Hugues is too wrapped up in Temple business to attend to it. He doesn't believe in the Brethren. If he did, he wouldn't have let it fade into nothing. He wouldn't have made an alliance with our betrayer. He wouldn't have sacrificed Scotland and he would have done more, perhaps the only man who could have, to stop Grand Master de Molay following his blind Crusade. Hugues is not my enemy, Robert. But neither is he my ally. The Temple is too fragmented to be guided from within now. We need to rebuild the Brethren outside those conflicting influences if we are to have a chance of protecting it from the king's ambitions.'

'I still do not see how we can do that on our own.'

'Not on our own. Philippe hasn't told me everything; Nogaret still doesn't trust me completely, but I do know who they plan to make pope if the Sacred College can be persuaded to support their choice. The king and his lawyer left Château Vincennes yesterday to meet him. They have something on him, I do not know what, but it is something they will use to coerce him. Nogaret sent men out months ago to search for a candidate who could be persuaded to help them achieve their plan. Their man is Archbishop Bertrand de Got.'

'What do you suggest?'

'I've met de Got before. He seems a reasonable man. Even as archbishop he is in a position of great power; as pope his power will be virtually absolute. If we can get him on our side and work with him against Philippe, he will be in our debt. Without the support of the pope we can do nothing to defend the Order and, in turn, without that same support, Philippe can do nothing against the Order. If we have an ally on the papal throne, we may even be able to stop Edward's war against Scotland once and for all.'

'And what about Scotland?' demanded Robert. 'What if, at the next announcement of an English campaign, you go charging off to save it and destroy your enemy? You admit it yourself, you still want revenge on Edward.'

'Scotland isn't my fight now. It is in the hands of other men. The Anima Templi is in mine, and yours. I want you with me, Robert, but either way I am going to do this. I will not let Philippe and Nogaret pull down the Temple, with my father and Everard's dream at the heart of it. You need to decide whether you can commit to this. You need to decide who you work for. Me. Or Hugues.'

28

Bordeaux Cathedral, the Kingdom of France

20 March 1305 AD

B ertrand de Got wandered the silent aisle between the rows, a gratified smile on his face. The youngest men of the cathedral chapter were bent studiously over their desks and the scriptorium was filled with the rhythmic scratching of goose quills on parchment, and the smell of oak gall ink.

'They are coming on well, your grace,' whispered the canon at his side. 'I believe most will soon be able to assist with readings during services.'

'Which passage do you have them copying?' The archbishop paused to peer over one of the men's shoulders.

'One of your favourites, your grace.'

'Ah, yes,' said Bertrand softly, scanning the neat black script. He closed his eyes. 'Rejoice greatly, O Daughter of Zion! Shout, Daughter of Jerusalem!' As he lifted his voice and the words echoed in the hushed hall, the young men turned in their seats. 'See, your king comes to you. Righteous and having salvation. Gentle and riding on a donkey, on a colt, the foal of a donkey.'

The doors of the scriptorium cracked open. A canon entered and hurried towards Bertrand, his shoes slapping on the stone floor. 'Your grace!'

'Hush,' Bertrand admonished, setting a finger to his lips.

The canon dropped his voice. 'Forgive my interruption, your grace, but there are men here to see you. I told them to wait, but they—' He turned, fearfully, as the clank of armoured boots sounded in the passage.

A group entered the scriptorium. Ten were royal guards in mail coats and blood-scarlet tunics. The eleventh, walking in their midst, was a short, slender man in a black robe and silk coif.

'Minister de Nogaret,' murmured the archbishop, swallowing back the dryness that rose in his throat. Behind him, the scratching of quills ceased, the young scholars all staring curiously at the imperious company. 'Continue with the lesson,' Bertrand ordered the canon. He hastened to meet Nogaret. 'Minister,' he called, trying to make his smile natural. 'This is indeed a surprise. What can I do for you?'

'I need you to come with me,' responded Nogaret, not bothering with any formal greeting or title.

Bertrand's smile vanished. He halted in front of the minister. 'Is there some sort of trouble?'

'There won't be, if you come with me.'

Bertrand was frowning, shaking his head. 'I have many things to attend to today; important meetings with the bishops of my province, who have travelled for days to see me. I cannot leave without good reason.'

'The reason, Archbishop de Got, is that your king wishes to speak to you on an urgent matter.'

'The king?'

'Lord Philippe is outside the city. He is expecting you.' Nogaret motioned to the open doors. 'Shall we?'

Bertrand's gaze moved to the soldiers, who stepped aside to let him pass. After a moment's pause, he followed the minister out of the scriptorium.

Half an hour later, after an agonisingly bumpy ride in a covered wagon, into which he had been ushered, alone except for two silent royal guards, Bertrand found himself in a wide green field, the city walls marching away behind him. In the centre, rising incongruously from the grass, was a lurid red pavilion. Bertrand grunted with discomfort as the guards helped him from the wagon. The chronic pain in his stomach, which he had lived with for some years, always seemed worse when he was anxious. He didn't speak, but allowed Nogaret to lead him into the pavilion, where he found King Philippe waiting for him.

Bordeaux Cathedral, the Kingdom of France, 23 March 1305 AD

'No. Absolutely not. His grace is not to be disturbed.'

'It is imperative we speak to him.'

'You will have to return tomorrow, request an audience.'

Will stepped back as the door slammed shut. He glanced irritably at the figure leaning in the shadows of the porch wall, chewing an apple. 'You might have said something. Backed me up.'

Wiping his mouth, Robert moved out of the gloom. He tossed the core into the deserted square. 'Well, I did say they wouldn't let us in, but you didn't listen. It is late. What do you expect? He's probably asleep.'

'It's only just past Compline,' responded Will, heading down the steps to the square and staring up at the cathedral, soaring dizzyingly above him, its walls bone white in the moonlight, gargoyles and angels perched ghost-like on their plinths. Beyond, gossamer wisps of cloud chased across the sky. 'We'll try another way.'

Robert followed, glancing around to check they weren't being observed, as Will moved silently alongside the cathedral wall. They were both dressed in woollen cloaks and tunics that hid their armour. There were doors set at intervals around the main structure, but Will ignored them all and headed instead for a stout entranceway in a high wall. It looked as though it bordered an open space, perhaps gardens or a courtyard. 'Servants' entrance,' he murmured, as Robert came up. He took hold of the iron ring and turned it carefully. The ring creaked, but the door didn't budge. 'Locked.'

'Even if you get inside, how do you expect to find the archbishop? For that matter, how do you know he even resides here? Many bishops have lodgings outside their churches these days.'

'Our friend said he wasn't to be disturbed.' Will had moved away and was staring up at the rough stones. 'He's in there. I'm certain.'

'Why don't we leave it until morning? A few hours cannot make that much difference.' Robert followed his gaze to the top of the wall. 'Christ, Will, we're not fifteen any more.'

'Lost your nerve?' Will's teeth flashed in the moonlight. He took a few steps back, then launched himself at the door, ramming his shoulder into the wood.

Robert swore as the sound echoed. A couple of doves flew up out of a cote, flickers of white against the black. Will tried again, grunting with the effort. On the third try, the lock snapped and the door sprang open. He grabbed it before it could slam back and entered quickly, flexing his bruised shoulder. Finding himself in a courtyard, he drew his sword. Large stones set at intervals in the grass formed a path, leading to a grand building that backed on to the cathedral. There were a few outbuildings and a cistern in the yard.

Pushing the door closed behind him, Robert followed Will, unsheathing his own blade. 'You never had it mended?'

Will was heading for a passage in the building ahead, into which the path of stones disappeared. 'What?' he murmured distractedly.

'Your old sword.'

The two of them pressed themselves up against either side of the passageway. As Robert stared down it, squinting into the gloom, Will glanced at the sword in his hand. The broken falchion was back in his room in the royal palace, wrapped in an old shirt inside a locked chest. For a long time, he had planned to take it to an armourer, certain that it could be restored. But he never had. There was something that felt wrong about it. He hadn't understood what until he had taken the blade out one day, not that long ago, to find tiny specks of dried blood embedded in the pits and grooves in the shaft. Scratching them off with a fingernail, he guessed they belonged to the last person he had killed with the sword: the unknown Templar at Falkirk. That the blade should remain broken seemed somehow fitting. He looked at Robert, feeling a need to explain himself, but just then hurried footsteps sounded, clapping off the passage walls.

A figure, clad in a grey, hooded robe, appeared. He held a blazing torch and was headed for the door they had broken. His cowl blocked his peripheral vision and he didn't see the two men until Will grabbed him from behind.

The man gave a cry and dropped the torch, which sputtered and hissed as it hit the damp ground.

'Take us to Archbishop de Got,' ordered Will, pressing his blade to the man's neck, firm enough to show he meant business, but not to draw blood. 'Do it!'

The man turned and walked unsteadily back the way he had come. Will moved in behind him discreetly keeping his sword point in the man's back. In this way, Robert walking at the other side, they made their way through the passage into moon-washed cloisters, across a lawn and into an imposing building. It was late and most of the cathedral's chapter were sleeping, ready to rise before dawn to sing in the office of Matins. They saw one other figure, passing the end of a corridor ahead, but when their captive hesitated, Will nudged him with the sword point, convincing him to keep quiet. Eventually, they came unmolested to a set of ornate carved doors on the upper storey.

'Please,' begged the man, hesitating outside. 'Do not do this.'

'Go on.'

With a trembling hand, the man reached out and grasped the handle. Turning it to flick the latch, he pushed open the door.

The chamber beyond was dark, filled with frankincense and dislocated whispering. His gaze moving over the shapes of furniture, a crumpled bed, chests, tall silver candlesticks, Will's eyes came to rest on a set of black drapes, embroidered with hundreds of gold crosses. As he approached, the whispering grew louder. Leaving Robert to guard their captive, Will went forward and swept one of the curtains aside.

There was a shout of alarm and a figure spun to face him. It was Bertrand de Got. He was kneeling in front of a small altar, draped with a white cloth, upon which were a smoking censer and a black Bible. A shaft of moonlight slanted into the recess from a pointed window, gleaming on the archbishop's tonsured head. His shocked gaze went from Will to Robert.

'Forgive me, your grace,' moaned the captive, sinking to his knees. 'These knaves made me bring them to you.'

Bertrand rose. He was dressed for bed in a long white shift. A large cross, encrusted with gems that sparkled darkly, hung against his chest. His hand went to it. 'Take this,' he said, holding it out to Will. 'It is worth a fortune. Take anything you want!'

'We're not thieves,' said Will gruffly. 'We've come to speak to you. We mean you no harm.'

When Bertrand's face remained full of fear, Will sheathed his sword. 'Have you had a visit from King Philippe recently?'

The archbishop's brow creased. 'What is this? Who are you?'

'Friends who do not wish to see the king take advantage of you.'

Bertrand swallowed. Finally, he turned to their captive. 'Leave us, Pierre.'

The man got to his feet. 'Your grace?'

'I will be all right.'

As if to confirm his words, Robert sheathed his blade. Needing no further encouragement, the man left the chamber. They heard his footsteps padding away down the passage.

'I expect he will raise the alarm,' said Bertrand, going to his bed and snatching up a velvet robe, which he pulled around his thin shoulders. 'Explain yourselves. How do you know of the king's visit?' He peered at Will's face in the blue moonlight. 'Do I know you?'

'I was in a council you attended in the London Temple about a decade ago and I've seen you a few times since then in the royal palace in Paris, where I have been a guest of the king for some years.'

'Are you one of Philippe's men?' questioned Bertrand, drawing his robe tighter around him, his voice hoarse. 'Is this some trickery?' He shook his head. 'What more does the king want from me?'

'You misunderstand me, your grace. I am not the king's man, nor an ally of his. I am here to help you, if you will let me.'

Bertrand pressed his lips together, then turned away. 'I don't know what to do,' he murmured. 'I don't know.'

'Just answer me this; did the king tell you what he wanted? His plans for you?'

After a long pause, Bertrand nodded. He sank on to the bed. 'He told me I will be pope,' he whispered. 'That he has agents in Perugia at this moment, organising my election.'

'Did he tell you why?'

'He said he had five obligations he wanted me to fulfil when I was crowned.'

'What were they?' pressed Will.

'That I would lift the excommunication order on Guillaume de Nogaret. That I would nominate cardinals into the Sacred College who support Philippe and France, provide papal funds to finance any ongoing struggles against Edward of England and the guilds of Flanders, and that I would formally denounce Pope Boniface as a heretic.'

'That is four, your grace,' said Robert, when the archbishop drifted into silence.

Bertrand looked up. 'And that I would dissolve the Order of the Temple, delivering its assets to Philippe and his heirs.'

'Jesus,' murmured Robert.

Will realised, by the shock in his tone, that the knight hadn't quite believed this was real until now. 'What was your answer?' he asked Bertrand.

'I said no,' Bertrand told them, angry all of a sudden. 'I said I would not corrupt the holy office in such a way. I said the Knights of the Temple were the only men left fighting for Jerusalem and I would not dissolve them!' He shook his head. 'But they told me if I refused they would kill him.' His face crumpled. 'Dear God, they have my son! The bastards have my son!'

Will exchanged a stunned look with Robert, then crossed to the archbishop, who had put his head in his hands. 'Where do they have him, your grace?'

'Not seven miles from here, in the house I bought for him.' Bertrand stared at Will, despair plain in his face. 'I cannot lose him,' he said, clutching at Will's hands. 'My beautiful boy. Please. I cannot!'

'What did they say would happen now?'

Bertrand heaved out a breath. 'They made me sign an agreement and told me that when I was crowned with the papal tiara and had fulfilled my obligations, my son would be returned to me.'

'We will help you,' Will said, thinking quickly. 'But in turn, you must help us. When the time comes, you must not give in to the king's demands.

You will not dissolve the Temple. You will protect the Order. As pope, you would be the only man who could.'

'No!' Bertrand was incoherent with terror, babbling his son's name. Somewhere outside, a bell began to clang, too early for Matins.

'Listen to me, your grace.' Will crouched in front of him, forcing the archbishop to look at him. 'Raoul will not be harmed. You will go along with Philippe's orders. Then, when you are crowned, we will liberate your son, removing the tool the king plans to use to manipulate you.'

'Liberate him?' Hope flashed across Bertrand's face. 'Then you can do this? Do this now?'

'No. Philippe must think he has your support. The point at which we rescue Raoul will be when it is too late and you are already crowned.' Will rose, the archbishop following him with dark, desperate eyes. 'This is the only chance you will have to save your son.'

'But Nogaret?' breathed Bertrand, jerking to his feet as footsteps sounded beyond the chamber, followed by voices, calling for the archbishop. Robert hastened to snap the bolt across the door. A moment later, fists began to pound upon it. Bertrand looked back at Will. 'I have heard Pope Boniface died of shock after the outrage at Anagni and the minister's treatment of him. And I have heard darker rumours, rumours that perhaps Pope Benedict didn't die naturally after all. Nogaret might do the same to me.'

'You have to trust me, your grace. Trust me and I will save your son.'

'I will,' insisted Bertrand, as the door burst open. 'I will!'

29

Château Vincennes, the Kingdom of France

9 April 1305 AD

P hilippe spurred his horse on, faster now, as they passed into the forest. The royal guards and advisors struggled to keep his reckless pace. Sunlight flashed through the trees, turning the well-trodden track into a path of gold. Philippe knew these woods well. He had grown up here, climbing oaks and chestnuts with his brothers, learning to ride and to hunt. He had flown his first falcon here, years before Maiden. There was freedom in such memories, so far from the burdens of adulthood and kingship, the endless politics and game-playing. Every time he rode this track to the château, leaving behind the chaos and filth of the city, he felt the fetters falling away, felt youth returning.

Today, without the constant burrowing itch of his hair shirt, the joy was complete. He hadn't worn the garment in almost a fortnight and his skin was starting to heal, the scars of mortification fading into pale webs across his back. Since his journey to Bordeaux had proved so encouraging, he had allowed himself a brief respite from his daily penance, which, prior to the meeting with Bertrand de Got, had become more frequent and severe. Now, freed from discomfort and worry, he could allow himself to delight in this homecoming. He could relish the warmth of the sun on his face and the fresh smell of the trees to either side of him, stretching into verdant shadows, thick with adventure. These were the woods his brothers and he had quested through, searching for boar and deer. These were the trees that had shaded him and Jeanne as they lay together, awkward in their first, tentative explorations, the trees he had watched his own children climb, their voices shrill with fear and exhilaration on the higher branches.

Catching a glimpse of the grey turrets of the château, Philippe slowed the horse to a canter, wanting to prolong his enjoyment. The day was breezy and bright, ideal for a hunt. He decided he would organise one tomorrow, just for himself, Sir Henri and a few hand-picked courtiers. He craved that sense of conclusion he felt at the end of a successful chase; the climax of the thrill when he loosed the arrow or the bird that would end it, sealing his victory. Politics so very rarely gave him that same satisfaction. Everything was so drawn out and convoluted. He felt, as king, that things should move when he wanted them to; people should bow and obey, fall to his will and bend to his whim. The protracted, shambolic business with Rome, the belligerence of Boniface and truculence of Benedict, had exhausted him beyond belief. Now, at last, it seemed as though he had got his way. Nogaret was abroad, making sure enough pressure was put on the cardinals in Perugia to get de Got elected; so long as there were no unexpected delays, he was finally on course to securing his realm and, more importantly, his own salvation.

Philippe smiled as he rode up to the château, not noticing the troubled looks the guards on the gates shared as he passed through, or the subdued manner of the squires who hastened from the stables to take his weary mount. It wasn't until the royal steward came out to greet him, along with his closest advisors, that Philippe halted, his smile falling away. He stared at their solemn, sorrowful faces and something clutched, icy tight, around his heart.

The king thought first of Isabella and Louis: his favourite and his heir. He must have spoken the children's names out loud, for the steward was now shaking his head and coming towards him.

'My lord,' he was saying. 'My lord, I am so very sorry. The queen—'

But the steward didn't get to finish, for Philippe was running past him, sprinting down the passageway, not hearing the calls at his back as he raced madly towards his wife's chambers.

The Royal Palace, Paris, 12 April 1305 AD

Water poured in streams from the rooftops, turning the grime that caked the streets to a grey sludge. The sky was leaden, clouds drifting heavy and low, swollen with rain. The towers of Notre Dame were lost in the murk and, beneath, the city lay trapped, people's heads bowed under the endless curtain, faces pinched with cold. Shop doors and shutters were closed against the chill, and just a handful of traders in the marketplace were hunched under the canopies of their stalls, calling listlessly to those who hurried past. The blue skies and burgeoning warmth of the past few weeks felt like a season ago. Winter, it seemed, had returned.

Will dismounted in the palace courtyard and looked around for a squire to take his horse, but other than a couple of distant guards the yard was empty and so he led the beast to the stables. He was sodden and splattered with mud from the hard day's ride, but discomfort wasn't foremost in his mind. He had spent the past few days perfecting the excuse he planned to give the king for his absence, but each time he played it through in his mind it sounded more and more like the lie it was. Before leaving for Bordeaux with Robert, he explained to Pierre Dubois that he'd received a message from William Wallace, ordering him to Lyons to meet a potential financier for the war. Dubois had noted this with preoccupied disinterest, but Will knew Philippe would be more inquisitive about his departure. For that reason he had been hoping to return to the city before the king. He might have, if not for events in Bordeaux.

When the canons of the cathedral broke into Bertrand de Got's chambers, he and Robert were seized and taken to a cell, where they were detained for several days. The chapter had persuaded the bewildered archbishop that they must be punished for their trespass and it wasn't until de Got came to his senses and managed to regain his authority that they were released without charge. With this delay and the rain that had swept in to hamper their journey, Will was certain the king would have reached Paris before them and would no doubt question him rigorously on his absence and the reasons for it.

Approaching the stables, Will found some grooms sheltering from the rain. They were huddled on bundles of hay, talking quietly. A couple of them jumped to their feet as Will ducked through the streams of water pouring from the eaves.

'Sorry, sir,' said one, taking the reins of his horse. 'Didn't see you there.'

Will looked around, struck by the silence and emptiness of the place, the grooms seemingly without master or duties. He stared through the sheets of rain out across the deserted courtyard. Come rain or snow, the palace yard was always crowded with people, bustling through on business. 'Where is everyone?'

The groom looked uncertainly at his comrades.

One, who was older than the rest came over. 'At the funeral, sir.'

'Funeral?'

The youth looked surprised. 'Of the queen, sir.'

Will sucked a breath through his teeth. On the heels of the shock came a slightly discomforting spark of hope. Surely this tragedy would delay

Philippe's designs for Bertrand and the Temple, giving him more time to put his own plans in place? He knew how close the king and queen had been. Then a finger of doubt laid its cool touch upon his anticipation. History had shown such deep sorrow could focus a man as well as distract him. He thought of Edward, who had grown only more ruthless in his bereavement over his beloved queen. He was, Will realised, simply thinking of his own grief after the death of Elwen, a grief that had plunged him into years of directionless torment. No. He could not anticipate what this would do to Philippe, or his plans.

'They're coming!'

Will turned as a young boy came scurrying into the stall. All at once, the grooms launched into a flurry of activity. Outside, Will heard the clapping of hooves in the wet. He moved into the rain to watch as the funeral cortège made its way into the palace.

First came the guards, blinking rain from their eyes as they rode into the courtyard, their uniforms sopping. Behind came the king, alone and on foot, his face poised somewhere between anguish and disbelief, rendering his expression almost blank. His black robes trailed behind him, coated with mud. Following him were his principal advisors, Pierre Dubois and Guillaume de Plaisans, the royal steward and his confessor, Guillaume de Paris. Of Nogaret, Will noted, there was no sign. After them came the children, Isabella small and lost, clutching the hand of her nursemaid and a single red rose. The handmaidens followed, Marguerite sobbing into her palm, Blanche at her side, supporting her. There was a host of other mourners: royal staff, bishops and clergy, dukes and dignitaries, all filing solemnly through the gates.

Within the line, Will glimpsed a thin, white figure in a black gown. He felt something wrench in him at the sight of his daughter, who looked so terribly alone in the midst of the vast crowd, stumbling along by herself. In a small sense, his single-minded determination to prevent the king from subjugating the Temple had been almost a relief, enabling him to ignore the rift that had widened into a chasm between himself and Rose. He had told himself that once he made sure the Temple was protected, he would turn his attention to his daughter. But he knew this was just another form of escape, and he had done altogether too much of that in recent years. She was his daughter, in love if not in blood, and that had never changed or diminished. It was his courage that had faltered.

It was that realisation that took him forward, his feet splashing through the puddles as he crossed to her. Rose flinched when he took her arm, but let him lead her out of the line, away across the courtyard. She seemed to be in shock, numb and compliant at his side, as he steered her through the royal gardens to a stone bench in a secluded corner, sheltered by a broad yew.

'You're wet through,' he murmured, as they sat. Realising he had nothing to dry her with, for he too was soaked to the skin, he settled for brushing back the strands of her hair, dark with rain, that clung to her forehead. Will's hand fell as he studied her face, her eyes staring and vacant, her skin pallid except for two hectic spots high on her cheeks. He realised he hadn't seen her this close in months, maybe longer. As a child, he had been struck by how similar to Elwen she was, but those similarities had since faded from her and she had now grown into her own face. It was a face filled with sadness and loss so profound it took his breath away. He gripped her frozen hand. 'Rose, I know you do not believe me and I have given you no reason to, but I never stopped loving you. If you believe nothing else, please believe that. I was scared.' He shook his head. 'No, I was selfish. I put my grief before my love. I let what happened to Elwen – to your mother, overshadow what I felt for you and what I should have done as a father. I do not expect you to forgive me. But I hope—'

'It was me.'

Her voice was so quiet, it took him a moment to realise what she had said. His heart pounded. She hadn't said no.

'I killed the queen.'

Will felt shock slam the hope out of him. 'What?'

She stared at the gardens, misty with rain.

Will gripped her shoulders, turning her to him. 'Rose, talk to me. What do you mean?'

Her gaze focused on him. 'I wished she would die so often. But I didn't want that.' Rose shook her head. 'I watched her die. Dear God.' Her face crumpled in disgust. 'The smell of that room. The smell of death as the fever took hold and her blood was poisoned. She was in so much pain and it was so very slow. We could do nothing. Nothing but watch.'

'Then it was a sickness?' pressed Will, not daring to feel relief yet. 'A fever?'

'In here.' Rose placed her hand low on her belly.

Now Will let the relief come. He sat back. 'Why in Christ's name would you say you killed her?'

'Didn't you hear me?' Rose stood, her face hardening. 'I said I wished it.'

'Why? Was she cruel to you?'

Rose went to walk away, but Will pursued her and took hold of her arm. 'Why did you wish the queen would die?'

'Because I love him.'

'Philippe?' he asked, after a long pause.

When she nodded, Will wondered grimly whether he had somehow been the cause of this; his abandonment driving her to seek affection at such impossible, reckless heights. The idea of his daughter wishing another woman dead in her fantasies about a man so dangerous and volatile, a man he was actively working against, was disturbing to say the least. Trying to push aside these deeper concerns, he focused instead on something he understood. 'Listen to me, Rose,' he said, coaxing her back to the bench. 'You didn't kill the queen by wishing it.'

'You don't know that.'

'I do. I once thought I had done the same to my sister.'

She looked at him.

'I never told you this, any of it. But it was the reason my father took me out of Scotland when I was a boy, the reason he joined the Temple as a knight and the reason I spent so many years trying to follow in his footsteps.'

He had her full attention now.

'My sister Mary and I were rivals, closer in age than with my older sisters. She was my father's favourite, which didn't help. I spent a long time wishing she would disappear, run away, get lost. I cannot recall if I ever wished she would die, but my feelings were clear: I didn't want to share my house or my father with her. I told you long ago that my sister drowned. What I didn't tell you was that I caused it.' Will looked away, unable still, after all these years, to look someone in the eye as he admitted this. 'It was an accident. We were arguing by the loch near our estate and I pushed her away from me, harder than I meant to. She fell and hit her head. I tried to save her, but I failed. It tore my family apart. My father left for the Holy Land the year after and I never saw him again. Him or my mother.' Will thought he saw a look of understanding in Rose's eyes, empathy even, but it was gone before he could be sure. 'I carried my guilt for years, perhaps I always will. But for a long time it affected almost every choice I made, leading me to execute the most deplorable, thoughtless acts, all in some misguided attempt at atonement. I didn't cause her death by wanting it, I caused it by accident. I know that now. But, Rose, I wasted so much on that false belief. I cannot bear to think of you doing the same.' Will grasped her hands. 'Do not bear this burden. Let it go. Your guilt, your fear, this' – he shook his head – 'hopeless love.'

Her face changed. It was like a wall going up. 'Hopeless? You think he couldn't love me?'

'Rose, I just—'

'Is it because I am too ugly to love?' She wrenched back the diamond-shaped sleeve of her gown to display her scars.

'Ugly?' Will stood. 'God, no. You're beautiful.'

'Because you caused this, *Father*.' She thrust her arm at him, her eyes now dry, cold as marble. 'Just like you caused your sister to die!'

As she ran, he reached for her, but his fingers caught only the back of her veil, which pulled free in his grasp, leaving him standing there holding it, watching his daughter disappear in the rain, feeling a fresh wound opening inside him.

The Royal Palace, Paris, 30 June 1305 AD

Rose hovered in the doorway, listening to the sounds coming from within the king's chamber: a rapid swish, followed by a sharp *flick* and a hiss of breath. Her back ached from standing there so long, leaning against the frame, her hand clutching the door to stop it banging in the warm breeze whispering through the windows, but still she refused to move, not wanting to leave, yet not daring to cross the threshold. Every once in a while she caught footfalls in the corridor and cocked her head to hear if they were coming closer. But none did. The royal apartments were quiet these days.

Following the death of their mother, the princes and Isabella spent most of their time with their nursemaid. Minister de Nogaret was abroad on business and the rest of the royal advisors were rarely admitted an audience with the king, the palace staff having learned to tiptoe around, never laughing or raising their voices. The only person Philippe had spent more than a few hours with had been his confessor, the fearfully devout Dominican, Guillaume de Paris. The dormitory seemed especially hushed and empty now Marguerite and two of the other handmaidens had left to serve the wives of the king's brothers. Rose, Blanche and one other remained to help with the children. There was already some hushed talk of the king remarrying in the future, but Rose knew that was the last thing on Philippe's mind.

These past months, she had stayed as close to him as she felt she could, creeping out of the dormitory to pick up his clothes when he tossed them carelessly on the floor, mending the stitching that was fraying on his favourite cloak, setting fresh flowers by his bed. They were all things that could be done by other people, things she doubted he even noticed, but she wanted – no, needed to do them.

Despite all her fantasies, the reality of the queen's death had sickened her. The very same desires that had sustained her for so long began to turn on her; the guilt and the shame swelling like a boil, poisoning her from within. At Mass, in the Sainte-Chapelle, she prayed more fervently than she ever had before, her eyes closed for the first time in years not in secret reverie, but in sincere penitence. The little tasks she performed for the king were not done because she wanted his affection. They were done in the hope of his forgiveness, a futile hope, she knew, since he had no knowledge of her thoughts or feelings.

Rose winced as a grunt of pain sounded through the curtains of his private chapel, louder now. His breaths were coming fast and hard, in time with the swish and flick. Each one made her flinch, as if she were the one being struck. Unable to stand it any longer, she opened the door and took a few steps into the room. She halted, caught in the mirror by his bedside, her image stock-still, hands clasped in front of her face, fingers pressed to her lips. Another *flick* distracted her and her gaze went to the black curtains, embroidered with the arms of France. Not allowing herself another pause, in which to think, to stop or turn around, she went forward and parted the curtains.

Philippe was on his knees in front of the altar. He wore no tunic and his bare back glistened in the daylight now flooding the recess, slick and red with blood. In his hand, he clutched a horsehair whip. The floor around him was spattered, as was the white cloth on the altar. His head jerked round, his eyes, blinking in the light, distant and feverish.

Rose dropped to a crouch in front of him, her dark blue dress spilling out around her. 'Please, my lord,' she whispered, reaching out to take the whip. 'Please, stop.'

Philippe let her close her fingers over his fist, but didn't relinquish his hold on it. 'Do you pray for me, Rose?' he asked, his voice hoarse with pain.

'Every day, my lord.'

'Do you think it will be enough? The prayers of my subjects?'

Rose shook her head, not understanding him.

Philippe stared blankly at the altar. 'My confessor tells me with enough penance and enough prayer I will hear it.'

'Hear what, my lord?' Rose hadn't taken her hand from his. The two of them were frozen together, their postures stiff and unnatural, her arm stretched out across him, her burns as vivid as his wounds in the pale light streaming into the chapel. The smell of his blood was overpowering.

'The voice of God.' Philippe's eyes swung back to her. 'So many great men, popes, princes, kings and scholars have spoken of it; that wondrous union, the ecstasy of being suffused with God's divine love, His voice like a bell, ringing in their souls. My grandfather made mention of it often, so my father told me. He said God spoke as a river inside him, guiding him, propelling him. But I have never heard it.' His brow furrowed. 'And if I cannot hear Him, surely it must mean God does not hear me? That none of my prayers has been strong enough to reach Him?'

Rose wanted to tell him that he needn't worry. She never heard God either, although she often felt Him up there, watching her, judging her. But before she even uttered them her words seemed like tiny whispers that could never be heard against the vast booming voices of such illustrious men.

Philippe, however, didn't seem to expect an answer, for he spoke on into her silence. 'Because of this, my queen is dead. I prayed to God to keep Jeanne safe while I was away, prayed to Him to make her well, but He cannot have heard me. Or else He did and chose to ignore me, to punish me.'

'No, my lord, I—'

'Things have been done in my name. Blood has been spilled and my confessor tells me the only way to make amends is to spill my own.' Philippe pulled his hand from hers and flicked the whip hard over his shoulder. The horsehair switched across his bloody skin.

'Please, my lord!' Rose grabbed his hand. 'I will pray for you. Let God hear me praising your name. Let Him know your penitence through me!'

He was breathing hard, sweat beading his face, but as she tugged on the whip, his hand uncurled, allowing her to take it and set it on the floor. Moving in front of him, her dress smearing the blood across the white stones, she bowed her head, pushed her palms together and began to pray.

At first, her words wandered aimlessly through her mind, then slowly they found a rhythm and began to build inside her into a flowing, if not coherent prayer, made up of promises and pleas, adulations, lines of psalms and repeated Paternosters. She prayed fervently and sincerely, hardly even aware of the king, kneeling at her back, his breathing slower, stronger now, filling the chamber along with the faint murmurs that escaped her lips. *May you forgive him his sins, O Lord, as you forgive us all.*

'Jeanne told me once that she wanted to dismiss you.'

Rose stopped, for a split second so caught up in her litany she thought it was God who had spoken. Her eyes snapped open as she felt Philippe shift behind her.

'She said that you desired me. That your affection was dangerous.'

Rose pressed her palms together so tightly her arms began to tremble.

'I laughed and told her she was being foolish. I said it would be a shame to lose such a conscientious servant over some girlish fantasy. I persuaded her to keep you for her sake, but in truth I enjoyed your adulation.' His voice was closer, his words whispering on the back of her neck. 'A subject should love her king, any way that love is expressed, whatever form it takes. I am pleased that you pray for me, Rose. I need you to pray for me.'

Rose felt his hands closing around her upper arms. She didn't want to breathe.

'Don't stop,' he murmured.

Her eyes fluttered closed and she tried to pray, but there were no words any more, just a rushing darkness that made her feel dizzy.

'My Lord King.'

They both started at the voice.

Guillaume de Nogaret was standing in the chamber beyond, his pale face framed between the gap in the black curtains left hanging open. The king stood and pushed his way into the room. 'Has your absence made you forget your manners, Nogaret?' he growled. 'Why didn't you knock?'

'I tried, my lord. But you obviously didn't hear.'

Rose had got to her feet. She felt Nogaret staring at her, cold and knowing. Heat rose in her cheeks. 'My lord,' she whispered, bowing her head and slipping from the room. Before she closed the door, she heard the minister speak.

'I learned of the queen's death on my way through France, my lord. I am so very—'

'I do not want your pity, Nogaret. I want to hear that you bring good tidings.'

'Then, my lord, let my news be a comfort. We secured two-thirds of the vote. De Got stands elected. He will be the next pope. The way to the Temple is clear.'

30

Near Bordeaux, the Kingdom of France

14 November 1305 AD

⚜

'Are you certain this is the right way?' Robert rose in his stirrups to survey the windswept fields. The leaves on the vines were brittle and yellow, the fruit long since plucked and turned into wine. 'Perhaps we should have gone left at that fork?' He frowned at Will, who was a few paces behind, looking back over his shoulder. 'Are you listening?'

Will nudged his horse forward. 'What?'

Robert looked past him down the track to where he had been staring. 'You're not still concerned?' he asked, eyeing the four men who were trotting their tired horses towards them. The men wore the same dark-coloured riding mantles as Robert and Will, concealing mail coats beneath. Robert exhaled roughly when he didn't respond. 'What else do I have to say to convince you?'

'I'll be convinced when we've done what we've come here to do.'

'They're good men, all. I've known them for years. They'll do what we need them to.'

'I'm more worried about them keeping their mouths shut afterwards.' Will urged his horse into a trot as the men drew closer. He could hear a couple of the knights talking quietly. They were all younger than he and Robert, probably by twenty years. They made him feel nostalgic. It felt strange to be back in the company of Templars after all this time. None of them was wearing the uniform, but they had a uniformity of conduct and of purpose, kneeling solemnly together by the roadside to say the Paternosters at each office, breaking bread to share at supper or passing around skins of water, one keeping watch when the others were asleep. He had forgotten what it was like to be part of a unit. He found he missed it.

'They're sworn to silence,' Robert assured him.

'You told them the Master of France ordered you on this assignment. What if they speak to him of it when you return to Paris?'

'They are following my orders, not his. But if you're that worried then perhaps we should tell them the truth? They know we're here to save the child of a local nobleman. What difference will it make if they know who the nobleman is and why his child is a captive of the French crown? At least they'll be fully aware of the gravity of the situation and our need to succeed.'

'The less they know the better,' responded Will. 'I won't run the risk of any of this getting back to Hugues, especially not my involvement.'

'Now we are getting to it.'

'What do you mean?'

Robert glanced back to check the knights were still out of earshot. 'This is really about Hugues, isn't it, this fear of anyone else finding out about the king's plan? Although I cannot tell whether you're keeping it from him because you're worried he'd punish you for your desertion if he knew you'd returned to Paris. Or whether going behind his back and getting me and others on board in secret is some sort of chance for you to punish him for taking your place. Either way, I think you could be risking the Order.'

'I've told you why I don't want Hugues to know of it.'

'We may have no choice but to tell him if this doesn't work,' murmured Robert. 'The archbishop is most likely being crowned as we speak. If we fail to save the child I have no doubt de Got will do anything the king demands, including handing him the Temple on a silver platter.' When Will didn't answer, Robert looked at the knights. 'And whatever your reasons for silence we couldn't do this alone. I told you to bring Simon into it, but you would have none of it.'

'I stand by that decision.'

'He isn't a fool, Will. He's been around both of us long enough to know we don't follow the same path as other knights. He helped you and Everard retrieve the Book of the Grail for Christ's sake.'

'He may have suspicions, but that isn't the same as knowing.'

'You told me you wanted to rebuild the Anima Templi, elect more members. We always had a sergeant as one of the twelve.'

'I don't want him to be part of this. That is the end of it.'

'Then what do you—'

'Listen to me,' said Will fiercely, turning in his saddle, his eyes fixing on Robert. 'You know as well as I the danger that comes with entering the circle. The danger, the solitude, the sacrifices we have to make. The Brethren have spent the past century in the shadows, working against our masters, using Temple resources to carry out our intentions, intentions that would be anathema to the Church and to the Order, indeed to most people in Christendom. Intentions that would most likely get us all executed. We've bled for this cause and we've killed for it. Simon would join us willingly, I know, but not for the cause. He would do it for me. He almost died following me to Scotland and I will not have his death on my conscience. He is certain to be promoted to stable master and I want him to have that. I want him to live out the winter of his life in the Temple. His home. That's part of what we're doing here, now, making sure men like Simon still have a home and a future.'

They rode on in silence, the sighing of the wind in the bare vineyards mournful.

'Do you still plan to go to Lyons, if we're successful?' asked Robert eventually.

'Yes. De Got will need to be told it has been done. Until he knows his son is safe, he remains at risk of being manipulated by Philippe. I will have to move fast. It will take at least a fortnight to reach the city.'

'Maybe I or one of the others should go? The king, his ministers, Rose, all of them think you're away in talks with Wallace. They'll all be in Lyons for the accession. What if someone sees you?'

'Rose isn't going,' said Will, in a quiet tone. 'I petitioned Philippe to have her stay behind. I said I was worried about her health.' He glanced at Robert. 'I know it was long ago now, but when you spoke with her that time, did she . . . ?'

Robert looked away when Will paused. 'Did she what?' he asked, a little defensively.

'Did she tell you about any feelings she had for the king?'

'Does she have?'

'There,' said Will suddenly, pointing towards a huge oak rising from a brown field in the near distance, with two hills beyond. 'Just as de Got described. We're going the right way.' He pulled the horse to a stop and slid from the saddle. 'We should find somewhere to hide the horses. We'll walk from here.'

Robert motioned behind him for the knights to dismount. 'I'm still surprised they kept the child at the house.'

'It's out of the way, self-contained; a perfect prison. The only one who knows of it is Bertrand and who would they imagine he would tell? The moment he does, he exposes his secret and endangers himself and the child anyway. The only reason he revealed it to us was because we knew the king was coercing him.'

Robert vaulted from his saddle as the knights approached. 'So we're in agreement? We cannot let the boy's gaolers live?'

'If we do, we could be identified. We have no choice.'

'I thought we'd seen enough death in the Crusades.'

Will stared down the track ahead. 'I fear it won't be the last blood we're forced to spill before this is over.'

Lyons, the Holy Roman Empire, 14 November 1305 AD

Bertrand de Got grabbed the arm of the throne and tried not to drop the papal cross as the litter swayed precariously, the bearers jostled by the surging crowds. The noise was overwhelming. Bertrand was glad of the canopy of stiff, brocaded silk erected over the throne that shielded him on three sides. Flowers and sprays of leaves were being hurled at him from the seething multitude, but judging by some of the weightier thumps these gifts made as they struck the cloth, they wouldn't all be gently received. There was a fire in his belly and acid rose bitter in his throat, but he kept the serene smile fixed on his face, waving now and then to the adoring congregation lining the road to the cathedral. All along the banks of the Saône they waited, trying to catch a glimpse of the new Vicar of God, arrayed in his ceremonial garments, bejewelled and imperious. Thousands had come to see their son, a Frenchman, crowned with the papal tiara. There were many from Gascony and Bordeaux, all pushing and shoving one another to get a better view, as fretful as a stormy sea. They were calling his name now, the name he had taken upon his election. He still wasn't used to it.

Clement V.

Coming from so many gaping mouths at once, it was an unholy roar.

Dark clouds were flying fast across the city of Lyons, in stark contrast to the snatches of blue sky between. The sun flashed in and out, its sweeping light turning the river to a sheet of solid silver, then disappearing again to leave the broad waters inky. Bertrand's fist, gripping the ferula, was oily with sweat inside his silk gloves. Under his flowing robes, his body felt hot and prickly, despite the glacial November wind. In the distance, he could see the white towers of the cathedral, framed against the backdrop of the hill that loomed behind it, the shadows of clouds climbing its sides, turning the trees from gold to black. The King of France and the cardinals of the Sacred College would be waiting for him there. But in the midst of this grand occasion, the pomp, the ceremony, the magnificent line of succession he was about to join, from the origins of St Peter down, all Bertrand could think of was his son.

It was nine months since he had seen Raoul. Nine months since King Philippe had met him in that red tent outside Bordeaux. He had barely slept in that time, each day hovering restlessly between rage, despair and hope. Today, the predominant feeling was hope. He would be crowned and either Campbell would do what he had sworn to or he, Bertrand, would give the king what he and that impious minister wanted. He had made this decision on the day they had come to him, with their demands and their threats. Whatever happened, he would not sacrifice Raoul, even if it came at the terrible price of sacrificing the very men who might yet fulfil his dream of the liberation of Jerusalem. There were other soldiers who could take the Cross. He would never have another son. Another miracle.

Up ahead, the mob was thicker. The road narrowed, caught between the riverbank and the bulging wall of a convent. Hundreds of people were crammed there, held back by royal guards. A great many had climbed up the wall and were perched on the top, feet kicking above the heads of those below. The jubilant cheers ringing out his name were fading behind him. The pitch of the crowd's roar was different here: louder, deeper. Bertrand opened his eyes. It was a sound filled with yells and shouts of protest, a sound of violence. At first, he thought it was directed at the guards who were barring the way, shoving people back to keep the road clear for the procession. Then, as he approached, he saw that the men and women shouting in anger were all looking at him. There were hundreds of them, fists raised.

'False pope!' they were screaming. 'False pope!'

They yelled the words in French, but even through the cacophony, Bertrand could tell this wasn't their native tongue. Here and there, he caught snatches of another language being hurled at him like the flowers. After a moment, he recognised it as Italian. He knew there had been unrest in Italy at his accession, many believing the cardinals were forced to elect him. People there knew of France's part in the violent arrest of Boniface and the king's subsequent demands that he be tried posthumously as a heretic, his remains exhumed and burned. Coupled with this, the rumours surrounding the untimely death of Benedict were growing. People were saying King Philippe was holding the Holy See to ransom. Bertrand couldn't blame them; he knew the rumours to be true. But all the same the sight and sound of that rage, directed at him, struck at his very core, leaving him quaking inside.

As the litter squeezed through the narrow gap the royal guards had created in the press, there were one or two thumps against the cloth canopy, much heavier than before. The litter lurched to one side as one of the men carrying it went down, struck in the head by a rock. The other bearers began to move faster and the mob surged forward. Bertrand glimpsed a royal guard slamming the pommel of his sword into a man's face. There was a burst of blood, startlingly red, and the man fell beneath the raised fists of those around him. Another went down, clutching his face, and another, as the guards started smashing their shields into the front rows, forcing them back, snapping fingers, breaking jaws.

The violence sent a shock wave through the crowd. People tried to move back, away from the guards, trampling on one another to fight their way free. Some stumbled to the ground, pushed under beneath a tide of feet and grasping hands. Men and women pressed up against the wall cried out in fear and pain as they were crushed. Those on the top reached down, trying to pull friends and family members to safety, but the wall wasn't strong enough to take so much weight. Here and there along its bulging line, stones began to crumble and dislodge. One man slipped and fell with a shout and shower of masonry into the mêlée below. There were more thuds and more shouts, louder and louder, until the thuds became a low rumbling, then a roar, as the wall collapsed in a cloud of dust and rock. Screams continued to tear through the air, even after the rubble subsided. Bertrand squeezed his eyes shut and tried to block out the terrible sounds behind him as the bearers carried him on, out of the chaos. His guts churned and the face of his son hung dislocated in his mind.

Near Bordeaux, the Kingdom of France, 14 November 1305 AD

Ponsard headed across the yard, cursing as his boots slipped in the muck. He stuffed a hunk of bread into his mouth and thumbed the crumbs from his chin as he approached the barn, looking around him. It was late afternoon and the light was dimming, the shutters closed over the windows of the house behind. Ponsard paused outside the entrance to the barn, squinting into the shadows that smelled of wet straw and dung. His gaze fell on a slender figure perched on a stool, milking a goat.

As he ducked through the door, the figure turned with a start. 'No, Marie,' said Ponsard, as she went to stand. He gestured for her to sit and crossed the barn, his heavy footfalls muffled in the straw. A few goats penned in a stall beneath the hayloft bleated nervously. 'Don't mind me,' he insisted, leaning up against a post, where a bridle hung from a hook.

Marie sat rigidly and bent forward, reaching under the animal.

Ponsard watched, his smile tighter now, as she squeezed and tugged the teats. Milk sprayed into the pail. Her gown was thinning, the linen almost transparent under her arms. He could count the ridges of her spine. Yolande had begged to be allowed into Bordeaux to get more supplies, but Gilles was no fool. He was the only one of them who had gone into the city in the past nine months and then rarely, a few times to collect supplies and once to meet reinforcements sent by the king.

Ponsard pushed himself from the pillar to see better. He noted how tense she was, how white and pale her fingers were as they pulled at the teats. Feeling something thicken inside him, he moved up behind her.

'Please, sir,' she whispered.

'Don't fuss, girl,' he murmured, when she recoiled from his touch. 'You know I don't like it.' Ponsard crawled his plate-sized hands from her shoulders down to her small breasts. He clutched at them greedily, kneading them. 'Turn around,' he ordered throatily, feeling himself quickly ready to spill. She was weeping, but did as she was told, shifting on the stool. He yanked up his tunic with fumbling fingers and unlaced his breeches. With his free hand he took hold of her jaw, positioning her. He halted, hearing something behind him. Jerking round, he expected to see Gilles or one of the others framed in the doorway. But there was no one there.

Ponsard stuffed himself awkwardly into his breeches. Putting a warning finger to his lips to keep Marie quiet, he crossed to the entrance, berating his recklessness. He'd been careless, going after the girl in daylight. If Gilles knew he'd abandoned his post, he'd crucify him. Ponsard peered cautiously out across the yard to the house. The glow of candlelight glimmered between the slats of the shutters, but the yard was empty. For a moment, he faltered, knowing he should get back to his duties. He could come for the girl later when everyone was asleep. But after a second's hesitation, hunger drove him back into the shadows of the barn.

Ponsard approached Marie slowly, letting his desire build, his hand opening his breeches. The shrill bleating of the goats drowned out the footsteps that came up, quick and quiet behind him. As the girl's eyes widened, he thought it was in fear of him and had no notion at all of the dagger that flashed in the air until it sliced across his throat.

Will went swiftly to the girl frozen on the stool. As her lips peeled back to let out a scream, he clapped his hand over her mouth and crouched in front

of her. 'It's all right. We're not here to harm you.' Her eyes drifted past
him to the dead guard spurting blood in a fountain across the barn floor.
Robert had sheathed the dagger and grabbed the man's arms. The other
four knights moved in to help haul him beneath the hayloft, one of them
scuffing straw over the blood. 'What is your name?' Will took his hand
from her mouth cautiously.

'Marie.'

Will smiled encouragingly. 'Archbishop de Got mentioned you. Listen
to me, Marie. We've come to free the boy, Raoul. I could use your
help.'

She was shaking her head. A trembling hand came up and pressed against
her lips. Her gaze was back on the guard. Robert and the others were
removing his weapons and scarlet and blue tunic, the gold fleur-de-lis on
the chest now obscured by blood. As the girl rose unsteadily, Will allowed
her to move past him to the dead man.

Marie stood looking down at his split throat, her arms wrapped around
her. Then she leaned over and spat on him. Wiping her mouth, she turned
back to Will, her face pale, but set. 'What do you need me to do?'

'How many other guards are here?'

'Seven. Gilles is their captain.'

'Are they all in the house?'

Marie nodded. 'Ponsard was supposed to be on watch, but he . . .' Her
eyes dropped to him and she sucked in a breath. 'Gilles and the others will
be downstairs, waiting for Yolande to bring them supper. Raoul stays
mostly in his room. They don't like him going out of the house.'

'This is good,' said Will, glancing at Robert and the knights to check
they had heard this. 'You've done well, Marie. I just need you to do one last
thing.' Pointing outside to the darkening yard, he told her quickly what he
wanted her to do.

Marie listened, looking frightened, but when he finished she nodded.

Will's smile faded as the girl slipped tentatively out of the barn. He
crossed to Robert and the others. 'Jean,' he said, gesturing to one of the
Templars, 'go into the yard and conceal yourself. When the guards come
out I want you inside the house. Find Raoul. Whatever happens, I want you
to get the child out of here alive. Understood?'

When Jean looked at Robert, the knight nodded. 'Those are your
orders.'

'You three, hide yourselves,' said Will to the others, as Jean headed out.
'Robert, you're with me.' He met Robert's eye as the two of them moved

to the door. 'That was a piece of luck, that guard caught off his post. Let's hope our fortune holds.'

From inside the house came sounds of shouting. They heard Marie's voice lifted in fear.

'There's someone in the barn! Please, come quickly!'

Robert hefted his broadsword. 'We don't need fortune.'

The two men crouched opposite one another a little way from the entrance, their cloaks making them melt in the shadows. Their faces, lined with age and scars of battle, one bearded, one bare, were grim, but determined.

Marie's calls were followed by heavy footsteps stamping across the yard.

'Who's in there?' came a gruff voice. 'Show yourself!' The voice faded slightly, as if the speaker had turned away. 'You. Go and find Ponsard. See if he saw anyone.'

Will's hand tightened around his sword as one set of footsteps echoed away outside.

A moment later, a figure appeared in the entrance, the red and blue of his cloak vivid in the gloom.

'The maid could have been mistaken, Gilles,' came a voice from behind the figure. 'Maybe it was a wolf?'

'She said she saw a man,' murmured Gilles in response, not moving. 'Damn this murk. I can see nothing.' He took a step forward, tensed and paused again, staring around him. The goats were bleating piteously. 'If you come out now, you won't be harmed.' Gilles moved further in, his stance balanced, poised for attack. Two guards followed him. Then a third. They spread out.

One man crept off to the right. He kicked over a bundle of hay, then shouted in alarm as something came hurtling towards him. 'Shit!' he cursed, laughing with relief as the goat charged out of the barn into the yard.

'Are you all right?' A fourth guard entered.

His comrade turned. 'I—' His words vanished as a much larger shape launched itself out of the darkness, eyes glittering. He got up his sword, just in time, as a blade swung in.

Will gritted his teeth at the impact of the strike. The man cracked his sword aside and dropped into a fighting crouch, as shouts echoed up all around them. The fifth guard hastened in to aid his comrades.

'No!' shouted Gilles, chopping fiercely at the Templar who leapt at him. 'Get the child!'

As the man disappeared, Will circled his opponent, his peripheral vision distracted by the jerking movements of men and weapons. The guard had a mail hauberk on beneath his long surcoat and mail gloves protecting his hands, as did he. No doubt he also wore some sort of mail or padded armour on his legs. Neither of them, however, had shields. Will had ordered the knights leave them with the horses. The Templars' large kite-shaped shields were too cumbersome a burden when attempting to move quickly on foot, unseen and in silence. He himself had learned to do without one during his time in Scotland, relying instead on the smaller buckler, used by infantry.

Abruptly, the guard lunged at his right side. Will knew at once from the clumsiness of the posture that it was a feint. As he anticipated, the sword switched left at the last second. He followed deftly and, slamming the guard's blade wide, punched out with his foot to throw an almighty kick at the man's stomach. As the guard doubled over, Will hacked his sword into his neck. The blade went halfway and stuck in the thick muscle. As Will wrenched it free, the guard sank to his knees with a bloody gurgle, dropping his sword. His hands started to come up to the wide, gushing wound, but Will finished him with a brutal two-handed cut of his broadsword.

Will turned, just in time, as footfalls sounded behind him. It was Gilles. The captain lunged viciously at him. After a couple of rapid blocks, Will realised the man was an expert fighter. The blade was a seeking, flashing thing coming at him from all angles. First his neck, now his thigh, a lightning-fast jab towards his groin, a whistling slash at his throat, a furious slice to his side. He forgot about everything around him, the grunts and gasps of the others, focusing only on stopping that sword from breaking through his defence and killing him. Gilles's blows were powerful. Almost every one knocked tiny shards of metal from both their blades that burst up in a shower of sparks between them. Within moments Will was dripping with sweat and feeling the strain in his forearm, the muscles locking tighter with every defensive block and countering strike.

Gilles's expression was rigid with concentration, but as they ducked and lunged closer to the entrance Will's face was lit by the grey twilight, and the captain's eyes widened. 'I've seen you,' he panted harshly. 'In the palace.' He hacked in. 'With the king!'

The captain's lapse in concentration was momentary, but it allowed Will to push his blade that little bit wider. He brought his sword round in a fluid loop that arced over his head to chop down at Gilles's skull in a move that would have cleaved his head in two, had it struck. Clumsily, but rapidly, Gilles recovered, whipping his own blade up to block. The two swords made a cross in mid-air as they clashed, before Gilles, snarling savagely, grasped the shaft of his sword in his free hand, protected by its mail glove, and slid it fiercely to one side. The blades screeched as they grated together. Gilles locked the edge of Will's blade against his quillon, then twisted down and to the side, pulling him off balance. As Will was thrown sideways, Gilles brought his sword up to ram the pommel into Will's face.

As his nose broke and tears blinded him, Will felt a faint rush of wind. He clenched in anticipation of the blow that would end him. He heard steel splinter against mail, the chink of rings snapping apart, a high gasping sound, then a thud. For a moment, he thought the pain in his nose was so intense it must have eclipsed the agony of the blade punching into him. But as he swiped the water from his eyes and staggered away, he saw Gilles on his knees before him, Robert's sword embedded in his back. Robert yanked the blade free and the captain sank into the straw.

Staring around him through his bleary vision, Will saw all the royal guards were down, although one of the Templars was leaning against the side of the barn, his face white, one hand clamped to his shoulder. 'With me, the rest of you. There are still two guards left.' Will nodded to Robert as they moved out into the yard. 'Thanks.'

'Well, I wasn't going to let you leave me with all the hard work.'

'Good point,' grunted Will, pressing his finger to one nostril to snort blood through the other. 'We'd all be doomed.'

They tensed as the door of the house burst open. But along with the candlelight that spilled into the yard came Jean, sword out before him. The Templar was followed by Marie, hugging a terrified-looking boy.

'Did you get the guards?' Will asked, crossing to the knight.

'Guards?' Jean shook his head. 'There was only one. He came after the boy.'

They turned, hearing pounding footsteps. A large woman, wielding a carving knife, appeared around the side of the house. She was panting hard. 'Thank the Lord! Thank the Lord you came!' Her eyes went to the barn. 'Are they . . . ?' When Will nodded, the woman bent forward, trying to catch her breath. 'I tried to stop the other one, but he took his horse and fled.'

Robert came over. 'One got away?' He looked worriedly at Will. 'Would he have seen us?'

'I don't think so. But still.' Will cursed beneath his breath and sheathed his sword with a stab. 'I hoped to have more time to cover our tracks.'

Lyons Cathedral, the Holy Roman Empire, 30 November 1305 AD

Philippe strode into the chamber, tugging off his gloves. 'You may leave,' he said tersely to the attendants hovering by the door. He stared at the figure sitting hunched on the window seat. His jaw twitched in anger, but he waited until the door clicked shut before speaking. 'You keep me waiting for two weeks and this is how you greet me? Not a bow or a welcome? Why have you denied my requests for an audience?' When the figure didn't turn, Philippe moved towards him. 'The cardinals tell me you have been ill and unable to accept visitors. But I see no sign of fever on you.' Still, the figure didn't look round. 'Answer me, de Got! Why have you denied me?'

The figure rose slowly, back-lit by the fiery sunset. He raised his head to meet the king's gaze. 'I am no longer Bertrand de Got. I am pope and you will address me with respect.' The king's eyes flashed with fury, but the pope spoke on. 'The cardinals told the truth. I have been ill. I apologise if this has disrupted your plans.'

Philippe faltered, thrown off balance by the pope's manner. It was as though he were speaking to a different person. This was not the feeble little man who had been led, terrified and cowed, to his tent outside Bordeaux, the man who had broken down at the news his bastard son was being held captive and would be killed should he refuse their demands. The man before him was apprehensive, certainly; that much was visible in the way he held himself, erect, but stiff, hands clutched at his sides. But despite his obvious tension, Bertrand de Got appeared stronger and more resolute than Philippe had ever seen him. It made him nervous. Did accession to the papal throne imbue these men with some sort of direct connection to God through the line of St Peter? Some holy power channelled through them, suffusing them with divine strength?

He cleared his throat and moved away, all at once fearful of looking into those dark, unblinking eyes, lest he see something greater and infinitely more terrible looking out at him. He now cursed himself for sending Nogaret back to Paris after the ceremony, but unrest over his recent taxes had erupted into violence in the city and he had wanted the minister there to help quell the situation. 'I accept your apology,' he said tautly. 'But now you are well, I want you to begin implementing the obligations you promised to fulfil upon your election.' Philippe paused to recall the advice

Nogaret had given him. 'First, and most importantly, you will recall Grand Master Jacques de Molay from Cyprus. We will need the head of the Order if we are to bring down the rest of it. Upon de Molay's arrival in the West, we will hold a council in Paris, attended by the three Estates, who will all have been briefed prior to the assembly. You will announce that the Temple has outlived its usefulness and that it has overburdened the people and the papacy in its futile attempts to reclaim the Holy Land. You will point out that the vast sums of money within the Temple would be better spent on creating peace in the West than on foreign shores, that the people of France will benefit greatly, that taxes will be lowered and our borders strengthened. You will then, as is your God-given right, dissolve the Order of the Knights Templar, transferring all its assets, possessions and funds to the French crown.'

Silence followed his words. Philippe frowned and went to speak, wondering if Clement had even heard him. But the pope spoke up, before he could ask.

'Are you finished, my lord?'

Philippe's frown deepened at that stilted tone. 'Yes, I am finished, but—'

'That is good, my lord, because I too am finished. I am finished being tormented by you and that poisonous serpent, Guillaume de Nogaret, finished being coerced and compelled, finished being threatened. I am pope, Vicar of Christ and God's voice upon this Earth, and I will be your pawn no longer. I will not meet your obligations and I protest against the validity of your agreement, which was signed under duress.' Clement's tone was rising, growing bolder. 'I will, under no circumstances, recall Jacques de Molay, when he and his knights are the only men fighting to uphold the dream of a Christian Holy Land. Did your sainted grandfather fight and die on those foreign sands for nothing? Will we surrender that dream so easily?' The pope shook his head. 'I will make it my mission to give as much aid, spiritual and financial, as possible to the Templars in Cyprus in order that they can continue this holy struggle.'

Philippe stared at him, stunned. 'You are gravely, *gravely* mistaken, if you think I will not do what has been threatened.' His hand jerked to the pommel of his broadsword. 'Do you forget, Clement? I have your son! I swear by God, I will kill him if you refuse me in this!'

'You will not,' breathed Clement, his eyes on the sword at Philippe's hip. 'My son is no longer in your custody. I received word this morning that he has been taken to safety. You will never find him and if you try I will do

what my predecessor, Boniface, had no chance to and excommunicate you.'
He crossed to the king, seeming to grow with every step, until Philippe was
forced to back away. 'You can say he existed to try to ruin me, but I will
deny it and your word is not enough these days, my lord. The people, *your*
people are growing dissatisfied with your rule and your liaisons with that
murderer, Nogaret. Already they are turning against you. Do you imagine
the men and women of Guienne have so quickly forgotten your brutality?
The arrests of the nobles and theft of their property? I know you have not
the money or the support to quell another uprising there, my lord. If you
attack me, you will regret it.'

Philippe was shaking his head, but he couldn't speak. He felt his back
come up against the wall. Those dark flashing eyes of the pope's were
boring into him, filled with accusation and wrath. Filled with God's
displeasure. It was all he could do not to put his hands over his face to
shield himself from that righteous glare.

'You have been infected by those around you. You have become as
faithless as that heretic minister of yours! You who have attacked two Vicars
of Christ!'

'No,' Philippe groaned. 'No. I was doing your bidding!' He slumped to
his knees, holding up his hands and clasping them together in supplication.
'I was doing it for you! For your people!'

Clement faltered at this answer. 'For me?'

But Philippe wasn't listening. He had closed his eyes, his hands upraised.
'Lord, forgive me! Forgive me my sins!'

Lyons Cathedral, the Holy Roman Empire, 1 December 1305 AD

'It is done.'

'Do you believe the king will accept it?' Will watched as the pope
crossed to the window seat. The man looked exhausted and seemed to have
aged rapidly in the time since Will had last seen him in Bordeaux. His red
silk robes dwarfed his small frame as he sat, folding his hands in his lap.

'I do not see that he has much choice. If I refuse to dissolve the Temple,
he cannot fulfil his ambition.' The pope looked up suddenly. 'My son was
unharmed?'

Will nodded impatiently. Clement had already questioned him rigorously on the boy yesterday morning. 'My men took him south to the village
as you instructed, with Yolande and Marie. Philippe will not be able to find
any of them.'

'Good.' Clement gave a tentative smile. 'My sister will take care of them.'

'So it is over? We have done what we need to secure the Temple?'

Clement glanced up, his brow furrowing. 'No. It isn't over. Not while Minister de Nogaret continues to poison the king's mind, turning him against the Church.'

'The king knows what he is doing, your holiness. Yes, Nogaret may be the one with the vision, but Philippe isn't a fool or a man of weak will.'

'Perhaps, perhaps,' said Clement, waving his hand as if this were unimportant, 'but nonetheless, I believe the king will be much less aggressive without that snake's influence.' He rose. 'I cannot touch Philippe, even my powers do not extend that far, not without causing terrible conflict in this kingdom. But Guillaume de Nogaret is a different matter. I could bring him to justice for his crimes against my predecessors, but rumours will not be enough. I need evidence.'

'I know for a fact that the king and Nogaret conspired to murder Pope Boniface. The king admitted it in a conversation with me, where he confessed his intention to bring down the Temple.'

Clement's face remained grave, but he shook his head. 'Your word isn't enough, not against these men. A Templar turned mercenary? The king has surrounded himself with men of the law, men of cunning. We will need more than the word of a deserter to confront them with.' He was pacing now. 'Besides, it is evidence of the truth behind Pope Benedict's death that I am more interested in finding. However despicable the act against him, Boniface made many enemies in the Sacred College; enemies who perhaps wouldn't be overly concerned to know he was murdered. Remember, half my college is made up of French cardinals who support Philippe. Benedict is another matter. He was liked by many and the rumours surrounding his untimely death are filled with anger and calls for justice.' Clement looked up at Will. 'Find me unequivocal evidence that Guillaume de Nogaret murdered Pope Benedict and I will move against him. With his removal from Philippe's circle, I believe we will all be safer.'

'I will have to be careful. As I told you, one of the royal guards escaped from the house.'

'You said he didn't see you?'

'I don't believe so, but this is a dangerous game. Nogaret has never trusted me. But I will do what I can to give him to you, if your holiness will continue to safeguard the Temple.'

'You have my word.' Clement crossed to a table where a jug of wine and two goblets had been placed. 'Now, let us talk of the Order. You said you were using Templars to help protect my son. Did any of them mention the Grand Master? His plans for a new campaign in the Holy Land?'

Will shook his head. 'The last we heard was that Jacques de Molay was trying to secure funding and support for a new Crusade, but that he hadn't met with much success.'

Clement looked disappointed as he poured the wine. 'Well, perhaps we might yet hear better news.'

'Yes,' murmured Will, 'perhaps.'

3 1

The Royal Palace, Paris

21 December 1305 AD

ᛘᛘ

'I cannot imagine how this happened, my lord.' Nogaret followed as the king pushed open a low door, half hidden by trailing ivy. Ducking through, the minister found himself in an unfamiliar place. They were on the very tip of the Ile de la Cité, the wall surrounding the royal gardens towering behind them. Ahead, the muddy riverbanks tumbled away to disappear beneath the Seine, swollen and grey after the winter storms. Three small islands rose out of the water, one after the other, like the humped back of some enormous beast submerged in the middle of the river. There was an old wooden footbridge that spanned the choppy water to the nearest island. Nogaret had seen the structure from the right and left banks, but hadn't known about the door in the palace wall.

'My father had it built,' said Philippe at his side, his eyes on the bridge. He pointed to the nearest island. Its yellow hump was wind-swept and bare, except for a few scraggly trees and a couple of river birds wading near the water's edge. 'He planned to fish from the Ile des Juifs.'

'My lord,' ventured Nogaret, trying to steer the king back to the matter at hand.

'I don't believe he ever did. The struggles of his reign prevented him. He was a feeble man, my father, led this way and that by the men he surrounded himself with and by his family, never thinking for himself, never doing what he wanted. He is hardly remembered at all by the people of this kingdom. All they recall is that his father was a saint.' Philippe turned to Nogaret. The cold wind lifted his hair. 'Is that what they will think of me when I die? That I foolishly and weakly let my ministers govern me? That I never did anything of consequence? Will I simply be the grandson of a great man?'

'You will be remembered as the man who united France,' said Nogaret adamantly. 'The man who led his kingdom into a new age of prosperity and order, an age ruled by men of reason, not blind faith.'

'I underestimated our new pope,' murmured Philippe, looking back at the forlorn island. 'Can the soldier tell us nothing of those who mounted the assault?'

Nogaret's expression tightened. 'He didn't see them. When he realised Gilles and the others were losing the fight, he fled. What the fool should have done was hide out near the house to get a clear look at the attackers. Now, I fear we will never know who they were.'

'I expect they were just mercenaries Clement paid to save his child.' Philippe wandered down to the bridge, the hem of his black cloak trailing in the mud. 'He had more backbone than I anticipated.' The king grasped the wooden handrail, but didn't step up on to the moss-coated boards.

'We could go after the child?' offered Nogaret, rubbing pensively at his chin. 'I am almost certain someone in Clement's circle will know where the boy has been taken.'

Philippe was shaking his head. 'No. It is over. Without the pope's support we cannot bring down the Temple.' He stared out across the bridge. 'My plans for the conquest of new territory will have to remain just that: plans. Without funds I can do nothing more.' His brow furrowed. 'Perhaps if we raise the taxes again?'

'It would be risky. The mood in the city and the rest of the kingdom is dark, my lord. The riots have only just been put down. The situation remains volatile.' Nogaret sighed roughly. 'The Temple is—'

'The Temple is lost to us,' interrupted Philippe, turning from the bridge and heading up the bank towards the door in the wall. 'That is the end of it.'

'There will be another way, my lord, I am certain.' Nogaret followed swiftly. 'We just need to think of it.'

'I have done enough thinking. My head is so full of thoughts it feels like it will burst. Just leave me.'

Nogaret went to say something, but fell silent, dropping back to let the king stride off through the royal gardens alone. Now wasn't the time to push Philippe. He would have to wait for the dust to settle before he tried again. This was a disaster. Bertrand de Got had seemed so ripe, so ready to be picked and pressed. But they had elected the wrong man again. Nogaret made his way into the palace, seething with frustration over the incompetence of the royal guards and the pope's sudden change of attitude. The

Temple remained their best chance of securing and strengthening the kingdom, but Philippe was right: without the pope's support they couldn't use the Order for their own gain.

The minister was so wrapped up in these thoughts as he made his way down the passage to his chambers that he didn't notice Will until after they passed one another. He stopped short and turned, eyes narrowing. 'Campbell?'

'Minister de Nogaret,' greeted Will, inclining his head.

'You're back sooner than I expected. I always imagined the journey to Scotland to be an arduous one.'

'I didn't have to go that far. I met with one of Wallace's generals in England.'

Nogaret's gaze moved to a square of parchment in Will's hand. 'A message?'

'From my sister by the hand,' replied Will, holding it up so Nogaret could see his name, scrawled on the front. 'It was waiting for me when I returned.' He smiled. 'I expect it will be a lengthy note on how many words my niece's child can now say and how many teeth the young one has. But I doubt any of it will interest you, Minister. How was the ceremony in Lyons?'

'There was some unrest,' responded Nogaret, studying Will's face and feeling suspicious, without knowing why. 'Twelve people were killed when a wall collapsed, but the pope was unharmed.'

'I presume the king will continue with his plans now?'

'There have been some unforeseen developments,' said Nogaret, after a pause. 'But this is not the time or the place to discuss them. I imagine the king will send for you in due course. I am sure he will want to hear any news you bring from England. We have heard very little from our neighbour of late.'

'I will be happy to oblige.'

Nogaret watched Will head off, before moving in the opposite direction, feeling his frustration building, a restless hum in his mind.

Philippe walked numbly down the passages of the royal apartments. Somewhere in a nearby room, he heard a young girl's laughter and guessed it was his daughter. The sound pierced him. He moved on, faster now, heading for his private chamber and solitude. The air in these gloomy corridors was icy, but he hardly felt it through the emotions that boiled inside him: a furnace of rage, despair and humiliation. He paused outside his room, palm pushed against the door, assailed by the memory of himself on his knees before the bewildered pope. He knew he had felt nothing but terror at the time, but almost immediately after he left Clement to make his way, defeated, back to Paris, he had felt a rising, flaming shame. How could he have let himself be cowed so easily? He opened the door roughly, then halted, his eyes on the woman who rose from his bed.

Rose stood in silence. Anger was scrawled across the king's face, drawn sharply in the lines that knotted his brow, etched in his taut mouth and jaw. She went to move, almost hearing him command her to leave, but stopped herself when she realised he hadn't spoken. Pushing the door closed, he turned back to her. It seemed like far longer than three months since she had seen him last. He had returned from Lyons the day before, but had been occupied in meetings.

'What are you doing in here, Rose?' Philippe asked, taking his gaze from her and removing his cloak.

She stared at it as he tossed it on the bed, wondering where he had been. The hem of the garment was coated with mud. 'I wanted to see you.' The words came out in a whisper. She had meant them to sound stronger. Philippe's blue eyes were wintry. She shook her head, realising how dangerous this was; how great a trespass. 'I . . . I apologise,' she said, stumbling over the words as she crossed the room. 'I will leave you.'

'Wait.'

She faltered, reaching for the door.

'Stay.' Philippe kicked off his boots and sat back on the bed, leaning up against the silk pillows. 'Sit with me.'

Rose moved slowly back, keeping her eyes downcast so he wouldn't see her emotions caught within them, naked and exposed. She perched awkwardly on the large bed, close to one of the carved wooden posts at the foot. His cloak, she noticed, was dripping mud on to the floor. Philippe had closed his eyes and rested his head against the wall. Unlike hers, his breathing was slow and even. As she watched, he moved a hand to the space beside him.

'Sit here.'

Rose bent to slip off her shoes. He moved his hand away as she slid over on to the place where it had been. She could feel every part of her: the blood in her cheeks, the trembling in her hands, the rapid pulse of her heart. She didn't think she had ever felt so alive or so terrified as she lay back against the pillows, as stiff as a board. She jumped, feeling something

icy against her knuckles and realised it was his finger. His eyes remained
closed as he brushed it unhurriedly, lightly up her hand, over her wrist and
under the sleeve of her black gown. She tried to close her own eyes, but the
feel of his dislocated touch in the darkness made her feel giddy. His
breathing had shifted its rhythm. All at once, he sat up. Removing the gold
circlet from his head, he placed it on the table by the bed and turned back to
her. He leaned over, planting his hands to either side of her. Finally, she
closed her eyes as his mouth came down to press against hers. She could
smell the river on him. After a time, he raised himself again. They stared at
one another, unspeaking, as he unlaced the ties at the sides of her gown.
Rose shivered as he pulled it from her. The air was freezing against her skin
and she crossed her arms self-consciously about her chest, one resting over
the other to cover the burn marks.

Philippe tugged his velvet tunic over his head and unpicked the thongs
that fastened the hair shirt in place. When it came away from his body, her
gaze traced the red-raw skin, following the lines the whip had made,
patterns of punishment and shame. Tentatively, she uncrossed her arms,
laying her own scars bare. She wanted to reach out and touch his web of
wounds. The queen's voice murmured in her mind.

All his veins on the outside.

His movements were quick now, impatient, as he pushed her thighs
apart, his hand going between them. His fingers were still icy. Rose wanted
him to slow, to be gentle. She wanted to whisper her thoughts, her fears
and wishes, to tell him how long she had waited for his attention. She
wanted him to kiss her again. But she didn't know how to command a king
and so she lay in frozen silence as he moved on top of her, his face flushed
and feverish. His eyes were shut. He didn't see her turn her head to mask
the wrenching, stinging sensation, didn't notice her hands splay and grip the
blanket. Rose squeezed her eyes together as she felt herself pulled apart,
but through the pain she heard him speaking softly. She twisted her head
closer to his to listen. After a moment, the whisper came again.

'Jeanne,' he was murmuring, as he ploughed blindly into her. '*Jeanne.*'

Will felt Nogaret's eyes lingering on him as he walked away down
the passage. He didn't look back as he turned a corner and headed for
his quarters, the folded parchment now soft and slightly damp in his
fist.

When he reached the small room, which had been home for so long,
he shut the door gratefully. There was a crack in the window that looked

out over a large courtyard and the chamber was freezing. The only items
of furniture, other than a locked chest in the corner upon which lay his
sword, hauberk and travelling cloak, were a stool and a table with a jug
of water and a few misshapen stubs of candles on it. He had returned
that morning to find a thin sheet of dust over everything, but now as he
ran a finger across the table and it came back clean, he realised the
servants must have been here. He wondered who else had noted his
arrival and felt all at once uneasy, as if the palace were full of watching
eyes, waiting for him to slip, to reveal himself. Forcing these thoughts
away, Will sank on to his pallet. He was an honoured guest of the king;
it was to be expected that people would notice his comings and goings.
He was just feeling guarded because of Nogaret's chilly reception, but
the minister's distrustful manner was nothing new. No one suspected
him.

He focused instead on the parchment in his hands. News from his family
was such a rare treat, he didn't want anything to spoil it. Smiling in
anticipation, he broke the wax that sealed it and pulled the pages apart. As
his eyes moved over the crumpled skin, his smile faded.

My dear brother,

*I hope this letter finds you well. Alas, I cannot say that all is well
with us, or ever will be again. I am sorry I have not written for so
long, but times have been hard and there has been scant occasion for
much other than the business of keeping alive. The harvests have not
been good and this in itself would be a hardship, but coupled with
King Edward's wars we find ourselves poorer and our larders emptier
than any of us could have imagined. John Balliol remains in exile in
France and we have given up hope of ever having a king upon our
throne again, unless it be the Hammer himself. We are at least
fortunate where we are in the north to have been spared from much of
the violence of his campaigns, although since the fall of Stirling Castle
to the English last year there has been little fighting. You may have
heard that the Scottish nobles were forced to yield to the king and
make a truce at that time, but what many outside our borders are
unaware of is that they were only granted their freedom on the
condition they hunted down the one man who still defied the English
king, your friend and general, Sir William Wallace. Even Sir David
Graham was enlisted in this cause, although of course he did no such
thing.*

The same cannot be said for others. Where the many men Edward sent out to capture Sir William failed, Sir John Menteith succeeded. He discovered Sir William was hiding out in a house in the woods near Glasgow with Gray. It is known that he and his men came upon them in the night. I am sorry to tell you that Gray was put to the sword. Christian can hardly speak for the grief of it. Sir William apparently fought and killed many of his captors, but they were too many even for him and in the end he was overpowered. He was borne in haste to Carlisle, bound to his own horse, and delivered to English nobles who took him south to London. It all happened so quickly that it was some time before we heard any of this in Elgin. David, however, was near the border on business with his lord and they made the decision to follow. I am still not sure what they intended to accomplish by this. I think my brave son hoped they would somehow be able to rescue Sir William. But as soon as they arrived in London they realised the futility of this. David says the city was packed to the walls with people from all over, come to watch. Sir William was under heavy guard and the streets around his prison were so crowded they couldn't even get near.

On the twenty-third day of August, Sir William Wallace was taken to Westminster, they say to stand trial, but I think you know as well as any of us the mockery of that. Sir William, who had never sworn fealty to the King of England, stood accused of treason to the crown. He was charged and the sentence passed that very day. David has told me some of what followed, but by no means all. I think he wanted to spare me the horror, which I know haunts him, even with all he has seen. When I start to think of it — the crowds, the heat, the terror of it — I feel sick to my soul. We have all seen blood spilled, too much blood, yet none of it compares with what was done to that beautiful, proud man on that day in London. I meant to write of it, but now I find the words fail me. I cannot write them . . .

The letter slipped from Will's grasp and floated to the floor, the lines of text dissolving, his mind filling in the sights and sounds his sister was unable to articulate.

He saw the baying crowds lining the streets from Westminster to the place of execution. Saw their raised fists and their red, open mouths. He heard the screams and shouts of abuse, the jeers and the laughter as the ogre of the north was paraded before them, naked and bound. He felt their spit hitting his face, their kicks striking his flesh. He smelled the stink of them, sweat sour with heat and excitement, all pushing one another, trying to catch a glimpse of the hated enemy. He sensed the deep gut-fear as the gallows loomed ahead, one empty noose, a sagging circle in the sky; not the end, but the beginning of agony impossible to comprehend. He imagined the stark loneliness of climbing that platform to look down upon a vast, seething sea. So many faces, so little humanity. He felt his hands secured behind his back, the bonds twisting and cutting with every movement, felt the roughness of the rope as it brushed his cheek, the immediate claustrophobic tautness as it was tightened around his neck. He heard the cheer of the crowd as he was hauled into the air by the black-clad executioners, breath snatched away, mouth opening, tongue swelling.

Will tried to block out the images as they came on, one after the other, mingling with Edward's voice calling down the years to taunt him from that cell in Stirling.

In this time, the bladder will void, then the bowels.

He tried to think of William Wallace as he had seen him last, four years ago, when they had said goodbye on the Paris docks. He tried to recall the feel of his strong hand gripping his own, the sight of that rare grin lighting up his blue eyes. But all he could see was his body, broken and abused, being cut down from that swinging rope, not dead, but gasping for the last vain threads of life to which he would cling as grimly and unrelentingly as he clung to his hope for liberty.

You will be laid out on a table, for all to see. A spectacle.

He felt the hardness of the bench beneath him, the silver, severing pain as his genitals were sliced away, with this act his manhood and his strength dismembered. He felt the rough tugging and pulling of the executioner's instruments at his chest and stomach. Dear God, let him have died at that point.

. . . every part of you removed and burned before your eyes.

Will rose suddenly. Going to the window, he planted his palms on the stone. Closing his eyes, he concentrated on the chill wind streaming through the crack. In his mind, he felt the final rip as the executioner plunged his hand inside to pull out his beating heart, his ears assaulted by the roar of the crowd as it was held aloft. He clenched his teeth and banished the images, focusing instead on the sight of Wallace climbing into the boat, the sweep and pull of the oars that took him out into the blue Seine. He had raised his hand, one last time, then turned his face into the wind, heading home.

Will dug his fingers into the stone. Now Wallace was gone, what hope was there left? For his home? His family?

Edward had won.

Will felt the old hatred, kept at bay with his struggle to save the Temple, slam back into him with savage force. Rage boiled up, black and bitter. He shouted and wrenched over the table, sending it flying, the jug smashing, candles scattering. Edward's arrogant, smiling face swept into his mind and he punched his fist into the wall. Turning, he pressed his back to it and slid to the ground, his breathing ragged, knuckles bloody. But even in the midst of his anger and despair, he felt another emotion stir, something raw, but strong. The face of Pope Clement filtered into his mind. If he delivered Nogaret, then perhaps he could strike a deal: the minister in return for a papal order forcing Edward to end the war? The raw feeling, he realised, was hope.

There was still hope.

Merlan Prison, the Kingdom of France, 25 December 1305 AD

The man crouched in the darkness, listening to the faint sounds echoing all around him: the distant jangle and chink of keys, a door slamming, a bolt sliding, a harsh cry that made him flinch. As he listened, he rocked to and fro, feeling his spine bump against the rough rock. He used to count them, these movements; each cold touch of the wall another number. One. Two. One hundred. Two thousand. It was a measure of time in a place without days or seasons. The sun didn't rise underground. There were only different shades of darkness, depending on how close the guards came with their torches. Now, he tended to lose count after the first few hundred. His mind would wander and he would forget how many times his back had met stone, drifting aimlessly within a memory.

Places and people were plain in these daydreams, but oddly leached of hues. Trees were black, sky ashen. Blue seemed impossible. In here everything was grey, his hair, his skin, the rags of his clothing, the walls and the floor, even the food, all of it grey and dirty, all except one colour. It was a bad colour; the colour of blood and sin and fire. The colour of the crosses on the guards' white mantles. It hurt his eyes as they towered over him, whips cracking, hurt his mind as it trickled hotly down his arms, raised to shield him from the blows. He had learned to fear it, learned the words he should not say by it. Painful words like guilt and innocence, punishment and blame. Heresy. Murder.

346 ROBYN YOUNG

A new sound sifted through the constant background hum of whispers and sighs, moans and whimpers. It was the sound of soft footsteps, coming closer. The man sat forward, the irons around his legs shifting. He cocked his head in the shadows, poised to listen. The footsteps stopped outside his door. He could see fire dancing beyond the cracks in the pitted wood and squinted in anticipation of its ferocious light. There was a rattle of bolts and the door opened. The light and heat of the torch bathed him, savage and beautiful. He held up his hands, only able to look at it from between the cover of his fingers. Behind the fire was the face of a young man. In his free hand, he held a bowl. The youth placed it carefully on the floor, only needing to crouch in the doorway the cell was so small.

The man peered tentatively over. Inside the bowl, he could see lumps of meat protruding from thick gravy. 'What is this, Gérard?' His voice was a croak.

'I brought you some leftovers from the kitchen,' whispered the youth. 'The guards have had their supper. They won't miss it.'

'Meat?'

Gérard nodded. 'We were sent a deer for the Christ Mass.'

'It is the Christ Mass?'

'Yes, sir. Today.'

The man sat back, resting against the wall, not daring to look at the bowl any longer. 'You had better take it, Gérard. If they find out, you may be punished.'

The youth paused, his face in the flames hovering somewhere between excitement and concern. 'It does not matter,' he said, after a moment. 'Today is my last day in this place. Tomorrow I am going to Paris. My father managed to secure me a place at last, just in the stables. But perhaps one day, if I work hard enough, I might be initiated.'

The man felt a wrench in him at the youth's earnest, eager face, so similar to a face he had once known and loved. 'Do not go, Gérard,' he said, holding out his hands to the youth. In the torchlight the welts around the bands of iron on his wrists were livid. 'Do not go to Paris. There are evil men there. Heretics.' His voice was rising. 'Murderers!'

Gérard looked around nervously. 'Don't say that, sir. You don't want the knights to hear any of that talk. You know what they'll do.'

But the man wasn't listening. He reached out and grasped the youth's arm, felt the warmth of skin, of another human, beneath the rough wool tunic. 'Then tell someone I am here. I beg you. Tell them I am innocent. That I am not supposed to be here.'

The youth snatched back his arm and stood, shaking his head. 'Quiet, sir. Don't let them hear you. Have your food now, before it gets cold.'

The door was hastily shut and the heat of the torch vanished. As the youth's footsteps padded quickly away down the passage, Esquin de Floyran sank forward on to his hands and wept in the darkness.

PART THREE

32

The Temple, Paris

7 November 1306 AD

The young man paced, fingers twisting and pulling at a loose thread on his tunic. The smell in the tack room was overpowering, made up of damp straw, fresh dung and tanned leather. He had never really got used to it. Reins dangled from hooks hammered into the stone walls and saddles were stacked neatly on rows of shelves. The vaulted ceiling was covered with funnel-shaped spiders' webs. He had never noticed just how many there were before, even though he had spent most of the past year in this room. He shuddered and backed away from an especially large web suspended above him, black with dirt and flies. He remembered walking into one down in the darkness of the prison corridors, the shock as it brushed like fingers over his face. The skitter of something across his cheek.

He started as the door opened and two men entered. One was the stable master, whose forthright face and easy smile were reassuringly familiar. The other was less comforting. The young man had seen the tall knight in the preceptory, but had never had cause to speak to him, except once when he'd called him sir while taking the reins of his horse. The knight had ash-grey hair and a hard, angular face, framed by a clipped white beard. In his long mantle and surcoat, a broadsword slung from his hip, he looked imperiously stern.

'Gérard,' said the stable master. 'This is Sir Robert de Paris.'

The young man bowed and tugged at the thread on his tunic as the knight studied him.

'Brother Simon says you have something to tell me?'

Gérard glanced uncertainly at Simon.

'It's all right, Gérard. You have nothing to fear from speaking the truth. Tell Sir Robert what you told me yesterday.'

Gérard fought against the voice that spoke up inside him, disagreeing with the stable master's words, whispering that he had everything to fear if

what he told was indeed the truth. But the voice belonged to a man whose
face still haunted him and Gérard knew he would not rest until he had done
what that man had begged him to do. He had lived with the knowledge long
enough, waiting, wondering who to share it with. Finally, several weeks
earlier, he confided in a fellow groom, thinking this would be enough to
ease his burden, but his friend had persuaded him to tell someone of higher
rank. Clearing his throat, Gérard began to speak. 'I was transferred to this
preceptory a year ago from the Temple's prison Merlan, sir, where my
father was a guard. There was a prisoner there named Esquin de Floyran.'

'De Floyran?' questioned Robert sharply. 'The prior of Montfaucon?'

'Yes, sir, he told me he had once been a prior.'

Robert looked at Simon. 'De Floyran disappeared three years ago,
around the time his nephew was found murdered. It was thought he had
something to do with the killing and fled fearing reprisals.'

Gérard shook his head. 'No. That isn't so. Esquin loved his nephew. He
told me Martin was . . .' He trailed off, then drew a decisive breath. 'He
said Martin was killed by knights.'

'Templars?'

Gérard looked again at Simon, who nodded for him to continue. 'Yes,
sir. From this preceptory.'

'How did de Floyran know this?'

'He was there when it happened. His nephew met him in a church to
confess he had been bewitched by heretics in the Temple who made him
practise obscene ceremonies. But his nephew was followed and killed.
Esquin thought because he was an official in the Order the men were
scared to put him to death so they sent him to Merlan instead. Perhaps
they hoped he would die in the prison.' Gérard looked down at his hands,
recalling the horrors he had seen there. 'Enough men did. It is a cruel
place, sir.'

'Tell me more of these knights. You say de Floyran's nephew accused
them of heresy?'

'That is what Esquin said. But he doesn't know who they were. The men
who captured him and killed Martin were masked. Esquin was taken for
questioning, he thought in the Paris preceptory, but he wasn't sure as he
was blindfolded.' Gérard paused when Robert cursed and pushed a hand
through his hair. 'He spent a long time in Merlan protesting his innocence,
sir. The guards beat him and tortured him whenever he spoke out, shouting
to any who could hear that there were heretics in the Order who must be
exposed and punished for their crimes. After many beatings he kept quiet,

telling no one but me.' Gérard shrugged. 'I think he felt he could trust me. When he knew I was leaving he begged me to tell someone.'

'Why did it take you a year to speak of this?'

Gérard avoided Robert's stare. 'I was scared if I told anyone the same might happen to me.' He looked swiftly at the knight. 'I couldn't bear to be sent to that place, sir. Death would be a mercy over that. But I had to say something. I keep seeing him in that tiny cell all hunched up in the dark.'

'You've done the right thing, Gérard,' Simon assured him.

'Brother Simon is right,' said Robert. 'But I need you to promise you will not speak of this to anyone else. You must leave it with us.'

'Of course, sir.'

'You may go.'

Bowing, Gérard made his way hastily out of the tack room into the welcoming sunlight. Already he felt lighter, having given up his burden to someone else.

Simon turned to Robert as the sergeant left. 'I thought you would want to hear that. As soon as he told me I was reminded of those rumours you asked me to listen out for among the sergeants. I have to admit,' he added, 'at the time I thought it was all very unlikely that there was any truth in what you were saying you had heard.'

'Well, to be honest, I came to the same conclusion myself. All the trails went cold.'

'Or went to Merlan.' Simon frowned. 'You told me Visitor de Pairaud launched an investigation. Why did he not know of Esquin de Floyran's imprisonment?'

'Any number of officials in this preceptory, the Master of France and the Marshall to name two, could authorise the incarceration of a senior knight. Hugues wouldn't necessarily have heard anything of it, especially if those involved were working in secret.' Robert shook his head irritably. 'Either way I cannot ask him about it. He isn't due to return from England for some time.'

'Gérard obviously believes what this prisoner told him and I suppose it's too close to the rumours you heard to be a coincidence,' murmured Simon, looking at the closed door. Beyond, came the whinnies of horses and the laughter of a couple of grooms. 'But Templars actually involved in heresy? It can't be true.' He studied Robert's grave face. 'Can it?'

*   *   *

Merlan Prison, the Kingdom of France, 19 December 1306 AD

Robert stared up at the grey fortress as he rode out from under the arched passage, his horse's hooves clopping loudly off the cobbles. There was a heavy clanking as the portcullis was lowered behind him, the knights who had let him pass moving back into position in front of the iron bars. The bleakness of the place was heightened by the dreary landscape. Barren fields surrounded the high walls, the soil dark as the winter sky where crows wheeled and cawed, circling the prison towers.

Robert had known of Merlan since he was a boy and his first impression fair matched the descriptions he had heard over the years, most of them uttered in the sergeants' dormitories in hushed, fearful tones. As he dismounted in the windswept yard, handing his reins to a black-clad squire, he recalled midnight stories of tortures inflicted upon prisoners, all of them men of the Temple who had broken oaths or disobeyed masters. After his initiation into the Brethren, he had some-times recalled those whispers uneasily, his mind lingering on the famous death cells: holes in the ground barely big enough for a man to crouch in, where the prisoner would be left in complete darkness, without food or water, until he died.

Slinging his pack over his shoulder, Robert climbed the steps to the entrance that yawned above him. Two knights standing sentry in the doorway looked him over in silence, hands resting on the pommels of their swords.

Robert nodded to one of them. 'I'm here to see a prisoner.'

'You have to talk to the steward,' replied the Templar, pointing through the doors. 'Second room on the left.'

Robert moved into a chilly passage, paused outside a door and rapped twice. Hearing an impatient voice calling for him to enter, he pushed through, having to duck low under the lintel. The room beyond was small and stuffy. A fleshy man was seated behind a table devouring a chicken leg and squinting at a skin covered in text, down which he was running a finger. His mantle was more grey than white and looked as though it hadn't been laundered in months. He looked up with a frown as Robert entered.

'Yes?'

'Good day to you. My name is Sir Robert de Paris. I've come from the Paris preceptory to speak to one of your prisoners.'

'Do you have a warrant?'

Robert reached into his pack and pulled out a rolled parchment.

Still frowning, the steward sucked his fingers noisily and took the scroll. After unrolling it, he glanced up quickly and peered past Robert as if expecting to see someone else behind him. 'Is Visitor de Pairaud here?'

'No, just myself.'

'Who is the prisoner?' When Robert answered, the steward looked instantly guarded. 'Esquin de Floyran? I was given strict instructions regarding his incarceration. No one but the guards of the lower cells is allowed to see him.'

'This warrant comes direct from the Visitor himself.' Robert pointed to the scroll, his finger hovering over the red seal stamped on the bottom of the order. He kept his tone forceful, but his unease was growing at the steward's dubious reluctance. Childish voices whispered that the death cells were just beneath his feet, reminding him that breaking into Hugues's office and using his seal was an extremely serious offence. Any minute now he would be found out, the floor would open and he would be sucked into oblivion, that darkness closing over him. He should have left this well alone. He never should have—

'Very well.' The steward rose stiffly. 'I'll take you down.'

Robert snatched up the scroll and followed the steward out of the stuffy room, aware of the sheen of sweat that had broken out across his brow.

Passing through a labyrinth of corridors and stairways, they made their way down into the lower levels of the prison. The passages grew narrower and colder the further they went and, after twice cracking his head on the rough ceiling, Robert was forced to walk bent forward, a hand pressed to his sword to stop the tip bumping along the wall. The steward seemed to have no problems at all, sliding his thickset frame almost gracefully through the bends and twists.

At last, they came to a recess where several pallets covered in blankets and a table and bench were set. A group of men, clad in the black tunics of sergeants, were seated at the table. A couple were playing draughts, the board bathed in the ruddy flicker of torchlight. They all stood as the steward appeared.

'Open de Floyran's cell.'

One of the sergeants took a torch from its bracket and unhooked a set of rusty keys. Moving past, he headed for a large black door, lifted the bar set across it and shouldered it open. A tunnel stretched away into darkness. Robert followed as the steward and sergeant made their way down. Doors were set at intervals in the wall to either side. The smell here was rank and every few paces his feet would squelch in something underfoot. He thought he heard a faint whimper behind one of the doors as the light of the torch swept across it, but otherwise the place was numbingly quiet. At the end of the passage, the sergeant and steward halted. A key was thrust into the lock of a door and the bolt tugged back to reveal a tiny cell.

Robert caught a glimpse of a huddled figure, hands raised over his face. The man's arms were as thin as twigs. Scraps of clothing hung from them and through the rags the knight could see a lattice of scars, some old and pink, others fresh. There were signs of infection in some of the wounds, yellow scabs bubbling up around mottled purple flesh. He realised that neither the steward nor the sergeant had moved. 'I must speak to him alone,' he told them, his voice thick with disgust from the stench.

The steward began to shake his head. 'No, that is imp—'

'I am here on the authority of Visitor de Pairaud,' said Robert harshly, holding up the scroll. 'You will attend to my requirements or the Visitor will look to you for an explanation as to why my business here was delayed.'

The steward's eyes narrowed, but after a barbed pause he nodded roughly at the guard. 'Leave him some light.'

Robert stepped aside to allow the sergeant to light a torch on the passage wall. As he did so, he thought of something he had forgotten in his concern that he wouldn't be allowed to see de Floyran. 'One last thing,' he said, as the steward made to head off. 'You said you were given strict instructions on the prisoner's incarceration. Who did those instructions come from?'

'I don't know who gave the order.' The steward gestured at the parchment Robert held. 'But it was stamped with the Visitor's seal.'

Robert just managed to keep his surprise from showing. As he stooped into the cramped cell, pulling the door to behind him, the prisoner shrank back against the wall. The man had lowered his hands now. In the glimmering torchlight coming through the crack in the door, he looked like a ghost. His skin, his eyes, his emaciated body: everything about him was pale and insubstantial. His grey lips were cracked and bleeding and his hair hung in knotted clumps around his face. As Robert watched, a black speck jumped on to Esquin's cheek, then disappeared back into the tangled mass. The man was probably alive with lice. While he was wondering what to say to this living corpse of a man, Robert heard a breathless rasp and realised the prisoner was speaking.

'Am I going to die now?'

The question sounded hopeful.

Robert moved from his bent position and crouched in front of him. 'No, Esquin. I've come to speak to you.' He kept his voice low, barely above a whisper, aware that the steward probably hadn't gone far. 'I need to know what happened to you. The reason you were imprisoned.'

Esquin shook his head fearfully.

'I mean you no harm. You have my word.' Robert exhaled, frustrated, as Esquin began rocking to and fro. 'We do not have much time.'

At this, Esquin let out a cackle of laughter.

Robert winced and glanced at the closed door. 'Gérard told me your story. But I want to hear it in your words.'

Esquin leaned forward, his chains clinking. 'Gérard? He is well?' He gave a toothless smile when Robert nodded. 'He is a good lad. He'll make his father proud.' His smile faded. 'But he won't. He is dead.'

'Gérard isn't dead, Esquin.'

'Not him, you fool!' Esquin hugged his scrawny knees to him. 'Martin.'

'Martin? You mean your nephew?'

'I won't tell,' Esquin hissed fiercely. 'You won't get him. He is safe now. Safe in the arms of God!'

'Please, Esquin, I need to know.'

'Need?' Esquin's pale eyes became slits. 'I need, brother. Need to get out of this hole.'

'That isn't possible.'

'Then you'll not get what you need from me. Take me out of here or you'll get nothing.' Esquin sat back against the rock, looking exhausted but adamant.

Robert wondered about threatening him, but didn't think he could cause the man any more pain than had already been done. 'I cannot. Not yet. But if your story is true then—'

'Guard!' shouted Esquin. 'Guard, I want this man to leave!'

Hearing footsteps coming down the passage, Robert cursed and glared at Esquin, who stared belligerently back. The knight got to his feet, bent double beneath the rock. In his hand was the letter with Hugues's seal. That mark gave him the authority to do what Esquin demanded. But there would be no turning back from this. If it was just the rumours or even just Gérard's testimony, he might have left this place now and never come back. But the order to keep Esquin isolated had come from the very office where his own investigations into possible heresy within the Order had been shut down and ended. He couldn't go back to the Temple with these questions unanswered. If he was to find out the truth behind these walls of silence, only the man in front of him could provide that.

The steward appeared with the sergeant. Robert ducked out of the door. 'Unchain the prisoner. I am taking him into my custody.'

'Come on.' Robert ushered the shivering man into the barn. Both of them were soaked through. Outside a crack of thunder rolled away to echo off some nearby hills.

Esquin started as lightning flared, turning the world stark white. He stood there, thin arms wrapped tightly around him, while the rain poured on to him through one of the gaping holes in the roof.

Robert had moved to the other end of the ruined barn, using the intermittent flashes to see by. The floor was covered with fallen timbers. As the knight kicked one of them, it crumbled apart, the wood rotten and desiccated. 'It is more sheltered over here,' he called, turning to Esquin. When the man didn't move, Robert crossed to him and took his arm. Esquin flinched, but let himself be led through the puddles. Robert shrugged his mantle from his shoulders and tossed it over a broken beam propped against a wall. He undid his sword belt, and pulled his surcoat over his head. As he went to pass it to Esquin, the man took a few paces back, staring at the garment as if the knight had just offered him something unpleasant or dangerous. 'It's dry,' Robert insisted. 'You'll catch your death in those rags.'

'No,' whispered Esquin.

It was the first word Robert had heard him say since they had left the cell in Merlan. Above them, thunder growled.

'I will not wear that thing.'

Robert looked at the mantle in his hands, its red cross almost black in the flickers of lightning. 'Very well,' he said gruffly, tugging the surcoat back over his mail hauberk. 'I'll find you something else. We'll want a fire.' After a slight hesitation, he picked up his belt and slid off the scabbard. 'Put your arms around that beam.'

Esquin stared at him.

For a moment, Robert thought he wasn't going to move, then, looking as pitiful as a maltreated hound, the man shuffled over to the beam and sat, lifting up his skinny arms. Feeling like a brute, Robert looped the length of leather under Esquin's hands and fastened it around the beam. With the man secured, he headed to the front of the barn, where he had tethered his horse, untied his pack from the saddle and drew out a blanket. After wrapping it around Esquin's shoulders, he set about gathering what he could of the drier timbers along with some scraps of old straw and brittle grasses for tinder. As he set the fire, Esquin watched in silence, his pale eyes glittering in the darkness between lightning strikes. When the first flames crackled into life, throwing light and the beginnings of warmth across them, Robert took a hunk of dry bread from his pack and tore half off for Esquin. Realising the man couldn't eat tied up, he loosened the belt and let Esquin pull one hand free. 'All right,' he said, as Esquin wrapped his toothless gums around the bread and sucked ravenously at it. 'I got you out of Merlan and probably damned myself to a cell in the process. Now it's your turn. I want you to tell me everything that happened before your imprisonment.'

Esquin removed the bread from his mouth. His gums were starting to bleed. 'I want justice,' he said in his lisping rasp. 'I want the men who murdered my nephew and did this to me to suffer for it. Will you help me achieve this?' He paused, when Robert nodded, looking suspicious, then began to speak.

Robert listened in silence to Esquin's story, from Hugues de Pairaud's blunt refusal to allow his nephew to return home, to their furtive meeting in the Church of St Julien le Pauvre, the appearance of the men in masks and his nephew's murder. When he had finished, Esquin sat there, the bread uneaten in his fist, looking exhausted beyond measure.

'You didn't recognise any of the men who apprehended you?'

'I told you, brother, they wore masks.'

'But what about voices? Names? Accents?'

'I had just seen them drag my nephew's body out of an alley. I was terrified. Grief-stricken. You ask me to remember the impossible!'

Robert raised a calming hand. 'Might you recognise them if you heard them again?'

Esquin's paper-thin brow crinkled. 'Perhaps . . .' All at once, he stopped. 'But no. That would mean I would have to return.' He shook his head. 'I won't return to that preceptory! It's crawling with heretics and blood-drinkers. Men spitting on the cross! Devil's sons!'

'You said you wanted justice.'

Esquin's eyes were bright and feverish in the yellow flames. 'I'll get it some other way. I won't return. I won't!'

Robert sat back, troubled. Without some idea of who was involved in this he wasn't sure what steps to take next, or what to do with Esquin for that matter. He wondered if there was a safe place where the man could be kept until he could find out more; perhaps speak to Hugues when the

Visitor returned from England? 'Get some sleep for now,' he said eventually. 'When the storm is past we'll head on. I want to get as far from Merlan as possible. The steward had no choice, but he wasn't happy about letting us go. I don't want him thinking he made the wrong decision and sending men after us.'

Esquin compliantly rested his head against the beam and closed his eyes. After banking up the fire, Robert wrapped his soggy mantle over him and leaned back, listening to the storm rolling around the hills and, between the crashes, the prisoner's uneven breaths.

Esquin opened his eyes. The fire had died down and the air was hushed and frozen. Across from him, the knight had his chin on his chest, which was rising and falling steadily. The sky between the jagged roof timbers was a pale, pearlescent blue. The sight of it made Esquin shudder. How long since he had seen sky? He went to move, then realised that both his hands were fastened to the beam. The knight must have bound him again while he was sleeping. Opening his cracked lips, he went to wake him, recalling the knight's worry that the steward of Merlan might send men after them. But he stopped himself before the words came.

Why should he trust this man, any more than he trusted his tormentors in the prison or the men who put him there? They all wore the same uniform. Esquin's eyes fixed on the hateful red cross on the mantle, his gaze watchful and brooding. What if this knight was deceiving him? Perhaps his gaolers wanted to find out how much he remembered before they finally killed him? Faced with death back in his cell he thought he would have welcomed it over the slow decay of years. But now, with the sky lightening outside and the icy morning creeping in around him with its promise of freedom, its promise of life, he realised he didn't want to die. He wanted to live.

Cautiously, Esquin reached out to the fire with his bare foot and teased out a smouldering shard of wood. Scrunching his toes over it, he drew it across the floor towards him. He halted as the fire shifted and the knight grunted in his sleep. When the man didn't wake, Esquin wiggled his hands, easing the strap down the beam, tugging it gently over knots and ridges in the wood. Finally, feeling sick with the exertion, he managed to position the belt over the smouldering shard, his head almost touching the floor. Slowly, the material began to blacken. He closed his eyes as the heat of it burned away the hairs on his wrists and his skin tightened and reddened. The smell of charring leather was acrid in his nostrils. At last, after what seemed an eternity, the burned strap broke apart.

Freed from his bonds, Esquin slipped across the barn floor. He paused in the ruined entrance, halted by the sight of misty fields stretching into grey-green distance, then carefully untied the knight's horse.

33
The Sainte-Chapelle, Paris
21 February 1307 AD

'My prayers are not enough.' Philippe's voice was muffled, his words spilling into his hands, clasped in front of his face as he knelt on the stone floor. 'Not enough.'

'Every man on this Earth, no matter the extent or severity of his sins, has the chance at forgiveness. If he is truly repentant.'

Philippe stared up at the man towering above him, whose black, floor-length robes made him appear dauntingly tall. His thin face was starkly white, framed by flint-grey hair carved into an austere tonsure, and a smell of incense came from him imbuing him with a certain sanctified air as if he were a small piece of the Church itself, broken off and planted before Philippe to judge and punish. At this thought, the king's eyes moved past Guillaume de Paris and fixed on the winged cherubs hovering over the lofty altar. He half expected them to climb down from their pedestals and stand before him, little gold eyes blazing with condemnation.

'Are you repentant, my lord?'

Philippe's eyes flicked back to the Dominican at the demand. 'You know that I am.'

'Does God?'

'What more can I do?' Philippe whispered, closing his eyes against his confessor's unforgiving stare. 'Every day I pray and do penance. Yet still I do not hear Him. Still He does not speak.'

'Perhaps your prayers are not sincere enough? Your penance not thorough?'

Philippe's eyes snapped open. 'Not thorough?' He rose. 'I have ripped myself into shreds for Him. For His love. What more does He want from me?' The king wrenched off his robe and picked at the thongs of his hair shirt. 'I have worn it ceaselessly for weeks! I have even slept in it!' His voice echoed in the silent chapel, shrouded in shadow except for a pool of candlelight which illuminated his chest with its sallow glow as he tore off the garment. 'Does this not please you?' he shouted, raising his arms and sinking to his knees in front of the altar, where the cherubs looked dispassionately down at his scarred body.

'You wore it ceaselessly, my lord?' Guillaume's voice was brittle. 'Did you wear it when you were with your whore?'

Philippe stared at him.

The Dominican went to him and crouched down, his grey eyes implacable. 'You may choose to hide your sins from me and from God. But you cannot hide them from your staff. The rumours are well known. You have been bedding a servant woman, yes?' When Philippe hung his head, Guillaume stood abruptly. 'How can I absolve you if you will not confess? How can God forgive you if you are not truly repentant?'

'I miss my wife. Miss her so terribly I can hardly bear to be near my children for the pain the reminder of her causes me. The servant woman is . . .' Philippe shook his head numbly. 'Solace.'

'Jeanne is with God, my lord. She is at peace. You must make your own peace, here in this realm, before you can join her. You must strive every day to uphold the Christian faith. Your people look to you to lead them.'

'My people? Everything I have done has been for them and still they hate me. When they light their candles in their churches it is always for Louis, never for me. The harvests are bad and they blame me. I raise taxes to secure their borders and they rebel against me. You know as well as I the mood in this city.' Philippe sat back, his voice thick with bitterness. 'It seems every time I make a proclamation these days there is a riot in the streets. But if God does not hear me, how will I make it into Heaven without the prayers of my people? I need them to love me, Guillaume.'

'You must not rely on others for your own salvation, my lord. You must submit fully and honestly to God's will, giving yourself up to Him to be forgiven. When your prayers and your penance are truly sincere, He will hear you. Of that there is no doubt.'

'There is time then?' murmured Philippe. 'Time for me to be pardoned? To feel God's love no matter what I have done?'

'Of course.' The steel edge had gone from Guillaume's tone, but his gaze remained uncompromising. 'These are troubled times, my lord. Now, more than ever, you must be an example to your people. You know my thoughts on the deeds of your lawyer, but Minister de Nogaret's fate is not mine to decide. For all his love of the law, he shall be judged in his turn by a higher court. But now the Church and France are no longer at war, I urge you to build upon the close relationship you have forged with Pope Clement for the sake of your subjects. Through your actions they will come to see what they too should be striving for.' The Dominican moved to the altar. 'They must be shown the true path; the path of the righteous. Vulgarity and irreverence are rampant in this kingdom. My Order mercifully halted the malevolent influence of the Cathars in the south, whose despicable sacrileges were consumed in holy fire. But with the fall of Acre it was shown to us how fickle the faith of many is, with their conversions to the religion of the infidel. All of us must work to ensure that such monstrous heresies are not spread again.'

'They won't be,' said Philippe flatly, sunk on his knees, weary now. 'Those of the Cathars who didn't perish during the Church's Crusade against them were forced into hiding. There would not be enough of them left to infect anyone.' He shot the Dominican a wilful look. 'I am sure Minster de Nogaret would tell you that.'

'Yet every day in my role as inquisitor, new offences are brought to my attention.' Guillaume turned back to him. 'Just this past week, I have been confronted by one such matter that has concerned me gravely. There is a man at our college in the city who is claiming that the Order of the Knights Templar is riddled with heresy.'

'What?'

'He arrived ten days ago, raving, half starved and begging for sanctuary. He spoke to one of my brothers, but when the seriousness of his charges became clear, I was informed. I have had several discussions with this man, who claims to have been imprisoned by members of the Order when he uncovered their involvement in certain depraved ceremonies. Apparently, his own nephew fell foul of these men and was murdered when he refused to obey them.'

Philippe had risen, his hair shirt and robe discarded on the floor at his feet. His eyes followed the confessor, who went to pinch out a candle that was dripping.

'The man displays obvious signs of torture and is clearly vengeful due to a long incarceration, and I am always wary of revenge as a motivation for men and women to alert us to possible heresies. I fear some in the past have been burned for the wrong reasons.' Guillaume de Paris inhaled briskly. 'But as the Dominican Order has declared, it is better to burn one hundred innocents than leave one heretic left standing to corrupt God's faithful.' He turned to Philippe. 'But whether he is just a malcontent, wishing to destroy his gaolers, or whether there is truth in his words, his tale is both convincing and extremely disturbing, and cannot be ignored. As the Temple lies beyond my jurisdiction I had intended to take this matter before the pope, but I did want to seek further counsel before troubling his holiness with something that may in the end prove false. Knowing your close relationship with Pope Clement, I hoped you might aid me in this, my lord?'

Philippe went swiftly to the confessor. 'I want to speak to this man.'

The Dominican's pale brow creased in surprise at the king's forcefulness, but he nodded. 'Your opinion on the validity of his claims would be most welcome, although I must warn you he is filled with rage and madness.'

'We will bring him here at once.'

Guillaume de Paris held up his hand. 'No, my lord. First we will finish your confession.'

After a pause, Philippe returned to his knees in front of the black-robed Dominican and began to list his sins, his clasped hands hiding an intense expression.

The Banks of the Seine, Paris, 2 March 1307 AD

'Listen, I can still find him given time.' Robert went to Will who had slumped on one of the eel pots littering the muddy riverbanks. 'At least we now know something is happening in the Paris Temple that needs to be investigated. De Floyran said he couldn't identify the men so to be honest his testimony isn't much use anyway and . . .' Robert stopped, seeing Will's expression. 'What is it?'

'I know where Esquin de Floyran is.'

'What? How?'

'Just over a week ago a man was brought into the palace from the Dominican College under heavy guard. The king and Nogaret spent several days in closed meetings with him, which the king's confessor, Guillaume de Paris, was privy to. It came to my attention because Philippe cancelled a feast and a hunt in order to spend time with this man. I wasn't told why he was there, but I did hear his name.'

Robert's face fell as he realised what Will was saying. 'Dear God. Why would de Floyran come back to Paris? He was terrified by the idea when I suggested it.'

'You said he wanted justice. If I wanted to accuse anyone of heresy the Dominican College is the first place I would go. Where better to get everything he needs? Food, shelter, protection. Revenge.'

'Christ.' Robert pushed his hands through his hair and paced the bank. A couple of boys were sword-fighting with sticks down by the water's edge. Their excited calls mingled with the piercing cries of the river birds swooping over the Ile des Juifs. 'Can you get him out?'

'He left five days ago with Nogaret under armed escort. They were heading for Poitiers.'

'Why there?'

'Pope Clement has been travelling around the kingdom visiting the provinces. He has been in Poitiers for some months. I imagine Esquin is being taken to him.'

'This is it, isn't it?' said Robert after a long silence, filled with the shouts of the boys. 'This is what the king needs to get what he wants. As soon as the pope hears de Floyran's testimony he will be forced to launch an inquiry into the Temple. A charge of heresy is serious when set against anyone, but against the most powerful religious Order in Christendom? His holiness will have no choice but to act.' The knight stared out across the Seine, turquoise in the dazzling spring sun. 'I should never have taken de Floyran out of Merlan.'

Will didn't say anything for a time. 'I wish you had come to me as soon as Simon alerted you to the sergeant's story.'

Robert shot him a defensive glance. 'I thought you would be occupied with other things.'

'Other things?' Will's face hardened. 'I've been trying to save my country and my daughter.' When the knight looked away, Will stood. 'You act as though I'm somehow to blame here. How could I have known any of this if you don't inform me?'

Robert faced him. 'The moment we returned to Paris after rescuing Clement's son, you disappeared back into the palace. You say you're still a part of the Anima Templi, but I've hardly seen hide nor hair of you this past year.'

'Pope Clement charged me with finding evidence that Nogaret murdered Benedict. If I do that he will continue to put pressure on Edward as well as safeguard the Temple from Philippe.' Will's voice was rigid. 'I am doing everything in my power to make these things happen. I have already persuaded Clement to send papal letters to England, demanding Edward cease his war against Scotland. After Wallace's execution this was my country's – my *family's* – best chance of survival. Can you blame me for taking it?' He didn't wait for Robert to answer. 'But I find myself on thinner and thinner ice. Since their plan for the Temple was halted, Philippe and Nogaret no longer need me in their circle and it has been all I can do to remain a guest in the palace, let alone keep close enough to them to uncover any evidence for the pope.'

'Do you actually believe you will be able to find proof of Nogaret's involvement in Benedict's death?'

Will was silent. He had known from the moment the pope charged him with this task how challenging it would be. It wasn't as if Nogaret would have left any kind of written evidence anywhere. 'I have to try,' he said, as much to himself as to Robert. 'I have to do what I can to keep the pope on our side. The king, however, is becoming ever more untrusting of me.' He let out a rough breath. 'I believe the main reason I haven't been evicted is because the bastard is bedding my daughter.'

Robert stared at him in disbelief. 'What?'

Will waved his hand and strode down to the water. 'I don't want to talk about it,' he said grimly when Robert followed. 'Just believe me when I say I am trying to salvage what I can of the Anima Templi's aims by remaining in Philippe's company, even though it is taking every ounce of strength I have left not to strangle the cur in his sleep.'

'Can you not take her out of Paris?' Robert asked quietly.

'And lose my last foothold?' demanded Will, the sunlight glinting in his eyes. Bending, he dug a stone out of the mud and flung it into the river. 'If I remove Rose from the palace against her wishes I think she will be lost to me for good. This way, I get to stay close to her and the king. Perhaps I am a fool, but I still believe my daughter might need me. I want to be there if that day ever comes.'

'What about Robert Bruce?' Robert ventured. 'Now Scotland has a new king, surely there is hope for your homeland at least?'

'The last I heard, Bruce and his followers had gone on the run. They had a victory at first, but it is rumoured Edward is gathering a vast army to send north, despite Clement's objections. If he has his way, Scotland's new king will be staring out across the Thames from a pike by the autumn.'

Robert watched the two boys chasing one another across the mud-flats, birds wheeling up in white clouds before them. 'I suppose it was naïve, but I thought when we returned from the Holy Land things would be simpler. Do you think we will ever see peace in our lifetime? Is it even possible?'

'More and more I think not. But then I remember Everard and my father and Kalawun, and all those men who believed it was, believed so completely they gave up everything they had for it. I have to hope that . . .' Will trailed off, shaking his head. 'What I hope isn't important right now. Whatever any of us wants will not matter if King Philippe has his way. Have you spoken to Hugues?'

'No. He is still in England.'

'Do you believe he had anything to do with de Floyran's imprisonment?'

'I cannot imagine he is involved in any of this,' replied Robert.

'But the order to keep de Floyran in isolation bore the Visitor's seal?'

'I think I proved that using Hugues's seal without his knowledge is possible.'

'That may be so, but we cannot ignore the fact that Esquin's charges bear a striking similarity to practices and tenets within the Anima Templi. Secret initiations. Drinking the blood of fellow knights. Spitting on the cross. All these things were detailed in the Book of the Grail.'

'Drinking blood?'

'The Book of the Grail was written on the orders of former Grand Master Armand de Périgord, who was also a member of the Brethren. According to Everard, the Grand Master had an obsession with the tales of Perceval and King Arthur and wanted a special ceremony for initiates into the Anima Templi that was different to the rituals of induction into the Temple. Everard wrote the Book to be Armand's new code.'

'I know this,' Robert cut across him.

Will ignored the interruption. 'Like other Grail Romances the Book was filled with unusual, even profane imagery, but unlike a simple story, it contained within its pages the aims and beliefs of the Brethren, which as we both know are as unorthodox as the Book itself. When Armand died in a Mamluk prison, the Book became obsolete and was never used, but some of the philosophies evoked within remained at our core. Remember how Everard always called Acre our Camelot,' Will added, when Robert frowned in question. 'It was all just allegory of course. No one was supposed to drink anyone's blood; that just symbolised brotherhood. But the Book wasn't some delicate Romance for ladies at court. It was dangerous, blatantly heretical in many of its themes and, what is more, it was evidence of our existence. This is why the Hospitallers stole it, hoping to expose us and, in so doing, bring down the Temple. It is also why Edward wanted it. With the Book in his possession, he could have used the threat of exposure to gain access to our funds. Everard always regretted not destroying it after Armand's death.'

'But who else would know this? You told me Everard burned the Book when you retrieved it. The priest has been dead for decades, and since your desertion the Brethren have been reduced to a handful.'

'There are one or two,' said Will, watching as Robert moved away. 'One specifically.'

Robert turned back abruptly. 'I've known Hugues since I was a boy. As have you.'

'I sent him Everard's writings before the fall of Acre. He could have gleaned things from those pages.'

'I cannot believe you would think him capable of murdering an innocent man and locking away another.' When Will didn't respond, Robert let out a sharp breath. 'You didn't see Merlan, Will. The man we know would never do that.'

The Castle, Carlisle, 11 March 1307 AD

Hugues de Pairaud followed as the page led him into the chamber. It was dark, the painted shutters closed over the windows, and it took the Visitor a few moments to see the figure propped up in the large bed, illuminated by the flames that billowed in a hearth. At the figure's nod, the page backed out of the door, closing it quietly behind him.

'My lord king,' greeted Hugues, bowing to Edward, whose face was feverish in the firelight. He was stunned by how old the king appeared. How old and frail. In the years since Hugues had seen him last, Edward's white hair had become thin and wispy on his crown, the bald patches creased and mottled. His cheeks were hollow and gaunt, his eyes sunk in their sockets, and he looked far beyond his sixty-seven years.

'Closer,' demanded Edward, his voice, although faint, still commanding enough to make Hugues step forward promptly.

'I am sorry to hear that you have been ill, my lord.'

'A fever, Visitor de Pairaud,' responded Edward tersely, 'nothing more. So, you received my summons eventually?' The criticism was plain.

Hugues inclined his head. 'I apologise that it took me so long to respond, but I have been occupied visiting the Temple's holdings in Britain.' He went nearer, feeling the ferocious heat of the fire. 'But I was glad to get your message, my lord, as I did wish to speak to you before I returned to Paris.'

Edward stared at him from out of the puckered folds of his pale eyes. 'Oh?'

'These past years have laid heavy burdens on us both, my lord: your struggle against the rebels in Scotland; my attempts to secure a base for the Temple. I know, when we first agreed to aid one another in our respective endeavours, that neither of us would have imagined we would be in the

same position after all this time. However, I would remind your graciousness that I have kept up my side of our agreement. The Temple fought for
you in two campaigns, during which we lost one of our most dedicated
Masters.' Hugues's voice tightened. 'Grand Master de Molay is still
encamped on Cyprus and despite my repeated requests that he return
to administer to the Order's growing needs in the West, he is adamant he
will remain there until support for a new holy war is forthcoming.' He
went closer to the fire, holding out his hands to the flames. 'I recently
received word that Pope Clement has endorsed the Hospitallers' planned
conquest of the island of Rhodes that they might secure a permanent base
for themselves. Their Grand Master has pledged to embark on a Crusade
once the island is under their control.'

'I fail to see what any of this has to do with me,' said Edward, his voice
dispassionate.

Hugues gritted his teeth, angered that Edward seemed inclined to make
this as difficult as possible. 'I had hoped, my lord, we could discuss the
terms of our earlier agreement and your promise to aid the Temple in
establishing a suitable headquarters.'

'I lie here on my sickbed with my coffers draining and my men spilling
their blood on battlefields as we speak and you have the temerity to ask this
of me?' Edward sat forward, his face strained. 'Who do you think you are
talking to, de Pairaud?'

Hugues stood his ground. 'We made an agreement, my lord.'

'Bah!' Edward sank back against the pillows, his laboured breaths rattling
in his throat. 'That agreement was made before my kingdom was blighted
by that whoreson Wallace and his bastard followers. Now, with Robert
Bruce arrayed against me I have neither the time nor the inclination to aid
you.' His eyes narrowed as he stared into the fire. 'I will have the Scots on
their knees before me if it is the last thing I do in this life. My wife and most
of my children have died around me during this campaign. I am left with a
son whose arm is as feeble as his wit. Who will wield the Hammer I have
forged against the insurgent north when I am dead? I can leave the task to no
one. I must finish it. I have not wasted eighteen years of my reign on this
endeavour for nothing.'

'Are you saying you will not help me, my lord?'

The king was silent. A log shifted in the hearth and a burst of sparks
crackled into the air. 'I am saying I cannot. Not now.' He paused. 'But if I
crush Bruce and his supporters, I will give you what you want.'

'Territory?' asked Hugues quickly.

'I would be willing to discuss the offer of a small area of Scotland as a benefice to the Temple, should this campaign prove successful. But I have a condition. It is, in fact, the reason I summoned you.'

Hugues waited.

'If I am to win through in Scotland I will need all the help I can muster from my subjects. I require the support of the barons to mount an effective campaign, the approval of my people whose taxes will pay for it and the endorsement of the Church from which I intend to levy further funds. This last requirement is proving to be difficult. William Wallace had the backing of Pope Boniface, who was my staunchest detractor in earlier campaigns. This past year his successor, Clement, has begun to take on a similar role. When I sent messengers to his holiness, replying to his letters of protest, my men discovered something very interesting. The pope, it seems, has formed an alliance with an old enemy of mine. The details of their acquaintance elude me, but the whys and wherefores are not important. What *is* important is that it is ended. That is where I require your help.'

'You want this enemy destroyed?' said Hugues, frowning.

'No. I want him captured and brought to me.'

'My lord, I am sure someone with your capabilities could find and detain this man quite easily without the need for my—'

'He is currently in Paris as a guest of King Philippe, where he has no doubt stirred up other trouble for me.' Edward's eyes bored into Hugues. 'The man is William Campbell.' When the Visitor didn't respond, the king nodded. 'I can see by your face that this comes as a surprise to you. I had wondered if you knew.'

'I thought him dead,' murmured Hugues.

'I had him in my custody in Stirling years ago, but he escaped. In the past Campbell has been little more than a wasp, an irritation. Now, his sting is starting to wound me. I want him destroyed. But by me, you understand?' Edward pointed a bony finger at Hugues. 'Bring me Campbell and you can have your piece of land, Templar.'

34

Franciscan Monastery, Poitiers

8 April 1307 AD

G uillaume de Nogaret smoothed back his thinning hair in the mirror
and pulled on his coif. He paused for a moment, staring at his pallid
reflection with a small, satisfied smile, before shrugging on his freshly
laundered travelling cloak. There was a knock at the door. When Nogaret
opened it, he saw an acolyte outside holding a basket covered with a cloth,
through which drifted a strong smell of cheese.

'His holiness said you required provisions for your journey back to Paris,
Minister.' The acolyte held out the basket expectantly.

'Give it to my squire.' As the man nodded and turned to leave, Nogaret
called to him. 'And while you're at it, make sure he has my horse saddled
and ready. I wish to leave right away.' Closing the door, the minister
finished packing his few belongings into a leather bag. When he was done,
he made his way out.

Striding swiftly along a gallery that looked down over an inner courtyard,
he heard faint chanting coming from the chapel, rising beyond the rooftops of
the friars' lodgings. Guessing it must be for the morning office, he halted to
listen, the sun warming his face. His smile deepened and he wondered at the
pleasure he felt at a sound that would usually grate on his nerves. After a
moment, he realised that his satisfaction wasn't at the friars' prayers; it was at
the fact that, for the first time, the Church had given him something other than
torment. His smile was one of victory, long awaited.

The feeling passed quickly, however, and by the time he made his way
out into the courtyard, the lines on his brow had settled into their well-
worn furrows. He had mistakenly believed he had succeeded before in
pursuit of his aim. That the pope had listened with mounting concern to
Esquin de Floyran's testimony when Nogaret had brought the former prior
to him was one step. That Clement had then, with some persuasion,
written the letter to the Grand Master of the Temple was another. Now the

message was winging its way across France and Esquin de Floyran was safely hidden all Nogaret could do was return to Paris, and wait to see if the next step was taken.

Crossing the cloisters and entering the building on the far side, he was making his way down a wide, sunlit passage when he saw three men coming towards him. They were some distance ahead and engrossed in conversation. The first was a friar in a grey hooded robe. The other two wore riding cloaks. Nogaret recognised one of them immediately. There was a second's indecision, in which he almost called out. But something stopped him. Instead, he slipped in through one of the doors that lined the passage and entered an empty chamber filled with writing desks. Standing close to the door, grasping the handle, he listened intently as the men's footsteps came closer. He caught a snatch of conversation.

'. . . but you are welcome to wait . . .'

The words faded into murmurs and the footsteps continued on. Nogaret eased open the door and saw the backs of the men moving away. His eyes lingered on the one in the centre, before they turned a corner and were gone from sight. Deep in thought, Nogaret almost knocked into an acolyte hurrying in through the cloisters. It was the young man who had brought him the basket of provisions. He grabbed the acolyte's arm. 'The two men with one of the brothers,' he said, pointing in the direction the three had gone. 'I want you to find out who they are and why they are here.'

'But—'

'Now,' demanded Nogaret. He held on for a second longer, his pinching fingers causing the acolyte to wince. 'Do it with care. I don't want either of them to know anyone was asking. Do you understand?'

The acolyte nodded quickly. 'Yes, Minister.'

'I'll be in the stables.'

As the young man moved off, rubbing his arm, Nogaret made for the yard.

His squire was there with their horses, the panniers filled with food and blankets, donations from the monastery. Curtly telling his squire to wait, Nogaret ducked into the shade of the stables. A couple of grooms were removing the saddles of two weary-looking horses. Nogaret knew the piebald stallion. The other was a powerful-looking destrier, with plain, but well-made trappings. He questioned the grooms on their riders, but neither boy knew anything. As the minutes crawled by, Nogaret's impatience hardened into a tight knot. The sound of chanted prayers had ended and the monastery was bustling into life.

Finally, a door in the building across the yard opened and the acolyte hurried across.

'Well?' demanded Nogaret.

'I spoke with Brother Alain, Minister. He said the men were asking if Esquin de Floyran was here. When they were told he had left, they requested to speak to his holiness.'

'Did you learn their names?'

'William Campbell and Sir Robert de Paris.'

'De Paris?'

'Yes. Did you want anything else before you . . . ? Minister?'

Nogaret was striding to his horse, not listening. He gestured to his squire and swung up into his saddle. 'Do not tell them I asked,' he told the acolyte, turning his horse roughly. 'That is a royal order.'

'Of course.'

As the young man hastened to open the gate, Nogaret glanced back at the monastery buildings. No doubt Campbell would soon discover he had been here, but that didn't matter. By the time he did, Nogaret would be on the road to Paris. He expected the men would be delayed for some while. Clement had taken ill several days earlier and was refusing all visitors to his private chamber in the monastery.

The minister dug his heels into the sides of his horse and rode through the gate, relieved he had trusted his instincts and hadn't called out to the Scot. He had initially thought the king must have sent Campbell, possibly with new instructions. But the second man, the one he didn't recognise, had stopped him, that and his distrust of Campbell.

Now, that distrust seemed more vindicated than ever. It blazed in his mind, fiery and righteous. Robert de Paris was the name of the Templar who freed Esquin de Floyran from Merlan. The way Campbell had worked himself so keenly into the king's trust, the unexpected appearance of the knights protecting Boniface in Anagni, the escape of Clement's child and the murder of the royal soldiers, these events were like arrows on a map all pointing towards the same place. Towards the Temple. Towards Campbell.

Franciscan Monastery, Poitiers, 23 April 1307 AD

'You have until Vespers.'

The friar shut the door behind Will and Robert, leaving them in the chamber, alone but for the ashen-skinned, emaciated man propped on a chair by the window.

The sight of him tempered some of Will's impatience, burning hot within him for over a fortnight. The pope looked as though he were hovering on the threshold of life, his face so pale it was almost translucent. 'I deeply regretted to hear of your illness, your holiness,' he said, realising that he meant it. Clement was his one true ally now.

'The worst has passed,' answered the pope, in a withered voice. He held a cloth pouch, which gave off a tart smell of herbs. 'Praise be to God.' He made as if to rise, then sank back with a sigh. 'Although I am still weak.' Lifting the pouch to his face, he took a sniff and grimaced. 'The infirmarer tells me this is to help the sickness, but I fear it might actually be the cause of it.' His bloodshot eyes focused on Will. 'The brothers told me you had come. I assume for the same reason as the king's minister?'

Will went to him. 'Where is Esquin de Floyran, your holiness? No one here would answer our questions.'

'Most of them know nothing of this matter. I spoke with de Floyran at length several weeks back, before the sickness gripped me. Nogaret took him after we were finished. He said he was moving him to a safe place, but did not trust me enough to tell me where, despite my insistence. Either it wasn't far from here or he had men waiting nearby to convey de Floyran, because the minister returned the same day.'

'What did Esquin tell you?'

'That there were heretics within the Temple who murdered his nephew and locked him in prison.'

'Did you believe him?

'He told a convincing tale.' Clement paused. 'But it was the testimony of one man alone, a man clearly fired by vengeance.'

'So you dismissed it? Sent Nogaret back to the king?'

Clement rose, using the chair to steady himself. 'I had no choice but to act. It was a serious allegation.'

'You know why they have brought this to your attention,' Will pressed, throwing a troubled look at Robert. 'This is what the king and his minister have no doubt been longing for; some spurious claim by which means they can steer their plans for the Temple.'

'Spurious?' Clement's voice sharpened. 'You can tell me for certain what de Floyran said is false? You have proof?'

'Whether it is false or not is surely a matter for the Temple, your holiness?' interjected Robert. 'The Order has jurisdiction regarding the discipline of its members. This is an internal matter. It should be investigated as such.'

'Exactly,' responded the pope, 'which is why I have sent a message to Cyprus summoning Jacques de Molay.'

'Did Nogaret demand this?' questioned Will.

'I made my own decision. In matters of heresy the final decision is always mine.'

The pope's irascible tone told Will he had indeed been browbeaten by the king's minister. Before he could think through the possible outcomes of this, Clement continued.

'Grand Master de Molay and his officials will be able to help me resolve this matter. Together, we will root out the truth or falsehood of de Floyran's testimony and deal with it accordingly. The king and his minister may see this as a route to the Temple, but I promise you, unless I deem it necessary, the Temple will not be damaged in any way. Besides,' added Clement, 'I dearly wish to speak to the Grand Master. It is long past time I received news from the East. I want to hear the plans for his Crusade and to see what I can do to support the Order.' He smiled faintly. 'Indeed, I consider this whole affair to be a blessing rather than a curse.'

Will said nothing, his unease merely heightened by the pope's assurances. He had always ignored Clement's evident desire for a Crusade, choosing to hope that the reluctance of rulers such as Edward and Philippe to take the Cross, along with Jacques's failures in the East, would render the pope's wish nothing more substantial than a dream. But now it seemed, either way the tide turned, a meeting between the pope and the Grand Master had the potential to lead to something more ominous. He wondered about going himself to Cyprus to warn Jacques not to attend the meeting, but the two-week head-start of the pope's message was discouraging and unless he told Jacques the truth, which in itself could damage the Order, the Grand Master would have no choice but to answer the pope's summons.

'Now, Campbell,' said Clement, his tone signalling the end of any further discussion. 'I want to know what you have found out on Guillaume de Nogaret. Have you uncovered any evidence on his involvement in Benedict's death?'

'I'm afraid not. Nogaret has cut himself off from me and since the death of the queen the king has closed his inner circle to the point where even some of his closest advisors no longer have his ear.'

'You should try to find something soon,' responded Clement pensively. 'Left to his own devices I fear that snake has enough venom in him to poison us all.'

The Royal Palace, Paris, 14 May 1307 AD

Will was in his room when he heard a soft tapping sound. After a few moments it came again and he realised someone was knocking on his door, but so quietly it was as if they were hoping he wouldn't hear. Crossing the chamber, he mentally rehearsed his lie about his recent trip to England, should the unexpected guest be Nogaret, and opened the door. 'Rose,' he murmured, too surprised to say anything else. Never once, in all the years he had been a guest in the palace had his daughter come to his chamber. He felt a rush of pleasure, but quickly quelled it, not daring to hope that this might signal some change in her feelings towards him.

Rose opened her mouth to speak, but nothing came. She tried again before a pained expression crossed her face and she turned and hastened away down the passage.

'Wait!' Will went after her and grasped her arm. 'Please, Rose. Come inside.'

She faltered, then reluctantly let herself be led to his room.

Will closed the door behind her and went to his bed, where his travelling cloak and sword were lying. He picked them up and dumped them on a chest. 'I've only just returned,' he explained, standing back and shoving a hand through his hair.

She perched on the edge of the bed at his gesture, planting her hands to either side of her, dwarfed by a voluminous blue cloak. 'I didn't know where you were.'

Will was struck by the desolation in her tone. 'I'm sorry.' He folded his arms and let out a rough sigh. 'But, to be honest, it didn't occur to me to tell you I was going away. I didn't think you would care to know.'

Rose looked at the floor and murmured something he didn't catch. She glanced up when he didn't respond. 'I needed you.'

Will went and sat beside her, trying to hold back the emotion that threatened to engulf him at those words. Tentatively, he took her thin, scarred hand in his, which was callused and thickly veined. 'I'm here now. Talk to me.'

'Philippe.'

She didn't say anything else for a long moment and Will wondered if she was going to speak at all when finally she did, her words stumbling, uncertain.

'He and I, we have . . . We are . . . Lovers,' she finished, looking at him with something of a challenge in her stare. When he said nothing, she continued. 'But he has changed in recent months. He has become cold.' Rose's eyes flicked away. 'Violent.'

Will's hand tightened around hers. He felt something clawing its way up inside him, something feral and ferocious, but he kept quiet.

'I am worried about what he might do next. I've heard things he is planning, things he speaks of with Guillaume de Nogaret when they think I am not listening. Father, I know he is intent on taking the wealth of the Temple for himself.'

'It won't happen.'

'You know of this?'

'For quite some time, yes. But he will not succeed. I will not let him.'

Rose shook her head. 'You do not know what he's capable of.' She bit her lip. 'He has so much anger in him. It scares me.'

'Then why do you still go to him?'

Rose snatched her hand from his and stood. 'How do I say no to a king?'

Will got to his feet, terrified she would run out of the door and out of his life yet again. 'I am sorry, that was careless of me.' He gripped her shoulders. 'Listen to me, Rose. You are right to be scared of Philippe. He is a vengeful, hard-hearted man, who will crush anything that stands in the way of his ambitions. But I understand your' – he gritted his teeth around the word – 'affair. For I know he can also be very charming and persuasive. I saw him as a useful ally for many years, before my eyes were opened by his cruelty. But it has to stop. You have to let me help you. Will you do that?' When she nodded, Will smiled and brushed her cheek with his finger. 'I can get you away from here. Out of his reach.'

'Where would I go?' she asked in a small voice.

'To my sisters, Ysenda and Ede in Scotland.'

'What about you?'

Will hesitated. He could think of nothing he wanted more than to take his daughter down to the stables, steal two horses and ride like the wind to the coast. They would find a merchant ship at Honfleur and he would sell his sword for passage. They could be in Scotland by June. 'I have to stay,' he said, the words some of the most difficult he had ever uttered. 'I have to try to limit the damage the king and Nogaret could cause.'

'How?'

'I have the confidence of the pope.' Will went to the chest where he had dumped his cloak and broadsword. 'He will ensure the Order is spared from Philippe's intentions.' Picking up his belt, he fastened it around his waist, adjusting the blade at his side.

She watched him worriedly. 'Where are you going?'

'I have to see Robert at the Temple. He was due to speak to the Visitor on an urgent matter and I must know the outcome. I will ask him to talk to Simon, explain that you need to get to Scotland.' He crossed to her. 'In the meantime, I want you to go to your room and gather your belongings. Make sure no one sees you. I will return for you in a few hours. I am hoping Simon will be able to help you secure passage down at the docks. But either way, I will make sure you are taken to safety.'

Numbly, Rose let her father escort her to the door. In the passage outside, she watched him stride swiftly away, swinging his cloak around his broad shoulders. Part of her wanted to call out to him, but fear and indecision won and instead she kept silent and walked back through the gloomy corridors to the halls of the royal apartments, bronzed by the early evening sun.

As she entered the king's chamber, Nogaret rose, his face flushed and impatient.

Philippe, however, remained seated, his expression coldly composed. 'Well?'

Rose turned her head, unable to meet their combined stares. She felt the door at her back, the wood cool and solid, felt shame uncurling inside her, bringing unexpected pain. Her father's face drifted before her, filled with concern and love. No one had looked at her that way in years. Not since Acre. Not since she was a child. Feeling sick, she glanced up, her gaze fixing on Philippe. She could see nothing of love in his face, only hard, unsympathetic arrogance. He was so inhuman. Even when he was inside her, his passion was icy and brittle. It was like making love to a statue.

'Speak, girl!' snapped Nogaret, making her start.

'He knows you wish to take the Temple's wealth,' she murmured, the words catching in her throat.

Philippe stood and went to her. 'This we know. What else did he say?' He gripped her chin, so she could look nowhere but into his eyes. 'Tell me, Rose, what else did your father say? Is he working against me, trying to thwart my plans? Is he in league with the pope?'

'Please. You're hurting me.'

His voice softened, but he didn't relinquish his hold. 'You have to think about what is best for you now, Rose. You have to think about who can take care of you. A father who abandoned you long ago? Or a king who can give you everything you need.' He pushed back the folds of her blue cloak and placed his hand firmly on her belly. 'I will take care of you.'

Rose looked down at his hand, cupping her stomach, already starting to swell.

When she had finished speaking, Philippe took his hand off her and let her slip past him. Rose entered her room and shut the door. Her sobs came to him through the wood.

Nogaret's face was alive with rage. 'That treacherous cur!' He paced the room. 'We should strip the flesh from him!'

Philippe went to the window and looked out. 'We have to find out exactly what damage he has done. Does anyone else in the Temple know of our plan, other than de Paris? How long has Campbell had Clement's confidence? Was the summons for Jacques de Molay even sent?'

'It was,' injected Nogaret, still pacing furiously around the chamber. 'I sent one of our men with the papal messenger to make sure.' He crossed to Philippe, lowering his voice. 'At least you can now rid yourself of two problems, my lord.' He gestured at the interconnecting door, beyond which Rose's sobs still sounded. 'Your betrayer and his daughter.'

Philippe glanced at him. 'No, she may still be of some use. We can use her as leverage if Campbell will not speak.'

'Oh, he will speak, my lord. He will speak until he runs out of words!' Nogaret's eyes narrowed. 'But his daughter remains an unnecessary distraction and that bastard she is carrying will bring you nothing but grief. What happens when it slithers out of her? An affair is one thing to explain away as sorrow for your wife, but a child will be—'

'Enough!' said Philippe, rounding on Nogaret. 'Bring me Campbell. Those are your orders. If he just left for the Temple, he cannot have gone far. I want you to intercept him. Take the palace guard.'

'And what then, my lord? When we have him in our custody and we know all that he has done against us, do we continue with our plan?'

Philippe's blue eyes glittered. 'If Jacques de Molay answers the pope's summons and returns to the West then we will make our move. In the meantime, we will make Esquin de Floyran's accusations public. Whatever Clement's personal feelings, he will be forced to act on the allegations if enough people demand it. After Campbell has been dealt with, I want you to start drawing up charges for the arrest of the Grand Master and his officials. As discussed, this will be based upon de Floyran's testimony, but it must be shocking enough to gain support from my subjects. Heresy is a wicked word, but we must not forget who we are dealing with. The Templars have two centuries of fame and might behind them. Their very mantle embodies the ideals of purity and innocence, they follow the Rule of a saint and are known as the warriors of Christ. The details of the charges against them will be all-important.'

'I know what to say, my lord.' Nogaret's voice was low. 'I remember what my father and mother were charged with.'

35
The Rue du Temple, Paris
14 May 1307 AD

W ill's breaths burned in his throat as he ran along the rue du
Temple. The sun had dipped below the fragmented rooftops and
spires and the narrow streets were dusky in the twilight. Some distance
behind him on the Ile de la Cité the bells of Notre Dame began the toll
for Vespers. The sound shuddered across the river, spreading out through
the city like a ripple as other bells joined it. Will tried to fix his thoughts
on the rendezvous with Robert and what the knight would have
discovered in his confrontation with Hugues, but it was almost impossible
to think about anything since his mind was so full of his daughter. Anger,
hope, fear, joy: all seethed inside him as he raced down the street amid
the harsh clanging of the bells, heading for Temple Gate. Part of him
dreaded Rose would change her mind and refuse to leave the palace in the
time it would take him to return. The thought made him sprint even
harder as he reached the gate, barrelling past a group of traders arguing
with the city guards.

He sped along the road that led to the preceptory until he reached a
grove of oak trees just outside the walls. Here he slowed and halted,
moving off the track. Sweat stung his eyes as he bent over, trying to catch
his breath. Ahead, the trees dissolved into shadows, but there was no sign of
Robert. Will straightened, wiping his face with the crook of his arm and
looked round, hearing hoof-beats. Five riders were cantering along the
road, dust kicking up behind them. Will watched as they passed, stones
skittering back on to the track in their wake.

'Campbell.'

He turned at the voice. 'Robert?' he called, squinting through the trees.
Seeing movement, Will stepped into the shade beneath the branches, twigs
crackling beneath his boots. He had gone only a short distance when a figure
stepped out in front of him. As his eyes alighted on the blade in the figure's

hand, Will reached for his sword, but even as he drew it he sensed motion all around him. He turned as four – no, five shapes lunged out of the trees. Wrenching the sword free, he swung it at the first figure, who parried deftly. A mailed boot smashed viciously into the back of his knee and he went down with a grunt, bringing up the sword to deflect a blow the figure aimed at him. But the strike was merely designed to keep him occupied so he wouldn't be able to avoid the second boot that rammed into his kidneys or the third that thudded into his back. Will shouted in rage and pain as someone stamped on his sword, pinning it to the ground, his fingers caught beneath it. He raised his free hand, trying to block the boots and fists all raining in on him. The last thing he felt was a crack against the back of his skull before the world went dark.

There was a heavy thudding sound, fast and low like a heartbeat. It echoed all around him. He felt as if he were gliding under water. The world seemed distant, hovering somewhere above him. Suddenly, he resurfaced. He was being hauled along a corridor, face down. There were flashes of torchlight and someone's cloak switched past his face. He felt hands around his arms, but his legs were free, his feet dragging behind him along the flagstones. The thudding, he realised, was the footsteps of those carrying him. He felt disorientated and weak, unable even to lift his head. He heard a door bang open, then felt draughty space around him. His captors halted. There was a harsh scraping sound, then a rush of stale air that reeked of bitter incense and they were moving again, down a narrow flight of steps, his feet dragging then dropping, dragging, dropping. Finally they stopped, somewhere warm, lit dimly by candles. He felt himself heaved on to a stool. Someone pulled his hands behind his back and rope was looped around his wrists. As an icy shock slammed into him, he gasped and lifted his head. Water dripped down his face and chest and as his vision cleared, he saw someone moving away, holding a pail.

Looking around, Will found himself in a gloomy chamber. Black curtains hung from one wall, in front of which stood a figure illuminated by the glow of candles and clad in a cloak sewn from hundreds of tiny circles of shimmering silk. As the figure pushed back the cowl, Will stared groggily at the face that was revealed.

Hugues de Pairaud's dark eyes looked back at him. The Visitor's cheeks were puckered with age, his once black beard now patchy and grizzled. He said nothing as he stared at Will, his gaze thoughtful, interrogative.

There was movement in the shadows. A second figure appeared, wearing a plain white mantle and a red mask with a stag's head painted on it; the same as those who had beaten him in the grove. The figure murmured something to Hugues, who nodded and looked back at Will.

'You've been in Paris all these years? How long has Robert known you were staying at the palace?'

Will swallowed with difficulty, tasting blood and soil. The smell of incense was pungent. 'What have you done with him?' he asked thickly. 'Where is Robert?'

'How did you poison him against me?' Hugues stepped forward. 'How did you get him to betray me?'

'You talk of betrayal as something terrible and yet it comes so easily to you.'

Will sensed someone come up behind him. A mailed fist slammed into the side of his head and he rocked back on the stool. Oddly, the shock revived him. Hawking blood out of his mouth, he looked back at Hugues, his gaze sharper. 'I trusted you, Hugues, that is why I elected you into the Brethren. I trusted you to understand what we were doing and to continue our aims, not pervert them.'

The masked man stepped in again, but Hugues raised his hand. 'You are the one who left the Brethren, Campbell. If it meant so much to you, you should have stayed. Still, it gave me the chance to do what needed to be done, what you never could have done. You and Robert were both so short-sighted. Everard, now there was a man who might have led us to greatness had he lived longer, a man who understood *fully* what the Anima Templi really is.'

'You know nothing of Everard, or his aims,' growled Will, anger pulsing through him at the suggestion he didn't know his old mentor and friend.

'No?' Hugues crossed to what looked like an altar and picked up something.

As he returned to the pool of light, Will recognised the leather-bound book Everard had kept, the record of his life.

'I think I know him quite well,' responded Hugues, flicking through the bound skins. 'I know he believed in sacrifice and that the price for freedom must sometimes be paid in blood. I know he believed in the authority of the Anima Templi and that it should, if necessary, steer the Order away from the influence of a Grand Master who thwarts our aims. I know he believed in the power of myth.' Hugues shook his head. 'He wrote the Book of the Grail. Did you learn nothing from that?'

'You cannot understand what you speak of.' Will watched as Hugues returned the tome to the altar. 'The Book of the Grail was destroyed years before you were elected into our circle. I've read Everard's writings. He was very careful that his words would only make sense to those who already knew of the Book and its content.'

'And they did. I learned the history of the Brethren when you inducted me in Acre and I learned of the Book and the story within from various sources: you and Robert, Brother Thomas in England, King Edward, although his thoughts on the subject were generally dripping with contempt. Over time, I pieced them together, well enough to understand the heart of the matter.'

'But you put the pieces back in the wrong order,' replied Will harshly. 'You distorted Everard's words. Men drinking blood? Knights spitting on the cross? Those were allegories!'

'They still are. Only now they are all the more powerful because they are truly meant.'

'In a story they are innocent. Enacted they are heresy.'

'Heresy!' scoffed Hugues. 'You are as stuck in the old ways as Jacques de Molay. No matter how much scorn he poured on Armand de Périgord's obsession with the stories of the Grail, Everard knew how powerful those ideas were. But he never used that power. He didn't have the chance. I have taken his and Armand's work and turned it into something real, not just some fantasy for grown men to pretend at, but something that can save the Order.'

'How in Christ's name is turning young, impressionable knights into blood-drinking sinners going to save the Order?'

'The blood is a potent reminder of our ties as brothers,' said Hugues, his tone intent. 'That is why Everard used it in his story of Perceval. I have simply taken it one step further and, in doing so, have made it that much more compelling. These knights' – he spread a hand to take in more shadowy figures at the edge of Will's vision – 'are true Brethren.'

'I doubt Martin de Floyran would think much of your idea of brotherhood.'

Hugues face fell. 'My men went too far that night. But they are fiercely loyal to me and to one another, and Martin's betrayal of our oaths wounded them deeply. It was my fault. He wasn't ready for initiation. Some men aren't.'

'And Esquin?'

'Another unfortunate sacrifice.' Hugues drew a heavy breath. 'We aren't sinners or heretics, Campbell. I believe in God as much as you do.

The men I pick for initiation into the Anima Templi come to this chamber to act out the journey of Perceval with me as their guide.' He gestured to his shimmering cloak. 'The Fisher King who leads them through their trials. They are asked to choose between two paths: the way of the old Order, under the Grand Master, a way of blood and violence and war, a way that will destroy the Temple, or the path to a new Order. But that new path is not an easy road. In following it they are betraying the oaths they took as knights, betraying their masters, their families even. To follow it they must trust me completely and I must trust them. They spit on the cross to prove their loyalty to me; to prove that when it comes to matters of the Brethren, I am the highest authority. Everard understood the power in these acts, or he wouldn't have written the Book of the Grail. That is why he called Acre his Camelot. The idea of men fighting to save a mystical ideal is more potent than men struggling to save a dusty scrap of land, isn't it?'

Will was shaking his head, incredulous. 'You've been initiating men all this time? Robert told me you were doing nothing. That the Brethren didn't even meet any more.'

'I once hoped Robert might join us, but I knew he was as entrenched in the old ways as you and Jacques. It is time for a new Order. A new Brethren. The Crusades are over, they were over the moment Acre fell to the Mamluks and while the Teutonics advance into Prussia to take land and wealth, and the Hospitallers plan their conquest of Rhodes, our own leaders stumble blindly about in Cyprus, still grasping for Jerusalem and a vanished dream. This is a time for building empires, for expansion, not wasting men and resources on futile holy wars. The world changed while you were trying to hold up a crumbling idea in the East. The kings of the West are busy gathering their power, building their realms. We need to do the same if we are to survive. We must change too and to do that we need a secure base in which to consolidate our strength. In time, we will stretch out our hand into a new age, an age of discovery and learning, peace and prosperity.' Hugues's eyes were shining in the candlelight. 'But I knew I could only change the Order slowly, from within, and so I began recruiting knights who would be loyal to me over Jacques and his Crusade.'

'So what do you intend to do? Invade a country with your personal army?'

'I do not need to. King Edward has promised to provide the Temple with an area of conquered Scotland.'

Will sat forward. His eyes narrowed with pain and anger. 'If he conquers it!'

'He will,' answered Hugues calmly. 'Robert Bruce and his followers have gone to ground and Edward's army marches north as we speak. It is the greatest force since Falkirk. Scotland will fall under English steel and the Temple will have its security, away from the turbulent centres of France and England, Germany and Rome.'

'You're a fool, Hugues,' murmured Will. 'Edward has fought for eighteen years to control Scotland. Do you honestly believe he will give any part of it to you? You've been blinded by your own fantasies and you've twisted the aims of the Brethren to suit them. This isn't what Everard, my father, Elias or Kalawun intended, what they lived and bled for. This isn't the Soul of the Temple.'

'It is now. You left, Will. You haven't been part of the Order or the Brethren for years. While you've been picking away at King Edward, a mouse trying to bring down a lion, I've been leading the Temple to a golden future.'

'A golden future? Right now, a message is making its way to Cyprus that will summon Grand Master de Molay to meet the pope to answer charges of heresy within this preceptory. King Philippe and Guillaume de Nogaret have been trying to gain control of the Order for years, to take its wealth for themselves. By your actions, you may have damned every man here.'

'Ridiculous. No one even knows of the Brethren.'

'Esquin de Floyran does and he is in royal custody.'

'That is impossible. Only I have the authority to free de Floyran.' Hugues stared at Will, realisation dawning across his face. 'Has Robert de Paris been more of a snake than I realised?'

'We can turn this around. I have the ear of the pope, but you must destroy all evidence of what you have been doing here. You must disband the Anima Templi and—'

'Disband it?' Hugues's face filled with suspicion. 'What game are you playing with me, Campbell?'

'No game, I swear—'

'Enough! I will not listen to these lies.' Hugues gestured to the men in the shadows. 'Get him out of my sight.'

'Shutting me away in Merlan will not change what is happening!' shouted Will, as the masked Brethren untied his hands and pulled him roughly to his feet.

'You're not going to Merlan. You're going to England. It was Edward's price for the Brethren's new territory: you, for Scotland.'

'Don't do this!' shouted Will. 'Don't do this, for God's sake!'

But Hugues was turning away and a hood was coming down over Will's face, cutting off his sight.

36

The Road to Carlisle, the Kingdom of England

1 July 1307 AD

The wagon bounced and rocked along the road. Will sat hunched against the side, feeling every jolt in his bruised body. Through the weave of the hood he caught flashes of brightness slanting in through the open back of the wagon. Judging by the sporadic glints of light and change in smell he supposed they must be passing through a forest. He had been trying for some moments to think where they might be, but time and distance were so distorted in his mind he simply had no way of knowing.

He had been taken from Paris on the night of his encounter with Hugues, his captors spiriting him down to the Seine, where they boarded a small vessel. Recovering slowly from the injuries he sustained at the hands of Hugues's men, he drifted in and out of consciousness. They kept him in isolation in the cramped, stinking hold, still blindfolded and bound, and it was only on hearing the cries of gulls over the slosh of water and creaking timbers that he knew when they reached the sea. He was dragged up on deck, gasping at the salt air and transferred to a larger ship at Honfleur, but before it could set sail a summer storm blew in along the coast, forcing the vessel to remain docked for several days.

Shaken beneath deck in the boiling waves that dashed the port, Will's thoughts settled on his daughter, presumably still in the palace. The image of her waiting for him, thinking he had abandoned her yet again, drove him into a frenzy and, yelling curses and threats at his captors, he struggled and kicked within his bonds until two men came down and methodically beat him into silence. Thereafter, the crossing to England passed in a haze. Arriving in London, he was taken to a building near the docks, where he spent a week or so chained in a cellar, surviving on bread and briny-tasting water, before finally being dumped in the wagon.

Listening to snatches of conversation during the ponderous journey north, he discovered that the thirty or so men conveying him were part of

King Edward's royal guard, following the English army on the march to Scotland with extra supplies. There were other carts with them on the road, but the one he was in was filled with barrels of sickly-smelling wine. The parched heat of the days seeped through the cloth, leaving him panting, sweating and mad for water, which he guzzled like a crazed dog whenever the guards thrust a bowl at him.

The glints of light flashing through his hood soon became a constant glare and Will guessed they must have passed out of the shade of the forest. The fertile smell of trees was replaced with the musty scent of dry grass and the soldiers muttered about the clouds of insects that plagued them. An hour or so later, Will caught a whiff of campfire smoke and began to hear the distant, incoherent hum of many people. The chatter of birdsong died away and soon the hum stretched itself out into proper sounds: dogs and horses, calls, laughter. The wagon trundled over fields and lurched to a stop. Will felt a shift in weight as two men climbed in. His arms were grasped and his stiff body yanked upright. He heard voices all around him, deafening after so long in relative silence. Suddenly, the hood was pulled from over his face and sunlight blasted into his eyes.

He was on an immense, grassy plain, covered, as far as he could see, by hundreds, possibly thousands of tents. Bright banners and pennants fluttered everywhere, a confusion of colour and emblems, many of which he remembered from the campaigns he had fought with Wallace. Knights and lords stood about in groups or else rested in open-sided tents, while squires and servants hurried between them like lines of busy ants. As the guards marched Will through the encampment, he saw a huddle of men working on mail coats, painstakingly linking each metal ring, the shirts silvery and supple as fish-scales in their quick-moving hands. There were cooks in stained aprons, labouring at fires, and a crowd of archers checking the flight-feathers on arrows under the watchful eye of their captain. Hugues had said the army was as vast as the one that destroyed the Scottish force at Falkirk. As he passed through its midst, Will thought it might actually be larger.

In the distance, near several grand-looking tents, was a regal scarlet pavilion. He felt a twinge in his gut as he recognised the golden lions on the banner planted outside. Behind it, the land rose gradually, but the incline and heat haze made it impossible to see what lay beyond and he had no real way of telling where they were. He realised the two soldiers were leading him towards a small cage formed of bound wooden stakes, guarded by men in royal livery. One opened the door and the soldiers shoved him inside. He had to bend double the prison was so low, the grass inside yellow and flattened. Four figures within, faces bruised and wary, stared at him as the cage door was shut.

Burgh-upon-Sands, the Kingdom of England, 3 July 1307 AD

Will tore ravenously at the leathery strip of meat. His mouth was full of blisters from lack of decent food and it hurt to chew, but if this was to be his last meal he was determined to savour it. It was late in the evening, the sky above the amber gleam of torches and fires a boundless blue. The sun had risen twice since he had been tossed into the cage and still the army hadn't moved from the grassy plain. It had, however, grown.

Over the past two days a stream of reinforcements had flowed on to the plain to swell the English forces, along with straggling supply trains. Infantry, faces burned dark by the midsummer sun, trudged wearily into the camp, bearing maces and axes, spears and shields, and nobles rode in, leading companies of knights. At night, when the rations were passed around, Will sat listening to the laughter and camp songs. These soldiers had fought the Scots for years. They knew the terrain and their enemy's tactics, and they were confident. The rumour was that Robert Bruce was planning to fight back, but the English dismissed his chances scornfully. Despite some early successes for Scotland's new king, Edward retained control of much of the country. Now, almost a decade after their terrible defeat at Stirling Bridge, his men had come again to make the rebel kingdom pay one last, bloody time.

Will had gleaned some of this information from his fellow captives. All four were Scottish scouts, two from Bruce's camp, who had been sent to spy on the English advance. They had been tortured for information on the Scots' whereabouts, but so far had managed to hold out, although Will wasn't sure for how much longer. One of the four had been taken away that morning. He hadn't returned. Between the creeping fear he felt, for his country and for himself, his thoughts travelled endlessly around what he had left behind. He thought of Hugues in his Fisher King's cloak with his army of masked soldiers, waiting in the Paris preceptory for the Hammer to flatten them a piece of land. He thought of Robert, one of his oldest comrades, most likely imprisoned or dead. He thought of his daughter, trapped in the palace, and of Pope Clement's message winging its way to Cyprus. He thought too of Esquin de Floyran, hidden in some royal tower, impatient to bring his gaolers to ruin.

'Campbell.'

Will swallowed down the last of the dry meat, seeing two royal guards approaching. One gestured to him.

'Out.'

Will crawled his way to the cage door, knowing it was futile to resist, and caught a staunch nod from one of the Scottish prisoners as the guards pulled him to his feet. English soldiers stared as he was marched between their campfires. One man spat at him. Will fixed his gaze ahead, realising his captors were leading him towards the scarlet pavilion.

The tent was sumptuously furnished with all the luxuries a king might require while on campaign: a bath, a couch, a table to dine at, servants and musicians to attend and entertain him. Despite this, the place seemed subdued, the lively confidence of the camp not reflected within the cloth walls, the attendants quiet and worried-looking. Will had time to sense this and to wonder what it meant, before he was led into a private compartment within the pavilion filled with a large bed, the four carved posts of which stretched up to the undulating red roof. Two braziers gave off heat and smoke, but very little light. There was a figure in the bed.

King Edward was almost seventy and wore his years like a faded mantle, hanging heavy around his shoulders. Will heard his breaths crackle like parchment, smelled piss and stale sweat. Gone was the arrogant expression, the forceful stare and regal bearing. In place of the king who had haunted his life was an old, incontinent man.

'Have you seen my army, Campbell?'

The voice still had power and Will heard something of the king's former self in that mocking tone. 'You cannot exactly miss it,' he responded, and received a punch in his kidneys from one of the guards for his insolence.

'You should look well upon it,' croaked the king, his bloodshot eyes gleaming. 'For it is the last thing you will see. Tomorrow I will do to you what I did to that bastard, Wallace. Then, with your entrails still reeking on the fire, I will lead my army into Scotland and—' Edward broke into a fit of coughing. One of the guards moved forward, but the king raised a trembling hand to halt him. He retched into a cloth, then drew a breath and fixed his watery stare on Will. 'The traitor, Bruce, and his ragged band will rue the day they ever thought to stand against me. They will be hauled from their horses and trampled in the fields, cut down in the hundreds, nay the thousands! Cut down to their sons and their daughters, down to the unborn children inside their whores. The soil of Scotland shall be cleansed with their blood and noble English towns set up in place of their mud-huts and tribes. Your own family, Campbell, will share this fate.' Edward leaned forward. 'I want you to know that before I execute you. I want you to know how they will suffer for your treachery. I want you to . . .'

Edward continued, but Will was no longer listening to the words. All he could see was the king's twisted face, the spittle flying from his grey lips. All he could feel was the hatred coming off him. It poured from every part of the king, black and bitter as pitch, stinking of frustration and impotence. Edward was bowed under with the weight of it. Will was filled with a rush of clarity as he realised that despite everything – the deaths of those he loved, the confusion and deception – he hadn't lost his soul. He could feel it inside him, blazing before Edward's choking, malevolent form. However strong his need for revenge, he hadn't let it poison him slowly over years. He knew, all at once, with absolute certainty, that even if Edward succeeded in Scotland, he would never now find peace. He had gone beyond that possibility a long time ago.

Edward's tirade ended in a violent outburst of coughing that had attendants rushing in with fresh cloths for him to hack phlegm into. 'Tomorrow, Campbell!' he was wheezing. '*Tomorrow!*'

Will was marched into the sultry night, struck by his revelation. Edward's coughs faded behind him as the soldiers returned him to the cage.

Most of the army was asleep, resting before the march into Scotland and the battle to come. Stars blinked, mirroring the low-burning campfires. Brushing aside the questions of his fellow captives, Will knelt and bowed his head. He prayed for his daughter and that she would learn he hadn't abandoned her, prayed she would go to Simon and he would help her escape Philippe. He prayed Hugues would see sense and Clement would hold his nerve, and prayed that Robert was still alive and Jacques de Molay's Crusade would fail. Once this was done, he lay down on the warm grass and closed his eyes. Even though he was afraid of what was to come, he knew the pain would only be transitory and in the end it would lead to something else, something far, far sweeter.

Tomorrow, he would see his father again and his mother. He would be greeted by Everard and Hasan and Elias, would clasp the hands of Kalawun and Owein. Tomorrow, he would be with Elwen. He would see them all with peace in his heart, knowing that in the end his path had been true.

But the next morning, no soldiers came to take him to a gallows. The hours after dawn crawled by and the army roused itself, men tending to their horses, breaking their fast. Gradually, the calm Will felt in the night faded into tension. He wanted it over. The waiting was pointless, maddening. But wait he did, all through that day and into the next, the sky above him turning from pink to gold to blue. The following afternoon, Will sensed a change in the mood of the camp. None of the Scots was taken for questioning and the guards who tossed in their scraps of food were tight-lipped and silent. There were no songs around the campfires, no coarse jokes and laughter. And still he waited.

On the morning of the fourth day since he was brought before the king a storm drifted in across the plain. He was sitting there, soaked to the skin, licking the rain from his lips, when he noticed movement in the camp. Will crawled to the bars and watched as a few companies headed off into the downpour, water plinking on helmets and shields. Over the next hour, more men began to move out. Some looked downcast, but others appeared relieved, neither of which seemed much like the bearing of soldiers about to head to war. In the distance, Will could see a huge crowd gathered around the royal pavilion.

Some time later, when the rain had moved north and the exodus from the camp had become a flood, all the companies threading their way southwards, a soldier came to the cage. He was dressed more plainly than the royal guards, their keepers until that morning. Opening the door, he motioned outside.

'You can go.'

The other Scots glanced at one another in astonishment, then scrabbled quickly out.

Will remained inside. 'Who let us go?' he called, as the man went to head off.

The soldier glanced back. 'The new king. He didn't want any extra baggage to take with him.'

Will felt his breath leave him. 'Edward is dead?'

'He passed this morning,' replied the soldier gruffly. 'His son succeeded him and ordered the retreat. He will not fight his father's war.'

As the man moved off, Will sank to his knees on the damp grass. He stayed there for some time, while around him the English army trundled slowly from the plain. Finally, he pushed himself to his feet and climbed the shallow hill, avoiding the red tent, where a crowd was still gathered. As he reached the top, he saw the fields falling away to become marshes and then a wide estuary. Beyond the water, dark gold in the storm-bruised light, the hills of Dumfries rose up. He thought of his family, beyond those hills. Given a second chance at life he wanted to see the living: Ysenda and David, Margaret and Alice, beautiful, red-haired Christian. The lure was tremendous. But he allowed himself only a moment's pause before he turned and, leaving Scotland shrouded in veils of summer rain, headed south.

37

Franciscan Monastery, Poitiers

18 August 1307 AD

'Your holiness.' Jacques de Molay's harsh voice echoed in the Chapter House. Going down on one knee, he took Clement's proffered hand and kissed the papal ring.

Clement smiled graciously. 'Master Templar, it is I who should be kneeling in the presence of the few brave men who still toil for the liberty of Jerusalem.' He lifted his gaze to the knights ranked behind the Grand Master.

There were around forty of them, all erect and austere in mail armour, broadswords slung at their hips, helmets clasped under their arms. Most were high officials or commanders in the Order. Clement recognised a few of the older members: the Master of France was close behind de Molay and at his side was the Master of Normandy, a flint-eyed, hook-nosed man named Geoffroi de Charney. The knights had been given the option of washing and resting before speaking with him, but had declined, preferring to meet him upon their arrival at the monastery. As a result, they looked as though they had all come straight from a battlefield, mantles stained, faces sun-browned and scarred.

Clement felt a twinge of regret that he had given in to Nogaret's demands and called these men away needlessly from their duties. But he was glad to see them. Their presence simply confirmed his own desire to ensure the continuation of the struggle for the Holy Land, flagging due to the dearth of enthusiasm from the rulers of the West. Perhaps now he would get the response he had so eagerly sought. Shuffling over to the cushioned seat the monks had set out for him, the pope gestured to the servants at the sides of the chamber. 'Bring our noble guests food and wine.'

The Grand Master's broad face, framed by coarse, iron-grey hair, retained its grim expression. 'Your holiness, my men and I have travelled long to answer your summons. In your message you said there was a grave problem within the Order. I myself know nothing of any trouble and so before I break bread with you I am anxious to hear what urgent matter has called me and my officials the many hundreds of miles from Cyprus.'

Clement faltered, taken aback by Jacques's terseness. After a pause, he nodded to the servants. 'Leave us. Tell the brothers we will eat later.' He shifted on his chair as the door closed and tried to recover some of his authority, discomforted by the dour silence of the knights lined up in front of him. He felt like an inept commander, being judged by his troops. 'Do you know of a knight named Esquin de Floyran?'

Jacques shook his head. 'I have many knights under me. I do not know them all by name.'

'That is the name of the former prior of Montfaucon, my lord. I was given a report by the Visitor some years ago detailing his arrest for heresy. He was imprisoned in Merlan.'

Clement glanced behind Jacques as the Master of France spoke up. 'That is correct. However, earlier this year de Floyran escaped the Temple's custody and was taken into royal protection. He protests his innocence and accuses the knights of the Paris preceptory who sent him to Merlan of heresy and murder.'

'Royal protection?' The Grand Master's brow furrowed. 'Why would de Floyran be offered this?'

Clement was careful in his reply. He hadn't yet decided how much to reveal to the Templars of Philippe's intentions for them. The last thing he wanted was to dash his hope for a new Crusade by causing the knights to turn from their efforts abroad in order to challenge the crown. 'The king was concerned and wanted to make certain de Floyran's accusations were unfounded. He is keen to see that the Temple's reputation remains untarnished. Both Lord Philippe and myself felt it necessary to recall you and your officials from Cyprus in order to conduct an investigation into this matter. After all, we do not want the people of the West to have any doubts over the honour of the warriors of Christ. They have been concerned enough since the fall of Acre.'

Jacques's frown deepened and the men behind him shifted restlessly, their expressions affronted rather than perturbed. The Grand Master, however, nodded to Clement. 'This is a serious allegation and will be examined to the fullest extent. I will speak to this de Floyran personally and judge his words for myself, then meet the men responsible for his arrest and hear their testimonies.'

'I am sure we can endeavour to make that a possibility.' Keen not to lose the confidence of the knights and heartened by Jacques's staunch response, Clement turned the subject to one of his choosing. 'The other reason for my summons, Master Templar, lies in my eagerness to hear of your progress in the East. There has been frustratingly little word from Cyprus of your endeavours, or plans for a new Crusade. Everyone I speak to seems adamant that this is still your priority, but they can tell me nothing else.'

At this, the Grand Master seemed to relax slightly, although his expression remained sombre. 'Since the fall of our last base on the island of Ruad to Mamluk forces, our progress has been hampered by the lack of support from the West. Even our own Order has been able to send us only the minimum of men and supplies, something I intend to rectify now I am here. As I told the rulers of the West when I made my progress through their kingdoms, a new Crusade will only succeed if everyone is behind it. Small armies without uniformity of purpose or the agreement of a clearly defined target will fail.'

Clement was unable to hide his disappointment. 'Then you are saying it will not be possible? I had hoped to hear better news, for I am determined to aid you, Master Templar.'

Geoffroi de Charney spoke up at this. 'We are grateful to hear your support, your holiness, but we remain certain that only by a coordinated move east can we push back the Saracens and regain the territories lost to us. We have been trying to secure the assistance of the King of Cyprus as well as help from the Mongol empire, but it takes time to bring about such alliances.'

Jacques nodded his leonine head at de Charney's words. 'What is needed is the whole-hearted alliance of a powerful king of the West. Have one such ruler take the Cross and inspire the people again, have him lead our war and I believe we can succeed. Perhaps the Lord Edward? Or King Philippe?'

'Alas, King Edward died in July. We received word of it barely days ago. He has been succeeded by his son, the Prince of Wales.' Clement's lips pursed. 'A man who I hear is more interested in feasts and unsavoury frivolities than holy war.'

The pope sat back as the knights took in this black news. He felt sunken. All his hopes of Jacques and his army of warrior knights making their plans, gathering their might, dwindled to this proud, yet worn-down band of men before him. The moment the cardinals of the Sacred College had placed the papal tiara upon his head in the Cathedral of Lyons, Clement had known, clear as a vision, that he was the pope to call Christendom to a new

Crusade. All his life had been leading up to that moment. Now, the dream of walking through the gates of that golden city in the footsteps of the Lord was fading before his eyes. He thought of the Grand Master's advice and heard the possibility in the words. But Philippe was the most powerful monarch left in the West and his concentration was occupied elsewhere.

The Royal Palace, Paris, 13 September 1307 AD

Rose sat swaddled in her blue cloak as all around her the Great Hall throbbed with noise and heat. On immense tables stretched between the scores of pillars ranked like an army of marble soldiers beneath the vaulted ceiling, the elite of the kingdom's nobility gorged themselves on the feast. Everywhere she looked, she saw mouths opening and slivers of meat, juicy with blood, being shovelled inside. A duke several places away told a ribald joke, while flecks of food flew from between his teeth and the ladies around him brayed with laughter. Stiff-faced lawyers and bejewelled bishops slurped at goblets of wine that stained their lips and teeth black, and everywhere silver plates glittered under mountains of food. At the heart of each table sat the crowning glory of the evening: a bloated pie stuffed with partridges, quails, larks and a dozen tiny sparrows.

A wide gash had been cut in the centre of the pie opposite her and Rose couldn't take her gaze off the rows of little dark bodies, slippery with fat, crammed inside its pastry folds. She could smell the eggs that had been mixed into the flour, pick out the sharp notes of rosemary and thyme. All her senses seemed heightened, fragile. The sound of a knife slicing through cheese to strike the board was an axe-blow, a bishop's booming voice a thunderclap.

'Rose, you have to eat.'

She glanced round to see Blanche staring at her.

The petite handmaiden nodded encouragingly. 'Just a mouthful or two.' Her murmur dropped to a breathy whisper. 'You have to think of the baby.'

Rose looked down at her stomach, hidden beneath the table and the folds of her cloak. Think of the baby? She could do nothing else.

Her belly was as taut as a drum and she knew that when she stood the eyes of most of the men and women in the hall would flick furtively to it. Hands, here and there, would come up to hide mouths as they whispered to their neighbours about the king's whore and her bastard child. Ladies would toss their veiled heads and lords would grin and make lewd gestures with their sticky fingers. The palace had never been a comfortable home for her, but she had never known it to be so hostile. Some nights, sweating in the darkness of the dormitory, she would lie there, stiff as a board, poised for the sound of footsteps approaching her door.

Once, shortly after she arrived in Paris, she had seen two servants carrying a litter of kittens out of the stables. She had halted, transfixed with pleasant wonder by the blind, soft bodies writhing in their hands, then, as the servants crouched by a pail of water, shock had tightened her skin. One of the worst things about it had been all the people who passed by, not even noticing the tiny lives being drowned in that bucket. When it was done, Rose crept into the stables to find the mother licking feebly at the blood on her fur and mewing for her children. She must have sat with that cat for over an hour, murmuring words of comfort and stroking her head until she slept.

If they came to take her in the night would anyone notice?

An image of her father hung in her mind. He used to be a shadow or a ghost, something vague that haunted her. How cruel fate was. His face, now he was gone, was painfully clear. Philippe had angrily denied killing him that night in May and had even accused her of his disappearance, but she knew the king was lying and her father was dead. Sometimes, she relished the violent kicks her child woke her with, each twist a punishment for her betrayal. Penance for her sin.

Rose's gaze moved to Philippe. The king was seated on the dais that spanned the far end of the Great Hall. The royal table, suspended above the rest of the crowd, was surrounded by his family: his brothers and his sons, now growing into handsome young men, and his beloved Isabella. Barely twelve years old, the princess was betrothed to the new king of England, Edward II, and was due to set sail early next year for the wedding. For months, Philippe, who had secured the profitable marriage in return for the restoration of Gascony to English hands, had hardly let her leave his sight, as if clinging to the last few precious moments of his daughter's childhood. To either side of the king sat his grey-faced confessor, Guillaume de Paris, and Nogaret. The placing of that table, its height, its remove, was designed to let everyone know the favoured positions of those around it. Philippe didn't need to tell her what he thought of her and his unborn child. Her place on the floor was plainer than words.

As she watched, Nogaret murmured something and Philippe nodded. He stood, his black mantle embroidered with white fleurs-de-lis falling around him, and a page hastened to draw back his throne. The minstrels ceased

their playing and, one by one, all the men and women around the tables
rose respectfully. Ignoring their bows and curtsies, Philippe headed for the
ornate doors that led to the royal apartments, Nogaret at his side, hurrying
to keep up. While the crowd seated themselves and the minstrels struck up
again, Rose remained standing. She felt Blanche's hand on her arm, but
shrugging it off, she slipped across the hall, keeping her gaze ahead so she
couldn't see all those faces turn to watch her go.

Through the doors the cool, hushed air of the passage was a welcome
relief. She passed quickly along an open gallery, the rain blowing across the
dark courtyard misting her face. It had been pouring for three days without
end and the palace grounds were swampy. Puddles gleamed like ink below
and the conversation of the guards moving in the compound was muted by
the thrum of water. Beyond the walls, the Seine was swollen up to its banks
and flowing fast, white flecks rushing in the darkness.

Heading into a wider corridor, Rose slowed as she approached the king's
chamber, partly to catch her breath, partly to arrange her thoughts. The
impulse that had driven her from the hall remained, but now she was here
she was scared. Philippe had become more and more distant these past few
months and she no longer knew his moods. But the feast this evening, with
all those unfriendly, judging stares, had confirmed her fear of just how
precarious her standing in the palace was and she desperately needed
assurance. For some weeks she had harboured the idea that the king might
allow her to go to the château at Vincennes, maybe even with Blanche now
Isabella was leaving; that he might let her have her baby alone, far from
court intrigue and the poison she knew Nogaret had been pouring into his
ear.

She could hear the two of them through the door. The king's voice was
pensive.

'You are certain Clement did as he was told?'

'The Paris officials should have already left for Poitiers.'

'Should have? I want to know for certain, Nogaret. You will find out.'

'Yes, my lord.'

'I want the Temple wide open when we come for them. I want the rank
and file separated from their leaders. Now that de Molay is in France we
must move swiftly before our plan is discovered.'

'It is all in hand, my lord. The pope and the leaders of the Temple will be
occupied discussing Esquin de Floyran's claims for some while. By the time
their assembly is finished our men will be in place and ready to act. The
summons for de Molay can be sent as soon as you command.'

Rose felt their words like knives, each one a cutting reminder of what she had helped to make possible by the removal of her father. How much ruin a few words could cause. She hadn't realised her own terrible power.

Steeling herself, she rapped on the door. The voices stopped abruptly. The door opened and Nogaret appeared. Behind him, Philippe stood by the hearth, the flames lighting his hard face. On a table beside him was a pile of scrolls, all bound in black leather cases. As the concern faded from their expressions to be replaced by irritation in Nogaret's and impatience in the king's, she understood how little she meant to them. They didn't even care that she might have overheard their conversation. She was so insignificant she might as well not exist at all. She opened her mouth to petition the king with her request, but all that came were words she didn't even know she wanted to say until they choked from her. 'Please, Philippe, tell me what you did to my father.'

Nogaret spun away with a curse.

The king's brow knotted. 'You dare to question me on this again?'

'My lord, I beg you.' Rose rushed into the room and went down on her knees before him. 'Tell me what happened that night and I will never speak of it again. I need to know.'

'Need to know?' snapped Nogaret, turning on her. 'I am almost certain it is because of you that Campbell isn't rotting in our cells! Did you warn him?' He grasped hold of her shoulder, his thin fingers pinching. 'Did you?'

Rose stared in shock as the king turned away and unhurriedly picked up a goblet from the table. She gasped as the minister's grip dug into her.

'Let her go, Nogaret,' Philippe said, after taking a sip. 'She didn't betray me. She knows what I would do if she did.' He drained the goblet and looked down on her. 'Don't you.'

Rose touched her bruised shoulder as Nogaret stepped reluctantly away, but her eyes didn't leave the king's. 'I wish I had,' she whispered, struggling to her feet. 'I wish to God I had warned him. I hate myself for what I did.' The words were out before she could stop them. 'And I hate you for forcing me to do it!'

Nogaret started forward, but the king held up his hand. 'Forcing you?' His mouth twisted. 'You were champing at the bit.' He moved to the table where the scrolls were piled high. There must have been dozens of them. Turning his back on her, Philippe gestured to Nogaret. 'I want these delivered to the Seneschals of France tomorrow morning.'

'What about your child?' Rose shouted, her hand clutching her stomach. 'Do you not even care for it?'

Philippe spun. 'Child? That thing inside you is no child!' His voice lashed out. 'It is grief, swollen and putrid. It is a boil. A cyst!' Rose stumbled back as he tossed his goblet aside and strode to her. 'By God, it should have been lanced when it was made, rather than allowed to grow into this monstrosity, paraded before me as proof of my sins!' He thrust her towards the door. 'Get out, before I decide to do it myself!'

Rose staggered into the passage as the door slammed shut. She struck the wall with painful force and slid down, feeling the baby writhe blindly inside her.

38

The Temple, Paris

14 September 1307 AD

It was past midnight and the city was a watery smudge of darkness, obscured by bands of rain. Here and there, flickers of torchlight in the windows of the taller towers winked out of sight as the downpour worsened, lashing the air in solid sheets.

Will crouched close to the roadside, the rain on his leather hood like the rapid drum of fingers. He blinked water from his eyes as he focused on the preceptory gate, visible through the swaying trees. Atop the gatehouse tower, the Temple's black and white banner twisted limply. Will made out the shadows of two men guarding the entrance, mail coats glimmering in the guttering flames of a torch. Keeping low, he crept into the tangle of bushes that ran rampant around the walls. The Paris preceptory was immense and it would usually take fifteen minutes to walk from the main gate to the servants' entrances at the back. In the gusting rain and dark and mud, it took Will almost an hour to negotiate his way through the undergrowth. By the time the brambles opened on to a path that led to a small gate in the sheer walls, he was exhausted.

After leaving the Scottish border, he had made it to London, surviving on berries, nuts and river water. In the city it took him almost a fortnight to beg passage on a vessel headed for France. This was the hardest part of the journey. The docks were crawling with whores, beggars and thieves, all trying to make a penny, feed themselves or escape the city. Without the fruits of the fields free to him, he was forced to pick through rubbish-strewn alleys outside inns and brothels to find food.

Finally, after a rough, uncomfortable crossing on a horse-carrier, he landed at Honfleur and followed the broad curves of the Seine to Paris. He hadn't shaved in weeks and his beard was as full as it had been when he was a knight. Crouching to cup water from a stream that morning, he had been struck by his reflection: crinkled green eyes staring up at him, hair, almost all grey, hanging raggedly around his sun-dark and battle-pitted face.

Ignoring the weariness dragging at his limbs, Will made his way up to the gate. He paused outside, listening, but only heard the roar of the rain. It was the dead of night, between midnight and Matins, and most men in the preceptory would be asleep. After trying the door, locked as expected, he crossed to a gnarled chestnut, the thick branches of which stretched over the wall. He was relieved to see it was still there. Once, many years ago, returning late from an errand for Everard, he had found himself locked out of the preceptory and, not wanting to be challenged by the guards, had shinned up the tree and down the other side. But he was sixty now, not sixteen.

Gathering his strength, Will hauled himself up and swung awkwardly on to the lowest branch. The leaves flurried around him as he climbed the next two, hands slipping in the wet. Straddling the fourth branch, he inched forward, until he could slide off and crouch on the top of the wall. As he paused to catch his breath, he sought a soft landing. The ground, a smear of black beneath him, looked a long way away. After a moment's hesitation, he gritted his teeth and threw himself out into space. As his feet slammed into the ground, he rolled with the impact. Coming to a stop, he lay on his back, staring into the rain and waiting for the scream of broken bones. When he felt no pain, he pushed himself to his feet.

Will jogged across muddy gardens, past the bakehouse and the fishponds, through the waterlogged orchards and into the servants' areas. It was all so familiar. Even in the dark, after all these years, he knew where he was going. The main preceptory buildings were rising in front of him. A few torches burned in windows and once he had to flatten himself against a wall as someone hurried across a yard in front of him, head bent beneath the storm. But otherwise the place was quiet and he made it unseen to the stables, the whickers of horses coming to him in the gloom. Just off from the stable blocks were the grooms' lodgings. Hoping he was right and this building still belonged to the stable master, Will headed for the door at the end. He pushed down the latch and entered.

The room beyond was warmly lit by a low-burning fire. A stool was set beside the hearth and a pile of bridles lay on the floor, next to a couple of tools. Will made for a set of wooden stairs that disappeared steeply above. He stopped, hearing the creak of a board. It was followed by a sleepy-sounding voice.

'Gérard? Is something wrong?'

'Simon, it's me.'

There was silence, followed by several heavy footfalls right above his head. Two feet appeared in the hole over the stairs, followed by legs, then the rest of Simon as he clambered down. He halted at the bottom.

Will couldn't help but grin at the sight of him. Simon's thatch of hair, grey like his own, was sticking up on one side where he'd slept on it, a piece of straw poking out of it, his nightshift rumpled and his eyes wide in the firelight.

'I thought you were dead,' Simon murmured. He embraced Will fiercely, though he was soaked to the skin and covered in mud. 'I sent a message to the palace months ago with one of the grooms, but he was told you were missing. Where in Christ's name have you been?'

'England. Listen, I don't have time to explain. I cannot risk Hugues finding me, but I have to know if Robert is here.'

'Well, Hugues isn't.' Simon's tone was grave. 'The Visitor and the rest of the officials left five days ago. A few weeks ago we heard the Grand Master was in France meeting with the pope. Hugues and the others were called to join him in Poitiers. Will, people are saying the king is accusing the Temple of heresy. Does this have anything to do with Esquin de Floyran? Did the prior really find heretics in the Order?'

'Have you seen Robert since May?' pressed Will.

'No. But I know where he is.'

'Where?'

'In the dungeon. I tried to discover why, but no one would tell me. To be honest, Will, the whole place has been in confusion. Now, with the officials gone and the rest of us left without any idea of what's happening it's impossible to find anything out. I tried to contact you, but when that failed there wasn't much more I could do.'

Will nodded determinedly. 'All right. The first thing is to get Robert out. I'm going to need him.' He met Simon's gaze. 'I'm going to need you too, old friend. Are you willing?'

'Do you need to ask?'

'No.' Will smiled slightly. 'But you might want to get dressed first.'

After tugging his black sergeant's tunic over his nightshirt and stuffing his feet into a pair of boots, Simon followed Will into the yard, splashing through puddles as they made their way to the tower that led down into the dungeon. There was no sign of any guards. Given the hour and the weather, Will guessed they would be in the guardroom or down in the lower levels. Pressing himself against the wall, he waited as Simon ducked in through the entrance, hair plastered to his head with rain. He heard his gruff voice come from inside, followed by that of another man. After a moment, footsteps came closer. A young knight appeared.

'Are you sure it wasn't one of the servants you saw, brother?' he asked, stepping reluctantly into the rain.

Will grabbed him from behind, locking his arm around the man's throat. The knight flailed and choked, trying to prise him off as he was dragged back into the tower. Finally, as his face began to turn purple, Will shoved him forward and cracked the knight's forehead against the wall. He dropped like a stone.

'Christ,' muttered Simon.

'He'll be all right,' said Will, grabbing his wrists. 'Get his legs, will you.'

Between them, they manoeuvred the unconscious knight into the guardroom.

'What happens when Rainier wakes up and remembers I was here?' asked Simon, as Will crouched down and removed his white mantle.

Shrugging off his muddy cloak, Will pulled the mantle around him, drawing the hood over his wet hair. 'Then he'll know there really was an intruder,' he said, taking the knight's broadsword. Will went first, heading down stone steps that spiralled into dank darkness. Soon, the way was lit by torchlight and a passage stretched before him. 'Wait here,' he whispered. 'I need you to watch my back. But try to stay out of sight. Your presence down here will be harder to explain away if anyone sees you.'

Simon hung back in the stairwell as Will strode purposefully down the passage, sword in hand.

He passed a recess where a few men lay curled on pallets, their snoring forms lit by a single nightlight. Ahead, at a trestle and bench, sat a sleepy-looking sergeant, head propped on his hand. Beyond, the passage continued on, with gaps cut out of the stone, each one covered with iron bars. The sergeant looked round at his approach. His face in the torchlight showed surprise.

'Sir Rainier? Is something wrong?' His gaze went to the blade in Will's hand, then back to his face, shadowed under the white cowl. He stood, reaching for his own sword, but Will sprinted the last few yards and slammed him into the wall.

He pushed his sword up against the sergeant's throat. 'Unsheathe your weapon,' he said, beneath his breath. 'Slowly.'

The sergeant did as he was told.

'Place it on the table.' When the sergeant paused, Will pushed the blade into his skin. The man winced and set his blade down. 'Now, take me to de Paris's cell.' Letting the sergeant edge away from the wall, Will moved in behind him, the blade poking firmly into the man's back.

At the third cell, the sergeant unhooked a set of keys from his belt. As he twisted one in the lock and pulled open the iron bars, a figure huddled on the floor of the cell sat up.

'So it's Merlan for me then, is it?' came a rough voice.

'Not yet,' Will murmured back, forcing the sergeant into the cell with a prod of the sword.

Robert stepped into the torchlight, his face filled with astonishment. Raising the sword, Will cracked the pommel into the back of the sergeant's head and, as the guard slumped, Robert followed him into the passage. He paused to snatch up the sword on the trestle and caught Will's shoulder. 'Will, I'm sorry. The moment I confronted Hugues he had me imprisoned and forced me to tell him where we were meeting so he could get you. I tried to hold out, but . . .' He looked away. 'I wasn't strong enough.'

'I understand. Now, come on.'

They went quietly by the sleeping guards in the recess, one of whom grunted as they flitted past. Simon loomed up in the stairwell, looking tense.

'Where's Hugues?' whispered Robert, as the three of them ascended. 'How did you get in?'

'I'll tell you when we're on the road to Poitiers.'

'Poitiers?' muttered Simon, glancing up at Will as he climbed. 'I would think that's the last place you should both be going.'

'The pope swore he wouldn't let the Temple fall into Philippe's hands,' responded Will, breathing hard as they neared the top. 'But I want to make certain he keeps his promise.'

'How do you plan to do that?' panted Robert.

'Somehow, we have to get Nogaret to confess to murdering Pope Benedict. I know it's a near impossibility, but it might also be the last chance we've got.'

The Royal Palace, Paris, 14 September 1307 AD

Philippe opened his eyes and sat up, uncertain what had awoken him. The candle on the table by his bed was shifting unsteadily in a draught coming from somewhere. He could hear rain falling in a torrent outside. Swinging his legs over the bed, he put his feet on the icy stones and walked across the chamber to pull aside the drapes. There was a slash of grey in the eastern sky. It was almost dawn.

Letting the drapes fall back, Philippe shrugged on his ermine-trimmed cloak and went to where a basin and jug of water had been set out. He was washing his face when a knock sounded at the door and Nogaret entered.

'My lord.'

Philippe straightened, patting his brow dry with a cloth. 'It is early,' he remarked, frowning. 'Why are you here?' His gaze went to a large bag that was slung over the minister's shoulder.

'I beg your pardon, my lord, but I wanted to collect these.' Nogaret headed to the desk where the scrolls were piled high. 'The sooner the messengers leave the better. This weather will slow them enough as it is.'

Philippe paused, nettled by Nogaret's eagerness and feeling the minister was taking control again. But he forced back his irritation, knowing the lawyer was right. For their plan to work the seneschals of all the principal cities in France must have received the order by the time the appointed day came. It was a delicate operation indeed. One slip here or there could mean the difference between success and failure and, when it came to the Templars, he'd had more than enough of the latter to contend with. 'Very well.' Philippe watched as Nogaret stowed the scrolls in the bag. As he took up the last, the minister frowned and muttered a curse. 'What is it?' asked the king.

'I must have lost count.' Taking the scrolls out, Nogaret totted them up out loud. 'No,' he said, looking up as he removed the last. 'There's one missing.'

'I checked them myself yesterday. You must have miscounted.'

Nogaret shook his head, but set about adding them up once more. Philippe came over as he fingered the last. Impatiently, the king picked through them, but the number remained unchanged.

Nogaret's face was troubled in the candlelight, as Philippe walked around the table scanning the floor. 'Could someone have taken one?'

Philippe glanced up. 'No one but the two of us knows what they are. Why would anyone take one?'

In the silence, Nogaret's eyes flicked to the closed door separating the royal chamber from the handmaidens' dormitory.

'No,' said Philippe. But his denial held little conviction. While Nogaret went to the door, Philippe's mind was filled by the look of hatred in Rose's eyes as he had pushed her from the room. Now the door was opening and

Nogaret was hastening inside, a candle beyond throwing his thin shadow up the wall. Even though the light was dim, Philippe could see that Rose's bed was empty.

The Royal Palace, Paris, 14 September 1307 AD

Rose ran down the corridor towards the Great Hall, her bare feet clapping softly against the marble. The embroidered drapes covering the arched windows swirled in the wind and in the gaps she could see a faint grey light. In one hand she held her shoes, too loud for these echoing passages. With the other she grasped the strap of the bulging bag that bounced against her back. Inside, her balled clothes muted any sound that might be made by the other contents: either the stiff leather-bound scroll or her father's broken sword, stolen from the chest in his room after he disappeared. She couldn't bear the thought of leaving some part of him in this place. If this was all that remained of him then this was what she would bury, when the time came.

She pushed open the doors of the Great Hall and slipped inside. Without noise and people to fill it, the vast chamber seemed to swell before her, the scores of pillars stretching into shadows like a forest of trees, bathed red in the bloody glow coming from the four massive hearths. Flitting between the columns, Rose made her way across the hall. Halfway across, she froze. To her left a dark shape was moving low to the ground. After a second she realised it was a large dog. Glancing warily at her, the beast slunk towards a fireplace and slumped in front of the embers. The servants must have left a door ajar and it had found its way in.

Rose continued, her hand clutching the strap of the bag damp with sweat. She had only gone a few paces when she heard a door bang up ahead, followed by footsteps. Ducking behind one of the pillars, she saw someone crossing the hall in the direction she had come from. When the figure passed one of the hearths, she picked out his face. Fear engulfed her as she recognised the pinched, waxy features of Guillaume de Nogaret. The minister had a bag over his shoulder that flopped loosely as he hastened towards the doors that led to the royal apartments. Philippe had been asleep when she crept in to take the scroll, but the only reason Nogaret would have to be going that way was to wake him. She had no idea if they would notice the theft, but when Blanche and the other handmaidens woke in an hour or so they would certainly notice her absence. She waited breathlessly for the minister to push his way through the doors and the moment they thudded shut she was off, moving as fast as her swollen belly would let her.

Rose stumbled up the flight of shallow stairs at the end that led to a door. As she shoved it open, fighting against the wind, an icy shock of rain struck her. After slipping on her shoes and pulling up the hood of her mantle, Rose halted on the steps. She had already memorised what she would say to the guards, but although there was a light in the guardhouse, she could see no sign of anyone by the gate that the tradesmen used and it was with a burgeoning sense of freedom that she hastened across the rain-drenched courtyard. She drew back the bolt, then snapped down the latch. One tug and the gate was open. The narrow streets of the Ile de la Cité stood before her like the entrance to a labyrinth, but she knew her way through the maze and splashed assuredly towards the street that led to the Grand Pont. Emerging on the riverbank, however, she was brought to a halt.

The Seine, surging high and fast through the night, had burst its banks and was a grey sea, wide and open before her, the chestnut trees that lined the river swaying like tall ships anchored in the churning waters. The flood was creeping outwards from its rushing centre, the waters lapping up to where she stood, the street disappearing ahead under the flowing tide. Rose bit back a cry of frustration at the sight of the bridge rising in the distance, where the ground sloped up again. Was God punishing her? Testing her? Flashes of biblical scenes went through her mind: the Red Sea parting before Moses, Jesus walking on water, Noah gathering his animals. But they were men with powers. She was a pregnant woman with a head full of fear and a heart full of guilt, her only hope of redemption the helpless life inside her and the scroll in the bag, lying heavy on her back.

Rose looked over her shoulder. She could return to the palace, slip the scroll back into the king's chamber somehow. Crawl into her bed. But even as she thought it, she remembered the rage in Philippe's face. *Lanced like a boil! Get out before I do it myself!* Do what? But she knew, deep down she knew. She had been a vessel into which the king had poured his anguish and despair. Being so empty, she let herself be filled by his blackness. To him, the child that kicked and dreamed within her was nothing more than a seed he had planted by mistake, a weed that needed to be pulled, but as it grew and she found herself nourishing something other than grief and anger, it had become something real. Something wonderful. She had found herself hoping for a boy. If it was she would name him William, and he would not have a life like hers. But if that was to be, she couldn't go back.

Rose turned and stared at the drowned streets before her, dark in the sullen dawn. The last thing her father said to her before leaving was that he would speak to Robert and Simon, ask them to get her out of Paris. The

Temple lay beyond the flood. Hope lay beyond. Steeling herself, Rose stepped into the freezing water and struck out for the bridge.

The water deepened quickly, reaching coldly up her legs to her thighs as she waded in. She gasped when the wind tossed back her hood and rain lashed her cheeks. Her mantle flowed behind, dragging her down and her gown mushroomed around her, making it hard to move. The Grand Pont loomed ahead, the water dangerously high beneath it, racing between the tops of the piers. Branches and debris swirled around her, catching in her skirts and whipping past her legs. Several times she stumbled on something hidden underfoot and almost dropped the bag. She could see a couple of people on the bridge, looking worriedly over the water. One man yelled at her to go back, but she carried on, almost swimming now, the bag perched high on her back. As she approached, panting with exertion, the man who had been yelling plunged down and came towards her, hands outstretched.

'Foolish girl!' he was shouting over the rush of water and the creaking bridge timbers. 'You could have drowned!'

As she grasped hold, he pulled her up on to the boards. Thanking the stranger through chattering teeth, she hastened along the Grand Pont. The banks were higher on the other side, the water only ankle-deep, and she quickened her pace as she entered the streets of the Ville, twisting through alleys, past squat churches where torrents of water spewed from the mouths of gargoyles. By the time she reached Temple Gate, her whole body was aching and she could do little more than lope awkwardly along. It was still early and the gates weren't due to be opened for another half-hour, but she pleaded desperately with the city guards and eventually, out of pity or impatience, they let her through.

She slowed her pace as she headed along the road, the preceptory before her. The slash across the eastern sky had widened and a dull gold light was haemorrhaging from it. The rain was easing. Rose grasped her side and came to a halt, wincing as the baby struggled. She was standing there, trying to catch her breath for the last slog to the preceptory's gate, when she heard a shout. It came to her faintly on the wind and it wasn't until it came again that she realised the sound was familiar. It was her name. She turned and saw four figures running along the road, the city walls rising behind them. Three were in scarlet and blue cloaks that billowed behind them. The fourth, sprinting at their head, was all in black with a white coif.

For a moment, Rose stood rooted to the spot. Realisation squirmed up through her shock and it suddenly seemed obvious that they would know where to find her. Where else would she go in this city for help? The shout came again, harsher now. It galvanised her. Turning, she launched herself forward, lungs and legs screaming. The Temple was coming up, slowly. Clinging to the bag, throwing a look over her shoulder, Rose was horrified to see how much the men had gained on her. She could pick out Nogaret's features in the seeping dawn. The minister's face was a mask of fury. She tripped on a rock, dropped the bag, snatched it up. The stitch in her side was a slice of agony.

The gate was ahead. Twenty yards. Fifteen. Ten. As she reached it, she threw herself against it, hammering both fists on the wood. 'Let me in! Please! God please, help me!'

'Get her!' came Nogaret's shout.

'*Help me!*'

A small door in the gates opened and she fell forward. Strong arms took hold of her. She saw the faces of two knights, surprised and concerned, then she was through. One of the men, seeing the soldiers come running, threw the door shut and swung a heavy bar across it.

The Templar turned to Rose as the soldiers banged on the gates. 'Who are you? Why are royal guards chasing you?'

'Please,' she panted, 'I have to see Sir Robert de Paris.' With trembling fingers she untied the bag and pulled out the scroll. 'He has to read this.'

The hammering came again. It was followed by Nogaret's voice.

'Open up in the name of the king!'

One of the knights started towards the door.

Rose shrank back. 'Please,' she whispered. 'He'll kill me.'

The knight's gaze went from the scroll to her belly, arching through the folds of her mantle. She raised her hand to her mouth in despair as he moved to the gate, but instead of opening it, he snapped up a board that covered a hole cut into the wood.

'What do you want?'

Rose heard Nogaret answer. 'The woman you have is a fugitive from the palace. She stole something that belongs to the king.'

'Do you have proof?'

'Proof?' spat Nogaret. 'I need no such thing! You will hand her to me at once or suffer the consequences!'

'I'm afraid, without an official warrant, I cannot do that. You see, the woman is on our property now and as our territory lies outside royal jurisdiction so does she.'

'Have you not heard me, damn you? She stole from the king!'

The knight paused, his face filling with dislike. 'King Philippe is very fond, it seems, of making unfounded accusations and so until you can bring us proof of this woman's crimes, I see no good reason to hand anything to you. Good day.' With that, he pulled down the board and crossed to Rose, ignoring the banging that started up behind him. 'Now, as I've just disobeyed a royal order, you had better tell me who you are.' He pointed to the scroll. 'And what that is.'

Rose pressed her lips together. 'I must give it to Sir Robert.'

'Sir Robert is in prison.'

Rose saw something pass across the knight's face. She thought it was anger, but it was gone too quickly to be sure.

After a pause, he nodded to his comrade. 'Stay here. I'll send you some reinforcements in case they try anything foolish. I'll take her to the officials' building.'

'There's no one there,' said his comrade, raising his voice above the shouts of the soldiers.

'I know,' replied the knight gruffly, 'but she cannot stay out here. The brothers will be waking for Matins any minute.' Gesturing for Rose to follow, he headed for a grand building.

They were almost at the entrance, Rose struggling to keep up with the knight's stride, when three men came barrelling out of a tower on the other side of the courtyard. Rose's face bloomed with hope as she saw Robert. The expression froze on her face as her gaze alighted on the man behind him.

Will came to a stop in the courtyard. He saw the knight first and alarm flooded him, but before he could get his feet moving again he registered the woman. She was staring at him, sinking to her knees on the wet ground, her ashen face crumpling in shock. Her coif was stuck to her head, hanks of wet hair coiling free around her shoulders, and her mantle was drenched and black with mud. But she was here. And unharmed. A faint prayer released itself from his lips. He took a few steps towards his daughter then faltered, his eyes on her distended stomach. Simon pushed past him, going quickly to where Rose had collapsed, something clutched in her hand.

Robert flicked the sword he had taken from the dungeon towards the knight, who had drawn his own blade and was pointing it at him and Will. 'Brother Laurent,' he called. 'I don't want to fight you. But I have to leave.'

Slowly, the knight lowered his sword. 'I'm not going to stop you, brother.'

Robert crossed to him, relief etched in his face. 'Thank you.' He clasped the knight's hand. 'I know you petitioned Hugues for my release.'

'I wasn't the only one.'

Will hardly heard their exchange as the shock drained from him and he rushed to his daughter. Simon had coaxed her out of the mud, but she raised her hands, dropping the object she held, as Will came towards her.

'No,' she was weeping. 'Please don't. Don't touch me. I betrayed you. *I betrayed you.*'

Not heeding her protests, Will enfolded her in his arms, remembering with piercing clarity the moment he pulled her to him at Acre after he thought he had lost her in the fire. It was the same wrenching love he felt now as he held her. Robert had bent and picked up the scrollcase she had let fall.

'She wanted to give that to you, brother,' Laurent was saying. 'She was being pursued by royal guards. They demanded we hand her over.' He glanced at the main gates, where the hammering had ceased. 'I think they've gone.'

Will watched Robert pull the scroll from its case, but didn't relinquish his hold on his daughter. 'There's writing on the side,' he said, as the knight turned it over in his hands.

Robert held it up, squinting in the gloom. 'To be opened by the Seneschal of Troyes on the evening of Thursday the twelfth day of October, and not before, on pain of death.' Glancing at Will, he broke the wax seal and began to read out loud.

A bitter thing, a lamentable thing, a thing that is horrible to contemplate, terrible to hear of, a detestable disgrace, a thing almost inhuman, indeed set apart from all humanity. This is the very essence of the matter that has been brought to our attention. I, King Philippe IV, have heard the testimony of upstanding and virtuous persons who accuse the men of the Order of the Temple, sorrowfully but truthfully, of the foulest of crimes. Like a wolf in the appearance of a lamb, these so-called warriors of Christ have sinned against God and deceived all of Christendom.

The brothers of this Order, it has been discovered, practise heresy and idolatry within their secret ceremonies and Chapters. More sickening still, they deny Christ and spit upon the cross. They engage in vile sorcery and devil-worship, and, eschewing the company of women, are encouraged to engage in the most obscene acts with one another. The Knights of the Temple defile the land with their filth, remove the benefits of the dew and infect the purity of the air. It is thus, with heavy heart, but firm hand that I, Lord of this realm, ordained by God, must act.

> *By my order, I command you forthwith to muster the officers under your authority for the arrest and detainment of all knights, sergeants, priests and retainers of the Temple, who reside within your territory. This is to be done at dawn tomorrow, Friday the thirteenth day of October, the year of our Lord 1307.*
>
> *Once the Templars have been imprisoned, you will install guards in their preceptories and holdings. All treasures, relics and records are to be collected and held securely until such time as they can be transferred to Paris. The Temple's property and all assets will henceforth be considered part of the royal treasury. After this is done, you will await further instruction from the crown.*
>
> *Scribed, on behalf of our gracious king by Sir Guillaume de Nogaret, First Lawyer of the Realm and Keeper of the Royal Seals.*

As Robert finished reading, Laurent moved away. He looked stunned, as did Simon.

Robert met Will's gaze. 'He doesn't have the power to do this, surely? The pope would have to authorise such an action.'

Rose turned her head, her cheek resting on Will's chest. 'The king was planning to send the messages today. There were many more of them in his chamber than the one I took. He intends to deliver them to all the seneschals of the kingdom.'

Will stroked her hair distractedly, feeling a mixture of pride at her bravery and disquiet over the danger she had put herself in. He was still reeling from the revelation that she was pregnant and it was hard to concentrate his thoughts, but he managed to marshal them after a moment. 'I think the king must be so assured he will have public support that he doesn't feel he needs Pope Clement's consent. In truth, if enough people demand an investigation into these charges the pope will have little choice but to endorse the king's actions. Remember, more than half the cardinals in the Sacred College are allied with Philippe. They can bring a great deal of pressure to bear on Clement.'

Laurent was frowning at Will, a stranger to him, but with a bemused shake of his head, addressed Robert. 'The Visitor, the Grand Master, all the officials are in Poitiers with the pope, attending to these very charges. I don't understand why the king is moving against us when an investigation has already begun.'

'A distraction,' said Will, before Robert could answer. 'They want to separate the officials from the rest of the knights. The dawn assaults will minimise the effectiveness of any resistance and without commanders to lead them the men will be cut off, disorganised.'

'Then is the pope part of this?' questioned Robert.

'I do not believe so. I think they are using Clement to keep the Temple officials occupied. I do not think it matters what the outcome of that assembly is, or whether the pope feels the Grand Master has answered the charges satisfactorily. The king plans to move against the Order whatever and such a bold action will not be easily undone. Once the Templars are in his custody it will be very difficult for them to muster any effective defence. I think, if it comes to that point, a full public trial will be inevitable.'

They fell silent.

'We've got four weeks before they come for us,' murmured Simon. 'What do we do?'

'There isn't time to warn everyone,' said Laurent. 'Not in every preceptory, but maybe if we gathered the knights who are here in Paris, perhaps fled to . . . ?' He trailed off. 'But we cannot. Not without the consent of the Marshall or the Visitor. I remember a story about a garrison of knights in the Holy Land who fled their preceptory when the Saracens came for them, leaving it undefended. They were stripped of their mantles. We cannot run.' His brow furrowed. 'I *will* not.'

'We need to warn the pope,' answered Will. 'I planned to go to Poitiers anyway.' He glanced at Robert. 'Once there I can speak to Jacques de Molay. The Grand Master must be the one to decide the best course of action. Your brother here is right: it will be chaos unless the chain of command is observed.' Will frowned, thinking quickly. 'There is one thing we can do now. We know the king's charges are based on Esquin de Floyran's testimony, but if they find no evidence to support that no judge could possibly pass sentence against the Order on one man's accusations alone. We know Hugues conducted the initiations here, so we need to destroy anything in this preceptory that might implicate the Order. We can make Philippe's task as hard as possible.' Will paused, a grim smile spreading across his face. 'And we can make his potential reward as uninviting as we can. I realise we cannot safeguard the assets contained in all Templar strongholds.' He spread his hands to take in the shadowy courtyard and the buildings around them. 'But we are standing in the richest preceptory in the world.'

'What are you saying?' questioned Laurent. 'Brother Robert, who is this man?'

Robert, however, wasn't looking at him. He was looking at Will, that grim smile mirrored in his own face. 'We take the treasury.'

'We'll need a ship and enough men to crew it,' said Will, ignoring Laurent's protests. He nodded to Simon. 'I want you on it. And you, Rose,' he added, looking down at his daughter.

'There are men in this preceptory I can rely on for that task,' replied Robert. 'Men outside Hugues's influence.' He turned to Laurent. 'Will you aid us?'

Laurent was staring at him in disbelief, but after a long moment he hefted his shoulders. 'We could perhaps have a ship ready by this evening, but—'

'Do it. I'll speak to the others before I leave for Poitiers.'

'I want you on that ship too, Robert,' said Will.

'What? No.'

'There is no one I trust more and someone who understands all that is happening here needs to make it out before the king's men begin the arrests. It doesn't require two of us to speak to the Grand Master and the pope.'

Robert was silent. 'Where do we go?' he said finally.

'Scotland. It is remote enough for you to remain hidden for as long as this lasts and now Edward is dead there should be little in the way of interference from England.' Will removed himself gently from his daughter's embrace. 'Go with Simon, Rose, and he'll get you some dry clothes. Stay with him and when it is time he'll take you to the ship.' He looked at Simon. 'When you reach Scotland, I want you to take her to my sisters in Elgin.'

'I'll make sure it's done.' Simon smiled faintly, as Will grasped his shoulder.

Rose hung back, staring at Will when Simon took her by the arm. 'Father . . . ?'

'There will be time, Rose. But not today.' Will watched as she moved off, looking over her shoulder. He turned to Robert. 'Come. We don't have long.'

'You'll need to check the dungeons,' Robert told Laurent. 'We had to put a couple of men down, but I expect they'll come around soon. Tell them . . .' He shook his head. 'Tell them anything.'

Together, he and Will sprinted across the courtyard to the officials' quarters.

The door to Hugues's chambers was locked, but they shouldered their way through. Will had taken a torch from the passage and the light spilled into the chamber before them. Other than Hugues's desk, the large armoire and a few stools and chests, the place was empty.

Will began picking through the parchments on the desk as Robert opened up the chests. 'Anything?' he asked, glancing up.

'Nothing. Just clothes.'

Will stared around him. 'This isn't the room I was taken to. He must conduct the initiations somewhere else.'

'The Chapter House?'

'No, it wasn't there. Anyway, that's too exposed. They would run the risk of being seen.' Will frowned, trying to remember. 'They took me down some steps. Narrow steps.'

'The dungeons?'

'I don't think so.' Will moved to the armoire and opened up the front. There was a goblet on one shelf, a Bible, some skins, a pouch filled with coins. Nothing incriminating. Frustrated, he went to turn away, then stopped. He could smell something. It was bitter and oddly familiar. He bent closer to the armoire, trying to think where he had smelled it before. It came to him suddenly. Will closed the doors and moved around the back of the armoire. The odour was stronger. His pulse raced as he felt a draught. 'Help me,' he called to Robert, sliding his fingers into the gap between the armoire and the wall.

To their surprise, the cumbersome object slid back easily, as if it had been moved many times before. Indeed, as they looked down, they saw marks scratched in the flagstones. Ahead, a narrow passageway disappeared down a set of stone steps. Glancing at one another, they headed in, Robert hefting his sword, Will holding the torch aloft.

They came out in a smaller chamber, where the stone was rough-hewn and unfinished. As Will moved the torch around, the flames danced across incomplete statues bowing from pillars, perhaps figures of saints or angels. There was a set of black curtains over one wall, which he recognised. He parted them to reveal a recess beyond, where a wooden dais had been constructed and a crude throne set upon it. The place had been scrubbed, but the bloodstains covering the walls and floor were unmistakable, as was the metallic odour that was barely masked by the stale incense.

'What is this place?' murmured Robert, eyeing a statue with the cross of St George chiselled into the shield it held. The head was blank and featureless.

'A private chapel, I think.' Will glanced at him. 'Perhaps a former Master ordered it built, but ran out of funds, or left for the Holy Land leaving it forgotten? It looks old.' He crossed to the altar. There were chalices and censers, skins scrawled with Hugues's hand. His fingers came to rest on a worn-looking tome that he recognised with a rush of sorrow. Everard's book.

Robert had opened a chest, one of several stacked in a corner. 'Jesus.'

Will stared at the misshapen monstrosity the knight held up. In the torchlight, the skull mask gleamed yellow, its long jaw bone thrusting forward, huge eye-sockets black and empty. As Robert turned it the image of a young man, carved deftly out of wood, was revealed. He turned it a third time and Will saw the face of an older man, lined and stern, threads of white hair hanging from its brow. 'Hugues said he was playing the part of the Fisher King in the initiations.' He crossed to Robert. 'I remember Everard saying the Fisher King in the story of Perceval is the embodiment of Christ. Of God.' He pointed to each of the mask's faces. 'The trinity. Father. Son. Holy Ghost.'

'Well, I always knew Hugues was ambitious.'

Will leaned over to look in the chest. He saw the glittering folds of Hugues's fish-scale cloak. 'We'll need to destroy everything.' He paused to light the candles on the altar with the torch, then sprinted up the steps to Hugues's chamber. There was a stack of logs by the hearth. He tossed a few inside, along with some of the skins from the armoire and set the torch to them. Leaving the flames to spring around the dry wood, he returned to help Robert.

The other chests were full of clothing; white mantles, strangely plain without their scarlet crosses, masks painted red with a white stag's head, a symbol of rebirth Will explained. There were also scores of books, all of them Romances, from the Grail story of Chrétien de Troyes, to writers and works Will had never heard of.

He and Robert emptied each chest, one by one, taking armfuls of books up to Hugues's chamber. The flames in the hearth spat as they devoured the pages. Parchments curled and blackened.

'We cannot burn all the clothes,' said Will, 'but we can stow them in the preceptory's wardrobe. They'll look like unfinished mantles.'

'What about these?' asked Robert, holding out the three-headed mask and the glittering cloak.

Will took them and threw them in. The fragile silk of the cloak caught quickly, momentarily turning the flames blue.

'And this?' Robert bent to pick up Everard's tome, which Will had placed on the floor.

After a moment, Will shook his head. 'Not that.'

Robert nodded, understanding. 'I'll take it with the treasury.'

With the last of the skins tossed into the fire, the two of them stood there, watching the smoke belching through the eye-sockets of the skull mask and forks of fire flicking from its mouth. As the Matins bell began to toll, they hastened from the chamber, leaving the mask to burn. Three faces vanishing in the roar of the flames.

39
The Temple, Paris
12 October 1307 AD

'I want to know everything,' demanded Jacques, sweeping along the palatial corridor. 'Do you hear me, Rainier?'

'Yes, my lord,' replied the knight, striding to keep up with the Grand Master, who had arrived at the Paris preceptory without warning several hours earlier, with the Master of Normandy, Geoffroi de Charney, four squires and two servants.

'Who did you say was involved?'

'I am not certain of all the details, my lord, but I believe Simon Tanner, the stable master, was in league with the man who assaulted me and freed Robert de Paris. They left a month ago with twenty of our men. I have all their names recorded. Myself and several brothers tried to intervene, but they outnumbered us.'

Jacques rounded on him. 'You should have lain down your lives rather than let them take it!'

'My lord,' conceded Rainier, hanging his head, still displaying a faint bruise where it had been slammed against the guardroom wall.

The Grand Master studied the young knight, his massive frame dominating the passage. 'Who organised the ship?'

'Brother Laurent, my lord.'

'And he is still here, you say?'

When Rainier nodded, Jacques's old eyes glittered. 'Bring him to me.' As the knight hastened off, Jacques thrust open the doors of his chambers.

'This is dire news, my lord,' said de Charney, entering behind him. 'What with the king's accusations and the pope's inquiry, the last thing we need is our own men working against us. There must be an explanation. It seems inconceivable to me that so many brothers would be involved in such an appalling crime.'

'We shall see, Geoffroi,' muttered Jacques, crossing to his desk, recently cleaned of the dust that had settled on it in a white blanket during his long absence. There was a jug of water and a goblet on it. Pouring himself a drink, he sat heavily on the chair behind. His hand shook as he raised the goblet and he frowned at the frailty. It happened often these days and he worried that it was the first sign of the decline of age, for he was in his sixties now. But perhaps it was simply the strain of the voyage from Cyprus.

Jacques had arrived at Poitiers in August, glad of the rest offered by his sojourn at the Franciscan priory with Pope Clement, circumstances notwithstanding, but it proved all too brief. A royal message had reached him barely days after the arrival of Hugues de Pairaud and the Temple's officials, summoning him to Paris. Telling the Visitor and the pope that he would return as soon as he had seen the king, who had promised to allow him to speak to Esquin de Floyran, Jacques had left with de Charney. As it was, the pope had fallen ill and was unable to continue the inquiry into the charges, and the summons seemed a timely opportunity for the Grand Master to speak to the king personally about the astounding accusations being levelled at the Order. Jacques had stopped for several days at the Orléans preceptory to celebrate the Feast of St Michael, but even so the journey to Paris had fatigued him further.

He drained the water. 'I would like to know why Sir Robert de Paris was imprisoned. He was on the progress I made through Christendom after the fall of Acre. I knew him well, but Visitor de Pairaud has known him since childhood. I cannot imagine what he could have done to cause Hugues to arrest him.'

'Perhaps this Laurent will know, my lord.'

Jacques grunted in reply and crossed to the window. He looked out over the courtyard, watching the men of the preceptory moving in the twilight: a sergeant leading a chestnut palfrey towards the stables, two servants carrying baskets of vegetables, four knights walking in a companionable group. His leathery brow creased as he thought of the crimes he and his men were being accused of. No, not crimes. *Sins*. The very thought of them struck at the core of Jacques's honour. That the warriors of Christ, who had toiled and bled for Christendom for almost two hundred years, could be considered heretics was beyond his comprehension.

The brief assembly in Poitiers, begun before the pope's illness, had turned up nothing and it seemed incredible to Jacques that all this trouble was caused by the accusations of one man. He had heard from some of the brothers today that the king believed the charges and had in fact made them public, but although the news disturbed him he chose to set rumour aside in favour of his audience with Philippe, planned for tomorrow. The Order had been through difficult times before. It was only twelve years ago that he was here in the West defending the Temple against Pope Boniface's suggestion of merging them with their rivals, the Knights of St John. If they stood firm, they would remain unbeaten.

Jacques turned from the window as a commotion sounded in the passage. He motioned to de Charney, who opened the doors. Between Rainier and another knight was a third man. He was shouting, struggling in their grip, but he fell silent as he saw the Grand Master, whose mantle was stitched with gold around the red cross at his heart.

'My lord,' he breathed, 'I heard you had come. I tried to speak to you earlier, but your servants told me you were occupied in meetings.'

'Why did you want to see me, Brother Laurent?' barked Jacques. 'To confess your guilt perhaps? Fall upon my mercy?'

'I wanted to warn you. A man left this preceptory several weeks ago to find you in Poitiers, but it seems he never reached you, as I do not believe you would have answered the king's summons, knowing it was a trap.'

'A trap?' said de Charney quickly. 'What do you mean?'

Jacques spoke over Laurent before he could reply. 'I want to know about the treasury. Who took it and where it was taken. Every last detail!'

'It was taken to protect it from the king, my lord. Last month a woman fled here from the palace. She brought an order for the imprisonment of all Templars in France on charges of heresy. My lord, the arrests are planned for tomorrow. The seneschals of the kingdom will be opening these royal orders this very night! If you have been called here by the king, as Brother Rainier said, then I am certain he intends to take you too. The man who freed Robert de Paris was supposed to have brought you this news, but as a precautionary measure twenty knights from this preceptory removed the treasury by ship to Scotland.'

'How do you know this wasn't some elaborate ruse concocted to persuade you to hand over the treasury?' demanded the Master of Normandy. 'Our men could have been ambushed. The treasury stolen.'

'I saw the scroll myself, Master de Charney. It had the king's seal upon it.' Laurent turned to Jacques. 'Believe me, my lord, what we did was in the best interests of the Order, though we broke the Rule most grievously in executing it.'

'Can anyone else verify what you are saying?' asked de Charney.

Laurent shook his head. 'It was agreed that we should keep it from the others so as not to cause panic. It was hoped Grand Master de Molay would return in time to make a decision as to how to proceed.'

De Charney glanced at Jacques. 'If he is telling the truth, my lord, then—'

'No,' growled Jacques, 'this is a misunderstanding. It has to be. King Philippe does not have the power to execute the arrest of a religious Order. Only the pope can do that and I know for certain his holiness has given no such command. I will meet the king as arranged and get to the root of this confusion and these lies.' He fixed Laurent with a baleful stare. 'Whether those who took the treasury thought they were doing right or not, I cannot condone their actions. Once these accusations have been laid to rest I will hunt them down and they will be punished, severely.' He nodded to Rainier. 'Take him to the dungeons. He can have a copy of the Rule to remind himself of our laws and the consequences of breaking them.'

'My lord! The king's men will be coming for us at dawn! We cannot stay!'

De Charney waited for the doors to close and Laurent's shouts of protest to fade before turning to Jacques. 'Perhaps it would be wise to leave the city,' he ventured. 'Just for tonight. We can—'

'No, Geoffroi,' said Jacques sharply. 'I will not be driven out of my own preceptory by rumour and panic. To do so would give these false allegations credence. How would it look if we ran? Would that not prove our guilt to our accusers? Would the people not think us cowards? We are Knights of the Temple of Solomon. We are God's sword.' The Grand Master's voice was implacable. 'I will not run before any enemy. To do so would mean the breaking of the vows I took upon my inception. I will defend this Order and my honour, even at the cost of death. I have stood in the desert before twenty thousand warriors, all intent on capturing or killing me. I will stand firm in the face of a few score city guards.'

The Temple, Paris, 13 October 1307 AD

It began with a deep thudding, like a slow-beaten drum. Birds flew startled from the dovecote, as the noise shattered the dawn hush. Horses tossed their heads and turned in their stalls, as grooms stumbled from their lodgings. In the kitchens, the cooks preparing the morning meal put down knives and glanced at one another. Servants stood uncertain, bundles of vegetables and braces of rabbits in their fists. The priests in the chapel, lighting candles for Matins, looked round, tapers flickering in their poised hands. Knights and sergeants rose from their pallets, shook drowsy comrades, pulled on boots and shirts. A few veterans of the Crusades, recognising the sound, snatched up swords, shouting for the younger ones to do the same. Men and boys poured into the courtyard, the sky above them a frozen, brittle blue.

Jacques de Molay, kneeling at his bedside, raised his head. As he stood, the rings of his mail coat clinked and settled into place. Unable to sleep, he had spent the night in prayer. Slowly, he crossed to where his broadsword stood against one wall. After sheathing the blade, he took his white mantle with its gold-edged cross and swung it around his shoulders. His hair and beard, silvery in the pallid light, hung loose and long as he strode out. He could hear doors banging and the calls of men, and above them all the boom of the battering ram striking the preceptory's gates.

Geoffroi de Charney met him on the ground floor. 'It seems Laurent was right, my lord,' said the Master, coming to his side. 'What are your orders? Do we fight?'

For a moment the Grand Master didn't answer. He paused on the steps outside his palace, his eyes on the men gathered before him. There were almost one hundred and fifty knights here, not to mention the sergeants and priests, and the large number of servants and squires, grooms and labourers. If necessary, they could hold off the king's men for months; mount an offensive from the walls to repel the attack on the gate, then settle in for a siege. But this wasn't Palestine. There weren't two centuries of slaughter between them and the men outside, just a grave misunderstanding and an arrogant monarch. 'We will not fight,' said the Grand Master, heading into the crowd, who parted before him. 'I will meet Philippe face to face to settle this matter. If we spill blood of the king's men here today we will only give him more cause to condemn us. We cannot be seen to be acting like guilty men. We will defend ourselves with our words and our actions, not our swords.' He walked to the gates where a group of knights were standing ready, swords in hands. The ram crashed against the wood, making it shudder. He heard the shouts of many men, along with the bellow of horses and the baying of dogs beyond the walls. 'Open the gates,' Jacques ordered two of the knights. 'Now!' he demanded, when they hesitated.

Together, they hoisted up the thick wooden bar that secured the entrance. Two others hastened to help and, between them, they pulled back the gates.

Outside, an army was waiting. Over two hundred royal guards were there, most of them mounted, along with a great number of officials and the city provosts. The soldiers at the ram, preparing for another strike, hung back at a shout from their captain. Others moved closer, crossbows trained on the Grand Master.

Jacques steeled his jaw and went forward, drawing strength from the knights gathering protectively at his back. Beyond the host of soldiers he could see a straggle of onlookers lining the road, watching with avid curiosity. They reminded him of crows, waiting at the edge of a battlefield. Movement to his left caught his eye and Jacques watched as a man in a black robe, trimmed with scarlet, trotted his horse out of the throng.

'Jacques de Molay?' the man called, looking down on the Grand Master from the height of his mount. He held up a scroll when Jacques gave a curt nod. 'By order of the King of France, you and your men are to be seized and your preceptory held in royal custody until a trial into the crimes you have been accused of has been conducted and a verdict reached. Lay down your weapons and tell your men to do the same.'

'Who are you to command this?' asked Jacques.

'My name is Guillaume de Nogaret,' replied the man, swinging his leg over his saddle and jumping down. 'I am Keeper of the Seals and First Lawyer of the Realm. You can read the order if you wish,' he added, holding out the scroll to Jacques.

The Grand Master's face hardened.

When he didn't take it, Nogaret gave a small smile. 'But of course, I forgot most Templars cannot read, can they? Well, then, I will have someone read it to you.' He snapped his fingers at an official.

As the man came forward, Jacques held up his hand angrily. 'Enough! I wish to parley with King Philippe.'

'His lordship does not parley with heretics.'

'Neither you nor the king have the authority to detain us or seize our property,' said Geoffroi de Charney, coming to stand at Jacques's side. His flint eyes regarded Nogaret with notable umbrage. 'Your royal order, whatever it may say, is invalid.'

Nogaret motioned behind him to a tall, grey-faced man dressed in the black robe of a Dominican. 'Friar Guillaume de Paris, as head of the Dominican college in the city, has the authority to arrest anyone suspected of heresy. This authority was given to the friars in their role as inquisitors by Pope Gregory IX, more than seventy years ago.'

'For laypeople, yes,' countered de Charney, 'but for a religious Order the pope must give his consent.'

'To my mind he has already given it,' responded Nogaret, 'by initiating an inquiry into the charges of heresy.'

'Inquiry?' demanded Jacques. 'It was little more than a conversation between myself and Pope Clement. His holiness is concerned to lay this matter to rest, certainly, but he does not truly believe Esquin de Floyran's accusations. He has told me himself what a grudge this man has against the Temple.'

'If this is so, you have nothing to fear from a trial. Your innocence will be proven.'

'We both know the task of the inquisitors is to prove guilt, not innocence.'

Nogaret met Jacques's gaze steadily. 'Stand down. My soldiers have been authorised to use force.' When Jacques didn't move, Nogaret gestured impatiently to the soldiers with the crossbows. 'Lay down your sword, or my men will shoot you!'

Jacques looked round, sensing his knights moving in at the threat against him. He went to call them to halt. But before he could get the words out, Nogaret dropped his hand and two of the soldiers with the crossbows let fire. One of the missiles slammed into the chest of a young knight, just behind the Grand Master. Jacques saw the man fly backwards and sprawl to the ground, sword clattering from his hand. Another went down, blood spurting around the bolt that caught him in the throat. There was a rush of motion as his men went to challenge the attackers. For a moment, Jacques stood rooted, his gaze on the two dead knights, mind filled with disbelief. It was a crime to insult a Templar and an offence punishable by excommunication to wound one. The sight of his knights advancing and Nogaret's men raising more weapons focused him. He would not allow this to become a massacre. '*Halt!*' roared the Grand Master, stopping them to a man. 'Lay down your weapons,' he bellowed at his knights. '*Do it!*'

One by one, the Templars placed their swords on the ground. As they did so, Nogaret smiled and motioned for the royal guards to enter the compound.

The soldiers were rough, pinning hands cruelly behind backs, kicking the knights to their knees or doubling them over with punches. Grooms, cooks and priests were treated in the same harsh way and cries of pain rose as the soldiers swarmed into the Chapter House and grand buildings of the officials, the tower of the donjon and the quiet chapel. They moved quickly, excitedly. For years, these men had grown up listening to whispers of the secret ceremonies of the proud, untouchable knights in their sinless white mantles, their prowess in battle and great deeds overseas, their immeasurable wealth. Now, the legends were bowed before them, humbled at last, leaving them free to pick through those treasures and secrets.

While the knights and sergeants were hauled away to rooms in the preceptory, now their prison, Jacques de Molay and Geoffroi de Charney were relieved of their mantles and bound to a cart, destined for the Louvre, the royal fortress on the banks of the Seine. Dawn had broken, clear and cold, but for the first time in almost two centuries the Matins bell did not ring out its call to prayer.

The Latin Quarter, Paris, 27 October 1307 AD

Will studied the buildings as he walked the winding street. Stores and workshops were crammed close together, the structures bowing over the muddy thoroughfare, ribbed with beams and painted in faded pinks and drab whites. In the distance, the dome of a church crowned the chaos of rooftops. Beyond, the sky was leaden, streaked with thin plumes of smoke. The air was chill and the people on the street were moving swiftly, swaddled in robes and mantles, breath misting before them. Most were scholars and priests from the many colleges that formed the focus of the Latin Quarter. Will was aware of how out of place he looked, his leather cloak shabby and stained, his hair and beard unkempt, his boots caked with dirt. The horse itself was conspicuous, a jet-black destrier Simon had saddled for him when he left the preceptory, and he sensed the curiosity of passers-by, where people tried to match the dishevelled man with the noble beast. He supposed, if anyone questioned him, he could try to pass himself off as a squire, though his age went against him. Forcing thoughts of excuses aside, he concentrated on the buildings. He didn't plan to linger long enough for people to challenge him. He just needed to find what he wanted and then he could go.

The journey to Poitiers had taken longer than he'd anticipated, the autumn storms slowing him down. Once in the town, he had kept off the main routes, knowing he couldn't afford to be spotted. Hugues de Pairaud thought he was dead, but Will had no doubt the Visitor would finish the job if he were caught. On making contact with a friar he knew from earlier visits, he discovered that he had missed Jacques de Molay by two days. The Grand Master had gone to Paris, leaving the Visitor and the remaining officials at the town's preceptory until he returned. Clement was seriously ill and despite Will's frustrated appeals to the friars, he wasn't allowed to see the pope until the day before the arrests were due to take place.

He had barely an hour's audience with the pope who, exhausted by his sickness, was in little position to offer him comfort or aid. He remained at the priory, hoping Clement would recover enough to make a decision as to how to counter the king's plans and it was there that he learned the Temple's preceptory in Poitiers had fallen in a fierce dawn assault led by a heavy contingent of royal guards. All the knights had been rounded up, Hugues and the other officials taken into royal custody and conveyed to Paris. The threat within the scroll confirmed and not knowing whether his daughter, Simon and Robert had managed to leave on the ship, Will implored Clement to write to the king condemning his actions and demanding the immediate release of the knights and their property. The pope agreed to meet the king as soon as he was well, but, frustrated by his lack of urgency, Will decided to return to Paris. He hoped, if he could bring something concrete to Clement, perhaps reports of the king's brutality or confirmation that he was taking the Temple's wealth for himself, that he might be able to rouse him to more immediate action.

When he reached Paris, he went straight to the preceptory, but finding the place crawling with royal guards he didn't dare get close. The city was buzzing with news of the Temple's fall. There was something ugly in people's interest. Some talked about justice, about the knights getting their comeuppance for losing the Holy Land. Others spoke of the charges, nodding knowingly to the butcher as they swapped money for meat, saying how they'd always thought the knights were up to no good. It was through this gossip Will learned that not all the men in the preceptory had been seized that day. People spoke of knights and sergeants fleeing through the streets during the initial chaos of the arrests. It was these fugitives Will had spent the past few days trying to find, which was why he was here in the Latin Quarter, staring at these buildings, looking for a sign.

Finally, he found it: a black door with a peeling golden cross painted on it. The shutters were closed over the ground-floor windows as it was still early. Leading his horse through the arched passageway in the side of the building, Will headed into a poky courtyard, with a stable block wedged against the back wall. A boy was out there, sweeping the yard. He glanced up seeing Will and his eyes widened as he looked the horse up and down.

'Where can I find the innkeeper?' Will asked, handing him the reins.

'In the kitchen,' replied the boy, turning the massive horse expertly and leading it towards the stables.

'Keep him saddled,' Will called, heading for the back door, 'I won't be here long.'

Two men inside the kitchen looked round, frowning quizzically as he entered.

One held a knife poised over a fish he was gutting. 'What do you want?'

'I'm looking for the innkeeper.'

'He's in front,' replied the man, slamming the knife down and taking off the fish's head. He jerked his thumb towards a door behind him. 'But there're no rooms if that's what you're after.'

Will moved past him into a dark, musty-smelling room where a scrawny man with carroty hair was manoeuvring a barrel across the uneven flagstones. He cursed as it caught on one of the benches that lined the room.

'Here, let me.' Will went over and took the other side.

The man looked surprised, but allowed Will to help him move the barrel over to where several others were stacked. He straightened. 'Are you here for a room? Because we're—'

'No,' Will cut across him. 'I'm looking for a couple of men I believe are guests of yours.'

'Oh?'

The man's tone was light, but Will caught an edge of tension in it. 'I think you know who I mean.'

The man gave a nervous laugh. 'How would I know if you don't give their names?'

'They're Templars.'

The man held up his hands, shaking his head. 'Sorry.' He was inching away from Will, towards the kitchens.

'I'm not here to turn them in,' said Will quickly. 'I only want to speak to them. Please. It's very important.'

The man started as he came up against a bench. 'Look, I'm just letting them stay here,' he said, his face in the gloom pale and frightened, 'just until they can escape the city. I've done business with the preceptory and the knights always treated me well. I felt I owed them when they came for sanctuary.'

Will nodded reassuringly. 'And when this is over you can be sure you'll be rewarded for your aid.'

The man faltered, then nodded to the stairs. 'There are four of them. Three knights and a sergeant. I've given them the top room.'

'Thank you,' said Will, heading for the stairs. The boards groaned as he made his way up past several landings, until he reached a door on the fourth floor, where the stairs ended. He knocked. There was movement in the room beyond, hushed voices. The door opened a crack and a face appeared.

'Yes?'

'My name is William Campbell. I am a friend of Robert de Paris and Simon Tanner. I need to speak to you.'

'I'm sorry,' said the voice, 'I don't know them.'

'Wait, Gui,' came another voice beyond, 'let him in.'

The door closed and Will heard a muted exchange. Finally, it opened fully, allowing him to step into the room. As he did so, a sword came up to his throat and he froze.

'Remove his weapon, Albert,' said the man behind him, kicking the door closed.

A young man with a broad, ruddy face unsheathed Will's sword. As he did so, Will glanced at the two other men in the room, both armed and ready to move against him if necessary. They had all shaved their beards, but there was a telltale white patch on each of their chins, where the sun hadn't browned them in years. Their clothes were coarse and ill-fitting, too long or short, and all of them had the watchful, wary look of the hunted.

'What do you want?' demanded the man called Gui, who still had his sword pressed against Will's throat.

'Information.'

'How did you find us?' asked Albert worriedly.

'A servant from the preceptory who made it out told me.'

Gui muttered a curse. 'I told you we shouldn't stay. If he could find us, that means the royal guards could. We need to get out of Paris.'

'How can we?' answered one of the other knights. 'We've no money and we're known in this city.' He tugged at his robe. 'Without a decent disguise we'll not make it past the watchmen on the gates. You heard what Martin said. They're questioning everyone trying to leave.'

'What information did you want?' Gui asked Will.

'Last month, do you know if a group of Templars left the preceptory? Robert de Paris and Simon Tanner would have been among them. They were supposed to be leaving on a ship.'

Gui said nothing for a few moments. Slowly he lowered the weapon, but kept the blade trained on Will. 'Yes. No one knew what was happening, or why they left, but later I heard it said they had taken the treasury. It was thought the Visitor must have ordered it.'

Will let out a breath. 'What about the day of the arrests? Can you tell me what happened? Has the king begun any kind of trial? Are the knights just being detained or are they being questioned?'

Albert shook his head. 'We don't know. The four of us were in the infirmary when the arrests began. When we saw the guards come in and kill several knights, we decided to run. We thought we should try to get to another preceptory to tell them what was happening.'

'It wouldn't have done you any good,' replied Will. 'This wasn't confined to Paris.'

Gui was frowning intently. 'Who are you? How do you know all this?'

'Someone who doesn't want to see the king get his prize,' replied Will. 'But in order to do that I need proof that the king is acting unlawfully in the arrests to take back to the pope.'

'The pope?' voiced Albert hopefully.

A low rumble of hoof-beats came to them, mingled with shouts of alarm. Will and Gui went to the window. A troop of royal guards was riding down the street towards the inn, people scattering out of their way. Will swore as they came to a halt outside, horses wheeling and stamping.

'Did you lead them here?' snarled Gui, turning on him.

'No.'

Words drifted to them. 'Open up, in the name of the king!'

'Shit!' Gui wrenched open the door.

Will followed the men, pounding down the stairs.

'The back!' Gui was bellowing as they reached the next landing. 'We'll get out the back!'

'No!' shouted Will. 'They'll have it covered. The windows! We might be able to climb on to the roof.'

But the knights ignored him and followed Gui headlong down the rickety stairs. Doors all along the hallway were opening, guests roused from their beds.

'What the hell is happening?' demanded one man, stepping out. He shrank back as Will came at him.

Pushing past him, Will entered the room and ran to the window. He cursed, seeing nothing but a long drop into the courtyard below. There were scores of soldiers down there, pouring into the back door. He heard shouting somewhere below as he sprinted from the room, down the hall. He tried one door and found it locked, tried another and shouldered his way in. A man leapt at him as he entered, swinging a bed-pot. Will ducked and lunged, kneeing him in the stomach. The man doubled over and a scream tore through the air as a woman vaulted from a crumpled bed. She was naked, her mouth peeling back in another scream. Stamping footsteps were coming up the stairs. Ignoring the woman, Will went to the window and thrust open the shutters. There was a ledge outside. If he stood on it, he might be able to reach the next building. He swung his leg up and over the sill, grabbing hold of the frame to support himself, just as three royal guards came running into the room. The woman's screams intensified as one of them caught Will by the hood of his cloak. He was hauled back into the room and crashed to the floor. One of the guards kicked him in the face and blood flooded the back of his throat. Dazed and choking, Will was dragged out of the room.

Spitting blood between his teeth as they lugged him into the street, Will saw the other men had been apprehended. Gui was on the floor, his face twisted with pain. A crowd had gathered, people spilling from shops and inns to watch the excitement. Someone cheered as Albert, who was struggling, was punched in the side and dropped to his knees.

'Another clutch of rats fleeing the sinking ship,' came a cold voice. 'Arrest the innkeeper and all his staff.' The command was loud enough for all the onlookers to hear. 'Anyone who harbours heretics will be dealt with in the same way.'

Will hung his head quickly, seeing a set of black robes sweep into sight.

'Who are they? Knights or sergeants?'

'I'm not sure,' replied the guard. 'But we'll know soon enough when we've got them locked away.'

'Indeed we will. Take them all to the preceptory.'

From under his lowered gaze, Will watched the black robes swish away. He felt himself being marched off, then that cold voice struck out again.

'Wait!'

Will tensed.

'That man there. Show me his face!'

Will tried to pull away, but one of the men holding him wrenched back his hair. He found himself looking straight into the dark eyes of Guillaume de Nogaret.

Nogaret's face showed disbelief, then the slow spread of satisfaction.

'Shall we take him with the others, Minister?' asked one of the guards hesitantly.

'No,' murmured Nogaret. 'This one can go to the Louvre.' His voice was thick with relish. 'I'll have a special cell prepared for him.'

40
The Louvre, Paris
31 October 1307 AD

ₘ

Will walked the cell floor, five paces forward, five back. For the past four days he had filled the hours that stretched into infinity in the cramped, airless space with these small acts of freedom. They hadn't bound his body and so he could make the choice to sit and think, lie down and sleep to save his strength, or pace to keep his muscles working.

The prison – four bare walls, no window, a blank door with a hole for his food to be shoved through – was a surprise. The way Nogaret looked at him when he was hanging between the royal guards, he had imagined beatings and tortures awaited him. In some ways, this nothingness, almost devoid of human contact, was worse. His anticipation of what was to come was now so heightened, his whole being seemed to vibrate with it and it took all his control not to let his thoughts spiral into madness. He had to stay calm, prepare himself, and so he walked, focusing on the simplicity of placing one bare foot in front of the other.

Some time later, the sound of footsteps echoed. Will halted, listening. They were coming closer. He guessed there were three, maybe four men, the chink of their mail unmistakable. He pressed his back against the cell wall as the footsteps stopped outside his door, heard a bolt rattle and snap back.

'Face the wall,' came a harsh voice.

Will hesitated, not wanting to show weakness, but there seemed no reason to disobey the simple order and so he turned. His back itched with expectation as the door opened and a cold draught brushed across him. He tensed as hands gripped his arms, pulling them back. Rope circled his wrists. He heard a man's breaths behind him as the pressure increased and felt the blood pulsing in his veins, his hands growing hot and prickly. He was jerked round and marched forward, two men to either side of him.

None of the guards spoke, to him or each other, as he was led from the cell through the prison. As he walked, Will tried to focus his mind down to a single point inside himself, a point at which threats or pain wouldn't be able to reach him. It was hard, his thoughts fluttering agitated within him. A memory of his daughter looking back over her shoulder as Simon led her away was followed by an image of William Wallace being cut down from the gallows. He gritted his teeth and forced them away, concentrating on the task of putting one foot in front of the other, just like in the cell.

The men holding him brought him to a stop at a door. As it was opened, Will felt a rush of heat and sweat beaded his forehead. The first thing his eyes fixed on was the immediate threat in the pitiless faces of the nine men he could see in the chamber. He recognised Nogaret at once. Other than the four royal guards who had escorted him, there were four more men, all clad in the black robes of Dominicans. He knew one by sight, a tall, thin man with chilling eyes. It was Guillaume de Paris, Philippe's personal confessor, and head of the inquisitors in Paris. As the door closed behind him, Will's gaze came to rest on a variety of items and contraptions, whose threat was more oblique and sinister.

There was a rope slung over one of the ceiling beams, near a triangular frame with what looked like a windlass positioned at the apex, a system of ropes snaking from it. In front of a coal-fire a blackened-looking board was propped beside a bowl of something oily. There was a trestle with some sort of metal funnel and a large jug sitting on it, and another table covered with a cloth, under which he made out the outlines of things whose identity his mind could only guess at. Worse than the objects themselves were the stains on the floor, some fresh, some old. He smelled blood and urine, faeces and sweat. Every splatter was an echo of pain, a scream or a whimper. It was a room of horrors, where a man would be shredded of dignity and humanity, stripped right back to the core of himself, to the blood and the sinews and bone. Distantly, he remembered Everard telling him about the tortures inflicted upon the Cathars, but the inquisitors had had a great deal of practice since those early days, refining their methods within the constraints placed upon them by the Church. Forbidden from spilling blood, unless it be done accidentally during examination, they had been forced to come up with ingenious ways of exacting suffering upon men and women accused of heresy, from whom they sought a confession. Limbs would be broken, burned, compressed, dislocated, all without a drop of blood to stain the Church.

Nogaret waited until Will had taken in the whole room before speaking. 'William Campbell, you have been accused of heresy. You will now be examined by the authority of the Church to determine whether or not the charge is true. You will be given the opportunity to confess your guilt and, should you be truly repentant, will be forgiven your sins. How do you plead?'

Will glanced at the other men, then back at Nogaret. 'How can I be guilty? I am not a Templar. I left the Order years ago. What evidence do you have that implicates me as a heretic?'

Nogaret smiled, seemingly pleased by this game. 'The confession of a high-ranking member of the Order implicates you.' He paused, studying Will. 'What is the Anima Templi?'

Will said nothing, but continued to meet Nogaret's gaze.

'Your silence surprises me, Campbell. The Visitor of the Temple, Hugues de Pairaud, told everyone in this room that you were the head of this organisation.'

Still Will kept quiet.

'In fact,' continued Nogaret, 'much of what de Pairaud said resonates with Esquin de Floyran's testimony, along with the testimonies of others, including the Grand Master.'

'That is a lie.'

'Is it?' Nogaret went to the triangular frame. 'Jacques de Molay confessed right here on the rack. He said he had denied Christ and spat upon the cross. He said he worshipped a three-headed idol in his Chapter meetings and encouraged other knights to do the same, and kissed brothers on the mouth and other parts of the body.'

Will noticed Guillaume de Paris's jaw twitch with disgust. One of the Dominicans crossed himself. In the heat of the torches and the fire, he felt sweat trickle down his spine. He could deny everything they were saying, he realised, and it would make no difference. Neither would a confession, not with Nogaret leading the investigation. But perhaps he could appeal to the humanity of de Paris, spare other innocent men this ordeal? At least until Pope Clement intervened. He focused on the tall Dominican. 'The Anima Templi does exist and I was once its head. It was never a heretical organisation, but one devoted to peace. Unfortunately, after I left the Order, a small number of men twisted our original aims to suit their own purposes. But, again, these men were not heretics, they were simply misguided. Their faults lie in greed and arrogance, not in crimes of faith and they should be judged by the only authority who has power over Knights of the Temple: his holiness, the pope. As I said, they were a small number only. Spare the rest of the brothers these tortures for they know nothing of any heresy, including the Grand Master.'

'Do you have the names of these few men?' enquired Guillaume de Paris sternly.

Will was thinking about how to answer when Nogaret stepped between them.

'Do not let him fool you. He is trying to distract us. You heard de Molay confess yourself, only yesterday.'

Will's eyes narrowed. 'Any man would confess to anything strapped to that,' he growled. 'Including you.'

Two stains bloomed on Nogaret's cheeks, but he checked himself before answering. 'I am pleased to get your confession so quickly, Campbell. It augurs well for the next set of questions I will be putting to you, for which the king requires an immediate answer.' He gestured to the guards. 'Strip him.'

Will stiffened as the guards came forward. His shirt was torn open. One of the others cut down the sleeves with a knife. He flinched as the blade nicked his skin. His breeches suffered a similar fate and then there was just the horrible vulnerability of his naked flesh. He remembered feeling something similar at his initiation into the Temple, only then there was the promise of reward at the end of the trial. Now, there was little to hope for.

As he was taken to the trestle with the metal funnel and jug placed upon it, Will could see water and other stains darkening the floor. His eyes moved over the instruments, although he couldn't tell what they would be used for.

'Where is the treasury, Campbell?'

'I have no idea. Ask the knights.'

'I have. Several of them tell me you were involved in its removal from Paris.' The minister's voice became a snarl. 'On the night your whore of a daughter stole one of the royal orders from my lord! I should have slit the bitch's throat when I had the chance!'

Will started towards him, but was yanked back and, at a barked command from Nogaret, hefted on to the table, one of the inquisitors removing the jug, another picking up the funnel. He struggled fiercely, but the other soldiers moved in and, between them, the four guards pinned him to the table, naked, his hands bound painfully behind him, arms crushed by his own weight.

'Where is the treasury?' demanded Nogaret, so close Will could smell his breath.

He twisted his face away, but one of the soldiers gripped his head. An inquisitor leaned over him and inserted the nozzle of the metal funnel into his mouth, pushing against his lips until they bled and he was forced to open them. Suddenly, the lip of the jug was hovering over him. His whole body convulsed with shock as a stream of water gushed into the bowl of the funnel. It flooded his mouth and poured down his throat, giving him no chance to swallow. More and more came, making him choke and retch, until it felt as though they were emptying a river into him. He couldn't breathe. He was drowning. This was it. He was dying and all the while Nogaret's voice grated in his ears.

'Where is the treasury? *Where?*'

The Louvre, Paris, 24 December 1307 AD

Will came to with a jolt as his cell door banged open. He tried to push himself up, but his body was weak with hunger and exhaustion, and before he could move, three guards were dragging him to his feet. One held a rough woollen tunic that was forced over his head and pulled down to cover his scarred body. Their hands felt like claws on his skin. He hadn't seen anyone in weeks and the shock of contact was painfully invasive. As they took him out, his dread swelled. They had gone far last time, using their instruments on the softest, most vulnerable parts of him, causing him to black out with agony. Now perhaps they would go further and he might not walk away from what they did.

Loud in his mind came Nogaret's voice, cruel and taunting, telling him how one knight, whose feet had been rubbed with fat and placed before a coal fire, was given the bones that dropped out of his feet in a bag to take back to his cell. Will's feverish thoughts had been filled with images of men, mutilated and limbless, crawling and whimpering in cells like his all across France. Nogaret had told him more than fifteen thousand members of the Order had been rounded up. Like many of them, Will had confessed to everything the king's minister wanted to hear, in an effort to end the pain of torture. During the session the inquisitors would put the words into his mouth and he would simply be required to agree, as they held him down and poured molten wax over him, or ran the flame of a candle up his bare thighs until he could smell his own flesh burning. The worst had been the rack, the ropes around his wrists and ankles attached to the windlass, which one inquisitor would turn, grunting with effort, until each limb was twisted to the point of snapping.

But even through the worst of it, part of him remained aware that these men needed to keep him alive. Nogaret believed he knew where the treasury was and as long as the minister kept believing that his life would not be put in danger. On the rack, Will told the minister the treasury had been taken to Cyprus, but shortly after, when asked to repeat the confession, he said Portugal. Nogaret was left not knowing which confession was false and which true. This frustrated the minister beyond belief and allowed Will one small victory in the midst of his torments.

Will now felt his dread fade into confusion as the guards escorted him up a set of steps. This wasn't the way to the torture chamber. After several turns through windowless halls, the soldiers approached a set of heavy doors. When they were opened, Will sucked in a breath as he was hauled out into daylight. It was early morning and bitterly cold, but he savoured its purity. Hearing voices and the clop of hooves, he looked around, feeling more awake and alert than he had in weeks. There were more soldiers out here and four wagons. Will spotted Nogaret and Guillaume de Paris. The minister looked tense and irritable. As his gaze moved over the crowd Will saw other shabby men wearing tunics like his, in between the guards. He recognised Jacques de Molay and Geoffroi de Charney. The Grand Master looked terribly frail and was being supported by two soldiers. He had lost a shocking amount of weight and his beard had been crudely hacked away. Will glimpsed men inside the wagons as he was forced up into one nearest to him. A handful of other prisoners, whom he didn't recognise, were compelled inside and after four soldiers climbed in behind, there was a crack from a whip and the wagons lumbered out of the yard.

Will caught the eyes of a couple of fellow prisoners, but no one spoke. They were all too aware of the royal soldiers sitting there, swords in hands. Trying to guess where they were being taken, he sat back as they passed out of the royal fortress. Once out of the yard, he could smell the river and hear the dawn chorus of birds in the trees along the banks. The air smelled of damp grass and smoke, and had never seemed so sweet. The wagon slowed briefly, then passed through a gate into the city proper. Will's apprehension built when they crossed the Grand Pont on to the Ile de la Cité, but rather than heading towards the palace, the wagon turned down one of the streets that led to Notre Dame.

In the little square outside the cathedral, Will and the others were ushered out by the soldiers. One man stumbled as he jumped down. Will grabbed him to keep him from falling, but no sooner had he grasped the man's arm than the guards were coming at them, shouting at them to keep apart. As Will pulled back, he collided with another prisoner. Recovering his balance, he found himself face to face with Hugues de Pairaud. The Visitor's face was ashen and gaunt, his hair and beard matted with blood, his lips blistered.

'I am sorry,' he breathed hoarsely at Will, as one of the guards pushed him forward. 'I'm sorry.'

Will stared after him as they were escorted up the steps into the dark maw of the cathedral. He smelled incense and heard the chanting voices of the canons singing the morning office as they were led into the Chapter House.

On a dais were three men in black and crimson robes, gold crosses, crusted with jewels, around their necks. As Will saw them, hope broke through his tension. By the resentment on Nogaret's face, he guessed the three cardinals of the Sacred College weren't here at the king's bidding. Perhaps the pope had finally intervened? He was jostled as the soldiers lined him and the others up in the centre of the room. The guards moved back, leaving the twenty-four emaciated knights standing alone before the judging stares of the cardinals.

After a moment, the one in the centre, an old, venerable-looking man, rose. He held a roll of parchment. 'We have been appointed by his holiness, Pope Clement V, to hear the case against the Order of the Temple.' The cardinal's voice strengthened. 'His holiness was most disturbed, as were we all, to learn that each of you has confessed to the appalling crimes with which you have been charged. With great sorrow, he appointed us with the grave task of judging those confessions that we might come to understand how such an ancient and respected Order could have fallen so far from the grace of the Lord.' He cleared his throat. 'Jacques de Molay, you will step forward while the charges against you and your men are delivered.'

There was a pause. Then, slowly, deliberately, the Grand Master moved. He walked awkwardly, with a limp that caused his face to crease with pain, but kept his head high.

The knights listened in silence to the one hundred and twenty-seven charges laid against them. On each, Will could discern Nogaret's hand. Indeed, the minister looked almost proud as they were uttered in the quavering voice of the old cardinal. The knights were accused of urinating and trampling on the cross at their inceptions, of adoring a cat and a three-headed idol, of keeping charitable donations for themselves and holding chapters in secret. Even through his anger and disbelief, Will understood the skill in Nogaret's lengthy indictment. He recognised charges that had been levelled at the Cathars, Jews and Saracens, all enemies of the Church; charges the public could easily understand, and fear. Some of the accusations were even true: the knights did hold their chapters in secret and only allowed professed members to read the Rule, something the Teutonics and Hospitallers would recognise. This lent a particularly damning element to the allegations. A lie was easier to swallow if coated in truth and Nogaret had artfully distorted the daily practices of the Order, many of which were well known, to fit the trial, rendering them suddenly suspicious.

Throughout the fifteen or so minutes it took the cardinal to read through the offensive list written on that scroll, Jacques de Molay kept his head raised. Hugues de Pairaud, by contrast, stared at the floor, his hands shaking at his sides. One knight collapsed, either from exhaustion or shock, and was left on the floor.

When he was finished, the cardinal looked up, his gaze on Jacques. 'You have confessed before the inquisitor, Guillaume de Paris, to all of these crimes. Do you maintain this declaration of guilt now, here before us?'

For a moment, Jacques said nothing. Then he lifted his hands and gripped the collar of his threadbare tunic. There was a tearing sound as he pulled, ripping the material apart with a grimace of effort, until he was standing bare-chested before the three papal commissioners. His back, arms and chest were criss-crossed with deep gashes, each one blackened and blistered. The inquisitors had gone to work on the Grand Master with pincers, designed to tear the flesh from the victim, but heated until red-hot, so as to cauterise the wounds as soon as they were made, thus preventing the forbidden spilling of blood. Some of the slashes glistened, still weeping, and Will couldn't imagine the pain the Grand Master must be in, even now, days after the injuries had been inflicted.

The cardinal's face paled. He raised a hand as if to cover his eyes, then dropped it and instead looked away. One of the two who had remained seated sat back, looking sickened. The other stared, appalled.

'I did confess,' said Jacques, his voice gruff, 'but I am only guilty of weakness. Like our saviour, in the moment when strength failed Him and He asked for His burden to be taken from Him, I gave in to my frailty. I told my torturers what they wanted to hear in order to end my suffering. But now let me make it right. Let me do what I should have done then and retract that confession, made in the confusion of agony.'

Nogaret's face was rigid. 'Your grace—'

The cardinal didn't let him finish. 'Minister de Nogaret, his holiness wants a clear and unequivocal admission of guilt before he agrees to the king's demands that the Order be dissolved.' He stepped down from the dais and crossed the hall. 'This' – he gestured at Jacques, looking horrified – 'cannot count.'

'The inquisitors are licensed, by the papacy, to use torture to extract an admission of guilt. Your grace, every one of these men has confessed!'

'And if we remove the clothes of each what will we find? I am sorry, Minister. I must inform his holiness that the confessions of these men cannot be judged with any accuracy, being made under such extreme duress.'

41

Franciscan Priory, Poitiers

26 May 1308 AD

℔

'Get out of my way.'
'My lord,' protested the friar, planting himself in front of the door, 'his holiness is not ready. Please. If you wait but a moment longer, he—'

'Move! Or I will have my guards arrest you for obstructing your king.'

The friar hesitated, looking distressed, but when two royal soldiers came forward at Philippe's command, he stepped reluctantly aside. Pushing past, the king forced open the door and strode inside.

As he slammed it shut, the figure in the room started. 'My lord Philippe,' murmured Clement. He was in the process of pulling on a crimson robe and struggled the rest of the way into it. 'What is the meaning of this? I was told you were waiting in the Chapter House.'

'I got tired of waiting,' responded the king, his blue eyes fierce. He stood head and shoulders above the pope, who seemed to have shrunk in the past year, his body curling in on itself, hunching over the pain that was said to plague him constantly these days. Philippe felt no sympathy. He had no desire to be here, having made the journey from Paris in record time, punishing both horses and men. His patience, worn down by the events of the past seven months, was thinning rapidly.

Philippe's action against the Templars had begun well, indeed far better than he could have hoped after Rose's theft of the scroll. True, the contents of the Paris coffers were still missing, but he had many hundreds of Temple properties in his possession despite this and Nogaret remained convinced that some knights, Campbell included, knew where the treasury was hidden. Jacques de Molay had confessed to the charges against him in a matter of days, the inquisitors surpassing their reputations, and after his declaration of guilt was made public the defence of the other knights quickly crumbled. As they yielded, one by one, to the

inquisitors' examinations, public and political backing for a full trial
against the Order grew. Clement had sent an incensed letter after the
initial arrests, demanding to know what he was doing, but Philippe,
secure in the knowledge that his subjects would support him, didn't even
respond. It was shortly after this that the three cardinals had arrived in
Paris, insisting on hearing the knights' statements.

When the cardinals took their report to the pope, Clement suspended
the work of inquisitors in France and, without his interrogators, Philippe
was forced to halt the proceedings. Attempting to counter the action,
confident of his own authority, the king summoned Masters of theology
from the University of Paris to pass their judgement upon the trial, but the
verdict, announced earlier that month, was not to his liking. A king, the
doctors had concluded, could only take action in matters of heresy at the
express wish of the pope. Which was why Philippe was here now, standing
before the belligerent Vicar of Christ, his blood boiling. 'I have had enough.
This ends, today!'

Clement shook his head. 'I do not know what you are talking about.'

Philippe bit back an overwhelming desire to unleash his sword and strike
down the bent little man where he stood. 'The Templars! I will not let you
get in the way of my intentions for them.'

'Your intentions?' The pope fastened the robe at his throat. 'Does that
not depend on their guilt?'

'Do not play with me, Clement,' warned the king. 'Do not forget it was
I who put you on the papal throne. I can just as easily remove you!'

Clement stared at Philippe. 'How? When the office of pope is one
elected for life?'

Philippe looked away, discomforted by the pope's scrutiny and feeling he
had said something he shouldn't have. Was Clement seeing through him,
right to the heart of his sins? Were the ghosts of his predecessors whispering
to him, pointing their fingers at the man responsible for their downfalls?
'We had an agreement, you and I. You signed a document, consenting to
five obligations, one of which was to dissolve the Temple and transfer their
wealth to me and my heirs.'

'That agreement, like the confessions of the knights, was made under
coercion. I signed it to save the life of my son, as we both know. So unless
you mean to have me killed like Boniface and Benedict, how exactly do you
propose to remove me from this holy office, my lord?'

Philippe's fear swelled at the accusation, but he forced himself to look
upon the pope's face, lean and withered by illness. 'Their deaths had

nothing to do with me. I am guilty only of attempting to arrest a heretic and blasphemer.'

'I fear for you, my lord.'

'I have expanded the territory and power of my kingdom, stood firm in the face of my enemies, but rewarded those loyal to me and to France. I am a good Christian king, Clement. You need not fear for me.'

'You have done nothing for your people and everything for yourself. You have taken them to war, yes, but against other Christian nations, not against the heathen in Palestine. You have misused your sacred office, putting men of evil character in positions of great power and have blighted the Church with vicious attacks against persons and property. You have devalued coinage, causing poverty and unrest, and moved deceitfully against the very men who have been fighting for Christendom across the seas. A good king, my lord?' Clement's voice hardened. 'Your grandfather, St Louis, was that. He took the Cross for the liberation of Jerusalem and led two Crusades. If not for the ambitions of his brother, I believe he would have succeeded, so great a man was he, fearless and gallant, devout and humble. You wield his memory like a sword, but that weapon is blunt in your hands. You are nothing like him, Philippe. All you share is blood.'

Philippe felt the words crushing him with the weight of truth. He moved away, his lips pulling back in a grimace of hatred, then turned back. 'I never went against the Temple deceitfully. You heard Esquin de Floyran's testimony. Heresy! That was his claim, not mine. No matter what you think of me, you cannot stop what I have begun, only hinder it. The people are demanding a trial.'

Clement spoke after a pause, clasping his hands behind his back. 'You are right. This process has gone too far to be halted. There will always be suspicion of the Templars now, even if they are given back their command. I cannot fail to see that. The people want to know if there has been heresy committed. They need answers and reassurance that their spiritual and temporal leaders are doing what is necessary to safeguard their kingdom from wickedness.' He nodded slowly, as if deciding something. 'The trial against the Templars will continue, but I will establish a council of commissioners to oversee it and make sure it is done properly. If enough evidence of heresy within the Order is found, I will dissolve the Temple.'

Philippe was staring at the pope, confounded by his change of attitude. 'And their wealth?' he ventured, trying to keep his voice steady.

Clement met the king's hopeful gaze. 'It will be transferred to you.' As Philippe let out a sharp breath, the pope lifted his hand, his face sober. 'On one condition.'

'Name it.'

'That you take the Cross and lead a new Crusade.'

42

The Louvre, Paris

8 September 1308 AD

W ill scrabbled back against the wall, throwing his arms up over his face as four men entered his cell. The light from their torches seared him and he cried out when two of them grabbed him. He was so thin they almost lifted him off the ground as they pulled him to his feet.

'I don't know where it is,' he rasped, as they forced him down the passage. 'I don't!' Will twisted against them, shouting the words over and over, but the guards barely broke their stride.

They came to a set of doors and dragged him through, into a dim-lit chamber. There was a desk in the centre with two men in official-looking black robes seated behind it. One had a quill in his hand, poised over a parchment. The guards stepped back, leaving Will alone in front of them. His support gone, he staggered, almost fell, then managed to steady himself and stood there swaying, but upright. Raising a shaking hand, he adjusted the filthy strip of cloth covering his right eye, loosened in the march from the cell.

'William Campbell?' enquired one of the seated men, in an arid tone.

Will looked round at the guards, standing behind him to either side of the door, then nodded to the official who had spoken.

'Please answer out loud.'

Will cleared his throat. 'Yes,' he said, swallowing painfully against his parched throat.

'The Knights of the Temple continue to protest their innocence, refuting the crimes they have been accused of. According to the papal commission established by his holiness Pope Clement, they have a right to defend themselves. Two members of the Order have been appointed lawyers for the trial and many brothers have pledged to support them in a public hearing. Would you be willing to stand before a tribunal and attest to your innocence?'

'I would,' said Will, his thoughts, until now suffocated with dread, beginning to clear. 'I would be willing.'

'You are certain?'

'Yes.'

The official scratched something on the parchment, then nodded to the guards.

Will felt his arms gripped. 'When will this happen?' he croaked, as the guards escorted him from the room. '*When?*'

But they didn't answer.

Back in his cell, Will slumped against the damp wall and slid down it, his gaze on the door. It was pitted with scars where he had banged and kicked and scratched at it, crazed with thirst, hunger, or pain.

It was almost a year since the arrests had begun, almost a year since they locked him in this hole. In that time they had tortured him beyond what he thought was possible for human endurance, taking him to the brink of madness. There were moments when he had prayed to God to end his suffering, to make his interrogators go too far. But the inquisitors always seemed to know the limits the body could take before it would give in to death and he lived through everything they did to him, the starvation and isolation, the threats and honeyed promises, the rack and the fire. He even survived the removal of his right eye, the inquisitors pinning him down and prising apart his eyelids, that blade coming towards him, closer and closer, until he was screaming and the metal was digging inside.

Some time ago, when the torture ceased for several months, he learned, listening to scraps of conversation from his guards, that the pope had intervened. His hopes lifted for a brief period, then faded when it became clear Clement had simply manoeuvred himself into a position of power within the proceedings, establishing a papal commission to oversee the interrogations, rather than halting them. The torture began again, albeit less aggressively whenever a cardinal was present, and Will's despair became complete when Nogaret told him the pope had sent letters to all the kings of the West, ordering the Templars in their territories be arrested, their property seized. He tried to convince himself the minister was lying; he had never told Nogaret where the Paris treasury had been taken and knew the lawyer was maddened by the fact he couldn't break him, but inside he had known the truth: Clement had abandoned them.

Until now.

Will tried to force his sluggish mind to think through what the proposed trial might mean. If the knights defended themselves publicly, the king and his men wouldn't be able to hide the fact that their confessions had been extracted with appalling force. Their plight had provoked the shock and sympathy of the cardinals. Might it do the same for others?

His thoughts were interrupted by the sound of footsteps approaching. He tensed, his heart pounding as torchlight flared around the edges of the door. The bolt clacked back. Between the cover of his fingers, Will picked out the faces of three or four guards, then someone was ducking inside his cell, torch thrust before him. It was Nogaret.

There was something greedy in the minister's thin face as he looked down at Will. 'I am glad to hear you are willing to defend the Order, Campbell. It means I can take one last thing from you.' Nogaret's expression shifted at Will's incomprehension, his eyes filling with rancour. 'Did you really believe I would give you the chance to defend yourself? You or the others?'

'Then it was a lie?' Will slumped back against the wall. 'Those men? What they said? Just lies?'

'On the contrary, it was true. Clement, fool that he is, is attempting to offer you the opportunity of a fair trial. He wants to be seen to be doing this properly, wants to be seen as the one in control, when he is just a puppet! He always has been.'

Will turned his head away, closing his eye to block out the sight of the minister's vengeful face. 'Why do you hate us?'

Nogaret appeared surprised by the question. 'I do not hate you, Campbell. You aren't important enough for me to waste such emotion on.'

'Clement then? Boniface? Benedict? What drove you to commit your crimes against them?'

Nogaret quickly pushed the cell door shut, blocking out the sight of the guards lingering in the passage. 'You should stop your tongue from flapping, unless you want it removed.'

'It is no secret, what you did.'

'And yet no one has ever convicted me.'

'Perhaps they won't in this life. But in the next —'

'Next?' Nogaret gave a bark of laughter. 'You have to believe in the next life to fear it.' His eyes narrowed and he crouched in front of Will, the torch flaring between them. 'You still believe though, don't you? Even now, you imagine God is up there looking down on you, loving or judging?' His voice dropped. 'My father and mother believed. Only they were

Cathars, not Christians. By the time I was born, the Church's Crusade against their sect had ended. The Cathar stronghold of Montségur had fallen, almost twenty years earlier, and their last resistance faltered soon after. My parents escaped the burnings and settled, like many others of their kind, in an anonymous town in the south of France. They pretended to be Christian, celebrated the festivals, went to Mass each week. But at night they would perform their heresies in secret. For years, I watched them lead these lives of deceit, terrified of being discovered, yet unwilling to give up their beliefs. I played the dutiful son and followed my father's example, but I never believed. I found their fearful rituals embarrassing.' Nogaret's mouth curled in contempt. 'All of us cramped together in a store-hold, my sister cupping her hand around a candle, my father whispering and sweating.

'I left when I could and went to university in Montpellier. I studied law, Roman and canon, and in doing so the secrets of faith were laid bare for me, rendered transparent. I could see how the Church manipulated and controlled, how its leaders benefited from the gullibility of its flock. My eyes were opened and I understood how I too, a man not of the cloth, but of the world, could use the law to get what I wanted, how state could become more powerful than Church. I was passionate, filled with knowledge. I made the mistake of trying to make my father understand; of trying to convince him he no longer needed these inane rituals. We argued and he cut me out of the family. Despite his past, he was respected in his community and he made his displeasure known by having me removed from an important teaching post I had been installed in at Montpellier.

'I did the only thing I could to discredit him and informed the Dominican college of his continuing adherence to the Cathar faith.' Nogaret paused, his expression distant. 'I wanted him to see that I was right, that the law was more powerful than any God. I imagined he would refute his beliefs, him and my mother, thought they would confess and beg to be pardoned. I wanted them humbled and humiliated, their absurd faith stripped from them.' His gaze focused on Will. 'Both of them refused to denounce themselves despite the tortures the inquisitors wrought upon them. They went to the pyres set for them along with my sister almost proudly. When the soldiers were lighting the faggots under them they began reciting the very prayers they forced me to say in that dark little store-hold, for all the crowd to hear.'

'So you wanted revenge against the Church?'

'Proof,' said Nogaret sharply. 'I wanted proof. Only man can condemn man. The Church proved that when they murdered my family. I proved it when I killed Boniface and Benedict.' He rose abruptly. 'And I'll prove it again when I bring down the warriors of Christ.' Turning, he thrust open the door. 'Bring him,' he commanded the guards.

As Nogaret strode ahead, the guards led Will behind him through the fortress, until they came to the main yard outside. There was a wagon and more than two dozen mounted soldiers in royal livery. It was night, the purple sky peppered with stars. Urged into the wagon by the guards, Will saw five pale faces turn to him in the gloom. Knights, he guessed, as the company began to move out.

It quickly became clear that they weren't heading into the city when the wagon turned north along a rough road that wound for several miles through starlit fields. Will and the other prisoners didn't speak or look at one another. He supposed they, like him, feared this was a final journey. In the silence, each man prepared himself, heads bowed in prayer or thought. Will centred on his father. He wondered what James had felt walking to his place of execution outside the Templar fortress of Safed, the parched ground dusty and hot beneath his feet. Will liked to think he was calm and walked with his head high, the Mamluk swords at his back not needing to force him on.

The wagon jolted off the track and into a field, where it rolled to a stop. The royal guards ordered the knights out and they jumped down awkwardly, one by one, into the long grass. In the distance, Will made out the walls of Paris, a paler shade against the backdrop of night. Closer, a line of oaks rustled in the breeze, boughs creaking. Around fifteen of the soldiers had remained mounted and were pressing out in a circle, their horses jostling and snorting. All had swords drawn and shields raised. What struck Will as strange was that they weren't facing their captives, but outwards into the darkness. Before he could guess why, he heard a fearful murmur and saw one of the knights staring at something obscured behind the wagon. Will took a few steps and realised what had captivated the man's attention. On the crest of a small hill, a short distance away, three shapes rose against the night sky, barbed and menacing. They were pyres, a stout central pole thrusting like a finger out of a bristling mass of twigs, branches and straw. Another of the knights, seeing them, crossed himself and began to pray.

'Secure the prisoners!' ordered Nogaret. 'Quickly. Two per stake.'

The silent calm the knights had displayed inside the wagon vanished. They began to struggle, but after a year in prison they were little match for the guards, who dragged them mercilessly up the hill towards the pyres.

'Why go to all this trouble?' demanded Will, when Nogaret moved in to help the soldier who had seized him. 'Why not just kill us in our cells?'

'Fool!' panted Nogaret, as Will fought him. 'Clement would never give us what we want if we murdered you in cold blood.' The minister staggered back, leaving the soldier to punch Will viciously in the side until he dropped to the ground. 'But Guillaume de Paris has, under Philippe's insistence, proclaimed all those who are willing to defend themselves as relapsed heretics. The law states that those who have recanted their confessions, who are deemed to be unrepentant heretics for whom there can be no salvation, can be transferred to secular authority for execution by fire.'

Will hung weakly on his knees, hands digging in the damp soil. Around him, the shouts of the knights were punctuated by the neighing of horses. Above him, Nogaret's voice continued, harsh and cruel.

'The king wants the Temple dissolved quickly. He doesn't want a public trial. This way, we get rid of those knights who are willing to testify, but we do it all within the confines of the law. Clement can do nothing!'

Will's fingers brushed against something hard, embedded in the soil.

'When your brothers learn what happens to those who retract their confessions, their feeble defence will crumble and my lord will have his prize.' Nogaret loomed over him. 'By the way, Campbell, one of the knights gave in to my questioning last week. A man named Laurent. He told me the Temple's treasury is in Scotland.'

Will felt over the object: a long, thin shaft that ended in a steel point. It was an arrow. For a moment he was astonished, wondering how it had got there. But his questions soon dissolved, overwhelmed by the feeling that the world and God were moving in perfect unison. That the arrow was meant to be here and he was meant to find it.

'Twenty knights took it, Laurent told me, along with a pregnant woman. That was Rose, wasn't it? When I find the treasury, I'll find her.'

Gathering the last of his strength, Will wrapped his fingers around the shaft. He had no illusion that he could make it from this field alive, but at least he could take Nogaret with him. This was how it would end. This was how it was supposed to end. Pushing himself to his feet, he lunged at the minister. Before he could strike, the night was filled with the screams of horses and men.

At once, everything was thrown into confusion. Will whipped round, hearing someone utter a rallying cry. A group of royal guards was riding towards the line of oaks. He saw motion in the undergrowth, black shapes rising, then two of the soldiers' mounts reared up and crashed to the ground, crushing their riders beneath them. There were more cries and flashes of steel. Will turned to where Nogaret had been standing a second before and saw the minister fleeing for the cover of the wagon.

'Guards!' he was shouting. 'I want them captured!'

The few soldiers who had dismounted were running to their horses. One man dug his foot in the stirrup and grabbed the saddle, but before he could haul himself up, something punched into his back and he arched backwards, his foot catching in the stirrup. His horse bolted, dragging him away across the field, scattering the soldiers in its path. Another man went down, dropping a torch, which blew flames across the ground.

'Just kill the prisoners, damn you!' Nogaret was yelling to the remaining soldiers who weren't yet in the fight. 'Kill them!'

Will saw one knight go down, stabbed by the soldier who had been hauling him towards the pyres. Then another. The other knights began to fight with renewed vigour. Hearing a rasp of steel behind him, Will jerked round to see a royal guard swinging back his sword to strike. An arrow came hurtling out of the night and plunged into the man's throat. He let his sword drop and fell back. Feeling light-headed with the exertion, Will snatched up the fallen blade, but before he could go after Nogaret, a figure came racing out of the darkness towards him.

It was a tall man with a flop of sandy-blond hair and a strong-boned face. He held a bow. Will stared at him, shock making his hand fall to his side, the sword tip striking the ground. Ten years had passed since he had seen that face. 'David?'

'Retreat!' one of the soldiers was crying out. 'Retreat!'

Nogaret was yelling hoarsely, ordering the guards back into the fray, commanding them to seize the attackers, but the night was filled with arrows and all the soldiers could do was raise their shields, wheel their horses around and ride back out of range. Another man went down, his horse tumbling over, caught in the rump by two arrows. Within moments, the rest were thundering from the field, abandoning the wagon and their prisoners.

Will, still staring at his nephew in amazement, hardly saw them go. As the young man embraced him fiercely, he felt himself flooded with relief.

'Are you hurt?' questioned David, stepping back and studying him in the agitated light of the torch still flaming on the ground. His brow creased as he saw the bloody rag covering Will's right eye. 'What did they do to you?'

Will checked his hand as he went to finger the bandage. He didn't like to touch it. Gazing around him, he saw other figures appearing out of the shadows of the tree line. They fanned out, examining the soldiers and helping the three surviving knights. One crossed swiftly to him and David.

'Is it him?' came an urgent voice.

The voice belonged to Robert. With him were six of the knights who had taken the treasury to Scotland. It took Will a moment to recognise them as none was wearing their Templar uniforms. Robert halted as he spied Will. 'Christ.'

Will took hold of his arm. 'Robert, why are you here? Why is David?' He shook his head. 'How?'

'We don't have time to explain, Will.'

Will didn't relinquish his grip. 'Make time,' he said, his tone implacable.

Robert hesitated, then nodded to the knights. 'Secure the area. I want to know those soldiers aren't going to return in a hurry. They were ready for us this time.' He turned to Will as the men moved off, bows primed. 'After leaving France we put in around the coast from Aberdeen. While the rest of the men stayed on board with the treasury, I went with Simon to escort Rose to your family in Elgin. It proved to be the best thing we could have done.' His gaze flicked to David. 'Your nephew was invaluable in establishing a safe haven for us.'

Will stared at David, struck with pride.

'We stayed in Elgin for a long time, waiting for you,' Robert continued. 'But when you didn't arrive we feared the worst. In the summer, word reached us that a trial against the Temple had begun in Paris. We came to see if we could aid our brothers in their defence.'

'Philippe is sabotaging it. He'll do anything to prevent the pope from interfering with his plans. If you are caught you'll be imprisoned, most likely executed.'

'We know,' said Robert grimly. 'But we don't intend to linger long enough. Tonight was to be our last attack.'

'Nogaret's done this before?' asked Will.

'Several times as far as we know. We were hiding in the city, trying to get information on who was imprisoned where and—'

'And hoping we could find you,' interjected David. 'But no one knew anything. We'd given up finding you alive until I saw you being led out of that wagon.'

'We discovered the royal guards were taking prisoners out at night to burn them,' Robert went on. 'We managed to intervene in one of these burnings and saved six men, but lost two of our own in the process.'

Will nodded slowly, the cause of the guards' tension now clear and the arrow's appearance not quite as miraculous as he'd imagined. He thought back over Nogaret's reaction and the readiness of the guards. 'My guess is he hoped to catch you if you tried again. He has been instrumental in tracking down Templars who escaped the arrests. He doesn't want anyone left to defend the Order. He wants—' Will stopped short, remembering the minister's final words, then started across the field to where Robert's men were making sure the soldiers were all dead. He checked the faces of the dead men, going between the bodies, Robert and David following. 'He must have been carried away by one of the soldiers,' said Will, rising quickly. He staggered and almost fell, before Robert steadied him. 'We need to find him.'

'No. We need to get you out of here,' replied Robert, gesturing to one of the men, who hastened over. 'Help him into the wagon.'

'He knows about the treasury, Robert. He knows it's in Scotland. He knows Rose is there.'

'He'll never find it, or her. I promise.'

Will was shaking his head. 'He knows my sisters live in Elgin. He knows where to look!'

Robert grasped his shoulders. 'They don't. Not any more. Will, please. We've got a ship waiting downriver. But we need to go!'

'Clement,' said Will. 'He might still help us.'

'I do not think so. While we were here we learned the pope has issued a bull, outlining plans for a holy war. It is rumoured Philippe will take the Cross for him. I suspect they have done a deal: the Temple in return for a new Crusade.'

Will was silent. 'Nogaret confessed to me in my cell,' he said finally. 'He admitted he killed Pope Benedict. Perhaps if Clement knew this it might convince him to end his alliance with the king.' He stared at Robert. 'It is worth a try, isn't it?'

After a long pause, Robert nodded. 'All right. I will make sure word is sent to Clement before we leave. After that, it is up to him. We can do nothing more.'

With David walking at his other side, Will limped across the grass towards the wagon, leaving the pyres unlit behind him.

Franciscan Priory, Poitiers, 24 November 1308 AD

Clement stood in the window, staring out over the moon-bathed cloisters. Behind him, his chamber lay in shadow. Earlier, a servant had offered to bank up the fire and light some candles, but the pope had declined the offer. It seemed somehow appropriate to remain in darkness this evening. In his hand was a piece of parchment, limp and crumpled. He glanced at the words, but his eyesight was poor these days and, anyway, it was too dark to see by. Still, he knew what it said.

There was a knock.

Placing the parchment on the window seat, the pope turned to face the door, feeling acid bubble in his stomach. 'Come in.'

When the door opened two figures entered. The first wore a grey hooded robe. He bowed low. 'Your holiness, your guest has arrived.'

Clement inclined his head. 'Thank you, Renaud. You may leave us.' As the monk backed out of the chamber, closing the door, the second figure remained in the shadows. He was tall and broad, that much Clement could discern from his outline. The pope cleared his throat. 'I take it your journey was without incident?'

'Your holiness, it is late and I have travelled far. Let us dispense with unnecessary pleasantries. Tell me why you have summoned me here.' The native accent behind his French was thick.

Clement nodded, but it was some moments before he could decide how to begin. 'Your family has not been treated well by the Church. My predecessor, Pope Boniface, was responsible for your downfall and you have suffered great loses, in terms of persons and property.'

'I do not need a history lesson. I am well aware of the hardships my people have faced.'

'Pope Benedict refused to lift the order of excommunication placed on you by Boniface. You have been a fugitive in France ever since, unable to return to your country or rebuild your life.' Clement paused. 'I can lift that order.'

The man's voice came to him, gruff with suspicion. 'Why would you do this?'

'I would consider it payment for services rendered.' Clement looked down at his hands, feeling his stomach churn.

The tall figure came forward, closer to the window. 'What services?'

Clement glanced at the crumpled parchment lifting slightly in the chill draught coming through the windows. He raised his head. 'That you end the life of the king's minister, Guillaume de Nogaret, for his part in the deaths of popes Boniface and Benedict.'

The figure said nothing. Clement just heard his breaths. 'Well?' he pressed, discomforted by the heavy silence. 'Is this something you would be willing to do?'

Finally the man stepped out of the shadows. Sciarra Colonna's black eyes glittered in the moonlight.

43

Argyll, the Kingdom of Scotland

20 December 1308 AD

♉

The horses hung their heads and ploughed on, threading their way beneath the dank canopy of trees, hooves splintering through frozen puddles. The sleet wind that had driven at their backs for most of the morning was easing and the company could now hear the distant drag and roar of waves ahead. The dark towers of the mountains that had been their marker for five days were hazy shapes far to the north, ringed with vaporous clouds. The largest peak, Ben Cruachan, squatted like a granite giant over the northern shores of Loch Awe. It was barely mid-afternoon and already evening was drawing in, spinning webs of shadow around them. The loch, which had turned from deep jade to glassy black, was still visible some miles behind them as the track climbed torturously towards the coast.

Will, slumped in his saddle and wrapped in a soggy, fur-trimmed cloak, had forgotten how short the winter days were this far north. On the sea-bitten west coast, they seemed shorter still. This wasn't a Scotland he knew. This wild kingdom of mountains and water was the realm of his forefathers. His grandfather, Angus Campbell, struck out from these lands and made a life for himself in the tame and fertile east, leaving four generations of Campbells to make their mark. Now a large and powerful family, with many different branches, some of which were highly favoured by King Robert, they owned a number of prominent castles in Argyll. Passing them on their journey south, his nephew recounting the history of each fortress and the names of the current lords, Will had begun to feel a strange sense of nostalgia. This was a place of kinship, of loyalties and family. The hostility of the landscape nurtured these things, binding people together in safety and shelter. It was a place where memories were honoured and blood ran deep. But the price for those bonds was its isolation. The way here was not an easy one, especially in winter, and for

Will, suffering a year of starvation and torture, it was the hardest journey of his life.

They had left the coast of France in September, Robert's company conveying Will and the thirteen knights they had saved from Nogaret's pyres to London, where two Templars were waiting with horses and supplies. Edward II had been slow to react to Pope Clement's letter insisting he arrest the Templars in his lands, but after growing pressure from the papacy and Philippe, he finally agreed to allow the inquisitors into his kingdom. The trial against the English Templars was well under way by the time the company docked in the Thames and it was with the sense of the hunted that they made their way north, plagued by snow on the hills and wolves in the forests. Once over the border, the terrain became ever more hazardous and they lost two men during one especially frozen night, but despite these physical hardships, Will found himself secretly eased by Scotland's impassibility. With every boggy valley they wound their way through, every grey skirt of mountain they inched themselves around, every sea loch that yawed around the next corner, he felt his enemies receding. It could take Nogaret a lifetime to find them here.

'We should be there soon.'

Will glanced round as his nephew manoeuvred his horse up alongside him, his face in the failing light ruddy with cold.

David smiled slightly. 'You look nervous, uncle.'

'I'm just weary,' responded Will gruffly, discomfited by his nephew's shrewdness. It was true. He was nervous. There were so many things that awaited him at the end of this unfamiliar track, the booming sea growing ever louder, so many hopes, any one of which could be fulfilled or dashed. He looked over his shoulder at the long line of travel-worn men stretching behind. 'I pray your mother has a pot big enough. There are a lot of hungry mouths to feed. Her husband's estate cannot house us all, surely?'

'Not indefinitely, no, but as I told you we'll find homes for the knights soon enough. I could use a few able men in Elgin and the King would gladly recruit more loyal warriors into his service, I'm certain. He has already accepted into his retinue seven Templars who arrived with Robert last year.'

Will saw a familiar look in David's face. It was a look of fierce pride that came over him whenever he was talking about Scotland's new king. On the journey north, he had heard David tell many stories of Bruce and his band of men, from his battles against Edward's forces to his ambitious campaign to unite all of Scotland beneath him, quelling the rivals who challenged his claim to the throne. The English might have gone, for now, but the scars of more than a decade of war remained, seeping unrest and the poison of family feuds that had welled up into civil war. Robert Bruce had been faced with a gruelling task, but from the respect the Scots in their company showed him, it seemed he was winning.

'But for now,' David continued, 'we'll be able to house most of them in this area. John is close with many families here.'

Will nodded, but said nothing. He was still getting used to all the changes that had taken place in his family and all the unexpected connections, not least the fact that seven men in this doughty company, who had risked their lives to free him, were kin.

At first, he had been scarcely aware of anything, hurt with exhaustion, too numb even to feel relief, but as his strength returned, his curiosity about his rescuers had been stirred. Other than Robert and the six former Templars, there were two spirited young men who were squires of David's, now the holder of a modest estate in Elgin, come to him through marriage. Will had listened in quiet amazement as his nephew, flushing with pleasure, spoke of his two children, who had stayed with their mother in Elgin, close to Margaret and her young family. Another marriage that had come as a surprise was that of his sister, Ysenda, to a widower named John Campbell, a well-respected knight from a minor branch of the vast family, who owned a large estate in Argyll. They met during King Robert's campaign in the north and wedded quickly, Ysenda moving south with him early in the summer. Two of John's youngest sons, rangy and chestnut-haired, were in Robert's company. But perhaps the greatest shock for Will was the introduction to his nephew, a man named Colin, who was only fifteen years younger than himself and a child of his elder sister, Ede. He had come with his three sons, all of them broad and black-haired, their faces holding echoes of James.

The emotion he felt, coming into this ancient land, surrounded by men of his blood, was overwhelming. He had spent most of the past twelve months thinking his life and everything in it was ended. To be here, now, knowing that in some ways it had only just begun, felt like a gift straight from God, but a fragile gift that he cradled warily, fearful of breaking it. David had told him he would be welcome, but he hadn't dared ask his nephew how he knew this and as they wound their way out of the trees and a wide dark sea filled the horizon, he felt doubts crowding in on him.

John Campbell's sons led the way confidently down the rocky cliff path, steering their horses expertly. The wind was raw and strong, snatching back their hoods and whipping tears from their eyes. Below, the sea crashed against the cliffs, spewing foam into the air. In the last of the light, Will could see a line of islands rising from the sea, some near, some distant, clouds rolling grey and low above them. Closer, just below in a sheltered cove with a natural harbour, was a little village. A dozen or more houses huddled around a chapel on a grassy bluff. He caught a whiff of smoke on the wind and heard the lowing of animals.

Skirting the village, John's sons urged their horses along a steep track that led halfway up the scrubby cliff to a much larger stone house, thatched with brown heather and ringed by a wall that enclosed several outbuildings, a barn, stables and a paddock. It reminded Will a little of his family's old estate. As they drew closer, he could see firelight winking in some of the windows. The front door flew open suddenly and a gaggle of children streamed forth, calling excitedly. John's sons cantered to meet them as a group of adults funnelled out behind the children. Their voices came to the men on the wind, sharp with joy. Will jumped down from his saddle as he saw one figure running towards him. It was Ysenda, her sandy hair streaked with silver, but her face flushed and youthful as she dashed across the scrubby grass to where he stood, rooted. Behind his sister, stepping from the doorway, one hand pushing back her red hair, was Christian, her eyes searching then fixing on him. There was Simon, his face, slackening with relief, now creasing in a broad grin. After Simon, came an old, white-haired woman who looked so much like his mother it pierced him. She was bent with age and obviously blind, being led out by a pretty young woman. That young woman, he realised with a jolt, was Alice, his niece. There were others he didn't recognise, calling to the men or hastening to take the reins of their horses. His eyes darted over their unfamiliar faces.

Then he saw her.

She was chasing a podgy toddling boy, who had teetered out behind the shouting children. As she scooped him up in her arms and planted a kiss on his pink cheek, Will noticed how full and healthy his daughter looked. He took all this in in a matter of seconds, then Ysenda was throwing her arms around him and grabbing at David, weeping and kissing them both. And all Will's fears fell from him.

Ile de la Cité, Paris, 21 December 1308 AD

Guillaume de Nogaret raised his hand to hide a yawn as he urged his horse across the Grand Pont, on to the island. It was late and the air was bitter, the cold seeping through his fur cloak, feeling its way into his bones. Frost dappled the riverbanks, sparkling in the silvery light of a pale half-moon. Behind Nogaret, two royal guards kept pace, nodding to the city watchmen on the bridge, who inclined their heads as the king's minister passed.

It had been another long day, his time divided between the preceptory and the Louvre, interrogating Templars. At least he had been rewarded with two deaths that evening. Some days, he would get nothing for his efforts, not even a confession, and his reports to Philippe were fraught affairs, the king increasingly aggravated by the protracted process, hindered further since the burnings had been forbidden.

After the attack in which Campbell escaped, Nogaret held two more executions, this time in the safety of the Louvre, but word somehow reached the pope that all knights who agreed to testify were being sent to the stake. When Clement threatened to suspend the work of the inquisitors if any more burnings took place without his authorisation, Philippe and Nogaret protested fiercely, saying they were acting within the law that stated unrepentant heretics could be burned if handed over by the Dominicans, but the belligerent pope remained unmoved and in the end they were obliged to continue with the slow process of torture.

Exasperatingly, it was usually the sergeants and servants who succumbed. Most of these men hadn't stood on a battlefield and had never even wielded a sword. They weren't trained for the sort of physical punishments and endurance that the knights were. Bewildered and frightened, many either very young or else frail and elderly, they were led into the torture chambers, where they were forced to accuse the professed knights of committing the crimes on Nogaret's list. Charged by association, these men faced lifelong imprisonment if they confessed, but more often than not they didn't make it out of the torture chamber alive. Neither they nor any of the knights who perished were allowed the last rites as they were dying, though all begged to be shriven. Instead, their corpses were dumped in unmarked graves on unconsecrated ground, a warning to those left not to resist the inquisitors' demands. In this way, the fifteen thousand men imprisoned across France were gradually whittled away, one month at a time. Unfortunately for the king, the ones left behind were Templar officials, commanders and battle-hardened knights, all of whom had repeatedly recanted the confessions they had offered up with their screams on the rack and the strappado.

Nogaret had tried everything his legal mind could conceive of to hasten the process whereby Clement would dissolve the Order and transfer the wealth to Philippe; such was the agreement the two men had come to. The trouble was the king was unwilling to take the Cross until Clement passed judgement upon the Temple and the pope was just as stubbornly insistent that the trial would be conducted fairly. Combined with this, the pope was often ill these days which created more lengthy delays. There was something of Nogaret's pride at stake in this now. Not only was the attack on the Temple his idea, but he had dedicated a great deal of time and effort to making it happen. Furthermore, he had been stung by Campbell's escape, which Philippe blamed him for, along with the fact that the treasury remained lost. He promised the king faithfully that when the pope dissolved the Temple he would personally lead a mission to Scotland to find the Paris treasury and destroy those knights who remained at large, along with Rose and her child. Philippe had sullenly agreed, clearly discomfited by the thought of his illegitimate son.

Nogaret was drawn from his thoughts by the sound of his name. At first, he assumed it was one of the royal guards, but as he glanced over his shoulder, he saw both of them had reined in their horses and were staring down one of the narrow side streets that tapered towards Notre Dame. He trotted back to them. 'What is it? Who called me?'

'It came from down there, Minister,' answered one, frowning into the gloom.

As Nogaret watched, he saw movement under the overhanging eaves of one of the buildings and a man came towards them.

'Who goes there?' called the guard, drawing his sword. 'State your business!'

Nogaret let a faint breath of surprise through his lips as the man came closer. 'Colonna,' he murmured, gesturing to the guard to lower his blade. 'This is unexpected. What brings you here?'

'I need to speak to you.'

Nogaret glanced at the palace towers rising ahead, then back at the Italian. 'It will have to wait until tomorrow. I have to report to Lord Philippe.'

'It is about Pope Clement. Trust me, Minister, you will want to hear this.'

Nogaret hesitated, but his curiosity was piqued. 'Very well.' He swung down from the saddle.

'Not your men,' said Sciarra curtly, when the guards made to dismount. 'I will only speak to you.'

Nogaret nodded to the royal soldiers. 'Wait here.' As Sciarra moved into the shadows of the street, he followed, picking his way around piles of mouldering rubbish. He started with a curse as several rats scurried away in front of him. 'Make this quick,' he said testily.

Sciarra didn't reply, but continued walking, past the darkened doorways of buildings as the street bent round to the right. Beyond the rooftops, the twin towers of Notre Dame glowed ghostly white in the moonlight. Finally, Colonna halted.

Glancing round, Nogaret saw his guards had now vanished from view. 'Well?'

Sciarra's breaths were coming quickly, each one fogging the air in front of his face. Nogaret felt a prickle of unease. His hand drifted to his sword. He was about to command the Italian to speak, when Sciarra answered.

'You left us to the wolves when you left Anagni, Nogaret.' His voice was low, trembling with suppressed emotion. 'I lost many men in the assault on Boniface. You promised King Philippe would restore our fortunes in return for our sacrifice. But no word ever came to me from you, or him. No pardon, no thanks, no riches. I wrote to the king, more than once, but I never heard anything from him. I then learned that Pope Clement lifted the order of excommunication on you for your crime against Boniface. For me, he did no such thing. One word from your king and he would have.'

Nogaret's unease vanished in a flare of anger. 'You brought me here to berate me? Damn you, Colonna. I do not have time for this!' He went to move off, then turned back, his face sour. 'Besides, you got what you wanted.'

'No!' snapped Sciarra. 'Revenge against Boniface was only part of what I craved. What I wanted was the restoration of my family's power: our strongholds returned to us, my brothers reinstalled in the Sacred College, the Colonna name lifted to its former glory.' His voice dropped again, full of bile. 'You betrayed us, Nogaret. You and your king.'

Nogaret saw Sciarra's gaze flick to the left, somewhere behind him. A rat darted past and he heard the crunch of footfalls on the frosty ground. Unsheathing his sword, he spun. Two figures were moving out of a doorway, coming straight at him. One held a length of something that looked like rope. Knowing he couldn't fight all three, Nogaret turned and lunged at Sciarra, who had drawn his own sword. The blades clashed in the stillness. Nogaret shouted for his guards, but as he parried Sciarra's strikes he heard no hoof-beats and guessed they were no longer capable of helping him. Dodging under one of Sciarra's swings, he straightened and kicked the Italian savagely in the stomach, sending him crashing backwards into a stack of rotten timbers. A dog began barking. Someone thrust open shutters in a house above and shouted for them to be quiet. As the other two men closed in, Nogaret began to run. Halfway down, he slipped on a crust of ice and fell forward, cutting his hands on the hard ground. His sword skidded away into the darkness. Jerking round, he saw Sciarra and his men racing towards him. With no time to grab his weapon, he pushed himself up and sprinted for the end of the alley. It was coming up quickly, the colossal towers of Notre Dame rising before him. Suddenly someone barrelled into him. He flew forward, sprawling on to his stomach with a winded groan. His attacker rolled off him, leaving him gasping. He felt hands seizing him, pulling him up until he was on his knees. His arms were yanked painfully back. Nogaret twisted away as he felt rope being wrapped around his neck. 'I'll give you what you want!' he panted, feeling the rope draw tight. 'I'll go to Philippe, tell him to talk to the pope, get you your pardon! I swear it, Sciarra!'

Sciarra crouched before him, his face pale in the moonlight, glistening with sweat. 'I already have Clement's promise of a pardon. All I need from you, Nogaret, is your last breath.' He nodded to the men who held Nogaret between them.

'No!' screamed Nogaret, but his cry was cut off as the man who held the rope began to pull. Nogaret felt his throat constrict. Rage billowed within him, towering and pure. Clement was his puppet! His instrument! He was *not* the master of his death! His fury was swiftly overwhelmed by panic as he started to choke. His tongue swelled and thrust out between his teeth. He began to convulse and the men holding him struggled. But they held on. As Nogaret's vision began to cloud, he saw Sciarra rising to his feet. Beyond, Notre Dame filled his failing sight, white and imperious, a soaring creation of man's unfailing devotion.

44

The Royal Palace, Paris

18 March 1314 AD

P hilippe stared into the mirror, while around him servants fussed and
bustled. In the depths, his reflection shimmered, the jewels on his
fingers catching the light streaming through the chamber's high windows.
Dust motes swirled in the slanting beams, glittering through ghostly trails
of incense. Raising a hand, Philippe adjusted his crown. He looked like a
painting of a king: perfect in his majesty, his floor-length robes of white
samite the essence of chastity, the simple circlet of gold resting on his
greying hair the embodiment of dignity. His smile was one of cold triumph
as the servants reverently unfolded a faded vermilion cloak, trimmed with
ermine. The ceremonial garment had belonged to his grandfather and now
he, Philippe, would don the mantle of a saint. As they placed it around his
shoulders, smoothing down the creases, and fastened the gold clasp at his
throat, his reflection became complete. He was ready. After seven years of
waiting, he was finally ready.

The trial against the Order of the Temple had been the most arduous
ordeal of his reign, indeed of his life, more fraught with delays and
frustrations than he could have ever imagined when Nogaret first conceived
the idea in the bowels of the Louvre. After the secret agreement forged
with Clement, Philippe had found himself in a tug of war with the pope,
who had grown more belligerent and stubborn the older and sicker he
became. Months of interrogations and examinations turned into years of
councils and assemblies, debates and fierce disputes. Nogaret's murder, still
unsolved, had been a severe blow to the king, but although he had lost the
trial's architect, the minister's notorious list of charges lived on, along with
Esquin de Floyran's damning testimony.

Knights were hunted down and rounded up from Cyprus, Portugal and
Spain, to Germany, England, Italy and Ireland. Across these kingdoms, the
initial shock and disbelief at the charges quickly gave way to outrage and

calls for justice, Philippe's ministers working hard to ensure the Templars
were left with no support. Clement insisted the properties and other assets
of the knights from these countries be sent directly to him, announcing that
in the event of the Order being dissolved, the wealth of the Temple would
be transferred to the Hospitallers. What wasn't so widely known was that
Philippe was to be elected as the new Grand Master of the Knights of St
John.

Finally, three years ago, Clement held a general council of the Church in
Vienne. It was called to discuss, among other matters, the pope's plans for a
new Crusade, but the only point in the lengthy proceedings of interest to
Philippe was the pope's delivery of a certain bull, *Vox in excelso*. For the
king, it wasn't the ringing endorsement of his actions he had hoped for, but
the outcome was nonetheless the same. Clement declared the Order of the
Temple not guilty of the one hundred and twenty-seven charges, saying, on
the advice of his papal commission, the accusations could not be proven.
However, he had gone on to say that due to the trial, the Order's
reputation had been so irrevocably damaged that it would be impossible for
it to continue serving Christendom and therefore should be disbanded and
the wealth it had procured over two centuries used to fund what the knights
had in the end been unable to accomplish: the liberation of Jerusalem.

For a long time after this, despite his pledge to the pope, Philippe had
fought against taking the Cross. He had no desire to risk his life overseas on
what he considered a fool's errand. His grandfather, among many others,
had met death on those foreign sands. But in the end, seeing no other way
to claim his prize, he had yielded to Clement's urgings.

Now, as he left his chambers and headed out, ministers and guards falling
in behind him, as he heard the distant roar of the crowds beyond the palace
walls and the beating of drums that pounded a rhythm deep inside him,
Philippe felt a surprising swell of exultation. It did not matter if he never
went on Crusade; many kings before him had taken the Cross and done
nothing more. What mattered was what his people thought of him on this
momentous day. What mattered was that he was following in the footsteps
of his grandfather, stepping out from the palace gates, the cheers of his
subjects a wave of sound washing over him.

At the head of the royal procession walked Guillaume de Paris,
Philippe's black-clad confessor, who had condemned hundreds of Templars
to death. At his side was the Bishop of Paris, crook held high, and around
them were many other dignitaries of the Church, prelates, archbishops and
bishops, all arrayed in garish ceremonial robes. Acolytes swinging smoking

censers sang hymns, their chanting voices lifting above the cacophony of the throng that lined the road from the palace to Notre Dame. Rosy-cheeked children dressed in gold robes, their heads crowned with laurel leaves, scattered fistfuls of rose petals before the king, so that with every step he took, Philippe walked on a fluttering blanket of red and white. Around him walked his sons and their wives, his brothers and their children. There were dukes and counts, princes and lords from across the kingdom, all with their knightly escorts garbed in silvery mail, helms borne under their arms. The greatest entourage belonged to King Edward II of England and his bride, Philippe's daughter, Isabella. The two walked apart from one another, Isabella with her handmaidens, Edward with his knights.

Royal guards bordered the road, pushing back the churning crowds. The king had decreed a week's holiday and all across the city servants had worked for days, stringing banners from buildings until the streets were a riot of colour. Sweets and gingerbread were tossed from the backs of royal wagons that trundled through Paris, followed by hordes of children and dogs. Taxes had been stopped for one week and there would be no toll on bridges. Philippe had made certain his subjects would come here to adore him on this day, showing all the nobles in his train how beloved he was by them. This was what his people would remember, not the soaring taxes and the poor harvests, the devaluation of coinage and the trial against the Templars, the massacre of the Jews and attacks on the Church. This day, Philippe was convinced, would be the one that would live in their minds forever. As he entered the great doors of Notre Dame, for the first time in his life he walked without fear into the house of God.

Inside, Clement and five cardinals of the Sacred College were waiting. The pope, a pale nub of a man, dwarfed in his robes, sat hunched on the papal throne before the altar, a plain gold cross in his shaking hands. As the lords and ladies spread out behind the king and the voices of the choir rose trembling to the distant expanses of the roof, Philippe went down on his knee, his grandfather's mantle flowing out around him. After the psalms were recited and the prayers offered, the pope leaned forward and the King of France stretched out his hand to take the golden Cross.

As his fingers clutched at it, Philippe felt himself suffused with a sense of holiness the like of which he had never felt before. He flushed with excitement expecting, at last, to hear God's voice pulsing through him, but before he could pause to listen, the nobles were moving in around him, pledging their support for his war against the Saracens. Philippe accepted their aid distractedly, his mind already focusing on his plans to divert the

Temple's wealth from the Hospitallers to his own coffers. With the ceremony done and his part of the bargain fulfilled, Clement would have no choice but to give him what he had promised. But before that pact could be consummated, there was one last thing to be done.

When the Order was dissolved, the Templars who survived the trial in France were either sentenced to imprisonment or else allowed to live out their existence in prayerful service in various monasteries. In other kingdoms, sentences were less harsh, the knights being given licence to do as they pleased, but as many had spent their lives in service to the Temple, their earthly needs cared for, there were few options open to them. Some became mercenaries, others beggars. The only ones on whom final judgement had so far been reserved were the surviving officials in Paris. Now, led through the hustling crowds who jeered and spat at them, they were brought to the steps of Notre Dame, where Clement was ready to pass sentence.

Jacques de Molay, along with Geoffroi de Charney, Hugues de Pairaud and Geoffroi de Gonneville, the Master of Aquitaine, were lined up before the pope. All were haggard and malnourished, their faces ashen with lack of sun, their hair and beards long and matted. Still, the Grand Master, whose massive frame was crooked with his injuries, kept his head raised as the pope began to speak in a quavering voice.

Despite the fact that the Order itself could not be proved guilty, the four men had admitted their culpability on numerous occasions. Therefore, Clement pronounced, all were to suffer harsh and perpetual imprisonment. Hugues de Pairaud and Geoffroi de Gonneville did not speak, neither man seeming to hear or comprehend what had been said, barely even able to hold themselves upright. Jacques de Molay, however, with a grimace of pain, rose shakily to his feet. Even on the lowest steps, beneath the king and assembled nobles, the Grand Master seemed to tower over everyone.

'The Order of the Temple was created to defend the people of Christendom. Its sons have bled for all of you on the sands of Palestine. It has been noble in its endeavours, gallant on the field of battle, honourable in its dealings, pure in its service to the Lord. It remains so to this day and shall forever more, if not in this kingdom then in the next.' Jacques continued, his old eyes boring into Philippe. 'The falsehoods that have been spun like webs around us by poisonous creatures will one day be swept away and the world shall see our innocence. I deny all that I confessed to, having done so only to end the pain of torture.' Lifting his gruff voice, he turned to the crowd behind him, which had fallen into a bated silence. 'I deny every charge that has been laid against me and my brothers. The Temple is innocent.'

Philippe watched on in fury as Geoffroi de Charney staggered to his feet beside Jacques to add his own denial to his Master's. De Pairaud and de Gonneville had so far remained silent, but the king wasn't going to give them the chance to have their say as well. The crowd were murmuring restlessly, excitedly. He felt their respect and adoration slipping away, replaced by curiosity, awe even at the sight of the impassioned Grand Master. Philippe crossed quickly to Clement, who was looking confused at the turn of events.

'Your holiness,' he hissed through his teeth, 'these two men are relapsed heretics. They must be dealt with swiftly, lest their infection spread. You must condemn them.'

Clement stared at him. 'Condemn them?'

'To the fire.' Philippe held the pope in his hard gaze. 'De Molay and de Charney must be passed over to my authority for execution. It is the law.'

Clement gazed back at Jacques, who had raised up his arms before the silent crowd and was standing like a crucified Christ on the steps of the cathedral. He closed his eyes. The Grand Master could have repented and saved his life, but he had sealed his own fate with this action. Philippe was right: it was the law. 'Very well,' he murmured.

45
The Royal Palace, Paris

18 March 1314 AD

T he lawns in the royal gardens were wet, the grass glimmering in the evening light. The rain that had swept across the city during the afternoon had moved slowly west, leaving the city drowned and bleary in its wake. The sun was low, caught between the base of a mountainous black cloud and the horizon, bathing the city in amber dusk.

The shadows of the men stretched long and thin as they moved through the gardens towards a small door in the palace wall, hidden by sodden veils of trailing ivy that dripped water on to their heads as they passed through in single file. Behind them, Notre Dame's bell began to toll, the sound shuddering over the island, but the streets of the Ville and the Latin Quarter remained eerily quiet, even as other bells began to join the call to Vespers. The citizens of Paris weren't on their way to prayer. They were lining the banks of the Seine in their thousands, their gazes all fixed on a bare island rising from the broad river, upon which a pyre had been built. The crowd, growing all afternoon as word of the pope's judgement went round, had been hushed, expectant. Now, as the men filed through the door on to the banks where the wooden footbridge spanned the waters, they began to whisper and murmur, eyes on the two figures within the company whose deaths they had come to witness.

Jacques de Molay and Geoffroi de Charney, stumbling out between the royal guards, had each been stripped down to a loincloth, their bodies displaying the ravages of seven years of torture. Both had been crudely shaved, their hair and beards hacked away, flesh scraped raw by the knives. Behind them came the Dominican, Guillaume de Paris, three cardinals and two executioners, hooded in black. They were followed by the king, who waited on the banks, while the company made their way to the bridge. Of the pope, there was no sign.

Jacques staggered and fell before he reached the bridge, his bare feet slipping in the slick mud. The soldiers went to haul him upright, but he shrugged away their clutching hands and instead grasped the rickety bridge posts and pulled himself up. The excited murmurs of the waiting crowds died away to quiet as the Grand Master put his foot on the boards and began to cross the river, each step taking him closer to the Ile des Juifs, and the pyre. Geoffroi de Charney limped in his wake, his pale face fixed on the Grand Master's scarred back. The guards' mail boots sounded hollowly off the wooden boards.

Once on the other side, the executioners took control, gesturing for the soldiers to secure the two men to the post that stuck up from the centre of the pyre. De Charney's legs gave out as they took hold of him. The crowds sucked in a breath and jostled one another to get a better look as the guards shouted abuse and grabbed at him. Turning, Jacques elbowed his way roughly to where Geoffroi had slumped. He crouched and grasped his brother's hands. The king started forward with a frown as the guards hung back uncertainly. No one on the banks heard what the Grand Master said, but when he was finished, Geoffroi struggled to his feet. Together, side by side, the two old men made their way unaided to the pyre.

A broad plank of wood had been laid over the packed heap of branches and straw. The soldiers led them across it to the central post, where the two Templars were bound, back to back, the stake thrusting between them. The pyre was high enough for everyone on the banks to see them, their faces tinged gold in the last of the light. The executioners headed down the plank, which was dragged away, leaving Jacques and Geoffroi alone. One of the black-clad executioners took a torch from Guillaume de Paris. As he shoved it into the straw that had been stuffed in between the branches and timbers, the crowd let out an approving roar. Smoke swirled and little orange flames sprung up around the wood. The second executioner took another torch and did the same on the other side. After lighting the four corners, the two men stepped back to wait and watch with the rest of the city.

The bottom of the pile began to glow, wood hissing, sparks spitting. The smoke grew thicker and the two men began to cough, their bodies straining against their bonds, but the executioners had been careful and the wood was dry enough to flame rather than smoulder. The king had instructed that they make it a slow fire with the minimum of straw, so that the men would burn rather than choke to death. At this point, when the heat from below began stinging the soles of their feet, victims would usually start to cry out; to protest or beg mercy, sometimes to pray, so it wasn't a surprise to the waiting crowd when Jacques's voice echoed across the water. But his words, when they came, were anything but expected.

'Before Heaven and Earth, with all of you here present as witness, I tell you the Order of the Temple is innocent.' The Grand Master's voice was hoarse from the smoke, but filled with an authority that silenced all who could hear him. 'Christ knows our innocence, just as he knows the guilt of those who have wrought these wrongs upon us. I tell you these men, these guilty men, will account for their crimes before the tribunal of God. For no man, neither king nor pope, can hide from the judgement of the Lord!'

There were no cheers from the watching throng, no taunts. Some people turned away as the flames rose higher, consuming the wood under the men's feet. On the riverbank, Philippe, his face pale, watched them burn.

Away on the left bank, opposite the island, two men in hooded cloaks looked grimly on as Jacques's words rang out. They were both tall and well-built despite their age, although one was leaning heavily on the stick he wielded, his grey hair pulled back from his face, sharpening the hard lines of his cheeks and jaw.

'It is as if he knows.'

Will glanced round at Robert's murmur. He had to turn his head fully to face his old friend, as a leather patch covered the scarred hollow where his right eye used to be. 'In a way, he does. He is innocent. God will be the last judge in this.'

Robert didn't take his gaze off the Grand Master and de Charney, now writhing in agony as the flames billowed around them. 'And us? Are we not somehow to blame here?'

Will looked back at the pyre. The blaze was reflected in the water between the bank and the island, turning the Seine to molten gold. 'No.'

Robert looked at him searchingly. 'That is the first time I've heard you sound so certain.'

'It was a long journey. I had a lot of time to think.' Will realised his comrade was waiting for more. 'All great empires fall, Robert. Nothing can stay the same forever. The world changes and those who refuse to change with it are destroyed by its convulsions.' He paused, frowning. 'That was something I do not think Everard understood. His beliefs were strong, stronger than mine have ever been, but ultimately constrained by the rigidity with which he held them. He couldn't see beyond the borders of his own ambitions, couldn't see that the world was moving in different directions, rendering some of his plans impossible. He always said the Anima Templi could only survive if the Temple did, that it needed the Order's money and resources if it was to continue its aims. I do not believe that. A dream isn't something that exists in bricks or organisations, laws or gold. Neither is hope. These things exist within us, waiting to be made manifest through our words and our deeds. We are our dreams, Robert, and they are us. It would be more true to say that the Soul of the Temple cannot exist without us.'

'Then you think we can continue?'

'We already are.'

Robert gave a sober laugh. 'I suppose you are right.'

Turning from the pyre, Will threaded through the crowd, using his stick to steady himself. Some of the wounds he had sustained in the king's prison had never properly healed and he was suffering from the voyage from Scotland. Robert followed, people moving back into the space they left. Once away from the main throng, Will handed over a pack he had been carrying.

When Robert took it the bag flopped open to reveal a snatch of white cloth, before he slung it over his shoulder. 'One last time,' he said quietly.

Will looked away. 'It doesn't seem right, you doing this alone. I should be with you.'

'I'm not alone,' responded Robert, nodding to two men waiting at the end of a street a short distance away, both dressed in the same woollen cloaks as he and Will. 'And no offence,' he added, cocking his head at Will's eye patch, 'but you're a hazard with a bow these days.' His grin faded. 'This has to be done. You made the right decision. We cannot risk another Crusade.'

'I know. But it feels more like vengeance today.'

'You know the price for peace, Will. It is always high.'

Will paused, thinking of Everard's belief that, sometimes, peace could only be bought with blood. For a long time he hadn't truly agreed, but after all they had been through these past few years it seemed the old man might have been right. He gripped Robert's outstretched hand. Will waited until his old comrade and the two men had disappeared from view, then moved off alone. Behind him, the pyre burned like a sun, the two men at the centre consumed by its light.

Dominican Priory, Near Carpentras, the Kingdom of France, 20 April 1314 AD

'I am afraid the journey from Paris weakened him beyond my skills to heal, your grace. Perhaps if he had remained at rest while the present bout passed . . . ?'

'He wanted to return to plan for the Crusade.' The cardinal's brow creased. 'Is there nothing we can do?'

'I would suggest,' said the physician quietly, 'that you pray for him.'

The cardinal nodded after a pause. 'I understand. Thank you.' He waited until the physician had been escorted away down the passage by two black-robed Dominicans before entering the chamber. Three other cardinals of the Sacred College were there, lingering around a large bed. They all looked round as he closed the door, their faces expectant. He shook his head.

In the bed lay Clement. The pope was breathing shallowly, his eyes hooded, the lids fluttering. He stirred as the cardinal who had entered moved to his side and took his hand. His face was deathly pale, the skin stretched taut over his bones as if there were nothing left between them; not muscle or blood. The disease he had suffered with for so many years had consumed him, eating away his organs and his strength until he was no more than an empty husk, with all his hopes and plans rattling inside him.

Outside, a bell chimed the afternoon office and doors banged in the distance as the monks filed to prayer. Clement's eyes flickered open. Staring past the bowed heads of the cardinals, he fixed on a picture hanging on the wall at the end of the bed. It was an image of Jerusalem, embroidered in silk. A tear slipped from the corner of his eye as his vision focused on the white and gold domes, crowned by their eternal sky. 'No,' he whispered, feeling his heart murmur uneasily. 'Not yet. I must see it done.'

'Your holiness?' said one of the cardinals, leaning closer to hear that papery voice.

Clement's head turned weakly to him. 'I promised Raoul.'

'Who is Raoul?' questioned the cardinal gently. When the pope didn't answer, the man glanced at the others, but they were shaking their heads in puzzlement.

As the Nones bell ceased its chimes, the pope's hand slipped from the cardinal's, his head sinking back on to the pillow.

Château Vincennes, the Kingdom of France, 29 August 1314 AD

Philippe urged his horse on faster, not waiting for the others to follow. The green wood ahead promised freedom and he was impatient for it. The white mare plunged keenly along the path that looped through the trees, her iron-shod hooves thumping up dust. The king settled into her rhythm, reins gripped in one gloved hand, the other crooked at his side, bearing a hooded falcon, the leash and jesses looped through his fingers. She was a young lightning-swift peregrine, a gift from his son-in-law, King Edward. Maiden had died the previous year and he hadn't flown a bird since, but he missed the chase and in recent months found himself dreaming often of the woods and river-flats of the royal estate. Sir Henri had trained the falcon and now they were ready, she and him, to test one another's mettle.

For months, he had been cooped up in Paris, feeling caged and restless. The death of Pope Clement had complicated matters, for while the pope had issued a bull decreeing the wealth of the Templars be transferred to the Hospital, no such document existed to attest to his decision that Philippe should be the new Grand Master of that Order. The king spent sleepless weeks arguing long into the night with Guillaume de Plaisans and Pierre Dubois, desperately seeking some resolution to the problem. Finally, the canny lawyers, in preparing to hand over the Templars' wealth and property to the Knights of St John, had drawn up a lengthy list of expenses and legal costs incurred during the king's seizure and collection of the assets. If the Hospitallers wanted the vast array of estates and small-holdings, they would have to pay for it. In the end, Philippe got everything he wanted. Clement's death freed him from the burden of an unwanted Crusade and the Hospitallers were slowly pouring money into his dried-up coffers.

As the king rode, he felt the sting of the hair shirt against his skin. Preoccupied of late, he hadn't worn it in quite some time. Above him, through the breaks in the canopy, the sky was tinged rose-gold in the east. It was still early and the sun was only just starting to rise. There was a heavy promise of heat in the air and mist rose from the dew-laden grass, turning the forest into an ethereal world of silver webs and shifting shadows. Birds cast themselves from the trees as the king thundered past. Hearing the barking of dogs somewhere behind him, Philippe glanced back over his shoulder. He couldn't see the company of courtiers who had been following him any more. Slowing the mare with a swift pull on the reins, he turned her sharply and cantered back the way he had come. He caught shouts and the bellow of a horn up ahead. Rounding a corner, he saw the company. They were crowded around the edge of the wood, staring into its depths. The huntsmen, who had been jogging on foot some way behind the horses, were straining to keep the barking dogs in check, the beasts pulling at their leashes.

'What is it?' Philippe called, approaching.

'They must have caught a scent, my lord,' replied one, whipping the hound with his stick to silence it. 'Deer, I reckon.'

'This close to the château?' questioned Philippe's son, Louis, doubtfully.

Philippe steered his horse to the line of trees and peered into the green gloom.

'What say you, my lord?' asked Henri, moving in alongside him. The old falconer smiled, his weathered face wrinkling. 'Shall we have our sport here or at the river?'

Philippe nodded to the huntsmen. 'Let the dogs go.'

The courtiers murmured excitedly, moving into position, as the huntsmen unleashed the hounds. The dogs streaked into the undergrowth, barking furiously. The chase was on.

Philippe went first, hurtling down the grassy bank that slipped from the track into the woods. Turning his horse skilfully, he ducked under low trailing branches, pulling his knees in as the mare whipped past the trees. The company followed, fanning out, each man finding his own path. Once again, Philippe left the rest behind him, none of them able, or daring to match his wild pace. As he rode, the mist swirling in his wake, he grinned savagely, filled with the thrill of the hunt. He was power personified, the master of all things: his horse, the killer on his wrist, the ground upon which he rode. He was king, worshipped and feared. He had beaten his enemies and watched them fall before him. He had expanded his kingdom and filled his coffers. God could not fail to notice him now. There was no one more powerful, or famed in all of Christendom.

Ahead, the barking of the dogs seemed to separate. He caught movement as the pack split and the animals sped in different directions. 'We have two scents!' he shouted, following the three dogs that had veered to the left. He rocked in the saddle as the horse vaulted a shallow stream. The woods behind and to his right were filled with the calls of the others as they spread out, each man wanting to be the first to catch sight of the quarry. The sounds were distorted, echoing through the maze of trees. Up ahead, the dogs' barking was louder, more urgent. Philippe slowed his mount with a tug on the reins as he entered a clearing. He couldn't see the dogs, but he could hear them, growling and snarling. Between two oaks the undergrowth was thrashing. Wondering if they had caught a boar, Philippe swung over the saddle and jumped down, still holding the peregrine poised on his left glove.

With his right hand, he drew his sword and went forward, cautious now. A cornered boar could be lethal. His horse circled behind him, snorting.

Golden light was flickering through the trees as the sun rose. The forest was alive with horns ringing and men shouting. It sounded as if the dogs had led them round in a circle. Philippe's brow furrowed in disappointment. Had he followed the wrong trail? He went closer to where the hounds were scrabbling. Parting the bushes he saw a dead deer, the dogs' faces buried in its guts. He was about to shout to the huntsmen, when he caught sight of a hole in the dead animal's side. It looked like an arrow wound. He straightened, his frown now one of anger. Poachers? On his estate? The undergrowth behind him rustled. The king turned.

Rising up out of the green and the mist were three figures. In the first rays of sun, their white mantles seemed to glow, the cross over each of their hearts as red as blood. One held a bow primed in his hands. It released, the arrow springing forth. Philippe watched its rapid trajectory, the nerves in his body firing into life, ready to send him lunging to one side. But the arrow was quicker. As its barbed tip plunged into his chest, the king hurtled back, his arms flinging wide. His sword with its golden pommel flew from his hand as he fell. The falcon shrieked, her wings beating the air and her leash pulling free. Philippe hit the ground and lay on his back, his breath shuddering between his lips, watching her soar into the blue air above him. Her small form spiralled up, moving further and further away, while he remained pinned to the earth, sinking further inside himself into nothing.

46

Argyll, the Kingdom of Scotland

2 November 1314 AD

T he calls of the children echoed sharply, catching in the wind and filtering back to the adults, who were wending their way slowly up the hill. Closer, the sea whispered and sighed, unfolding itself across the sand then dragging back. Will paused on the crumbling cliff edge, the raw breeze flurrying around him, whipping the stiff grasses against his legs. The sun had set, but the western sky was still glowing, the tumbling line of islands that shaped the horizon black against the gold.

Some days, he would sit out here for hours. After so many years of uncertainty to be able to see everything before him was a comfort. Yet within those confines, change was a constant. The sea could shift from green to grey in an instant and mists would roll in unexpectedly over the bracken hills to cast a white net across the lochs, some of which were so deep they cradled mountains in their depths. The summers were glorious, the nights light and mild, but the winters were brutal. Community meant something here, unlike the anonymous sprawl of London or the twisting labyrinths of Paris. It reminded him in some ways of Acre, the same barren beauty and white sugar sands, people clinging together on a rocky strip of coast, reliant on one another for survival. Everard would have liked it here, as would Elwen.

Will felt a hand on his arm.

Ysenda smiled at him. 'Are you coming inside? It's going to be cold tonight.' She glanced round as her husband put his arm around her.

John Campbell nodded to Will. 'It was a good service, I thought.' He looked up hearing his name and his brown face crinkled as a young boy came racing down the hill towards them.

The boy came to a breathless stop, tossing his hair from his eyes. 'Can we get some more apples from the store?'

'What for?' asked John, groaning as he hoisted him into the air.

The boy was whip-lean, but tall for his age. Sometimes, Will saw glimpses of Philippe in his face, which for a time had disturbed him, but the more he had come to know his grandson, those fears had dissipated, since he couldn't have been more unlike his father in temperament.

'For the lamb's wool. Christian says I'm to make it.'

John's smile broadened. The drink, made of roasted apples, ale and nutmeg, was a favourite in the household. 'That sounds like an important task for one so young.'

'I can do it.'

'I'm sure,' said John with a chuckle, letting the boy down. 'Perhaps your grandfather can help?'

Will nodded as the boy's eyes darted hopefully to him. 'I'll be up soon, William.'

Ysenda caught his eye. Taking the boy's hand and with her husband's arm still slung around her waist, she led them towards the house, following the rest of the children and adults up the darkening path.

'You'll soon not be able to do anything without him, you know.'

Will didn't turn. A cold hand threaded through his and he closed his eye as his daughter rested her head on his shoulder. For a time they stood there, neither of them speaking.

Finally, she gave his hand a squeeze. 'I had better help prepare the feast.' Rose paused, wrapping her cloak tighter around her as the wind snatched it back. 'I'll set the place for them.'

Will stared out across the sea as his daughter followed Ysenda and the others.

It was a night of celebration. Tonight they would drink to the close of the year and thank God for their blessings. But it was also a night of sadness, a feast for the dead, when all souls were remembered. In chapel that evening they had said prayers for the departed and an extra seat would be set at the table in honour of those who had gone before. Tonight, the air was thick with their memories. Here on this cliff edge, with the gold light fading to blue, he could feel them thronging around him: his mother and father, Elwen and Owein, Everard and Elias, William Wallace, Jacques de Molay, even Garin. He stayed there for some time before heading up the track, his stick tapping the ground.

As he neared the house, Will heard David's voice, clear and strong, coming from inside. His nephew had arrived a week ago, alive with stories of King Robert. There had been further skirmishes with England over the past few years, but Edward II wasn't the warrior his father had been and in a decisive battle at midsummer, Robert Bruce had driven the king and his men back across the border. These events seemed a long way away to Will, out here on this remote coast. It was a time for younger men to forge out histories for themselves, to become legends. For him, it was a time of reflection. Last year he had started to add his own words to those begun by Everard, the old yellowed parchments eagerly soaking up the ink from his quill. It didn't seem important these days to keep the secrets of the Anima Templi so closely guarded, indeed it felt more appropriate that he finally tell the truth and so he wrote freely about the Brethren, about the men of the Temple, and its Soul.

Will was approaching the door when he heard the thud of hooves. Turning, he saw a horse moving swiftly up the cliff path towards him. Brow furrowed, he squinted into the gathering gloom, trying to make out the rider. His frown deepened as he heard his name come to him over the rumble of hooves. Suddenly, he knew who it was.

As Robert reined in the horse and slid stiffly from the saddle, Will called over his shoulder through the open door and went to meet him, flooded with relief at the sight of his old comrade.

'It is done,' said Robert quietly, when Will greeted him.

John was in the doorway. 'Set another place!' he bellowed, as Will and Robert followed him into the house, one of the servants hastening to take the knight's weary mount.

'I brought these with me,' said Robert, hanging back in the doorway and holding out the pack he was carrying to Will. 'It didn't seem right to burn them.'

Will took the pack and looked inside.

His grandson's face appeared around the kitchen door. 'Christian says you're to help us.'

'Did she now?' Will smiled. 'Tell her I'll be there shortly.' He gestured Robert to an empty room off the hallway. As they passed the kitchen, Will caught a glimpse of his grandson climbing up on a stool to reach the table, where Christian and Rose were slicing up a pile of wrinkled apples. Ysenda was crouched before Ede by the hearth and Simon was talking with David, who was pouring out two jars of ale.

'Will you tell him?' asked Robert, as they entered the empty room. The servants had stoked the fire and the flames roared in gusts of wind, filling the chamber with the peppery smell of burning wood. 'Your grandson?'

Will closed the door. 'About his father?' He turned to meet Robert's gaze. 'In time, yes. He deserves to know where he came from. There have been too many lies in this family.' He crossed to a chest by the window. Opening the pack, he withdrew the three folded mantles and placed them inside the chest, next to Everard's book and the hilt of his father's broken sword that Rose had saved from the palace.

'It doesn't seem like much to be left with, does it?' murmured Robert, looking over Will's shoulder. 'Not after two hundred years.'

'It isn't all.' Will glanced at him. 'We still have the treasury.'

'Have you decided what to do with it yet?'

'I'm not certain that is for us to decide,' answered Will, after a pause.

'Who then?'

'Those who come after us.' Will stared into the chest at the broken sword and the white mantles. 'Those of the future.'

'And us? What will we do now?'

Will shut the lid and stood. 'Let us speak of that tomorrow.' He put a hand on the knight's shoulder and smiled slightly. 'Tonight we feast.'

The two men left the room side by side, Will leaning heavily on his stick. Together they entered the warmth of the crowded kitchen, enveloped by a host of welcoming voices and the ring of laughter.

AUTHOR'S NOTE

Back in 1999 I was sitting in a bar listening to two friends discussing the Templars. I'd never heard of them, but was instantly intrigued by the idea of these warrior monks. Some months later, I came across *The Trial of the Templars*, by historian Malcolm Barber, which detailed the downfall of the Order. I read it in one afternoon and by the time I had finished I knew I had to tell this story. I initially embarked on a stand-alone novel, but the more research I did into the knights, the more I discovered of the richness of the period: the Crusades, the rise of the Mamluks, the politics, the courtly dramas, and before long the book became a trilogy. Starting *Requiem* last year, it felt as though I had come full circle, the Templars' end being the story that inspired it all. I was exploring the voices of characters who had been in my mind for almost a decade, but I was also writing what is perhaps the best known of the three periods covered in the trilogy.

As with *Brethren* and *Crusade*, I have made slight changes to the history, mainly chronological, but as much of the narrative in *Requiem* is based on real events and people I thought it useful to note some of the places in the story where fact and fiction meet. Most of the alterations are in the form of the simplification of events that either went on for much longer or were more complex than portrayed. As a historical novelist you often have to make a judgement call as to whether to keep the history exactly as it was or to change it to make it more interesting or accessible. This becomes even more necessary when you're covering nineteen years in one novel.

I have, for instance, simplified the war between France and Flanders, although events such as the Matins of Bruges, the French defeat at Courtrai and the alliance between Edward I and Guy de Dampierre are all based in fact. The uprising in Gascony against French royal forces occurred in 1303, not 1302 and Bertrand de Got was in Rome at the time. Philippe IV did expel the Jews from France, but not until 1306 and his grandfather, Louis

IX, was canonised a little later than portrayed. Boniface's bull, *Clericis laicos*, was issued in February 1296 and *Unam Sanctam* in November 1302. Guillaume de Nogaret died around 1313, rather than 1308, and although Philippe did take the Cross it occurred a year earlier than portrayed. The king himself died in a riding accident in November 1314.

So as to keep a level of consistency in the hierarchy of the Temple I have avoided the introduction of certain officials who would, in reality, have been important figures in the Order, such as the Master of France. Sometimes there were long gaps between a post being filled after one man's death and it wasn't uncommon for an official to hold two positions at once. Hugues de Pairaud was Visitor and Master of France for a time.

Incredibly, the attack on Pope Boniface VIII in Anagni, led by Guillaume de Nogaret and Sciarra Colonna did happen and in much the way I have described (there are even reports that suggest they arrived to find Templars guarding the pope), but again I have condensed the sequence of events so as to keep the pace. It has been speculated that Boniface's convoy, fleeing the town, may have been attacked by Colonna's men, but this isn't known. What is known is that the pope died in Rome several weeks later. Some say he went mad, others that his heart gave out over the shock of the assault. It is not clear how his successor, Benedict XI, met his death, although one report states he died after eating poisoned figs and it has been theorised that Philippe and his lawyers may indeed have had a hand in this.

With regard to King Edward's first Scottish campaign, John Balliol didn't renounce the French treaty until July and Edward received word of this in Perth, not Edinburgh. Balliol then appeared before the king at Montrose to be stripped of his royal tabard and Edward's famously contemptuous remark about a man doing good business when he rids himself of shit was apparently uttered as he crossed the border into England in the autumn of 1296. Likewise, on the Scottish side for the campaign of 1297, details have been tweaked. William Wallace was attempting to relieve Dundee in August and it was from here, rather than Selkirk Forest, that he advanced on Stirling. He had, however, spent much of the previous month in the Forest, gathering his army and training his men, and he often used it as a base.

The proceedings against the Templars were an incredibly protracted and complicated affair, which, although fascinating and indeed what drew me to this story, doesn't lend itself to a fast-paced narrative. For anyone wanting to read the whole story, I would seriously recommend Barber's *The Trial of the Templars.* Much of what I have chosen to portray in the narrative, however, is based in fact, or at least conjecture.

One chronicler states that Philippe IV secretly met with Bertrand de Got before he became pope and persuaded him to fulfil certain obligations. Modern scholars, in the main, dismiss this, but whether fact or fiction it is clear the king went to a great deal of trouble to have a hand in the election, ordering Nogaret to pressure the Sacred College to elect someone sympathetic to French royal policy. I invented Bertrand's son, although the archbishop was accused of having an affair with a local noblewoman. Esquin de Floyran, a rather obscure character, was a Templar who had been imprisoned and who first accused the knights of heresy, writing to both King Philippe and King James of Aragon supposedly with evidence to support his claims, but his nephew, Martin, is fictitious. The establishment of the papal commission and the knights' defence occurred later in the trial, as did the systematic burning of knights outside Paris. What happened to the Templars' famed treasure isn't known, although it is thought that around twenty knights escaped the initial arrests in Paris and may have had some warning. Where these men went and whether or not they took the treasury with them has been the subject of fervent speculation throughout the centuries.

The Order of the Temple was never found guilty of the one hundred and twenty-seven charges against it, Clement only dissolving the organisation because its reputation had been so severely damaged during the trial. It was a different story for the officials. Jacques de Molay and Geoffroi de Charney were burned at the stake in March 1314 as relapsed heretics. De Molay's famous judgement against king and pope has echoed down the years to us and although we have no way of knowing if the account is purely apocryphal, Philippe and Clement were both dead within that year. The Capetian dynasty, of which Philippe had been so proud, ended in scandal and disaster, his three sons dying in rapid succession.

The Templars in France and elsewhere admitted most of the charges levelled at them, but their confessions were extracted during horrific tortures and many of the knights recanted these confessions once they had recovered, including de Molay and de Charney who went to their pyre protesting their innocence. The charges against the Order bear striking similarities to those the Cathars were accused of, as well as other groups that became targets of the Church's war on heresy. If you wanted public opinion on your side in the Middle Ages, stirring up people's fear of sorcery and devil-worship was an effective way to get it and Philippe and his ministers proved more than once that they were incredibly adept at this sort of propaganda. There is one charge, however, that does crop up again and again in the trial and almost always around the figure of Hugues de Pairaud: the charge of knights spitting on the cross. One theory for this is that it was a practice adopted by some in the Order as a form of obedience test. The truth behind the trial and the motivations of those involved will probably never be known for certain, but whatever really happened it does say something for the character of the Templars that these warrior monks in their sinless white mantles continue to live on so vividly in our conscious-ness almost seven hundred years after their exit from this world.

Robyn Young
Brighton, July 2008

CHARACTER LIST

(* denotes real figures from history)

*ADAM: cousin of William Wallace

ALBERT: Knight Templar

ALICE: daughter of Ysenda, Will's niece

*ANDREW DE MORAY: Scottish noble and leader of the Scottish rebellion

*ANTHONY BEK: Bishop of Durham

*BENEDICT XI: pope (1303–4)

*BERNARD SAISSET: Bishop of Pamiers, accused of heresy by Philippe IV

*BERTRAND DE GOT (1264–1314): Archbishop of Bordeaux, then accedes papal throne as Clement V in 1305

BLANCHE: handmaiden to Jeanne de Navarre

*BONIFACE VIII (1234–1303): pope (1294–1303)

*BRIAN LE JAY: Master of the English Temple

*CELESTINE V (1215–96): pope (1294)

*CHARLES DE VALOIS: brother of Philippe IV

CHRISTIAN: sister-in-law of Gray

COLIN: son of Ede, Will's nephew

DAVID: son of Ysenda, Will's nephew

*DAVID GRAHAM: Scottish noble, son of Patrick Graham

DUNCAN: first husband of Ysenda

EDE: sister of Will

*EDWARD I (1239–1307): King of England (1272–1307)

*EDWARD II (1284–1327): King of England (1307–27)

*ELEANOR OF CASTILE: first wife of Edward I, Queen of England

ELIAS: rabbi

ELWEN: wife of Will, died in Acre in 1291

*ESQUIN DE FLOYRAN: Templar Master of Montfaucon

EVERARD DE TROYES: Templar priest and former head of the Anima Templi, died in Acre in 1277

GAILLARD: squire of Bertrand de Got

GARIN DE LYONS: former Knight Templar in the service of Edward I, killed by Will in Acre in 1291

GAUTIER: French royal soldier

*GEOFFROI DE CHARNEY: Master of the Temple in Normandy

*GEOFFROI DE GONNEVILLE: Master of the Temple in Aquitaine

GÉRARD: Templar sergeant

GILLES: French royal soldier

*GODFREY BUSSA: captain of the papal guard

*GRAY: companion of William Wallace

GUI: Knight Templar

*GUILLAUME DE NOGARET (–1313): lawyer and royal advisor to Philippe IV, Keeper of the Seals from 1302

*GUILLAUME DE PARIS: Dominican and confessor of Philippe IV

*GUILLAUME DE PLAISANS: lawyer and royal advisor to Philippe IV

*GUY DE DAMPIERRE: Count of Flanders

HASAN: former comrade of Everard de Troyes, died in Paris in 1266

HELOISE: lover of Bertrand de Got

HENRI: Master Falconer to Philippe IV

*HENRY PERCY: English noble

*HUGH CRESSINGHAM: English royal official, treasurer of Scotland under Edward I

*HUGUES DE PAIRAUD: Visitor of the Temple

ISAAC: Jewish merchant

*ISABELLA: daughter of Philippe IV and Jeanne, marries Edward II of England in 1308

*JACQUES DE MOLAY: Grand Master of the Temple (1293–1314)

JAMES CAMPBELL: Knight Templar and father of Will, executed in the Holy Land in 1266

*JEANNE DE NAVARRE: wife of Philippe IV, Queen of France and Navarre

*JOHN BALLIOL: King of Scotland (1292–6)

*JOHN BLAIR: chaplain of William Wallace

JOHN CAMPBELL: Scottish knight, second husband of Ysenda

*JOHN DE WARENNE: Earl of Surrey

*KALAWUN: Sultan of Egypt and Syria (1280–90)

LAURENT: Knight Templar

*LOUIS IX: King of France (1226–70), canonised by Boniface VIII in 1297

MARGARET: daughter of Ysenda, Will's niece

MARGUERITE: handmaiden to Jeanne de Navarre

MARIE: servant of Bertrand de Got

MARTIN DE FLOYRAN: Knight Templar, nephew of Esquin

*NICCOLO: Italian noble

OWEIN AP GWYN: Knight Templar, former master of Will, killed in Honfleur in 1260

*PATRICK GRAHAM: Scottish noble

*PHILIPPE IV (1268–1314): King of France (1285–1314)

PIERRE DE BOURG: French noble

*PIERRE DUBOIS: lawyer to Philippe IV

*PIERRE FLOTE: lawyer and royal advisor to Philippe IV, Keeper of the Seals until 1302

PONSARD: French royal soldier

*RAINALD: captain of Ferentino

RAINIER: Knight Templar

RAOUL: Bertrand de Got's son

*ROBERT BRUCE: Earl of Carrick, King of Scotland (1306–29)

ROBERT DE PARIS: Knight Templar and member of the Anima Templi

ROSE: daughter of Will and Elwen

SAMUEL: Jewish moneylender

*SCIARRA COLONNA: Italian noble

SIMON TANNER: Templar sergeant

STEPHEN: an Irish warrior

THOMAS: Knight Templar and member of the Anima Templi based in London

WILL CAMPBELL: Templar Commander and head of the Anima Templi

WILLIAM: son of Rose

*WILLIAM WALLACE (c.1270–1305): Scottish knight and leader of the Scottish rebellion

YOLANDE: servant of Bertrand de Got

YSENDA: youngest sister of Will, mother of David, Margaret and Alice

GLOSSARY

ACRE: a city on the coast of Palestine, conquered by the Arabs in 640. It was captured by the Crusaders in the early twelfth century and became the principal port of the new Latin Kingdom of Jerusalem. Acre was ruled by a king, but by the mid-thirteenth century royal authority was disputed by the local Frankish nobles and from this time the city, with its twenty-seven separate quarters, was largely governed oligarchically.

ANIMA TEMPLI: Latin for 'Soul of the Temple'. A fictional group within the Knights Templar founded by Grand Master Robert de Sablé in 1191, in the aftermath of the Battle of Hattin. It is formed of twelve Brethren, drawn from the Order's ranks, with a Guardian to mediate during disputes, and is dedicated to achieving reconciliation between the Christian, Muslim and Jewish faiths.

BERNARD DE CLAIRVAUX, St: (1090–1153) Abbot and founder of the Cistercian monastery at Clairvaux in France. An early supporter of the Templars, Bernard aided the Order in the creation of their Rule.

BLACK STONE: in Arabic 'al-Hajar al-Aswad', a sacred relic set in the eastern corner of the Ka'ba in Mecca, held in place by a silver band and kissed or touched by Muslims during the rites of pilgrimage. In 929, the Karmatians (Ismaili Shi'ahs) took possession of the Black Stone and carried it out of Mecca, effectively holding it to ransom until its restoration twenty-two years later.

CRUSADES: a European movement of the medieval period, spurred by economic, religious and political ideals. The First Crusade was preached in 1095 by Pope Urban II at Clermont in France. The call to Crusade came initially as a response to appeals from the Greek emperor in Byzantium whose domains were being invaded by the Seljuk Turks, who had captured

Jerusalem in 1071. The Roman and Greek Orthodox Churches had been divided since 1054 and Urban saw in this plea the chance to reunite the two Churches and, in so doing, gain Catholicism a firmer hold over the Eastern world. Urban's goal was achieved only briefly and imperfectly in the wake of the Fourth Crusade of 1204. Over two centuries, more than eleven Crusades to the Holy Land were launched from Europe's shores.

DESTRIER: Old French for warhorse.

DOMINICANS: the Order, whose rule was based on that of St Augustine, was founded in 1215 by Dominic de Guzman in France. Guzman, who promoted an austere, evangelical style of Catholicism, used the new Order to aid the Church in eradicating the Cathar heretics. In England they were known as the Black Friars, in France the Jacobins. The Dominicans, who continued to grow rapidly after Guzman's death, eschewed the luxuries enjoyed by many in the priesthood and were highly educated. In 1233 they were chosen by the pope to root out heretics and official inquisitors were appointed. By 1252, inquisitors were permitted to use torture to obtain confessions and many Dominicans became active members of this newly established institution which would become known as the Inquisition.

ENCEINTE: an enclosure within or area of a castle, or other fortified place.

FALCHION: a short sword with a curved edge, primarily used by infantry.

FLANDERS: a county in the Low Countries, famous for its cloth industry. Throughout the medieval period the kings of France sought to impose their authority over the county, which was often an ally of England. The resulting unrest led to the rise of the merchant guilds and eventually to open revolt, which climaxed in the defeat of French royal forces at Courtrai in 1302. Flanders was eventually annexed by the Duke of Burgundy in the fourteenth century.

FOSSE: a ditch or moat.

GAMBESON: a coat made of leather or quilted cloth.

GASCONY: a region in south-west France that became part of the duchy of Aquitaine in the eleventh century, then after the Treaty of Paris in 1258 came under the authority of the English kings who ruled the duchy of Guienne, which was then divided from Aquitaine.

GRAIL ROMANCE: a popular cycle of romances prevalent during the twelfth and thirteenth centuries. From this time, the Grail, the concept of which is thought to be derived from pre-Christian mythology, was Christianised and adopted into the Arthurian legend, made famous by the twelfth-century French poet, Chrétien de Troyes, whose work influenced later writers such as Malory and Tennyson. The following century saw many more takes on the Grail theme, including Wolfram von Eschenbach's *Parzival*, which inspired Wagner's opera. Romances were courtly stories, usually composed in verse in the vernacular, which combined historical, mythical and religious themes.

GRAND MASTER: head of a military Order. The Grand Master of the Templars was elected for life by a council of Templar officials and until the end of the Crusades was based at the Order's headquarters in Palestine.

GUIENNE: a duchy in south-west France, with Bordeaux as its principal city. Guienne was ruled by the kings of England, as vassals of the French king, after the Treaty of Paris in 1258, but following the death of Louis IX, English authority in the duchy was disputed by the French.

HAUBERK: a shirt of mail or scale armour

KINGDOM OF JERUSALEM: the Latin Kingdom of Jerusalem was founded in 1099, following the capture of Jerusalem by the First Crusade. Its first ruler was Godfrey de Bouillon, a Frankish count. Jerusalem itself became the new Crusader capital, but was lost and regained several times over the following two centuries until it was finally reclaimed by the Muslims in 1244, whereupon the city of Acre became the Crusaders' capital. Acre fell in 1291, signalling the end of the Kingdom of Jerusalem and of Western power in the Middle East.

KNIGHTS OF ST JOHN: Order founded in the late eleventh century that takes its name from the hospital of St John the Baptist in Jerusalem, where it had its first headquarters. Also known as the Hospitallers, their initial brief was the care of Christian pilgrims, but after the First Crusade their objectives changed dramatically. They retained their hospitals, but their primary preoccupations became the building and defence of their castles in the Holy Land, recruitment of knights and the acquisition of land and property. They enjoyed similar power and status as the Templars and the Orders were often rivals. After the end of the Crusades, the Knights of St John moved their headquarters to Rhodes, then later to Malta, where they became known as the Knights of Malta.

KNIGHTS TEMPLAR: Order of knights formed early in the twelfth century after the First Crusade. Established by Hugues de Payns, who travelled to Jerusalem with eight fellow French knights, the Order was named after the Temple of Solomon, upon the site of which they had their first headquarters. The Templars, who were formally recognised in 1128 at the Council of Troyes, followed both a religious Rule and a strict military code. Their initial *raison d'être* was to protect Christian pilgrims in the Holy Land; however, they far exceeded this early brief in their military and mercantile endeavours both in the Middle East and throughout Europe, where they rose to become one of the wealthiest and most powerful organisations of their day. There were three separate classes within the Order: sergeants, priests and knights, but only knights, who took the three monastic vows of chastity, poverty and obedience, were permitted to wear the distinctive white mantles which bore a splayed red cross.

MAMLUKS: from the Arabic meaning *slave*, the name was given to the royal bodyguard, mainly of Turkish descent, bought and raised by the Ayyubid sultans of Egypt into a standing army of devout Muslim warriors. Known in their day as 'the Templars of Islam', the Mamluks achieved ascendancy in 1250 when they assassinated Sultan Turanshah, a nephew of Saladin, and took control of Egypt. Under Baybars, the Mamluk empire grew to encompass Egypt and Syria, and they were ultimately responsible for removing Frankish influence in the Middle East. After the end of the Crusades in 1291, the Mamluks' reign continued until they were overthrown by the Ottoman Turks in 1517.

MONGOLS: nomadic tribespeople who lived around the steppes of eastern Asia until the late twelfth century when they were united under Genghis Khan, who established his capital at Karakorum and set out on a series of massive conquests. When Genghis Khan died, his empire extended across Asia, Persia, southern Russia and China. The Mongols' first great defeat came at the hands of Baybars and Kutuz at Ayn Jalut in 1260, and their empire began a gradual decline in the fourteenth century.

PALFREY: a light horse used for normal riding.

PARLEY: a discussion to debate points of a dispute, most commonly the terms of a truce.

PRECEPTORY: Latin name for the administrative houses of military Orders, which would have been like manors, with domestic quarters, workshops and usually a chapel.

RULE, THE: the Rule of the Temple was drawn up in 1129, with the aid of St Bernard de Clairvaux at the Council of Troyes, where the Temple was formally recognised. It was written as part religious rule, part military code and set out how members of the Order should live and conduct themselves during their daily lives and during combat. The Rule was added to over the years and by the thirteenth century there were over six hundred clauses, some more serious than others, the breaching of which would mean expulsion for the offender.

SARACEN: in the medieval period, a term used by Europeans for all Arabs and Muslims.

SENESCHAL: the steward or chief official of an estate. In the Temple's hierarchy, the Seneschal held one of the highest positions.

SIEGE ENGINE: any machine used to attack fortifications during sieges, such as mangonels, trebuchets and espringales.

SURCOAT: a long sleeveless garment, usually worn over mail or armour.

TAKE THE CROSS: to go on Crusade, a term derived from the cloth crosses that were handed out to those who pledged to become Crusaders.

TEUTONIC KNIGHTS: military Order of knights, similar to the Templars and the Hospitallers, originating in Germany. The Teutonics were founded in 1198 and during their time in the Holy Land were responsible for guarding the area north-east of Acre. By the mid-thirteenth century they had conquered Prussia, which later became their base.

VISITOR: a post within the Temple's hierarchy created in the thirteenth century. The Visitor, who was second only to the Grand Master, was the overlord of all the Temple's possessions in the West.

SELECT BIBLIOGRAPHY

Baigent, Michael and Leigh, Richard, *The Inquisition*, Penguin Books, 2000

Barber, Malcolm, *The Trial of the Templars*, Cambridge University Press, 1978

Barrow, Geoffrey W.S., *Robert Bruce and the Community of the Realm of Scotland*, Edinburgh University Press, 1988

Bryant, Nigel (trans.), *The High Book of the Grail: A Translation of the Thirteenth-Century Romance of Perlesvaus*, D. S. Brewer, 1978

Campbell, Alastair of Airds, *A History of Clan Campbell Vol. 1: From Origins to Flodden*, Polygon at Edinburgh, 2000

Chancellor, John, *The Life and Times of Edward I*, Weidenfeld and Nicolson, 1981

Cummins, John, *The Hound and the Hawk: The Art of Medieval Hunting*, Phoenix Press, 1988

Delon, Monique, *The Conciergerie, Palais de la Cité (Guide)*, Monum, Éditions du Patrimoine, 2000

Fawcett, Richard, *Stirling Castle (Official Guide)*, Historic Scotland, 1999

France, John, *Western Warfare in the Age of the Crusades, 1000–1300*, UCL Press, 1999

Grabois, Aryeh, *The Illustrated Encyclopedia of Medieval Civilization*, Octopus, 1980

Houston, Mary G., *Medieval Costume in England and France, The 13th, 14th and 15th Centuries*, Dover Publications, 1996

Mackay, James, *William Wallace: Brave Heart*, Mainstream Publishing, 1995

Maurois, André, *A History of France*, Jonathan Cape, 1949

McNair Scott, Ronald, *Robert the Bruce, King of Scots*, Canongate, 1988

Menache, Sophia, *Clement V*, Cambridge University Press, 1998

Nicholson, Helen, *The Knights Templar: A New History*, Sutton Publishing, 2001

Prigent, Serge, *Paris: Dates, Facts and Figures*, Éditions Jean-Paul Gisserot, 2006

Read, Piers Paul, *The Templars*, Weidenfeld and Nicolson, 1999

Tabraham, Chris (ed.), *Edinburgh Castle (Official Guide)*, Historic Scotland, 2003

Upton-Ward, J.M., *The Rule of the Templars*, The Boydell Press, 1992

Walker, Jim, *Berwick Upon Tweed, History and Guide*, Tempus, 2001

Weir, Alison, *Isabella: She-Wolf of France, Queen of England*, Pimlico, 2006

Wood, Charles T. (ed.), *Philip the Fair and Boniface VIII, State vs. Papacy*, Holt, Rinehart and Winston, 1967

Zacour, Norman, *An Introduction to Medieval Institutions*, St James Press, 1977